The Banker

by Cheng Naishan

Translated, with Introduction, by Britten Dean

CHINA
BOOKS
& Periodicals, Inc.
San Francisco

Map of Shanghai 1940--pg. 14

About the translator:

Britten Dean earned his doctoral degree from Columbia University in East Asian Languages and Cultures. A professor at California State University, Stanislaus, since 1967, he has published extensively in the field of Chinese history, and translated a book of Cheng Naishan's short stories in 1989, entitled *The Piano Tuner*. Here he again brings to us the flavor and humor of a language and culture as different as China's.

Cover design by Linda Revel

Copyright © 1992 by Britten Dean

No part of this publication may be reproduced, stored in a retrieval system, or transmitted, in any form or by any means, electronic, mechanical, photocopying, recording or otherwise, without the prior written permission of Britten Dean, California State University, Stanislaus, Turlock, CA 95380

Library of Congress Catalog Card Number: 92-055038

ISBN 0-8351-2492-4

Printed in the United States of America

Introduction

The Banker is set in Shanghai during the period of Japanese invasion and control from 1937 through 1945. Shanghai was a complex city. Forcibly opened in 1842 to foreign trade and cultural influence, it grew rapidly in size and population to become one of the world's major cosmopolitan centers. By 1937 there were two distinct sectors—the foreign and the Chinese. The former comprised the International Settlement and the French Concession, both under foreign administrations and protected by foreign arms. Here were the stylish foreign shops, the great American and European business houses, the broad parks and quiet residential neighborhoods with their western street names. The Chinese sector, seemingly a different world, included densely populated South City (the original walled city), Zhabei, Hongkou, and other districts, all under Chinese administration only ill-protected by inadequate national armies.

More than just a gripping story, *The Banker* is good history. The family is a window on society, says the author Cheng Naishan, and family history is the most valuable kind of history. Thus, chronicling her own prominent family offers insights into the nation. Cheng painstakingly went about her task of collecting material, and she was in a unique position to do so, for the Zhu Jingchen of the novel is no less than her own grandfather, Cheng Muhao. "Cheng Muhao, born 1898; 1913 joined Bank of China; Bank of Communication (Manager); Bank of China—Hong Kong Branch (Advisor); Bank of China—Head Office (Director)." So reads the entry from a Who's Who in Hong Kong. Cheng Muhao moved from the countryside to Shanghai as a teenager with only a fifth-grade education and began what would become a distinguished seventy-year career with the Bank of China. Like so many other business-class families, the Cheng family migrated to Hong Kong in 1949 when the communists came to power on the mainland. Although his children and grandchildren returned to the mainland in 1956, Cheng Muhao himself wisely remained in Hong Kong to continue his banking career.

Besides fictionalized family members and friends, many fully historical personages also strut across Cheng Naishan's stage, from the urbane Peking opera star Mei Lanfang to the gangster-turned-philanthropist Du Yuesheng, whom Cheng faithfully describes from authentic eye-witness accounts. The broad lawns of missionary-operated McTyeire School for Girls where the author's mother was a student, the chaos produced by the Japanese invasion which the Chinese armies, for all their unexpected valor, could not repel, and the notorious Chinese collaborationist headquarters at No. 76 Jessfield Road whose dank underground dungeons can still be seen today—all this too was real and has been faithfully and vividly recorded in the pages of Cheng Naishan's epic account.

The granddaughter was able to visit the 89-year-old retired banker in Hong Kong in 1986, and for three months she listened while this unique insider source, whose memory remained keen to the end, recollected his days in Shanghai under the Japanese. She also collected material from her own uncle and aunts, who figure in the novel as Zhu Jingchen's son and four daughters. Cheng Naishan thus knows whereof she speaks, and The Banker provides a stunningly accurate portrait not only of her own family but of the times as well, both the small details of everyday life and the larger currents of social and economic change.

The Banker is her first full-length novel. It reveals two aspects of Nancy Cheng's outlook that can be found in many of her works. One is her general approval of the business class and the positive contribution it has made to China's economic and social development over the years. The other unique element in Cheng's work is her sympathetic treatment of Christianity.

The Banker is Cheng Naishan's first novel of a projected trilogy chronicling three generations of the Cheng family: from the rise to prominence of the banker himself, to the trials of his self-indulgent offspring following the establishment in 1949 of the communist regime, to, finally, the fate of the third generation—that of Cheng Naishan herself—in the aftermath of those "historically unprecedented days of madness," as she calls the Cultural Revolution.

What place will the business ethic and Christian piety have in the new society following the communist triumph in 1949? The uncertain conclusion of the novel leaves the answer in doubt, though history will show in the subsequent volumes of the trilogy that they fared ill.

Chapter 1

I t happened to be April 1, 1937, popularly referred to in the West as April Fool's Day, and it had arrived on the campus of Shanghai's prestigious McTyeire School for Girls.

As the bell sounded for the start of classes, the girls, notebooks under arm, clad in their green silk school uniforms, began moving in twos and threes across the green, and filed into the lecture theater at its end. They were the third-year students of the senior high school—the graduating class, and they all detested this home economics course.

Exclusive girls' schools like McTyeire regarded home economics equally important as English, and while it was not one of the academic majors, it did seem to be even more helpful to the students in becoming models of femininity and the McTyeire spirit in their worlds after graduation. Consequently, whether the school administration or the students themselves, none dared to neglect this subject. The school regularly invited outside authorities in various fields to give lectures at the school.

The topic of today's home economics lecture was the "Prevention of Common Children's Ailments," and probably some old lady would come to recite her scripture. The girls particularly disliked lectures by these elderly women doctors or nurses, who mumbled on endlessly yet permitted not a peep out the audience below. Really, classes like these were veritable disasters.

"Dean Shen is actually very far-sighted, having already anticipated the need for a class in the prevention of children's ailments, as if upon graduation when we step through McTyeire's portals we'll be occupied with..." And with that patter, one of the girls heaved a disgruntled sigh and began humming the "Wedding March." She was Ju Beibei, who, though wearing the same green mandarin dress uniform as all the others, pulled it especially snug around the waist and let her fluffy permed curls fall to her shoulders and puffed up her chest, evidencing an allure and fashion which did not altogether comport with her student status. Luckily, however, McTyeire was operated by a comparatively open-minded and flexible American missionary board, for otherwise the school would have been unable to accommodate such a student as she.

"The way I see it, it might just be you, Ju Beibei, who will be the first to hear 'Here comes the bride, all dressed in white!' In the entire class you're the busiest with phone calls and telegrams." One of the girls, Zhu Juanmin, with beautiful almond-shaped eyes but without a trace of the classic charm, who possessed a beauty that revealed intelligence but a certain hauteur as well, ridiculed her from aside.

"Don't be silly! I'm not going to get married. Once you're married, you're like merchandise that's left the store—it's not worth a cent! I'm a confirmed celibate." Ju Beibei raised her arms and, like the Grape Fairy of legend, gracefully pirouetted in the narrow corridor—a practiced movement, yet not lacking in charm. Caught off guard, an elderly instructor in his long gray gown who happened just then to pass by, very nearly had his glasses swept to the floor by those gracefully swinging arms.

"Such frivolousness!" The old instructor quickly adjusted his glasses, his eyes falling against his will upon Ju Beibei's bosom pushing tight against her dress, then quickened his pace and went on. With that, another girl rushed ahead a few steps and pushed open the glass front door for him, and said softly, "Take care, Mr. Syu."

Mr. Syu looked at her fondly. "Thank you, Syi Zhishuang," he said, nodding warmly, and he went through the door and headed upstairs. At that point the other girls in the corridor burst out in uncontrollable laughter. Some among them began a pretentious declamation of an earlier lesson: "I pass through the world moving westward, at length to come upon the old cottage; the sun is then setting over a troubled pool of chilly, mournful water..."

This Mr. Syu, who taught Chinese, was McTyeire's only teacher who wore a long gown, and its only male teacher, too. He came from nearby Chingpu county and held the provincial-level academic degree under the old Ching dynasty examination system, and somehow or other had been engaged by the school to teach Chinese. One can easily imagine how tiresome and uninteresting it was teaching this subject to these westernized young ladies, the more so for such a shabby, old-fashioned scholar as he. The girls just couldn't take him seriously, and in his class they would secretly read English novels or do knitting work out of sight beneath their desk tops. "Don't bow and scrape for a bushel of rice," the saying goes, but this Mr. Syu, when confronted with life's hard realities, swallowed his pride and endured humiliation, and stayed on at McTyeire precisely because it paid a significantly higher salary than most middle schools. Thus he became the perennial butt of these insensitive girls' jibes.

"You oughtn't to be joking that way," Syi Zhishuang admonished her classmates. "Mr. Syu is such a learned man, and elderly, too. Don't tease him so. We'll be graduating soon; we should try to leave each other with a good impression."

Syi Zhishuang—with a plump and light-complexioned squarish face, with small but beautiful glistening eyes whose bright pupils darted about—was a very lively young lady. Although at eighteen she still retained a certain childish air, she was certainly a beauty in embryo. Add to that a soft, perfectly round chin which lent to her good looks an appealing degree of matronly gentility, and no wonder that from their housemother, "Night Owl," on up to Mr. Shen the dean of studies and even the foreign headmistress Miss Perry, Syi Zhishuang was everyone's favorite.

A studious girl, Zhishuang scored well in English and received excellent grades in Chinese, especially her compositions, which the Chinese teacher Mr. Syu often selected as model essays to be read aloud in class. On account of this she was chosen editor of McTyeire's 1937 class yearbook. At McTyeire, a good-looking, hard-working student enjoyed enormous prestige, so when she delivered this admonition to her classmates, they immediately quieted down and silently filed into the lecture theater to wait for some tedious lecture to begin.

Treading audibly, Dean Shen entered the hall leading a tall, young gentleman wearing a white sharkskin suit.

"I should like to present Dr. Peter Gao..." The words had scarcely issued from Mr. Shen's mouth when a student rushed in requesting him to go out, presumably because some class was giving the Chinese teacher a hard time and the dean was needed to put out the fire.

The atmosphere in the hall seemed suddenly buoyant on account of this young gentleman, for who could have guessed that Shanghai's celebrated Dr. Peter Gao was this dapper young man. Just see how Ju Beibei, now sitting so erect, had her tantalizing bright eyes riveted on him. But he was completely composed. Smug, even. Just see how his left palm rested on the lectern, how his right hand, pushing aside his opened jacket, was casually thrust into his pocket, the perfect model of a dashing gallant. He smiled a slight smile, and in fluent, Oxford-accented English began his lecture. "Young ladies! I must be awfully dumb to lecture at this institution on the prevention of common children's ailments, for I now await the day when you raise your own precious children to be healthy and plump, thus bringing the avenue of my livelihood to a dead end."

The girls broke into giggles.

His handwriting was as stylish as the man himself, and just as he was tall and slim, so he drew his f's, t's, and l's long and slender.

Before long, having scribbled the chalkboard full, he pulled from his pocket a crisply starched, pure white handkerchief, snapped it open with a flick of the wrist, held it against his nose and mouth as protection against chalk dust, and then stood sideways to the chalkboard and erased it. The maneuver was executed with an elegance and style that subdued every one of those supercilious girls.

The girls looked at each other in speechless wonderment as if to say, "Did you see that?"—"I sure did!"

Zhu Juanmin and Syi Zhishuang were such inseparable friends that their classmates referred to them as "this half" and "that half." Juanmin had just now surreptitiously slipped a note to Zhishuang: "Does this chic Mr. Gao meet your 'black bench' requirements?" (As it happens, in Shanghai dialect, "black bench" is pronounced just like the English word "husband," so the girls always said 'black bench' when they wanted to refer to a future marriage partner.) And Juanmin methodically drew a sturdy little bench followed by a big question mark.

Zhishuang took the note and casually read it over, looked up at the man on the stage, took stock of his westernized, slicked-back hair and marvelous aplomb, then bent over the note and scribbled her reply: "This is no mere 'black bench,' this is a full-length sofa, and one would at the very least have to get matching furniture, add cushions...far too extravagant. Too much for me to handle."

Juanmin took the note back and had to cover her mouth to suppress a burst of laughter.

The more the gentleman at the lectern spoke to the roomful of girls the more enthusiastic he became, and the further he wandered from his subject. "...Life, in fact, is brimming with all kinds of philosophic principles, and these philosophies of life can be explained by the same theorems used in science. For example, 'for every action there is an equal and opposite reaction,' 'opposites attract, likes repel'..." Having arrived at this point in his lecture, he realized he was meandering like a trackless trolley, so he hurriedly put on a serious expression and added: "Therefore, if you bear in mind these scientific phenomena, you can avoid many of life's unfortunate accidents. For example, when you are cuddling your infant and a heavy object falls from the sky, you avoid it by simply moving against the direction of the wind, because a falling body will be deflected by the wind in a parabolic line. Once you understand this principle, irrespective of whether you are avoiding a falling flower pot or a falling bomb, it's all the same." And having spoken, he raised his hand to the chalkboard and drew a long arc from top to bottom, revealing in the process dazzling platinum cuff links accenting his fresh white shirt.

The bell signaling the end of class sounded, much to the girls' surprise. How fast the hour had gone, they thought, as they watched the gentleman daintily brush the chalk dust from his hands. "My lecture," he said with a sly smile, "doesn't solve any problems. If you really have problems that require attention, you'll have to come to the Peter Gao Clinic. And one other thing. My name is Mr. Feng. Feng Jingsyao, Dr. Peter Gao's assistant. Dean Shen did not have a chance to finish his introduction. But fortunately, today is April Fool's Day, which provides me authorization for playing this practical joke on you young ladies."

He left the lecture hall leaving the class in an uproar, and by the time the girls had recovered their senses and rushed to the windows, the tall, white figure had already crossed the tree-lined walkway and soon turned a corner and disappeared.

Juanmin exhaled a long stream of air, overcome with a vague disappointment. "I did think it strange that a pediatrician of such stature could be so young!"

*   *   *

At four o'clock the students had free-time activities. The McTyeire School for Girls, under the jurisdiction, as it was, of a wealthy American mission board, had the finest of dormitory facilities. There were only two or three girls to a room, and each floor was furnished with two commons rooms which the girls took turns keeping clean and tidy—a responsibility which both molded the girls' sense of taste and made those who'd never had to do a lick of work in their lives apply themselves to daily household chores.

The commons room was always bright and clean. Two sofas, of differing size and style, were arranged at opposite ends of the room, and a large oak dining table, spread with a lace tablecloth tatted by the girls themselves, was placed next to one wall. Piled atop the table were sheaves of manuscripts, and Zhishuang had her head buried in them, hard at work. As editor of the 1937 McTyeire school yearbook, she was busily preparing drafts for the press so the yearbook would be out by graduation, just three months hence.

During free time after class the girls liked to bring their textbooks or their embroidery work into the commons room to sit and chat. Today's talk seemed to center on that youthful counterfeit of Peter Gao.

"He speaks beautiful English, with a marvelous Oxford accent. With panache like that he could easily set himself up in a law practice. So why of all things," asked a puzzled Juanmin, "did he chose pediatrics?"

"It's easy to make a name for yourself as a pediatrician," someone interjected. "But for a lawyer, you won't have any backers if you don't come from a good background. Shanghai has as many lawyers as hairs on an ox, so how can you just go out and make a name for yourself? A lawyer without a reputation is a lawyer who won't earn enough to eat."

"That gentleman lacking backers?" said Ju Beibei, piquing their curiosity. "That's just gossip." And she thrust out her ample bosom.

"So what prominent family does he come from?" Juanmin, as the very daughter of Zhu Jingchen, a mover and shaker in Shanghai financial circles, unique in serving both as president and a permanent member of the board of directors of the privately owned Cathay Republic Bank, likewise considered herself to be a young lady of fame and fortune and consequently was rather in the habit of talking down to others from a high perch.

"My guess is that this Mr. Feng is from the prominent Feng family which lives on Rue Bourgeat. The patriarch of the Feng family in Hangzhou successfully fought off Japanese buccaneers in the last century, so the emperor granted him 10,000 acres of prime farmland plus 10,000 ounces of gold. That's how they acquired their wealth." Ju Beibei was the class celebrity when it came to social contacts, and she seemed to be a walking Who's Who which recorded something or other about the confidential financial histories of all of Shanghai's distinguished families. "But I've heard that within just three generations," said Ju Beibei, chattering on, "this Feng family was pretty much right back where it had started from, and except for one or two grandchildren who went abroad to study, most of them just liked to stay home and live off their capital. Then, decades ago, the family split up, and I don't know what branch of the family the Mr. Feng we saw today belongs to."

"Um..., does he have a wife?" Juanmin, who had been listening in awe and veneration, finally ventured a question.

"What's that? Well, if you make me a present suitable for a matchmaker, I'll go and make detailed inquiries for you," said Ju Beibei, eyeing her classmate.

"Oh, stop your gibberish!" Juanmin flushed deeply, snatched up a cushion and threw it at Ju Beibei, except that it brushed past the pile of manuscripts Zhishuang was working on and flew right into the high-cheekboned face of a girl who had throughout been sitting at the end of the table silently buried in her needlework. She good-naturedly pushed the cushion aside, but Zhishuang jumped up and demanded, "Hey, what about my papers! You not only don't help me with the yearbook, you people are actually causing me trouble. Really, after you're through with your dinner, you don't have anything to do. Oh, by the way, Ju Beibei, did you ask Hong Fung to do us that favor?"

Hong Fung was one of the hottest movie stars of the day. The McTyeire yearbook needed to bring in a lot of advertising, and movie stars had broad social contacts including acquaintances among business people, and because Ju Beibei was on very close terms with Hong Fung, Zhishuang had asked her to handle all the advertising work.

"A big movie star like her is never at home. Whenever I call, no one answers. But I'll give it another try now." Ju Beibei went to the telephone in a corner of the commons room and dialed the number.

Zhishuang turned her head, and her gaze fell upon that girl with the protruding cheekbones.

"Liu Tsaizhen, how about your article on 'Thirty-seven's most liked and least liked'?"

"I still haven't figured out what to write," she replied plaintively.

Liu Tsaizhen was the daughter of the influential cotton yarn manufacturer at Nantong, 100 miles or so inland, and because she had transferred to McTyeire only recently, she still smacked slightly of the out-of-town rustic. And her English proficiency was below average to boot. Thus, in manner and deportment she always betrayed a wooden dullness which, among this bevy of spirited, modern girls, inescapably connoted only a very modest family origin. Whenever the talk turned to why she had been able to transfer to McTyeire, it was concluded that because the linen and cotton material for the school's spring and summer school uniforms had always been provided on preferential terms by the Liu family-owned Bounty Textile Mill, the school administration for its part granted admission on preferential terms. In any event, in academies which hitherto had claimed to remain aloof from worldly considerations, one nowadays could hear not only the sound of student recitations, but the jingle of silver dollars as well. That someone might spend money to acquire a diploma from a well known school was nothing so very exceptional.

"That won't do at all." Zhishuang, noisily shuffling through a sheaf of papers, spoke to Liu Tsaizhen in an officious, uncompromising tone. "You'd better get it all figured out today. Otherwise our yearbook won't be ready by graduation day, and it'll be all your fault. Are you ready to accept that responsibility?"

All people by nature have a touch of imperviousness whereby they bully the weak even while fearing the strong, and the sweet-faced, sweet-tempered Zhishuang was no different. She was not from a wealthy family. Her father, though educated in England and now assistant manager of the credit department of Cathay Republic Bank, went strictly by the rules and, unlike many in the banking industry who tried to make extra money on the side, had never once used the bank's money to speculate in gold or securities; he relied only on his salary to get by, which kept his family in no more than modest comfort. But because most of McTyeire's students if not rich at least enjoyed elite status, Syi Zhishuang had during her six years at the school been placed in the midst of privileged young ladies, and on not a few occasions had silently cried herself to sleep because she lacked an expensive fur coat or a diamond ring. A haughty girl, Zhishuang preferred to leave her fingers bare than to stoop to adorning herself with second-rate jewelry, for, just as in her studies, she strived to be number one and would not be satisfied with number two. Her good looks, not to mention her intelligence and academic record, allowed Syi Zhishuang to rank among McTyeire's outstanding students, but in her heart of hearts she harbored an aching resentment towards those rich girls. Fortunate she was, then, to have encountered the countrified Liu Tsaizhen from an upstart family, at whom Syi Zhishuang on whatever pretext could take verbal jabs.

Seeing everybody's gaze concentrated on her, Liu Tsaizhen felt distinctly ill at ease. She put down her half-finished runner, and bit her lip. "I like most of all to crochet runners," she said, looking down at her needlework.

Zhishuang and the others stifled their giggles and pressed her to tell what she "liked least."

"Like least? I least of all like history exams," she replied in all earnestness. "The genealogy of the English royal family is harder to understand than the genealogy of the eighteen generations of my own family tree. I'll never ever get it straight."

"Okay, okay!" interrupted Zhishuang, suppressing her giggles. "Just get that 'most liked, least liked' article finished up and everything will be fine. It's a natural for our yearbook."

Meanwhile, Ju Beibei had gotten her call through. Zhishuang perked up her ears to catch every word.

"...Hong Feng, would you be kind enough to give me some help? As you know the money to produce our 1937 class yearbook has to come from advertising, and the cost of paper is so high these days...Now, you're a big star, so if you'd put in a good word for us with the owners of the well known stores like Greenhouse Fashion Boutique and Comfort Shoe Emporium, that'd do it..." Catching Juanmin giving her a wink, Ju Beibei smiled back. "I'll bring a couple of classmates around to see you in a day or so. One is my good friend Miss Zhu Juanmin, the daughter of Zhu Jingchen who runs Cathay Republic Bank. She positively worships you. And the other one is the editor of the yearbook. If you'd give them autographed pictures of yourself..."

A delighted Juanmin nodded vigorously.

Juanmin picked up the phone as soon as Ju Beibei hung up. Juanmin had lost her mother at fourteen and to console her bereaved father, she had of her own initiative as eldest daughter taken on the household responsibilities. From managing daily expenditures to the hiring and firing of servants, she handled everything with perfect competence, just as if she were the lady of the house herself. Thus, even though she lived in the school dormitory, she frequently called home to check up on household affairs. Everyone praised her as clever and capable, a perfect replica of her father, President Zhu.

"Is that you, Fagun? This is Miss Zhu. Let me speak with my younger sister." A glance at her pretty, clearly edged lips curled downward in a scowl, and at her nose, held high in haughtiness, revealed her sense of proud self-importance.

*   *   *

That evening, with the lights-out bell soon to ring, Zhishuang wearily closed her heavy tome on British history, yawned a long yawn, and said to the befuddled-looking Liu Tsaizhen next to her, "This history stuff is all just rote memory. That's as much as I can help you."

A few minutes still remaining before lights out, Zhishuang took a shower, then twisted a big white towel around her head, rather resembling a turban of tulle such as an eighteenth-century French noblewoman might wear.

"Oh, Zhishuang, you're so pretty," Juanmin exclaimed; "just like those shots of Greta Garbo in Grand Hotel."

"More like one of those Sikh policemen, seems to me," returned Zhishuang, adjusting her towel headdress.

This was a spacious room with three beds arranged along the east wall, each with a silk mosquito netting hung over it. Before Liu Tsaizhen had transferred in, there had been just the two roommates, Juanmin and Zhishuang. At this moment, from the farthest bed, draped with its mosquito net, came the sound of Liu Tsaizhen's light snoring.

"She sure can sleep," said Zhishuang, gesturing toward the bed emitting the husky sound. "From the 'Wars of the Roses' on down, her knowledge of English history is just one big jumble. If she doesn't pass her history, she won't get her diploma."

"It's not just history she'll flunk. I think she'll flunk English and economics, too. No way she'll be able to graduate this year. She sure is lucky though—nothing ever bothers her. Just listen to that snoring," said Juanmin with an envious sigh.

"What's wrong, Juanmin," asked Zhishuang in alarm, hearing her friend sigh so heavily. Had she not perhaps been moonstruck by that Mr. Feng Jingsyao?

"Earlier, on the phone my sister told me Daddy and Miss Pu have come to a decision." As Juanmin spoke, tears welled up in her eyes.

Juanmin had known bitterness in her life, all right. Referred to as a "precious daughter," when still a youngster her mother had died, evidence of the fact that life is never perfect.

"Don't be upset." Zhishuang hugged her friend from behind and gently comforted her. "Your father's only in his forties and his career has been so successful, could you really still count on his going on forever like this without remarrying?"

"Of course not," she murmured, "but..." But she couldn't articulate the whys and wherefors of it.

"Don't be upset; it was bound to happen sooner or later," said Zhishuang trying to buck her up in a soft voice.

"Whenever I think of that Pu woman, who wants to take the household keys right out of my hand, I get too angry for words."

"Well even if Miss Pu had not come into your home, that doesn't necessarily mean you'd still want to stay and take care of the house for the rest of your life," said Zhishuang patting her friend's hand.

Juanmin snorted. "You think getting married is all so important. I bet you've fallen for that doctor, haven't you. Hm, I wonder if he really is from the Feng family, the way Beibei said."

Indignation showed on Zhishuang's face. "Well I certainly would never settle on that westernized whelp!" And with that she parted the mosquito netting and climbed into her bed.

"I kind of like him, actually." Juanmin talked into the mirror as she curled her hair around paper curlers.

Zhishuang stuck her head out of the mosquito netting. "I've said before what I think of that kind of 'black bench.' Only Ju Beibei's type has the qualifications for making a match with him."

Just then from outside the door came the sound of keys clanging on their ring, followed by a stern voice announcing lights out—it was "Night Owl" making her evening round. This housemother actually had a very literary-sounding name, but the girls all called her "Night Owl." It was not only her dark, fleshy face, round as a ball, and big round eyeglasses, but her owlish habits as well which suggested the sobriquet: during daylight hours she was never to be seen, but appeared only when the corridor lights came on, adjusting those thick, round glasses and busily getting about her work.

"Humph. She's forever telling us to maintain quiet during night hours, but it never occurs to her that her own key ring makes the biggest racket of all," grumbled Juanmin as she turned off her light. "Clang clang clang—just like a blacksmith."

After a long while, not hearing Juanmin get into her bed, Zhishuang poked her head out from the mosquito netting and checked: there she was, a dressing gown thrown over her shoulders, standing quietly on the balcony, lost in thought. At this season in this climate, outdoors was still disagreeably chilly. The moon had slipped behind a cloud, and offered only indifferent illumination. Juanmin's beautiful almond eyes sparkled in the dim light. "Do you think that...that Ju Beibei is pretty?" she said, without turning her head.

"Well, at least her style and manner aren't bad," Zhishuang answered, "and she's a very sensible girl."

"Don't you think that today's lecturer was pretty impressive?" asked Zhuanmin with feeling. Suddenly realizing she had spoken too loudly on so still an evening, she quickly covered her mouth with her hand and anxiously looked around, but detected nothing save the monotonous splashing of a nearby fountain.

Zhishuang was quite unaffected. "I don't know why," she smiled, "but it seems just like looking at a pretty dress in some shop window—maybe when I see it I really like it, but I certainly don't plan on actually acquiring it. There's probably a lot of reasons for that—maybe it won't fit, maybe the color won't go well with my skin, or maybe it just doesn't match my personality. Yes, that's it, my personality."

"I don't care any about that," said Juanmin, as she slumped against the cold stone balustrade. "If I liked it, I'd want to buy it, and even if I couldn't get into it and just locked it away in the trunk, I'd still want to buy it, and having bought it, it would be mine."

Zhishuang didn't say a word as she joined Juanmin in leaning against the railing, gazing into the distance. Perhaps because she was not from a well-off family, she was in so many ways much more practical than her friend, which ruled out her getting moonstruck about anything.

The clouds dispersed and a circle of brightness illuminated the tranquil paths graveled with crushed porcelain and the flower beds edged with low shrubs. These were the McTyeire grounds that so enchanted countless numbers of Shanghai's young ladies.

Zhishuang had lived here for six years now, from junior high through high school. The McTyeire campus was like a window through which she could glimpse a whole new lifestyle of splendor and elegance and she had already become accustomed to it. In three more months she would be leaving this place, but she hoped that, just as she would obtain her diploma, she would also achieve the qualifications whereby she could forever enter this social stratum. She was unsure whether she would succeed, but she would apply herself with unflagging effort.

"Minny, what do you plan on studying in college?" Zhishuang asked her friend.

"Journalism."

"A woman, running all over the place as a reporter?" Zhishuang shook her head again and again. "You're not the Ju Beibei type, you know."

"What's gotten into you today, always setting me against Ju Beibei?"

"What I mean is Ju Beibei is real good at getting around, but you haven't any knack for that at all. So how can you be a reporter? And besides, for a woman...Well, a reporter has to be rushing around everywhere." Zhishuang spoke with some trepidation at the thought of it.

"So what? I'll get to know a lot of people by rushing around, and rushing around is something you can get used to. St. John's has a good journalism department. And what about you?"

"I'm going to study home economics."

"Good heavens, what's worth studying about home economics? Isn't it just teaching you how to cook and keep house? It's the same as training a maid."

"Don't talk rubbish. I've always felt I was cut out to study home economics. 'Home economics'—the very term suggests that one will never be far from her home, unlike a news reporter flying about all day long." Such were the words on her lips, but in her heart Zhishuang all along recognized that home economics alone would provide her the most reliable assistance in entering that stratum of life which she cherished. There was another consideration, too. Every year McTyeire sought from among that year's college-bound graduates one or two of exceptional character and academic achievement to engage as future teachers at the school. Any woman who could gain employment at such a seat of learning as McTyeire would of course enjoy great prestige. And coming, as she did, from a family of the salaried class, she naturally had to consider the difficulties of seeking employment after graduation. Judging from her own careful observations over the years, McTyeire was overstaffed in English and history, while in home economics, science and music there remained hope for employment. And among these subjects, she was most interested in and most confident about home economics.

"Hm...I'm just anxious to get away from home," sighed Juanmin. "The farther the better. When that Pu woman steps across the threshold of the Zhu home, I'm certain the day will come when I won't be able to live there."

"That's an easy problem—just get married," Zhishuang kidded her. Juanmin put her arm around her shoulder, and the two broke out into a giggle, and then suddenly stopped.

The fragrance of the flowers wafting up in the moonlit night became thicker and heavier, like an intoxicating fog, gradually enveloping them in its shroud. It was the eighteenth spring of their life, and they thought that all their springs would be this way—fragrant, gorgeous, intoxicating, and, yes, full of hope.

SHANGHAI
1940

Hongkou

INTER-

Huangpu River

Cathay
Republic
Bank

The   Bund

Sichuan   Rd.

Jiangsi   Rd.

*South
City*

Small East Gate

NATIONAL

Garbage
Bridge

Tibet Rd.

Great
World

Rue Hennequin

Zhabei

Race
Course

Rue Bayle

Suzhou Creek

R.R. Station

Avenue Rd.

Bubbling Well Rd.

Edward VII Ave.

Avenue Foch

Avenue Joffre

FRENCH

Moulemein Rd.

YWCA

Seymour   Rd.

CONCESSION

Hardoon
Garden

←To Nanking

SETTLEMENT

West District

Hart Rd.

Robison Rd.

Facility
Village

Jessfield Rd.

McTyeire
School

Bubbling Well Rd.

Jiaotong
Polytechnic
University

St.
John's
U.

Jessfield
Park

To Hangzhou →

Chapter 2

An old Buick carrying Zhu Jingchen, president of Cathay Republic Bank, slowly turned into quiet, secluded Rue Bayle.

Just to the west was the New Temple to the City God, and nearby on the east was Great World Entertainment Center. Yet Rue Bayle itself was entirely free of the incessant noise of those bustling adjacent districts. By no means a broad avenue, both sides were uniformly lined with sturdy homes of bluish-gray or red brick construction, whose design included stained glass windows with sturdy wooden louvered shutters to provide seclusion to those within. On this avenue, in the early decades of the century, one found the residences of Shanghai's rich and famous.

Few pedestrians were about. A spotlessly clean private rickshaw darted out from a lane, its side lantern banging against the chassis. A woman in maid's dress with a youngster in hand occupied it. The child was impishly kicking the runningboard bell, "ding-ding, ding-ding" as the rickshaw crossed the street until, passing out of earshot, tranquillity was restored to the scene.

"Keep going straight ahead, Ayi, and let me take a look," said Zhu Jingchen, leaning forward toward his chauffeur. "I'm not sure I remember which house it is."

It had been quite some time since he had last come to this neighborhood. Previously, when he had just started with Cathay Republic as a trainee, he had come to this neighborhood with the senior apprentice to present New Year's gifts to the bank's depositors. In those days horse-drawn carriages still came down these streets. The great gates lining the avenue, with their delicately chiseled stone gateposts and large pendant brass-ring knockers, had frightened and humbled him.

"Each sixty-year cycle involves a great change," or so the saying goes. In fact with the passage of just these twenty or thirty years, great change had come to this street, and whether it was because the Zhu Jingchen of today was no longer that young apprentice or because the newly rich had been gradually settling in West District, at any rate in Jingchen's eyes great change had come to this street. The wooden balustrades—their paint long since peeled, and the heavy shutters—now pulled tightly shut, were but two indications that the street's former power and panache had waned, and Jingchen was much affected.

As the car approached a towering, arch-shaped gate of western style, Jingchen tapped the driver's seat-back: "Yes! This is it."

It was the Liu family residence. Mr. Liu, the Nantong cotton industry tycoon, had acquired his wealth during the Great War, when he single-handedly managed Bounty Textile Mill. But in recent years, as a result of large-scale dumping of British and Japanese cotton goods in China, one cotton mill after another had unfortunately met with bankruptcy. Many in the business community thus now regarded the cotton industry as fraught with danger and were disinclined to invest in it further. According to the local records of Changzhou, a well known textile manufacturing center, one bankrupt mill owner commented, "In writing the history of this county, the phrase 'citizens are advised against operating cotton mills' must certainly be included," which is sufficient to demonstrate businessmen's lack of confidence in engaging in the textile industry at that time.

Old Mr. Liu had retired at the height of his career, terminating once and for all his Nantong enterprise, and shifting his investments to Shanghai real estate. A few years ago the entire family had moved from Nantong to Shanghai and lived on the proceeds of those investments. Old Mr. Liu was now advanced in years and had gradually withdrawn from active affairs, leaving their management entirely in the hands of his "only son" Liu Tongjun. (To be sure, there was a group of petty-minded evil-tongued outsiders who bruited it about that this only son had actually been adopted from a foundling hospital; whether this is so or not, I do not know, and it is not worth exploring further.)

Cathay Republic was a private commercial bank, and, as such, many of its employees had their origins in the traditional counting houses, and were well acquainted with the old merchants in the neighboring provinces, among whom Cathay had had dealings with Bounty Textile

Mill, which indeed, could be said to have been one of Cathay's best customers. But with the retirement of old Mr. Liu, dealings between Cathay and the Liu family had begun to flag.

On the present occasion the young owner of Bounty, Liu Tongjun, had specially sent a note inviting Zhu Jingchen to a tea party. These "tea parties" were new-fangled things. Up to now Jingchen had known only "dinner banquets," or, perhaps, some host's "tea reception" at a tea-house. But to hold a "tea party" at home Jingchen felt to be rather infantile, too much like some amusement his daughter at McTyeire might indulge in. Jingchen had never imagined that the young industrialist of the Liu household would himself fool around with any such new-fangled function.

This Liu Tongjun, although about the same age as Jingchen, did not yet really amount to anything on his own; he just relied on his father's reputation and resources to win undeserved acclaim throughout the city of Shanghai as the ostentatious young master. Ordinarily Jingchen would not take much notice of a profligate like him, but since he had personally extended so sincere and earnest an invitation, Jingchen would use the opportunity to get to know him a little. And it might be advantageous for Cathay to attract idle capital into its coffers by forming a connection with so prominent a family as this.

A servant, already waiting at the gatehouse, led Jingchen through a courtyard, gravelled in a striped pattern, and on into the house.

The Liu residence was a hybrid Sino-Western structure with spacious, high-ceilinged rooms—a central section of three main rooms on each floor, plus two wings. Even during summer's hot spell, a cool breeze gently blew, making electric fans unnecessary. Jingchen had a great fondness for this style of Sino-Western architecture—light and spacious yet restrained, consistent with the old convention of not indulging in a conspicuous display of one's wealth.

The ground floor reception room was surfaced in square green tiles, furnished with elegant marble-inlaid mahogany furniture, and decorated with hanging wall scrolls, such that the overall effect was one of a well-to-do and prominent family.

The servant led Jingchen through the reception room and on upstairs, where Liu Tongjun was already waiting for him at the top of the staircase.

"Well, well, I've gotten Tycoon Zhu to come here. The God of Wealth himself!" And he ushered Jingchen into the main parlor. It was furnished in a contemporary western style altogether different from the reception room below: low, semicircular couch upholstered in black leather with peachwood frame; fireplace mantelpiece adorned with a buxom western nude holding a clock on high, whose pendulum swung back and forth across her shoulders; overstuffed wingback chair centered in front of the fireplace (as an imperial throne might overlook an audience hall), apparently reserved for the exclusive use of Liu Tongjun; on the south wall, pleated window drapes held back with gilded tassels. The entire room was light and spacious.

Liu Tongjun was well into his forties, but waved a high pompadour into his hair in the faddish "airplane" style, wore a fashionable Hong Kong style blue-striped linen shirt matched with white slacks and embossed white pointed-toe shoes—the perfect image of some flashy entertainment quarter entrepreneur. In the business world such attire would surely give the impression of a man deficient in reliability. Yet, as a person he was thoroughly modest and amiable, without that overbearing hauteur associated with wealthy scions.

"In years we are the same generation, but in ability, Mr. Zhu, you are my senior. Today we have the pleasure of your company for midday refreshments, which certainly is a great honor for me."

And saying this, Liu Tongjun introduced to Zhu Jingchen each of the several guests. Among them was a certain Mr. Gao, well known in Shanghai as president of the International Club, and although supposedly concerned exclusively with horse racing, tennis, and such (that is to say, unengaged in any proper line of work), he actually was in great demand everywhere. His appearance on this scene was apparently to provide the customary moral support to the host, Liu Tongjun, for otherwise there seemed to be no one in the parlor of a stature sufficient to "exhort the troops to victory," as it were, and that, after all, just wouldn't be right. The others present, so far as Zhu Jingchen could tell, were just ordinary business colleagues, invited solely to enliven the scene. But one among them, a young man with glasses, possessing an air of refinement and astuteness, dressed in a traditional man's long gown of gray fabric, was sitting quietly in a corner and clearly seemed to be of a different caliber; Zhu Jingchen could not restrain himself from taking a good look at him. Liu Tongjun immediately introduced the young man: Tsai Liren, a graduate of Nantong College of Textile Industry and recently engaged by Liu Tongjun as the factory's engineer and concurrent manager.

Factory? Jingchen was taken aback. Hadn't Bounty Textile Mill ceased operations? Where had the present "factory" come from?

"To be perfectly honest, Mr. Zhu," said Liu Tongjun, coming straight to the point, "I want to 'beg a bowl of rice' from you."

It seems that a textile mill located at the inland city of Hangyang was to be put up for sale and Liu Tongjun was interested in acquiring it.

"This mill has seven or eight thousand spindles and about one hundred looms of standard dimension. The selling price is only 300,000—cheap."

Three hundred thousand for a textile mill was cheap, all right. But since the 1931 Mukden Incident when the Japanese began their invasion of Manchuria, Japanese goods had been sold cheap, even dumped in Chinese inland markets. And in the wake of the Japanese attacks on Shanghai early the following year, the Shanghai economy was so depressed that even Liu Tongjun's father had been forced to "lower the curtain and leave the stage"—in short, to retire from the world of business altogether. But now he was itching to take some kind of initiative, such as even reestablishing his factory in the interior. But if this came to be, how could the enterprise at so distant a location be properly managed? Could it be that zeal had the young Mr. Liu a little befuddled?

"I've been mulling it over. I'm a few years too late to make a go of it in the Shanghai area. By the looks of it I'd never squeeze in here, so I don't think I'll even try to. I might as well go inland and start an enterprise there." Liu Tongjun picked up an abacus and began clicking the beads as he elaborated. "I've already done the figuring for it. The ginned cotton used in the weaving process comes directly from the inland villages, and the most important sales of cotton yarn are also right there in the inland market places. So, by setting up a factory in an interior location, savings can be realized in the process of transforming the raw material into the finished product, right? Moreover, there are also regional price differentials. The purchase price of cotton in the interior can be lowered a little below the coastal areas, while the selling price of yarn can be raised a little. So isn't there also a profit to be realized in the buying and selling? And what's more, foreigners occupy a powerful position in Shanghai, so rather than compete with them let's run off and forget 'em. And also, because of cheaper materials and lower production costs in the interior, if we really want to compete with foreigners, we can go all out and slash our prices and still be able to make ends meet." And with that, he clicked a few more beads on his abacus.

Hm, this befuddled zealot made some sense. "But," Jingchen mused aloud, "does Hangyang have electrical generation facilities? It's not like Shanghai, you know, where electricity is supplied by the power company. . . "

"Well..." The young man, who had been silent throughout, now ventured a remark. "I went there and looked around. There's a coal mining operation near Hangyang, so we could resolve on our own the matter of generating electricity. Of course, it would be rather a nuisance."

"The biggest advantage in setting up a factory at an interior location is that labor is much cheaper than in Shanghai. One Shanghai worker is the equivalent of three or four rural workers." Liu Tongjun rattled the abacus, disarranging the rows of beads.

"You've done quite a job figuring on that abacus. But, Mr. Liu," countered Zhu Jingchen, "factories aren't concocted at will simply by flicking abacus beads. First things first: does it make sense to set up a factory in a far-off place beyond the reach of your authority? Besides which, Shanghai has the International Settlement with its own Municipal Council, whereas in the interior bandits will be running wild and sharks will be trying to fleece you—do think you can handle problems like that?"

"We've already thought of these things," laughed Liu Tongjun. "Here, this is Mister Gao," he said, affectedly using the English term. And Mr. Gao, who had been sitting without uttering a word, reserved and haughty, nodded slightly in the direction of Zhu Jingchen. Lin Tongjun continued with an air of self-satisfaction. "Mister Gao has already introduced to me the manager of the Overseas Bank of Belgium, and we've already concluded favorable discussions with him. They will appoint one of their nationals to reside permanently at our factory, thereby authenticating Bounty as a Belgian enterprise. The cost for that service will be 50,000 yuan."

Hm, this International Club president really did have some talent; no wonder he had made the big time in Shanghai business. And even if Liu were more arrogant than he already was, Jingchen would still want to exchange pleasantries with him, for on some future occasion he might prove useful. Jingchen offered his business card to him.

"Do you think this transaction can go through?" asked Liu Tongjun in English. Afraid the conversation might turn to other topics, he cast an inquiring glance at Zhu Jingchen.

Although Liu Tongjun was positioning his chessmen with great skill, he still hadn't really qualified for a loan from Cathay. He'd have to move with utmost care and caution.

"The Japs have created a huge market for their textiles. Are you sure you can outdo them? Besides just lowering your prices, will the quality of your product beat theirs?" Jingchen directed a piercing gaze at the young owner as he looked him up and down.

"On this matter," said Liu Tongjun, turning toward Tsai Liren, "let me have Mr. Tsai provide an explanation. As our chief engineer, he is of course very knowledgeable."

Tsai Liren was a tall, slender man whose pale complexion lent him a certain bookishness, yet without any trace of pedantry, and he spoke with unhurried assurance.

"As to quality, I have complete confidence that we can manufacture a good product. We've formulated strict proportions in the use of constituent materials, and have actually increased certain amounts. For example, sixteen skeins of yarn, each of 80 strands, normally make one bundle of 10.7 pounds. In our factory, we'll weave yarn of 10.9 pounds per bundle, with 83-strand skeins. What does give us some cause for concern now is the loom operators—they're not as well educated or skilled as the workers you can recruit in the Shanghai-Zhejiang area. So we'll strengthen our quality control with a reward and punishment system—bonuses for good workers, fines for bad ones. This way, there'll be no worry about not producing good yarn."

Jingchen stroked his chin as he sized up this young factory manager for whom he was developing real appreciation.

"This Mr. Tsai of ours was at first apprenticed to a craftsman, then he worked in a textile mill for a while, and after that studied on his own. Later he entered the Nantong Textile Institute. This is the sort of person I really like." Seeing Jingchen's admiration for his assistant, Tongjun was much pleased. "his engineer and manager of ours illustrates that overseas study is not a necessity, but what is essential is a knowledge of the entire production process and the larger social environment."

What Liu Tongjun said made sense. When employing people, one must seek this type of realistic person of genuine talent and practical education. Nowadays in hiring at Cathay, it seemed the new people simply had to come from Shanghai University, or from St. John's. Consequently, the new batch of young employees, because they came from families, if not wealthy then at least elite, which were able to get them into Shanghai University or St. John's where they would win showy degrees, were such as would never make it to the top but would never be willing to work at the bottom; they refused to be a nobody, they all had to be a somebody. Consequently, it was like hiring a Buddhist monk who demands respect but won't do any work. Such a situation should never be allowed to develop. The better suited were young men of Tsai Liren's stamp.

Realizing that Liu Tongjun had engaged this factory manager, Jingchen felt a good deal easier about the proposed bank loan, but he still somehow felt that Liu Tongjun, the young prodigal, was, in the last analysis, unreliable. He'd better be careful still. So, in an unhurried manner but with the same uncompromising tone of voice, he inquired further.

"Cathay Republic Bank naturally takes as an obligation assistance to domestic industry and resistance to foreign economic encroachment. Within a few days I'll send someone from the bank to Hanyang to look the site over. What's your company's book value?"

Liu Tongjun smiled slyly, but then went on to explain with candor. "It's no easy matter these days for textile mills to raise funds. Recently we placed an order for weaving and spinning machinery from England, so we should have at the very least 700,000 in operating capital to adequately meet our needs. Our book value is 800,000, but in reality we've raised only 400,000 and that's just not enough money to go around." And again he smiled his crafty smile. Jingchen now realized he'd greatly underrated this foppish young heir, whose astuteness and ability were concealed behind the countenance of a scatterbrained profligate.

"Cathay charges interest on its loans at 1% per month, payable quarterly."

"Couldn't you give more favorable terms?" asked Tongjun, as he began the bargaining process. "Confidentially, a certain Mr. Gong, assistant vice-president in the credit department of Bank of China," he said, dropping the name of the well-funded quasi-government bank, "is watching me like a hawk. They've agreed to extend us a long-term low-interest credit secured on Bounty stock," (he paused momentarily to register Jingchen's reaction, then continued) "but I haven't yet replied to their offer. And the reasons I haven't can be stated candidly and simply. First, my father has always reposed great confidence in Cathay where he's been a long-time depositor. Second, I myself have an inherent dislike for dealings with anyone named Mr. Government. It's easy to figure out what's going on inside the mind of Assistant Vice-President Gong and his people: make the loan and acquire shares, then start meddling and penetrating our company. They've already used this tactic to gain control of a lot of enterprises. That assistant vice-president, Mr. Gong, is full of clever tricks, and his only thought is to get rid of the adjectives in his title and become the president. I can't stomach his type, and I don't relish having any Mr. Government meddle in my business. So today, quite aside from approaching you about a trifling loan from Cathay, I also wanted to invite you to buy shares in the firm. To put it plainly, I have full confidence in Bounty's future. I've already talked with our board of directors about it, and if any of them are uneasy about the future of Bounty they can convert the stock shares to deposit funds, for I am confident that after one or two years the capital will be recovered." Having said this, he patted Jingchen on the sleeve, and with an air of confiding in him, spoke on. "The great difficulty for us is that we don't have our own bank. National finances are at present entirely in the clutches of the Mr. Government types, and while in fact there's an ocean of idle private capital, we can't get the assistance we deserve. Actually our two enterprises—your bank and our mill—could cooperate beautifully with each other, and once Bounty hits its stride it would be the very foundation of Cathay Republic Bank. The fact is, for a country to be strong and prosperous it simply must promote industry, and the development of industry relies on support from the financial community, and the financial community in turn can thrive only if business and industry provide a solid foundation."

What Liu Tongjun said was right on track, even if it did have the flavor of a trade association pronouncement. But the great difficulty was, words that might be right on track when transformed into action all too often get derailed, and a derailing might end up in a disastrous failure. Since the Japanese attack on Shanghai in 1932, the city's financial markets had been extremely skittish—like "a gamebird startled by the mere twang of a bowstring." And when the banks gave out big loans, because of the continual devaluation of the currency, when it came time for banks to collect on large loans they had extended, what they recovered was in reality quite limited. This being the case, Jingchen had determined as an interim policy that Cathay would rely only on its well established depositors and postpone the development of any new accounts. But now, he was himself on the verge of breaking his new rule, so he must treat the proposal with the utmost prudence.

Jingchen expelled a pensive stream of cigarette smoke.

Liu Tongjun had good reason for his self-confidence. Since the 1931 Mukden Incident, a Chinese boycott of Japanese goods had sprung up and now had reached a high tide, giving hope for sales of Chinese-manufactured textiles. Then too, since the government's substitution of the new paper currency for the former silver yuan system, ordinary citizens in the towns and cities throughout the country would tend to make purchases of merchandise that could be stockpiled—and cotton yarn and cloth were just such sorts of merchandise. Every issue invariably had two sides to be considered, and looked at from this angle, Zhu Jingchen might well seize the present opportunity.

"Cotton was originally introduced into China from India, but there is no way to ascertain the date when China actually began its own cotton cultivation. Although Japan has a well developed textile industry, Japan itself lacks the raw material and therefore must rely on cotton imports from China. Other countries—Germany, France, and the United States, for example—also regularly use coarse Chinese cotton flannel. Hitherto cotton was exported in large quantity. What's strange is that in recent years the amount of cotton exports has been steadily decreasing, and yet with the Yellow River and Yangtze River areas under Japanese influence, the import of raw cotton and cotton manufactures is actually increasing year by year." The young engineer-manager Tsai Liren was carrying on an animated conversation to one side with Mr. Gao of the International Club. "Of course there are many reasons for this," Tsai continued, "the most important being, in my opinion, that the Chinese people lack a concept of nationalism. They're like mice who can see only what's under their noses, and seek only the immediate advantage. Businessmen practice deception and have almost completely lost the confidence of the people, who now desire only foreign goods, if reasonably priced and of good quality. Because of this, products from the Bounty Mill need but satisfy these two conditions—confidence and affordability—and for sure we'll be able to start winning back..."

Behind the gaze from Tsai Liren's thin face were eyes which, though not large, sparkled with calm confidence: here was a capable young man, talented yet modest. How Zhu Jingchen wished his own son were such a man!

Jingchen arose and walked over to the fireplace. In all fairness, Cathay Republic Bank had in recent years managed to achieve success one way or another, and had attracted a goodly amount of idle capital, and it definitely needed to find a reliable manufacturing enterprise in which to put its money. Furthermore, that young factory manager Tsai Liren had the bearing of a competent leader.

"In regard to this matter, I'll convene a meeting of the board and discuss it with my colleagues. Once we arrive at a consensus, I'll send someone from the bank to take charge of bookeeping operations and assist in financial affairs."

What? He still wants to supervise our finances? Well, all right. Liu Tongjun retained his composure and adopted the strategy of "feigning friendship to snare the prize." Putting on a smile, he said, "Let's take some refreshments now. We've just hired a chef from Yangzhou—a city famous for its fare, you know. His cooking is quite acceptable." Saying which, he rang the bell and ordered the dishes served.

Jingchen, sensing that the conversation was approaching a climax, would not abandon the pursuit. "We can discuss a long-term, low-interest loan. But...let's all give a little. Starting this fall, Cathay is planning to offer to all new depositors who open accounts of ten yuan or more a large linen handkerchief bearing the words CATHAY REPUBLIC BANK. I hope Bounty would subsidize the expenses incurred for this service."

While Liu Tongjun hesitated, Tsai Liren came forward and readily assented. "Yes. We can stitch along one edge a small label bearing your bank name, and, as our advertising fee, as it were, indicate on the label that the handkerchief is the 'Silver Dollar' brand produced by the Hanyang Division of Bounty Textile Mill."

"Well then, what will you use as collateral for a bank loan? Priced securities or real estate?" Jingchen, satisfied he had bargained them down cheap, maintained a poker face and calmly put forth his second question.

Liu Tongjun instantly leapt to his feet and, half in jest, half in earnest, exclaimed, "Well, Tycoon Zhu, indeed! You're a jumbo thirteen-row abacus incarnate. No one can out-calculate you."

"Even if I am a thirteen-row abacus, when have you ever fallen so much as one bead behind me? Anyway, the beads are metal and hard to move, so I must say it's a very stingy abacus." He crinkled his eyes into a smile at the repartee.

Liu Tongjun thought for a moment. "Would it be satisfactory to Cathay," he offered, "To secure the loan with that home on Hart Road? It's in an excellent section, the 'Golden Corner,' they call it."

"Fine. That's settled then. Close as brothers though we are, we can still strike a deal like businessmen." Jingchen chuckled: in an instant they had reached an agreement orally. Liu Tongjun called the butler in to open the champagne, and as the corks popped one after another, the tense, never-yield-an-inch atmosphere abated and the air turned animated and amiable.

"Mr. Zhu, when will you be a bridegroom?" asked Liu Tongjun with a mischievous grin. "Would you like me to introduce a young lady to you?"

Since the death of his wife, everybody had been most concerned about Zhu Jingchen's remarrying. But as Jingchen was strongly disinclined to talk of private family affairs on an inappropriate public occasion, he merely smiled in reply.

To his surprise, however, Liu Tongjun, now feeling the effects of drink, launched into a prolix oration. "You're afraid that if you invite a new wife into the house, your freedoms will be restricted? Never mind about that. A man has to keep a wife at home in any event, for otherwise home is like a face without eyebrows, and that just isn't right. As the folklore has it, a wife is like a salted croaker, not fresh, unfortunately, but which, like any cured fish, if kept carefully won't spoil and won't give your reputation a bad smell. But a concubine is like a flatfish—nice and fresh, and when asleep in your bed she looks real big and has great appeal; but when she's up and about, one sees how thin she is and how little there is to her, and behind your back people will make unflattering remarks that belittle your reputation. Women outside the home are even more difficult to turn to your advantage. A friend's wife, for example, is like a goldfish, and however beautiful she may be, a gentleman may look but not touch, for the glass goldfish bowl stands between him and the prize. Absolutely the worst kind are prostitutes. You don't dare touch them. They're like blowfish—savory in aroma, delicious in taste, but they're poisonous. If you're not careful with them, you'll come down with a bad case of syphilis, and..."

And he burst into laughter even before finishing his sentence. Although rather coarse, being coarse it was humorous, and Jingchen joined in the merriment.

How he admired these private businessmen. When it came to making money, they could really use their heads, and nothing, even though they might play around with dance-hall girls or indulge in wisecracks, could deflect them from their pursuit of business goals. But a person who made his living in banking had ever to be concerned with that all-important word "credibility" which impelled him, wherever he went, to appear of a formal and serious mien, for to appear otherwise might adversely affect his calling and his future.

"We were all married the old-fashioned way. At eighteen I became a muddleheaded bridegroom, without the foggiest notion of what it was all about." Liu Tongjun scratched his head, sighing as he spoke, his words concealing a touch of sadness.

"Not the foggiest notion?" someone chimed in. "With a new child coming into the world every year without fail, I should say you had a very clear notion of what it was all about." The company had another good laugh. Jingchen glanced at his watch. To remain longer, he felt, would both waste his time and prove a bore. He made an excuse and bade his farewells.

As the host was accompanying Jingchen through the downstairs courtyard, a young lady wearing the McTyeire dark green school uniform happened to walk in from the opposite side. Liu Tongjun introduced her as his eldest daughter Tsaizhen. Since Jingchen himself had an only son who was this year to graduate from the university, he did entertain, though perhaps only half consciously, a certain interest in daughters from suitable families. But one glance at Tsaizhen and he felt that here was a young lady of very ordinary looks without a trace of great-family manners, yet with an erectness of posture showing her to have been cast from the same mold as Liu Tongjun.

Emerging from the Liu residence, Jingchen had his chauffeur, Ayi, drive him directly to the Cotton Exchange to check market conditions. Just now the cotton textile market was extremely bullish: no wonder Liu Tongjun was willing to jump in with so much confidence. It appeared that the venture might well succeed. He decided then and there, that in order to reduce the time for the return of capital and to avoid currency depreciation, it would be best to sign an agreement with Bounty for a loan repayable in stock. Thus he could on the one hand make a low-interest loan to Bounty while on the other acquire shares in textiles, and he could still follow through on the deal for handkerchiefs to be turned out at Bounty's expense, allowing Cathay to save on its own advertising expenses. Of course whether in the end this transaction would make or lose money, there was no one who could speak with complete assurance. Life was, after all, a journey filled with chance opportunity, and doesn't everybody like to play at games of chance?

Rain began pattering down, not big drops—more like a misty drizzle.

"Drive over to Ferry Road," he said to his driver.

A bank employee had died. As president and a member of the board of directors, Jingchen could have acted as if it were no particular concern of his, and just dispatched his secretary, Mrs. Zhong, to present his business card and offer a pension to the deceased family, and that would be the end of it. But Jingchen had always considered that, while it may not have been obligatory to put in an appearance at a colleague's wedding, a funeral or encoffening ceremony did require his presence to show the sympathy of the bank staff.

Bankers are said to eat from silver rice bowls, so lucrative their profession is assumed to be, but it is by no means the case that the rice bowls in their hands are made from silver. Take, for example, this long-time teller, Mr. Fan, recently deceased at forty-odd years of age. Thinking back on it, Zhu Jingchen recalled that he and Old Fan had started at the bank as trainees in the same year; one had risen to president, while the other, tragically, had remained a bottom-level employee. A son of Old Fan had been pursuing his studies at Shanghai College of Commerce which doubtless placed a heavy burden on the father, who last year began coughing up blood and, quite unexpectedly, endured only one more year before he just up and died.

The Fans lived on a narrow, shabby alley. Right smack at the alley entrance was a public urinal whose stench on a drizzly day like this hung heavy in the air. Waste cooking water and garbage clogged the back-door gutter of noodle shops and was overflowing everywhere, mixing with the rain water. It was spongy and sticky underfoot, and positively nauseating to Jingchen, who felt no interest in determining any further what made his footfall so squishy.

A wood gate, its slats hanging all awry, was banging in the wind. The Fans lived in a type of two-story alley house which had small, poorly lit rooms. Jingchen groped his way to the front parlor where incense was burning, and saw only that all the furniture had been piled up against one wall to transform their cramped living quarters into a funeral parlor. The deceased, wrapped in a burial shroud, was laid out on a bier, his head oriented toward the south. Right nearby was a rosewood side table for holding the incense paraphernalia. There was barely enough room to pass between the corpse and the side table, yet that was the only passageway into the room. So small was the room that the bier was pushed up right against the frame of the casement window, which made it impossible to swing the two sashes all the way shut, thus leaving a crack in the middle. As the light rain pattered against the window panes, Jingchen noticed that some fell in through the crack onto the spotless shoes of the deceased, and, having now rained for some little time, his black shoes were covered with beads of moisture.

Tears welled up in Jingchen's eyes as strong feelings of compunction came over him: the lives of Cathay's workers were so very harsh; at the very least the bank should operate an employee dormitory to make things easier for them.

Old Mr. Fan was stretched out on the bier, his eyes tightly shut, his face wearing that same harried, tired expression as in life. Jingchen's overall impression of him was a gaunt-shouldered man hunching over his abacus on the teller's counter, the way he had passed his entire life—a life both ordinary and impoverished.

"Sleep well, Old Fan," Jingchen spoke to the corpse; "sleep well. You are so very tired."

On this rainy day, darkness gathered early. Light from a street lamp in the narrow alley penetrated the murky curtain of rain, which seemed like tears of sorrow, passed dully through the rectangular panes of the windows and on into the room. And light from a table lamp dimly illuminated the room as rain drops continued their ceaseless patter against the glass. It gave one a bleak and chilly feeling. The corpse's shoes were again covered with a sheet of moisture. Jingchen lacked all courage to look at Mrs. Fan. She had already been completely overcome by grief, and two sons, not yet grown up, were pressing up against her. Fatherless children, widowed mother—what terrible desolation.

The back door creaked open, and a young man, tall of stature, holding a dripping oilcoth umbrella, came in. He was the deceased's eldest son, Fan Yangzhi, the very one who was studying at Shanghai College of Commerce. It would seem that the household had now only him alone on whom to depend for sustenance.

Jingchen spoke briefly with him conveying sympathy, for which Fan Yangzhi thanked him, with an expression neither obsequious nor supercilious. He noticed, without directly looking, that Jingchen placed an envelope on the table—an envelope containing pension money.

"It's extremely kind of Mr. Zhu to come here personally on a rainy day like today. If your father—may his soul rest in peace—only knew of it, he'd be so comforted." Mrs. Fan was speaking to her son, displeased that he did not show more humility before Mr. Zhu.

"Yes, indeed. When Father was still alive, Mr. Zhu, he often spoke of how in the beginning you and he were both trainees. Back then you used to call at New Year's and eat dumpling soup with us. Later on at every New Year's Dad would always have Mother fix Ningbo-style dumplings and if you had continued to come, Dad would have been so happy, and would have had so many things to talk with you about."

The nerve! Fan Yangzhi was clearly blaming Jingchen for not having shown more concern for his father while still alive. Little might one think that the honest and diligent Old Fan could have raised a son so acerbic as this! Jingchen raised his eyes and sized up the son, who returned the gaze with equal reserve.

Having no further interest in staying, Jingchen awkwardly bade farewell and left.

On the way back he began thinking again about that bank employees' dormitory that had all along been troubling him. A few years ago the board of directors had had the same idea—build Cathay's own housing complex in order to improve the living standards of bank employees. Jingchen had actually located a lot of about one and a half acres out Robison Road way beyond the International Settlement; but it was priced at that time at about 3000 ounces of silver and the cost of construction would bring the project's cost to about 60,000 altogether—a figure which was too large, so in the end the deal was not completed. Furthermore, in recent years purchasing power had been steadily dwindling, for-sale and for-rent notices on empty buildings were appearing with increasing frequency, so that to have undertaken then a large housing construction project would have been like throwing money away. Pity Zhu Jingchen was not God who could give aid without expecting repayment, but an ordinary banker who could not use Cathay's money for pure philanthropy.

The rain fell more heavily and soon became a downpour. Poor Fan; alas, even in death he had not found peace.

Chapter 3

Liu Tongjun's wife, Ruan Syimei, used the third floor parlor as her private room. Because the Liu house had been specially planned and built for them, even the third floor was spacious in its design. A high-quality teak furniture set had been custom made by Mao Chuantai Furniture Co. to fit the room dimensions; that was twenty years ago when she was a new bride and when the furniture was the very latest style. Ruan Syimei, now thirty-six, with delicate features and smooth white skin, was actually a handsomer woman than her daughter Liu Tsaizhen. The Ruan family was prominent in Suzhou, and as a youngster Ruan Syimei studied at the exclusive Jingyuan Girls School in Suzhou; at sixteen, muddleheaded, she married into the Liu family of Nantong. Everyone said it was a perfect match—the two families being of comparable economic and social standing. Syimei alone thought it a thoroughly imperfect match: her husband was forever out drinking and fooling around with dance-hall girls. Fortunately he'd never brought a concubine into the house to be planted before her very eyes all day long, and she'd heard that he didn't have a permanent mistress somewhere else either. So let it be—she was happy enough that inside the house itself she was the only one who counted.

At this moment she was sitting at a tea table with just her maid, Ahsong, chatting as she folded pieces of tinfoil paper to be used as ritual money. The Lius were very attentive to tradition, and at year's end there were sacrifices to be made to deceased ancestors too numerous to enumerate, and however much tinfoil paper she had, she never seemed to have enough. She was wearing a mandarin dress of silver-gray silk with black polka-dots which clearly revealed the protruding abdomen of a woman already five months pregnant.

"Mr. Liu hasn't returned yet? Who knows where the hell he may have run off to this time," said Ruan Syimei with a frown. Being pregnant she could afford to flaunt her temper and act the spoiled child. Pity was, only the chambermaid Ahsong was here to pay her heed.

"To celebrate the reopening of Bounty Mill today, Mr. Liu is hosting a banquet at the International Hotel. But I really must tell you, ma'am," continued Ahsong, affecting a troubled expression, "you're a little bit too easy going. On occasions like these, you need to, well, be forthright in making your position known, and not let anyone think you're not the real thing. When all is said and done, you're still Madam Liu." And Ahsong stuck her thumb up to show she was the number one lady in the house.

But Mrs. Liu languidly gestured in disagreement, pointing to her stomach. "And go out into public in this condition?"

"Ma'am," Ahsong protested, "going out when you're pregnant like this is just the way to show your pride and spirit."

"Mom!" Liu Tsaizhen had returned home for the weekend from school and, as was her habit, had come to her mother's room to pay her respects.

"Oh, you're back." Since her marriage, Mrs. Liu had been having children almost yearly. She had already given birth to six, and each new one was simply handed over to a nurse—six children, six nurses—who alone looked after the child's welfare, while she herself had come to resemble an old layer hen, which, after laying an egg, was totally unconcerned and made no further inquiries. Thus, after this long a period, her feelings toward the children were so thoroughly dilute that none of the emotion associated with what people call "maternal love" was aroused in her. That is why Mrs. Liu kept folding her tinfoil without so much as looking up to her eldest daughter. It was actually Ahsong who maintained a sporadic conversation about school matters, like how's the food, what's it like studying that foreign Bible, and so on.

Mrs. Liu pressed her temples with her fingertips, complaining of a headache. Ahsong knew that madam was irritable. Trying to ingratiate herself, she glanced at the chime clock in the corner and exclaimed, "Oh, it's almost time. I'll turn on the radio. Today they're doing that Shaosying opera, 'Liu Yi Rescues the Dragon Maiden,'" and she eagerly twisted the dials. Mrs. Liu began humming along. Liu Tsaizhen seemed now to have been set aside and forgotten, but to leave would not be right, while to stay would be awkward.

"Mrs. Yang has come accompanied by Miss Yu," someone announced.

Mrs. Yang and Mrs. Liu were both mahjong partners and Shaosying opera enthusiasts, and both their husbands liked to chase skirts. Whenever the two women got together, they'd say, practically in unison, "I'm so angry..." and there followed a long heart-to-heart talk. Miss Yu was now a star in the popular opera in Shanghai, specializing in young male roles. People called her the "Little Diva" and a staging of "Liu Yi Rescues the Dragon Maiden" had become all the rage. Her elegant stage make-up and flamboyant costuming enthralled Mrs. Liu, who every day, from her reserved fifth-row center seat, cheered her on, and had sent backstage to her every day a huge basket of flowers. Little had she thought that today Mrs. Yang would bring Miss Yu here to her home. In an instant Mrs. Liu livened up.

"Show them in. Be quick about it!"

Then, realizing her daughter was still standing there like a wooden pole, she impatiently dismissed her. After that she sent Ahsong off to fetch the two suits of colorfully brocaded theater costumes for young male roles, which she had bought for Miss Yu.

Tsaizhen knew that ever since her mother had become so fond of Miss Yu, she had all the more diminished in her mother's eyes. And so she tactfully withdrew.

Tsaizhen and her younger sister went to the west wing. She also had an elder brother, Rubin, who was studying law at Shanghai University. The Liu family favored the son and denigrated the daughters, and Rubin was indulged like a little emperor, and changed his girl friends with kalidoscopic speed. Consequently, even on weekends she rarely met up with him.

Seeing that it was only about four o'clock, she reflected that at school it would be just the hour for free activities. Although she had no gift for social small talk and, furthermore, knew that her classmates rather looked down on her, nonetheless she preferred living at school, where, at the very least, she could hear all the latest gossip. It wasn't at all like at home which did have quite a few people, where, indeed, the family reunion dinner on the lunar New Year's Eve would require two heavily laden tables. But on ordinary days it was each person for himself, and even the servants, if you didn't ring the bell for them, were never in sight. The whole house lay in vast stillness.

Liu Tsaizhen sat down at her desk and pulled out her homework. While she felt she had gradually managed to fit in with life at this pretentious private school, the studies themselves were still a real strain. But she felt that if she just kept applying herself, then she would in future...well, it would be a good future and a much better life than she now had.

It certainly was no easy matter getting through her English lessons, only then to be assailed with history. What a headache. The textbooks were all the original English-language editions, so it was difficult enough just reading them let alone understanding the contents.

"Tsaizhen." Only a camera hanging around his neck was all to be seen of Rubin, who called in to her from outside the door. "Mom wants you," he said with a secretive expression.

"Whose picture were you taking?" asked Liu Tsaizhen inquisitively.

"Mom and Miss Yu, that opera singer. Mom bought two sets of stage costumes for her. I used a whole roll of film shooting them from every angle. Our mother sure likes to spend money for that Miss Yu. Today, even besides those two new costumes, she gave her a really fine pearl-inlaid bracelet. She doesn't even treat her own daughters as well as that."

How true it was. Liu Tsaizhen hung her head in silence.

"You're too kind. Why don't you sisters go and have it out with her?"

"What good would that do?" replied the timid Tsaizhen. "She never wanted us in the first place."

"What do you mean it wouldn't do any good? If you confront her, she'll notice you more, but if you say nothing, she'll think you don't exist at all," said Rubin impatiently. "You'd better get on up there; she's calling you." Rubin hesitated a moment, then said with hidden meaning, "It's time you went and confronted her; you can't let yourself be a lump of dough to be kneaded by someone else."

No sooner had those words left his lips than Ahsong popped her head in at the door to urge her on. "Miss Tsaizhen, Madam is calling for you."

Mrs. Liu's room still had the uncleared remains of refreshments on the table. The guests had already departed, yet a heavy fragrance suffused the atmosphere—a fragrance quite unlike those to which Tsaizhen was accustomed at McTyeire. The McTyeire girls also applied perfume, but of a gentle aroma, agreeable whether subtle or obvious. Tsaizhen couldn't stand the perfume that assailed her nostrils now, and as soon as she stepped into the room she sneezed violently.

"Tsaizhen. Mrs. Yang has invited us to Kangle Restaurant for dinner tomorrow. She's making a match for you," announced Mrs. Liu when Tsaizhen appeared. "The young man is from the Li family which owns the Yuanfeng Counting House. Their home is on Great Western Road, an enormous wood-frame structure. Their garden alone is like walking into Jessfield Park with all those trees..."

Liu Tsaizhen was stunned, for it certainly had never crossed her mind that she needed to find a husband. If her classmates at McTyeire learned of this, especially her roommates Syi Zhishuang and Zhu Juanmin, there's no telling how they might rib her.

"No..." she said in a practically inaudible refusal. Then, recalling her brother's urging her to "have it out" with her mother, she plucked up her courage and announced, "I'm planning to go on to college."

"What? Go to college?" And her mother stared at her uncomprehendingly, as if she were listening to a tall tale. "You actually want to go to college? What for!"

What for? Tsaizhen couldn't answer.

"Here, there's a few steamed dumplings on the table still hot. Why don't you eat them." Perhaps because she'd had matters to discuss concerning her daughter today, Mrs. Liu exhibited seldom seen concern.

The steamed dumplings were half cold and hardly steamy, but Tsaizhen was disinclined to defy her mother, so she took a perfunctory bite of one and found it flavorless.

The mother continued her questioning. "Why should girls go to college just to learn a lot of fancy ideas?"

Tsaizhen could not come up with any convincing reply. She just felt the reason was so simple, just like buying cloth—whether it was sixty cents per foot or eighty cents per foot or one yuan per foot: if she liked it, well then, she bought it. That was the reason. And since she could afford college, why not go to college?

"Mr. Liu? Did you go and ask him in?" Mrs. Liu addressed her impatience to Ahsong. "A moment ago we heard his car honking; why is it he hasn't come up yet?"

"I think we should talk about it again after I've completed college." Liu Tsaizhen forced herself to take issue with her mother, but unfortunately she spoke too softly for anyone to hear.

There was the flop-flop of slippers and Liu Tongjun came in, draped in a patterned dressing robe of satin brocade, a cross expression on his face.

"What is it? I've just gotten back from a dinner party and haven't even had time yet to smoke a cigarette," he said.

"There are family matters that also require your attention. Tsaizhen is nineteen now, and Mrs. Yang came to call shortly ago..."

The name had no sooner been uttered than Liu Tongjun broke in irritably. "That damned Mrs. Yang again—social scum, as low as a stage actress. You'd do well to have less contact with the likes of her. And you'd do well to have less contact with that opera person, too.

Those people are as bad as con artist criminals. You just now gave her costumes and jewelry, didn't you? Fine thing. I kill myself trying to make money while you wildly spend it till I haven't a cent left. However much I make, it still is no use..."

"Strange," said Mrs. Liu, arms now akimbo; "the money I use is the money from my dowry and my own relatives. Do you control that? And for your part, you fritter away all kinds of money on those dance-hall girls of yours at the Pleasure Gate and have I ever so much as muttered one word in protest? Shit!"

To allow his wife in the presence of his daughter to ridicule him openly was more than Liu Tongjun could accept. The veins stood out on his neck as he shot back, "The money I make I'll spend anyway I choose. You think the bit of money you brought with you from your family would last your whole life? You really thought that in coming into my Liu family you were moving into a gold mine, didn't you?"

"Huh! You still have the nerve to boast of 'my Liu family?' Who in all Shanghai doesn't know that you, Liu Tongjun, weren't adopted from an orphanage? A bastard child, baseborn and fatherless."

Ahsong and Tsaizhen had by now quietly slipped away. In the corridor Tsaizhen again bumped into Rubin bounding down the stairs with a tennis racket in his hand.

"It's all your fault," she scolded. "You told Daddy that Mom had given some things to Miss Yu, and that's got them arguing again."

Rubin laughed with unconcern. "We'd better let Dad keep the reins on her, otherwise she'll give all our money away for nothing. Mom's really out of it. If I were Dad, I never could have taken to her."

"What talk!" exclaimed Tsaizhen resentfully.

"Let them have a good fight," Rubin laughed. "If they're fighting, won't they forget all about that matchmaking business?"

Tsaizhen returned to her room, but had no mind for homework.

"Out!"

Through the opened window came an affectedly sweet voice using English to call an out-of-bounds ball. The voice belonged to a neighbor girl, who was playing tennis with Rubin in the back yard. The girl was wearing white slacks, which outlined her long graceful legs to good advantage. From time to time she emitted laughter like a string of silver bells. But Tsaizhen couldn't figure out what she found worth laughing about.

The steamless steamed dumplings she'd just eaten were now causing trouble in her stomach. Fortunately Tsaizhen was not one of those sensitive and thoughtful young ladies, for if she were and considered her situation carefully, she might have realized that the entirety of her nineteen years of life was just like that bowl of dumplings: meticulously prepared but unpalatable withal. And just as she had mindlessly gulped down those dumplings, so too she had mindlessly accepted the unpalatable life God had arranged for her.

Chapter 4

Felicity Village was a residential area of what are called "new-style alley-houses" located in the Robison Road area, whose construction was just completed in 1931. Consequently the rows of brown brick property walls with their decorative white brick strips were still very fresh and new. Leading up to the front door of each home was a flight of three red-brick steps, and the brass address plate above each main gate was still bright and glossy. While these homes could not compare with the luxurious mansions of the rich, they did nonetheless count as creditable residences of Shanghai's upper- middle class.

A short, chunky fellow with a sunburned face, leading a teenaged country girl, came up to the door of the house at No. 25.

"Now you just keep in mind, people of our class can only go in by the back entrance. Being a maid for people is nothing easy, so you just pay attention and learn your job and everything will be okay for you. Otherwise, instead of escaping from life's misery, you'll just get sent back to the countryside to work in the fields." Such was the advice of Lu, a custodian in Felicity Village.

From the open kitchen window came the sounds of cooking, and a heavy white cloud fragrant with frying fish curled outward, so appetizing that the fellow couldn't resist taking a few sniffs.

The fellow called in softly through the kitchen window, "Mrs. Syi!"

"Hey, Lu's here!" The back door opened with a creak, and there at the stove with a spoon in her hand stood Mrs. Syi, wearing an apron over her checked mandarin dress.

"Mrs. Syi, you called me. What can I do for you?" Even though it was only the kitchen, Lu did not presume to go right in and sit down, but stood beside the sturdy work table, hands at his sides.

Just at this moment Mrs. Syi was absorbed in dealing with the two carp in her wok. Each a good foot long, as soon as the flesh came in contact with the hot oil, their stomachs bulged way out. Mrs. Syi carefully lifted them with her spatula, then, bright faced from the hot stove, she looked up and instructed the oldish maid, Zhou, "Next time, if you just put two pieces of straw about an inch long underneath the fish, it'll keep the skin from burning." She next spooned up some of the juice to taste, then distributed mushrooms evenly around in the pan.

Lu speculated to himself: if little Lianzi here can just learn at the hands of this able matron for two years, she'll have it made for sure.

"You'll have to pay close attention," said Lu to the girl. "These Shanghai people have made cuisine an art, not like you country people who just cook it done and figure that's all there is to it."

"Hm, this little lady seems bright and lively; is she a relative of yours? Has she come to Shanghai just for the fun of it or to earn her living?" Mrs. Syi carefully placed the fish onto a purple-edged white platter as she took stock of the girl. Although she had sun-darkened skin, she had delicately chiseled features, and one rather liked her just at first sight.

"This is a niece of mine, little Lianzi. She hasn't seen much of life, but she's an honest girl," said Lu, putting in a good word for her. "I hope you'll keep an eye out for her, and if you'd help by recommending her when some suitable family might be looking for a maid, well, ma'am, I certainly would be most thankful to you."

Mrs. Syi let out a sigh, for by any normal measure she herself ought to have such a helper at hand who could run errands and help with this or that; Zhou, after all, was stuck in the kitchen cooking three meals a day and washing and wiping—quite unable to leave that work, in addition to which there was this three-story house that had to be kept clean, and buying rice and oil and salt and kindling, running around delivering little presents to friends: for all of that she needed a helper. But unfortunately, nowadays didn't every family have to be extra careful with its money? So then, about this girl, she dared not even think about hiring her and so her own life would unavoidably be just a little harder.

"Lu, prices these days are out of whack," said Mrs. Syi, shaking her head back and forth with a pained sigh. "Before, when I got married, one ounce of gold was worth eighteen silver dollars, but now things are bad and everybody is ringing their hands just trying to make it from one day to the next."

"Gosh, if people like Mrs. Syi have such tales of woe, then how can the likes of us possibly eke out a living?" Lu was saddened by the knowledge that her favorite niece's hopes would come to naught.

"Lu, could I trouble you again today? Zhishuang won't be returning home this Sunday so I want you to take her some things to eat. If you'd just be good enough to hurry off now, the food will still be hot."

The residents of Felicity Village were far removed from the owners of grand mansions, and most did not have maids and butlers, so whenever some errand might come up, it was the normal practice to request one or another of the Felicity Village custodians to get it done.

Another voice now called at the back window; this time it was Mrs. Tsao, who lived just across the way. Mr. Tsao also worked at Cathay Republic Bank, where he and Mr. Syi were from the beginning both department heads. Because Cathay did not operate its own dormitory, employees of specified rank were paid a extra sum by the bank as a housing allowance, and each employee himself found accommodations that would be appropriate to his professional status and personal reputation. By chance Felicity Village, located in the Robison Road area had been constructed not long before. But in early 1932 when the Japanese were in the midst of an attack on Shanghai, real estate went into a slump, so as an inducement the landlord agreed to rent the houses with no payment for the first six months. The Syi and Tsao families thereupon moved in and took up residence and found the places practical and convenient so that neither ever entertained any thought of moving out. But during the last few years, because he had studied overseas and spoke fluent English, Mr. Syi inevitably won rapid promotions, so a certain unavoidable ill feeling existed between the two neighbors. Yet the Syis and Tsaos were cultured and respectable people, and outwardly the two families got along with each other very cordially.

Mrs. Tsao was holding a dish of pickled vegetables. "Mrs. Syi, I've just opened a crock of home-pickled potherb mustard greens. Zhishuang is coming back today, so I picked out some for her to try. At that foreign school she goes to they probably don't get delicacies like this."

And sure enough, the greens heaped on the fancy decorated dish were a fresh, almost transparent green, and meticulously garnished with bright red shredded chili peppers—colors and flavors matched to perfection.

"Why, thank you, Mrs. Tsao. It's very kind of you to think of her. As it happens, though, she said she isn't coming back this week. Graduation is coming up soon so they're busy at school with choral practice and other things, so she's really too busy to spare the time to come home. Anyway I was just about to send Lu off with some food. Lu, take this dish along too. Pickled vegetables are particularly refreshing on days like these."

Mrs. Tsao cast her gaze on the platter laden with two foot-long carp. "Does Zhishuang really have an appetite as large as that? Can she polish off two fish?"

"Neither she nor her roommate, the Zhu daughter, is returning home. The daughter's mother is dead and Mr. Zhu is such a busy person. I imagine there isn't anyone who might think of sending a little food to her, so I thought I might just as well cook up a double portion so the girls can have a pleasant meal together."

"Yes, of course. The daughter of the bank president requires special consideration all across the board," replied Mrs. Tsao with deliberate ambiguity. Mrs. Syi understood her temperament was just this way, though her character was not bad. So she simply smiled and took no offense.

"That's fine, Lu. Now hurry off so she'll get it still hot. Here's money for the rickshaw fare going and returning, and here's a little extra to buy yourself some wine." Mrs. Syi had always been a generous, open-minded person, and always tipped servants very liberally.

Lu set off, happy with the extra pocket money he'd earned. Mrs. Tsao judged the color of the sky and, figuring her husband would soon be leaving work, bustled back home.

With approaching summer the days were gradually lengthening and even now as the clock chimed five, the sun still shone bright. This was the bank's closing hour. Mrs. Syi undid her apron, and standing before the big dressing mirror in the corridor, smoothed back her hair.

She was one of those women whose age is difficult to guess. Her hair, coiled into an S-shaped bun, was still thick and glossy black, while her skin was smooth and white—a woman apparently thirty-odd years, not yet forty, just the age you'd expect for a housewife. Yet her movements and her dress seemed rather too elderly for that. Exquisite jade earrings—two droplets of green—very appropriately distinguished her status as wife of an assistant vice-president. Their ground-floor parlor furniture of intricately carved mahogany was immaculately clean and polished to a lustrous red. Their belongings, even if not luxurious, were certainly not without taste, and betokened a household whose circumstances were on the rise.

When at leisure, Mrs. Syi was fond of sitting in this room and, adopting the eye of an outsider, would critically scrutinize with utmost objectivity this precious world of hers. She would chide herself time and again: this really doesn't add up to much, there are plenty of homes more opulent than this. She was in fact a thousand percent content with her own present situation, and the reason she was always producing these vague feelings of unease—dread, even—was that she sensed her life to be too fortunate. It brought to mind the adage, "When the moon is full it can only wane." This dread dissipated only when she was surrounded by her husband, daughter and son. Regrettably, each of the family had his own affairs so that she was alone at home during much of the day. Consequently this mysterious dread gnawed away at her vexiously and without let-up. Mrs. Syi had never learned to read, and so was unable to take up books and newspapers to while away her leisure hours. Of course she could listen to the radio, but her husband did not like listening to Shaosying opera, Kunchu opera, and things of that sort, recognizing that these had appeal only to mere residents of alley houses. And so she did not indicate her own liking for such music, and even when her husband was not at home, she still did not listen to those programs. Her husband had already reached the level of assistant vice-president, and so she had to have something of the bearing of an assistant vice-president's wife. She was not literate and had had bound feet during her youth—matters largely beyond her control. But in other respects she tried her utmost to measure up to an assistant vice-president's wife. That her husband did not ignore her was her great good fortune, but, given these deficiencies in her background, she felt she had always to be careful of sensitivities, and do nothing to undermine her husband's reputation.

She was bent over her work, stitching soles onto cloth shoes, when she seemed to hear the indistinct sounds of the neighbor's door opening and closing as the husband was welcomed home from work, while her own home remained all too desolate and cheerless. She looked up at the sky: the slanting rays of the sun were already disappearing in the west. Today her daughter was not returning, her son was at rehearsal for a school play, so that this weekend evening would be lonely and cheerless, and now with no sign of her husband's return, she began to feel anxious.

Then of a suddden came the familiar sound of jaunty footsteps approaching the front gate, and before she knew it, she heard the clink of the key in the lock, and in came Zhishuang.

"Well, little girl, how is it you're back? Didn't you say you wouldn't be returning? I even went to the trouble of having Lu take some food over to you. How come you've changed your mind on the spur of the moment without even so much as telephoning first? How many times have I told you, when something comes up, give us a ring. It's so convenient and..."

"What a pain!" Zhishuang didn't seem very happy today: she was wearing an angry expression as if to say "You owe me a lot but I'm getting only a little," and she stomped upstairs in a huff. A moment later she could be heard yelling to Zhou to heat the bath water, to get her slippers, to...

Well, Mrs. Syi had to admit, it was she who had raised this daughter, so she had to put up with her. If in the future her son might take as a wife a woman of this sort, mother would certainly thank son not to bring her home. To invite into one's family a young woman requiring the pampering and respect due the goddess Guanyin—who could put up with that? The fault lay entirely with Mr. Syi who had spoiled her: sending her to that expensive school; in this lane there was only one girl—Zhishuang—who went to such an expensive school. What was the point? She studied to broaden her outlook, only to ruin her temper!

Some time after, she heard the sound of shoes being wiped on the mat outside the door: Mr. Syi had returned. He scuffed his shoes back and forth a few times, opened the door and came in.

Syi Zhensyu was a man of great refinement, wearing a faille-cloth Western-style suit, carrying the jacket in the crook of his arm, not yet having had the time to remove from his sleeves the two black sleeve garters; his glossy hair was combed back not one strand out of place. Compared to his wife, he was a good deal younger and much more stylish. But today his face seemed to wear a worried expression.

Mrs. Syi handed him a steaming towel. She had already sensed that her husband had something on his mind, but she was not anxious to press him.

She waited until he had changed into shorts and a short-sleeve shirt, and put on straw sandals, then brought him a bowl of lily-bud soup, which she had cooled in water from the public well. Finally she sat down next to her husband, and, leaning toward him, picked up a big Ningbo fan made of banana leaf and gently wafted it for him. She then began a sporadic account of her day.

"...Zhishuang—that girl! She said she wouldn't be coming home this week, so I went to the trouble of sending off Lu with some food for her, only to have her return after all..."

Syi Zhensyu sipped the refreshing soup. Her patter seemed somehow like a slowly running stream trickling over his brow, and finally the tension in his knitted eyebrows relaxed. As the saying goes, with a worthy wife in the home, all affairs will proceed smoothly.

"Oh by the way, today Lu brought over a girl from Yangzhou. A pretty girl with an intelligent face. I really thought of hiring her. Next year Zhishuang will be studying at the university and coming home every day. You have no idea just how troublesome that daughter of ours is. All her dresses need ironing, all her shoes need polishing... With just Zhou and me, we'd never have the time to give her the least bit of help! But on second thought, I just let it go. Let's wait until then to consider it. If we take on another servant," she continued, leisurely figuring the accounts, "our expenses for water and electricity will go up, not to mention the increased monthly expense for wages..."

"Well, in my view," Mr. Syi interrupted, "there's no need to save such a small amount. Pretty soon I'll be traveling inland on business, and I'm afraid it'll be for quite a while."

"What? You have to go on another business trip?"

Because he was the only bank employee who had been a genuine overseas student studying economics, he was given heavy responsibilities at Cathay, and was regularly sent to other cities to represent the bank in loan negotiations and other matters. Unfortunately ever since the January 28th Incident of 1932 when the Japanese attacked Shanghai, everyone was on edge, and Syi Zhensyu was, after all, in his mid-forties, so that to have to go off once again caused Mrs. Syi much unease.

"There's little help for that. The rule at Cathay is, 'The able get overworked, while the inept sit back and relax.'" Zhensyu's resentment began to spill out, for he had never been pleased with this state of affairs.

Because Cathay Bank had made loans to Bounty Textile Mill and had acquired some of its stock, the bank's credit department wanted to have someone make an on-site visit to ascertain the strengths of the company, and, while he was at it, to take care of some matters dealing with agricultural loans in the same area. This mission fell to Assistant Vice-President Syi.

"It's beyond my comprehension why the bank, which employs plenty of energetic young people, should of all things send an old man like me. What's Mr. Zhu thinking of? What's the idea of keeping those young people in reserve like concubines? It's not as if he were aging whisky." Syi Zhensyu angrily rapped his fan against the arm of his rattan chair.

"Well, then, the president has great respect for you," said Mrs. Syi to console her husband.

"I've taken on all kinds of assignments like this and people are actually saying nasty things about me. You know what Sky-Tile next door is saying behind my back?" The more he spoke, the more agitated

Zhensyu became, as he motioned with his lips in the direction of the Tsao home.

The "sky tile" in question referred to none other than Tsao Jiusin. Small pox had left a few scars on his face, so his colleagues jokingly likened him to the mahjong "sky" tile whose design somewhat resembled pockmarks, and from long usage it had simply become his nickname, now absent of any derisive connotation.

"He says that because Mr. Zhu's eldest daughter and Zhishuang are such good friends, that whenever cushy jobs come up, the president selects me for them. Heaven knows these assignments are a damn pain, but I can't refuse them when my turn comes up. Anyway, to get back to my point, when Sky-Tile's turn comes for one of these jobs, he just can't manage them. These outdated people from counting house backgrounds can't even write ABC, so getting them to handle loan business would be as useful as having a dead crab do it."

The employees at Cathay had always been divided into two camps: those who had studied overseas or who had majored in commerce and banking at Chinese universities, and those who had had apprentice backgrounds in the traditional counting houses and had worked their way up through the ranks. The former knew English and had a solid grasp of economic principles, while the latter were conservative old-timers who, because they were well connected with the merchants and manufacturers in the business world, possessed their own undeniable abilities. Consequently neither camp would yield to the other and there was constant contention between the two.

Zhensyu continued his angry account. "I just can't understand why so savvy a man as Mr. Zhu should actually willingly keep on that bunch of old, muddle-headed staffers!"

"But," he said, changing the subject with a certain self-satisfaction, "this time will be a good trip. In Hanyang the bank operates a training class, and I'll be going there to lecture to the trainees. The eighty-yuan salary supplement is no big deal, but at least it shows the bank has no qualms about my qualifications to handle the assignment. So presumably I won't have any trouble later on getting promoted to associate vice-president. But don't talk about any of these things to Mrs. Tsao next door. You women are all alike—once you get going, you can't stop talking until you've pulled your heart right out of your chest and revealed everything in it!"

"Watch what you're saying!" retorted Mrs. Syi irritably.

"Another thing. When I'm away this time, it may be that some depositors will take advantage of the opportunity to come with presents and ask for favors, but don't you accept any presents, not even a single thread. And if they still keep pestering you, well, don't pay any attention to them; it'll be enough if you just tell them to look me up personally. Understand?"

As assistant vice-president in the credit department, Mr. Syi did not lack for businessmen and industrialists who came with presents and entreaties, in hopes that when it came time to negotiate loans the terms might be a bit easier. But Mr. Syi had no recourse in such circumstances but to be absolutely unequivocal.

"What's this? You think you married me only yesterday?" retorted Mrs. Syi angrily. "Oh, just because we country people can't read, so we don't know anything that's going on, huh?"

When his wife spoke self-righteously, her expression was endearingly petulant. Mr. Syi couldn't help reaching over to caress the smooth, creamy skin on the nape of her neck. Not a few of his colleagues felt sorry for him because of his marriage, and there were even those well intentioned fellows who tried to think of ways of tricking him into revealing his true feelings in order to authenticate that his marriage was a misfortune. Who could have guessed that his wife was in fact worth more to him than gold itself.

"Don't get angry. Let's just be a little careful, that's all. By the way, have you noticed? Our daughter has grown into quite a graceful maiden. Later on she'll probably cause us a good deal of worry. This year she's planning on starting college, which is fine by me. We'll certainly want her to study at one of the missionary schools, like St. John's University or Shanghai University or maybe even send her abroad to study. And she still has to take life's big plunge into marriage... We'll all have to be very careful about considering her best interests. And Chengzu keeps growing up, too. In matters like these we can't engage in speculative investment, but we can't treat them as just ordinary business either. I've got to be as conscientious as possible—try to earn a little bit more in salary and work like an ox for our children."

"It's so hard on you," Mrs. Syi said to her husband with genuine sympathy.

Mr. Syi patted her hand lightly. "If this year I can get promoted to associate vice-president and keep working until retirement age, I should certainly be able to rise to division manager. That way when I finally get my retirement payment, it will be a very considerable sum. And once I have it in hand I'll exchange it for U.S. dollars and put it in the bank. That way we'll be secure in our old age. We'll be free enough to go on a trip abroad—I'll take you to see my old school in England, and the room I lived in."

Mrs. Syi leaned against her husband's shoulder and felt a wonderful peace of mind. That a woman of such ordinary looks who could not read a single word could have found so fine a husband as this must have been a good fortune bequeathed from a previous reincarnation, and precisely because she enjoyed this excess of blessings she also felt a degree of unease lest her good fortune be snatched from her.

"Chilin's here." And Zhishuang led in a tall young man, stalwart of build. Chilin was a nephew of the Tsaos. His family lived in Baoshan, ten miles or so north of Shanghai, but with only an acre or two of land to rent out, it wasn't easy making ends meet. Consequently he didn't have the wherewithal for outside lodging, so he lived with his aunt's family, where he had been from junior high school right on through college, from which he was now soon to graduate. An adult man of twenty-some will always encounter numerous inconveniences and dissatisfactions when living with another family, but financially hard-pressed as he was and with his younger brother soon to start college, Chilin simply had to put up with the situation and be as attentive as possible to others' sensibilities. Fortunately his uncle, Mr. Tsao, was a man of generous disposition, who could get along very nicely in a delicate situation, and had thus for these several years accommodated himself well to the circumstances. During vacations Chilin worked as an English instructor for part-time students to earn a little extra spending money, and recently he'd also found a job at the Verity Chemical Works. Every weekend when Zhishuang came home, Chilin, busy or not, always came over to sit a while. Mr. Syi was sharp enough to be able to sniff the wind with cold objectivity and sense what was going on: Chilin had thoughts for Zhishuang. But Zhensyu was a man of the modern school, after all, and had no mind to interfere in his daughter's marriage affairs. Anyway, he could rest quite at ease, he knew, for his daughter, shaped by McTyeire's edifying influence for fully six years, was herself amply capable of handling these important rites of passage.

"You two sit downstairs here; we're going on up. Chilin, why don't you have supper with us." And as he spoke, Mr. Syi, very much in the English style, let his wife go ahead of him, as the two parents proceeded upstairs.

"Your dad sure has a nice manner about him," said Chilin.

"Nothing like your uncle, all day long with his brass water pipe in hand, 'gurgle-gurgle' smoking away—the stereotypical Shaosying businessman."

Frequent visitor as he was, Chilin without asking took out a cigarette from the cigarette tin and lit up. "At first you weren't supposed to be coming back this weekend," he said with a smile, glancing at her. "Then when I seemed to hear you calling at the gate, I thought I must have been mistaken, so I listened again, and sure enough it was your voice. Really I had no idea..." Suddenly realizing he was being overly voluble, he quickly broke off in embarrassment. He had a full face, just as he was solid of build, conveying a sense of firmness and steadfastness, which, complemented with full lips, made people immediately assume him to be kind and amiable. Just look at his neat canvas tennis shoes, the muscular shoulders pushing tautly against his white shirt, the white sailcloth slacks outlining long legs strong and sturdy. Someone unacquainted with him might take him for an athlete, and in fact, as a member of his university baseball team, he was indeed an athlete of sorts. The expression in his eyes, however, was quite unexpectedly kind and gentle, even bore a trace of timidity and melancholy.

But Zhishuang paid not the slightest attention to any of these things, as she gesticulated in her fit of pique.

"Boy, did I ever get hopping mad today." As the resentful Zhishuang began her account, tears began to form in her eyes.

"What happened?" The melancholy in his eyes gave way to a masculine self-confidence.

"I'm the editor of our school yearbook, and I'd already contracted with Continental News to do the printing for this year's issue. We agreed it would be bound in linen and printed on coated paper. Before the contract was finalized the guy I discussed it with gave me a lot of sweet talk and agreed to everything I asked. But as soon as it was signed, he turned his back on us. They didn't even do the proofreading—said we had to proof it ourselves. Today I went to the publisher and looked up the head of their commercial department and he was so nasty, he practically bit my head off. How is it possible to have such bad people? Four thousand yuan to print the yearbook and that doesn't even include proofreading. Who ever heard of such a thing! And besides that, they changed the linen cover to cardboard cover!"

But Chilin roared with laughter.

You might say the two of them had grown up together. When Chilin had come to Shanghai to take the high school entrance exam, she was a pigtailed kid of just seven or eight who all day long liked to play at "building house" by her back door. Since Chilin's family was by no means well-off, he studied intermittently for over five years to finish the three-year curriculum at Maihen High School. And because from time to time he had to drop out and do a stretch of work in order to get the money to resume his schooling, Zhishuang had the impression he was not a student at all but a person who had long been out in the world of work. Thus, by extension, she felt that Chilin was almost a generation older than herself. However, at a time when one was eighteen and the other ten, the older took not the slightest notice of a silly little girl "building house" or "kicking the shuttlecock" or some such, but when it came to 28 years and 18 years, how everything then became so very delicate. With the passage of time Chilin began to realize that completing his education would be increasingly problematical, while for Zhishuang, quite aside from her natural grace and nobility, time seemed like a sculptor's chisel, fashioning her more beautiful and radiant with each passing day. All of that rendered Chilin at once transfixed and disappointed, for in his eyes she rather resembled a ballerina slowly fluttering on tiptoe out of his reach until finally the day would come when she would disappear from his stage altogether. But every time she called him familiarly by his given name, "Chilin," it would summon new courage and hope. He was, after all, still just twenty-eight and an honor student at prestigious Jiaotong Polytechnic University, so he never imagined that he might not win her, particularly when she was sitting so very close to him affecting the manner of a helpless victim.

"You just marched down to the newspaper office and opened negotiations?" asked Chilin suppressing his laughter.

"Juanmin went along with me."

"If you two girls think you can discuss business with them, you're really no match for that type. Those newspaper people are used to discussing issues with people of all sorts, so how can you two manage to get from them what you want? Next time, let me go along with you."

"There isn't going to be a next time—I'm graduating now," said Zhishuang sorrowfully.

"Hm. That's going to be a great 'turning point' for you," said Chilin, using the English phrase, for educated people of Chilin's day liked to sprinkle their speech with a little English. "Presumably, if you hadn't in fact taken the entrance exam for the journalism department, it would have been the sociology department, wouldn't it? How come you're not going to study science?"

"Well..." Zhishuang hung her head. Running her fingernail along the seam of the sofa upholstery, she spoke without any great assurance. "Well, I really liked home economics..."

"Humph! Home economics," Chilin gesticulated contemptuously. "What good is it for you to study that stupid home ec stuff? Unless you marry some social celebrity or some big businessman, you can't put that stuff to any good use."

His condescension got her ire up. "So you despise me because I can't marry some celebrity or public figure?" she retorted. "Well, I will marry one just to show you."

Her childish outburst provoked his laughter, but beyond his laughter, he could not fail to realize that the Syi family had expended a large amount of capital in sending her to so aristocratic a school as McTyeire precisely in order subtly to mold her into a future woman of stature.

"I'm sorry," he said dolefully. "I was just thinking that if you were to pass the exams for the engineering department at Jiaotong Polytech, some time you and I might go abroad together to study. I'm going to try to make the government fellowship quota and leave first, and then later when you're able to leave, I'll be able to meet you when you arrive in the foreign country. I'll be able to help you with all the procedures for admission to the foreign university."

"I don't want to study science. It's too demanding. And for the time being I have no notion of studying abroad. After I graduate from the university," she continued with a smile, "the first thing I intend to do is heave a big sigh of relief. If I rush overseas to continue my studies, I'll just be studying myself to death. And furthermore, it would be awfully hard on Daddy. After I graduate from the university, first I plan to work for a while, and supposing if later on I still want to pursue advanced studies, I'll assume the responsibility myself so Daddy won't have to shoulder the burden. There's my little brother Chengzu, you know, who will be burden enough for him. After I graduate in home economics, maybe I can get a position at McTyeire. Today the dean of studies, Mr. Shen, seemed to hint at that." To be sure, the dean of studies had spoken with her that day.

Fresh from her bath, Zhishuang's body gave off the cool fragrance, one moment subtle, the next pleasantly obvious, of her scented western bath soap, which seemed to reveal all the better her unsullied charm, recalling to Chilin the poet's line, "Raised secluded in her chamber, unbeknownst to man at large." And yet it had never occurred to him that this thoroughly delicate Zhishuang was also thoroughly scheming. She was no longer the little girl sitting at the back door playing house. And she might change even more in the future: who could say, indeed, what her ultimate transformation might be?

Zhou came in with some watermelon. The melon had been submerged in the well-water and was now wonderfully cool and refreshing. This was the first shipment of watermelon from Guangdong province in the south.

"Tomorrow's Sunday; what do you have planned?" asked Chilin tentatively as he bit into his watermelon. "In the afternoon at Great

China they're showing a Shirley Temple film. Shall we go see it together? ...Take Chengzu along with us?" Lacking any confidence, he tacked on that last sentence.

"Take him along—what for! Twelve- or thirteen-year-old boys like him are the biggest pain in the neck." And unexpectedly Zhishuang shot him an angry look.

"OK, so let's not take him," said Chilin, somewhat encouraged.

"I don't like Shirley Temple films. Seen one, seen 'em all. Wait a minute, I'll get the newspaper and look at the movie ads."

Zhishuang was apparently very interested in seeing a movie, and hurried to the dining room in back to look for the newspaper.

"Zhou, are you rinsing your dinner rice?" From the back door came the Shaosying-accented voice of Sky-Tile Tsao.

Having just finished bathing, Tsao Jiusin was dressed in cool, rustling linen, with leather sandals on bare feet, and being a near neighbor he had just moseyed on over dressed as he was as if he were a member of the family.

Tsao Jiusin was a Shaosying opera fan. Every day after work he would order a rickshaw for himself and go off to a third-rate theater near Garbage Bridge where he had recently begun helping in the rehearsals of the Daban Opera Company of Shaosying as an unpaid scenarist and director.

"Ah, Chilin's here, too. Say, tomorrow's Sunday; why don't you come to the theater and lend moral support to your uncle's directing efforts?" Saying which, he tore off for Chilin a few tickets from a strip he'd brought along.

"Of course I'd love to go and give encouragement to the plays you put on." Chilin, readily assenting, had no choice but to accept the tickets.

Zhishuang just then rushed back in from the dining room with a newspaper in hand. "Tomorrow the International is showing Dark Journey."

"Those foreign films aren't very interesting. Why don't you come and see the opera I'm staging. It's called 'The Russet-Maned Stallion.' What a noble ring that title has. It was originally called 'The Eastern Campaign of Syue Pingguei,' but isn't that too banal? Now that I've revised it, you see, it really isn't the same." The more he talked, the more enthusiastic Sky-Tile became, and he merrily headed up the stairs uninvited to call on Mr. and Mrs. Syi.

"Do you really have any appetite for that theater at Garbage Bridge? Be careful not to bring back any bedbugs with you," said Zhishuang with a sneer. How could a privileged child such as she possibly understand the meaning of the proverb, "When living in another's home, one must be defferential?" As her contemptuous gaze swept over him, Chilin felt he had been struck by a bolt of lightning. Wiping away the sweat on his brow produced by this embarrassment, and he sullenly took his leave.

From the upstairs corridor came snatches of Tsao Jiusin singing a Shaosying tune.

Zhishuang muttered a vulgarism in English, and angrily flopped down on the sofa. The university had no dormitory accommodations, which meant she would have to endure the lifestyle of these unadulterated urban commoners, and yet, because of her six years at McTyeire, she could not endure the conditions which confronted her.

The smell of hot lard came from the kitchen. "Zhou!" called Zhishuang with a frown. "How many times have I told you to close the kitchen door when you're deep-frying!"

Unendurable. Absolutely unendurable. When in the future Zhishuang might have her own home, it would be nothing like this. The maids in her home would wear fresh white aprons with flowered borders and would have had specialized training. Her home would be decorated with fresh flowers year round, just like the commons room at McTyeire. Even if her room had to be in an apartment building in the beginning, at least it would be in a private residence in the French Concession, and definitely without the likes of the insensitive neighbors here who just scuffed into your home with thongs flopping on their feet.

But alas, who could really tell what the future had in store?

"Zhishuang." Chilin had come back. "Next Sunday, Polytech and Shanghai Electric Company will have a baseball match, and I'll be playing in it. Why don't you and Chengzu come and watch it."

"Chengzu again?" she shot back angrily. "Why of all things do you want me to drag him along? I'm not his babysitter, y' know." Zhishuang was in bad temper and she vented it all on Chilin. Incredible: Chilin could be such a pain she just couldn't stand it. Incredible!

Chilin forced a smile and left.

Zhishuang put a record on the victrola—"Home, Sweet Home"—and suddenly felt her spirits had hit rock bottom.

Chapter 5

Juanmin was wearing a colorful satin mandarin dress with high collar and tight-fitting waist, which delicately delineated the lines of her figure and instantly added several years' maturity to her appearance. She was in the east dining room inspecting the wine goblets one by one against the light, and, sure enough, discovered a few among them with cloudy surfaces.

"Hey, what's going on here, Fagun?" She addressed her question with a light-hearted laugh to the white-gowned butler, standing there motionless with hands at his sides. Yet with a careful eye she was scrutinizing the glasses under the lamp light, and found a smudge no larger than a grain of rice on one of them, which made Fagun, already in his fifties, feel prickles up and down his spine, such was his uneasiness.

"I instructed the kitchen maids to polish each one individually with emery powder," he said weakly.

"It's not your fault. You're old, and naturally your eyesight isn't too sharp, so you didn't find the smudges. Fortunately the guests haven't arrived, because if they saw this, wouldn't bad talk start circulating? But, it does seem the Zhu family lacks a lady of the house, what with not even being able to get a few goblets washed right. You'll have to embarrass the maids about their sloppiness, Fagun." She pointed to several goblets she'd picked out. "I'll have to trouble you again to have the maids wipe them clean, and bring them back. And don't let them be careless about it. It will be sufficient to tell them once; if I have to tell them a second time, everyone will be quite uncomfortable."

Nodding repeatedly, old Fagun placed the glasses on a silver serving tray and hurried off to the kitchen in back.

Juanmin was now left alone in the large dining room, and once more closely inspected everything from the arrangement of rice bowls and chopsticks to the fresh flowers, making sure Fagun had not slipped up anywhere, and only then did she go out of the room, leaving the door ajar behind her. She started up the stairs to see how her sisters' preparations were progressing. As she was ascending the stairway, the heavy keys she was holding clinked against each other with a crisp metallic sound in rhythm with her footsteps, reminding her of the school's housemother ("Night Owl," they called her), whose key ring sounded like a coppersmith at work, as she clanged up and down the pathways. She felt an indefinable cheeriness. Although she was just a girl, this clanging key ring hanging from her waist caused the servants to regard her with obedience; among her sisters and even her older brother she enjoyed prestige, and she was without doubt a very competent household manager for her father.

Lu, the maid, was rushing down the second-floor corridor. She had not yet changed into her prescribed white tunic and black pants. Juanmin called the maid up short. "What's going on here? This late and still not changed into your serving uniform? The guests will be here any minute."

"I've just come from helping the youngest daughter with her bath," offered Lu in timid self-defense.

"Why only at this hour did it occur to you to get her bath ready? What were you doing before?"

"The youngest daughter just woke up."

"You couldn't wake her up earlier? How old is she and how old are you? She's just like a candle—if someone doesn't light her, she doesn't shine." And having lectured Lu right to her face, Juanmin went on up to the third floor. She understood perfectly well that she was in an especially bad temper today, but it was also perfectly clear that a woman having nothing to do with this home would be bursting into it; and what qualifications did that woman have other than she might become the ready-made Mrs. Zhu? That was just too easy for her.

The third floor had three rooms in a row, all facing south. At the east end was Juanren's room—he was the oldest of the five children and the only son; in the middle Grandmother had her bedroom; while the four daughters had the west room. Walking past the piano room, Juanmin heard the heavy sounds of piano music: her second sister, Juanying, was practicing. That she could actually have a mind to play the piano at this hour!

In looks, Juanying and Juanmin were exactly alike, though Juanmin didn't have her younger sister's graceful bearing; yet by this small difference, one could immediately sense that the two sisters differed greatly indeed.

Juanying had since childhood been brought up by her grandmother in the countryside, and not until she was in the sixth grade did she come with her grandmother to Shanghai, and by this time, whether she was with her father or even with her brother and sisters, she always felt a certain estrangement, an estrangement that time had done nothing to bridge. Quite aside from that, in her studies she did not measure up to Juanmin and only with much effort did she manage to pass the exams for a third-rate high school and even there her record was very ordinary, which only increased her feelings of unease and inferiority before her father. After her mother's death, she really should have taken a greater interest in household affairs and attempted to help her elder sister with some household duties, but unfortunately in temperament she was not Juanmin's equal in either forcefulness or shrewdness, and thus became prey to the domestic staff's disposition to "bully the weak and fear the strong." Furthermore, the servants knew that this particular daughter was not a favorite of her father, and so they gradually pretended simply not to hear her when she called or were dilatory in carrying out her instructions, while whatever Juanmin had to say, they dared not delay or put off. Consequently, it developed by degrees that, whether it was bringing a new domestic into the household or deciding the Sunday menu, the views of the eldest daughter had always to be consulted. In this way Juanmin took on the role of housewife, and notwithstanding she returned home but once a week, the entire Zhu household (which, taking in everyone from high to low, was quite a few people) came under her very orderly management, and her father thus came to favor her even more. Fortunate for Juanying, then, that by nature she did not enjoy taking on responsibilities, and was all too glad to be left to relax with nothing to look after. Yet this was just the period in one's life when the emotions are at their richest and most require loving consideration, and so she had dedicated her ardor entirely to religion. She was a devoted Christian. Most of her time she spent in the church, or, if not there, then in the piano room.

"Sis, have Juanwei and Juansi finished dressing?" Juanmin looked at Juanying, who, even though there would be dinner guests, was only wearing a dark green poplin dress and a light yellow wool sweater—refined in color, to be sure, but since this was in fact the day of their father's engagement, such dress was really rather too plain; nor had she curled her thick jet-black hair, which, not unlike many pious Christian women, was tied into one very thick braid coiled on top of her head, making her look on the whole rather dull-witted. Juanmin, very mindful of appearances, was concerned that if her sister should thus show herself in company, it would reflect very ill upon the dignity of the Zhu family.

"Sis, why don't you wear the claret-colored dress? The one we both had made last year for Grandma's birthday. Your skin is a little sallow recently, and looks even more so wearing the dress you've got on now. Quickly now, go change into the other one." And so saying, she half pulled, half pushed her out of the piano room.

In their bedroom, twelve-year-old Juanwei was just then combing ten-year-old Juansi's hair. In temperament Juanwei very much resembled Juanmin, and although Juanwei was merely twelve, she was very clever and sensible, and was quite able to function as Juanmin's helper.

Juanying got the claret dress and went into the bathroom. Looking at herself in the door mirror, she felt that, set against yellows and greens, her own face, even if not very pretty, did reveal delicacy and worldly detachment. Yellow suited her perfectly, she knew, but not wanting to harm her amiable relation with Juanmin, she reluctantly changed into the claret dress. The fact is, claret concealed a subtle gracefulness Juanying possessed. Juanmin, nonetheless, thought that her sister looked much better in the claret dress. Juanmin hoped above all else that the four sisters, each a finer child than the next, would afford not the slightest pretext to fault-finding by the new woman, in order that the new woman might nominally assume the title of "Mrs. Zhu," but would lack any practical maternal role toward them.

"Are you all dressed now, young ladies?" Jingchen, hearing only muffled twittering within, knocked lightly on the door.

Zhu Jingchen at home preferred to dress in traditional Chinese clothes. On this occasion he was wearing a long, plain white silk gown, white silk socks, and Chinese-style cloth shoes. His strong facial contours and his bright piercing eyes set off by thick eyebrows betokened a man of great ability, one successful in his enterprises.

"You just take care of picking up Miss Pu." And more hubbub could be heard from behind the door.

Although Zhu Jingchen had four daughters and just one son, for some reason he was fond only of the girls. Perhaps it was because his son, as was possible with any male, would become a competitor, adversary even, and moreover he had seen with his own eyes too much of life's malice. Thus he felt that daughters were really more ingenuous and lovable. On those rare occasions when he could relax at home, he would give himself over to his daughters' diversions—squirting water on him, combing his hair up into a flat pile in the latest "waterbag" style, daubing the tip of his nose with soap foam, or making him sing an aria from some Peking opera. In the midst of his busy and tense schedule of duties these were wonderful moments of domestic bliss.

"All right, I'll go pick her up now," he replied submissively to the closed door, and he hitched up his gown and headed downstairs. Turning the corner at the landing, his eyes fell on the mahogany grandfather clock standing against the wall. He frowned anxiously: how was it his son had not yet returned? Juanren, in his last year at the university, had gone to Wusi for three months' training with his artillery battery and was to have returned today. It was precisely to await the return of his son that he had delayed until today inviting Miss Pu to his home.

Just at this moment, in fact, a young man in military uniform was walking toward the Zhu residence, and although only with the rank of private, his medium build and cultivated demeanor gave to this mere soldier the unmistakable air of a spirited and talented young man that set him apart from the ordinary run of draftees.

He pursed his lips and cheerily whistled "Yankee Doodle," swinging his arms snappily back and forth in time—one, two, one, two—as he stepped along in a martial gait.

It was his son, Zhu Juanren. Whether intentional or unintentional he knew not, but in any case the pronunciation of the two names—father's and son's—sounded very similar, indeed, in the Shanghai dialect, identical. But in reality father and son were poles apart. The son was a senior chemistry major, and would graduate this summer.

"Juanren, help please. Give your uncle some help."

Suddenly, a shabbily dressed beggar skulked out from around the corner of the block, and thrust an outstretched and unspeakably filthy hand, with fingernails fully a half-inch long, right in front of him.

Juanren was taken aback, seeing before him only a sallow face touched with blue, emaciated into a triangular shape, with tangled hair; standing close by, as he was, his body exuded a very disagreeable odor.

Juanren opened his mouth to say something, but just could not bring himself to say "Uncle."

"Oh, remember when you were small, how I used to hold you... Now your uncle hasn't eaten a thing for two whole days..." This fellow kept pressing toward Juanren, who kept stepping backward until he'd backed himself right up against the property wall, and the beggar pressed even closer to him.

"I...I don't have any loose change on me. Honest, I don't!" Juanren's martial sternness deserted him instantly. "You know my father doesn't usually give us spending money...," he said tremulously as he plunged his hands into his pants pockets. He fingered a few bills in his right pocket—money his father had given him to use during his spell of training, money, he'd been instructed, not to be frittered away and, if spent, certainly to be accounted for. Consequently, he had not dared spend any of it; but of course when on military exercises there really wasn't any place where he could have spent it.

"I don't have any. Really, I don't..." Feeling the money in his pocket, his whole body seemed to get feverish, and his denials became increasingly unconvincing.

"Juanren, you mustn't be like your father whose conscience has been devoured by dogs. Think about your dear departed mother instead."

Juanren pulled a bill from his pocket and, trying not to look, thrust it into the grime-etched palm. The man's eyes brightened; even the red scar on his face brightened. He grabbed the bill and held it tightly in his fist, then noiselessly slipped away.

Juanren straightened his coat and adjusted his cap, and, wiping the beads of sweat from his forehead, walked over to the large metal entrance gate to his house and rang the bell impatiently.

"Coming, coming!" And Old Chang the gatekeeper rushed to open one of the gate wings. "Ah, it's you, Master Juanren," he said, panting. "I've just been waiting for you."

Juanren took the front steps by twos and threes, only to come up face to face with his father. How the scene recalled Dream of the Red Chamber where Bao Yu feels like a timid mouse whenever encountering his father, the cat. Although not so serious as the fictional scene, still, Juanren, nervously shifting back and forth from one foot to the other, felt very much constrained. For Jingchen had always been serious in both word and deed toward his son, and very strict. And no wonder, for he knew the world was rife with unworthy heirs.

"Father."

"Well, the training's over." Zhu Jingchen looked over his only son: three months out in the open under the sun had given Juanren a strong and healthy look; and in field jacket and leggings he stood erect and smart. Seeing the martial bearing his son had developed, Jingchen felt an inner comfort, indeed felt moved enough to want to show his son a measure of paternal affection, yet unexpectedly the words that issued from his mouth seemed more like a boss interrogating a subordinate, which even he felt to be excessively impersonal.

"I trust you didn't spend your money foolishly?" Since banking was his very livelihood, whenever Jingchen opened his mouth it was always about money, just as ordinary people might talk about the weather as a conversation opener.

Juanren knew his father would ask for an accounting, yet he also knew his father did not do this out of stinginess. According to his father's principle, all evil occupations—eating, drinking, and making merry—required the expenditure of money. Having no money, one could not indulge in evil occupations.

"No, I didn't misuse any money...," replied Juanren, glancing uneasily at his father.

"Oh?" Jingchen had intended the question only casually, but now he surveyed his son with a vigilant eye.

"Just now at the gate, I bumped into Uncle...He stopped me, and insisted I give him some money...I didn't happen to have any loose change, so I just shoved a bill at him..." The more he spoke the less self-assured he became, and that model of martial bearing a moment ago had now disappeared without trace.

"Humph. It never takes more than a couple of coins to send a beggar on his way, but you're really extravagant—he just sticks his hand out and you put a bill in it. With a soft-hearted fellow like you for a son, I'll be reduced to begging too!" Jingchen was not given to issuing loud rebukes, but on this occasion even though his scolding was not loud, it was of such severity as to make any listener's hair stand on end. In this respect, Juanmin was rather like her father.

"If you have any genuine intention of making a good reputation for yourself," he said, "you'll have to figure out a way to earn money for yourself, and if you want to achieve anything in life, you first have to learn how to make money. Period."

"I...um...I didn't have the heart to refuse him," Juanren mumbled in self-defence. "Uncle said he hadn't eaten for..."

"Uncle? What uncle of yours is he? His own wife even refuses to recognize him, while you still claim him as your uncle? He says he hasn't eaten, but in a city the size of Shanghai, there's always work to be found so he could get food into his stomach. I've told you before, people like him are a bottomless pit—even if I gave him our entire house, it probably still wouldn't be enough for him." Juanren, hit with this salvo of criticism right in the face, stood stock still, head hanging.

It was the son who was probably correct. An uncle is always an uncle, and this uncle was the cousin of his own mother, but regrettably had brought no credit to the family; he was addicted to opium and to dog racing besides; he'd lost every job a bank had ever proffered him;

he was an uncle who had ruined his own family so that his wife in the end had no recourse but to grit her teeth and throw him out to become the companion of street beggars, and he constantly came to the Zhu residence to panhandle. Jingchen, knowing he was already beyond salvation, concerned himself only that the domestics and his children give him not a cent, for otherwise he would come to depend on them day in and day out. But Jingchen was well aware that his son would still feel too ashamed to disregard the uncle's entreaties. This Juanren—how was it he was so utterly unlike his sister Juanmin? How wonderful if only brother were sister, and sister brother.

Beads of sweat stood out on Juanren's forehead. He was a tenderhearted soul. Jingchen believed that while he himself was by no means harsh, an impartial judgment of Juanren during recent years forced the conclusion that he was weak-kneed, softhearted, and wishy-washy, a young man who knew only sympathy and submission, a young man who would never make much of himself in life. Jingchen was very uneasy for his son.

"You, don't you know the world's a battlefield? You can't be softhearted and achieve anything. And just for sticking his hand out you give him the equivalent of two silver dollars. In the beginning when I was apprenticing I made only four dollars every month, and at that, I had to save money so I could get a decent New Year's present for your grandmother. Next year you'll already be graduating and going out to work, and yet you're still so simple-minded as this? People may look upon you kindly now, but that's only because of my reputation."

The son just stood there, head hanging, uttering not a sound.

"Now hurry on in and wash up. Within the next few days you should take some time to call on Mr. Bei. You're going to have to find employment on your own and not rely on me to do it for you. Pretty soon you'll be graduating and out in the world on your own—you'll have to be more wary about things. Now off with you."

Juanren left, and his dismayed father watched him disappear from sight. In all honesty, though, he had to admit his son really wasn't bad at all: he got straight A's, didn't waste his time in dance halls or gambling dens—what more could he ask? But then he recalled the young factory manager, Mr. Tsai, whom he'd met at the Liu residence: although he was only a few years older than Juanren, didn't he seem far older in experience? Far more capable in managing affairs? There was a man who could meet the challenges of running a thousand-spindle textile mill! In trying to assign blame for this quirk of fate, Jingchen could only blame his son for having led too comfortable a life. If Jingchen had done what he'd thought best, he would have sent the boy off to apprentice in a business after high school graduation and before he'd started college. Let him first do menial work every day: dumping chamber pots, boiling tea water, and wiping counters, to purge him of his superciliousness. Then let him enter the university. That was the old way of apprenticeship, with its own standards and rationale. Unfortunate it was that such practices were now no longer fashionable. But even if such were still the practice and the son of Mr. Zhu the bank president went in perfect anonymity to seek a business apprenticeship, he much feared not one employer would be willing to take him on. He shook his head and walked toward his Buick. Juanren watched as his father hitched up the front of his gown and eased himself into the car, settled himself in the seat, and then drew in his legs, shutting the car door behind him. How unlike those clods who just climb in through the car door with their bottoms sticking up in the air in a frightfully ungainly posture.

His father, of course, was a successful man, and a successful man in all his actions and activities embodied ineffable attractiveness. Whenever Juanren and his father were alone together, the son always felt inferior, even though Zhu Juanren's battle with life had not even begun yet.

Entering the parlor, he saw his sisters all dressed up—pretty as "bouquets of flowers and piles of brocade."

"Look, here's Juanren in uniform," said Juanwei, as she cocked her head to take an appreciative look. "Real smart. Military dress is very becoming on you."

But Juanmin frowned as she hurried him on. "All right. Be quick and get out of that tiger-stripe camouflage—it looks terrible. When Miss Pu sees you shortly, she must think of you as the son of the dignified Zhu Jingchen, and how could such a son be a common soldier?"

"Don't look down on us soldiers," returned Juanren with a stern expression. "Just now our troop trucks drove past the Japanese encampment in Hongkou on the city outskirts. Today the military training for university students for all Shanghai was completed, and so there was a steady stream of trucks loaded with troops like me coming back. And some of those Japanese looked pretty nervous, figuring we were troops specially transferred in from all around..." Juanren's self-confidence grew as he talked on. "We purposely sang at the top of our lungs, 'We're ready to die the cruelest death to serve the motherland; fight on, fight on! When shells and bullets whistle by, we fearless men will stand our ground; fight on, fight on!...'" And he sang it aloud.

"Are the Japanese really likely to provoke war with us?" Juanmin asked skeptically. "Can there be a repetition of the 1932 incident when they attacked Shanghai?"

"Can't say for sure. But you girls do nothing all day long except go to the movies or sing hymns—how could you know about the gravity of the international situation?"

"This spring wasn't Kong Yangsi appointed special emissary to attend the coronation of the new king of England? And afterwards went to the United States to have discussions with Roosevelt? It's hard to think the U.S. and Britain have no way of dealing with the Japs. They can prevent a Japanese military offensive against us, can't they?" Juanmin actually had always been much concerned with current events.

"What would be the use of that!" retorted Juanren with a wave of his hand, as he scoffed at his sister's absurd naiveté. "The Japanese don't give a damn about the United States or Great Britain, and with the European situation itself getting more tense by the day, the U.S. and Britain simply don't have the leisure to be looking out for the Far East." Juanren felt that his military training had broadened his horizon considerably, and he spoke with real confidence.

"You need to understand that the situation is very unfavorable," he continued. "Did you know that the Japanese garrison in Peking recently held a mutual friendship party with Song Zheyuan, the commander of the 29th Army? The Peking mayor, Chin Dechun also went. And although they called it a 'mutual friendship party,' in fact it was a ploy to intimidate us. The Japanese began waving their swords around, so Song Zheyuan chose a person to compete in a martial arts contest; then some of the Japanese, feeling strong with liquor, actually lifted General Song and then Mayor Chin right up into the air. The Chinese side was just as rude and took two senior Japanese officers—Matsutakara Takayoshi and Miyazaki Shima—and lifted them up. Things sure were getting tense."

"So what happened after that?" The girls were all listening in rapt attention.

"After that? Well, it'd be too tiresome to relate the whole thing." Seeing his sisters' expression as if they were listening to a mere storybook tale instead of a serious international incident, he was really disinclined to talk further. They were just girls, after all, who knew nothing beyond dressing up and going to the movies. So to talk further with them was simply pointless.

"Well, I will tell you that today," said Juanren changing the subject, "I bumped into Uncle at the front gate. He seemed very pathetic, so I gave him some money, and wouldn't you know but what Dad gave me a bawling out..."

"Goodness, you still regard him as an uncle?" exclaimed Juanmin with a contemptuous wave of the hand. "What do you want to pay any attention to him for? Daddy's chased him off any number of times, and so has Old Chang, so he'd never dare come and actually ring our doorbell."

"It used to be he'd wait for us when we went to school and when we came back, standing there at the gate. At first I guess he figured I was too young to know how to put him off, so he came up and began pestering me. But I told him I'd yell for the police, and he stopped it." Juanwei, who had just started junior high school, gestured with her hands and shrugged her shoulders in the manner of the French as she chipped in a remark, acting just like a westernized young lady. "After three occasions like that, he just didn't come pester me any more. You have to be like Daddy, otherwise he'll have his eye out for you from morning till night, and how can you just let that go on? Of course Juanying isn't hard-hearted enough to do that either, but then she's a Christian."

"You silly girls—you pray all the time yet you're still so mean," said Juanren icily, thrusting his hands into his pockets. After being squeezed into a troop truck and jolting through the towns of ill-clad, dull-eyed poor people, then experiencing three months of military life in the field eating out of a tin messkit and wearing sweat-stained khakis, to return to the company of his lively, charming sisters, rather affected in their elegance though they might be, he felt a touch of surprise and estrangement to the point of unease.

"It's not that I'm soft-hearted," said Juanying, fiddling with a box of matches, "but when a person has sunk so far as to beg, it doesn't matter how unclean or useless he may be, he's still worthy of sympathy, particularly for someone whom for years I called 'Uncle.' Before he fell into degeneracy, Uncle was a man of talent who had a fine hand for calligraphy. And he was very kind and endearing, too."

"Yes. I remember when I was small, Mother would take me to Uncle's calligraphy studio to amuse myself. Back then, Uncle had great gambling luck, and used to pull out from inside his gown whole piles of copper coins and give them to me." As Juanren spoke on his expression saddened somewhat. "Uncle was a very good employee at the bank in those days, bought a house on Baikal Road, and everyone in the family treated him like a regular person. Who could have guessed he'd become addicted to this evil habit."

Juanmin looked at the grandfather clock, clapped her hands, and jutted out her aristocratic chin to indicate that the conversation might now come to a conclusion. "He's beyond our salvation; even Daddy can't save him. This is a social problem."

"Humph. You're talking just like a Communist," said Juanren, pointing an intimidating finger at her.

But Juanmin just sighed heavily and said, "If I were a man, I'd really like to fool around with politics."

"Join the Communist Party?"

"Any ol' party, just so I could distribute leaflets, do clandestine work, deliver intelligence. Exciting stuff like that." Juanmin became quite animated as she spoke. "Just now when you were talking about that 'mutual friendship' ploy—I'd have been thrilled to have been in on that... When I think of the life I live now—studying, eating, sleeping—what a bore!"

"Enough," Juanren interrupted impatiently. "While we were on training, we did catch a few Communists. It was at Fudan University. The messhall wasn't very sanitary and as a result some of the troops came down with cholera. Some Fudan students—lots of them are Reds, you know—refused to go out for drill and agitated the entire body of student recruits not to drill."

"You refused, too?" asked Juanmin with much interest.

"I didn't dare. One can get involved in hubbubs like that any old time." Juanren took a few karate chops at his own neck. "You'd really get the book thrown at you. And sure enough Song Syilian was in a terrible rage. He was in overall charge of our training regiment, and he nabbed a few of the student ringleaders right on the spot and locked them up."

"Wow!" the girls exclaimed.

"Hey, is it true what they say that Song Syilian looks real dashing?" asked Juanmin, apropos of nothing in particular.

"Dashing!" Juanren stood erect and squared his shoulders. "A model of martial bearing, and very dignified. One day in the field I happened to bump into him and some aides on inspection tour. There I was standing right in front of him, so I felt I just had to snap to attention. I reported to him that I was a student trainee in such-and-such company, battalion, and regiment. And lo and behold he drew his own pistol from his waist and told me he wanted to watch me shoot some targets then and there. I was so nervous as I took the gun I just fired one shot without even taking aim, and then gave the gun back to him. Then he told me to go back to my unit, so I slipped away like I had greased shoes on."

The girls roared with laughter. When Juanmin had regained her composure, she remarked, "If I'd been you, I'd have been especially careful to let him watch me shoot several rounds so he'd remember that this Zhu Juanren was from such-and-such company and was a real good shot. That was a real opportunity for you."

Juanren just shook his head. "Forget it. It didn't mean a thing."

"How could it not mean a thing?" Juanmin arched her eyebrows as she took issue with her brother. "It could have been a great opportunity for you. It had, as we say at McTyeire, 'social potential,'" she said, using the English phrase.

"The episode might seem to you girls to have some potential, but not for us men. Oh yes, when we were on training this time, we started a basketball competition, and for some reason or other the referee was very one-sided, which got the two teams into an argument, and one of the trainees—a student at Chingsin Catholic High School—got real agitated and struck the referee, though only a light blow. Fortunately, just then Song Syilian came rushing out and immediately summoned all the trainees together and with everybody looking on punished the Chingsin student with twenty-five blows of his swagger stick. Right across the buttocks."

"Oh my gosh. How painful!" screamed Juanwei.

"The pain was only secondary. He'd completely lost face."

"Did he cry?" asked Juanwei.

"Mere crying? He howled!"

"That's terrible!" exclaimed Juanmin, sticking out her tongue.

"That's what I'm telling you. When you encounter a big shot, the best thing to do is to slip away like you've got greased shoes on." And with that, Juanren authoritatively brought the discussion to a conclusion.

"Oh! Juanren's back." Their grandmother, having finished her nap, had moseyed in to find out what the excitement was all about.

Old Mrs. Zhu, well into her seventies, was wearing a subdued, loose-fitting, mandarin dress of rippled silk, and on her large feet (large only because they had never been bound) jade-colored cotton socks matched with dark slippers embroidered in silver. She still walked with a lively step. Because her son had been lucky in life, she was a warm-hearted, well nourished woman whose face radiated perfect contentment.

"Grandma, you're up." Juanying greeted her and, taking her by the arm, helped her into a high-backed rattan chair, then placed a decorated porcelain teapot and a small spittoon on the end table next to her. Old Mrs. Zhu was fondest of the second sister, Juanying, because she most resembled her mother who, whatever came up, had always maintained a marvelously even disposition. And her mother had also been old Mrs. Zhu's favorite daughter-in-law, so that now she in turn favored Juanying, a sort of spiritual sustenance, as it were, for the old lady. But being excessively fond of Juanying, old Mrs. Zhu would not feel contented unless Juanying were present to help with whatever was at hand. Consequently Juanying was much busier than she might otherwise be, and was kept pretty well tied up; but then she was a quiet, gentle soul with no particular outside social interests. Her school work did suffer though, and, unable to get into a top academy like McTyeire, she was studying at a less prestigious school.

"Now let me think. Where did this soldier come from?" The old lady squinted through her spectacles at her grandson. "Seeing you in camouflage khakis makes me think of your father's brother—this year he'd be fifty, six years older than your father. Pity I don't even know whether he's dead or alive," she said, bringing up a subject she'd brought up before a hundred, perhaps a thousand times. "During those years when your father was still working in the Feng residence and coming home only once a year, his greatest concern had to be the food right in front of him, and the rest of family had to depend on raising silkworms to get by. But as luck would have it, one year we got nothing but a crop of dead cocoons. Your father happened just then to come down with spells of fever and chills, his forehead was burning hot and we didn't have the money to call in a doctor. Your uncle had gone out very early that day to work in the mulberry orchard, or so I thought. Who would have known that by noontime he had already changed into a khaki uniform, placed a sack of rice on the floor in front of me and kowtowed three times. That was the warlord period with turmoil everywhere, and some recruiters had come to our village, and whoever was willing to throw on a camouflage combat uniform could receive two bushels of rice. But even though there wasn't any food in the house, he just shouldn't have joined the army all on his own; whatever was to be done, he ought first to have discussed it with your father. But your uncle in an instant pulled himself away from me, turned around and left, and what a pity the uniform he was given was so baggy it flapped in the wind like an old gown. He was only fourteen then. No sooner had he left than I rushed into the town, only to learn that they'd already moved out...Not so much as a letter and I've no idea if he's dead or alive..."

Juanmin noticed that it was getting rather late, and was afraid that if Grandma talked on, she would become more distressed and end up ruining everybody's good mood. Anyway, letting the servants hear these stories was not a good idea, so she quickly diverted the old lady from her topic by discussing the evening's menu with her. At this point, they heard a couple of honks of the horn as their father's Buick approached the main gate, and the shepherd dog, Lily, scampered down the stairs to wait at the front door for him.

Pu Zhuanlin was well into her thirties and might be reckoned an "old miss"—a spinster. She was graceful and fair complexioned, yet well filled-out and healthy of appearance. Her jet-black hair, was combed back into a large flat bun held in place with a clasp studded with Mikimoto pearls, and though everyone referred to her as Miss Pu, in fact she already had a certain matronly air about her.

Miss Pu's family formerly owned a well established foreign antiques business. It was said that the Pus were collateral descendants of the famous Pu Songling, author of Records of the Strange, and while this had never been carefully authenticated, presumably because these Pu descendants were so wealthy and had brought no disgrace to their illustrious forebear, the connection was widely recognized by the public to be true.

Miss Pu was a graduate of Jinling Girl's College where she had majored in sociology and for a time was deeply involved in women's rights and other social causes, and even now was in charge of the public relations section of the YWCA. And precisely because of this her life had reached an impasse, for no man would much want to take for his wife so socially active a woman as she.

At the moment she was sitting close to Jingchen, who was concentrating on his driving. It gave her a considerable sense of security to be sitting next to so capable, successful, and high-class a gentleman as he. Reflecting on it, she smiled a smile of satisfaction. As the car took a turn, she intentionally brushed against his shoulder. Thinking she wanted to say something to him, he turned his head toward her and raised his eyebrows, while keeping his eyes fixed on the driveway ahead. Zhuanlin pursed her lips into a smile and murmured softly, "I'm so happy. Everything is just wonderful."

Jingchen smiled too, and reached across to squeeze her delicate and graceful hand, and she returned the pressure. Although he had a son already over twenty, regarding love between the sexes Jingchen seemed only recently to have begun to savor its delights. Now that he had sorted out his business affairs and achieved success, everything seemed to be going very smoothly for him.

Old Chang came bounding out to open the big iron gate and Jingchen, still holding Zhuanlin's hand, stuck his head out the car window and introduced him: "This is Old Chang!"

"Thank you," she smiled, nodding in acknowledgment. Old Chang was the gatekeeper, and Zhuanlin had enough social experience to know that eventually she would inevitably be troubling him to open the gate and close the gate, so it was well to show him courtesy. Traditional families always were careful to distinguish between master and servant, while foreigners advocated courtesy and equality toward subordinates; Zhuanlin rather favored the latter. Courtesy toward one's servants produced results better than giving them a little more money.

But Zhuanlin was a stranger to Lily the shepherd dog, which tactlessly barked and growled at her.

"Hey, hey—this is your future Mommy," said Jingchen as he opened the car door and pulled Lily in onto his lap.

Lily remained on the alert and kept right on barking at Zhuanlin. Zhuanlin controlled her annoyance, since the dog was Jingchen's pet, and patted it a few times on the neck, while thinking to herself, "So this is the payment I get for marrying Bigshot Zhu!"

The car proceeded in along the thickly graveled driveway, and in the light of the headlamps, Zhuanlin could make out that the flower garden appeared unkempt, apparently for lack of a hired gardener. But the velvety lawns beyond the driveway were fresh and still in the dim light of the moon, which lent to the surroundings a particular charm all their own. At the end of the gravel drive stood a three-storied English manor-style residence, originally the home of a Spanish businessman, which, following the owner's announcement of bankruptcy, Zhu Jingchen had been urged to buy, furniture and all, by Cathay's late president, Wei Jiusi. Back then West District was still an undeveloped area, and thus the selling price was really quite reasonable; and precisely for that reason he'd snapped it up. In his heart of hearts, though, what he really preferred was the design of the Liu house: a structure of mixed Sino-Western style, set well back from high property walls, solid and secure yet without being conspicuous. But finding such a dream house was no easy matter. Fortunately Jingchen had been raised in poverty and was not at all fussy about where he lived. If the truth be known, deep down inside Jingchen didn't even believe in home ownership: a home was something you got stuck with, for whatever the exigencies of the times, you could neither take it with you nor put it in storage. For so imposing a personage as president and board member of Cathay Republic Bank, however, if he did not own a home that fully measured up, well that would damage the reputation of the bank. And Cathay did, after all, loan him the money to purchase it.

The downstairs parlor was furnished with a French-style sofa set upholstered in a long-since faded blue and ivory satin, a leftover of the former Spanish owner. It had certainly never occurred to Pu Zhuanlin that the residence belonging to the financial world's eminent Mr. Zhu would be quite like this.

Fagun the butler was there to greet them in all due earnestness. As he was indeed the butler, it behooved Pu Zhuanlin to accord him a certain prestige, the better to avoid in future being put off at every turn with an annoying, "That's not the way it's done here." Thus Zhuanlin gave him a reserved nod of the head.

The elderly Mrs. Zhu was assisted into the parlor by all five of her grandchildren. Zhuanlin had seen many grand occasions in her life and had whirled around the dance floor of many a foreign consulate. So it would certainly be easy enough to cope with Jingchen's mother, an illiterate old lady reared in hardship: to while away spare moments in her company and chat a bit would be quite sufficient to keep her happy. And to those five children she accorded even less regard: she engaged each in polite exchanges without in any way compromising her own dignity. She had comments for everybody: for the old lady, were her teeth sound and how did she pass her idle hours; for Juanren, did he have any plans for studying abroad after graduating, whereupon she recommended several of the top-flight schools like M.I.T. where, she said, fellowship aid might be arranged; with Juanmin, she had even more to talk about, since she herself was a McTyeire alumna and many of her friends at the YWCA were teachers there. Juanmin was only tepid in her responses, however. Yet Zhuanlin took no offense, for it is no easy thing to be a stepmother to a seventeen- or eighteen-year old girl like her. Fortunately sooner or later the day would come when she would marry and leave the household. Right down to the youngest child, Juansi, Pu Zhuanlin remained attentive, patiently amusing her as the two sat at the piano for a four-hand version of "The Merry Farmer."

"What affectation!" Juanmin eyed her icily as she cursed her silently.

Seeing how adept Zhuanlin was at these social amenities, Jingchen urged her on, and old Mrs. Zhu, too, was warm and encouraging. A parlor, after all, was a place to gather for lively amusement, for mixing together. The small talk concluded, the old woman and the four daughters dispersed, each to her own affairs, leaving behind only Juanren who as eldest son could not very well leave, but must stay to help entertain the guest. Luckily Zhuanlin conversed easily, never at a loss for words, and she felt not even momentary awkwardness. It was natural that they should talk of Juanren's plans after graduating.

"The economy is bad now. Commerce, industry, office work—employment opportunities are scarce; no one's hiring." Juanren sat with his elbows propped on his knees as he spoke with some embarrassment.

"Why do you want to go job-hunting by yourself? Wouldn't it be enough to have your father just make a few phone calls? He knows so many businessmen, how can you worry one of them won't take you in?" Surprised by Juanren's circumstances, she turned her eyes inquiringly toward Jingchen.

Jingchen nonchalantly packed tobacco into his pipe bowl. "I've long since told all five children," he said calmly, "that I'll see them only through college. After that, whether they study abroad or seek employment here, they're on their own."

"Dad's right in this," Juanren agreed, cracking his knuckles. "That's the only way I'll ever develop my abilities when I'm on the job. Otherwise, whenever anyone hears I'm the son of Mr. Zhu the bank president, they'll find some soft, meaningless work for me, and what I studied will just go to waste."

"Precisely." Jingchen felt comforted that Juanren understood the pains his father took to help his son. "At the bank, we've never hired the children of big shots. When such people are hired they're always a drag on their fathers' own reputations. And you always have to be a little more polite to them, which is of no benefit to those young people either. It's easy to damage their careers, and easy also to provoke the resentment of colleagues, which just makes it difficult to remain on good terms with them. So, I've made it clear to my children long ago: if you would not saddle me with these kinds of problems then I, for my part, would not create these kinds of problems for you."

What he said made sense, but...Zhuanlin took a good look at Juanren—delicate featured, cultured, handsome—and could only feel that the father was excessively harsh toward his one and only son. "Wouldn't it in fact be better, then, to send him abroad for study?"

"More study?" Jingchen shook his head. "And the money?"

"What an ungenerous father you are," said Zhuanlin aloud, while at heart she groaned, oh, this Jingchen—the longer I live with him the more an incomprehensible stranger he'll become, and I'll never know what he's really thinking.

"It's not being ungenerous," returned Jingchen. "For a person in his mid-twenties still to be sitting in class going to school, and still requiring his father to support him—what kind of prospects do you think such a person can have?"

"You're simply wrong about that," Zhuanlin retorted. "Now is just when you have to look at a person's educational level. In my brother's company, most of the department heads had to have studied in

America, while those who'd studied in Europe can only rise to section chief, and the ones who'd studied in Japan are at the very beginning level, while the graduates of Chinese universities are practically the equivalent of odds and ends. If this trend continues, more and more emphasis will be put on academic degrees..."

Juanren was beginning to feel that, adult man though he was, he was rather unfit to act as host; that his father and this stepmother no more than a few years his senior should right to his face be arguing about his proper disposition was something of a humiliation. Furthermore he'd already been planning soon to find work, and, for better or worse, support himself. So he hurriedly came to his self-defence. "I intend first to work for a period of time to accumulate experience, and if I should in future go abroad for study, it will be even more beneficial."

At this point Fagun entered to announce the arrival of Miss Yi.

Not yet in her thirties, wearing expensive gold-framed octagonal glasses, the woman who entered was dressed in a woolen, greyish-blue striped mandarin dress and there was a very bookish appearance about her. She had been an assistant to Jingchen's younger brother, Jingwen, during his student years in Germany, but because Jingwen had a legal wife back in the countryside, the Zhu family, from old Mrs. Zhu right on down without exception, referred to her as Miss Yi, even though she and Jingwen lived together openly, to indicate the distinction. This Miss Yi came from a prominent family of north China (her father was a foreign service officer in the northern government), and why she fell for an impractical intellectual like Jingwen is anybody's guess. Willingly abandoning everything, she followed him no matter what, never complaining that Jingwen had a wife and children or that he had not a cent to his name.

Ever since boyhood Jingwen had been a studious type and had scholarships all the way through high school, after which he passed the exam for a government fellowship to study in Germany, where he majored in chemistry. Unfortunately, in today's world where everyone was bent on instant success and personal advantage, chemistry was a pursuit which consumed both money and time, and as a result, since returning to Shanghai from eight years of overseas study, he had not once found work. Later, on the strength of Miss Yi's own family reputation, she found a position for him at a missionary hospital as lab technician, while Miss Yi herself took a job at a girls' high school teaching chemistry. Thus, although the two had work entirely different from their academic specialties, still their combined income was well above the average—not enough to get rich on perhaps, but at least enough to live on comfortably and without financial worry. Yet,

Jingwen, of all people, could not content himself with this career, for he could not get out of his mind the urge to make some new scientific discovery, and he threw away God knows how much money for chemicals and equipment for his experiments, while transforming the bathroom of their apartment into a virtual chemistry laboratory. And always the pungency of hydrochloric acid and the stink of hydrogen sulfide produced by his experimenting suffused the surroundings. The neighbors complained unendingly and the very clothes he wore from top to bottom were eaten through from the splatter of chemicals. Ten years ago he finally asked Miss Yi to withdraw all the money given to her by her parents and, through Jingchen, got a loan from Cathay Republic Bank, and along with some friends established, with himself as manager, Verity Chemical Works near Zhoujia Bridge in a dirty, factory section of the city, which produced bleaching powder and caustic soda. The investment in this plant was considerable, but there was no assured market for its products; indeed, the British firm of Brunner, Mond & Co., Ltd. had filled every nook and cranny of the Shanghai market with good quality, low-priced products of its own chemical plant. How could the rude facilities of Verity Chemical Works be a match for that? When the Verity products came out, it was only by relying on a few of Jingwen's old schoolmates who worked in the chemicals industry and also by relying on Jingchen's reputation that a few businessmen were talked into buying some of the stuff. Thus the plant earned a small return, but after deducting costs for materials and replacement parts, for land and facilities, et cetera et cetera, there was precious little profit—hardly enough to muddle through on. Jingwen and Miss Yi went on as before squeezed into their apartment, and while everyone referred to him politely as "the proprietor," he was in truth an impoverished proprietor in debt up to his ears.

Recently Jingwen had quite unexpectedly run into a former classmate who had studied in Germany; he was now employed by a Swiss chemicals firm and was doing exceedingly well. He greatly admired Jingwen's passionate will to succeed in industrial applications and had specially invited him to his own plant in Switzerland for observation.

"Miss Yi, has Jingwen fixed a date for his return? I understand the poor fellow's been working like a ox from morning till night; he really ought to try and go out and relax. But," Jingchen joked, "he'd better be careful: those European girls are so darned attractive he might be enjoying himself too much and forget to return. He's been gone a month now, hasn't he?"

Miss Yi occupied a position which in practice differed little from an ordinary mistress, yet the entire Zhu household, aside from referring to her as Miss Yi instead of Mrs. Zhu, otherwise regarded her, daughter of a distinguished family, as she was, and one who had herself studied abroad, with the respect and cordiality fully commensurate with the role of Jingwen's wife. Jingchen in particular, being an open-minded, cosmopolitan sort, looked upon her as his proper sister-in-law.

Miss Yi could not be said to be beautiful. Yet she was creamy complexioned, soft-spoken in speech, possessed captivating dimples, and had about her an exceptional aura of amorousness. She pulled a letter from her purse and handed it to Jingchen. "Jingwen asked me to give this to you," she said. "The main thing with this trip to Switzerland is to try to utilize the waste ammonia which the plant discharges in the production process and convert it to ammonium sulfate. But the color of the nitric acid synthesized in the laboratory wasn't exactly right, and they're afraid no one will want to use it. So he's gone to his schoolmate's plant for on-site inspection."

"At present," she continued, "that former schoolmate of his is general manager of the Swiss Nitrogen Engineering Co., which has already set up ammonium sulfate plants for the production of fertilizers in Japan and the Soviet Union. On this occasion, Jingwen is engaged in discussions with him about securing their help in improving the facilities at Jingwen's plant. The Swiss company does not itself sell machinery or equipment; instead it offers planning services, provides blueprints, assists in the selection of machinery and supervises its installation, offers guidance on plant operations, and so on. After a few negotiating sessions, we all recognized that this firm was reliable and they were very willing to help..."

Zhuanlin shot a glance of amazement toward this outwardly unprepossessing woman who assumed the role of regular wife, and whom from the start Zhuanlin had looked down upon with all her heart, only to discover now that she was actually a wife of ability and education, precisely a wife such as foreigners term a husband's "secretary and helpmate."

Jingchen opened the letter. His brother's handwriting was like the man himself—a calligraphy so careless it might have been scribbled by some Daoist wizard, as if you were free to make out the characters to mean whatever you wished them to mean. Fortunately Jingchen was quite proficient in his brother's scrawl.

"A few close friends and I," the letter went, "are planning to improve and enlarge the plant in order to develop China's international standing from its present humiliation; we have no other course than to vigorously develop our country's science and industry. People nowadays are too concerned with commerce, real estate, and stocks, and while these do yield easy profits, the climate is liable to sudden and unpredictable change. Quite aside from those uncertainties, I feel it unconscionable to engage in business which brings no benefit to the nation as a whole. I hope, Jingchen, that you will be able to lend a helping hand, and join with us in the planning of this enterprise, so that even if we do not achieve success, we at least need not feel ashamed before our country and people. I anxiously await your favorable reply. Sincerely... "

Jingwen was still of the same old temperament, putting his heart into everything he said, and what he said made sense. But what Jingchen found irritating was that so many ideas of which he spoke so sensibly, proved upon implementation to be utterly senseless. Weren't some people just like that: too daffy to change direction until they bumped their very noses into the wall at the end of a dead-end street. Jingchen silently crumpled the letter into an ashtray and heaved a long sigh. "'He who does not know himself will attempt enterprises beyond himself.' In China the chemicals industry is a dying endeavor. He has no understanding of the times."

"Jingchen, if you bought some shares in his company, it certainly wouldn't unduly burden Cathay Republic. The bank's reputation is exceptionally good, and if you took the lead in investing in the company, others in the financial community would surely respond. Our plant is already on file with the Ministry of Industries so it's impossible for it to be some irreputable, fly-by-night operation..." Miss Yi, slender as she was, looked even more delicate in her blue-grey striped dress, yet she stood erect and pressed her argument. "The Swiss company has a lot of equipment which it sent us practically for free, and this presents a wonderful opportunity for Jingwen."

"Dad," interjected Juanren, "I'm wondering about working for a while in Uncle Jingwen's chemicals plant. I think it would be a good idea both as a learning experience and for my personal development. The most important thing is that I could study something of practical value."

"He who does not know himself will attempt enterprises beyond himself." Jingchen turned his piercing eyes on his son as he repeated the adage.

"It's meaningful work precisely because we'll be doing something no one's ever done before." Well, Juanren was young and, convinced by what Miss Yi had said, had the manner of one who was itching to have a go at it. "Uncle Jingwen and I went over initial figures for his plans in some detail. According to those figures, China's present cultivated area is approximately two hundred fifty million acres, and if you figure that each acre will use ammonium sulfate fertilizer valued at ten yuan per year, that amounts to a two billion five hundred million yuan annual expense to the national economy. Rather than let the British firm of Brunner-Mond engage in a business of this magnitude, it would be better to let the Chinese themselves do it. And this two and one-half billion yuan has to be exchanged for foreign currency of equivalent value before it can be actually used to purchase the foreign product. And how does China come up with so large an amount of foreign exchange? In my view Uncle Jingwen's efforts have a great deal to recommend themselves."

"Young Master Zhu." Jingchen impatiently interrupted his son's discourse. "You can't figure the accounts like this. Of China's four hundred million peasants, how many today know enough to use ammonia sulfate fertilizer when they plant their fields? You've just been out on military training and broadened your experience of society. Now tell me, did you see any country people using chemical fertilizers? Aren't they all still just spreading night soil on their fields?"

Miss Yi smiled. "But, Jingchen, aside from rural poverty, another reason peasants don't use chemical fertilizers is that they don't know how. Last month I took four people to the Chingpu-Baoshan area where I sought out a few old land owners and gave them some bags of fertilizer for them to try out, and instructed their hired hands in its proper application. They were very happy to use it. The countryside has its share of educated people too, and they were of course able to help us explain things. The main problem now is the poor quality of our own product which puts us at a real disadvantage. We'd be delighted if Juanren could come to work for our plant. However, our plant is the chemicals industry, which can't be compared with the consumer industry, and can even less appropriately be compared to a foreign commercial enterprise. If Juanren comes to work for our plant, the salary and benefits would of course be modest to the point of hardship, but in terms of experience he would certainly learn a great deal. Well, let's talk more about it later." She cleverly spoke only half of what she had to say, and then kept her silence.

Jingchen had her stay for dinner, after which she had to leave, for the next day first thing in the morning she had to go to Syujiahui where their factory was conducting a training class, and Miss Yi was in charge.

"Uncle Jingwen and Miss Yi certainly are exceptional people," Juanren remarked admiringly. "I heard that once when there was a hydrochloric acid spill at their factory which threatened the neighbors, the police used it as a pretext to come and extort fines from them, and

Miss Yi had to deal with the situation all by herself. Finally she sold some jewelry to pay compensation and bring an end to the matter."

"Strange. Why didn't she try to get me to help her?" Jingchen wondered aloud.

"She told me that unless the situation got totally out of control she was disinclined to trouble you with it...Dad," continued Juanren in an imploring voice, "Uncle Jingwen and the others are thinking out a comprehensive plan to go into production of electrolytic salt and liquid alkali in order to solve the raw materials problem by ourselves, and achieve a product that's completely Chinese. So I really would like to go to Uncle Jingwen's factory and work in industry."

"Didn't the German firm of Bayer Pharmaceuticals already have a position waiting for you? Why are you shilly-shallying about it?" Jingchen swept his eyes majestically across his son. "If you want to learn by experience, you can do that anywhere. Your Uncle Jingwen's plant plainly lacks any assurance on the two crucial matters of having adequate capitalization and a market for its product. Furthermore, this kind of chemical product is closely linked to the Ministry of Industries which means there's the nuisance of cultivating contacts with government officials. This company of his simply has no prospects, so why on earth would a young man like yourself want to travel down that dead-end street? How can succeeding in industry be as easy as all that? You can't even play a simple poker hand well, so how can you possibly manage a chemical plant with your limited qualifications? Juanren, I might as well lay my cards on the table right in front of you today: I entertain no extravagant hopes for you—it will be good enough if you can simply be self-supporting. Nor do I count on you to bring honor to your ancestors, for it's plain to me you are not made of such stuff."

These remarks caused Juanren acute embarrassment, especially as they were uttered in the presence of his young future stepmother. He sat awkwardly for a moment then left in a depressed mood.

Pu Zhuanlin, a spectator in this little family drama, could not help but feel apprehensive, for it would be no easy matter to fill in as stepmother in a family so extensive and complex as this! Yet she still would give it a try and be a competent Mrs. Zhu—Mr. Zhu's secretary and helpmate.

In an intimate gesture, she put her arm on Jingchen's shoulder, and with mixed coquetry and seriousness she said, "Jingchen, what your brother says in that letter really does seem reasonable. If a privately owned commercial bank whose motive is profit should actually invest in a chemical fertilizer plant beneficial to farming, even though the present enterprise presents certain risks and the possibility of profit not very great, yet it's good enough to allow Cathay to enhance its reputation, and so in my view this matter could be done successfully."

Zhuanlin, who had always been engaged in social activities of one sort or another, had cultivated a very persuasive tongue. Unexpectedly Jingchen patted the hand she was resting on his shoulder. "This is different from the work you perform for the YW," he said, "where it's sufficient to rely on simple enthusiasm. Investing capital in a sulfuric acid amine plant jointly with several other banks requires dealing with members of the government who shamelessly seek to line their own pockets, and that would make it all the more difficult for Cathay to maintain its policy of working closely with private business and keeping the government at a distance. Furthermore, if you go take a look at the homes where our employees live, you'll know why I've always wanted to build regular employee housing, and that requires holding on firmly to the money the bank earns, not frittering it away on risky investment schemes. Letting a starry-eyed academic like Jingwen take Cathay money so he can fiddle with his beakers and flasks would hardly be as worthwhile as using the money to buy land and construct employee housing." Jingchen paused a moment, and added, "Furthermore, I refuse to become the butt of ridicule that my brother has taken advantage of his association with me."

Zhuanlin sensed that her remarks had caused Jingchen to rebound, and he showed not the slightest regard for her feelings and that rather displeased her. Moreover the displeasure showed clearly in her facial expression.

"Oh, while I think of it, Zhuanlin, there is something I should make very clear to you at the outset." Jingchen seemed not to have noticed the displeasure in her face, or perhaps we should say, he feigned not to have apprehended the unhappiness signaled by her compressed lips, her reticence and reserve. "You met all five of my children, didn't you?" he said in a tone of some gravity. "In addition there is my mother, nearly eighty. I'll be entrusting them all to your care. It will suffice if you look after each of them carefully. In other matters, particularly my business affairs, you needn't trouble yourself or get involved."

What was this he was saying? Zhuanlin could not keep the anger from burning in her eyes, and her heart pounded violently.

Jingchen looked at his watch. "Dinner will probably be served soon. Shall we go into the dining room?" he said, making as if nothing were the matter.

Zhuanlin rose to her feet without uttering a word, let him take her arm, and headed into the dining room. The outcome of her relation with Jingchen was now certain and so there was no further need for him to be overly solicitous; indeed he had never been particularly solicitous toward her. She understood that even if there was something she was unhappy about, she could only humble herself and accept her position, and do what he had just instructed her to do. She had no other alternative. Even so, the title "Mrs. Zhu" in Shanghai's high society still had a very nice ring to it.

At the dinner table, Zhuanlin conducted herself with perfect composure and spoke in appropriate and dignified terms, fully consistent with the status of someone bred to be a "Mrs. Zhu," yet from her slightly knitted brow and her unsmiling lips, one sensed she already no longer possessed that same easy gratification with which she had entered the house a little while ago.

Similarly at the dinner table, Juanren showed subtle signs of depression, and the atmosphere throughout the meal was heavy—sometimes more so sometimes less so, but heavy throughout. Yet Jingchen seemed oblivious to all this: the people clustered around this dinner table were eating food provided through his labor, and did not everybody therefore have to heed his words? Contrary to the rest, there welled up in his heart a feeling of self-satisfaction.

But Jingchen seemed born for a life of hard work. He hadn't had more than a couple mouth's full from his first bowl of rice than Fagun, the butler, called him to the phone.

"Mr. Zhu..." From the other end came the flustered voice of the day's officer-in-charge at the bank. "This afternoon from four o'clock on, there's suddenly been a large number of customers coming to the bank to make withdrawals. Right now the main lobby is swarming with people."

Jingchen clapped his hand to his forehead. He glanced over at the family crowded around the dining table, then spoke softly into the receiver. "Wait a moment; let me talk to you from my study." He said a word to Zhuanlin, then hurried to his study and again picked up the phone.

What all bankers feared most was a bank run. Because a bank's funds were mostly circulating outside, if by chance all of a sudden turnover stopped and deposits could not be withdrawn, then the bank's reputation was finished.

"Mr. Zhu, don't you think we should close early?" the other end pleaded tentatively.

"Definitely not!" roared Jingchen, silencing the other end. Milktoasts of that ilk were unwilling to accept even the slightest risk, and when the next time staff had to be reduced, he would remove them. "If there's not enough distributable cash, then transfer funds from another department."

"The other departments are also under pressure," came the despondent reply.

It certainly was a case of "disaster following hard upon the heels of distress," thought Jingchen. There hadn't been any particular demand for withdrawals recently, but, strange to say, as soon as Cathay lent out a large sum to Bounty Textile Mill and bought a large amount of its stock, both reducing the bank's liquidity, there just happened to be a run on the bank. For sure there was someone here trying to create mischief.

"Is there anyone with you now?" asked an alarmed Jingchen.

"Don't worry, I'm alone."

Jingchen muttered to himself—still two hours to closing time, not much cash in the vault, but probably enough to get by on; when things get to this extremity you have to resort to uneconomical stopgap measures, but let's just get through today and then I'll think about what to do next. Tomorrow at noon he would go to the stock exchange and talk with his banking colleagues and try to borrow some short-term cash. Thus considered, he instructed his officer-in-charge. "Allow a free hand in paying out funds. All demands for withdrawal must be honored, no matter how much. You hear me? It's absolutely impermissible to create difficulties or intentionally delay processing customer requests. Those are my orders."

This bank run had come very suddenly without the slightest forewarning, as if someone was intent on creating difficulties. In recent years, Cathay Republic Bank had prospered wonderfully, especially since its loans to Bounty and purchases of its stock, even though it had not been a very long time. But just as Liu Tongjun had expected, he had reaped profits from the very beginning, and on that account it was unavoidable that he invite the jealousy of his fellow bankers who wanted to do him an evil turn.

There was no comparing a modern bank with the old-style Chinese banks—the counting houses, for when they ceased operations and went bankrupt, their owners used to be put in a cangue and exposed to the public, and their property would be assessed and liens placed on it. Yet on the other hand, if Cathay Republic Bank started going downhill while under the stewardship of Zhu Jingchen, he'd have to hide his face in shame for the rest of his years.

So agitated was he that a pencil he was gripping in both hands snapped right in two. He looked dumbly at his palms, reddened from the pressure he'd applied, and tossed the two pieces on the desk. Then he took out a cigarette and sat smoking silently in the darkness.

"Chenny," referring to her son in her familiar down-country way; "are you busy?" The door was quietly pushed open and old Mrs. Zhu came in.

Jingchen snapped on the desk lamp, instantly suffusing the room in a soft glow. Mrs. Zhu sat down in an easy chair before his desk and looked at him with worried eyes. In the lamp light the wrinkles at the corners of his mother's mouth and eyes were as close and numerous as a spider's web. Oh, how difficult it was to be a human; how very difficult. If Jingchen should live to his mother's ripe old age, he knew not how many more times he might live and die.

"Nothing special, just a minor complication at the bank," he said reassuringly.

Old Mrs. Zhu kept her worried eyes fixed on him.

"It's really nothing, Mother. I feel quite embarrassed the way you're staring at me. I've lost a tooth on this side and just haven't had time to go get it fixed. I'm just like an ugly old man."

"Silly boy," she said lovingly. "When you were newborn, you didn't have a single tooth in your mouth, but your mother never tired of looking at you all the same."

Jingchen's heart warmed. In all the world only a mother could love a son, however he might change, even if, like his cousin-in-law, he sunk into beggary; still she loved him.

His eyes burned with emotion.

"Come, Mother, let's go back downstairs." And he turned off the lamp.

Chapter 6

Still a half-hour until opening time, Zhu Jingchen stepped through the main entrance of Cathay Republic Bank. He was wearing a double-breasted suit in a light-colored faille, with a matching light-blue bow tie with dark-blue polka dots, giving him very much the air of an astute and dignified banker. During banking hours he always wore western-style suits. He recognized that western attire was a suit of armor which could strengthen one's image, for his own mettle and self-confidence were representative of the mettle and reputation of the bank he managed.

Originally the Italian Chamber of Commerce Club, this building had been put up for public auction following the Great War. At that time Cathay Republic Bank was already prospering and needed to enlarge its quarters and consequently it bought this renaissance-style structure.

The lobby's marble floor was polished to a mirror-like luster every morning. Arranged at the bases of the marble columns around the four sides were overstuffed chairs upholstered in red velvet, and running the length of the lobby was a row of potted palms about the height of a man, like a rank of guardsmen standing straight and tall. How very imposing! Jingchen alone felt, stepping into the building just as he had been doing for twenty-some years now, that it was excessively sumptuous and insufficiently dignified, too reminiscent of a first-class opera house and too unlike a solemn and august financial institution.

Too resplendent and too fussy in ornamentation, the building tended to intimidate small depositors, disinclining them to enter the place. But, as the saying goes, "small accumulations become large." Although the deposits made by these small savers were not large in amount, there were large amounts of this type of person. Jingchen had looked on helplessly as these people walked up to the Cathay entranceway but not go inside, and he felt sick at heart. Cathay was not a government bank; what it depended on was the money in the pockets of Shanghai's ordinary man on the street. It was precisely for this reason that Jingchen was firmly opposed to posting the customary Sikh guard at the bank's entrance. Even robbery was preferable to stationing one of those Sikhs, whose snobbishness was itself enough to cause his revenue source to dry up.

Jingchen looked forward to that future day when Cathay Bank under his management might own a new building of his own design—simple and dignified in outward appearance while at the same time embodying the accomplishments he had himself achieved for Cathay, which together would determine a solid architectural style worthy of the admiration and respect of his successors.

Since business hours had not yet commenced, the red velvet rope was still looped across the entrance of the main lobby, but there was already a considerable number of customers milling about on the portico, impatiently eyeing the big grandfather clock inside. Acquaintances were quietly talking among themselves, their solemn reserve holding in store a certain restlessness and anxiety. All the while other people were crowding up the steps to the bank in a steady stream.

Those customers who recognized Zhu Jingchen sized him up dispassionately from aside, straining to determine Cathay's present financial strength from the expression on his face. Jingchen, reserved in attitude, strode purposefully into the main lobby of the as yet unopened bank. His heart inevitably beat a little faster, for this frenzy of withdrawals had been going on unabated for days.

With the president himself arriving at work a half-hour early, the bank employees also were all on board at this time.

Flanking the entrance to the main lobby hung two calligraphic scrolls by a famous artist bearing Cathay's motto: "Helping industry and commerce, serving citizens and society." The same two phrases were also printed on the bank's customer account statements and on bank receipts.

As the employees rose to their feet to greet their president, Mr. Zhu returned the greeting with a gesture of clasped hands. "These past several days there have been a great many withdrawal customers," he said, "and all of you have been very busy. In a few days, I shall thank you all in a more concrete way."

The arrangement of the banking floor had a distinctive feature all its own, for the bank officers did not occupy separate offices, but rather were seated in a horseshoe-shaped arrangement in front of the tellers' counter. The desk of the business department head was the same as that of the other employees, and likewise displayed a nameplate identifying the officer and his function in order to facilitate response to customer inquiries.

"Possibly there will be even more withdrawal customers today," he said quietly to the business department head. "Please keep close supervision of the personnel and make sure they don't get irritable; they should do everything they can to shorten the customers' waiting time, and by all means they must not intentionally create difficulties for the customers making withdrawals. In the event of withdrawals in large amount, it will do simply for you to OK them with your signature—there's no need to treat it as a matter of any particular gravity. Our operating principle is this: a withdrawal request must be honored whether the sum be large or small." Having finished with his instructions, he took a turn around the tellers' counter. Spotting what appeared to be a small puddle of water over on the lobby floor, he was about to have it mopped dry lest a customer accidentally slip and fall, when, upon closer inspection, he realized it was just the natural veins in the marble flooring which from a distance resembled water streaks. His concern alleviated, he left the main hall.

"Mr. Zhu, you're arriving at work earlier every day," remarked Luo, the elevator operator. He was born in the same year as Jingchen, though it was clear their destinies were altogether dissimilar. At first Luo's job was serving tea to the gentlemen on the staff, but now that he was getting on a little in years, Jingchen could not bear to assign him to lugging a heavy teakettle around, and so transferred him to the elevator. Cathay now had two elevators: one was an automatic imported from Germany, but most of the older employees preferred the manual elevator.

The president's offices were on the nine-story building's top floor, and no sooner had he stepped out of the elevator than his secretary Mrs. Zhong announced, "Tsao Jiusin, chief of the business section, would like to see you, sir."

"Thank you. Ask him to come in," replied Jingchen as he proceeded into his private office.

The room was hot and stuffy. As he pushed open the heavy louvered shutters, he could see that on the main steps below so large a number of customers was already waiting for the bank to open that passersby stopped to stare. News of how Cathay Republic would cope with this rash of withdrawals would instantly circulate through every street and alley of Shanghai.

Jingchen's big oak desk was placed at right angles to the window. Pressed under its glass top, right in the middle, was the bank logo in the form of an old Chinese coin—round with a square hole in the center—bearing the following motto written in the hand of the late founder and chief executive himself, Wei Jiusi:

> If business slumps we take no risk
> Nor are we flurried when it's brisk;
> Cathay's transactions with the public
> Regard this coin to be symbolic:
> The round outside means flexibility,
> The inner core is four-square honesty.

Someone timidly knocked at the wide open door.

"Come in," said Jingchen in an authoritative tone.

Tsao Jiusin got his start in the traditional counting houses doing "outside work"—attracting new customers, inquiring about market quotations, and the like—and even though he was now employed in the modern banking industry, he still wore his traditional ankle-length blue silk gown and cloth shoes, still let the nail on his left little finger grow an inch long, and still kept close at hand his brass water pipe—the perfect picture of an old-style banker from Shaosying. Because he was skilled in the use of an abacus and was well connected in financial circles, it was his job every day to go to the clearing house to balance the bank's overages and shortages.

"Mr. Zhu," he said, bowing and lowering his voice, "there is a certain assistant vice-president at Cathay who is taking advantage of fluctuations in the priced securities market to engage in secret insider trading, and he has made enormous profits. Many of our colleagues at other banks, having become aware of this, are unwilling to lend us funds."

"Who could have such audacity as this?" asked Jingchen angrily.

"Who else could it be?" Sky-Tile Tsao forced a smile as he dropped his hint.

Jingchen scratched his cheek and instantly was speechless. The person in question was a relative of and recommended by Li Dengpeng, chairman of the board of directors and owner of a low-key supporter of Cathay, Good Faith Counting House. Recently Jingchen had come to understand from Liu Tongjun that an uncle of his was Mr. Gao, the manager of the International Club. "If in your dishes dwells a rat," so the saying goes, "you daren't assault him with your bat"—sometimes evildoers had to be endured for fear that bringing them to justice would cause even more harm. From this point of view, where there's no breeze there can be no waves, so there had to be some schemer blowing up this tidal wave of withdrawals and then capitalizing on the difficulty Cathay found itself in. What was to be done? There seemed nothing for it but to suffer in silence.

Tsao Jiusi shifted his weight back and forth, as if he had something further to say.

"Mr. Zhu, Mrs. Fan—the widow of Old Fan who recently passed away—asked me to request a favor of you, whether it would be possible to employ her eldest son, Fan Yangzhi, as a trainee. Old Fan was utterly impoverished, and the family now simply can't get by." Tsao spoke with urging in his voice.

Fan Yangzhi? Jingchen recalled the imperious young man that rainy day in his gloomy front parlor.

"He's studying at Shanghai College of Commerce, and still has two years until graduation. He's now planning to work for a few years to save some money, and then continue his studies. His educational level's quite high." As he spoke, Tsao Jiusin handed to Jingchen Fan Yangzhi's letter of self-introduction. It was written in a fluid and elegant calligraphy.

"Damn! Business conditions are so unfavorable just now," exclaimed Jingchen despairingly. Cathay had recently invested heavily in government bonds and in property; how could anyone have known that following the Japanese attack on Shanghai in 1932, the value of government bonds would plummet and that real estate values would also be affected, and no sooner had business recovered its vitality than Cathay was hit with this bank run, and for every additional person hired into the bank, another salary would surely have to be paid out, thus exacerbating the bank's financial crisis. But Old Fan had been one of Cathay's old-timers who after all had to be treated with special consideration. "All right, then; I'll ask the personnel department to see if they can't somehow arrange a position for him." And having said this, he wrote his name across Fan Yingzhi's letter, whereupon Tsao Jiusin thanked him profusely and left. This Shaosying banker might be old fashioned, but attaching such importance to human ties was rarely to be seen in the foreignized Shanghai of today.

For the entire morning, Jingchen felt he were sitting on a carpet of needles, so agitated was he. There was a limit to what was in the bank vault, and now there was this insider trading scandal; if by chance his colleagues in the banking profession should refuse to help him with cash loans to balance his accounts at the end of the day, that would be very troublesome indeed: "as helpful as a dead crab," the saying goes—no help at all.

It was not easy enduring until noon when all the member banks of the Shanghai Bankers Association would meet at the clearing house on Hong Kong Road to balance accounts. Jingchen felt he could not just sit in his office waiting for reports to reach him, so he ordered his driver, Ayi, to get the car ready, and he hurried directly to Hong Kong Road himself.

As the car turned onto Jiangsi Road, the flow of traffic and pedestrians became congested. A feather duster to bring out the metal's shine was stuck in the back of every rickshaw, the glass globes of every side lamp were wiped spotlessly clean, and their bells were ringing in high spirits, as they all raced down the street, each vying to be ahead of the others. Most were the rickshaws belonging to the various banks, each carrying its clearing house representative to participate in the account balancing. At this season of the year the noonday sun was blazing hot, and the rickshaw coolies, bare-armed with opened shirts, were shouting for the swarming crowd to open up a passage for them. The human current along the route welled up like a tide against the buildings lining Hong Kong Road.

Among the pedestrians there were even more wearing western-style fedoras along with traditional long gowns who were hurrying along on foot under the hot sun. One need but look at the middle finger of their right hand, around which was wound a paper certificate folded into a narrow strip, to know they were delivering their bank's statement. These were the aides popularly referred to as "barefoot bankers." Although they too wore long gowns, they could not be reckoned "long-gown bankers" (as employees of the traditional counting houses were customarily called), because they were not members of any bank's formal staff. Rather, they were a vestige of the "pole porters" who in the old days used to carry silver bars on their carrying poles. Back then when the counting houses balanced accounts, a porter, just as the term implies, would shoulder his carrying pole and deliver the silver. Later the system was improved: certificates replaced the transport of silver specie, and "pole porters" became aides commonly called "barefoot bankers."

The bankers met here every day to balance their receipts and disbursements. Those who had deficits had to register a debit with their colleagues to even the account, and if the cash on that day could not meet the sum and the accounts could not be balanced, the bank would simply have to cease operations until it could get itself in order, or even close its doors for good. Those banks with a surplus, on the other hand, gave credit to their counterparts, earning thereby a certain amount of interest. Otherwise they would "go rotten," as it was termed. On these occasions every minute, every second was crucial if one was not to be at a disadvantage.

Jingchen had Ayi stop at the corner of Sichuan Road and Hong Kong Road. He remained seated in the car, his arm resting on the opened window, observing in the distance the tense commotion and noisy voices at the entrance of the Banking Federation Building, where the clearing house was located.

Jingchen silently stuck his head out the window and expelled a stream of cigarette smoke, squinting his eyes against the blazing midday sun. Hot and tense, beads of sweat moistened his forehead.

Three cigarettes later and still Sky-Tile Tsao had not emerged. How much money would Cathay lose during this storm of bank withdrawals? How would its reputation be affected? In order to force himself to calm down, Jingchen shifted his gaze to the street scene. Just ahead was the Hong Kong Road street sign which recalled to mind when, at fifteen having first come to Shanghai to learn a trade, he saw street signs like "Sichuan Road," "Hankou Road," "Jiujiang Road," and actually thought that if he followed Sichuan Road he could get to Sichuan Province, and that Jiujiang Road would take him to Jiujiang, because in the countryside he'd only heard the terms "main road" and "side road." Then with the speed of a finger snap, twenty-nine years had flashed by, and everybody was saying he had prospered, had achieved success. And yet, looking at it now, it was not necessarily so! A president who managed his bank into closure and liquidation would be likened to a monarch who lost his realm: quite aside from the ruination of his present lifetime, the ignominy would be remembered forever.

Sky-Tile Tsao appeared, panting for breath, his pock-marked face glistening. As expected, Cathay's deficit was substantial and the bank had to borrow, but this pulling together of funds in order to survive a daily crisis was no long-term strategy. At the present daily interest rates on borrowed funds, Zhu Jingchen would lose money anew with each passing day, and as the days and months accumulated, interest would be added to interest with consequences he dared not even contemplate. Enough! Let's just get through this day and worry later about the others.

When he got back to the bank and pushed open the door to his office, he discovered Juanmin and another girl seated in the easy chairs waiting for him.

"Daddy, will you give us some help real quick?" said Juanmin with a petulant pout. "This year's school yearbook still lacks a little funding, so how's about you have Cathay buy advertising space in it? Oh, this is Syi Zhishuang, our editor and also head of the advertising department. My very good friend."

With Cathay already stretched to the limit, how could he have any thought of incurring advertising expenses?

"Mr. Zhu," said Zhishuang, smiling her sweet dimpled smile. "This year, the job of editing the yearbook happened to fall on me. I'm going to be graduating so this is the last time I'll be working on the yearbook, and I hope I can do a good job with it."

This young lady was marvelously poised, with a full face and big bright dancing eyes which revealed intelligence devoid of shrewdness—a thoroughly likable person. It would be unthinkable to refuse a request from such a young lady as this. As a matter of fact, Cathay might well train a couple of young women to drum up more business. Seeing a woman as intelligent and quick-witted as she, any big depositor would agree to any request. Unfortunate it was that even today career women were still few in number; women with practical ability and a high level of education did not like those inconsequential, decorative "flower vase" jobs, as they were derisively referred to, and even women who did like those jobs always seemed to lack qualifications and education for them.

"As a matter of fact, this year's yearbook has a slight connection with Cathay Republic Bank." As she spoke, Zhishuang pulled a spring binder from a large sailcloth bag she was carrying and slipped out the already printed table of contents for the yearbook when "plunk," a piece of Butter Queen candy caught in the binding fell out onto the desktop. Startled and embarrassed, she placed it in front of Mr. Zhu. "Here, have some candy," she said, making the best of it. "For the yearbook's 'Favorite Literary Work' department," she continued, "I've selected Lao She's story, 'The Bank Withdrawl.' Doesn't that give our yearbook a connection with your bank? The story was written when Lao She was teaching at Jilu University—the Christian college in Shandong. I have a copy of it. You just relax in your office, don't you? So when you have nothing to do, take a look at it. It may well inspire you in your bank work."

What? How can this girl possibly think that I just relax in my office? Jingchen looked straight at her. She smiled apologetically. "Forgive me," she said. "What I meant to say was...um, when you are relaxing..."

Jingchen contained his laughter as he glanced at the story and inquired, "How did you happen to choose 'The Bank Withdrawl'? Do you have a special interest in banking?"

"Well, my father is employed at Cathay and he recommended this story to me. He said the sort of thing described in it was very common, and even happened at his own bank. The whole story is written with great realism. It's a fine work."

"Your father is...?" Learning that this was the daughter of Syi Zhensyu, he could see the similarity in appearance. Syi Zhensyu's daughter was quite remarkable, at once attractive and gracious.

He opened his desk drawer and straightway wrote out a check for her. As the saying goes, "When fleas abound, its pointless to scratch; when debts abound, one more won't hurt." He'd put off worrying about it all until later.

"Thank you, Daddy," exclaimed Juanmin using her English. She felt her father had greatly boosted her stature, and she leaned across the desk and gave him an audible buss on the cheek. In those days such conduct was affectedly westernized, and Zhishuang, watching from aside, was rather embarrassed by it all.

The overjoyed girls took their leave. Jingchen sat in his place, looking out the opened door at the two receding green school uniforms, like two green leaves fluttering gracefully down the long gloomy corridor.

Jingchen looked at the piece of candy on the desk. Warmed in her bag on a hot day like this, the candy had already half melted. He unwrapped it and popped it into his mouth, casually picked up "The Bank Withdrawal" and began reading. And as he read on he felt more and more that this story was a vivid and forcefully written satire on the bureaucratic mentality. He was so moved that he scribbled instructions on "The Bank Withdrawal" suggesting it be represented in the bank's own newsletter, *Cathay Garden*, as a warning to bank employees. He was just about to ring for Mrs. Zhong when she knocked softly.

"Mr. Zhu, Mrs. Wei is here. Will you see her?" Fifty-year-old Mrs. Zhong performed her duties with consummate ability. Jingchen was averse to employing young women as his secretaries, the better to avoid idle gossip.

Mary Wei, nee Luo, was the widow of Cathay's founder and former president. A woman of spirited personality and good looks, when she happened to be strolling in the neighborhood, she might drop in Mr. Zhu's office to relax and chat for a while. In intervals between heavy official business, to pass a little time in light banter with so attractive a woman was by no means objectionable. But on this particular day he simply was not in a leisurely frame of mind. Nonetheless, he said politely to Mrs. Zhong, "Ask her to come right in."

Mrs. Wei had deposited in Cathay Republic the entire amount of money which Mr. Wei had left her, withdrawing only the interest for her own use. She thus counted as one of Cathay's most important individual depositors, and it would hardly do not to exchange pleasantries with her.

There was a light knocking at the door, almost pianistic in its quality. He recognized it immediately as Mrs. Wei's.

Mary Luo Wei, also in her forties, was wearing a sleeveless black and white mandarin dress with a maple-leaf pattern, which revealed full, creamy shoulders. Her jet-black hair was combed back into a large flat bun, held in place with a hairnet studded with tiny star-like pearls. Although a beauty past her prime, in her graceful bearing she was just as she always was.

"Ah, Mrs. Wei. How is it you are getting younger all the time!" Jingchen pushed his chair back and stood up.

"Oh, please, please, Mr. Zhu." Mrs. Wei drew off her white gauze gloves, in the process purposely brushing against Jingchen, who was instantly enveloped in the scent of Chanel No. 5. Mrs. Wei had been born into a family of only modest means which owned a coal briquette shop. After graduation from high school, she passed the exam for employment at Yongan Company as a salesgirl at the writing pen counter. Stunningly attractive, she soon had something of a reputation for herself, and was dubbed by hack writers at a local tabloid which wrote her up, as the "Queen of Pens." Her detractors, on the other hand, referred to her behind her back as the "Briquette Babe." After the loss of his first wife when he was close to sixty, Wei Jiusi, always a frequenter of the gay quarters, formally took Mary Luo as his wife. As Mrs. Wei for over twenty years, she learned the outward ways of a cultured wife, but she was at bottom connected to her origins, and among close acquaintances some of her actions and manners smacked inescapably of her former years as the bewitching Queen of Pens.

"On hot days like today, if you have business please just give us a call," said Jingchen, fixing her a cup of jasmine tea with his own hand. "No need to trouble yourself running over here personally."

She took a sip of tea. "I've come especially to see you. Isn't that allowable?" she said glancing at him slyly.

"To the contrary, I fear only that you would not come to see me, Mrs. Wei." Such were the words on his lips, but he returned to his chair, thus interposing the desk between himself and his guest. With people popping in and out so often it was not worthwhile laying himself open to gossip by sitting close beside her.

Wei Jiusi had doted upon this wife, but lest the children by his previous marriage treat with contumely their youthful stepmother, Mr. Wei not only left her a very considerable amount of money, he specially summoned Jingchen to his deathbed where he entrusted everything—wife and property alike—to Jingchen's care. As a matter of fact, even without the entreaty of Mr. Wei the Cathay Republic president, Jingchen would have been more than happy to look after so attractive and intelligent a woman as Mrs. Wei.

On rare occasion he would play mahjong with her. How adorable those soft creamy hands of hers, with five little dimples on the knuckles dancing before his eyes as she mixed the mahjong tiles. Jingchen could not resist hooking his little finger around hers. At such times Mrs. Wei would smile faintly and look at him with smiling eyes, too, bringing an intoxicating confusion to his heart. Notwithstanding, for a variety of reasons, he did not let his manner or relationship toward her exceed the limit, although Mrs. Wei for a time had really hoped she might marry him after he'd lost his own wife.

Seated opposite him, her gaze fell upon a glittery frame on the windowsill holding a photograph of Pu Zhuanlin. In recent years, Jingchen had taken to copying the style of the presidents of the big foreign banks, like the British Hong Kong and Shanghai Banking Corp. or the Deutsche Asiatische Bank: in one corner of the office a picture of the family, next to which a small cut-glass flower vase holding a single pink carnation.

"Jingchen, when will invitations be sent for the wedding banquet?" Her slender fingers took the cigarette Jingchen offered and leaned forward to catch the flame of his cigarette lighter. From behind the smoky haze her expression was one of pampered indolence.

"I'll wait until autumn to start thinking of that. It's just too hot these days to get fired up about marriage. Like today—not even noon yet and it's already this hot." Jingchen strived to treat his upcoming marriage with offhanded casualness.

Mrs. Wei, cigarette dangling from her lips, reached out quite without asking and picked up the picture of Zhuanlin.

"This young lady," she remarked, appraising the likeness, "is certainly interesting looking. I hear she's from the Pu family of Suzhou. Her elder brother was in the first group to study abroad under the Boxer Indemnity Fellowship Program, and later was appointed to a diplomatic post overseas..."

This breezy, self-assured hauteur of hers provoked in Jingchen a certain displeasure.

"What is it you wish to speak to me about, Mrs. Wei? Now before it gets too busy, I can help you with your business. But it will shortly become hectic and I'm afraid I may then not have that liberty." Politely but with cool detachment he interrupted her, courteously reminding her not overly to occupy his time.

Mrs. Wei drew in on her cigarette and flicked off the ash, hesitating. "Um...Jingchen," she finally began, "that little sum of mine...I mean the money which Mr. Wei left me...well, I'm thinking...I'd like to withdraw it."

Jingchen was dumbstruck. Not only was Mrs. Wei's account of considerable magnitude and relatively inactive—a bank's ideal account—but if the widow of the bank's founder himself, Wei Jiusi, were to withdraw her funds, how could this not undermine Cathay's very foundation?

He looked at her in astonishment. Could it be that, having heard of his marriage plans, she was seeking revenge? But on second thought, it couldn't be that, for there had never been any agreement between them, indeed they had never even spoken of marriage. But when a woman feels wronged, she is capable of anything.

"Mrs. Wei, your late husband worked tirelessly so that Cathay Republic could be what it is today..." Jingchen rose and stepped over to her, one hand resting on her chair back, the other on its arm as he bent over her to speak.

She regarded him calmly. "But he's no longer with us today. 'When the tree falls, the monkeys scatter,' they say; so too, when an influential person like my husband dies, former friends and associates go their own way. No one seems to think I exist any more. And I have to be mindful of my own interests. Since the conversion from the silver standard to the national currency, there's been economic depression and silver inflation. If I keep my money on deposit and try to live off the interest, its value will gradually erode. That just isn't worthwhile. It would be better to withdraw the money and go into business or buy securities in order to provide a healthy cash flow."

As Jingchen weighed these words, they seemed less her own than those of someone else instructing her what to say. Nonetheless, he retained his patient temper. "In that case, Mrs. Wei," he urged, "could you wait a few days before making your withdrawal? So you won't get swamped in the wave of withdrawals these past few days. Rest assured I shall not treat you unfairly. Even supposing, for the sake of argument, that Cathay is indeed experiencing some untoward contingency, your funds—both principle and interest—will in any event suffer no diminution. You may have full confidence in what I say."

She stubbed out her cigarette in the ashtray. "If today the words of President Chiang Kaishek cannot always be relied upon," she resumed in an uncompromising tone of voice, "how much less so your own words, sir." In that instant Jingchen apprehended the full truth of the phrase, "life's harsh realities," for even this woman, who on countless previous occasions had gazed at him with tenderness and affection, could now so mercilessly turn against him.

"It's difficult to imagine what business you could take up," said Jingchen, speaking rather sternly. "Foreign bullion exchange? Securities transactions? I advise you to dampen your enthusiasm, for prices in this sort of business fluctuate widely and could ruin you. Mrs. Wei?"

"Naturally I won't be personally involved in the trading," she said with a careless shrug of the shoulders. "A friend will be helping me."

"A friend helping you? Who?"

"Mr. Gong, an assistant vice-president at Bank of China."

"Him?" he asked as if she had some explaining to do. "I'm sure he's very keen on all this."

"Perhaps before long, Mr. Zhu, you'll be addressing me as Mrs. Gong," she said, adjusting her hairnet.

"He..." This man Gong who had in recent years been madly scurrying around, now for some reason or other had all of a sudden become quite smug. He must be eight years younger than she, and if he married her, clearly it would be for reasons other than mere matrimony.

"How's that? Do you consider that I am unworthy of him?" She drew her lips into a scornful smile. "I can say quite honestly that everyone wants me to marry him, and if I deposit my money in that other bank, what of it?" (Hearing "that other bank," a cold chill penetrated Jingchen to the very marrow.) "What's more, Gong would like to have more cash available to engage in business. You are also aware that a law-abiding banker trying to live on his meager salary would be hopelessly impoverished." She spoke the truth, all right, it was just that he didn't know if that Gong fellow would appreciate her kindness.

"Mrs. Wei," said Jingchen with real sympathy, shaking his head. "He is not worthy of you. Truly, he is not worthy of you."

Outwardly she smiled a light-hearted smile, but her eyes concealed an inner gloom. "Tell me then, who is worthy of me?"

Indeed, who was worthy of her? She, the precious daughter of mere coal-briquette shop owners; she, the salesgirl standing behind a fountain pen counter. What's more, it would be her second marriage with two kids—two "oil jars"—in tow at that. Among men with status and position, who would want to marry her?

Jingchen felt he ought to say something more to her, but he really couldn't think of anything appropriate. He rang the bell for Mrs. Zhong and instructed her to escort Mrs. Wei and help in the transaction of her business.

Jingchen stepped over to the window. Below, there was still a throng of people crowded about the bank's entrance, and he could suppress neither his sense of unease nor the perspiration wetting his palms. How was it this bank run had come upon him so abruptly and so viciously? It seemed to be intentional, for it could not possibly result from simple bad luck.

Chapter 7

At the corner of Bubbling Well Road and Seymour Road stood a Spanish-style apartment building, which Juanm in ahead and Zhishuang behind were just entering.

The elevator wobbled up toward the seventh floor. Its operator, sort of an oldish fellow, was wearing a neatly pressed silk shirt and trousers.

"Seventh floor. You're going to see Miss Hong Fung?"

Hong Fung was as popular an entertainment idol as Zhou Shuan, and her rendition of "One Summer Evening" had catapulted her to fame overnight.

Juanmin held her head high and ignored the elevator operator, while Zhishuang, unable to wound his sensibilities, smiled at him.

"Movie stars, movie stars." The elevator operator intoned every syllable with flourish and exaggeration, then grinned mischievously. "Where do you find time to visit movie stars? They always work nights, and sleep right through till at least four or five in the afternoon."

"But now it's almost ten," said Zhushuang, "and she must be up."

"How can well behaved students like yourselves bring discipline to the lives of these movie stars?" As he spoke, he picked up a large bundle of letters from his stool. "Here. Give these to your movie star. Every day there's a pile of letters like this. People seem to have a large appetite for writing fan letters."

"Oafs like him—why pay them any attention," said Juanmin to Zhishuang when they'd stepped out of the elevator. Juanmin made extremely fine distinctions of rank, which even Zhishuang at times felt to be excessive.

They rang the doorbell, and heard a mincing voice inquire within, "Who's there?"

The two girls looked at each other in confusion and were able to reply with no more than a "It's me."

"Is that you, Mannuo? Why've you come so early?" The voice inside perked up. "Wait a sec."

"This voice doesn't sound much like her movies," said Juanmin. But Zhishuang felt an indescribable anxiety, more so even than going into an examination hall.

Inside could be heard rustling sounds, followed by the shuffling of slippers, and, it seemed, a man's voice besides.

The slippers shuffled right up to the other side of the door, where she was probably surveying them through the peephole and, discovering she was wrong, asked nervously, "Who is it?"

"We've come with an introduction from Ju Beibei."

"Oh, you're the Zhu daughter?" The voice behind the door immediately adopted a politer tone. "Please wait a moment."

More rustling was heard from behind the door. It seemed somebody was hurrying into another room, shutting the door with a bang.

The front door opened. Hong Fung, wearing a yellow searsucker bathrobe with a black design and bright red leather slippers, welcomed them in with a giggle. She totally lacked the manner of a movie star. She took the bundle of letters, no more than glanced at them, and set them on the hallway table.

"Excuse me," she said. "Yesterday we were filming right up till daybreak today. I just got up and haven't had a chance to straighten up the room."

This stuffy apartment was of the type which had one large central room; off one end of the entranceway was the kitchen, the other end the bathroom, and right in front the main room, which faced south and had a balcony. A door off the bedroom, apparently leading to the bathroom, was at this moment closed, but inside the splash of the water faucet could be heard; the footsteps of a moment ago had doubtless gone in there. In any event these single-main-room apartments were cut up into just such a layout as this, which allowed not the slightest leeway.

"Sit down. Which one of you is Miss Zhu?" asked Hong Fung, all smiles. Zhishuang discovered she was far from being as good looking as in her films; indeed, her skin was coarse, though she did have beautiful eyes and her lips arched into a lovely smile.

Hong Fung seemed to know quite a bit about Zhu family affairs: Zhu Jingchen's fiancee, Zhu Jingwen's romantic history—she knew it all.

And yet this was not so surprising, for in Shanghai small things weren't so small, while big things in fact were nothing very special, and in being bandied about and circulated sooner or later everything came to have some connection with everything else, and how much more so when it was a popular movie star and a prominent banking family.

In her films this star, if not the daughter of a noble family, at least portrayed the daughter of a wealthy family, who in almost every scene was ornately dressed and richly made-up. Unexpectedly, then, Zhishuang found the real-life Hong Fung to be no more than this. The room could boast no more than a cream-colored French-style furniture set, a pair of armchairs, and a low coffee table scattered with the previous night's cups and saucers and a half pack of cigarettes.

"Here's a copy of our current yearbook, with thanks for your assistance, Miss Hong. If you hadn't come to participate in our commencement exercises, we would all have regretted it a great deal." And Zhishuang handed Hong Fung a copy of the yearbook, while Juanmin stood there gaping at her.

"Your rendition of 'Fishing in the Bright of Day' has much more feeling than Wang Renmei's, yet without that cloying sweetness of Zhou Shuan's. Speaking of Zhou Shuan, isn't she the illegitimate child of a nun?" queried Juanmin, expressing a long suppressed mysterious feeling she had about the film world.

But Hong Fung smiled wanly. "The film world is full of rumors. Whenever a few people blow on a chicken feather it gets transformed into a soaring pheasant." And she began chatting with them as she smoked a cigarette.

Although she was a movie star, her conversational style had none of the vulgarity associated with her profession, and the two girls listened eagerly as she entertained them with one interesting account after another about the pleasures and hardships of her life in the entertainment world the way it really was. All the while, however, behind its tightly closed door the bathroom refused to be quiet, and there issued from it a constant stream of gargling noises, spitting noises, and the particularly obvious noises of urination and toilet flushing. Hong Fung, true to her movie world origins, just sat there in complete nonchalance while the two girls squirmed awkwardly in their chairs.

Soon, fortunately, the bathroom door at the end of the hallway could be heard to open, followed in a moment by the soft opening and closing of the apartment front door, and the bathroom now finally had quieted down.

The girls also felt they should say goodby. Hong Fung presented them each with an autographed photo about the size of a picture postcard, which the girls accepted with profuse thanks as priceless treasures.

The same old busybody took them down on the elevator.

"Well, then, was the movie star good-looking?" he inquired with a meaningful smile.

The elevator wobbled down to the ground floor, the door opened, and there stood a stylish young man with a handsome face waiting for the elevator.

"Dr. Feng!" exclaimed a pleasantly surprised Juanmin.

Mr. Feng turned toward them, smiling broadly. "You young ladies are..."

Zhishuang was rather reserved of personality, while Juanmin lacked all inhibition, and how much more so considering her long-time crush on Feng Jingsyao. Juanmin said with great poise, "We're from McTyeire. You gave a lecture there this spring." Then, after a pause, she asked nervously, "Oh, you've come to see Miss Hong, too?"

"Yes, the movie star. Don't girls just love movie stars!" he said with a noncommittal smile. "Bye-bye," and he stepped into the elevator.

"Let's go," said Zhishuang, tugging at Juanmin. But Juanmin just stood there motionless, watching the indicator lights flash on as the elevator proceeded upwards, coming to a stop finally at the seventh floor where Hong Fung lived.

"You go on ahead. I forgot my handkerchief at Hong Fung's," replied Juanmin, as she pressed the elevator button.

"Juanmin, you can't just go up there. Be reasonable, won't you?" Zhishuang understood that Juanmin was having a flare-up of her childish temper. "People will make fun of you."

Juanmin didn't care about that and willfully stepped into the elevator.

"Wha'd'ya forget?" asked the old elevator operator.

"That gentleman just now—didn't he go to Miss Hong's apartment?"

"There's eight families live on that floor. How do I know which one he went to?"

Juanmin got out of the elevator and gave Hong Fung's doorbell a long ring, then rang it several more times and still nobody responded. Again the elevator could be heard clunking upward, and Zhishuang came out and grasped Juanmin's hand.

"You're crazy, Juanmin." Zhishuang was stunned to see Juanmin's face flushed a deep red and breath coming in short pants.

By now too embarrassed to ride yet again the nosy old man's elevator, Zhishuang with her arm around her friend walked all the way down, floor by floor. "Juanmin, you just can't do this. Even if you do like him a lot, you can't do this," she said exhorting her friend.

Juanmin frowned deeply but said not a word.

As they emerged from the main entrance, they noticed newspaper boys waving a just-published extra and calling out in loud voices some big news event.

"Miss, Miss, read about it in the extra...," and a newsboy shoved a paper under Zhishuang's nose. Carelessly glancing at it, she was struck by the huge and imposing black headline: "Japanese troops on pretext of soldier's death bombard Marco Polo Bridge in Peking outskirts; Chinese garrison forced to engage the enemy..."

"Juanmin!" Zhishuang shrieked.

They only now realized that people in the street were all knotted into groups of three and four eagerly reading the extra. Even the rickshaw coolies along the street, rather than looking for customers, had pulled up into a line, several coolies bunched around one who could read, listening to the news as it was read aloud one word at a time.

"Oh my god, it's finally come to war. It had to happen."

"Zhang Jingjiang and Hu Shi have rushed to England and the U.S., but to no avail."

People were milling about on the street discussing the news, some so agitated that they shouted in the middle of the street, "Letting the Japs keep taking our territory is no solution!"

"Let's quick get back home!" said Zhishuang, timidly pulling at Juanmin. Girls such as they—youthful and inexperienced—always reckon that home is the safest place to be.

Chapter 8

"**M**rs. Syi, could I borrow some cooking wine?"

Mrs. Tsao, a small wine cup in hand, had come in through the back door and into the Syis' kitchen. Mrs. Syi then and there had Zhou, the maid, pour out a cupful of wine for her. Mrs. Tsao retrieved the cup but, far from showing any intent of leaving, began to strike up a conversation. "Any news of Mr. Syi? With the hostilities in the north now, conditions are none too safe. It'd be better to tell him to return early and be done with it."

"How could he do that? He's on official business." Mrs. Syi smiled good-naturedly, though worry was etched in her forehead. "Didn't the bank send him, after all?"

"By the way, Mrs. Syi," said Mrs. Tsao, bending close to her ear, "have you heard the stories? They say Cathay's business has gone sour and people are lining up like crazy to withdraw their money. I keep a jewelry case in the bank's safe deposit box—do you think I should take it out? What if something happened to the bank? Then there wouldn't be even so much as a soup bone left to me. Have you seen the papers? Just recently a Cathay vice-president was reported to have taken depositors' funds and used them for speculation. When foul-smelling scandals like this get circulated, people lose faith in the bank and want to withdraw their money. I'm terribly anxious about all this."

Mrs. Syi was stunned; she looked around at Zhou, then took Mrs. Tsao into the parlor. "You'd better discuss this matter with Mr. Tsao, and not talk irresponsibly about it."

"Humph, what's to discuss? Cathay's just like my husband's ancestors—he wouldn't dare be disrespectful to either. But look, since the outbreak of hostilities with the Japs, everybody's anxious. In such circumstances the most peace of mind comes from having your money and valuables clutched right in your own hands!" No sooner had she settled her bottom into the easy chair than she started grumbling. Then she suddenly leaned forward and with great mystery whispered into Mrs. Syi's ear. "They say that Bank of China is going to raise interest rates by twenty percent. Twenty percent!"

"Mrs. Tsao," replied Mrs. Syi gently rebuking her, "Your husband and my husband are both Cathay employees. The bank is doing well, and when the bank does well, we do well, too. 'The boat rises with the tide,' you know. Some people there are fabricating rumors about Cathay, but if we simply take the approach of patiently explaining the truth to people, how will it be possible to undermine the bank's foundation? One jewelry case in your eyes or my eyes looks terribly important, but for a bank it is no more important than a sesame seed or a green pea. Even if the bank were to fold, still it wouldn't gobble up such trifles as you or I might have in safe deposit. Yet if at this moment when there's a run on the bank and you anxiously go and get caught up in the heat of things withdrawing your funds and retrieving your jewelry, people would start talking about how Cathay employees themselves have no confidence in their own bank—even that would be a small matter. But if by chance people's slander reached the ears of President Zhu, then that would certainly not be good for Mr. Tsao."

What Mrs. Syi was saying made sense, and Mrs. Tsao was somewhat reassured yet she still couldn't keep from heaping abuse on her own husband. "It's all the fault of that senseless old man of mine—anything and everything he wanted to keep in the bank. Previously, valuables were safest when clutched in our own hands, yet he of all people was itching to deposit our whole house and all with Cathay..."

Later, having seen Mrs. Tsao out, Mrs. Syi herself began to feel uneasy. Her husband had no choice but to stay all the while at the Bounty Mill site inland, and although Zhishuang was eighteen, she hadn't the slightest interest in these matters, and Chengzu was still in junior high, so all day long Mrs. Syi didn't have anyone at home she could talk to. But in so important a matter as withdrawing her funds from Cathay, she was utterly unwilling to rush presumptuously into action on her own. Turning it over in her mind, she decided to have Zhishuang write her father and put these questions to him. Pity the mails inland were so damnably slow!

"Mother, Mother, some rich gentleman has come into our lane. His own private car has driven in and stopped." Chengzu who happened just then to be in the lane playing kick-the-shuttlecock, came scurrying in through the back door calling to Mrs. Syi. Only twelve or thirteen, Chengzu was already wearing western-style shorts with suspenders and calf-length socks, affecting an altogether westernized appearance. But unfortunately, this lane was just a third- or fourth-class residential area, where one might well see privately owned rickshaws, but hardly ever a privately owned sedan.

"There's no need to make such a fuss about it, you little devil. A guest is still just a guest." Mrs. Syi scolded her son, yet she too was surprised and wondered who it might be; she did not have to wonder for long, however, for a knock was soon heard at the front door.

"Zhishuang, Zhishuang, have you finished dressing? Come down right away." It turned out to be Zhishuang's good friend Zhu Juanmin. How was it she had come by car today, something she had never done before. Mr. Zhu was always very frugal in everyday life, and during all their years at McTyeire when returning home Saturdays and going back to school Sundays, Juanmin and Zhishuang always went together by bus.

"I'm coming, Juanmin." Having fixed herself up most attractively, Zhishuang descended the stairs feeling self-important. "Mother, I won't be back for supper," she said without even bothering to turn toward her mother.

"With food at home, you're still going to eat out? Why spend the extra money? Miss Zhu is no stranger here, so why not just eat here?" Mrs. Syi was a housewife of the old style who, while not altogether old fashioned in her social conduct, did always consider frugality as her natural vehicle.

"Gee, Mother, here we've been killing ourselves studying for the past six years, and now we've managed to get a moment of rest before we go to college where there won't be any time for relaxation—just four straight years without a break, and still you won't let us go out for a good time." Zhishuang scowled as she turned on her childish petulance. And just then the car waiting at the front door honked its horn impatiently.

"Oh, Miss Zhu is still waiting at the front entrance. Quick, open the door for her and ask her into the parlor to sit a while." Mrs. Syi only then realized that Zhu Juanmin was still locked outside, and was just hurrying over to let her in when Zhishuang quickly moved toward the door. "Forget it," she said; "I'm going out instead." In truth, Zhishuang was loathe to ask Juanmin into her own home, although it's not that she'd never come to call before. But Zhishuang always felt that once Juanmin had come in to visit, the balance that ordinarily existed between them would undergo a palpable, even if subtle, transformation, and it would be a long time before the imbalance could gradually be righted. Juanmen herself may have been quite unmindful of all this, yet Zhishuang, for her part, was extremely mindful. Moreover, she was unwilling to let her mother chat overly much with Juanmin, for fear that this old-style housewife of a mother would make a fool of herself in the presence of the extravagant and ostentatious Miss Zhu.

Moving gracefully, Zhishuang made her departure. This Zhishuang—it's all because her father doted on her. Syi Zhensyu had been studying overseas when he learned that his first-born was a girl, and he said that even though she was a girl, she would be raised like a son and would go to the best schools. All right, then, from kindergarten through high school she was a student at McTyeire School for Girls, where the friends she made were all daughters of important Shanghai families. Just see how this private automobile—so inappropriate to the Syis' status—had come to pick her up. Zhishuang was a very pretty girl and broad-minded, too, but still, just the product of a salaried household. Eighteen this year, nineteen next—how fast the time was flying by. When Mrs. Syi was eighteen she had already given birth to Zhishuang. As it happened, a frost had fallen that day so the new father chose the name Zhishuang—"angelica frost." The family had to tighten its belt to send her to so elite a school as McTyeire, for quite aside from tuition, the other expenses (like the various functions involved in commencement exercises which alone required from first to last eight new dresses) were of a magnitude for which the term "sinful" might well be applied. Yet Mrs. Syi feared that in so assiduously complying with her daughter's every need, Zhishuang would still not be content with her lot, would still not be happy. And later on her troubles would be greatly multiplied. Heavy at heart, Mrs. Syi heaved a sigh.

Juanmin was wearing a gaily colored silk mandarin dress—peacock blue and purplish rose with a touch of bright red—but because she possessed an inherently dignified beauty, she not only did not appear cheaply vulgar, her slender figure was set off with a greater stateliness and gentility. Zhishuang could not but secretly admire Juanmin's boldness in her choice of colors, which, come to think of it, was related to her character.

"How thoughtful you are today!" Seeing the well polished Buick parked there in the lane, Zhishuang actually felt a little constrained.

"It's my brother. He's just learned how to drive so he's been itching to get behind the wheel. Daddy's been using the bank's car for the past few days, so my brother snuck out in our own car to satisfy his craving. We were only too happy to drive here and pick you up." As Juanmin spoke, she rapped the car's rear end a couple of times and began scolding her brother.

"What do you mean by honking the horn like that? I've never before known you to have so irritable a temperament. If you're this impatient, you'll never get any girl friends!"

Zhishuang only now noticed the face of a young man sticking out the window of the driver's seat, who had almond-shaped eyes just like Juanmin. This, presumably, was Juanmin's older brother.

Juanren conducted himself as the progeny of Cathay Republic Bank's president ought, assuming several degrees of arrogance, especially towards women. And, indeed, there were not a few young ladies, extremely desirous of becoming his wife, who were always trying consciously or unconsciously to attract his attention. Consequently this only abetted his disdainful bearing toward women. But at this moment when Zhishuang broke into a dimpled smile and nodded to him, he actually felt a little flustered; he hurriedly opened the car door, stepped out, and greeted her with gracious courtesy.

Zhishuang was to be a college student in the fall, but she was too impatient to wait, and was now already doing her hair up in the latest fashion, adorning her ears with red jade earrings bright as two little red beans, and wearing a white linen dress with red polka dots—the perfect model of the graceful and refined daughter of a great family. To be perfectly honest about it, today's young ladies are insufferably vulgar if they are the daughters of petty households; or, if they are the daughters of families with a modicum of social status, then they puff themselves up with an air of importance. And those of Juanmin's type—well, you just can't stomach them. On the other hand, young ladies like Zhishuang—cultured and poised—were they not too seldom seen?

Since Zhishuang had been a dormitory student throughout her years at the girls' academy, she was still unused to mixing socially with men and thus could not avoid a certain bashfulness. Juanren opened the car door for them, took his own place in the driver's seat, then with a flourish slammed his door shut. Zhishuang's heart fluttered—here, clearly, were the manners of the son of the quintessential great family.

The engine had just started when from the back seat Zhishuang said softly, "Wait a second."

"What is it?" asked Juanren, looking back.

"Oh, never mind," she seemed to say to herself. Then with an apologetic smile, "Let's go."

Just then turning into the lane ahead was Chilin on his bicycle pedaling toward them at a leisurely pace. Zhishuang had thought to call a greeting to him, but today for some reason or other, she really didn't want him to know that she was being taken for a drive by a gentleman driving his own car. She sensed he might not be very happy about it.

With that special hauteur of one belonging to the private automobile stratum, Juanmin zipped down the lane in his 1936 Buick, brushing by Chilin's bike, horn honking cockily.

"Just look at that driving technique!" exclaimed Juanren, smiling smugly. "Well, ladies, what's on your entertainment agenda?"

"Let's first go to the movies, then go for a spin, and after that have dinner," said Juanmin.

"And how about you, Miss Syi?" asked Juanren, looking back at Zhishuang.

"Anything's fine with me," she smiled.

Juanren was in fact a very good driver. His two fair-skinned hands held the steering wheel lightly, neither tense nor slack, and he controlled the vehicle with facility. He was positively elegant. The rear-view mirror reflected the lower half of his face: straight nose and thin, well defined lips. Fortunately the line of his chin was rather rugged, otherwise the face would have been discernibly delicate and somewhat feminine.

Juanren began merrily whistling "Yankee Doodle." He had already found a position at German-owned Bayer Pharmaceuticals making one hundred silver dollars per month, where his duties consisted of promoting its pharmaceuticals in the Chinese medical community. It was a cushy job—he didn't have to sit in an office from nine to five and the salary and benefits of a foreign firm were exceptionally good, what with a company-provided rickshaw to and from work and allotment of two suits of clothes both in spring and summer in order to help maintain the appearance of this foreign firm's staff. All this could not but allow Juanren the swell headedness that attends those who enjoy success while young. He congratulated himself in finally following his father's advice in not working for his uncle at Verity Chemical Works, but rather at this foreign firm where the work pace was relaxed and the salary generous.

The car drove leisurely through the French Concession where the shop windows along the bustling streets were already displaying the latest summer clothing fashions—cotton dresses sheer as a cicada's wing, requiring a silk petticoat to set them off. All the dresses seemed to require petticoats, a clever scheme by which shops like these might relieve people of even more of their money.

A summer gloaming: the green trees swayed in the cool, whispering breeze, signaling a chilly evening coming on, and although it was already close to six, the horizon was a roof-tile blue and still bright enough to sting the eye, yet flashing neon lights lining the street had already begun to vie with each other. At the entrance to a department store two clerks on a bench in front of a counter were reciting aloud the comic dialog, "Little Scatterbrain," which drew a large cluster of idle passersby to the store's entrance.

"Hm, it's been a long while since I've meandered the streets; I've been as away from things as a country bumpkin. With bustle like this, why is Daddy always lamenting business is bad," Juanmin wondered aloud.

"Dong...dong...dong..." The clock atop the Customs House building was chiming the hour in large bold sounds with a lingering shimmer.

"Oh dear, another day is almost gone." Zhishuang recalled how time seemed to have been stuck when she was living in the McTyeire dormitory waiting (waiting forever, it seemed) for Saturday to arrive; now she had taken leave of her high school years but for the time being had not yet stepped through the portals of the university. For the entire summer there was neither homework nor church services and although she felt relaxed and happy she did sense that she was just frittering away her time; and as the clock chime assailed her ears, she couldn't repress the feeling that she had lost something.

Outside a western-style coffee shop two waiters were in the process of taking down the blue and white striped canvas awning. "Would you care for some coffee?" asked Juanren pleasantly.

Zhishuang's heart skipped a beat. She had never before gone into a coffee shop. By custom girls went into coffee shops only if in company with a male escort. But girls like Zhushuang were not supposed to mix much with young men and so she had never had this opportunity.

"Drinking coffee at this early hour? The night life hasn't even started yet!" said Juanmin languidly, fanning herself with her handkerchief.

The traffic light ahead turned red and two sweethearts, hand in hand, crossed the street brushing past the front of the car; the young lady's eyes glanced enviously into the car window. Zhishuang too, in that instant, felt infected with the conceit of being in the automobile stratum.

⋆   ⋆   ⋆

"Dong...dong...dong!"

The Customs Building chimes also wafted into Cathay Republic's Small East Gate branch. This branch was a four-storied structure of red brick, to outward appearance plain and practical. At the time when construction of the Small East Gate branch was in the planning stage, Jingchen much preferred business premises which in appearance were of simple dignity, and because the customers in the Small East Gate area would be mostly lower middle class people of modest means, a building of extravagant design would inevitably cause those everyday city people to feel inferior and overawed.

Due to the storm of withdrawals during the past few days, the entire bank staff had extended their working hours, though comparatively speaking, the secretarial staff upstairs would be rather less pressed than the operations personnel. Hearing the Customs Building clock sound the hour, the typists, the scribes, the accountants all pushed their work aside and got ready to go out for supper. Normally the bank provided only the noon meal to its employees, but now, what with the extended business hours, the evening meal was also provided, in the form of a cash salary supplement which allowed the employees to eat out in a restaurant. The Small East Gate area had plenty of inexpensive restaurants serving good Shanghai-style food, so as soon as the dinner hour arrived the office people went out in groups of twos and threes to the restaurants to eat. But in one corner of the room there was a young man still poring over the work on his desk.

"Supper time, Fan," said a colleague.

"Take a break, Yangzhi," said another.

"I still have a little more to do, and that'll be it," replied Fan Yangzhi with a smile. He waited until the circle of colleagues had all left, and then took out a tin of cooked rice, poured some boiling water over it to warm it up, then took out a jar of pickled radish. Since the death of his father, he had become the pillar of his household, and had had to drop his studies and find work in order to maintain the family. To save money he took the bank's supper subsidy and gave it to his mother for household use, himself bringing from home every day a tin of cold rice which he ate with hot water added. Raising the lunch tin to his lips, however, a sour smell tingled his nostrils. Damn, today the door of the office cabinet was closed and the rice had spoiled. He angrily punted in a couple of mouthfuls: after all he had to get something into his stomach. It wouldn't be worthwhile getting a stomachache, however, so he dumped the remainder of the rice onto some scrap paper, crumpled it up and threw it into the wastebasket. But a healthy chap in his twenties has a strong digestive system, and Fan Yangzhi's stomach was growling so loudly it seemed to be singing a tune—"The Empty City."

In order to forget his stomach, he again took up his writing brush, dipped it in the ink and resumed his transcription of the day's checks.

Having finished their dinner, the other workers gradually returned, picking their teeth as they exchanged information they'd picked up outside about recent market conditions of concern to banking.

"They say that some of our shareholders got real angry, but Mr. Li, at a supervisors' meeting today, pounded the table and lectured them on the old virtues of 'sincerity in speech and resoluteness in deed,' which underpin the credibility of the banking industry—since we take in people's money, we are obliged to let people take it out any time they want to. He also talked about how the total of Cathay's share capital was increasing, so how could anybody still be saying the bank was ridden with problems? Was there any hanky-panky in the account keeping? Where had the cash gone to? Had someone been embezzling funds? It was pretty heavy talk."

"In any case the ledgers are all open, so let Mr. Li send someone to check them." Fan Yangzhi jumped to his feet as he made this comment, for he was young and felt this Mr. Li's remarks were very insulting. "Why doesn't he go inquire of his own nephew? Whoever's at the bottom of this hanky-panky—trading negotiable securities in these fluctuating market conditions—will make an ill-gotten fortune, but he'll pretend to be innocent like everyone else!"

Those who made their living at Cathay felt fortunate to have such good jobs—"eating from silver rice bowls," as they say—and, consequently, tended to be careful, circumspect people, obsequious even, who never dared openly criticize their own boss, so that now all of a sudden hearing Fan Yangzhi singling out Mr. Li by name for criticism, they were all quite at a loss; but because Yangzhi was a straightforward man who spoke his mind, they secretly felt pleased.

"Have you seen the tellers' counter downstairs? The withdrawal customers may not be actually clamoring to get in, but it's still plenty active. Even so, it's not so bad as the run on the big four national banks in June 1935 during the silver crisis," said one worried old-timer. Banking's unpredictability had struck terror into the hearts of these employees, and if by chance the bank should have to bang its doors shut and go out of business, where could they possibly find new work?

"It's tough, all right. The vault cash has now already dwindled nearly to insolvency, and if we brace ourselves again to approach our colleagues in other banks for loans, presuming on our friendships, we could probably get some; it's just that, considering Cathay's standing in Shanghai, if we rely for a long period on our fellow banks to support us with their credit, it would do that much damage to our bank's reputation," another worker said uneasily.

"Did you hear what they're saying about how the head office in order to attract depositors is allowing accounts to be opened with just one yuan? The other banks are all snickering at Cathay for outright panhandling. A gentleman came in this morning, took out one hundred yuan and said he wanted to open a hundred one-yuan accounts. Wasn't he really intent on just pestering us? But we gave him one hundred accounts anyway. We were already up to our ears in work what with this bank run when in comes this guy to make trouble for us—those tellers were mad enough to curse their own mothers!"

"It'll be tough for Cathay to survive this crisis."

There was a collective sigh, for all were burdened with anxiety: if something untoward befell Cathay, they might well find their rice bowls in risk of being broken—might well be out of a job.

Fan Yangzhi dipped his writing brush in the ink. "I really don't understand," he said, "why we just don't accept government shareholding. Banks everywhere have to have government backing in order to provide stability. How can it be good for us the way we're now 'digging out the east wall to patch up the west wall?' Whether modern banks or traditional counting houses, if they're not run the way they're meant to be run, they'll simply go out of business just because they're too caught up in this bank run!" Having thus spoken he realized his writing brush was an old one with a ragged tip which just wouldn't pick up the ink well; he got up and went to the General Affairs Section to get a new one.

The General Affairs Section, which handled the receiving and issuing of stationery supplies, was under the charge of a Ningbo gentleman in his fifties, a gaunt-faced, sallow-skinned man whose responsibilities in life, by the looks of him, were far from trifling, but whose stature in the bank was much like those "old junior trainees" who had come in with old Mr. Fan and who in old age would still be just clerks. This elderly gentleman ought to have been regarded with sympathy, but the insincere smile on his face and the fawning manner about him invariably made Yangzhi feel most uncomfortable; he tried, therefore, to minimize his contact with the man. At this moment, the Ningbo gentleman was earnestly involved in soaking a new writing brush for the head of the Paying and Receiving Department. An unctious smile on his face, he was saying to the department head, "This is an excellent weasel-hair brush—just look at its tip..." Yangzhi withdrew in disgust to one side, waiting until the department head had taken his pen and left before approaching.

Would he have guessed that the gentleman would actually hand him the used brush which had just been brought in for replacement? "This is a used brush," said Yangzhi angrily.

"A used one works just the same, doesn't it? You young people don't know what frugality is." And the gentleman went back to his work, ignoring Yangzhi.

"Damn it," he exploded, pounding the counter, "who says some people can get weasel-hair brushes while I just get somebody's hand-me-down brush?"

"Huh! Wait till the day comes when you're a department head, and don't be talking about using new brushes now." The "old junior trainee" sneered, incomparably pleased that there was finally an apprentice on the staff whom he could bully. "And you'll have your own sedan then, too."

"You servile bastard!" Yangzhi was in such a huff, he grabbed the used brush, snapped it in two and threw the pieces right at him. The elderly gentleman was himself on the verge of an angry outburst when he saw Zhu Jingchen standing in the corridor, who signaled to him to replace Fan Yangzhi's brush with a new one. Knowing he was in the wrong, the old gentleman quickly fished out a new brush and gave it to Fan Yangzhi. In signing for it, Yangzhi, still agitated, scrawled his name over fully three lines in the receipt book, then spun around and stomped off.

"Mr. Zhu, just look at today's young people," the old gentleman whined to Jingchen, who had come up to the counter. "No respect for their elders."

Jingchen smiled. When he himself had apprenticed, he too had taken a lot of such demeaning guff. He recalled the day his wife had given birth to Juanren: after he'd gotten the news he was anxious to get back home to see how mother and child were doing, so he rushed in to ask permission to leave work a couple hours early, only to encounter, quite unexpectedly, such a gentleman as this one, who smiled derisively as he sucked on his water pipe, finally opening his mouth to say, "So what's the big deal when a nobody like you acquires a son? It's not as if there were a fortune in property you were waiting to transfer to his name, so why on earth must you act so irrationally? Wait until the work day is over to go home and see your wife and child. That'll be early enough." Jingchen was rendered speechless by the rudeness of those remarks, but, unlike Fan Yangzhi, he of course could not slap the counter or pound the table. But ever since that time he'd secretly resolved to struggle to make a fortune and transfer it to his son. Of course, that was a minor incident twenty-some years previous, but in the end, even though he had not made a huge fortune, he had at least become, to his relief and elation, the head of Cathay Republic Bank. Zhu Jingchen could understand Fan Yangzhi's outburst only too well.

"Yes, but there's something else I might add to that," said Jingchen to the luckless old clerk in all seriousness, "—the shopkeeper's motto, 'fair and honest in all our dealings, with young and old alike.'" Jingchen then asked if the young man was a new employee. "His face seems vaguely familiar," he remarked.

"That's Fan Yangzhi, the son of Old Fan," replied the other with a touch of condescension.

Jingchen started—no wonder this young man had such a temper. When Jingchen had been present at Old Fan's mourning, he had gotten a taste of Fan Yangzhi's overbearing behavior. Young people possess a degree of arrogance—it's a symbol of their ambition—but it should not be excessive. Jingchen perused the ledgers Fang Yangzhi had made: he wrote a graceful hand, not a stroke misplaced—a very impressive job.

Jingchen walked slowly toward the records room. This morning after the supervisors' meeting, he felt like going to all the offices and departments for personal observation, to see how the bank run was affecting each of them in terms of cash reserves and conditions generally. For there was no gainsaying Cathay Republic was in the midst of a serious crisis, and there were some outstanding loans that were now very risky—borrowers who would "take advantage of the fire to loot the house:" they would not repay their loan when it matured but would rather surrender to the bank their now depreciated loan collateral. In such an eventuality the circulation of funds would obviously become even more of a problem. With things as they were now, the best policy was simply to calm people down. In addition, each board member one after another had taken out his private savings. But Mr. Li, knowing that blame for the present crisis lay partly with his own nephew's misconduct, would have to show some generosity by taking fifty thousand U.S. dollars of his own money and place it with the bank, where it could function both as a cash reserve and as a reassurance to anxious depositors. It would thus be possible, one hoped, to weather the present crisis.

Jingchen had not yet entered the records section when he heard Fan Yangzhi saying, "If they'd invited me into their supervisors' meeting, I'd have told 'em straight out, 'You'd damn well better allow government purchase of our stock, otherwise Cathay Republic will fold up overnight, and then what'll we do?'"

"Allow a government buy-in?" The query came from Tsao Jiusin, quietly smoking his water pipe, who, as it happened, was today auditing accounts at the Small East Gate branch and was now on break sitting in the records office. "Wouldn't that be like sucking blood from an open wound? Naturally if we rely on government stock purchases, we'll have lots of money and an authoritative air, but from that day on Cathay Republic will be a living corpse led around willy-nilly by a ring in our nose." As a man of some years who had seen it all, this Tsao Jiusin, despite appearances as a kindly Shaosying banker type, in fact displayed keen insight. Jingchen was afraid that by barging in he would interrupt their debate, and yet he really wanted to sound out the range of opinion among his colleagues, so he just stopped where he was and eavesdropped.

Fan Yangzhi yielded not an inch. "Modern banks like Cathay," he pressed on, "ought in the last analysis to be more progressive than the old-style counting houses. The purpose of financial institutions is to attract capital in order to finance industry and commerce. Quite aside from that economic mission, the modern banks must embody a social conscience and conviction. Cathay Republic may be a private commercial bank, but at the same time we have an obligation to help realize a higher standard of living for our four hundred million fellow citizens. We can't become just the private pocketbook of a few big shots while regarding with indifference the interests of our depositors. Moreover, if we pull the rug right out from under ourselves by refusing to accept a government buy-in, then we'll really have to rack our brains to find the cash for our coffers to survive the present bank run. And if it came to that, our business aims would certainly undergo great change, putting us inevitably on an altogether different course which, as I see it, would get us into the malodorous business of stock quotations and market speculation. And furthermore, who knows but what we won't be inspired by those audacious third- or fourth-rate private banks to start keeping double sets of books ourselves? And if we go to that extreme, Cathay's reputation may truly be said to be destroyed."

"This young devil," someone retorted, "certainly has an unrestrained mouth to pour out sharp words such as these. Cathay Republic Bank treats you so well, letting you fill in your father's vacancy, and you still can be so harsh."

This Fan Yangzhi not only had a sharp tongue, he was also very volatile of personality, a man easily roused. Had he perhaps not been one of those campus radical types giving speeches at every turn? If indeed he was such a type, that was really quite a nuisance.

"You're wrong. I earnestly wish Cathay Republic were in the hands of the younger generation like me so that we might embody the true spirit of the bank's motto, 'Helping Industry and Commerce, Serving Citizens and Society.' That's what concerns me so much."

It was an awfully bookish sentiment, but among bankers, for whom the smell of money was everything, the flavor of such innocence as this was hard to come by.

"Young man," broke in Mr. Tian, quite unfazed, "let me tell you something in all frankness. Mr. Businessman admittedly seeks profit, but that does not exceed 'what's mine is mine.' Mr. Government, on the other hand, is insatiable—'everybody's is mine,' he says. It's been like this throughout time. Once you get involved with Mr. Government, it's just like being bound hand and foot, and when it's all over, far from no longer being able to say, 'Serving Citizens and Society,' the reputation of Cathay Republic Bank itself will have been completely devoured and we will have become just a part of the government bank. Period." And how right he was!

"But with matters having gotten to the present predicament," put in a timid young lady, "besides just steeling ourselves for resistance, don't we really need to have a workable plan?"

"How can there be no way out of this? They think just a handful of managers are the only people with brains, but if they were to ask me..." Tsao Jiusin's own brain, it seemed, had come up with a solution, and what followed was accompanied by the gurgling of his water pipe. Well, bankers like him, with their origins in the counting houses, had wide social contracts, circulated easily in financial quarters, and were much sought after, so who knows but what he might not really be able to contribute some worthwhile ideas.

Jingchen cleared his throat and pushed open the half-louvred door and went in, greeting the company with hands clasped before him. "Everybody is doing his best to think of ways to preserve Cathay's reputation and independence—Mr. Fan is young and principled, Mr. Tsao is experienced and savvy. I'm really very touched." With this he brought calm to the room, and then briefly related what had gone on in the supervisors' meeting. He then urged them on with these instructions. "I must again trouble you to strive to the fullest extent of your abilities to attract funds into the bank from a broad range of people, that we together may rescue Cathay. I alone haven't the ability to do it, but I was elevated to the position of president by my colleagues on account of my reliability. In the coming days I shall still be depending on your help." As he spoke his gaze swept across the employees, one by one, seated at their desks, until his eyes fell on Fan Yangzhi. Jingchen was startled to realize that his cheekbones were exceptionally prominent, which instantly called to mind the lore of the physiognomy books, "Cheekbones protruding beyond the skull attest to a person contrary in heart," and he couldn't help raising his guard against him a little, for this young man might well prove overbearing in immodest displays of his considerable abilities.

"Mr. Zhu, you're wanted on the telephone," called a voice from outside.

As Jingchen started for the telephone he signaled to Tsao Jiusin to wait for him in the reception room.

"...Mr. Zhu, every time we lay in gold, it gets immediately drawn out—devoured by Bank of China." The voice on the telephone sounded harried. "The news has already gotten out that Cathay Republic Bank is losing its original capital."

"No matter, we'll throw in more," replied Jingchen with outward calm, though inside he was much troubled. He put down the receiver and was about to move on when it rang again. It was as if ghosts from the underworld were trying to drag him to his death. The latter call was from his secretary, Mrs. Zhong, conveying the news that the third son of the Feng family had passed away.

Even before the bereaved family had published an obituary, it appeared they had hastily dispatched someone to the bank with the news so that Jingchen might know how things stood.

The Fengs had been the employer of Jingchen's father. In those days Hangzhou's well-to-do families could be counted on the fingers of one hand, but since the Feng patriarch had rendered meritorious service by suppressing Japanese pirates (the "Jap dwarfs," as they were contemptuously referred to back then), the emperor conferred on him official rank and granted paddy land, whereupon the family fortunes abruptly soared. What's comical, when you think about it, is that old Mr. Feng originally was simply a common soldier helping to protect the port city of Hangzhou. On one occasion he happened to be squatting on his haunches moving his bowels and leisurely puffing on his pipe, when, having gotten half through his business, he vaguely made out a band of people putting ashore at the edge of the bay. As they gradually pressed toward the gate tower in the city wall he could see clearly that they were Jap dwarfs, whereupon, without taking the time to sound an alarm or even to pull up his pants, he rushed over to a nearby cannon emplacement, squatted down just as before and reached out with his pipe to the touchhole and set it off. The explosion killed half the enemy while the rest, figuring there were more armed troops along the parapet waiting for them, turned and beat a hasty retreat back to their ship. Thus Feng the old patriarch established his meritorious record with no more effort than it takes to relieve nature. The Feng mansion in those years, very much like the Jia family estate in Dream of the Red Chamber, occupied fully half a block. It was in this Feng residence that Jingchen's father had worked as a servant doing odd jobs.

For a time when they were boys, Jingchen and his younger brother, Jingwen, lived in a dank ground-floor room of the Feng residence. Once when the two boys were fooling around outside the firewood room, old Mr. Feng—the father of the third son who had just now passed away—chanced to come by and inquired of them why they were not studying instead of idly playing here. He only then learned that they were so poor they had never had a bit of schooling. So he immediately let them start studying at the Feng family's private school. When children of poor families are thrown in with wealthy children getting their lessons without paying a cent, there will always be friction and taunting, of course, but at least Jingchen and his brother did not grow up to be illiterates. Jingwen proved a particularly hard-working student, scoring first in his class year after year; he was recommended for admission to City High School No. One in Hangzhou, and later passed the exam for a government Boxer Indemnity Fellowship to study abroad, and though today he had still made nothing of himself, there was no denying he was indeed the holder of a Ph.D. degree. Jingchen, for his part, was accepted into Cathay Republic Bank as a trainee on the strength of a letter of recommendation from the Feng family patriarch, who was a former schoolmate of the bank's founder, Wei Jiusi. For these reasons, then, the Zhu family owed the Feng family a great debt of gratitude.

Jingchen hurried out of the records section and went into the staff lounge, where he found Tsao Jiusin holding his water pipe waiting for him. "Oh, I'm terribly sorry, Jiusin," said Jingchen, clapping his hand to his forehead. "With two phone calls right in a row, I'm afraid I've kept you waiting. I've been busy all afternoon and here it is now nearly seven and I haven't even had supper yet. Let's go out together to eat."

Jiusin had already had his dinner, but he understood Jingchen's real meaning, so he hurriedly tucked his fedora under his arm and went out with Jingchen.

In the boisterous downstairs dining room of Tonghe Restaurant quite a few laboring-class people were drinking and playing their loud finger-games, but as one proceeded up the colorful ceramic tiled stairway it became secluded and elegant. Jingchen, who was fond of the strongly flavored dishes, was a frequent guest here. The waiter appeared, greeting them with a smile, and led them to a private room at the very end of the corridor.

"It's been very busy at the bank lately, and it's been a long time since I've had a chance for a chat with you." Jingchen kneaded his brow in a gesture of utter exhaustion, then perked up his spirits and leaned toward his old colleague. "Jiusin, my friend, you're my senior in years—you've been around a lot and seen a lot...what do you think of Cathay's situation?"

Ah, here was Jingchen's talent at work, the talent that had enabled him to climb from trainee to the exalted position of president. To be perfectly candid, Tsao Jiusin was so old when he finally got a department head appointment, his beard practically reached the ground, and people like Mr. Syi, of the same age but higher ranking, objected to his vulgar manners, while the snobbish younger employees objected to his rustic demeanor. Today Zhu Jingchen invited Jiusin alone for a chat in a private room in Tonghe Restaurant, knowing that in Tsao Jiusin's decades at Cathay he may not have realized any conspicuous achievements, but he had worked indefatigably at many thankless jobs.

Jiusin cleared his throat and began. "Since the founding of Cathay Republic in 1905, the bank has weathered many vicissitudes and experienced several predicaments—the 1911 Republican Revolution, then the depredations of the warlords, then the Northern Expedition in 1927...and all the while the government has been watching for its chance to become a shareholder, though never with success. But if, sir, at the present juncture when the bank is in your hands the government should actually succeed, well then..." And he trailed off into a sardonic snicker.

Jingchen got his meaning and nodded.

The waiter lifted the curtain aside and came in with the food. Except at formal banquets Jingchen never took a drop of drink, so the dishes were being served directly. Jiusin had already eaten, although, as a matter of economy, only a bowl of noodles, so when now a dish even of simple fried pork slices was placed on the table, his appetite instantly revived. He took a morsel in his chopsticks and chewed it noisily. When he withdrew his chopsticks from his mouth, a thin, glistening thread of saliva like a strand of rice-flour noodle clung from the tip of his chopsticks to his mouth. The strand broke in a moment and congealed on the chopsticks, and Jiusin then again stretched them toward a plate of fried eel...Watching it all, Jingchen felt a wave of nausea overtake him, but he said nothing. Benighted souls like him of counting-house origins lacked any sensitivity to their surroundings, quite unlike the new breed of college graduates who had studied abroad and were very mindful of bearing and form. Syi Zhensyu, for one, was not in the slightest like this, but always wore trim western-style suits, highly polished shoes, and a fresh white handkerchief in his pocket.

These two strains of employees—the old style and the new style—had always formed themselves into two main camps at Cathay, and since Jingchen headed a single bank, he had to walk a tightrope between them, forever striving to maintain his balance and keep things on the level. Because he himself had begun as an apprentice and had worked his way up step by step to president, he held no such thing as a university degree in banking or in business: his academic record, as it were, was a shrewd knowledge of people gained with his own two eyes. As a consequence, emotionally he was rather inclined toward those employees of the old style, cautious and conscientious people, loyal and hardworking, unlike the university graduates and overseas students clutching their sheepskins, with their supercilious I'm-better-than-anyone-else attitude and their affected urbanity. He well knew, however, that with the increasing competition in the banking industry today, any bank which relied solely on its savings business would be bested by its rivals. Consequently banks had perforce transformed themselves into institutions whose present-day business was largely trust accounts, and as a result the new-style employees had become the nucleus of Cathay's operations. But Jingchen throughout displayed neither favor for the one nor disdain for the other but rather strived to allow them each to utilize to the fullest its own strengths: the new-style staff were mostly assigned to the various types of secured loans, to bookkeeping, and to paying and receiving; the old-style staff, because of their broad social connections, were asked to handle the bank's external activities, to seek additional subscriptions of capital, and to attend the daily clearing house sessions to pick up money market news. With this division of labor the two camps could at least on the surface exploit their strengths and maintain a peaceful coexistence.

Avoiding the area contaminated by Jiusin's chopsticks, Jingchen also took a piece of eel, still listening intently to his views.

"Thus considered, regarding a government purchase of our stock," Jiusin continued, emphasizing his remarks by tracing his chopsticks along the clean white tablecloth, "we might go through the motions of talking with them, but we should still act according to the lesson of our late founder, Mr. Wei: 'Be close to businessmen and keep officials at a distance.'"

"Yes, but..." Jingchen interjected, but Jiusin waved him to silence.

"There are now two approaches open to our forces. One approach concentrates on recalling outstanding loans, accumulating idle capital into savings accounts, and in recalling our silver dollars; the only other approach lies in quietly engaging in speculative activities to bring in some money in order to get us through the crisis. But in so doing we'll have to be cautious in the extreme and not let a word of it leak out..."

Jingchen forced a smile as he puffed away on his cigarette. Presently he said, "I've already been doing that. The damn thing is there's someone inside who's making trouble and if he thereby undermines the bank..." And he explained the whole situation to Jiusin.

Jiusin was completely taken aback. Resorting at this time to throwing in the bank's gold reserves could only mean the situation was out of control and that this able president sitting opposite him really had no idea which way to turn. Indeed, "the commander-in-chief had lost his mount!"

"Endlessly propping up the bank like that simply isn't the way to do it." Tsao Jiusin already had a plan of his own in mind, but he bided his time. He took a leisurely sip of fish soup, noisily chewed his sparerib, and after a long while finally said, "Actually, it's not so difficult—just secure the services of some Shanghai power-broker who can come in like a weighing-rod weight and squash things, and there won't be any more problems."

"Huh?" Suddenly Jingchen's heart felt buoyant. "But this heavyweight...he can't be an official or a businessman—he's got to be someone fair and impartial who'll weigh the situation evenly. Where do we find someone like that?"

"Well, there is someone."

"Who?"

Tsao Jiusin turned his chopsticks around and with the dry end etched the character "Du" on the tablecloth.

"Mr. Du?"

"Mr. Du. He's the director of the Shanghai Bankers Association. If we ask him to come forward and say a few words, that would be sufficient to stabilize the situation."

"I'm afraid I may not be on good enough terms with him," said Jingchen a little doubtfully.

"I think Mr. Du would be quite willing to help a man of your prestige, sir. I know him to be a man who, once he's set his mind to it, can get his money back from anyone. Yes, he'll be willing to help. Just the other day I heard someone remark that Mr. Du had publicly expressed his admiration for you."

"Well..." Jingchen hesitated. "If we trouble a big shot like him, what sort of a thank-you gift should we figure on?"

"They say he's fond of antiques."

"Well...I've no idea about that." Now Jingchen seemed even more unsure.

But Jiusin just chuckled. "That old melon-head," he replied, recalling Du Yuesheng's fruit-shop origins; "he doesn't know a thing about antiques—can't tell good from bad. Just give him any old thing and you'll get by very nicely."

Isn't it true that "ginger grows spicier with age." Looking at this old banker Tsao Jiusin, one could only wish there were a lot more like him.

"Jiusin, my friend, there are not many older people still at Cathay today. In everything I still have to ask you to take the helm. Today's young workers have the book learning, all right, but in experience they're pretty shallow. I've already instructed Mrs. Zhong to notify the accounting department to increase your monthly salary by fifty yuan starting next month. Since we're not having wine with the meal, let me substitute tea so I can toast you a cup."

Tsao Jiusin beamed in reply.

Emerging from the restaurant, Jingchen drove directly to the Feng house on Hart Road.

The summer days lasted particularly long. Near eight, dusk was only now gradually spreading its canopy, and in the twilight the brilliance of scattered street lamps dispersed the gathering darkness. Wafting from the open window of someone's house came the shrill tones of a Chinese fiddle. Everything seemed to convey the bleakness people tend to associate with sunset and dusk.

Jingchen had long since heard that after the break-up of the Feng family, the third son had himself brought along his brothers' concubines to live in the house he'd purchased in Shanghai. Realizing that their circumstances were far from favorable, Jingchen had never paid a call on them lest it only prove embarrassing, yet he did send gifts of some value at New Year and other festival days, which might be taken as a face-saving form of material assistance. Just think of it: this proud third son, who in former times had enjoyed new clothes and rich foods, who had never lacked for crowds of enthusiastic hangers-on, now lay dead and neglected in this miserable alley house.

A centipede, they say, may die but it never falls down; so too old families still stand after suffering mortal injuries. Until the time of the Northern Expedition in 1927, the Feng family still had a cash fortune of over two million in addition to its real estate holdings. Before his death old Mr. Feng, who tried to plan everything carefully to avoid having his heirs bring discredit to his name, arranged matters in detail for them: he took personal possession of all his property (over one hundred pieces) and deposited a very considerable amount of foreign currency in a foreign-owned bank; even if his stock investments should come to naught, he figured, there would be rental income, and even if that was used up, the rural branch of the family still owned fifty or so acres of paddy land. Truly, his love of family ran very deep, and he lavished all his energies on it. Inevitably, however, the Feng household declined. "Troops in defeat are like a mountain crumbling," they say, and the Fengs' decline was like a mountain torrent irresistibly rushing downward. Reflecting on these things, Jingchen could not avoid a certain commiseration with his fellow man. His heart suddenly sank. At this time Cathay confronted adversity and Jingchen did not know if he would survive. If not, the Zhu family would meet with the same fate as the Fengs today. Would seeking out Mr. Du really help? No, Cathay must never fall, for if one day there were no more Cathay, then he, Zhu Jingchen, would become a worthless nobody. He often likened himself unflatteringly to a ham cord—the cord itself wasn't worth a cent, but because it suspended a succulent ham, the cord was no longer simply a worthless cord but was an integral part of the price of the ham. Yet once the ham hanging from that cord was consumed, the sodden string was only worth chucking into the garbage!

"You silly boy, when you were just born you didn't have a single tooth in your mouth, but your mom loved you all the same..." That's what his mother had said to him that evening in his study. It did seem that in this world only his mother loved him unconditionally, while all others, including wife and children, bore him only a conditional love. He would not fail; no, he absolutely would not fail.

The Feng residence was a 1910s two-story westernized structure of red brick, which, by the time it had come into the Feng family, presumably had passed through several other families. At the black-lacquered main gate, stained and discolored, Jingchen rang the bell; it was opened by a maid wearing a dragon-head patterned gown of delicate white fabric. The Feng family may have fallen but the pretensions of a great household had not in the slightest been compromised, such that mourning habit for the maid was still indispensable.

She had evidently long been in the Feng's service, for as soon as she looked at Jingchen's business card, she bowed to him with great courtesy, and ushered him into the house.

The bedroom of the deceased was on the second floor. From the disarranged, now incomplete set of mahogany furniture, Jingchen could still vaguely remember the graceful elegance of the family's former life. The air was laden with the odor of burning incense and sacrificial tinfoil money, creating a plaintive and gloomy atmosphere.

A few scroll paintings decorated the east wall, none from a famous hand, however, and on a high stand stood a bulbous crackleware vase, likewise a cheap antique, retained merely to serve the purpose. One could confirm at a glance that the Feng family had sold every last thing of value, and possessed nothing of any worth.

Jingchen took a few steps toward the bed. Parting the mosquito-net draped around it, he beheld the third son—the deceased—dressed in a simple old silk gown, with a thin and faded embroidered silk coverlet pulled over him. The body had not even been properly wrapped in a shroud. The sight grieved Jingchen, who had to fight to hold back the tears that were welling in his eyes. He stepped over to the mahogany desk at the south window, took out his checkbook, tore out a large denomination check and signed his name. All the while, quite unmindful of the mournful occasion, canaries and warblers kept in four bird cages ranged under the window were merrily chirping away.

"Funeral expenses for the deceased third son—I'll take care of them," he said, as he held out the check not quite knowing to whom to give it. The women in the room were all of different ages, but he could not distinguish who was wife, who daughter, and who concubine or maid.

With a rustling of their robes and gowns, the room's occupants instantly kneeled down before Jingchen. Oh, if Mr. Feng's soul in heaven could only see these unfilial offspring, how grieved he would be.

"Mr. Zhu, as my father's eldest son, I promise to repay this money in full."

A young man with a long handsome face, and the only one in the house wearing western clothes, emerged from the cluster of mourners and approached Jingchen.

An eldest son who is to inherit the family property may well assume the grand posture of "scion and successor," but considering the jumble of stuff remaining to the Feng family today, this young man blandly puffing himself up as scion and successor in fact was saddled with a life of debt. One might gaze upon his imposing appearance and his aristocratic bearing, but there were none of the extravagances of an aristocratic family, for he was unfortunately fated to have had as his father this good-for-nothing. How Jingchen pitied him.

"Um...well, son..." Jingchen started to mumble something but couldn't go on. He had intended to inquire about his place of employment, but on second thought there were plenty of his ilk—descendants of great houses ending up as opium-smokers and freeloaders, so to spare him embarrassment he checked himself just in time.

"I'm Feng Jingsyao," the young man said, introducing himself, "assistant at the Peter Gao Clinic in Huamao Apartments."

Good enough; the young man at all events was a son who could at least earn his own living.

Jingchen took his leave, and Feng Jingsyao, in his capacity as Feng family eldest son, saw him to the front gate.

"Mr. Zhu," he said as they were crossing the courtyard, "I shall repay this money on behalf of my father."

"We'll talk about it later," replied Jingchen to comfort him. He reflected on the cluster of women still in the household, for whom time seemed to have stopped in the 1910s, perhaps because that was the period of the Feng family's greatest splendor. Each and every one of this bevy of wives, daughters, and concubines had "golden lilies"—tiny bound feet—and a few of them were only teenagers; all of them, it would seem, were unable to part from their maids and servants and amahs. But in the days to come... Yet Zhu Jingchen could only feel he was somehow letting them down. As the saying goes, "One helps another in emergency, but can't deliver him from poverty."

Feng Jingsyao hurried ahead to open the gate for Jingchen, and waited there until he had gotten into his car. Quite a fine young man, really. Alas, people speak of their own writings as the best, but speak of another's wife as the best. How could it be that in his heart of hearts Jingchen felt that not his own but another's son was best? Consider the several young men he'd met just during the past half-year—Tsai Liren, the manager of Bounty Textile Mill; Fan Yangzhi, the son of Old Fan; and now this Feng Jingsyao, the descendant of a great family—all showed greater strength than his own Juanren.

*   *   *

Juanren, meanwhile, his enthusiasm unabated, was still driving his sister and Zhishuang around on their little excursion.

"Well, how about it, my driving technique isn't bad, eh?" Juanren spoke smugly as he turned the steering wheel.

"Quite good enough to be our chauffeur," replied Juanmin, affectedly leaning her head against her brother's shoulder. She took pride in her brother's refined manner. "Later on that will be very convenient for me."

"Humph. You'd really have me be your chauffeur?" he teased back. "Why not tell your future matchmaker to find you a taxicab driver. Wouldn't that be even more convenient?"

Driving along Seymour Road, the car turned into Hardoon Garden, a fashionable residential area. There one beheld low red brick walls uniformly lining the street, behind which stood one after another small and exquisite two-story foreign-style homes. One could catch occasional glimpses of their rust-colored tiled roofs nestled among dense, lush sycamores. The brass mailboxes on their front gates and the brass door knobs, too, shone brightly in the moonlight. Beams of amber light stole out through louvered windows, and the strains of a piano wafted out on the breeze, lingering only a moment before flying away with the wind. This midsummer evening scene recalled to Zhishuang's mind the special peace and contentment of a snowy night before Christmas, and the exotic atmosphere recalled the McTyeire School's aristocratic lifestyle to which she had now accustomed herself.

She leaned against the back seat as she gazed enviously up and down at these residences.

Hardoon Garden! To live here would allow her to make perfect use of what she had learned at McTyeire and the lessons she'd scored highest grades in—flower arrangement, social activities...She did not like having venetian blinds, which bore too obvious a similarity to the medical clinics of Japanese doctors. She preferred to decorate with floor-length French-fabric drapes of a miniature flower pattern (the kind she'd once seen pictured in Life magazine), with easy chairs widely spaced for the best effect, and of course the indispensable floor lamps; a large console-style radio was also a necessity, covered, of course, with a doily of punchwork lace.

"Are you getting tired, Miss Syi?" inquired Juanren considerately. "Shall we go back?"

Without even being aware of it, Zhishuang had closed her eyes and lost herself in thought, or, more accurately, daydreams. She thought it a little silly of herself. But was it really just dreaming? Was she not now obviously sitting in the Zhu's comfortable automobile, settled into the soft seat, driving through the quiet and exclusive residential neighborhoods of the French Concession, with the evening breeze caressing her and the fragrance of fresh green grass diffusing the atmosphere? None of this was a dream; it was real.

She languidly stretched her legs and lifted her head, and realized that Juanren was looking at her in the rear-view mirror with some concern. Without rhyme or reason she felt her face flush. "I guess I am, really," she replied awkwardly. "It's gotten late. Perhaps we should go back."

"Hey, we haven't gone to the Mandarin Club yet. You meanie, Juanren. You're going back on your word!" Juanmin, her appetite for entertainment still unsated, raised a voice of loud complaint.

"What future husband would ever dare settle on so unsatiable a young lady as you?" said Juanren.

"How strange. Why must some man settle on me?" retorted Juanmin, genuinely agitated. "Why must we women always just sit and show our faces, waiting for some man to come along and pick and choose? How come it's the men who can come up to us with a bunch of flowers and say 'I love you,' while we women, lest the man to whom we might think of saying 'I love you' just brush past us, can only put on an act and say to him, 'Isn't the weather lovely today'?"

"Really, Minnie," asked Juanren half seriously, "is it possible that you yourself have fallen into the cobweb of love?" Juanren sized up his sister through the rear-view mirror. Zhishuang had but to steal a surreptitious look at her friend's expression to know exactly that she was telling the truth and to know exactly whom she meant. Zhishuang could not help making comparisons between the person sitting right in front of her and the person in Juanmin's heart, Feng Jingsyao. Zhishuang actually retained no more than a vague impression of Mr. Feng and only a general sense that he was stylish, handsome, tall...But although the man right before her eyes, Zhu Juanren, was also upper class, good-looking, and considerate, he was real, 100% real, even to the wave the barber had so carefully worked into his hair; and his reality, moreover, was present fully within Zhishuang's field of vision. That having occurred to her, she lifted her eyes to steal a look in the rear-view mirror, where he too, unexpectedly, was looking at her. Their eyes met; he winked at her and made a face, which erased her embarrassment. She smiled pleasantly.

With no flashing neon lights in this area, the stars overhead shone with particular brightness. From the little flower gardens in front of the house gates came the continual drone of locusts, now rising, now falling. "What a beautiful evening!" exclaimed Juanmin. "It's so close inside the car, why don't we get out and take a stroll. It's a rare thing in bustling Shanghai to experience such quiet solitude as this." And as she spoke, she opened the car door and jumped out, quickly followed by Zhishuang, while Juanren parked the car and jogged back to them.

The three walked along in silence, save for the sound of their footfalls on the pavement. Juanren felt relaxed and happy and, as was his habit, could not resist pursing his lips and whistling a tune, the ever popular "Santa Lucia," whose moving strains undulating across the emptiness of the street were the more beautiful for the solitude of the surroundings.

A foreign lady happened then to open the gate of one of those homes to walk her dog—a cute little puppy with a pure white coat, which immediately scampered over and ran around the threesome time and again. Zhishuang, in particularly high spirits today, knelt down and patted the silky fur on its head, and the dog responded to the caresses by licking her hand. How pleased she was that this strange dog should be so friendly to her, which she felt to be a particularly good omen.

Juanren bent over Zhishuang and played with the pup, inquiring in English of the woman, "Is it a boy or a girl?"—the question westerners customarily ask, he thought.

"Oh," the foreign lady said proudly, "it's a very obedient, pretty little fellow!"

"Aha, then no wonder it's showing so much interest in this pretty young lady," he said in Shanghai dialect to Zhishuang leaning close to her, not knowing at all why he was so full of witticisms tonight.

"All right, all right," said Juanmin who was feeling rather left out in the cold. "I'm getting chilly."

Juanren only now realized his sister was angry with him. He hastily put his arm around her shoulder and laughed, at the same time casting a glance at Zhishuang as if to say, "Hey, we've been giving my sister the cold shoulder," implying that the two of them—Juanren and Zhishuang—already had developed some tacit understandings between them.

Around the corner of the narrow street ahead could be heard the sound of metal against metal, "ping pi-i-ing ping, ping pi-i-ing ping," a strong rhythm which reverberated through the empty street.

"Is that someone selling cotton candy?"

It was indeed a cotton candy peddler, standing all alone in the shadows cast by a street lamp, who preferred to knock the candy oven with a spoon to attract business rather than calling out his product.

Munching snacks along the street was something the girls would never do, but for some reason or other this evening they all felt like indulging themselves a little.

"Shall we have some?" Juanmin asked enticingly.

"Let's!" exclaimed Zhishuang, nodding unambiguously.

"Okay, I'll treat you," and Juanren started toward the peddler's cart.

"Wow," said Juanmin, teasing her brother; "what rare generosity we're seeing today."

"We'll buy our own," said Zhishuang. She felt her face flush with embarrassment, sure that Juanren's generosity reflected fondness for her; she and Juanmin rushed over to the handcart. Juanren hurried along with them.

As they approached, they discovered that the cotton candy peddler was a White Russian. In appearance not more than forty or so, he was wearing a battered cap and had a once white apron tied around him. They watched as he switched on the motor underneath the heating pan and the contraption began whirring round and round; then he added a spoonful of sugar syrup to the flat-bottomed pan and slowly gossamer-like threads of sugar began to form from it, gradually filling the bottom of the pan and fluffing up, just like wisps of smoke hovering in space, and then the air was suffused with its sweet fragrance.

Buying cotton candy on the street like this—how it seemed so much like a distant dream.

Giggling, the girls paid their money, and giggling they held their huge cones of cotton candy, while the peddler just scowled throughout. Zhishuang noticed when he took the money that his fingers were slender and fair, the hands of a pianist, it might seem. She couldn't help but take another good look at his face, half-hidden behind the cap which was pulled down to his eyebrows, but it was too shadowy to make out anything very clearly.

"What a strange fellow, scowling as if he were eating uncooked rice—how will he ever make money that way?" muttered Zhishuang as she nibbled at the candy.

"Can't say for sure, but it looks to me as though that White Russian might be a duke or a count. See how he stands so erect—a man of disciplined upbringing!" exclaimed Juanren.

As Zhishuang listened, she thought of those hands so like a pianist's, and couldn't help looking back at the man. He seemed intent on pulling his cap even lower, standing on the dimly lit corner leaning against the lamp post, banging his spoon against the pan trying to make his living.

"How pitiful," said Zhishuang. She thought of the period of the French Revolution when aristocrats were sent to the guillotine.

"What of it? That's the way revolution is—either you eat me or I eat you." Juanren affected a know-it-all expression. "At our military training in Suzhou, we seized a few communists."

"Communists? What were they like?" Zhishuang's interest had been piqued.

"Whether in fact they really were communists, I don't know. They seemed to be from Fudan University."

"There's a lot of communists at Fudan," said Zhishuang, putting on a disdainful air. "That's why at McTyeire nobody ever takes the entrance exam for Fudan. That kind of school has political activities going on day and night—how can anyone get any studying done there?"

"But maybe our country needs to have a change of government," said Juanmin. "If the same government always runs the country, what's the distinction between that and the old emperors who ruled the realm?

The emperor was overthrown decades ago, but the Chinese people are still here and just as poor." Her agitation increased as she went on. "I'd really like to meet a communist and ask him to please tell me what means they are preparing to use to change the poverty of the Chinese people."

"What means? Won't it be like what they're doing in the Soviet Union now?" interrupted Zhishuang. "The nationalization of all property. But the common people in the Soviet Union are still poor. Couple years ago when that film star Butterfly Wu toured the Soviet Union, there were crowds of people the whole time gaping at her wanting to buy her fur coat, her camera, even her watch and gold Parker pen—that's the tragedy of Russia after it went communist— terrible shortages."

"But the Russians were poor from the beginning—it's the poorest country in Europe. If the foundation is poor, there's just nothing they can do. You can't turn out wealth just by turning out the old regime. You can only distribute equitably the money of the rich, but even that's limited. When all is said and done, there are still a lot of poor people. Think of it like this. Originally there was one chocolate bar in the possession of one person and there were nine other people with nothing to eat. So there's a revolution, and the chocolate bar is divided among the ten people. But since that little bit is all the chocolate there is, by the time it gets divided into those ten mouths, there's only a tiny piece, and of course everybody is still poor. You need to find a way to make more chocolate bars—then you'll have the basic means to eliminate poverty. And that," said Juanren, "is what may be truly called 'revolution.' Otherwise, you've got to call it a 'rebellion;' you can't call it a 'revolution.'"

"Gosh, Juanren, you sure do explain it well." Juanmin was quite taken by surprise.

"That's how a trainee from another school explained it to me at camp."

"Was he a revolutionary?" asked Juanmin, her eyes lighting up.

"Who knows. Underground party people keep poker faces."

"Rebellion, revolution! Whenever I see those words I feel so ill at ease. Do you still remember our history textbook illustrations about the French Revolution? The aristocrats were lined up in a long, long line waiting to be guillotined, and their children, still too young to understand what was going on, were lined up too, playing with their hobby horses." As she spoke, Zhishuang couldn't help again looking back at the White Russian engaged in so meager a trade, and, feeling a little chilly, she wrapped her arms around herself.

"And so that's why you're studying home economics instead of social studies," said Juanmin with a laugh.

"Could China produce a proletarian revolution like that?"

"That's what you call, 'having eaten your fill, there's nothing to do.'" Juanren felt it to be thoroughly comical. "Even if it's a genuine revolution, it won't affect us personally. We're not bureaucrats nor are we capitalists. We're just part of the intelligentsia. Say, why don't we talk a little about something else. Tonight is really a beautiful evening." And having said that, his eyes, almost unintentionally, fell upon Zhishuang, and Zhishuang smiled back. She felt so happy to have discovered for herself this glorious and unsullied emotion, an emotion she had never before experienced. But for the time being she did not want to probe further.

Chapter 9

By the time Jingchen had returned home it was already nearly ten, and he felt weak and weary. But when he discovered that his newly purchased Buick was not in the garage, doubtless because Juanren had taken it out for a joyride, he was instantly in a fury.

"How many times have I told you, when that son of mine comes on just his own say so to take my car out, don't open the gate for him."

"He went out in the company of Miss Juanmin. He said that she..." Old Chang the gatekeeper felt himself to be in an awkward situation.

"Who pays your salary, anyway? Do I pay it or do they pay it?" As he had in the past, Jingchen yet again unloosed his anger at him. "What do young kids have to do with driving cars! Next time you find him trying this, you tell him his father does not allow him to drive the car!"

Jingchen went into the house and on upstairs. Passing by the piano room he could hear the jerky sounds of scale practice; he didn't know whether it might be his third or fourth daughter, but he didn't want to distract her by barging in; he passed on and went into his mother's room. There he encountered his second daughter, Juanying, combing her grandmother's hair. Juanying was by nature a quiet girl who even on her holidays just stayed at home all day long in the company of her grandmother.

"Mother, the third son of the Feng family has passed away." Jingchen spoke wearily as he sank into an easy chair near the door. "How pitiful. The family has been reduced to ruins; there's nothing left, not even the wherewithal to get proper burial garments."

The old lady shook her head and thumped her chest in bewilderment. "Oh my, a family with so much property as they had now in ruins? Before, just mention the Fengs of Hangzhou and people would gasp in admiration! In all honesty, though, while the sons of the old patriarch were honest people who didn't gamble or smoke opium, still they really didn't know how to conduct their financial affairs very well."

"Isn't that quite enough to bring ruin? The old boss himself never paid any attention, and the household ran up bills willy-nilly; it was every day money going out and none coming in. Sooner or later the family would meet with ruination." He shook his head as he spoke. "The Fengs to this very day just like always keep a houseful of servants, maids, and mistresses...Figure it for yourself, Mother: how much per day does it cost for that one expense alone? You can't blame anyone except the unworthy later generations!" At this point he couldn't help casting a look at Juanying standing there, mindlessly running a fingertip over the teeth of the comb, time and again from one end to the other then back again, like a mousy daughter-in-law.

Juanying was a girl of gentle, complaisant temperament and reticent too, whom Jingchen had always regarded as utterly bland, but at this moment when by chance she and Jingchen came face to face, he realized that he had always been rather cold and indifferent to her and he suddenly felt a twinge of conscience. He stretched his hand out and stroked her on the neck and really wanted to find something to talk with her about, but feeling the pliant flesh of her neck suddenly stiffen (which both of them sensed very keenly) the two abruptly felt awkward. It was obvious that these were emotions which could not have been feigned. Fortunately, Jingwen and Miss Yi happened to come in at just this moment; Jingchen hastily withdrew his arm and sighed an inward sigh of relief.

"Jingchen, is Juanren still working for that German firm, Bayer? What's he doing there? Sales engineer? Sounds impressive, but it's nothing more than riding around comfortably in a rickshaw going from one medical clinic to another peddling stuff like aspirin or antacid. This kind of work even a junior-high school student could handle, yet here's Juanren with a chemistry degree from a prestigious university actually fooling around with errands like that. A clear case of 'putting great talent to little use.' Of course the salary and benefits are good, what with special allotments for rickshaw fares, clothing allowance for neckties and leather shoes, a settling-in housing allowance...Jingchen, by letting Juanren take this job you can bring him no harm economically. But you never considered that sacrificing ten-odd years of education and specialized training in exchange for idle errand work would itself be very harmful to him!" Jingwen always assumed a person's undertakings to be the inspiration of genius, and he firmly believed that since his own undertaking was scientific study, science was surely worthy of reverence.

Although he had studied in Germany and traveled once to Switzerland, Jingwen had never been much infected with foreign airs: he still just dressed in a rumpled suit and usually lacked a fresh shave, yet he wore a proud and indomitable expression.

"I can't make any arrangements for him. I don't have that kind of talent. But I'll look around for some kind of position for him. He could work in a factory as a technician. Technician at Verity Fertilizer Plant." Jingwen, legs crossed, lazily blew smoke rings as he spoke.

"Verity Fertilizer Plant?" Jingchen didn't quite comprehend. Just then Miss Yi, who up to now hadn't said a word, laughed.

Miss Yi was the daughter of a prominent family, and yet, surprisingly enough, she accepted many hardships in helping her husband make that great discovery which never seemed to happen. Because a chemical reaction usually had to proceed without interruption, she helped him by observing the state of reaction, recording its progress, analyzing its components, busying herself among the flasks and beakers and alcohol burners, very often throughout the entire night. A small back room had become their laboratory, and time and again their hands suffered chemical burns, and their lungs often were so irritated by the acrid fumes of hydrochloric acid or the nauseous odor of hydrogen sulfide they could hardly breathe. These were still minor matters, but when the noxious fumes diffused in all directions, when the neighbors on all sides began talking about it, that was a real annoyance, and then this delicate, this exquisite Miss Yi was again indispensable in visiting the neighbors one by one to apologize in her stiff, Peking-accented Shanghainese. Heaven only knows how Jingwen had managed to get a wife like her. Sometimes Jingchen was a little jealous of him for his marvelous good fortune, and if he himself, the illustrious and imposing President Zhu of Cathay Republic Bank, should ever choose a young woman in her twenties to be a new Mrs. Zhu, she would be just like her. In fact, however, who among those young ladies willing to become his wife, including Pu Zhuanlin herself, was not attracted by his bulging wallet and sonorous title? If during the present bank crisis he should get pummeled black and blue, then those women who had originally prepared to march down the aisle with him would assuredly, every last one of them, go into hiding.

"Jingchen," she said, "the funds for Jingwen's chemical fertilizer plant have been accumulated and now everything's ready, and we've already located an old factory lot on Route du Père Froc. It'll be a simple and inexpensive operation; we're planning within the next few days to put up the buildings and move the equipment in." As she spoke, Miss Yi looked at her husband with infinite pride. Miss Yi was not pretty by any means, but, being a woman intellectual with a small and pale triangular-shaped face, with hexagonal wire-frame glasses, with cheeks faintly dabbed with rouge, she nonetheless possessed great charm. Little wonder, then, that Jingwen was disinclined to live with his first wife, Ying; he had bought her a home in Hangzhou and let her live there with their children, thus avoiding any awkwardness over the status of Miss Yi.

"Have you resigned your hospital lab technician job? How will you manage your expenses?" Jingchen always felt a little sympathy for him.

"I do hope you'll honor us with your presence, Jingchen, on the day we formally begin operations." Miss Yi gazed at Jingchen with boundless expectation, then with loving sympathy turned toward her own husband. "These past several years Jingwen has lost all of sixteen pounds. It took him over three years in that back room just to produce a few grams of ammonium sulfate."

"I'm not going to sell out myself any more," said the proud Jingwen, pulling up his suspender straps which were forever slipping off his shoulders.

"Managing an enterprise can be a very involved affair," said Jingchen thoughtfully, "and there are a lot of racketeers out there, too. It's far from being the sort of work that the likes of you, now without any position or financial resources, are qualified for. You've gotten loans from three banks, and if once you should be unable to repay those sums, that will be an extremely serious matter."

"Don't worry, Jingchen," said old Mrs. Zhu as if she had a plan all worked out. "Remember when you two boys were at the Feng mansion in Hangzhou? The accountant read your palms for you, and when he finished he right away bowed to your father and told him, 'Mr. Zhu, your two sons will in the future be very remarkable—one is destined for high rank, the other for wealth.' But now it seems Jingwen is to have the wealthy destiny. Can't say for sure, but Jingwen may in the future prosper more than you. Now they're investing with others to start this plant, which means the prediction is coming true."

How could Jingwen and his wife, who had both studied abroad, believe in such superstitions? All this auspicious talk, while very pleasant to the ear, was, after all, just talk. Yet Jingchen felt uneasy at heart—this sort of amusement could not be totally believed yet could not be altogether disbelieved either, and it might just be that Jingwen would meet with some great good fortune.

"Well? Shall we bring Juanren into it? Then I shall really be able to learn from true talent. I also want to bring my three sons in. The younger generation of Zhus will thus with one mind and a united effort bring forth a great enterprise into the world..." Jingwen was positively bubbling. "This may truly said to be a case of 'pupils surpassing their teachers.'"

"Exactly, Jingwen. That proverb carries a great truth." Old Mrs. Zhu was also in high spirits today, and voluble, too. "Now off you go—fetch your children in here and bring along Ying too. After they've made their fortune, they'll build a large house and the whole family can live together in wonderful harmony, never mind who has precedence over whom. You know the saying, 'When all the family farms together, the earth produces wealth forever'."

This rash outburst caused Miss Yi alternately to blanch and to flush. Jingwen quickly diverted his mother onto a different subject. "Mom, you've got it wrong again. Managing an enterprise isn't the same as doing business. The amount of profit is not the important thing. What's most important is the development of China's chemical fertilizer industry so we don't have to rely on foreigners."

"How can you not talk of profit?" Jingchen cut in icily. "What capital do you control to engage in an unprofitable venture? According to law, an inventor has patent rights. It's not a matter of courtesy."

"Yes, of course, we need to consider that, but the problem first and foremost is to get the fertilizer plant into production!"

Blood brothers though they were, in temperament, alas, they were poles apart. Jingchen was weary of disputing with him; after all both were men well into their forties, not three-year olds.

Jingchen went off by himself to his study. Checking his watch, he thought he'd still telephone to Chian Sinzhi, asking him to put in a word with Wan Molin, the Du mansion's steward, to make an appointment for himself to call on Mr. Du and pay his respects.

Jingchen could be reckoned a man of broad experience, naturally adept in social intercourse, always conducting himself with ease, but in this instance, he really did feel a measure of timidity and was far from sure of himself.

After Auntie Lu, the maid, had tidied up the bathroom, Jingchen, pajamas in hand, went in to take a bath, thinking all the while of his appointment with Du Yuesheng.

Despite his origins as a fruit peddler, this Mr. Du was now one of Shanghai's moguls, such that not only did prominent figures in the financial world like Chian Sinzhi or Syu Maotang cater to his whims, even Chiang Kaishek had to sing his praises. But in interviews with the board chairmen of every private commercial bank, however insignificant, Du Yuesheng felt a certain deficiency of self-confidence, a lack of self-assurance. A hooligan of his background, no different from a waterfront bum, was capable of anything once he'd turned against you. Getting hassled a little hardly counted; the big fear was that Du Yuesheng would ply all his connections and one day really cause trouble, far beyond what Gong, that assistant vice-president at Bank of China, was doing right now.

Jingchen filled the bathtub half full of water and got in for a good soak. Outside the closed bathroom door he could hear his third daughter, Juanwei, in the corridor lecturing Auntie Lu.

"How could you forget to lower the blinds on the west window of the parlor? The sun has been shining right in all afternoon and the furniture upholstery will all fade. I've told you so many times I feel embarrassed about it. People who know me understand, all right, but people who don't know me must think I'm terribly crabby, nagging the whole day long..."

Only fourteen years old, but Juanwei could really lecture the maid—not in a loud voice, but with each syllable virtually flung in her face. Listening to her tone Jingchen thought it all too obvious she's another Juanmin, and he couldn't keep a smile from his lips.

Weren't people inexplicable just this way—in order to satisfy their self-respect, the higher ranked took it out on the lower ranked. The master scolded his butler, the butler scolded the maids, the maids scolded the hired girls, the hired girls scolded vagrants...The whole world was this way—one rank devouring the next rank. If you intend not to be devoured by others, you've got to make yourself so strong that no one can swallow you up. But sometimes you've got to use cajolery combined with threats, or, if worse comes to worst, you just have to burrow into a dog's hole and stay out of harm's way.

Chapter 10

The Du mansion was located at No. 216 Rue Hennequin. It was by a cursory glance ordinary enough: a front building in Chinese style, similar in layout to the Liu residence on Rue Bayle, was connected by a covered walkway to a rear building, a western-style structure of three stories, each of three main rooms. A manservant wearing a black summer-weight silk gown courteously ushered Jingchen to the east room of the rear building. The room, refreshingly air-conditioned, was furnished with a mahogany desk of Chinese design and some upholstered chairs of various sizes. By the looks of it, it was Du Yuesheng's office.

Jingchen didn't care to sit by the air conditioning vent, so he chose an easy chair in the corner, tucked up his thin gown and sank back into the chair importantly, tapping his fingers on the arm as he quietly waited.

In so large a mansion as this the domestic staff would naturally be quite numerous, but, strange to say, the place was silent and solemn with everything in perfect order; the household was certainly very capably managed. Jingchen took a look at his watch—already past eight. The Du mansion was like a late night market—even at eight o'clock in the evening, nothing was going on yet, and who knows at what hour the dinner meal might be served. Normally one would feel somewhat awkward about coming to call at this hour. In setting up the meeting, Chian Sinzhi had said that Jingchen's business was of the utmost importance, and that he was most eager to secure the assistance of Mr. Du. As luck would have it, however, since the Marco Polo Bridge

Incident in July, when the Japanese began their invasion of North China, Mr. Du had set about organizing the Shanghai Relief Committee. So busy was Mr. Du in collecting medical supplies, one might think Shanghai would itself soon be at war. Busy as he was, then, it had been no easy matter for Wan Molin to squeeze Jingchen into the schedule.

Presently a shadow fell across the open doorway, and Jingchen nervously jerked himself erect: sure enough into the room swayed a wizened, wrinkled man—Du Yuesheng. Jingchen sprang to his feet and bowed respectfully toward him, while Du replied with repeated gestures to resume his seat. Jingchen had once met Mr. Du when, accompanying old Mr. Wei, he had gone to Pudong New Bridge to convey congratulations upon the completion of the Du ancestral temple, but with all of Shanghai's notables and nabobs in attendance, Jingchen had been very much on the sidelines. But on the present occasion he could say he was in Mr. Du's very close proximity. He was wearing an ivory colored long silk gown, with gray silk socks and Chinese style cloth shoes—all very refined and cultivated. It's just that his smooth white face was covered with a layer of dull greenish yellow—produced, as any insider could instantly tell, by opium smoking.

The two settled into their chairs. His speech thickly accented with his native dialect, Du Yuesheng began courteously with the usual civilities. "It has been many years now since Mr. Wei passed on, and well it is, Mr. Zhu, that you have continued his work so satisfactorily. Now Cathay Republic Bank enjoys the highest reputation among private banks in all Shanghai. I'm sure the present run on your bank has made you very busy."

Whether intentional or not it was hard to say, but Du Yuesheng himself had clearly chosen his subject of conversation, thus sparing Jingchen the effort of beating around the bush trying to find a suitable conversational gambit. Presumably news of the predicament confronting Cathay had circulated throughout Shanghai, and Du Yuesheng could pretty well understand why Jingchen had come, so he took the initiative in broaching the subject. Jingchen felt that Du Yuesheng was really a fine person and a very understanding person. Jingchen availed himself of the opening and came straight to the point: Cathay's predicament was due to excessive pressure from Bank of China.

Du Yuesheng listened attentively throughout Jingchen's exposition, then pondered for a moment. "Bank of China is the most prestigious of the government banks," he began, "and Cathay Republic Bank the most prestigious among the private banks. Twenty years ago the joke circulating around Shanghai was, 'The God of Wealth deposits in Bank of China, while devils of more modest means prefer Cathay.' At present I am a permanent member of Bank of China's board of directors and I was an old friend of Cathay's Mr. Wei. The two parties have been mutually acquainted for many years, have had good relations with each other, and both were friends. I could not have anticipated that today there would exist between these two institutions such bitter enmity. It grieves me to speak of it."

That seemed to be a tactful refusal to help. But Jingchen was an intrepid soul, and Du Yuesheng, in a matter of such moment, could not very well make casual promises. So Jingchen again smiled again and pressed his request.

"In fact Bank of China is making life for Cathay quite difficult and they certainly are intent on causing our collapse. Since the run on Cathay began, we've been in deep distress. From the very founding of Cathay in 1905, we painstakingly built up our enterprise for many years, and though our achievements may be modest, at least it can be said that Cathay has established a solid foundation, so that if it goes bankrupt while in my hands, where in all of Shanghai could I hide my face? Thus, Mr. Du, I have come to request you in some little way to give me your help."

Du Yuesheng took a sip of tea, pulled out a hanky to dab his mouth and smiled modestly. "And where do I have such great ability as that? Basically I'm just a thief in scholar's garb, so people view me with some trepidation. Now, as a lowly earthworm fixed up as a dragon, I have some standing in society, but whether or not a person cares to accord me any respect is really quite up to him. Although I may be a director at Bank of China, a banker like yourself knows full well a director has no real authority, and even less so in the case of a government bank. I'm mere window dressing, nothing more."

Jingchen immediately grasped the implication of these remarks, but, painful as it was, made one last lobbying effort. "In that case, may I at the very least, sir, request that you honor Cathay Republic Bank by accepting a seat on our board of directors to enhance Cathay's prestige. It would be quite sufficient if you would help us in just this small way."

Du Yuesheng declined repeatedly but finally indicated that Cathay was a private bank with a good record, that should it one day fail it would seriously affect the Shanghai financial community, and that he could not very well look on with folded arms in face of such a possibility.

"Now, in the wake of the Marco Polo Bridge Incident, the situation is very volatile," said Du Yuesheng with a serious expression. "In my view it is entirely possible that Shanghai will be caught up in the war. And if this further destabilizes the financial markets, Shanghai will be in utter chaos." Jingchen thought these remarks to be sensationalist exaggerations intended only to parade concern for the nation's welfare and nothing more, and consequently he merely nodded his head as if it were polite small talk without taking the remarks to heart.

"That being the case," Du continued, "I feel morally obliged to help. Unfortunately I'm friends of both parties, so at most I can only offer my advice. We are all colleagues in the financial community and we should regard as most important service to people and society. As regards sitting on the Cathay board of directors, that is absolutely out of the question." Again, Du Yuesheng feigned refusal to accept the post. Jingchen pondered a moment and sensed the implication of Du's remarks to be that he was agreeing to help. But a big shot has to put on the airs of a big shot, so for the moment he was unwilling to consent to a directorship at Cathay. Provided that Du would consent to speak with the perpetrators at Bank of China, however, that would be favor enough. Not wishing to press him further right now, Jingchen excused himself and took his leave. Du Yuesheng saw him to the door. "In my opinion," Du reiterated, "sooner or later Shanghai will be caught up in war. We've got to be a little more alert about everything!" Jingchen readily agreed, then took his leave.

Emerging from the Du mansion main gate, Jingchen was greeted with an evening breeze. He felt a chill along his spine and his skin suddenly got goose bumps. Only now did he realize that his back was bathed in sweat. Inside it had been palpably cool with the air conditioning on, so that presumably his sweat came not from warmth but from tension.

Utterly exhausted, he flopped into the back seat of his car with the feeling he had not an ounce of strength left in him.

This neighborhood was comparatively unfrequented, and as the car moved through the dark and desolate streets, without even being aware of it they'd come out at the Sichuan Road bridge where a crowd of ragged vagrants was collected, and as soon as a rickshaw or pedicab began crossing the bridge, they'd rush out vying with one another to help push the vehicle up the steep incline and then wait for some coins to be tossed their way, whereupon they'd swarm around fighting among themselves to pick them up, quite unmindful of the din of horn honking by cars trying to make their way through.

"Hey you guys, you trying to get killed? There's no lid covering the river if you get knocked off the bridge!" Ayi, the driver, stuck his head out the window to curse them, then turned toward Jingchen apologetically, "Those devils don't consider that they just might really get run over and then there'd be a young fella gone forever!"

Jingchen squinted his eyes into a smile. "Just relax, they're certainly not likely to get run over. Those devils scramble around with such agility, even if you tried to run them over, you'd never manage to."

Of course Ayi could never have imagined that the formidable financier sitting in the Buick had himself once been such a ragamuffin pushing handcarts over the bridge. That was in his spare time after his apprentice work—a youngster without much sense trying to earn extra pocket money. If in those days he had pushed handcarts all the time, surely the bank would eventually have noticed. And if that had happened he would certainly have been fired, in which case he would doubtless have sunk to the level of street tramp. And if it had been like that, Zhu Jingchen naturally would never have come to occupy the position of president of Cathay Republic Bank. But would he have become a second Du Yuesheng, who'd gone from fruit vending to gangsterism to respectability? Jingchen smiled, for he believed he would never willingly spend his life as a pauper. As Jingchen watched the street scenes gradually become more animated, he recalled, rather like a motion picture, one scene after the other of his visit with Du Yuesheng. This Mr. Du knew how to acquit himself masterfully. In manner he was gentle and refined yet clear and concise. Here was a man of surpassing intelligence. Presumably, in return for putting in a few helpful words for Cathay, appointing him an honorary director would be more than enough. And with that gold-lettered sign on his desk who would dare cause trouble for Cathay? Well then, Bank of China, that ought to change your tune! But then a big question mark suddenly flashed into Jingchen's mind: since all the trouble arose from Bank of China and since Du Yuesheng was likewise a board member there, if he were indeed concerned about the stability of Shanghai financial markets, he could long since have put a stop to that Mr. Gong; so why wait until Zhu Jingchen came to call and make the request? Moreover, Du Yuesheng had hinted about a directorship: could it be that he himself had been singing the tune? Had he perhaps composed it? Don't forget, Du Yuesheng himself had established the profitable Huizhong Bank. Now Jingchen felt goose pimples form over his whole body and his palms became wet with sweat. Stop it, stop it; he was being just like that Liu Tongjun who paid in silver a fifty thousand dollar gratuity to that Belgian firm for the use of its flag—an insurance policy, as it were, like a tiger skin for draping around his factory to scare off government predators. The important thing was to send to Mr. Du with all possible dispatch the certificate of appointment to the board, lest some hitch develop in the meantime. The following day Jingchen, in the company of Mr. Li, personally went again to the Du mansion to deliver the letter of appointment, and also sent around two servants bearing a large Ming Dynasty crackleware ceramic vase as an expression of Cathay's appreciation. Du Yuesheng as before made a show of refusal, but after repeated entreaties by directors Zhu and Li, he reluctantly agreed to serve in the post, but only on two conditions: first, he would not go to the bank to perform any duties; and second, he would accept no salary.

"Agreed, agreed." Jingchen readily accepted the arrangement. No difficulty was posed in his not going to the bank for work, and as for not accepting a salary, that was a mere ego-boosting gesture of magnanimity. But it was indispensable that Cathay find some other way to provide the expected gratuities. He would take his own monthly salary of one thousand yuan as president and send every penny of it to the Du mansion. Now finally after so many days of personal anxiety, Jingchen felt a measure of reassurance. Du Yuesheng for his part could pat himself on the back, while Bank of China for its part would at least not be able to take advantage of Cathay's difficulties to cause further trouble. Little did Jingchen expect, however, as he was contemplating the peaceful sleep he could now enjoy, that the rumble of cannon would fill the midnight air, that the northern sky would be red with flames.

Chapter 11

On the evening of August 13 Japanese forces launched surprise attacks on both the South City and Zhabei districts, which lasted almost the whole night. All roads connecting the Chinese districts to the International Settlement and French Concession were cut off by barbed-wire barricades.

The several storehouses and properties located in Zhabei which belonged to Cathay Bank sustained varying degrees of damage, and a small number of Cathay employees, rendered homeless and destitute by the bombing, fled with their families in the middle of the night to refuge in the bank building. On the morning of the 14th, Jingchen convened an emergency meeting of the operations department, following which he directed the South City and Zhabei branches to place all stock certificates and customer account documents in safe-deposit boxes and move everything to the head office, located in the International Settlement. It was also arranged that the homeless employees be settled for the time being in a nearby hotel. As soon as Jingchen had heard the sound of the midnight bombing coming from Zhabei, he immediately rushed to the bank to take personal charge of all the arrangements and preparations. Now already noon of the following day but without giving a moment's thought to having some lunch, Jingchen again went personally down to the vault for another careful look, though he knew full well that Cathay's underground storage vault was strong and dependable, indeed, bomb-proof.

Its massive door was fully a half-foot thick, and as soon as the door opened one felt a wave of cold air blow across the face and heard the whirring sound of twelve German-manufactured dehumidifiers along the walls running continuously day and night. Stacked in neat piles in the vault were precious antiques, Persian rugs, old books, and so on, while closely packed along the four walls were the depositors' rented safe-deposit boxes ranged side by side. Jingchen slowly paced around the four walls; the sound of his footfalls echoed drearily. To say that this large underground fault was "worth the price of whole cities" was indeed no exaggeration, for the documents, the antiques, the jewelry preserved within were priceless treasures. With Shanghai now fallen under enemy attack, bringing damage and destruction to factories and businesses, Jingchen surveyed the room and contemplated the neatly ranged safe-deposit boxes shining under the electric lights, and felt a responsibility bearing down on his shoulders so heavy he could scarcely catch his breath. Although Cathay Bank was situated in the International Settlement, it was in the proximity of Zhabei and South City where the flames of war were rising skyward. All things considered, there was little cause for peace of mind.

Returning to his office from the underground vault, Jingchen had not yet had time to light up a cigarette when he heard the sound of an explosion close enough to rattle the window panes. Jingchen sprang to his feet, throwing aside his unlit cigarette. As if a powerful typhoon had just begun to blow, the outside air was whistling furiously. He rushed to the window and looked out: the street below was a sheet of broken glass, and in the direction of the Bund black smoke was belching skyward.

Just then the telephone rang, and the steady alto voice of Mrs. Zhong calmed him down. Secretaries like her were rare indeed.

"The bomb hit in the area of Huizhong Hotel," she reported, "and the shop windows in the Sassoon Building were completely blown out. Luckily enough, everything's safe and sound here at the bank—just some second- and third-story windows shattered by the force of the blast. No employees or customers were hurt."

"Thank you, Mrs. Zhong." Still shaken, Jingchen pulled out a handkerchief and wiped his forehead. As if to confirm the concern he'd felt a moment ago in the underground storage vault, the International Settlement itself was subject to bombing after all. Jingchen's thoughts suddenly ran to the bank branches at Basyan Bridge and Jingan Temple, and in order to reassure the employees there, he immediately had Ayi drive him over there to check the situation.

The day was uncommonly hot. Fire trucks and ambulances, their sirens screaming, were snaking endlessly through the littered streets, rendered nearly impassable by roof tiles and broken bricks. Some distance away he saw the twisted beams and shattered glass of the Palace Hotel, its windows blown out, giving the impression of eyeglasses with lenses removed. He viewed in stunned disbelief the crumbled walls and piles of debris.

"Yes indeed, we've been caught up in war!" Seated in the car, his face pale and strained, Jingchen suddenly thought of the Du mansion on Rue Hennequin and Du Yuesheng's remarks about the current situation; at the time he had thought that Mr. Du was simply bandying words about, but now Du's estimate of the situation had unexpectedly proved accurate.

Shanghai people are customarily carefree and unhurried, and even if bombs are falling right overhead, they still retain their composure. In the vicinity of Great World Entertainment Center, it was bustling as always with a sea of people and a stream of cars and carriages.

"Look! Those are our airplanes!" exclaimed Ayi, who had caught sight of them in the rear-view mirror.

Sure enough, on the blue horizon two black dots were swooping in toward the street, the roar of their engines clearly audible, as the people on the street paused to look up. Even bus passengers stuck their heads out the windows, hands shading their eyes, and looked up into the sky.

In the intersection just before Great World, the traffic signal turned red and Ayi pressed down on the brake pedal. Watching the two planes in the rear-view mirror, he urged them on. "Get 'em, get 'em! Kill those Jap bastards! Chase 'em into the Huangpu River! There's no lid covering the Huangpu! Get 'em!..." In the rear-view mirror one of the airplanes was rushing downward—one could almost make out the wing insignia—and just then a little black something fell from the tail section.

"Watch out!" yelled Ayi, and before Jingchen knew what had happened, Ayi pushed the accelerator pedal to the floorboard and Jingchen's Buick shot past the red light and through the intersection like an arrow, and just in time, for almost simultaneously Jingchen heard from behind a deafening explosion. The car lurched to a stop, and then there was a silence so deathly it was suffocating. Jingchen felt there seemed to be only he and Ayi left alive in the whole world. Was it really possible that Judgment Day had arrived? Uncertainly, he looked back and beheld through the rear window an expanse of thick billowing smoke, and only then did the world seem to revive. Suddenly from all around could be heard mournful cries.

Ayi stepped hard on the gas, but the car wouldn't budge. He got out to check. After a moment he stuck his head in through the window, his face drained of color. "Mr. Zhu," he said, "two bomb fragments have slashed the tire, so it can't move."

Jingchen gazed at Ayi's terror-stricken face, and was just about to ask why he looked so terrible—was he perhaps injured, when in fact Ayi shook Jingchen hard by the shoulders and asked, "Mr. Zhu, are you all right? You're not hurt, are you? Why do you look so bad?"

Ambulances and fire trucks now came rushing down the smoke-filled street one after another in a steady stream, their screaming sirens and clanging bells mixing with the sound of whistles as policemen tried to maintain order and with the cries of the pedestrians to form a terrifying cacophony. As the acrid smoke began to disperse, Jingchen turned his head and looked, and could not help but gasp in horror. The traffic light, the metal pole on which it was mounted, and the platform where a Sikh policeman had been directing traffic, had one minute ago occupied the middle of the intersection but had now all vanished, while just to the south a crater some ten feet deep and twenty feet across had been blown into the street.

"I've got to go to the Basyan Bridge branch to check on our employees there." Jingchen opened the car door, and only then discovered the rear tire had been completely caved in and the car was leaning to one side. What a close call it had been!

The street was strewn with the smoldering wreckage of vehicles, and everywhere one saw the bloody and mangled bodies of the victims, most dead, some still writhing.

The front entrance security grill at Cathay's Basyan Bridge branch had already been rolled down, and it was deathly quiet within. Though scarcely half a block from where the bomb had hit, the bank apparently had escaped damage; Jingchen closed his eyes and offered silent thanks to Heaven. He went in and spoke reassuringly to the branch personnel. Making an exception to the rule, he directed the branch close early so the employees could return home and spare their families further anxiety.

★   ★   ★

At about eight p.m. on the same day at the Syi home in Felicity Village, everyone was in a panic. Mrs. Syi, whose hair previously never showed a misplaced strand, was sitting in a parlor rattan chair, her hair disheveled, her eyes swollen and puffy from crying. Mrs. Tsao was at her side offering consolation

"Everything is fated to be this way, there is no one who can be blamed, and you're not a palm-reader..."

"I must have been out of my senses. I didn't send Zhou earlier and I didn't send her later, but of all things exactly at three o'clock when she woke up from her nap. Some inscrutable god or ghost made me send her out to the market to buy a ham. If I'd just let her nap a little longer, then she'd have avoided that fateful moment and she'd still be living...Oh my god, why did she have to wander over to Great World of all places?"

Zhou had been killed at Great World Entertainment Center, but because she had with her a letter she'd just received from the countryside, rescue team volunteers could locate her address and they had come to the Syi home to inform them of the tragedy.

"...Poor Zhou had been with us for nineteen years. How will I ever be able to break the news to her husband in the countryside!" Mrs. Syi was wailing all the while she was talking.

Mrs. Tsao signaled with her eyes for Zhishuang to get her mother a handkerchief, as she kept trying her best to offer consolation. "Now don't be talking yourself into the blame for something that you just couldn't have helped. The most you can do is to burn some ritual mourning money for her sake and send her husband some money to satisfy your obligation to the servant's family."

Zhishuang was dumbstruck. When Zhou had gone out not long before, Zhishuang was a little miffed at her about something or other but now, remembering how she had gone out the door carrying a shopping basket and holding an umbrella as a parasol, how could it be that suddenly they'd be talking about getting killed in an explosion? She had been so alive just minutes ago.

"Zhishuang, I need to go to the bathroom," said her little brother, Chengzu, timidly. "Come with me. I'm afraid." Zhishuang took him upstairs, and as they passed Zhou's small garret room, Zhishuang herself felt a little afraid, too.

All the newspapers next day reported that a Chinese "Cloudbreaker" fighter plane attacking a Japanese warship had been hit by enemy antiaircraft fire, so the pilot decided to attempt a landing at Hongchiao Airport on Shanghai's outskirts, and in order to lighten the aircraft he intended to drop his bomb in the racecourse in the center of the city, but for some unexpected reason in fact dropped it in the intersection at Great World.

Nine days later when Syanshi Company also sustained a bomb explosion, the hitherto unperturbed Shanghai natives now finally felt they were really at war, and their predisposition of trusting to luck now (hard to imagine though it might be) gave way to terror.

Felicity Village was located in the Chinese section of Robison Road, and the neighbors right before Mrs. Syi's eyes had all escaped helter-skelter into the foreign sector to seek safety with friends and relatives. She had always promised herself that when it came time to die, she would die in her own home. But now with the rumble of exploding bombs coming from the Chinese areas of the city, she too was fearful, and as luck would have it, her husband was again away from home, leaving her alone with the two children. And she was anxious, for as long as bombs could not see where they were supposed to hit, anything might happen. Her next door neighbors, the Tsaos, had all fled to a relative's home in the International Settlement. It was fortunate that in her present state of utter shock, Mrs. Syi had a brother who was concerned about her, and had come to urge her and the family to flee. By that time Mrs. Syi had seen most of her immediate neighbors leave, and at nighttime it had become deathly still in the vicinity, so she also came to the decision to lock up the house, take the children and seek temporary refuge with her brother.

Mrs. Syi was originally from the provinces, where her family was once reckoned as being of considerable means, but later they were robbed by bandits, sapping the vitality of the family, which further declined owing to the eldest son's general ineptitude. The financial foundation of the family thus become weaker and weaker. Finally the eldest son—Mrs. Syi's brother—sold off that portion of the family property which was in the countryside and bought a home in the Pinecloud neighborhood near Moulmein Road, where he started a small general store fronting the main street, and the family managed to accommodate itself to a new way of life.

A small structure of two stories each with two main rooms, part of which was given over to the store, the house was plenty crowded with the family of six living there, and now came the Syi family of three and their servant girl. One felt there wasn't even room enough to turn around. And how was Zhishuang to survive these days without a flush toilet or running water for the bathtub? Who could blame her for going around with a worried brow and a long face all day long?

"You have to make allowances, dear." Mrs. Syi was sensible of Zhishuang's discomfiture and couldn't refrain from trying to help with advice. "How many families do you suppose there are in Shanghai like us who have to get by in these conditions? But compared to the refugees who have to live in the streets, you should be content with your lot."

At McTyeire, Zhishuang's eyes had everywhere beheld the daughters of the wealthy and powerful, so how could her mother's comments in this instance make any impression? Most unbearable of all were the evening hours after dinner. To save electricity her uncle kept just one light lit in the back parlor. It was a 25-watt bulb suspended above the eating table, and everybody sat around this table, each occupied with his own activity. With such noise as this it was impossible to read with any hope of its sinking in. And as for conversation, with petty tradesmen for relatives Zhishuang found it impossible to converse. So every evening when she finished her supper, she just carried a stool upstairs to the verandah and sat there blankly.

One evening, when Mrs. Syi had gotten quite tired of seeing Zhishuang's apathetic expression, and when only a maid happened to be about, she gave her another talking to.

"In all events, you must at least go through the motions of talking a little with your uncle and his wife. After all he is part of your grandmother's family. As a person, well, to be perfectly honest about it, your uncle hasn't been very successful, but he still is, after all, your uncle..."

"Well, aren't I polite to them? Don't I always speak to them whenever I come and go? What else do you a want me to do? Get down on my knees and bow to them?" Zhishuang had no patience for her mother's harping and ridiculed her outright.

"Now Zhishuang..." Her aunt's elderly maid couldn't let her go on. "We country people have a saying. 'The poorer the in-laws, the more they come to visit'—to show they're as good as the rich relatives. Your mother understands that clearly enough. The tie of relation can never be broken. You should always remember this saying. This is your grandmother's family..."

Zhishuang, stomping her feet, burst out angrily. "Mother and I are having a talk and we don't need you to butt in." And having said that, she stormed out, slamming the door behind her.

Mrs. Syi could only heave a sigh. Her daughter's experience had deepened, her horizons broadened, and the prestigious school where she had studied and the upper-class friends she had made there were putting a widening distance between her and her mother. Mrs. Syi really couldn't comprehend, having spent so much money to send her to such an expensive school, what the point of it all was. Just look at her brother's daughters: they'd never gotten much schooling, but in the house and in the store they attended to things with utmost care, and whatever they were told to do, they'd reply with a ready "yes." Had it not been for her husband's insistence, Mrs. Syi would never have wasted their hard-earned money in sending her to so expensive a school.

That evening under the electric bulb, the Syi son, Chengzu, was practicing his calligraphy—required homework given him by his father. The women had finished up the dish washing and other household chores and were also gathered under the light making padded vests—volunteer work to clothe the troops fighting the Japanese. All the while one heard the steady sound of bugs bumping against the glass globe of the dim bulb. Were it not for the war, this would be a very peaceful evening indeed. Since her marriage Mrs. Syi had had precious few occasions to enjoy so extended a visit with her brother and sister-in-law.

"What wickedness! Those damn Japs went on a rampage of burning and killing in the Luodian area," said Mrs. Syi's brother indignantly as he opened the newspaper. "So many wounded troops are waiting along the Peking-Shanghai line, it's impossible to get them all to hospitals!"

"Oh," the sister-in-law moaned. "I wonder how much longer it will be safe here in the International Settlement. What sins did we commit in our previous reincarnation that this lifetime should be spent fleeing one disaster after another? First it was fleeing the warlord Sun Jiafang, and now we have to flee the Japanese. When will we ever again be able to enjoy a peaceful meal?"

"By the way," Mrs. Syi's brother broke in, "when does Zhensyu get back? There are some things I've been waiting to discuss with him. Now that Du Yuesheng is serving on the board of Cathay Republic Bank, Cathay seems to have stabilized at least on the surface, but I'm still uneasy—afraid the bank's just putting on a brave front to obscure its real vulnerability. Do you think I should really keep my small savings in Cathay? Especially with the current situation so chaotic? Wouldn't it be better to take some money out and buy goods to hoard?"

"When my husband's not at home, I'm like a deaf person who doesn't know anything. But as a general practice, Cathay's property holdings, not to mention its other assets, are so vast and extensive, I don't think it's merely putting on a brave front. Furthermore, with the turmoil and chaos of war at present, the safest place to put your money is in a bank. A few years ago Zhensyu took me to see the bank's safe-deposit vault and it was so big and strong you could really say it was indestructible."

"That's true, I guess," her brother said, nodding in agreement. "There's an old saying that goes, 'a rich man may look poor, but he still has a load of money in reserve.' Cathay is a big bank with big assets; I guess I shouldn't liken it to a little store such as we run. The slightest wave will sink us. Keeping money in the bank is still the least worrisome. Du Yuesheng must have had his good reasons for not earlier joining the board of directors. He seems to have been able to get things settled down."

Chengzu had been listening in rapt attention to his lively exchange. His mother patted him on the head and told him to finish up his homework.

"I've already finished," replied the boy.

"It's still early. Study a bit more. Here, take this book and read it." Mrs. Syi grabbed a book and handed it to him. She herself did not know how to read, didn't even know if a book was right side up or upside down. Seeing that she happened to pick up Romance of the Three Kingdoms, Chengzu took it without a murmur of protest and began to read with real relish.

Mrs. Syi resumed her conversation. "But now I've come gradually to understand the vanity of ever increasing one's wealth and property. It's only this thing right here," patting her head, "that's real—bandits can't rob it, bombs can't blow it off. So whatever happens, the most important thing for a child is to study hard." Having gotten to this point, she recalled Zhishuang's arrogant manner and felt a sudden pang of emotion, a bitterness, of which she could not speak, so deep was her disappointment.

Meanwhile, Zhishuang was sitting glumly on the verandah, fanning away the mosquitoes as she brooded on her problems. The staccato sounds of frequent gunfire could be heard from the northern part of the city, where General Sye Jinyuan's troops were resisting. Why was this world changing so quickly? That evening strolling in front of Hardoon Garden, giggling as they ate cotton candy, petting that sheep dog with its pure white coat: thinking back on it now, it seemed like a dream.

One day Juanren, quite on his own, had asked her to go out with him again, but she'd declined. Of course Zhishuang, steeped, as she was, in her McTyeire values, could not just perfunctorily go out with a man to a few movies or for a few strolls, as if that alone were sufficient to conclude a contract. Quite to the contrary, she hoped that after every contact he had with her he would feel she was definitely not going to be easily won, and although she might not be the daughter of a prominent family, she was nonetheless from an honorable family, and she would soon be a student at Shanghai University; and having come from a top-flight school like McTyeire, she certainly wasn't going to get giddy in the head just because he was the son of bank president Zhu. Of course no one would regard the Syi family as poor, but in comparison with the Zhus, a great gulf separated them. And just now she actually had to be staying with this very inconsequential uncle of hers. If ever Juanren should burst in on her here, Zhishuang would be positively mortified. The more she thought about it, the more agitated she became—especially with all these mosquitoes buzzing around her. In a fit she lashed out at them with her big banana-leaf fan. "Darn, how can a person get mad all alone in the dark!"

The verandah door opened and Chilin came out, wearing a khaki uniform and having very much a martial bearing. Zhishuang had not seen him for quite some time. Nor had she even thought of him. But now that he had abruptly appeared before her eyes, she realized she was really very happy he had come to call. It was as if her hopes had been realized.

"Chilin, why have you been so long in coming to see me?" She pouted like a neglected child suddenly seeing a long-absent relative; her eyes reddened. "Living here, I don't have a soul I can talk to."

"Well, haven't I come? What's the situation here now? You're still turning on your childish temper." Chilin took the fan and rapped her on the head. With Chilin here, Zhishuang felt quite at ease. She had the sudden feeling that if some day in the future everyone in the world should treat her with cold indifference, there would always be one person who would not leave her out in the cold, would not turn his back on her, and that person was Chilin. "These past few days I've been at the army hospital helping in the relief work," said Chilin. "It's a terribly gruesome scene."

"Could we have a repeat of the January 28th Incident when we beat back the Japanese attack on Shanghai in 1932?"

Chilin looked at her as if she were still living in a protected world. There were so many things he just couldn't explain to her.

"In view of present conditions," Zhishuang said, "the school doesn't know when classes can start." She gazed mournfully into the night sky, still reverberating with the incessant sound of gunfire, like strings of firecrackers going off. Never had it occurred to her that the college life she had so long anticipated would commence just at the time of war. Those damn Japs had messed up her whole life, her peaceful home, her studies, and, what's more, messed up that newly formed...still hazy yet somehow beautiful...what should she call it...friendship perhaps— Zhishuang was a little superstitious and preferred to conceive of things in terms somewhat less than the reality; they somehow seemed better that way.

"Well, what do you think? Can Shanghai be defended?" she asked. The Chilin in her heart possessed great wisdom and ability; he knew everything.

"The troops under Sye Jinyuan have high morale," he replied. "I imagine they'll be able to hold out for a while."

"Hold out for a while?" she asked, disappointed.

"Well look. We gave up the three Manchurian provinces, and in the Marco Polo Bridge Incident the government allowed itself to suffer a terrible humiliation. And what good has forbearance like this done the army? Or done us ordinary people?" As Chilin spoke, he looked out silently into the inky night sky.

"At all events the Japanese won't enter the International Settlement, will they?" she queried. Hitherto, Zhishuang had never been much concerned with current events, and on the McTyeire campus anecdotes about British royalty and gossip about Hollywood stars seemed of more concern to her than national affairs. But now she had come to a pass where she could not but concern herself with such matters.

"Shanghai University is in the Japanese-occupied zone," said Zhishuang, practically in tears, "and I don't know now if it's even possible to study there."

"And the Japanese are occupying some countryside, too," added Chilin in a depressed tone. "My mother and brother don't know whether they'll live through it."

"Oh, I'm sorry." Zhishuang in sympathy patted his hand resting on the stone railing. Rarely did she find it easy to consider others. But Chilin's family lived in the port of Baoshan ten or twelve miles north of Shanghai, and had doubtless suffered greatly with the outbreak of hostilities: how could she not feel some concern for him? There were more than just her own annoyances.

"It's nothing. These days there's plenty of people like me who've lost contact with their families. With a war going on, nobody can help you no matter who you ask. You can only depend on everybody putting forth their greatest effort and win victories a little earlier and bring the war to a conclusion a little earlier. That's why I've joined the Red Cross Rescue Team—to do all I can. But actually, even after the summer's over, I don't think school will be able to start for a little while. In fact you could get involved in some relief work yourself, so you won't just have to mope around home day after day."

"No, I can't do that sort of thing." Zhishuang shook her head emphatically. "The sight of blood makes me faint, and besides who can say but what these refugees may not have fleas. You'd better be real careful. If you get those fleas yourself, it'll be very annoying."

Chilin gave her a little punch, a little punch both loving and resentful. He had no extravagant expectations about this pretty, headstrong girl, only the hope that while he was forging his path through life, she would stand by and watch him sympathetically.

It was getting late in the season, and the evening breeze carried the first touch of cold.

"Chilly? Shall we go downstairs?" asked Zhishuang.

"No." Chilin took off his olive-drab jacket and draped it over her shoulders. "No, there's too many people down there. Let's just sit here a while longer."

She could feel his body warmth in the jacket, and it carried a trace of the pleasant smell of cigarettes; suddenly strong feelings of sorrow and tenderness welled up within her. If Chilin said anything further to her, she believed she might very well find it difficult to bear. Fortunately Chilin said nothing, just sat there silently smoking...

Downstairs, Mrs. Syi's sister-in-law was asking her about Chilin. "The gentleman who came a moment ago—is he Zhishuang's boyfriend?"

Mrs. Syi sighed a heavy sigh. "Well, I certainly think well of the young man—honest and hard-working. But we're living in the Republican era now, not the old dynastic era, and so what parents have to say about this sort of thing doesn't count. When that daughter of ours buys material for a dress, she's so picky and choosy it takes forever, and I guess she's too picky and choosy to ever settle for this Chilin. Now Zhishuang has gotten in with a new crowd of friends, you know, and all of them come from Shanghai's most prominent families. For example, that Miss Zhu who came last time is the daughter of Mr. Zhu the banker. Well, they're the best of friends and that's raised her sights much too high."

"Well, since she's not figuring on getting married, how come she seems to be so hot on him?" Her sister-in-law seemed to have trouble comprehending the notion, while her two daughters, bashfully busying themselves with their needlework as if embarrassed at hearing things they were not supposed to hear, sat with pricked ears not missing a word.

"That's the way these new-style girls do it," remarked Mrs. Syi disapprovingly. "She hasn't the slightest desire to marry him, but she does want to maintain a natural and friendly relationship. If she really has settled on him, she's keeping it a closely guarded secret. And it really does rather disturb me that I don't even know if she really may have settled on someone. She's not a child any more. When I was her age, I was already a mother."

Listening to this, Mrs. Syi's sister-in-law just kept shaking her head. "I'm too old to understand these new ways," she said. "My two daughters, at all events, go by the old rules—attended a few years of school, learned how to read and write a little so they can read the newspaper and keep accounts—and that's good enough. But when it comes to housework, you can see for yourself they're real good at that.

In the future when the situation improves a little, I'll ask you to find good solid husbands for them, husbands who might work in a bank, in fact, like Mr. Syi. I'd be very satisfied with a match like that."

As Mrs. Syi listened, she was carefully sizing up her two nieces sitting under the light meticulously engaged in their work, one a few years older than Zhishuang, the other roughly the same age, both wearing simple dresses of foreign fabric, their hair permed into curls—young ladies who, quite aside from being pretty, possessed the sweet demeanor of beloved daughters of a modest family, adaptable to circumstances and content with their lot. With such daughters as these, parents need feel no anxiety; at most they need but find a well-off family for them to marry into. But a daughter like Zhishuang never allowed worry-free parents. She'd once overheard Zhishuang say to her own father that when she graduated from college, her private academy would invite her to return and teach there. Although she was the new breed of woman, and while there were young ladies who sat at desks or taught school, yet for the daughter of a respectable family every day to run around openly trying to earn her own living, well, wouldn't people take jabs at her parents for being unable to support her? Now a few of the neighbor girls were indeed going out to work, but in most cases because their fathers had died and they had to support their families and care for their younger brothers and sisters. Even admitting that Mr. Syi was urbane enough to be unconcerned with other people's taking jabs at him, still might not Zhishuang's future in-laws themselves gossip about it? How could one guess how tolerant or forgiving other people might be? Everybody was talking about how Zhishuang had made friends with an extravagant young man who had his own automobile. This sort of thing was worrisome, but Mrs. Syi was too old-fashioned to ask her daughter about it directly. According to Mrs. Syi's way of thinking, the Syi family need not be envious of people who owned automobiles, since such people tended to be very snobbish, but what she was afraid of was that Zhishuang's past would earn the contempt of others.

Soft footsteps could be heard on the stairway. Chilin came in to say good-bye to the family. He was a well mannered young man—sincere, conscientious, respectful; it's just that his family was of meager resources, and right now one didn't even know if his family in the countryside was dead or alive. What a pity. Otherwise, he would make quite a satisfactory match for Zhishuang, and the two of them had grown up together since they were small. The most important qualities to seek in conjugal life were kindliness and congeniality.

"Zhishuang, dear." Mrs. Syi called to her daughter, who was about to slip quickly upstairs again after seeing Chilin off. "Come over and take a look at how your aunt has done these linings over. You're a big girl now; you should try to learn how to do this kind of work. It'll come in useful later on."

Zhishuang's aunt was from Huzhou, and all Huzhou people were experts at working silk wadding. Just watch her rough, chafed fingers nimbly tearing and gathering, pulling the silk floss into sheets thin as cicada wings, piling one layer upon another. Having meticulously pulled out the snarls, she said to Zhishuang, "You're a lucky girl—there's no need for you to learn how to do this sort of work. The better you are at working, the more tired you get from too much work. It's really best not to know..."

She was interrupted again by rapid bursts of gunfire.

"They're still fighting over there at Garbage Bridge," said Mrs. Syi, inclining her head toward the sound.

Zhishuang remembered the day when Sky-Tile Tsao had a whole string of theater tickets and invited everybody to see the Shaosying opera he was directing, "The Russet-Maned Stallion." The troupe was apparently right there in the theater when the present battle broke out and who knows whether or not the theater had been destroyed.

She suddenly recalled with a lump in her throat those many hum-drum evenings which she had found so utterly boring—the sound of Suzhou parlandos drifting over from a neighbor's, the flopping of Tsao Jiusyin's leather slippers, Zhou in the kitchen softly humming a tune from a popular Chinese movie...Thinking of all this now, these sounds gave one a sense of security, a taste of consolation and stability.

"If we build it up with another layer of silk wadding to make it thicker," mumbled Mrs. Syi as she worked on a lining, "they say it'll even stop bullets! If Buddha will bless and protect this young man from rifle bullets, the sooner we'll push those loathsome Japs out of here, and ourselves peacefully return to our mothers. Why are some people so merciless when we're all born human beings equal from the start!"

Oh, those murderous Japanese!

Chapter 12

With fighting underway, foreigners and well-to-do Chinese families living in Zhabei and Hongkou, as well as landlords living along the Shanghai-Nanking and Shanghai-Hangzhou lines, all came fleeing to the international sector of Shanghai, for during the chaos of war there was no other appropriate place to keep the large amounts of valuables they had on their persons. Banks, precisely because they were trustworthy and safely located in the international sector, were attractive repositories of such people's wealth, and department stores and other such businesses which previously had been on the brink of collapse, now sprang back to life due to the large influx of people into these foreign havens. All of this was for the banking community a welcome rain after a long drought. And no more so than for Cathay Republic which had endured so prolonged a withdrawal crisis; but it had managed to remain solvent, and now with Du Yuesheng on its board and with the sudden changes wrought by war, the long lines of withdrawal customers had become long lines of depositors, such that Cathay had finally come from adversity to prosperity, had turned crisis into stability. And before long Syi Zhensyu sent the welcome news from the interior that Bounty Textile Mill had sold out the very first production run of cotton yarn, and because many of the textile mills in Shanghai, located, as they were, in the Chinese sections, had been reduced to rubble, Bounty's large-scale production had caused the value of its stock to rise dramatically, and accordingly Cathay's coffers soon began to fill.

A close call, thought Jingchen. Whenever he recalled the run on Cathay, he invariably felt a certain fear and he still broke out in cold sweat. It was like two people in face-to-face confrontation: the first to blink, even if by only a fraction of a second, will experience completely different results from the other.

Just days following Japan's attack on Shanghai—the "August Thirteenth Incident," Verity Chemical Works, where Jingwen worked, ceased operations and the entire workforce was let go. But gradually, within a month or so, Jingwen, believing boastful newspaper stories, mistakenly assumed Chinese forces were sufficient to withstand the Japanese and that it was possible with another successful campaign, like the Wusong-Shanghai action on January 28, to conclude the war before much longer. Because Jingwen had just recently borrowed a large sum for equipment modernization, he was eager to resume operations, and already by the middle of September had begun recalling workers so he could start up the machinery and resume production. Who could have foretold that by October the Japanese, assessing the unfavorable developments in the military situation, would revise their strategy: make a landing at Jinshanwei, south of Shanghai on Hangzhou Bay, outflank the Chinese army's rear lines, and sever the Shanghai-Hangzhou railroad. Ivory-tower intellectual that he was, Jingwen did not pay much attention to current affairs, didn't listen often to the radio, and was by temperament stubborn as an ox, so that other people's advice never sunk in. Consequently even in the present circumstances he still did not issue any notification for again suspending operations. True to the adage, he managed to remain "ignorant of the disaster staring him in the face," as he preoccupied himself with the bustle of plant operations.

It happened to be an early Sunday morning. Fagun the butler knocked lightly at Jingchen's bedroom door.

"Sir, your brother's wife has fled with her children to Shanghai from the countryside. She telephoned from the dock, asking if Ayi might be sent with the automobile to pick them up."

"Telephone my brother right away." Jingchen jumped out of bed and threw on a robe. "Don't waken Ayi," he added; "he didn't get to bed until very late last night. I'll go myself to pick them up."

"I've already telephoned to Mr. Jingwen's home; nobody answers."

"Try the plant. I wonder why Miss Yi isn't at home."

Fagun hesitated a moment. "Just now when I was out at the market," he said, "people were saying the Japanese had shelled indiscriminately in the Zhoujia Bridge area, but I don't know if Mr. Jingwen was able to make it out safely from the plant."

Oh my god! And there are a lot of workers in the factory besides just my brother, Jingchen thought to himself. No way of knowing if the plant actually got hit. Jingchen had advised Jingwen not to be in such a hurry to resume operations, and of course he hadn't listened. But for right now, the important thing was to pick up his sister-in-law and her children. The chaos of war indeed: a woman forced to flee with her children was no light matter.

A hurried bite of breakfast, and Jingchen was off to pick up his sister-in-law.

Today happened to be the day the newly hired gardener had come for a trial, and on that account Juanmin had gotten up early to watch him hoe weeds, then make a flower bed, and, satisfied with that, haggled for a long while before finally deciding on his wages, and by the time everything had been settled, it was already nearly ten o'clock before she'd gone inside for breakfast.

If there were no guests, the Zhu family normally ate their meals at the large, old-fashioned mahogany table in old Mrs. Zhu's room, for she liked the lively atmosphere. Today there was in addition a tailor's work table set up by the east window. Juanmin thought this most odd: how was it that without consulting her a tailor had been called in for some work? And just who was it who had engaged him in the first place? And to do what? Just as she was mulling over how to broach the matter tactfully to her grandmother, Juanmin caught sight of several bundles of silk fleece and fabric piled in a corner, and realized that the old lady was making winter uniforms for the troops with material which Juanying, a thoroughly devout Christian and active in social work, had gotten her church to donate. The old lady, spectacles perched on her nose, was getting ready to set to work. Seeing Juanmin come in, she asked affectionately, "What's taken you so long to have your breakfast? The porridge is all cold."

A big pot of pasty rice porridge was on the table, along with three side dishes—preserved eggs with grated cured meat, soy-flavored pickles, and fried peanuts. The sight of these three dishes made Juanmin scowl. Reluctantly she ladled a half-bowl of porridge for herself as she replied to her grandmother's query. "Today the new gardener came on a trial basis, so I had to watch him and talk with him about his wages. The guy seems awfully dull-witted, but actually he's as sharp as they come, so from the very beginning you have to nail down every little detail with him lest he try something funny later on. Right at the start he wanted me to pay him fifteen yuan a month, said the Lius gave him fifteen a month and their gardens aren't even as big as ours. I beat him down to seven yuan. Even though our gardens are half an acre, still the work isn't anywhere near so fussy as the Lius'." Juanmin's face radiated excitement as she spoke—she loved haggling over prices, an activity in which she found boundless pleasure despite the fact she was at bottom indifferent to a savings of just a few yuan.

"Don't give him a hard time for just two or three yuan," the old lady said impatiently. "That's sinful."

"You don't understand, Grandma," said Juanmin, pushing aside the half bowl of inedible porridge and rising to her feet. "This kind of person is terribly cheap. If you're polite to them, they just feel it's their due."

The old lady's maid, Zhao, came in to clear away the breakfast things, and Juanmin exploded angrily at her. "It's like putting out the same offerings to Buddha day after day—pretty soon you can't stand the sight of it any more. Didn't I tell you yesterday to add a dish of omelet slivers and shredded ham mixed with shredded agar? So where is it?"

"Miss Juanmin, with the fighting going on these past few days, the streets are full of homeless city people plus refugees fleeing the countryside. How can I find a stall selling eggs?" Zhao explained herself carefully, and Juanmin, knowing she was in the wrong, dropped the subject.

Just then Liu Tongjun's son, Liu Rubin, telephoned. Rubin and Juanmin had met once when the two families got together for a dinner party, and he had been telephoning constantly ever since. Today's gardener had been recommended by Rubin, which gave him yet another pretext for calling. First he feigned interest in the gardener's work then changed to the real topic, namely inviting her out for coffee. Juanmin declined every way she knew how, and finally hung up unceremoniously.

Granted the young Mr. Liu was a man of striking appearance and an outstanding student at Suzhou University, whenever Juanmin thought of his crass sister, Liu Tsaizhen, she lost all appetite for the brother. Because Juanmin was the daughter of an imposing family and, what's more, was charmingly attractive, she had had from early on many suitors, but she found each and every one of them unappealing: such young gentlemen, including her very own brother, seemed all to have been cast from the same mold, and except for being able to finger through a few piano pieces or to throw a few English expressions into their conversation, what else were they any good at? She had encountered many of this type and, just as when one eats too much tinned butter, it cloys to the point of nausea. Weren't they just flaunting their fathers' prestige? Only a person like Zhishuang, the daughter of a family one step her social inferior, could ever get a crush on men like these. That evening when Zhishuang seemed so attracted to Juanren, wasn't the naked truth really that she was attracted to the Zhu family reputation? Who would have thought that a refined and elegant girl like Zhishuang did not understand true love.

Juanmin went into the piano room and drearily leafed through the scores; she lifted the piano lid and picked through the melody of "The Maiden's Prayer."

Suddenly she heard Fagun downstairs at the house entrance talking with Old Chang the gatekeeper. "Mr. Zhu has gone to pick up Mrs. Ying, and it's hard to say when he'll be back. Did the caller give you his business card? Oh, Mr. Feng Jingsyao. Must be the son of that Feng family."

What! Feng Jingsyao! Juanmin's heart leapt and the piano playing broke off.

"Ask him to be seated in the parlor. Quickly, now!" Juanmin stuck her head out the piano room door and yelled downstairs, then dashed into her bedroom and combed her hair, inspected herself in the mirror, freshened her rouge, but sensing it wasn't too natural quickly took a piece of tissue and wiped it off, accidentally wiping away the touch of rouge that had already been there, then hurriedly fixed it up again, and ran down the stairs two and three steps at a time. In the parlor a tall slender man with hands clasped behind his back was just bending over a glass case admiring the cut-glass knick-knacks left behind by the Spanish businessman who had lived there before, when, hearing footsteps, he turned around to see, much to his surprise, a young lady. Moreover, he remembered where he had seen her before.

"How do you do. I am my father's daughter." No sooner had she said that than she realized how stupid it was. "We've met before," she hurriedly added.

"Hm. Is that so." Evincing no enthusiasm at having met her before, he merely smiled politely a wan smile.

He was wearing a blue-checked linen shirt and white slacks.

"Please sit down." Juanmin waved generously toward the sofa. Her six years at McTyeire had certainly not been in vain. "Father has gone out to pick up my aunt; he'll be back momentarily." She seemed to have become aware without having made any effort to do so that this striking Mr. Feng was originally from the Feng family of Hangzhou, and, again without knowing why, she all of a sudden felt relaxed.

"Did you know that since the war started in Zhabei we've all been talking about you every day," offered Juanmin with a charming smile.

"About me?" Feng Jingsyao seemed a little unnerved.

"Well, the last time when you came to our class in home economics and taught us to avoid bombs, I told everybody here that all they had to do was to run toward the tail of the airplane, not in the direction it was flying. So everybody, even the gatekeeper, Old Chang, has been repeating it all day long: Mr. Feng says to run toward the tail..."

Feng Jingsyao laughed heartily. He felt that this young lady was really very appealing, and without conscious effort the two fell into very agreeable conversation.

Before long Jingchen returned with Ying and her three little children. After arranging for their rooms, he came into the parlor. Immediately Feng Jingsyao courteously rose to his feet and greeted him. "Mr. Zhu!"

Clearly Feng Jingsyao had come to call on some sort of business. Perhaps to borrow more money? That could be a bottomless pit. Jingchen was beginning to feel a little ill at ease—was it or was it not to borrow money? Jingsyao glanced over at Juanmin, who gave not the slightest indication of leaving the room, and hesitated to broach his business.

"Juanmin, hurry upstairs and help your aunt get settled in," her father instructed, and with the greatest reluctance Juanmin got up and went out.

In the corridor just outside the door she bumped into Juanying who was craning her neck eager to see what was going on. "So this good-looking gentleman has come to see Daddy. At first I thought he was your boyfriend," whispered Juanying full of disappointment.

In the parlor Jingsyao took from his briefcase a small, cloth-wrapped package and opened it, revealing a piece of cocksblood stone big as an inkslab, deep red and wonderfully lustrous, which even Jingchen, who was no great judge of gems, realized to be quite out of the ordinary.

"I'm told this is something which has been handed down through the generations of the Feng family, so that even when my father fell on hard times, he was loathe to turn this into cash. Thus it passed into my hands." Jingsyao fidgeted with the stone as a wry smile played across his lips. "I really should pass it on in turn to my descendants. Chinese tend to be rather particular about that sort of thing, but I am a son not destined for good fortune, and in addition I have inherited my father's mountain of debts, so what meaning does this priceless treasure have for me?" Jingchen examined the stone which Jingsyao wanted to sell him—it was authentic but how could one put a price on it? There wasn't a low figure for this sort of thing, and the upper limit might go into the thousands or even tens of thousands; if he named an excessively low figure, he would clearly be suspected of taking unfair advantage of a man already assailed with problems, while if he named an overly high figure, it would be hard justifying the expenditure to buy a mere curio.

Surprisingly, however, Jingsyao held the stone in both his hands and respectfully offered it to Jingchen. "During the past few years," he said, "I'm afraid my father has not brought much credit to the family and I, his son, have little ability, and thus the family resources have been dwindling daily. So it is all the more fortunate that you, sir, have provided us with discreet support. Now my father has passed away and even his funeral expenses had to be borne by you. While it is not idle exaggeration to say that the debt I owe you could never be adequately repaid, I do want to bring things to a conclusion, and so for that purpose I beg you, sir, to be so kind as to accept this cocksblood stone as a token of my gratitude."

Now this was something Jingchen had not at all expected. Just as he was about to decline the gift, Jingsyao again pressed it on him saying, "You can't possibly refuse, sir, for otherwise I'll never feel at ease, for it is my character not to like to owe people anything."

Seeing him speak with such determination, Jingchen realized he had given the matter a great deal of thought and he would certainly not lightly retract his offer. "All right, then, let me keep it here for you until it may be convenient for you to retrieve it." So saying, his fingertips played over the stone and he could not restrain from exclaiming in admiration, "This is a treasure."

Now that Jingchen had accepted the stone, Jingsyao seemed greatly relieved. The Feng family had already divided its resources among the separate branches, though in fact there had been little worth dividing; it had been just a matter of selling the house and dividing the proceeds among family members to let each make his own living. Jingsyao used his portion to repay some of his father's debts, then provided for his mother and sisters to return to the Hangzhou countryside, where they could get by relying on income from their paddy land. Expenses would be less in the countryside, unlike Shanghai where you had to spend money for everything.

"I had long ago told my father that some of the girls in the family should be sent to a western-style school for girls, which would at least have provided them the skills to make a living. But Father didn't listen and the girls themselves didn't take any initiative, so now they've become old-fashioned young ladies of a backward era. And because they don't have any dowry, even marrying them off will be difficult." As he spoke, Jingsyao wrung his hands in futility. Fortunately Jingsyao had come into the world a few years earlier when the family fortunes had not yet dwindled to their present level, thus allowing him to study abroad. Having once contracted the foreign fever, however, Jingsyao found himself ever more out of step with the antiquated lifestyle of a large household. Consequently, for many years he had been living alone away from his family in a rented apartment, and only now on the occasion of his father's passing had the force of blood relation brought him back to attend to family affairs. Originally he'd considered his separation from the family to be irrevocable, but, to his surprise, his father had left so many outstanding financial obligations, which by Chinese tradition had now to be borne entirely by the eldest son (the more so in this case, for he was the only son), that he could hardly just walk away from them as if they were no concern of his. And with only his job as a pediatric clinic assistant to rely on, it would be difficult indeed to repay those debts in full.

As they parted Jingchen, much moved, patted this proud but straitened young man on the shoulder. At the very least a person must accept the responsibility that during his own lifetime he will do nothing that would bring disgrace to his descendants.

Jingchen saw him out and as they came to the front door he saw Juanmin playing with Juansi on the entranceway steps. Spotting Jingsyao coming out, Juanmin grabbed her sister by the hand and came over, smiling a charming smile.

"Dr. Feng, would you mind looking at her throat? She's had a bad cough the past few days."

In the bright sunlight Jingsyao checked Juansi, and finding absolutely nothing wrong simply instructed her to drink more water. Just as he was about to leave, Juanmin stopped him again. "Dr. Feng, if she doesn't seem well later on, I'll bring her to your clinic."

"Please do. Here's my card." And as he handed his business card to Juanmin, he realized how very attractive she was, her innocent, adorable face looking up at him with boundless expectation. Perhaps he should say something to her appropriate to the occasion, some little witticism to make her happy. That was nothing difficult for him. But (and he didn't know why) he said nothing. He just bowed courteously toward her, and left.

Jingchen cradled his little daughter in one arm, and pressed his forehead to hers to see if he could feel a fever. "Tell Papa now," he said affectionately; "is your throat sore? Do you have a fever?"

Juansi curled the fingers of one hand through her father's hair. "I don't have a cough," she said, "and I don't have a sore throat either. Minnie really just wanted me to have the doctor take a look. That's all."

Jingchen started. Turning toward Juanmin, he discovered her standing on the steps gazing absent-mindedly after the disappearing form of Feng Jingsyao. He did not disturb her; instead he led Juansi up into the house.

The table in old Mrs. Zhu's room was spread with silk wadding. Juanying, Auntie Ying, and Mrs. Zhu's maid were all at work making vest linings. Auntie Ying was five years older than her husband Jingwen, and an old-fashioned woman besides, so she looked very much his senior. What with her hair pulled back into a bun and her cheeks without a trace of rouge, if she hadn't been wearing a mandarin dress of expensive poplin, one would have assumed she was herself a maid. Little remained of the normal distinctions between master and servant. Her fingers, long accustomed to such household work, deftly picked at the wadding as she spoke resentfully of her recent experiences. "Those damnable Japs. They killed, they burned, they pillaged—no different from rural bandits. They ripped out the doors and flooring from our home to burn as firewood. The village head, Mr. Yeh, whose family had been scholars for generations, had his paintings and books either burned or stolen... Those Japs were merciless!"

"For a country as big as ours, how come we can't beat a few Japs!" The old lady clucked her tongue and shook her head.

"Speaking of soldiers, it's just sinful. As I was coming here, all along the railway were lines and lines of our wounded soldiers, and there was no way to get them all to the hospitals. Broken arms, broken legs, they just lay on the embankment calling for their mothers..." And on she went.

Once on the subject of war, the old lady recalled how, many years ago, the family was so straitened her eldest son, Jinghao, left to join the army, and for nearly thirty years with never a word from him, she didn't even know whether he was dead or alive. In the mother's eyes, he was forever either the stalwart uniformed soldier or the frolicsome little boy. Now, for all she knew, he might be one of those severely wounded troops lying on the embankment calling to his mother... The old lady's eyes reddened as she sighed heavily. "I've lived into my seventies, and all my life I've never understood why when Chinese fight other Chinese they are so cruel. One moment it's Sun Zhangfang's army, the next it's Bai Chongsi's. But when it comes to fighting the Japs, our armies can't seem to do anything except get routed. By the looks of it, the Japs are even more vicious now than they were back in 1932 when they attacked Shanghai. More and more refugees are fleeing into the International Settlement. Juanying was saying that the refugee shelters are too full to accept more people. The streets and doorways throughout the International Settlement are packed with refugees, and when autumn comes what are these people going to do?" The old lady spoke with a sorrowful heart.

Juanying looked at the clock, and started picking off the bits of floss sticking to her clothes. "Grandma," she said, "I've got to go out for a while."

Juanying was participating in her church's volunteer relief work at the refugee shelter, and she went there every day to put in a few hours, and during the past few days with the shelter particularly busy, she had been working so hard she had developed bags under her eyes.

"This granddaughter of mine," said the old lady heavily as she watched Juanying disappear. "Seeing how she hardly ever says a word and how she wears such a pitiable expression, she's just like her mother in character—from morning till night burying her head in churchly matters, singing hymns, donating money, doesn't even perm her hair but winds her braid instead on top of her head like a nun. Really," the old lady moaned, "she doesn't give me a moment's peace of mind."

"Is it possible she'd become a nun? We really ought to try to stop that." Auntie Ying was also a little concerned.

"She can't become a nun because she's joined the Protestant church, not the Catholic church. The problem is she's too single-minded about the church, and I'm afraid if she keeps wasting her time with it, she'll end up an unwanted old maid." The old lady took off her spectacles.

Unexpectedly her remarks touched a sore spot in Auntie Ying who heaved a long sigh and said in a faint voice, "She might do well to become an old maid. It would be very pleasant having no one's business to mind except one's own. With a husband in name only, is there any real difference between my life and an old maid's? Not to mention having to drag the kids along all my myself, and the hardships suffered along the way. When I got to Shanghai, fortunately Jingchen came to pick us up in his automobile, otherwise I really would have had to scream for help. I'm not at all familiar with Shanghai and all the streets leading into the International Settlement have been fenced off with barbed wire—it was all very frightening. That heartless Jingwen—if it weren't for the children, I'd prefer death in the countryside to my present vile lot!"

The old lady herself felt that her daughter-in-law had been mistreated, but what else could have been done? In the beginning it had been impossible for her sons—one a student, the other apprenticing in a Shanghai bank—to provide the slightest help, yet the family was still tending a few acres of mulberry trees and there were still the silkworms to be raised, but with only herself and old Mr. Zhu to rely on, how could just the two of them handle all that work? Consequently very early on they arranged marriages for the sons and moved the new daughters-in-law into the country home. They were both several years older than her sons, for country people preferred the wife to be the older for no other reason than being older they could work harder. How could they have known then that the elder daughter-in-law was destined to die young, while the younger had never been to her husband's liking, and the old lady always felt sorry for them.

"Enough of that, Ying. What's so unusual for a man to have one or two concubines? When they were small, the Feng family's accountant read the palms of both Jingchen and Jingwen, and said one had a noble destiny and the other a rich destiny, and now Jingchen has made all this money. But as for the noble destiny, the way I see it, now that Jingwen has his factory going, mightn't a rich destiny be in store for him too? I've already told him if he makes a fortune he'll have to build a large house and you and Jingwen and his concubine can all live together amiably and happily. Then wouldn't your hardships really be all over?"

"Just let me get the children raised up and then he'll have nothing more to ask of me." As she spoke, Auntie Ying's eyes reddened.

"Don't take it so badly. Women are born to suffer. Fortunately Jingchen is a warm-hearted man, and he always sent money to us in the countryside without fail. If I were to tell your fortune, all things considered, you are particularly..." The old lady, as she always did, dug deeply into her store of experience and insight in order to help her daughter-in-law conquer her distress, but how could she know that the more she talked the more distraught Auntie Ying became.

"Why isn't Jingwen back yet?" complained the old lady, annoyed at his absence. "I sent Juanren to go look for him at his plant, and even Juanren hasn't come back yet. Really now!"

But as it happened, just then the maids out in the hallway could be heard to say, "Is that Mr. Jingwen just arrived? His wife has been here for some time now."

In came Jingwen wearing a rumpled jacket badly eaten from a hundred chemical spills, a dispirited look on his face. He flopped into an easy chair at the foot of the stairway. His eyes teary, he said to Jingchen, who had come down to greet him, "Finished, it's all finished. When all is said and done, I have watched my own funeral."

What had happened was that earlier the same morning Japanese heavy bombers had conducted dawn saturation attacks on the Zhoujia Bridge area in the western suburbs at a time when the workers had to be on the factory floor to tend to a production run then in process; when the workers heard the thunder of explosions it was already too late to run to safety. In an instant the plant was a mass of flame and smoke—the workers couldn't find their way out, and everywhere there were horrible cries of anguish. The whole plant went up in one great sea of flames.

Jingwen, who was five years younger than Jingchen, seemed to have aged overnight—his temples had grayed, and his eyes, otherwise just like his brother's, lacked the latter's bright, piercing quality.

Full of sympathy, Jingchen sat down next to his younger brother, though inwardly rejoicing that, precisely because there were no guarantees, Juanren had not joined Jingwen's enterprise. He hadn't studied anything about technology and he would not have earned enough even to put food on his table.

"Really, it's all over. I had only enough time to salvage a high-pressure electric circulating pump and some platinum filters. The shipment of Swiss machinery we'd just received and hadn't even uncrated yet—all that's destroyed too." Jingwen buried his head in his hands—hands which, like his clothes, were pockmarked by the accumulation of chemical splatters—and sobbed.

"Is Miss Yi all right?" asked Jingchen anxiously.

"Right now she's visiting the families of the workers who got killed and injured, trying to console them. The workers positively despise me, so I can't possibly show my face. Damn, it appears to be all my fault, but only God knows why it really happened."

"You never listened to me. For the sake of pursuing gain you risked starting up operations, only to meet with this terrible tragedy. You can't shirk the blame," said Jingchen in a stern rebuke. "That's why I've said you can't be so damn single-minded about this. Whatever endeavor it is, you've always got to proceed prudently, keeping your nose to the wind so you won't be caught off guard."

"How could I have foreseen that our forces would collapse at the first blow? I always figured that if only there were another successful campaign like the one that beat back the Japanese after the January 28th Incident, then..." Jingwen blew his nose as his voice trailed off, full of regret.

"Jingwen!" His mother had poked her head into the upstairs hallway and was calling down. "Your wife has come. In chaotic times like this for a woman to flee here with her three children is a terrible hardship. Be a proper husband and stay with her a few days. I'm not permitting you to go running off again during such times. Fagun, tell Old Chang to take care of the front gate and tell him I said he's to make sure Jingwen stays here a few days and he's not to open the gate to let him out. And Zhao," she said, turning to the maid, "tell them to arrange the south guest room on the third floor so Jingwen and his wife can stay together."

"Mother, that's out of the question," said Jingwen jumping to his feet. "There's a pile of work to do at the factory."

"And that's out of the question, too." The old lady was now pulling Jingwen upstairs toward her own room.

"All right, Mother, that's enough," said Jingchen, putting in a word for his brother. "Jingwen won't go out to his factory. Honest."

"Then starting today, why don't you spend some time visiting with your own wife." And having said that, she summoned her maid and Juanmin out of her own room, pushed Jingwen in and closed the door behind him, stopping just short of locking husband and wife together inside.

"Fine. Now let's go. What are you doing waiting outside?" The old lady shooed Jingchen and the others off, then she too left, well satisfied that her interventions had been to very good effect.

"Poor ol' Uncle Jingwen!" said Juanmin, who couldn't help gasping in astonishment at her grandmother's decisiveness.

"I wonder why you don't sympathize instead with Auntie Ying," said Jingchen. "She's been in the family twenty-one years now, living all that time alone in the countryside."

"Daddy," said Juanmin in all seriousness, thinking to turn his argument to her account.

"What is it?"

"Promise me that later on if I get married you'll let me make my own choice."

Jingchen silently regarded his daughter's innocent almond eyes, at first thinking she was just joking, but seeing her imploring look, he could not help but nod his head repeatedly in assent. Juanmin's concern was by no means idle. The Zhu family now no longer counted as one of Shanghai's great families, though of course it was still of the upper class. The president of Cathay Republic Bank: well, how many people would like to associate, indeed even curry favor, with him? It was just that Zhu Jingchen himself had never given the slightest thought to getting in good with the influential and powerful by manipulating marriage ties. Just the day before yesterday Liu Tongjun sent a matchmaker around to say on behalf of his son Rubin that he favored Juanmin. To be sure, a marriage tie between Cathay Republic Bank and Bounty Textile Mill would be a good arrangement. Prospects would be advantageous for both parties—one might liken such an arrangement to a tiger which had sprouted wings. But right now, seeing Jingwen and his wife Ying forcibly kneaded together, who wanted to separate but were unable to do so, who wanted to reconcile but were incapable of it, now also with Juanmin's having so clearly expressed her own mind, Jingchen realized that it was a marriage proposal which he could not bring himself to broach to her.

Sitting in old Mrs. Zhu's room Jingwen and Ying silently viewed one another. Finally Jingwen backed down and timidly withdrew his gaze, quietly asking, "Are the children all right?"

"They got pretty tired along the way, but I've already given them baths and sent them off to bed."

"They didn't even wait to see me," said Jingwen with a touch of regret, for it had been years since he'd seen his three young children.

"They're quite accustomed to life without a father, so it never occurred to them to wait for you. They were sleepy."

Jingwen did not reply, nor did Ying expect him to. She bent over her work picking at the wadding. Because she had for many years been working to support the family, her knuckles had become swollen and discolored and protruded in a most obvious manner. He recalled when she had just become a bride that these two hands and her arms too were smooth and creamy. He was eighteen then—just an impetuous kid, while she was already twenty-three, for according to the rural custom most families liked the wives to be older than the husbands. There stood lovely Miss Ying in the light of the red candles at the wedding ceremony, and whether from his nervousness or some other reason beyond his ken, Jingwen's chest began to heave: those rosy lips of hers, those knowing eyes...This now matured woman was brimming with those enchanting qualities, yet she was reserved, not flaunting, like a piece of red-hot wrought iron, motionless yet emitting energy even while remaining absolutely motionless. Finally he could restrain himself no longer. Though he had in the beginning resolutely opposed this marriage, later, not wanting to hurt his mother, he decided to himself first to preserve her virginity and eventually to let her have her freedom—he was only eighteen and he thought in simplistic terms. But life is by no means like doing arithmetic problems, which can be readily solved step by step as easily as splitting bamboo.

One day when he happened to be on the school athletic field involved in a spirited game of soccer, indeed just when he was being held down and pummeled in fun by his classmates for his own hell-raising playing style, a worker came up to tell him that someone from his home in the country was in the reception room to see him. He was surprised, and thought that his mother must have taken ill, so he hurried to the reception room only to find an old neighbor with a basket of the traditional red-dyed eggs on his arm; the neighbor offered repeated congratulations: Lady Ying had borne him a son and Jingwen's mother had asked him to bring him the good news. At the time Jingwen was just itching to kick that basket of eggs right out of the fellow's hands. As it was, he convinced the old neighbor to take the eggs back with him.

On the playing field, his schoolmates were still waiting for him so they could resume the game, but he had now lost all interest in it.

Returning home on vacation, Jingwen found Ying, fully recovered from childbirth, had become even more delicately beautiful. He could not resist her, and now abandoned altogether his earlier plan of abstinence. Consequently not long after he had returned to school, his second son arrived.

Later, there was Miss Yi. But he was unwilling to have people regard Miss Yi as his mistress or concubine. Because of this, after he returned from overseas study, he arranged for Miss Yi to settle in Shanghai, while he returned alone to the countryside, thinking he would discuss matters with Ying and bring their marriage to a conclusion.

In anticipation of that, he had written his wife explaining the entire situation. But she seemed not to have taken the slightest offense, for as soon as he stepped into the courtyard, she came right out to welcome him, and waited for him to take off his coat so she could hang it up for him. He thought he'd ladle out some water to wash his face in, when she poured it for him, and brought him a new cake of soap besides.

As evening came on the weak flame of the oil lamp dimly illuminated the bedroom. She bent over their old-fashioned mosquito net-draped four-poster and adjusted the bedding, expressionless, unemotional, unblushing, arranging the quilts into a large sleeping bag... Her arms were no longer creamy, but her jet black hair retained its glossy sheen. Rural women were not in the habit of wearing brassieres, and with every motion her protruding breasts were never still. Consequently his passion was suddenly aroused so strongly that he himself felt he could not overcome his own astonishment.

This situation went on for several years and even he himself felt it thoroughly contemptible, yet he could not but return once every year to the country home. Eventually, at a time when he had come to despise his own conduct, it happened that he took employment at a missionary-operated hospital. There wasn't much vacation time at New Year and consequently for a good many years he didn't return to the countryside at all. His idea was that after a brief period of quietude, things would simply resolve themselves. It was still his way of using mathematical solutions as models for human existence. As a result, his life became a shambles.

And now: she was still the same—sitting so close by him yet without either excitement or indignation. But she was no longer that commanding, red-hot branding iron and she could no longer excite in him any passion.

Silence. Broken only by the sound of bugs colliding against the glass globe of the lamp.

"There's work to do at the plant, but I can't go out," he fretted. "Some workers were killed in the bombing today, and the factory is in ruins..."

With the outward tranquillity he knew so well, Ying fixed her eyes on him without excitement or resentment, but her fingers kept nervously picking at the silk floss. "I've come here, and you still want to leave."

"Anyway being here with Jingchen is just like being at our own home; Mother's here too, and..."

He darted a cautious glance at her out of the corner of his eye: still that same frozen expression. At bottom she had not the slightest understanding of the magnitude of the catastrophe he had just been through.

★   ★   ★

In her room old Mrs. Zhu was merrily chatting away with Jingchen. "Anyway, I've done a good thing today by bringing about a reunion between those two, so from here on out the three of them can live together. You go now and tell Old Chang that no matter who comes to call for Jingwen, he's to say that his wife is in Shanghai and that he has to be with her. Tell him I said so."

"Um, Mother, Jingwen's plant really has sustained damage and a number of his workers were killed in the explosions. Things are in a terrible state. If you keep Jingwen locked up and just let Miss Yi attend to things, well, how can a mere woman cope with all that?"

The old lady listened. But she just sat there blankly, not uttering a sound

"Mother," continued Jingchen quietly, "matters between Jingwen and Ying—you needn't overly worry yourself about that; that's just the way things are. Just think of it as the Zhu family bringing up a another daughter."

"And let the people back in the countryside start talking? He got an education, he got wealthy, he set up a factory, but he doesn't want the wife who's stuck with him through thick and thin. Well, that's just not right." The old lady pursed her shriveled lips and looked very serious.

"Let them talk it out together. Jingwen never did get wealthy, and anyway, you never listen to what people say back in the village." Jingchen smiled and patted his mother on the shoulder as he spoke, and then left.

Old Mrs. Zhu looked around the empty room. The expensive mahogany furniture set had been specially bought for her by her son, and visitors from the countryside were invariably envious of her good fortune. But how could those outsiders know that this lucky air of hers sometimes blew ill winds. Her son had attained sudden wealth and was filial, but unavoidably humored her along as if she were a little girl. Everybody in the entire house, everybody, from servants to granddaughters, just humored her along as if she were an overaged little girl. Who would have known that in years gone by this old Mrs. Zhu was famous throughout the surrounding villages as a woman of real ability.

The sky darkened, and the dark-colored furniture seemed to shroud the room in gloom, and a fear welled up in her which she had never before experienced. Old Mrs. Zhu had no particular analytical ability, so even if she had tried to analyze the trepidation she now felt, it would have been for naught. She just felt that it was because she was old and that the family had nothing it needed to trouble her about, that when she had something to say there wasn't anybody who wanted to listen.

From first to last she had never figured out why Jingwen was unwilling to have any contact with Ying. A man might have a legal wife, but he could also take concubines—this posed no moral difficulty whatsoever. But to spurn his first wife after having become wealthy, well, that was despicable. True, Jingchen had just said that in Jingwen's plant a lot of workers had been killed and that these were very difficult days for Jingwen as boss. Was this not deservedly called retribution? As this notion flashed through her mind, a chill pierced her to the marrow. Entrusting her luck to the ancestors, her two sons were now in Shanghai and had done very well—Jingchen unquestionably so, and Jingwen, for better or worse, had in all events started a factory. According to the rural wisdom, having clawed his way to wealth a person must thereafter stress right speech and moral conduct lest otherwise he incur the ancestors' wrath. Jingwen's coldness toward Ying was thus simply unjustifiable.

In fact during the past few years old Mrs. Zhu had been troubled by an apprehension that allowed her no peace. Normally she ought now to be enjoying her blessings free from any such apprehensive feelings.

The door opened quietly and Ying came in, stood there blankly a moment, then sat down next to old Mrs. Zhu.

"Has Jingwen gone out?" the old lady asked.

"That Miss Yi telephoned for him to go out." Ying was biting hard on her lips to prevent their trembling, her face expressing tragedy without resentment; Mother Zhu felt further pangs of conscience.

The old lady struggled to put on a smile, picked up the teacup by her side and, eyes closed, took a sip. "Wait until the present battle is past. Then you and I will return to the countryside and raise silkworms just the way we used to. If you're not around getting involved in these quarrels, they won't bother you, right?" This suggestion was offered quite spontaneously: the old lady had decided to retreat from managing the affairs of that couple and submit everything to the will of Heaven. And having said it, she looked full at her daughter-in-law, and in that look both seemed to have concluded a contract.

Ying, whose lips had been trembling throughout, now lost control, and quickly pressed her hand to her mouth.

"It couldn't have been helped," Mother Zhu said, her lips also quivering. "Women are born to suffer, and illiterate women are born for even greater suffering. I only wish we both could renounce the world a few years early."

Chapter 13

Autumn was well advanced and the evening breeze bore a definite chill.

The clock on the Customs House building had just chimed five in the afternoon, and the Cathay employees finished up the work at hand and prepared to leave. Cathay's survival of the recent bank crisis had actually greatly boosted its reputation, and its employees, like the proverbial boat which floats higher with a rising tide, were all in an upbeat mood. The war had forced the Small East Gate branch temporarily to shut down its operations, and its entire staff had been transferred to the main office.

The office Fan Yangzhi now occupied included high-ranking bank officers—"Assistant This" and "Associate That"—who in excited anticipation were now combing their hair or shining their shoes with a wastebasket scrap, looking at each other as if to say, "Let's go!" and out they started.

As they passed by Fan Yangzhi, head still bent over his work, one among them patted him on the shoulder and said, "Hey, Fan, we're going to the Great Shanghai Dance Hall for a little 'um-pa-pa, um-pa-pa'. The big dance star Mimi is doing a stage show. Tang here says he's treating. Young people should go out and have outside activities."

Without waiting for Fan Yangzhi's reply, the fellow named Tang stopped the others with a mischievous grin. "Don't hassle Fan; the guy's still a Boy Scout. He's still got to seriously improve himself for a few years so he can add 'assistant' or 'associate' to his title, and then he can go to the dance halls with calm confidence." The fellow's spiffy appearance hardly suited his uncouth tongue.

A few of the conservative, old-fashioned bank employees instantly affected a condescending expression toward the others. "Fan," one of them said, "don't pay any attention to them. Anyway, they're just extravagant young men who happen to enjoy the backing of powerful patrons. When something goes wrong they're the types who make things even worse when they try to fix it. Don't you learn their ways."

Of course Fan Yangzhi would not possibly associate with those people. When the office was finally empty, he took out from his drawer a copy of A Tale of Two Cities in the English original and began reading. His home was so cramped and the light so dim, there just was no place to read, so he usually stayed alone in the office after work and read—for self-improvement and also to save electricity and enjoy peace and quiet.

"Yangzhi, you still slaving away?" A man of thirty-some years pushed the door open and came .in. It was Syu Zhiyong who worked in the trust department, a graduate of Yanjing University, educated and interesting, whom Fan Yangzhi had greatly admired from the first. Zhiyong's family home was in Manchuria, but following the 1931 Mukden Incident when the Japanese started invading Manchuria, he'd lost contact with his family. Having no relatives in Shanghai, he too often remained behind after work alone in his office reading books or practicing calligraphy. Thus he and Fan Yangzhi had become close friends.

"Are you going to the Children's Refugee Shelter tonight?" he asked Yangzhi

Since the Japanese invasion of Shanghai, people had started a "National Salvation Dollar Donation Campaign" in which individual contributions were collected by banks and newspaper offices, and Yangzhi thus had dealings with the various anti-Japanese relief organizations when he turned over these contributions to them, and he himself sometimes went in the evening to help out in the relief work.

"Please look up Zhu Juanying. We have a load of medical supplies ready to ship across the Yangtze to help our troops. Miss Zhu and the church are quite familiar with the situation. Can you ask her to see if she can get the church to find a way to help ship the supplies?"

Zhu Juanying did volunteer work at the Children's Refugee Shelter, teaching the youngsters singing and reading, and recently had had frequent contact with Fan Yangzhi. Yangzhi had always felt that this Miss Zhu with her modest and amiable manner, her features expressing a certain melancholy, dressed in refined simplicity, who in no sense resembled the daughter of a wealthy family, participated in this relief work with genuine enthusiasm.

"Ship across the Yangtze?" Yangzhi was astonished.

"Chinese troops occupy both the northern and southern bank," said Syu Zhiyong with a knowing wink of his small, intelligent eyes.

"Ship across the Yangtze," mumbled Yangzhi doubtfully. "Ship across the Yangtze where?"

"To Yangzhou. A missionary there is in on it with us, and that being the case it would be safest to have the church here send it out. This really will be working for God."

"Okay." Fan Yangzhi put his book back, pushed away from his desk and started out.

"Wait a second." Syu Zhiyong handed him two Chinese Marxist works published in the 1920s—Ten Lectures on Social Science by An Ticheng and The History of Social Evolution by Tsai Hesen. "You've got to read foreign books, but you've got to read Chinese books, too," said Syu Zhiyong, patting him on the shoulder. "So many Chinese these days go through life with blind eyes. That can't be called real living, it can only be called existing. Man must live up to his full measure, not just muddle through life."

"A lot of people do just muddle through," remarked Fan Yangzhi. "But there's no security today for people muddling through with one eye blind and the other one closed. While we watched helplessly, our armies retreated from Zhabei and Jiangwan, and then from Zhenru and Dachang, yet the papers just keep publishing rubbish about it. 'Luring the enemy in deep,' they say, or 'choosing advantageous terrain to facilitate mass annihilation of the enemy.' How can ordinary people not ask, how damn far do we have to retreat before we get to that advantageous terrain? If it's really luring the enemy in deep, why don't we have orderly retreats instead of utter routs? And one more thing. There are still a few men in our office who like to idle away their free time by fooling around with dance hall girls. Really, it's unthinkable!"

The more he talked on, the more agitated Yangzhi became. "To tell you the truth, if it weren't for my family burdens, I'd refuse to earn my living by working for this bank. But I don't have the heart to let down my sickly old mother and my widowed sister, and a younger brother and sister still pursuing their education. The food you eat bought with this bank salary is unpalatable; it always makes you feel somehow you've sold yourself to the bank; it dulls the spirit. If you're sharp-witted you sell off the springtime of your youth, in the end to be transformed into a rosy-complexioned, radiantly smiling gentleman such as you see in advertisements for malted milk extract. And if you're dull-witted you'll be like my father, who burned himself out with overwork to his dying day, when he was still just a superannuated errand boy. I'm awfully naive, I guess, thinking that just because I'd gotten a college education majoring in economics I might sometime in the future be able to bring real reforms to Chinese society. How could I have known that during our recent bank crisis I finally saw that everybody practiced fraud and deception, cunningly seizing every opportunity for personal gain, yes, even in these hitherto highly respected banks. But even I who have studied economics have absolutely no way to change things. The so-called ideal of using education to reform the people and change their ways may be convincing to those who already have education, and be the cherished ideal of those who are far from it. But university graduates the likes of me, impoverished and powerless—where is there any place in society where they need us to make a mark?" And having gotten it off his chest Fan Yangzhi felt relieved.

Syu Zhiyong listened attentively throughout, then smiled generously. "Yes, right now there is a place. Ask Miss Zhu about those medical supplies."

*   *   *

Since fares were charged according to distance traveled, to save money Yangzhi had always walked a portion of the route before catching his bus. But on this day, having particular errands to do in the evening, he took a trolley directly back home from work.

Turning into his roughly cobbled lane, he became progressively troubled. The cause of it was his home, which was like a heavy shackle tightly constraining him. If he could have it the way he wanted during this serious national crisis, he'd unhesitatingly rush off to the front lines. But news from the front lines was invariably terribly disheartening.

In the gloomy parlor of the Fan home stood a big brass bed hung with linen mosquito netting—the most lavish of the home's furnishings, and also the sole remaining indication of a once imposing family.

"Our daughter has never remarried." Old Mother Fan, now close to sixty and infirm, but retaining the delicate features of her earlier years, was propped up on the bed. She waved her hand in a meaningful way as she spoke solemnly to an elderly relative sitting at bedside. The water tap beyond the courtyard was gushing forth its white stream as Fan Yangzhi's still young but already widowed older sister squatted there rinsing rice for the evening meal. Her daughter, just three years old and carefree, was sitting on the high threshold nibbling away at some dried potato flakes, her sparkling black eyes fixed on the briquette stove placed in the narrow alley, on whose gray-blue flame a pot of red bean soup was stewing, suffusing the air with a savory sweetness.

Since Fan Yangzhi had replaced his father as family head, he had been working at Cathay's Small East Gate branch, where his intelligence and diligence had brought him several salary increases. He had thus finally rescued his family on the brink of desperation, though he had definitely not become its savior. For example, he had not been able to alter the destiny of this young widow.

"Mother," he said softly, after the relative and would-be matchmaker had left. "Sister's only twenty-eight and customs today aren't the same as they used to be. She should start a new life for herself. In my view she's completely capable of choosing a suitable man for herself."

His mother retorted with unexpected anger. "What! You object to your sister and niece eating any more of your food, so there's no longer enough room for them?"

"Mother, what are you saying!" Yangzhi was so upset he started stamping his feet, but old Mrs. Fan carried on with her own notion.

"In the beginning a sister of your paternal grandfather—your third great-aunt—had her husband die on her before she'd even moved into her new family, and your great-aunt at that time was only seventeen years old, yet from that moment on she actually wore mourning the rest of her life. A great family must always deport itself like a great family... " She spoke in short pants, as her hands pressed down against the long-faded quilt cover, whose embroidered butterfly pattern was now quite threadbare.

A few thin rays of the setting sun filtered in obliquely through the lattice of the room's only window. This was the gloomiest time of the whole day, dull and cheerless, but because there was still sunlight it was too wasteful to turn on the lights, and Yangzhi felt enshrouded even more tightly in a suffocating cloud.

He couldn't wait for supper, so his sister filled a bowl with the thick red bean soup for him, topping it with two heaping spoonsful of sugar.

"Sister," Yangzhi could not contain himself from asking softly, "why are you so resigned to wasting away your youth forever in this house? You're still just in your twenties." His sister was wearing a simple lined mandarin dress, and her forehead was already faintly creased. It pained Yangzhi to see a face aged so prematurely; before, his sister's face was wonderfully attractive, and her skin faintly dark but very fine and smooth, earning her the childhood nickname "Dark Peony." Regretfully she had not yet graduated from high school when she married the man to whom she had been betrothed by her grandfather even before she'd been born—forced into marriage for the sake of maintaining "great family" appearances (even though it was no longer great), and, more importantly, to lighten the burden of her husband's father. Three years after the marriage, her husband died and his family upbraided her for bringing bad luck to him, and she found intolerable the constant abusive language. Later, the husband's family split up. She took with her some scant belongings and sought refuge with her mother. Time flew by and very soon Fan Yangzhi's sister would be thirty, but day after day she just idled away her life in the gloomy parlor. Alas, for a woman liberated for so many years, how could she still have such hardships!

"Sister," he whispered, glancing over at his mother who was resting quietly. "What I was just talking with you about, give it some thought." In fact, he had already requested Zhu Juanying to see if she could find some work for his sister at the YW; the pay needn't be a lot but his sister could at least avail herself of the opportunity to get out of this oppressive house or even, perhaps, to get acquainted with some people to her liking. But his sister merely forced a smile.

The sky had by now darkened, and the room could be illuminated with a fifteen-watt lamp. Too dark outside to see much, some kids in the courtyard came inside for their horseplay. Yangzhi's younger brother, still in high school, also came back home; he too had the habit of staying at school to finish as much of his homework as possible before returning home because the home environment was definitely no study environment. The kids who'd come in started complaining they were hungry, just as his brother was about to continue his homework at the table; his sister told them to wash their hands and faces as she took care the food cooking on the stove didn't start to burn. There was also their ailing mother on the bed who had to be given her medicine. The room was a scene of confusion. Yangzhi practically ran out of the place.

"Yangzhi, thank Miss Zhu for her thoughtfulness. You see? How can I possibly get away to take a job? If it weren't for this family... " And she threw up her hands in resignation as she saw her brother off.

Yangzhi stepped sullenly out into the narrow alley. The street lamps provided only fitful illumination for him, who was the only soul about. The doors and windows of the houses along both sides of the alley were tightly closed, and as he walked past his own house, a faint and gloomy light shone through that small latticed window and the sound of chopsticks could be heard clinking against their rice bowls. Alas, precisely on account of this family, his father had worked himself to the bone, he himself had, contrary to his convictions, changed his own career goals, and his sister was resolved to sacrifice her own youth: it could be justly claimed the family had done its very utmost. This family so weighed down, so riddled with wounds—why was it that Fan Yangzhi could neither shoulder its heavy burden nor cast it aside!

He suddenly felt cold drops on his face: it had started to rain.

Turning out from his alley into the larger cross-street, he saw refugees all along the street huddled under the large projecting eaves to escape the rain. This was the International Settlement, formerly a place of quiet tranquillity, but no longer, as the refugees fled to it in ever greater numbers such that the emergency shelters were reportedly already full to bursting. And presently winter would be upon them, and what would these people do then? The shelter Fan Yangshi headed for was originally the gospel hall of a small Christian church. The downstairs rooms of the church and adjacent gospel hall had been linked together and opened up as a make-shift refugee shelter specially for the housing of children fourteen years and under who had become separated from their parents. In one corner of the shelter a piece of fiberboard (formerly the church bulletin board) partitioned off a temporary office for the volunteer staff.

At this moment just one person, Chilin, was seated in the office, reading the newspaper. Of stalwart build, he seemed very awkward in so cramped a space as this. His shift ought to have been over now, but his relief, Zhu Juanying, had not yet shown up, so he was obliged to wait until the night person, Mrs. Wu, arrived before he could leave. Seeing Fan Yangzhi come in, he brightened up, happy to have someone to talk with to relieve the boredom.

"Chilin, how come you haven't left yet?" asked Fan Yangzhi, shaking the rain from his hair. "Is Miss Zhu in class?"

"That pampered daughter—who can say for sure about her. She's too busy going dancing or going to the movies. Doing emergency relief work is for her no more than just keeping up with the latest fashion. Not so much as a telephone call from her, and when I telephoned to her place, she wasn't in. Fortunately Dr. Feng has come to do physicals, otherwise how could I have managed all the little whelps by myself?" Chilin was very much out of sorts. This Miss Zhu, of such commonplace appearance, was very meticulous in the performance of her tasks. If only it were not she but Syi Zhishuang who came five times a week to teach the refugee children singing and literacy, well, how much better that would be! It was from that consideration, or perhaps vague feeling, that he was always taking out his anger on the blameless Miss Zhu, as if she had snatched away Zhishuang's job.

"Miss Zhu isn't that kind of irresponsible person. If she's late there's got to be a good reason. I hope she hasn't had some sort of accident." Fan Yangzhi looked out the window at the ever increasing rainfall, and began to feel a little uneasy.

"What accident could she have!" objected Chilin. "Young ladies of her type have their own private automobiles, or at least private rickshaws. And this is the International Settlement, y'know." Then he suddenly remembered something. "By the way," he asked, "that opening you learned of for a spare-time night job at the newspaper—is it still available?"

"You want that kind of job?" replied Yangzhi. "Proofreading is terribly tiring. I can't get through it myself."

"How can I be compared with you? You've got something coming in every day and can actually eat from the banker's proverbial silver rice bowl. But I'm in a financially awkward situation. With the war on my family has cut off its financial assistance, and employment is very hard to find. And for the time being I don't plan to leave Shanghai, but being in Shanghai you inevitably spend money every time you turn around. These past few days I've been particularly tight for cash." Chilin was just lighting up a cigarette when he heard the childish noises of those wretched kids on the other side of the partition. He crushed out the cigarette.

"You still haven't had any news from your parents in Baoshan?" asked Yangzhi with concern. "If I were like you," he added, "all alone in the world, with no worries and with no one around, I'd certainly take off and go to the government-controlled area. After all, what's worth being so attached to Shanghai?"

Chilin looked up and was about to say something, but in the end said nothing. What could he say? To say that in Shanghai there was a girl—intelligent, pretty, and a little imperious—and although there was absolutely no hope for him with her, still he would happily wait for her...he hoped that one day when he had accumulated enough money he might go to England to study and, having earned a degree, return to some position, preferably in a British firm, and find an apartment and settle in his parents, and then, bouquet in hand, say to that adorable girl, "Come, everything has been made ready for you." This is why he was so attached to Shanghai. Perhaps this was what is called a rare treasure?

One of the kids on the other side of the partition apparently just couldn't handle the stethoscope exam, which gave him a giggling fit as if someone were tickling him.

"Just listen. Kids don't know what worry is," said Chilin wistfully. "Before, when I was living at home, my father kept a concubine, and so there was always a lot of ill-feeling and argument, and I wished then I could grow up quickly and leave home to go to college, and then everything would be just fine. How could I have known that when I came to Shanghai I'd be staying the whole time with my aunt and uncle, and though they're nice people, I just can't consider their politeness to be my good fortune and I always have the feeling of being a stranger living under someone else's roof. So I really had my heart set on going to a big-name university and in the future having my own career. Then everything would be just fine. But it turned out to be much tougher than expected getting into college, so my prospects are still just as uncertain as ever!"

"Yeah, I've always figured too that once I got into Cathay Republic Bank and got hold of that silver rice bowl, my prospects would be infinite. But come to find out that grand Cathay is a battlefield where the higher-ups exploit the weaker. The president feeds on the vice-presidents, the vice-presidents feed on the assistant v-p's, assistant v-p's feed on section chiefs—one level feeding on the next lower until they're so stuffed they can hardly breathe. Don't just look at all of their trim western-style suits—the work they perform couldn't stand up to public scrutiny. Like the president, Zhu Jingchen. As a plasterer he's a top-notch artisan—everything is fixed up into ship-shape condition, clean and shiny, winning on that account a nice reputation for himself. You'd hardly expect he was involved in under-the-table deals, manipulating intrigues among the staff, in cahoots with the enemy—that's President Zhu. He's a real fox, all right. During the fighting when Cathay was knocked down, it bounced right back up. So it's obvious that war isn't necessarily everybody's misfortune. What's strange is that Miss Zhu really isn't a bit like her father." Recently, for some reason or other, whenever Fan Yangzhi met fellow relief workers like Chilin, he took pleasure in talking with them of Zhu Juanying, and the very mention of her name always made tender thoughts well up inside him.

Chilin, noncommittal, scowled abstractly. From the direction of Garbage Bridge came the familiar sounds of gunfire. The national armies had by now completely withdrawn to the west, leaving only forces under Sye Jinzhi still resisting.

"Those are General Sye's troops," said Chilin.

"An isolated force engaging the enemy isn't strong enough to win," said Yangzhi despondently. "This defense to the death is little more than a hollow attempt at recouping national pride, when the truth is, it's a national tragedy."

At this point Feng Jingsyao and an International Red Cross doctor came in, having finished up their work.

"It's very good here—we didn't discover any fleas. We've discovered fleas at other refugee shelters, though, so you still need to be careful." As the foreign doctor spoke with a satisfied air, he washed his hands under the tap and was just about to pull down the towel that hung above the sink to dry them when Feng Jingsyao surreptitiously tugged his sleeve; he immediately pulled away, and took out his own handkerchief to wipe his hands.

"Are you going back? We can give you a lift part way in our car," said Feng Jingsyao politely in English to Chilin.

Chilin declined icily. Feng Jingsyao followed the foreign doctor out and got into his mud-splattered car.

"He actually faults us for unclean towels," said Chilin contemptuously, "while he himself is positively nauseating. Looks like a western bastard, but he's obviously a Chinese just spitting out a foreign language."

"You'd really better return now, so as not to keep your girlfriends waiting," said Yangzhi jokingly. But Chilin actually heaved a long sigh and said, "It has gotten late; I'd better go back. It's just that there never has been a girlfriend waiting for me. You probably don't realize that for people of my class it is considered quite good enough simply to have employment and enough food to eat. In this society of ours now even love must be categorized as an extravagance!"

He put on a rain hat and left. Large-framed as he was, he had to stoop to pass through the low doorway. Fan Yangzhi felt a wrong on his behalf.

"Auntie Zhu..." A five- or six-year-old country lad holding up his trousers stepped into the room. "My pants are falling down...the button fell off..."

Now this put Fan Yangzhi at quite a loss. He picked up some paper clips from the desk. "Here, try to make do with these, sir." But when the little boy saw the shiny things, he thought he was going to be given an injection, so, holding onto his pants, he instantly turned around and left, only to bump full into Mrs. Wu, who worked nights and happened just then to be coming through the doorway. This Mrs. Wu used to work at a night school in Zhabei, but later when the school was bombed and her home bombed as well, she herself became a refugee and she came here to help. Mrs. Wu was a native of the backward northern area of Jiangsu province; she had a thunderous voice and sloppy eating manners, but a kind heart. Yet the child was, after all, very small and stood in great fear of her. Because of this, when Yangzhi asked Mrs. Wu to sew on a button for the boy, the little kid bolted out of the room.

"Your pants are going to fall down, sir!" Yangzhi grabbed hold of him and paper-clipped him together, the clips sticking out this way and that.

"Why don't you go back now, Mr. Fan?" urged Mrs. Wu. "What a fright I had," she continued. "Just now outside two men were crossing Baidu Bridge and because of the rain they forgot to bow to the Jap sentry there, so he cuffed them right across the face."

From outside now came the sound of quick, short footsteps, and Juanying, shielding her head from the rain with her handbag, burst in, soaked through.

"You're here!" exclaimed Yangzhi in relief.

"I'm terribly sorry to be late. I found fleas in a lot of other emergency shelters, so I helped them with disinfectant showers; some of the volunteer cleaning people are awfully careless, and if you don't keep a close eye on them and make sure they disinfect everything, they might just as well not do any work at all, and on top of all that I couldn't find a pedicab anywhere." As she spoke, she quickly pulled out a music book from her handbag and was about to give the children their singing lesson.

"You can relax a minute. Mrs. Wu is right now getting them to wash their faces and feet." Yangzhi, noticing Juanying's lips were purple with cold, busied himself pouring a glass of hot water for her. He then pulled down the towel for her to dry herself off; it was supposed to be white, but used by everyone, as it was, it was badly soiled, and he involuntarily hesitated to pass it to her. Juanying smiled at him gratefully and herself pulled down the dirty towel and started wiping the water from her.

"How come it's so late and you still haven't left?" she asked with a smile. As she clasped the glass in her two hands, Yangzhi discovered that her fingernails also were blue from cold.

"I have a favor to ask you. There's a load of western medicines that somehow needs to get transported north. Could you ask the assistance of someone in the church who might like to help? We want to ship it to northern Jiangsu... " Yangzhi watched her expression closely for a reaction, and beheld only those eyes under her thin eyebrows, eyes neither particularly big nor particularly black, but eyes serene and limpid, looking back at him. He went on. "It would be best that a foreigner be personally involved... "

"I'll do my best," she readily promised.

Because she replied so off-handedly, Yangzhi was still rather anxious.

"You won't have any problems with that?"

Again, she spoke with composure. "I'll think of a way so there won't be problems. In our church there's a gentleman who has close connections with the International Red Cross; they've got a steamer, the Buddhist Cross, which presumably the Japanese wouldn't dare interfere with." It seemed that Syu Zhiyong had been right in placing his confidence in her.

The rain grew heavier. Overhead the bare light bulb soaked the room in its dim glare. The two sat across from one another at the narrow desk. Normally a boy and a girl sitting silently like this would be, unless they were sweethearts, extremely awkward. But on this occasion, sitting opposite the gentle and refined Juanying, opposite those thin eyebrows and those serene eyes, to his surprise Yangzhi felt not at all ill at ease, indeed felt that the suffocating cloud long oppressing his heart was gradually dispersing. Her eyes were placid and serene not because she was ignorant of affairs or escaping reality, but rather because of her own goals, her own beliefs. In the present chaotic conditions, people who had beliefs were truly fortunate, and Yangzhi was very interested in probing her beliefs, although at the same time he felt that to accept them would be very difficult for him. How he envied her!

She raised her glass with both hands as a child might, and took a sip; the electric bulb edged her coiled braid in a halo of light, and while she certainly could not be reckoned a beautiful woman, she was very sweet. "Uh...the sound of gunfire around the Fourth Route Army's supply warehouse certainly is obvious. Daddy was saying today that Mr. Yan Esheng of the Chamber of Commerce had received a telephone call from the Fourth saying that the national flag that Yang Huimin had sent them was too small and unsuitable for flying on the top story of the warehouse building, and asked the Chamber to find some way to send over a big flag. If they do that, our refugee children here will all be able to see it."

"Auntie Zhu, my buttons have fallen off." That same sun-darkened chubby kid holding up his pants came moseying in.

Juanying stooped over and took a look at the crazy-looking paper-clip job. "What do you think you're doing with all these paper clips?" she queried.

"That gentleman fixed it," the boy mumbled.

"Gracious, Mr. Fan!" Juanying laughed aloud. Yangzhi had never seen her laugh like this, a laugh that was so infectious Yangzhi himself had to join in.

Juanying took out needle and thread from the drawer, knelt down and sewed the buttons on. The rain was now dripping into the rain gutters and beating against the window panes—a rain which in this season made you feel the chill. Just listen to it splashing down the rain gutters!

Because of the moisture and the cold, a thick layer of fog misted the windows. In the dim light Yangzhi quietly watched Juanying nimbly fly through her work as the boy obediently leaned against her knees, and it occurred to him that if at this moment a stranger happened to look in through the window, he would certainly consider this a family of three. No sooner had this thought flashed across his mind than he felt his own cheeks start to burn.

"Done." Juanying bit through the thread, patted the little fellow on the bottom, and was about to rise to her feet when she let out a painful cry and tumbled onto the stool. It happened that just before at another emergency shelter when she was sterilizing things, a pan half full of boiling water had spilled on her thigh, raising two nasty blisters.

"Oh, oh, let me take you to a hospital; you need to take care they don't get infected," Yangzhi said anxiously. She turned her back on Yangzhi and lifted her dress to inspect the injury.

"I've got to give the children their singing lesson." She quickly let her dress drop back, took her music book and limped into the main room. In a moment from the other side of the thin partition came the sounds of a little treadle organ, followed by the pleasing voice of Juanying. She was a choir member at Muen Church, and had been receiving voice training.

> Don't wait for big things ere you show your light,
> And don't wait until your light can shine to far-off lands;
> Right before your eves you can shoulder lots of tasks
> To brighten the little place you are right now...

Her clear and steady voice, despite her deceptively weak frame, showed Jyanying to be strong in will and resolute in her pursuits.

> Slow of step and frail in strength you're loath to
> do the task;
> Yet if a single soul might hear your song, your song
> must needs be sung;
> For with these humble hands you can do the will of God.

The children sang along vaguely, only half understanding the words, but in any event the singing was just a way to cheer them up. The childish, immature voices were moving, even melancholic to hear.

The lesson over, Juanying discovered Yangzhi still waiting.

"I'll walk with you to the hospital to see about your leg."

Juanying thought a moment. "All right," she said. How charming she was; how she could make one feel relaxed and at ease.

Luckily not very far away there was a hospital. Having treated her, the doctor commented in a way that made them both feel extremely awkward. "For the next few days, don't let your wife exert herself too much with housework. Fetching bath water and such—you ought to help out more with things like that, sir."

By the time they'd left the hospital it was already nearly eleven.

"You can't go back alone; let me go with you," said Yangzhi.

"What's the matter in going alone? I'm always alone." She spoke defiantly, yet she could not suppress a slightly doleful expression: yes, she was really still a child.

"But today I'm here, and I just don't feel comfortable letting you go back alone." Yangzhi hailed two rickshaws, and, one behind the other, they headed for the Zhu home.

The rickshaws rolled through the streets at a steady pace. Because it was raining, their canopies were raised and the passenger was shielded in front by an oilcloth curtain as well. The streetlights penetrated the seam in the cloth—a thin sliver of light that just fell on Juanying's creamy white face. Because she had finished her lesson with the children and with the hospital visit also behind her, the nervous taughtness she had earlier felt had dissipated, and now, in fact, she felt utterly drained emotionally. Drops of rain, big as soybeans, pattered against the canopy, and from behind she could hear the soft splashing of Yangzhi's rickshaw following along; and all of a sudden her heart filled with tranquillity and satisfaction, as when a ship finds safe haven during a storm at sea.

"Which one?" came the hoarse voice of the rickshaw coolie from beyond the canopy.

Juanying quickly straightened up and lifted aside the curtain, but the murky rain had rendered nearly unrecognizable this street normally so familiar to her. She pulled herself together and called to the coolie to stop outside her gate.

A large puddle had collected just before the front steps, and light from the gatepost lamp shone brightly on its surface, giving the impression of a bottomless pool.

"I'll help you across," said Yangzhi.

She leaned cautiously on his arm as he helped her down from the rickshaw. Looking at him with those placid eyes he already knew so well, she bade him good bye.

He stood there watching her as she covered her head with her handbag and, half-tiptoeing, half-limping, started for the heavy iron gate of her home.

The gate clanged open. She turned around and looked, looked at him still standing there; she seemed rather surprised, but the gate was already open, so she disappeared inside.

Yangzhi just stood there blandly, the raindrops pelting his head, dripping off the ends of his matted hair.

He could see through the iron railing atop the property wall to the three-storied English-style residence, the windows of each floor brightly lit. Ah, so this was the home his colleagues at the bank always referred to as "The Zhu Mansion."

Yet that solitary, refined, melancholy young woman was actually the daughter of that awesome Zhu Jingchen. They seemed to be two people utterly unconnected with one another, and lest they find some small bit of connection, they apparently would not look for it.

"For us, love is an extravagance."

That's what Chilin had said.

"It can't be that way," Yangzhi said to himself, as he rubbed his cold, wet hands.

"The rain's coming down hard, sir. Do you still want the rickshaw?"

The rickshaw coolie, a threadbare coat thrown over his shoulders, had come around, hoping for another job.

Riding in rickwhaws—that's what was extravagant!

Yangzhi shook his head. Water-soaked leaves squished under foot as he hurried toward the trolley stop.

Chapter 14

Books tucked under her arm, Zhishuang followed the crowd
spilling out of the big Commerce Building located in the
bustling downtown area. Because of the war several of Shanghai's
prestigious universities had moved into the International Settlement,
and now held classes in this office building.

"Miss Syi," called a student chasing after her from behind. An
affected fourth-year student who wore a fashionable suede leather
jacket, he'd recently had his eye on Zhishuang. "Great China's showing
a Vivian Leigh film..."

Zhishuang declined with a dignified reserve. She would never
casually strike it up with any such male student of unknown origins.

Emerging from the building onto the noisy main street, she followed
along with the throng through the International Settlement, where, in
spite of the war going on, the shops were doing a brisk business.

Zhishuang was finally able to take off that dark green school uniform
she'd worn for nine years. Now she was wearing a purplish woolen
mandarin dress with a short jacket of off-white cashmere, and, with
those lecture notebooks tucked under her arm, she was every inch the
college student. Regretfully, however, the campus life to which she had
so looked forward at any of the universities—the ever-fashionable St.
John's University, the courtly formality of Shanghai University, the
romantic ambiance of Great China University, the insufferable
arrogance of fourth-year students—all this was now distorted beyond
recognition by war. Not even the campuses remained: everybody was
now crowded into the noisy shopping district to listen to lectures, and

when the bell rang the students flooded into the room with a whoosh and at the next bell they squeezed out of the room with another whoosh, while the students themselves never quite got around to forming meaningful friendships (the relation of one to another resembled the indifference among passengers on a public bus), to say nothing of group spirit, save, of course, for those romances between men and women students which would take forever to recount.

She checked her watch. It was still early and she had no taste for returning to her uncle's insufferably crowded home. She only now understood the extraordinary patience Chilin had exercised in living for so many years with his aunt and uncle's family.

A large roasting pan was set up in front of a nut shop along the street, and just now roasted gingko nuts were being sold. A shop clerk, his face flushed from the roasting fire, was dexterously turning the nuts as he barked his product: "Right here, tasty roasted gingko nuts, each one nice and big; girls eat them and your tits grow bigger, boys eat them and your balls grow bigger!"

The fellow's jocular appearance induced passersby to stop and appreciate the humor of his crude patter, and no one seemed upset by his vulgarity. This spirited, cheerful shop boy piqued Zhishuang's recollection of the White Russian selling cotton candy that evening in Hardoon Garden. It had been a scant few months, but thinking back on it now, it seemed like a very long time indeed. Juanmin had always been rather narrow and intolerant, and from that evening on, because Juanren had been excessively warm to Zhishuang and had scarce paid any attention to his own sister, Zhishuang seemed suddenly to have grown distant from her. Then, later on, when Zhishuang moved in with her uncle in the International Settlement, the two girls seemed to have even less contact with each other. And her other classmates at McTyeire also seemed abruptly to have disappeared from the scene. Now she was all alone in her comings and goings, left to while away her long-anticipated college years with utter lack of interest.

Zhishuang bought a bag of gingko nuts, climbed to the upper deck of a trolley and sat down in the back, aimlessly eating the nuts as she gazed out at the street scene. Although it was considered a serious breach of etiquette to eat snacks in public, she was now indifferent to everything; neither did she have to wait for the housemother to announce dinner nor did she have girlfriends who might regard themselves superior. Now, the male college students were actually wearing their raincoats as they swaggered into the classroom, for there was not even a coat hook there. Well, this was wartime, and anything was permissible.

Zhishuang found a perverse satisfaction in audibly cracking the gingko shells, a moment of conscious rebellion affording her a vague happiness. The nutmeat was indeed soft and tasty, jade-colored, slightly translucent.

"Well, isn't this a nice treat," said someone in a soft voice, sitting down next to her.

"Why, Chilin, it's you!" Glancing down at the gingko shells piled on the hanky she'd spread on her lap, Zhishuang felt a little embarrassment.

"Where you going? Back home?"

"No idea," she shrugged. She felt empty at heart. Just a few months ago at McTyeire her beauty and intelligence could still earn the admiration of her teachers, and it was not mere braggadocio to say that her reputation was school-wide. How unlike today—without friends, without social life, without anything at all! Somehow she'd have to exert all her strength to accommodate herself to this odd college existence.

"Zhishuang, this Saturday evening at the YW there's going to be an outdoor fund-raiser, and they need some girls to help with the charity sales. I'll try to find a place for you. The work shouldn't be at all hard for a McTyeire girl." Chilin hoped in all sincerity that Zhishuang might concern herself with the relief work. At this time of national crisis, it was inconceivable to him that any young person could actually remain indifferent, yet Zhishuang was indeed such a person.

"Oh, I've got to review for my courses. The biggest headache studying home economics is nutrition, which requires organic chemistry. Those formulas are as uninteresting as tortoise shell markings. What a pain." She scowled unhappily.

Chilin said nothing further.

The trolley clanged past Great World Entertainment Center. The shopping area was particularly crowded with people, the reason being a mammoth three-ton shark on exhibition, for which a huge advertisement was hung above the Great World entranceway.

"It's amazing that people in this city can be in such a buoyant mood. It's only been a few months since Great World took that bomb explosion, but you'd think they'd forgotten all about it." Chilin spoke with anger in his voice.

"Well then, Chilin, I'll go," said Zhishuang, as she carefully dumped the gingko shells back into the paper bag.

Chilin was a little embarrassed, though. "Don't put yourself out. Only if you really feel like it." He'd been feeling recently that because of his increased uncertainties and worries he'd become very short-tempered and had actually lost all capacity for sympathy with his fellow man. And Zhishuang, of course, took as her principle in life not to tolerate other people's intrusion into her own affairs; thus, what right did Chilin have to interfere with her? What did he mean to her?

★   ★   ★

Saturday evening came. The broad lawn of the YWCA on Bubbling Well Road was decorated with lanterns and streamers, and a lace-covered horseshoe-shaped counter adorned with flower arrangements was all set up. The fountain in the pool was shooting skyward, flower petals and fallen leaves floated on the water's surface, and light from the colorful lanterns flickered off the column of water in a rich splendor that gave the fountain a life of its own.

Along the balcony of the main building a temporary stage had been erected and a band of musicians dressed in white tuxedoes with black bow ties was already seated on its left side. This evening was witnessing a social function of impressive formality. Under a padded sleeveless jacket, Zhishuang was wearing a silvery satin mandarin dress edged in real silver piping, recalling a fresh, crisp lily; walking with a deliberate step, she entered the grounds, accompanied by Chilin. A large silver tray was placed at the entrance where the guests might leave their business cards. Since Zhishuang and Chilin were still reckoned as social nobodies, they of course had no cards to toss on the pile.

"How very formal it is!" exclaimed Zhishuang, letting out a long stream of breath. Although her training at McTyeire had been well rounded, still now was the first time she had personally participated in anything like this, and she could not avoid some slight nervousness.

"That's all right. Anyway we've just come to do volunteer work. You just relax; tonight I'm your 'partner,'" said Chilin, self-consciously using the English word, and he patted her reassuringly on the shoulder.

Zhishuang glanced at the silver tray. She noticed among the business cards those of Hong Fung the movie actress, Liu Tongjun the owner of prospering Bounty Textile Mill, Mr. and Mrs. Joo Meisyan who had just established the International Red Cross Soldiers' Hospital, and many other prominent Shanghai citizens.

The fund-raising booths displayed all kinds of intricate needlework, dish after dish of lotus aspic and other such delicacies—all made by YW volunteers. One could see at a glance that those behind the sales tables doing the volunteer work were all pretty young ladies. Many faces seemed vaguely familiar, presumably students at McTyeire or at sister schools. Not a few of them were with their mothers—women obviously of the new breed, socially active women who seemed to know every one of the guests and many of whom were themselves public figures. And, in situations like this, it was very possible that they were also attentive to marriage prospects for their daughters. Zhishuang's mother, however, was of the old school of women who confined themselves to the home, and that being the case, Zhishuang could choose her own path in life all by herself, and therefore would have to build her own self-confidence.

Chilin introduced Zhishuang to a woman director at the Y.

Zhishuang strove to follow her along with a dignified, self-assured stride. After a few steps she looked back at Chilin; he was still there, his eyes watching her attentively.

"You needn't worry about me," she signaled to him with her eyes.

"Wishing you a pleasant evening," he replied silently with his eyes.

Zhishuang was led to a booth offering artificial-flower breastpins. After a few words of explanation, the woman went off. Before she had even taken stock of the girls at the sales tables around her, someone came over and tapped her on the shoulder.

"Zhishuang!" said the enthusiastic voice.

Hey, it was Ju Beibei! Having divested herself of that dark green school uniform, Ju Beibei was so much prettier and charming—her hair, which now fell gracefully to her shoulders, was held in place with a marvelous amethyst clasp; she was wearing a high-collared dress of purple velvet, snug-fitting white elbow-length gloves, and around her neck a chain of pearls each as big as a kernel of corn, which caused Zhishuang, herself by no means unsophisticated, to stare in amazement. Gracefully holding a wine goblet, Ju Beibei inquired, "Where have you been hiding since graduation? I haven't seen you even once." Ju Beibei pouted irritably as she cocked her head and said, "You're still the same—you haven't changed a bit."

Zhishuang felt like retorting with a "You, too!" but realized that would be too disingenuous. No longer in her schoolgirl clothes, the Ju Beibei of today assumed perfectly the manner of a frivolous socialite.

"You're so pretty," said Zhishuang. Ju Beibei had indeed grown prettier. "What college are you going to? I'd heard that you were preparing to take the entrance exam for a sociology major. I think you're well suited for that."

Quite unexpectedly, the hand holding the wine goblet began trembling involuntarily. "Right now," Beibei stammered, "I'm studying at...um, let's call it 'Domesticity University.' One of my classrooms is right here, you know—there are so many things to study. What purports to be sociology—" and she shrugged her shoulders very much in the foreign manner "—with the war on, everything's a mess—the refugee emergency, unemployment, school closures—there's a huge pile of all kinds of social problems. I'm astonished by it all. It wasn't worth it walking into that trap. To put it crudely, sociology as a discipline belongs in the same category as shark's fin soup—first of all you have to use chicken stock to bring out the seafood flavor, but if the stock is weak or if you just use plain water, the soup will be watery and it's pointless to put in the shark's fin. Sociology's the same way—it's an exercise in futility if you don't have the basic strength to solve social problems."

Zhishuang felt that Beibei, whom she had not seen for several months, had become rather coarse in her speech. She was staying at home and didn't have the look of someone who had work to do, but that expensive pearl necklace she was wearing really puzzled Zhishuang. As far as Zhishuang knew, the Ju family fortunes had long since declined, so how could she afford so costly a piece of jewelry?

"And what about Juanmin?" Ju Beibei remembered Zhishuang's "other half," not suspecting their friendship had now become a matter of ancient history.

"For the time being I'm staying with relatives in the International Settlement, so I haven't run into her for a long time," said Zhishuang circumspectly.

"I've heard Juanmin is running after that handsome Dr. Feng just as hard as she can. A real romantic, and still with that same old boldness of hers." Beibei sipped at her wine, and asked about other former classmates at McTyeire, a few of whom were at the same university as Zhishuang, but due to the exigencies of wartime, the university had been dismantled into separate divisions, each with its own classes, in addition to which the university was on the unit-credit system, which meant students didn't necessarily have to attend class every time. As a result most of Ju Beibei's questions had to go unanswered. To think that during the scant half-year since graduation she had already lost all trace of her former roommates and school friends was inevitably a bitter disappointment.

"Hey, know about Liu Tsaizhen? She's married! Got married to the son of Mr. Li, the real estate tycoon. I think her father-in-law is here tonight." Ju Beibei's eyes searched the throng. "I caught a glimpse of the old fogy just a moment ago," she mumbled, "wearing an out-of-date long gown."

Zhishuang entertained not the slightest interest in Liu Tsaizhen's father-in-law, but she did feel it most unfortunate that Tsaizhen had married so early. "No wonder she didn't appear for the graduation exam. There was only a month or so to go and if she had taken the exam and passed and gotten the diploma in hand before marrying, then whatever might happen she'd at least have that diploma."

"Well, the Lis are an old-fashioned family. They don't even approve of girls living away from home in school dorms, so what do they care about this diploma? You know the old saying about ugly women being lucky so long as they have a rich husband, so don't pay any attention to Liu Tsaizhen's very ordinary face when she's been so lucky with money. Her own family is wealthy—their Bounty Textile stock has been in high demand the past few days—and her husband's family has accumulated a lot of property. Really, she's the number one woman in our class. The Li home is on Rue Mercier. It's absolutely huge! The gardens running along the property walls alone are as imposing as Jessfield Park." Then, abruptly switching the subject, she said, "That woman over there coming this way, she's Pu Zhuanlin, the public relations director at the Y. Did you know that she'll soon become Juanmin's stepmother? She's an old maid, awfully picky and choosy, but she finally got chosen. She's coming this way..." As she spoke, Ju Beibei turned on a courteous, though not excessively deferential, smile, as seemed appropriate to the occasion. It had only been a few months since Zhishuang had seen her, but Ju Beibei had learned a lot.

As Pu Zhuanlin passed by the sales booths, she greeted one after another the young ladies who had come to help her, and the mothers accompanying them as well. Her make-up was applied with restraint and she held herself with graceful dignity, yet she was one of those women whose natural simplicity in fact derived from painstaking effort. A lined, black lace mandarin dress with mid-length sleeves under a blousy and gossamer-thin ivory cashmere cape, and a square diamond brooch centered at the neck opening of her dress all betokened the graceful affluence that suited perfectly one who was to be the wife of a prominent banker.

"Miss Ju, it's so very kind of you to trouble yourself on our behalf this evening." She smiled as she shook her hand, at the same time taking Zhishuang's hand as well. Pu Zhuanlin's hands were wonderfully warm and soft; from time to time she held them with fingers interlaced against her bosom in a gesture rather affecting a singer's stage mannerism.

The band started playing "Ave Maria" in an expression of people's hope for peace and brotherhood, and the evening had begun.

Pu Zhuanlin as mistress of ceremonies of course delivered the opening remarks. Amplified over a P.A. system, her voice seemed to have a somewhat husky, metallic quality which conveyed an authority not to be ignored.

Gazing at her, Zhishuang recalled Ju Beibei's aphorism, excessively earthy, but not without some truth: "Sociology is shark's fin soup—if you don't have a good chicken stock to carry the flavor, it's an exercise in futility." This Miss Pu was to be married to Zhu Jingchen. So now one could justly say that here was a woman who had found scope for her abilities. She appeared to be a woman of substantial ability, one who could fill the role of Mrs. Zhu with great credit. Ah, Juanmin had now truly met her match, yet it made little difference, for sooner or later she'd be getting married and moving out anyway. The question was, would Juanren be able to get along with so capable a stepmother? When, in a twinkling, another few months had passed by, would Juanren still remember that evening? If he should again telephone to Felicity Village only to be answered by an endless ringing of the phone, he would know she didn't live there any more, but would be inquire about her present whereabouts?

One look at Juanren was enough to prove that he was not a man of ability, but he was gentle of breeding, not at all like Dr. Feng that day who was so completely westernized. She'd heard Juanren had found work with a foreign firm, and at work he was still the respected son of Mr. Zhu the banker; and he was so handsome a man there would be many interludes like the one that evening when they bought cotton candy. Zhishuang's thoughts were all ajumble as she concentrated her gaze on Pu Zhuanlin, yet she had not heard a word of what she was saying.

Pu Zhuanlin kept up her flow of exhortatory remarks of the type "give of your wealth if you are wealthy, give of your strength if you are strong." People had heard this sort of thing a great deal, so they were not paying

overly much attention. Some were quietly chatting with their neighbors, while others unreconciled to respectful silence were craning their necks trying to spot acquaintances.

At this moment a gentleman wearing a dark purple silk crepe gown stepped into the entrance, a man of exceptional dignity. His appearance provided a momentary surprise to the gathering, and not a few of the guests nodded to him in greeting, and he responded, gesturing with clasped hands to them one by one, smiling broadly and sincerely.

"Zhu Jingchen of Cathay Republic Bank."

"He can sure hold his head high now, the way he managed to withstand that bank crisis. He's a real survivor."

"Investing in Bounty Textile Mill was exactly the right thing to give him a boost now—he saw perfectly that having so prosperous a business behind Cathay, he could walk with even greater self-assurance..."

Such was the hushed whispering among the guests.

Zhu Jingchen had never before shown any interest in such modish, westernized activities as this, and, to be perfectly honest about it, he had never expected Pu Zhuanlin would be so inordinately enthusiastic about such things, for they took both time and energy, and when it was all over and done with, they'd wish they'd taken in just a little more money—so what was the point of it all? Zhuanlin was mistress of ceremonies today, so he had no choice, really, but to come and lend moral support. Besides, there were a lot of big shots here tonight, and he could use the occasion to sound them out about business conditions.

"...And I believe that by your presence here this evening you, compared to others, are putting out more effort and are exhibiting more concern, which will greatly enrich our society. Because here today are gathered the ablest people from all walks of life..." As Zhuanlin brought her speech to a conclusion, the crowd responded with enthusiastic applause.

Following that, the charity sale was opened, while the choirs of the YWCA and YMCA began their musical program. Since the retreat of the national armies to Free China in the western hinterland, even in Shanghai's International Settlement the foreign authorities were cautioning anti-Japanese patriotic groups not to be too conspicuous, and quite a few groups had in fact already been disbanded. Because of this, most of the numbers comprising this benefit concert were simple hymns, meant to convey, however, condemnation of the war and the aggressors.

Chilin himself was on the evening program. Looking around from backstage while waiting for his turn to go on, he saw how very briskly the charity sales were going at Zhishuang's stall—so much so she could hardly handle all her customers—and he felt a great sense of satisfaction. He sensed that he and Zhishuang had finally become measurably closer to one another, and, moreover, that he was able to make her happy. And precisely because he was fond of Zhishuang, he could not tolerate her attitude of utter indifference to the war, so wrapped up was she in her own little world.

As the charity sales began, the guests started chatting among themselves, and their topic did not stray far from the war situation and its outcome. Because Jingchen had displayed heroic qualities during the recent bank crisis, he was looked upon as a skillful strategist, and was soon surrounded with people seeking his advice.

At a stall selling soda pop, however, came bursts of unrestrained laughter—Liu Tongjun was flirting with one of the volunteer girls.

"My conditions for buying soda pop," Liu Tongjun was saying, "are very numerous. First of all, young lady, I want you to open it for me..."

"Of course. The cost of opening one bottle is two hundred yuan." It was Ju Beibei in her purple dress, smiling profusely. "And if you pay two hundred, I'll even feed it to you."

People collected around the soda pop stall watching the merriment.

Liu Tongjun's Bounty Textile Mill was highly profitable. Since the August Thirteenth Incident when the Japanese invaded Shanghai, more than half of Shanghai's five thousand-some factories had been destroyed in the fighting, but Liu Tongjun, out-witting the opponent, had established his factory inland and it had not suffered the slightest damage. Now he was frequently shuttling between Hong Kong and Shanghai and his inland factory, busily coming and going, his face weather-beaten and his body grown thin, but obviously just as high-spirited as ever.

"Good, only two hundred yuan!" Money is courage, the saying goes, and Liu Tongjun had made a fortune, so in conduct he had become bolder than ever, and did not scruple in playing the spendthrift. Just see how he pulled his billfold out and pealed off two hundred yuan and slapped it down on the counter, then watched with merry eyes as Ju Beibei uncapped the pop bottle with her dainty hand and offered it to him.

"No, I want you to feed me," said Tongjun, closing his eyes.

"If you substitute milk, then I'll feed you," she fussed, her arms planted on her hips.

"Isn't that clown your Liu Tongjun? He's a bit much." Pu Zhuanlin had slipped over to Jingchen's side, and addressed him with a frown.

"Never mind. That volunteer girl you asked to help out is a real social butterfly herself, so you can't very well blame others for what they do, can you? What you want is for the people here to clean out their pockets, and there's no need to be concerned much about anything else." Indeed, the more there were of such "foolish fatheads," thought Jingchen to himself (he was tactful enough not to say it aloud), who tried to puff themselves up by throwing away their money, the more profit the fund-raiser would rake in.

The soda pop stand was getting yet more boisterous, as Liu Tongjun, seemingly glued to the spot, was acting the fool, putting the onlookers in a fine mood and bringing roars of laughter to them all. That was characteristic of Liu Tonjun—the more he got people laughing, the headier he himself became. But to Jingchen's thinking, the larger one's enterprises became, the more one should cherish a good image, for only then would other businessmen retain confidence in the future of those enterprises.

"Tongjun, my friend!" Jingchen called him over.

Liu Tongjun, clasping the pop bottle in his two hands, his face flushed bright red, stepped over to Jingchen's side.

"Tongjun," said Jingchen, only half joking; "don't forget who you are, and be careful lest someone lodge a complaint with your wife against you."

But Liu Tongjun was intent on his merry-making. He stuck his thumb up jauntily and said, "This Ju Beibei has real pizzazz. Anyone with eyes can see that the way she keeps getting them to slap their money down, for sure she'll be able to make it in the world. Mark my words: within a year she'll be famous throughout Shanghai."

"If you're really in the mood for fun, nothing can compare with keeping a concubine..." The others continued teasing Liu Tongjun, but Jingchen, realizing that that just wasn't the way to behave, tried to change the topic of conversation.

"Looking at the present situation, although the fighting has been going on only about three months, Shanghai already has been reduced to an isolated island. I recall only a few days after the Marco Polo Bridge incident in July I called on Mr. Du, who reminded me that it was possible war might come to Shanghai. It never occurred to me he was as prescient as the ancient strategist Zhu Geliang, who could foretell great events without even emerging from his thatched cottage! If people had just listened to him a little when he was screaming at everybody not to be so fuzzy-headed, things would be better now."

One among them, a short, fat gentleman of very unremarkable looks, heaved a long sigh and said in Cantonese-accented Shanghai dialect, "My factory at Tsaohejing was completely taken over by the Japs for their headquarters. If I'd known they'd do that, I'd have burnt the factory to the ground myself rather than let those Japs in there to ruin it." The speaker was Syan Guansheng, owner of Guansheng Gardens, whose production facilities had been completely ruined, and although its managerial and sales offices, located, as they were, in the International Settlement, fortunately still existed, he was nonetheless able to rely only on the uncertain support of makeshift handicraft workshops, which made eking out an existence extremely difficult.

"Still, didn't you show great foresight, Mr. Liu?" said someone in the group with an admiration bordering on jealousy.

"What foresight? I succeed by farting harder than anyone else." Liu Tongjun scratched his head, and affected a guileless innocence—his magic weapon to lure the unsuspecting into his clutches without their ever knowing it.

The prospering Bounty Mill was without doubt the beacon light among factories and businesses at that time, and it may have been precisely because businessmen realized the wisdom of Liu's strategy too late to compete with him that Bounty's reputation had risen to such great heights. Jingchen rejoiced in his own initial good judgment when he decisively extended a large loan as the first stepping stone by which he could gradually insinuate his influence into the company, and the agreement he'd concluded with Bounty, which secured the loan on Bounty stock shares, doubtless was even more advantageous for Cathay's control of the company; if he could just make further loans to Bounty along the same lines, Jingchen need not worry he'd be unable to manipulate Bounty. And if Cathay Republic Bank could control Bounty, its own strength and reputation would take a giant step forward.

Jingchen pulled Liu Tongjun aside. "Tongjun," he began, "you've enjoyed success from the very beginning, and now you are following up your successes with real energy building up a large modernized enterprise...Mr. Syi of Cathay Bank, who's stationed at Bounty, reports that the Chinese textile industry now uses all motor-driven machinery, but that at Bounty you're still using steam-powered machinery to drive the overhead shafts; that not only wastes coal, but if suddenly the flywheel belts should go slack the machinery operating off them would of course all come to a halt, which would be a great drawback. You know the old adage, 'Fine craftsmanship requires the artisan first sharpen his tools.' So why not enlarge the present factory and install motorized equipment? Once again, we can cooperate in the project with Cathay offering loans on favorable terms. How about it? Are you game?"

"Bounty has only just recently become profitable, and if we immediately start to expand, each new project will require ever more capital." Tongjun tapped his fingers against the pop bottle. "Does this kind of investment really pay off?" he asked rhetorically. His point was well taken, and for the moment Jingchen could offer no reply.

Just then a gentleman wearing an expensive linen sport coat walked by; spotting him, Liu Tongjun shot out a hand and stopped him. "Ah, Mr. Gong. Let me introduce you. This is Mr. Zhu of Cathay Republic Bank. You are both indestructible gods of wealth."

Enemies, they say, are bound to meet on a narrow road, making confrontation unavoidable. Jingchen and Mr. Gong, that assistant vice-president at Bank of China, had had a few indirect run-ins before, but they had never actually met face to face. Now, quite unexpectedly, they were meeting right here. But Zhu Jingchen was a broad-minded man, and he understood that all people had the same unavoidable fatal flaw—they had to eat. That condition, in the normal course of affairs, was productive of all kinds of competition, even enmity, and how much more so since Zhu Jingchen had not been unseated by the other party. Because of this, he extended his hand with a pleasant smile. "Ah," he said, "how pleased I am finally to meet you! You've married, I hear. Is your new wife here with you?"

"Aa...she's not feeling well..." replied Mr. Gong somewhat awkwardly. He was tall in stature, practically like a clothesline pole, with high, sharp protruding cheekbones, and a harsh, shrewd-looking face: one wondered what Mary Luo Wei (or, as she should now be called, Mrs. Mary Luo Gong) saw in him.

So there they were, the three of them standing together each holding his drink, each with his own secret ledger of thoughts, and for the moment each at a loss for words. Finally Jingchen managed some small talk when he spotted a familiar face. "Say, isn't that Sye Baosheng, the owner of the Fairyland Dancehall?"

"He seems to be quite cheery about something," Tongjun chimed in.

"Speaking of Sye Baosheng makes me think of the movie actor, Wang Jiting, years ago. Sye Baosheng was then just a mere attendant of his. Now Wang Jiting's star has dimmed and I hear he's looking all over for Sye for help, but Sye's just turning his back on him," said Zhu Jingchen with a mournful sigh. Since seeing with his own eyes the decline of the Feng family, and having been through a business crisis himself, recently he was often overcome with grief, though he was unable to articulate the reason why.

"Really, other than possessing an actor's face, this Wang Jiting is worthless. If he had to rely on brawn he couldn't even be a fireman, and if he had to rely on his brains, he couldn't even make it as a letter-writer for illiterates. Who'd ever willingly let a guy like that free-load off him? And to think that back then Wang Jiting had that booming imperious voice, and all day long recklessly drove around in his carriage. And on top of it all, had that theater-actress wife of his, Yang Naimei. To flatter her, he wouldn't just throw flowers at curtain-call, he'd toss a three-carat diamond ring onto the stage. The gods would never allow such a person as this to escape ruination. That's why they say, within just three generations a person who has worked hard to make his money without ever taking advantage of anyone will probably produce an incompetent descendant who'll squander it all and make you penniless." Mr. Gong spoke in an unhurried manner, smiling wanly, every sentence a jab at Jingchen.

Liu Tongjun now saw an opening to ask for news from the higher-ups. "Tell me, Mr. Gong," he inquired, "why it is that the Ministry of Finance has come up with this new folderol recently—high efficiency spindles now have a lower tax rate, while low efficiency spindles have a high tax rate. The guy who thought up this stuff probably doesn't have to worry about where his next meal is coming from, but for us businessmen it's created so many obstacles we can hardly move. What's going on?"

"The Department of Taxation drew up the regulations as they are, and they must have had their own reasons." Because Mr. Gong worked in a government bank he always strutted about and put on airs, and anyone who really tried to toady up to him only abetted his overbearing arrogance. Just listen to his long-winded officiousness as he prattled on. "Confronting the present national crisis, industry, commerce, and banking must each regard the citizenry as most important, and it is only right that one not forget, on account of mere profit, the struggle for national salvation in the face of Japanese aggression. Now Joo Meisyan of the Ningbo Citizens Association has contributed an airplane, and Dian Yunchu, proprietor of Tianchu Factory, has also donated tens of thousands of gas masks to be sent to the front lines. You two gentlemen are well known in Shanghai business circles, and presumably have been giving money in not inconsiderable amounts. How many National Salvation War Bonds have you subscribed for?"

Liu Tongjun, quite taken aback by this question, rather awkwardly put him off with, "Of course I'd never let myself lose face by not subscribing!"

Jingchen just gazed in silence at the foam clinging to the side of his beer mug, and after a long pause said icily, "It's not simply a matter of giving of your wealth if you are wealthy or giving of your strength if you are strong. It's rather that there are instances where the government has to provide clear explanations to the people. For example, where exactly has the government been spending its national defense money? Why is it that equipment for the troops is so inferior? German mountain artillery is inappropriate for use in Shanghai, fighter planes purchased from America are used surplus, even the rifling in the cannon barrels on Italian bombers is worn smooth...And the airplanes that were presented to Chiang Kaishek on his 50th birthday? How is it not a single one has actually been seen? If you don't arrest those who are taking advantage of their position to practice fraud and corruption, but just single-mindedly ask people to buy war bonds and donate

money, people may indeed do so but they won't be happy about it."
Zhu Jingchen's remarks really expressed the sentiments of everybody.

Liu Tongjun rose unambiguously to the occasion. "Indeed. It's not
that we're stingy, it's just that when we donate money we want to see
results."

Zhu Jingchen switched the topic of conversation. "Mr. Gong," he
said, addressing him directly, "you have yourself presumably subscribed
for a number of war bonds, and Mrs. Gong has a considerable private
savings, all of which I have handled for her. That being the case, you
yourself must be quite well fixed for cash."

"What talk! What is my wife's is hers, what's mine, mine. I don't live
off any woman." Mr. Gong was much discomfited by Jingchen's
comment, even if words of defiance came to his lips. Spotting a curio
dealer acquaintance, Gong executed a fighting withdrawal, excusing
himself and leaving the little group without a moment's more delay.

"Now he's drawing a curio dealer to add to his winning hand,"
sneered Jingchen.

"Hey, you really don't know? That devil's famous as a dealer in what
you might called 'used goods,' as a lover of 'excavating artifacts.'"
Tongjun smiled slyly, then pressed close to Jingchen and with a lewd
expression whispered into his ear. "He especially enjoys looking for
widows older than he is and this time the wife he's hunted up must be
eight years his senior. Now isn't that excavating artifacts!" And so
saying, Tongjun screwed up his face and laughed aloud.

Jingchen might have joined in with a chuckle, had not Mary Luo's
smile of sorrowful resignation floated up before his eyes. "Well, tell me
then, who would be suitable for me?" He could feel only a lump in his
throat, blocking any chuckle.

". . .That stone was deposited with the bank as security on a loan,
and at the time I had it appraised by an expert, who said it contained
high quality jade. How was I to know that later on some stone masons
would come in who, quite on their own, said the stone could not
possibly contain jade and that I'd really gotten taken in. So I had the
stone moved into the restroom to use as a footing for the urinal..." Mr.
Gong was over there pointing to his foot as he related his story with
gusto. "But as it happened, the dampness of the restroom made the
stone's texture get crumbly. Then one day when one of the employees
had just stepped onto the footing he heard a loud 'cra-a-ck,' and the
stone just broke into two pieces, and lo and behold we finally
discovered that at its core there was a chunk of dark green—and that
was the piece of high quality jade. So you can see from this that by
sheer accident..."

Jingchen listened as Mr. Gong and the antique dealer merrily chattered

on, and he couldn't help drawing inspiration from the story. Were not business management and jade quarrying very much the same? First you must have real ability and you must also have patience, but those two together were worthless lacking a suitable opportunity. Jingchen turned toward Tongjun to continue the conversation just now interrupted. According to government banking regulations, banks were barred from direct involvement in mining enterprises, and because of the financial constraints imposed on people during this era of war, Jingchen was concerned that there might be no outlet for Cathay's funds. Consequently he was planning to separate Cathay's trust department from the bank and set it up independently as Cathay Trust Company, for the nominal purpose of enlarging its trust management operations, but in reality for the purpose of engaging in the mining industry. Of course that would be a form of deception. But if Cathay could control Bounty Textiles, which presently enjoyed such high prestige in the marketplace, Cathay could undoubtedly strengthen its own foundation, thereby further enlarging the scope of its economic activity. Thus, like a rolling snowball, Cathay could amalgamate with other enterprises to become an economic organization of cartel proportions, which in turn would enhance Jingchen's personal strength.

"Tongjun, my friend, let us hasten our step toward victory. Cathay Republic is a purely commercial enterprise—a 'Mr. Businessman,' you might call it—and your Bounty Textile Mill is also a privately financed business. If the bank were to establish a Cathay Trust Company, mightn't we cooperate further with one another? In view of the present situation," he continued, "manufacturers and businessmen all over are focusing their attention on Canton and Hong Kong. The British stand behind Hong Kong, and in my estimation the Japanese are unlikely to make a move there, so investment in Hong Kong could serve to preserve our funds and also be a stronghold from which to plan further development...I imagine you too would like to reserve some leeway for yourself, and at a timely moment move your funds to Hong Kong and set up your own sales outlet or a branch factory."

These remarks rather quickened Tongjun's pulse, but he replied somewhat uncertainly. "That young Mr. Tsai on our staff happens not to be in Shanghai just now, and furthermore transferring funds is no simple matter. Won't there be trouble if we profit illegally from a purchase of Hong Kong currency?"

"We're old friends—if there's any problem I'll always be right there to fix it up," replied Jingchen, tugging at Tongjun's sleeve in a friendly gesture.

"Well, let me think about it."

As Tongjun walked off still holding his soda pop bottle, Jingchen watched him with a wary eye to see with whom he might next strike up a conversation. Liu Tongjun, now rich and successful, had become popular with everybody—a hunk of succulent flesh everybody wanted to take a bite of. But the first person to have felt sure Liu Tongjun was fully capable of pulling off his lucrative schemes was Zhu Jingchen, and when the succulent morsel reached his mouth, he would certainly not allow someone else to snatch it away. He saw that Tongjun had walked over to an elderly gentleman in a long gown and was whispering to him on the sly. It suddenly occurred to Jingchen that this gentleman was the celebrated and monied Mr. Li, who was Liu Tongjun's new father-in-law; no wonder Tongjun did not jump just now at the prospect of a loan: he had his own private depository. Well, forming connections and bringing others over to your side through marriage was one way to manage things, all right, and if Juanmin hadn't made her views clear beforehand but had instead consented to marriage with the Liu son, it would have been a good thing for both the Zhu and Liu families. Jingchen was to blame for pampering his daughter and allowing her to be so headstrong.

At her charity booth Zhishuang was so busy she could hardly catch her breath. There were precious few like Liu Tongjun who would pay two hundred yuan for a soda pop; by far most of the guests just bought one artificial flower for one yuan (which did not harm their economic health) and pin it on their front to indicate "I've been here today and spent some money," after which they needn't dig into their purses again. Thus it was that Zhishuang was too busy for socializing. When, then, one gentleman came up to her and said abruptly, "I'll buy ten silk flowers," she could not help but consider it quite unexpected, and she raised her eyes to see who the generous guest might be, only to discover Juanren standing there, wearing a spandex sports jacket with black slacks and a black necktie; shoulders squared and looking very handsome, he seemed to have descended from heaven to appear before her very eyes.

"I spotted you some time ago, but I was too busy to say hello." He just stood there, very pleased, "I haven't seen you in a long time, not since that evening...already so many months ago...Well, you're busy, so I'll just sit over there and wait for you. Don't leave—I'll have my eye on you." And he bought a cup of coffee and sat down at a small round table nearby.

As the eldest son, indeed, the only son, of Zhu Jingchen, Juanren had no lack of opportunity to become acquainted with pretty girls, but unfortunately he was timid by nature and was afraid of his father, as a result of which in relations between the sexes he was always extremely reserved. Moreover, his sisters, though not jewel-like beauties, had indeed grown up in a rich household, had studied at high-class girls schools and had developed personal refinement and elegance, which together raised Juanren's aesthetic standards to very high levels, such that he would not so much as cast a glance at women evincing even a hint of the commonplace.

He ordinarily would not be much interested in this type of social function, but unfortunately his firm's foreign owner had received an invitation, and he was of course aware that the event's sponsor, Miss Pu Zhuanlin, was to become Mrs. Zhu. Moreover, foreigners are avid boot-lickers, and so the foreign owner had asked Juanren to accompany him. Luckily enough, once inside he was at long last able to see Syi Zhishuang again. Ever since making Zhishuang's acquaintance that evening, Juanren had found it hard to forget her charming grace, but he had been too lacking in self-confidence to follow up with any determination. After receiving a polite refusal from Zhishuang over the phone, he had thought several times of writing her and asking her out, but he was always afraid she'd just look down on him for it. In comparison with his father, successful in his undertakings and well known for his competence, Juanren judged himself as more and more resembling the character Pigsy of fiction who looked into the mirror only to see a very unflattering self-image. It had not occurred to Juanren there might be a chance encounter with Zhishuang here this evening, and seeing her pleased expression he clearly felt that she was likewise equally happy to see him, and this also encouraged his self-confidence. So he sipped his coffee with a happy heart as he patiently waited for her work to end.

"Mister Zhu," someone said in English. His boss, Mr. Heintz, was taking a turn around the grounds and had walked up to him. "Let's find your father; I'd like to meet him."

Juanren had no inclination to get up. Seeing that Zhishuang was still busy with her work and afraid she might think he'd broken their date, he removed his sports jacket and draped it over the back of his chair to indicate he was going only for a minute to introduce his boss to his father.

From a distance, Zhu Jingchen caught sight of his son wearing a pointed-collar, charcoal-gray woolen shirt—an attire altogether out of place for such a formal occasion as this. How could he be so inattentive to the details of good breeding? In the midst of brooding over this, his son led the foreigner over to him.

"Father, this is my employer, Mr. Heintz of Bayer Pharmaceuticals." Juanren provided a distracted introduction, impatient, as he was, to look back in Zhishuang's direction to see if she was still busy.

"Your son is doing very nicely at my company. He really acquits himself splendidly in his position as sales engineer. We're considering your son for promotion to head of the sales department." Mr. Heintz spoke to Jingchen in the most appreciative tones.

Jingchen smiled appropriately. "It's only right," he said, "that young people put in their best effort." Yet inside he realized perfectly well that the traditional doctrine, "excellence in scholarship leads to power and influence" had been supplanted by today's stratagem, "wealth through commerce leads to power and influence," and that this foreign businessman's praise for Juanren was for no other reason than Juanren's relation to Zhu Jingchen, the president of Cathay Republic Bank.

They exchanged a few pleasantries, and then Jingchen, turning his head, discovered his son had neglected his own boss to wander off he knew not where. Oh that Juanren—already a working man for some time now, and yet still so lacking in sense. What could Jingchen do but swallow his bad luck and hold in his anger while continuing to engage Mr. Heintz in small talk. Thus engaged, he happened to catch sight of Juanren devoting himself to conversation with some young lady, a comely young lady, to be sure, poised and elegant, whom he seemed to recognize. Then it finally dawned on him—she was Syi Zhensyu's daughter who with Juanmin had come to his office one day to sell advertising space in the McTyeire yearbook. Juanren, that devil: in everything else a pace behind other people, in making girlfriends he was actually a self-taught expert with a very discerning eye. Jingchen gazed over at his son with both resentment and fondness.

Then quite without warning, an acquaintance, beer mug in hand, came up and opened a conversation. "Mr. Zhu, you've a good son there—a fine-looking young man with a promising future. Does he have a girlfriend? I've come with a marriage offer. The second daughter of Mr. Li the construction magnate is just twenty-eight and a student at St. John's University. If the Zhu and Li families were united in marriage, the God of Wealth himself would be praying to you."

Jingchen smiled noncommittally, and cast another glance toward his son only to discover this time that he and Miss Syi had both disappeared without a trace.

"...And the government just keeps repeating the same old thing like a broken phonograph record—in times of peace prepare for war, in times of peace prepare for war..." Liu Tongjun's loud voice could be heard with perfect clarity all around. He was a wealthy man now and he talked without restraint. "To be blunt about it, when have we ever had a day of peace? We suffered during the January 28th Incident, and we at first thought the present hostilities would be like the previous one and within a month or two at most everything would settle back to normal, so how were we to know this time was the preparation for a prolonged war of resistance. My factory had already placed an order with Japan for a shipment of textile-weaving equipment, but now with the war on I haven't had any word about it at all. It's been just like throwing money away for nothing."

"Did you take out insurance?" someone asked.

"I paid the first installment," he continued in the same loud voice, "but was disinclined to pay the second. Things aren't the same now. Now the banks are all bad and don't want to take any losses during the present war-time disruptions. Especially when it comes to ocean transport—if you don't have insurance the banks simply refuse to issue bills of exchange. The big shots at the American-Asiatic Underwriters Corporation are getting real fat off their profits this time. The heavier the fighting the more they take in."

Keen-eared Jingchen knew perfectly well which of those remarks were meant to go in one ear and out the other, and which were supposed to hit home. He tossed his head back and drained the last of his beer, filed Liu Tongjun's remarks in his memory and, expressionless, left the place unobtrusively.

★   ★   ★

After finishing his number on the program, Chilin quickly changed out of his stage clothes and bounded over to Zhishuang's booth only to discover the sales had been concluded; looking in all directions and not finding a trace of her, Chilin became a little worried. Because her booth had finished early, had she perhaps left ahead of him? The hour was already late, and going back home alone...Chilin couldn't keep calm. Fortunately a modish young lady wearing a purple dress just then brushed past, and he recalled it was she who had been chatting with

Zhishuang for quite some time when the charity sales opened. He chased after her.

"Oh, Miss! Syi Zhishuang..."

"Oh, her?" Ju Beibei was implying more than her words said. "She went off with young Mr. Zhu some time ago."

"Someone was with her? Well, that's good." Chilin was relieved, and he realized his relief was not at all feigned but absolutely genuine: Zhishuang had someone to see her home.

Many years later, when Chilin himself had a son and daughter, he marveled that his own emotions toward Syi Zhishuang could have been so restrained, and only then did he understand that it had been love, but a love tempered by his intellect.

A half-hour previous when Zhishuang had sold the last of her velvet flowers, she slipped out with Juanren. Juanren could hardly wait until she had finished, so, seeing still over twenty flowers on her table, he just bought them all up himself in one fell swoop that Zhishuang might get away from her duties a little earlier. Anyway, Juanren was now making over one hundred yuan a month at Bayer Pharmaceuticals and his father did not interfere with his right to manage his own salary, and furthermore the household in no way relied on his one hundred yuan. Thus he could parade his wealth just as much as he wanted.

Out on the street colorful lights were gaily flashing, and there was not the slightest trace of war to be seen—it was the scene of a prosperous nation and a contented people. Juanren suggested they go to the Mandarin Club, where there were no dance hostesses, to sit and chat.

Suddenly, from inside the YWCA compound the melodious tones of a male quartet came drifting out, and Zhishuang remembered then that Chilin had told her that he was going to perform this evening in a quartet. Quite unconsciously she stopped and listened.

"What is it, Zhishuang?" asked Juanren uneasily.

"Let's not go to the Mandarin," she replied. She felt that if this evening she willfully went out on a date with Juanren it would be an extreme embarrassment to Chilin. But when she saw the expression of disappointment and anxiety on Juanren's face she could not help but soften. "All right, then, let's do go," she said considerately.

The lonely street running in front of Hardoon Park was at this time of night particularly secluded. The street was blanketed with fallen sycamore leaves, rustling as the evening breeze blew them along. It was a moonless night, nor were there any stars to be seen behind the canopy of graying clouds, so the neon lights of Tsangzhou Restaurant and the Mandarin Club all the more caught the eye. They were only a few hundred yards away, but in contrast the street here was enveloped in the deep stillness of night, with hardly a soul afoot. Once in a while, some women would pass by arm in arm, carrying their lunch boxes as they headed for their night shift. Homes lined the street in a uniform arrangement, their large projecting eaves running all the way around to the back entrances where red-lacquered toilet buckets were queued up quietly waiting to be dumped, while from behind latticed windows came the occasional strains of local opera or parlando recitations or popular songs—the perfect picture of middle class urban society. All of this brought to Zhishuang's mind her uncle's home where she was staying, which was so typical of the lives in these alley houses it was positively unbearable to her. Fortunately they were soon to move back into Felicity Village.

"This section is my old stamping ground," said Juanren with nostalgia in his voice. "Before, we used to live in that lane right there. Back then there was always an old fellow at the head of the lane selling gumdrops. He could make them into all kinds of shapes and figures. The thing that made me as happy as Pigsy carrying his wife around piggy-back was every day when I got out of school and came walking into our lane yelling 'Mom!' all the way. It was Mother's habit to be busy at that hour with kitchen work near the rear entranceway. Hearing her answer through the back window with a big 'Hello!' made me feel a great sense of relief, because if she had been out shopping or playing mahjong and no one answered me, I wouldn't be able to concentrate on my homework or even enjoy playing. When it got to be dusk around six o'clock, I'd go out to the head of the lane and wait for my father to come home from work, and if he happened to be in a good mood, he'd give me a copper or two and I'd go buy some of those gumdrops to eat..."

"Yuck, how unsanitary."

Zhishuang was touched by Juanren's chatter about things that were so deeply moving to him. But for some reason or other Zhishuang was reluctant to indicate her own feelings, and that is why she scowled and spoke as she did.

"Well, I never got a stomachache from it. Nothing like my littlest sister who gets diarrhea from just eating too many watermelon seeds. Back then, even though we had a pretty hard life, being small we didn't think it was bad, in fact the whole family being squeezed into one room was really fun. And Dad wasn't so busy then the way he is now, and not so strict with us either...After Mother died, when I came home from school there wasn't anybody to answer me from the back window." As Juanren continued to pour out his heart, she was very pleased to be able to listen to him.

"How old were you when your mother passed away?"

"About ten."

"About ten—old enough to know the meaning of death," said Zhishuang with sympathy.

"I knew, all right. So I've always felt that my own childhood was not all I could have wished. A youngster without a mother just can't be happy. I always felt that compared to other kids, I was lacking in something, and that there was no way to compensate for that something. But now I think...I don't think I lack anything compared with the others..." And as he spoke, Juanren's bright gaze fell on Zhishuang. Zhishuang made as if she hadn't understood, and lowered her eyes to inspect the tips of her shoes.

The two walked along silently a way and Juanren spoke again. "I'm really quite a weak person; I'll never accomplish anything great in my life. I have an uncle who, before he got addicted to opium, was a copy clerk in an office building on Second Avenue, and my impression was he was a very kindly man. Because he didn't have children of his own, he was particularly fond of Juanmin and me. We were always going to his office to play, and he'd buy some Shaosying-style chicken porridge for us to eat, and take us to see Chinese opera. Later on he started smoking opium, lost his job on account of it, couldn't go back home, and sunk to a life of begging. He'd constantly wait by our main gate...The police would chase him off, the gatekeeper Old Chang would chase him off, even Juanmin would chase him off...But me, I just could never bring myself to be so heartless, and as a result, of course, I alone never seemed to be able to free myself of his pestering. My sisters all laughed at me for letting myself walk right into his trap..."

Having gotten to this point, he seemed to lack the confidence to go on, and he cast an anxious glance toward Zhishuang. "I'm afraid I'm not very good at talking," he said in an exceptionally thin voice. "Am I bothering you? Perhaps Juanmin has already talked to you of my uncle."

"Oh, I really enjoy listening. Most men when they're with women just like to boast about themselves, and brag about how good they are or about how rich their families are or about the famous relatives they have...You're not at all like them." Zhishuang lifted her eyes and looked right at him as she spoke. In the obscurity of the evening dark, her gaze was so very kind, yet touched with a certain shyness, that Juanren's heart flooded with tenderness.

"Well, that depends on the woman you're talking with. When I'm at the office with the other women around, I can brag too." Juanren touched Zhishuang's fingers, trying to hold hands with her. But she quickly withdrew her hand, cold from the evening breeze.

"And here I've been saying what a fine person you are," she rebuked him, "but now I see it's just pretense. If you talk nonsense like that again I won't pay any attention to you any more. Anyway, I should be going home. Darn, how come there's not a single rickshaw around here!" she said with some embarrassment. Then she began calling into the broad emptiness of the street, "Rickshaw, rickshaw!"

"No need to make it sound like you're screaming for a fire engine," continued Juanren with a happy smile. "There's not a trace of a rickshaw in this neighborhood. Let's walk to the corner of Hart Road and take a look."

Still feigning peevishness, Zhishuang paced along, not uttering a word,

while Juanren, in high spirits, maintained the conversation without a break the whole way. When they came to a narrow side street with red brick walls on either side, he halted.

"Hey, Chunping Lane. Remember? Twenty years ago the stories in the cheap tabloids that shook all of Shanghai—daughter of wealthy family runs off with family's rickshaw coolie. When that story exploded, we were still living on Hardoon Road, and every day we'd pour into Chunping Lane to watch the excitement. Reporters from the tabloids were all over the place, while the people involved in the affair stayed inside behind lowered blinds and locked doors and never said even a word about it...Back then, this area figured as high-class society news...and what a drag! Those old-fashioned girls were to be pitied—usually they didn't have any social life, and they probably never had any opportunity to meet men, and so she just fell for her own rickshaw coolie..."

"I don't think you can say that," Zhishuang countered. "That girl enjoyed a respectable position and never needed to worry about basic necessities or to understand the world outside the home, and so she began to spin all kinds of romantic fantasies so that when she saw a person she didn't just see his money or see his social position, she really just saw him as a person. So what I think is, that rickshaw man was certainly a truly outstanding human being."

"Well, you've got a point there. It's just like Juanmin. You know about it? She's crazy about some doctor in a pediatric clinic—the son of the destitute Feng family. But the way I see it, provided she herself is perfectly happy with the situation, other people probably shouldn't poke their noses into her business. What do you say?"

Zhishuang felt it difficult to reply, so she just smiled.

"Your business...aren't there too many people who are trying to poke their noses into your business? Fortunately...I'm not a rickshaw coolie." Juanren's sparkling eyes looked full at her.

"Really, I refuse to pay my attentions to you any more." And she turned her head the other way, spotting, as she did so, an empty rickshaw passing slowly by. She scrambled into it, and waving her hand toward Juanren, said to him, "Thank you for buying all those velvet flowers."

"May I come again to have a date with you?" asked Juanren anxiously, grabbing the back of the rickshaw.

"Telephone me. Next week we're moving back to Felicity Village," she called over her shoulder in a bell-like voice.

Juanren looked after her fondly as she disappeared into the darkness. How wonderful that so charming and respectable a girl as she should have developed a liking for him. Clearly, he thought, he wasn't at all the luckless incompetent that people supposed.

Chapter 15

When you want time to pass quickly, they say, it seems to pass slowly, and when you want it to pass slowly, it zips right by. Well, however that may be, since Shanghai had become isolated by war, already an entire year had slipped by.

A Cathay board meeting was presently in session. Jingchen, amid a chorus of opposing voices, was proposing bank policy to cope with these extraordinary times.

"...And now the war against Japan has entered a period of prolonged stalemate. A number of areas are suffering saturation bombing from Japanese warplanes, and what will happen to property belonging to businesses and individuals is utterly unpredictable. Many enterprises will urgently need to get insurance protection. In my view, today's Cathay is entirely capable of setting up an insurance division. The fact that we were able to withstand the prewar bank crisis is sufficient proof that Cathay's reputation in the community is extremely good, and that's the best capital there is if we establish an insurance business."

A skeptic interrupted. "If we offer insurance against war damage, will we be able to compete with American-Asiatic Underwriters Corporation? Their insurance premiums are set at just fifteen percent."

"We could insure for even less than theirs—just ten percent. I have a detailed report here which was prepared by our accounting staff, and Cathay could accept business at that premium." Jingchen was never unprepared, and therefore as he presented his views, he confidently pulled out the report which summed it all up at a glance, and everyone was of course eager to take a look at it.

"But American-Asiatic has had so much more experience than us in the insurance field. If we compete with them for customer accounts only on the basis of a low ten percent premium, that doesn't necessarily mean we'll succeed." These cautionary remarks came from Liu Tongjun, recently appointed to the board of directors.

Jingchen's self-confidence was unshaken. "Due to the critical situation we face at present," he responded, "many in the banking industry are unwilling to undertake insurance operations, and in my opinion it is quite true that 'something scarce is something precious.' So let us avail ourselves of this opportunity to charge boldly ahead by lowering the profit margin and increasing sales. After all, people are always anxious to get things on the cheap, and provided our price is low and our product good, we need not fear for lack of customers. While Cathay's experience in the insurance business admittedly cannot compare with American-Asiatic, we can openly announce to the public what Cathay's financial assets are. We could engage the services of Shanghai celebrities and the chairman of the Native Bankers Association, who, along with representatives from Cathay's board of directors and accounting department, could come to Cathay on a given day each month to open the vault and announce publicly the extent of our cash on hand and our market reserves: that will win the confidence of people from all walks of life. In my opinion we should pay close attention to these matters. In the wake of Shanghai's wartime occupation many businessmen and manufacturers here are being very innovative and are moving their operations south to Canton and Hong Kong, so now is just the time they are anxious to take out insurance. Let us not lose this opportunity, for it will never recur!"

"My dear friend," said one of the directors with a touch of derision in his voice; "you certainly know how to spot an opportunity. The fiercer the fighting the bigger your plans to expand business."

"There's nothing strange about that." Zhu Jingchen rebutted his critic gracefully. "Each person must follow his own path. The national armies are withdrawing but we can't very well withdraw along with them. Isn't it being said about the anti-Japanese resistance that those who are wealthy should give of their wealth, and those who are strong, give of their strength? So if we don't make any money how are we going to give of it for the resistance?"

Just then Mrs. Zhong came in, an anxious expression on her face.

The situation was this. Cathay had a loan account with Yuesheng Iron Works, which for the last several years had been losing money and was long overdue in meeting its loan repayment obligation and was even unable to pay wages; then came the invasion of Shanghai, and

Yuesheng collapsed altogether. Accordingly, Cathay took possession of the factory, which had been pledged as loan collateral, in payment of the debt, and during the past few days had been engaged in trying to auction it off, but if the start-up price were too low, the bank would not be able to recover its losses. And as a matter of fact, with the present situation as it was, it was not an opportune time to be conducting this sort of transaction. Then, quite unexpectedly, the workers' union at the factory sent representatives to Cathay petitioning the bank to allow the ironworks to maintain operations, for otherwise the workers would be without any means of support.

"Damn!" Jingchen angrily banged his teacup down onto the table. "Must it be that Cathay take on this kind of responsibility? Absolutely incredible! You tell them that Mr. Zhu himself is on the verge of losing his means of support on account of this factory. After the equipment has all been auctioned off, I'm going to use the land to construct housing, because housing is the only thing that makes money now."

"The representatives are in the reception room waiting," Mrs. Zhong reminded him gently.

"Well let them wait, because in any case I can't accept their position. If I see them, I'd still tell them the same thing. I'm busy now. The next item on our agenda, gentlemen, is the matter of establishing a Cathay branch in Hong Kong. What with the move south by business and industry, I consider Cathay could unquestionably do a thriving business in loans and investments in Hong Kong ..."

"I think, however," Liu Tongjun reminded him, "that we'd better go and check it out. If the situation there becomes disruptive, it will be very disadvantageous for us. The Communists are now very active, and who knows but what there may not be some right here at Cathay, and if they should collaborate with Communists on the outside, wouldn't that be a dangerous oil leak for us."

Jingchen maintained his same air of unconcern. "What can a few ignorant workers accomplish? The ideogram for 'worker,' after all, looks like the ideogram for 'dirt.' If they want to make trouble for themselves, that's none of my business—they're not my workers. And as for whether Cathay may or may not have any Communists, I'm disinclined to investigate. Provided they don't make any trouble for Cathay, it matters little to me whether they sing to the Communists' tune or to the Naionalists' tune. But if they cause trouble for Cathay, then whatever their tune is, I won't let them through the door."

Another director objected. "About this Communist-Nationalist business, I think you need to be reminded not to be too blasé. The Bankers Recreation Club has a lot of activities—a benefit basketball tournament one time, a native products charity bazaar another time; they write articles and edit their own newspaper, and they do singing programs and put on plays with more of their propaganda messages. The more they waste their time with this sort of activity, it's difficult to avoid having the employees be distracted from their real work. So let me remind you, Mr. Zhu, not to let the Cathay employees join in too much in these sorts of outside activities. One can't guarantee there are no Communists right here. I'm just afraid that one day a disturbance will erupt providing an opportunity for some people to bad-mouth the bank."

Those comments made sense. And yet the director who made them was the owner of Good Faith Counting House, Li Dengpeng, whose nephew, a Cathay department manager, had used his uncle's reputation as a Cathay financial backer to engage in unauthorized speculation in the sale of negotiable securities for his personal profit, thus provoking talk that Cathay engaged in unethical business practices. During the depositor withdrawal crisis, Cathay had had great difficulty borrowing cash from its sister banks, which allowed Bank of China to exploit the situation to its own advantage. Up to now, however, Jingchen had avoided a confrontation with the department manager in question for fear it might prove more costly than it was worth: "If in your dishes dwells a rat, you daren't assault him with a bat," as the saying goes. There had been many times when Jingchen had thought of taking drastic action at the bank to root out, without exception and irrespective of rank, nepotistic connections—between uncle and nephew, or brother and brother, or father and son: he would not permit them to work together at Cathay, so that he could maintain better control of the entire workforce. Unfortunately this Li Dengpeng had the biggest name, and relying on his financial power, he was virtually unmoveable. Moreover, he and Liu Tongjun had now formed an alliance by the marriage of their children, which made them an impregnable fortress. It smelled of cliquish self-aggrandizement, and how could he, Zhu Jingchen, alone change it all? In helpless resignation, Jingchen could only tell them resentfully, "If they participate in more of these social activities, they're really beyond reproach and the bank's reputation can't be harmed. But if they do exploit their official position to fatten themselves at public expense, then it's definitely a case of one rat-dropping spoiling the entire pot of soup!"

"If it can be determined through reliable evidence that there really are such persons, of course they should be dealt with very severely. We can undertake an investigation!" Li Dengpeng knew perfectly well the bank lacked the gumption for that; in fact he was just trying to rile Jingchen.

Seeing the exchange between the two men getting a little off track, Liu Tongjun quickly came forward to smooth things over. "This business of starting up an insurance operation—we'll have to advertise it extensively. Nowadays whenever you say 'insurance,' small businessmen automatically think of American-Asiatic, so... "

He was in mid-sentence when Mrs. Zhong again came in. "That group of factory workers is now actually staging a sit-in in the bank lobby, and they're surrounded by people listening to their complaints. It's really a very awkward situation."

"Let's call the police," someone said as he headed for the telephone.

"Hold it!" called Jingchen, and he quickly followed Mrs. Zhong down to the first floor.

There in the main lobby, sure enough a large group of people was milling about, and others were moseying in off the street to watch the excitement. One of the workers was saying in a thick upcountry accent, "Each of us is just getting a half-month's wage and is being told we don't need to come to work any more; the owner said he's broke. Well, a broke owner who auctions off his factory still has money by the tens of thousands, and us workers are broke too, without enough to even put food on the table."

His plaintive story won the sympathy of the onlookers, and Jingchen was agitated about the nuisance this commotion was causing. Just as he was mulling over whether to call the police, he caught sight of a young man wearing the black Cathay uniform who was in discussion with one of the factory workers, and on second look he saw it was Fan Yangzhi.

"Mr. Fan." He quickly motioned Yangzhi toward him. "Telephone to the police station. This is a bank and it's unsafe for this crowd of people to be congregated here."

"What's the point," Yangzhi replied, smiling. "They're in such pitiable circumstances, I was just now offering them encouragement." And having said that, he went back to the throng and said, "Friends, workers! Just as you can't eat porridge if it's too hot, so too, you can't accomplish anything if you get too heated up. If you want to blame someone, then blame those damn Japs for starting the war. Now with the ironworks owner bankrupt, the bank would like to help but is unable to; it's a situation where there really isn't any remedy. But I've learned that after the factory equipment is auctioned off, housing will be constructed on the site, and construction always means odd jobs. So for those of you who are young and strong, you might want to go there and keep your eyes open. If you can get some odd work to do, somehow you'll manage to get through this period..."

These remarks calmed them down, and indeed Fan Yangzhi had gone about it in a most conscientious manner. Now that they had quieted down, Jingchen saw his chance. He stepped over to them, and, continuing Fan Yangzhi's approach, he said, "What Mr. Fan has just told you expresses my feelings, too. In fixing blame for this, we can only blame the government's weakness in allowing Jap aggression. In many ways Cathay would really like to help, but we just can't. A bank collapse can't be compared with a business bankruptcy. A bank collapse affects the entire business community, and because of that, bankers, just like chess players, are sometimes forced to sacrifice a minor piece in order to save a major piece. The ironworks is in debt to us but it doesn't have the financial resources to repay its loan. Consequently, we've had to take possession of the factory in order to maintain the functioning of the bank. There's an old saying that goes, 'He who cannot accept minor setbacks will surely bring his major plans to ruin.' The present wartime economy is very unstable, and I hope you'll be kind enough to make allowances for that."

Seeing Jingchen speak with such understanding, the workers could say little more. Jingchen himself had lived through days when there was no food to eat and no roof over his head, and deep down he was much moved at the workers' plight. He really would have liked to give them some emergency money, but, thinking it over, that was a subject better not broached, so he let it drop. At this moment some young bank employees appeared who encouraged the workers to leave, and as they did so, the curious bystanders also dispersed. Fortunately the police had not been summoned.

"Mr. Fan, thank you very much," said Jingchen, stopping him.

"Thank me for what? You should really thank that group of workers. They're the ones hit hardest and yet they were very reasonable." Yangzhi spoke with genuine feeling.

"What is it that brings you to the main office today?" Jingchen did not want to dismiss him peremptorily and leave, for that would too obviously be like "using a person when there's work to be done but ignoring him when there's none," so Jingchen wanted to chat with him a bit. "I had to deliver some report forms," he replied. "And while I was at it I notified some of the younger employees of the singing practice this evening. I hope, sir, that when we give our performance you'll be good enough to come."

"Mr. Fan," asked Jingchen a little hesitantly, "are you a member of the Bankers Recreation Club?"

"Yes, I am. It provides me the opportunity, in the company of friends, to study and broaden my knowledge, and I take part in a number of group activities."

"I understand perfectly that young people always seem to have a certain fondness for such activities, but you ought to be clear about the present situation. Being young, it's difficult to avoid being carried away by your emotions, and if by chance there should be some outbreak of trouble...well, you know the bank's rules and regulations, and should the time come when...well, I'd have no recourse but to... "

Jingchen spoke with genuine goodwill, yet Yangzhi remained silent. Jingchen pressed on with his remarks. "In this world where there are more workers than jobs, it's not easy even for me to earn my livelihood, so you had better be very cautious, and in the future of course there'll be hope for a promotion. Your father was an old-timer at Cathay, and by the looks of it you'll get along even better; you're still a young man, and provided you're earnest in your work... the prospects are unlimited!"

"Thank you very much for your concern," said Yangzhi in acknowledgment, and his squarish face broke into a broad smile, revealing intelligence and ability. Suddenly a bit of old lore popped into Jingchen's mind: "Cheekbones protruding beyond the skull attest a person contrary in heart." Standing face to face, as they were, Jingchen surveyed him closely.

"I still have a few papers here to take care of, Mr. Zhu. Will you excuse me?" Fan Yangzhi put the question courteously in his soft-spoken way, raising a bushy eyebrow as he did so. Jingchen suddenly had the feeling that what he had just said was rather clumsy, for Fan Yangzhi did not at all appear to be a person easily convinced by mere chit-chat.

★   ★   ★

By the time Jingchen returned home, it was already dark enough to turn the lights on. Zhuanlin was alone in the gloomy downstairs sitting room working at her knitting as she waited for him. They had celebrated their marriage ceremony in the spring of the present year, and Jingchen, who by nature disdained ostentation, used the occasion of war to dispense with all unnecessary formality. On that account, however, Zhuanlin bore an unending grudge, yet Jingchen affected ignorance of her unhappiness. There's a saying that goes, "The more Granny spoils her songbird, the crankier it becomes." Jingchen certainly did not want to become that granny. He was busy enough with his work outside, and if his wife at home became cranky, it would just bring trouble upon himself. "How is it you don't have even one light on?" Jingchen came in and, very much in the western style, kissed his wife on the neck.

"Why not save a little on the electric bill? In a household like this with over ten people old and young alike, the monthly expenses are enormous." Saying one thing, Zhuanlin seemed to be hinting at another.

The fact was, recently Jingwen's several grown children had one after the other come to Shanghai, both to flee the disorder of war and to pursue their college education; in addition, of course, there was Jingwen's legal wife, Ying. And the lot of them was here in the Zhu household, eating and sleeping, which naturally increased household expenses considerably. As a great family, the Zhus deemed it unseemly to haggle over every penny, a principle which Zhuanlin well understood. To tell the truth, however, it was not the extra bit of money that gave her such a headache, but rather the feeling that the household was such a complex multitude, from old Mrs. Zhu and the five children of the first wife on down to the in-laws and nieces and nephews; every day when meals were served, two tables had to be heaped with food, and Zhuanlin, in the role of the new Mrs. Zhu placed amidst this throng, far from feeling she was the brightest object in the heavens felt instead she was drowning in the depths of an extensive household. Her husband did not usually come home for dinner during the week, and even when he did, he chatted with his mother and chatted with his own children and chatted with the nieces and nephews, never quite making it around to Zhuanlin, and when he finished eating, he went to his study to receive phone calls or listen to the radio or make notes about market conditions, and it was not until the middle of the night that he finally came into the bedroom. His time was already so precious, yet it had to be divided among so many people, and he seemed loathe to neglect any of them so none of them would feel offended, with the sole exception of Pu Zhuanlin herself.

Jingchen was intelligent enough to know what was on his wife's mind, of course, so he took the present occasion to sit down beside her. "I come from an impoverished background," he said kindly, "and how remarkable it is that I could become so successful. And if I am able to look after my brother's family, then look after them I shall. Jingwen is a pitiful soul—has talent but never found the opportunity to use it..."

"How odd. I didn't say a thing other than being a little more frugal. The household expenses have increased and the paper currency doesn't buy so much now as it used to." Zhuanlin had been appeased, but she still was a trifle angry. Jingchen chuckled at her little fit of pique. He understood perfectly when he needed to yield a bit to his wife, or let her grouse a little when she needed to.

"These past few days you've been so busy with setting up the Hong Kong branch, you've hardly put in an appearance at the dinnertable..." Zhuanlin carefully started to bring the conversation around to the main point. She rarely had the opportunity to speak her intimate thoughts with Jingchen, but now, she sensed, was just such an opportunity.

"Of course, opening a branch bank is no small matter, and it keeps me pretty busy," said Jingchen apologetically, kissing her behind the ear.

"Well, the post of branch manager..." said Zhuanlin.

"Syi Zhensyu would be best suited for the job, I think." With his finger-tips Jingchen caressed the silky hair behind her ear, speaking as if for her benefit, but actually conjecturing to himself. "He did a beautiful job when he went to Bounty Textiles this time to arrange payment for goods, and he's got an excellent command of English... Hey, how come all of a sudden you thought to ask me about this?" He straightened up and looked hard at his wife.

"My brother..." Zhuanlin shrugged her shoulders and said nothing further, letting her gaze and quivering lips speak the rest.

"Zhuanlin." Jingchen got up and paced about, his hands thrust into his pockets. "Let's you and I agree to a simple little compact, shall we?" he said with great sternness. "You are now Mrs. Zhu and to you I have turned over my entire household with its ten-plus persons—high and low, old and young, everybody—and you have the last word there. But the bank is my business and you are not to interfere in any matter, large or small. So that's settled now."

She was so stunned by her husband's uncompromising severity that she felt a certain involuntary fear.

Sensing he'd spoken with undue gravity, Jingchen sat down again beside Zhuanlin and explained things in kinder tones. "You don't appreciate how difficult it is for me to sit in the president's chair with a thousand pairs of eyes riveted on me. What's more, I've always greatly disapproved of father and son or uncle and nephew or brother and brother working in the same place. So how can I myself be the first to break the rule? Frankly speaking, to have occupied that chair at Cathay Republic for so many years without being unseated has been no mean feat. There are lots of people waiting for me to make a fool of myself or to stumble..."

"If it can't be done, that's okay. What need is there for such a long-winded speech!" Pu Zhuanlin gathered up her knitting and rose to her feet. "I've got to see to getting dinner on the table. The son of my family's old wet nurse brought us two chickens from the countryside today, so I told the cook to stew them over a slow fire until you got back for dinner."

"With so many people, a broth-stewed chicken will never be enough. It would have been better to have the cook stir-fry two platters of spicy diced chicken to stretch it a bit."

"You're impossible. For all I know you must have been a miser in a previous reincarnation." Both irked and affectionate, Zhuanlin threw him a disdainful look. "There aren't many people for dinner tonight. Juanren's not here, Juanmin's not here, and Juanying isn't here either; and Miss Yi came to pick up Jingwen's children and their mother. So on purpose I instructed the cook to set just one table for us."

Zhuanlin was about to go out to take charge of dinner preparations when Juanmin's maid—Auntie Lu, they called her—came in. She had served in the Zhu home longer than any of the other maids, and seemed to have become the head maid.

"Madam, Mr. Chian from Lufuchang's Silverware Shop has come. He's seated in the back parlor right now." And having said that, she just stood there silently with her hands at her sides, unwilling to utter a single word more.

Zhuanlin was dumbfounded. She couldn't figure out what Auntie Lu had in mind by stabbing her at this particular moment with that particular news. What was someone doing here from Lufuchang's? She'd never gone there to order jewelry, nor was it likely the daughters without first asking their father would have a silversmith come to the house. Since Zhuanlin had married into the Zhu family, Juanmin had never once briefed her about anything; she had just thrown the heavy key ring onto Zhuanlin's bed with a fierce expression, figuring that household management had now been transferred to her, and with that lifted not a finger to help, waiting instead for Zhuanlin to grope her way through everything all by herself.

The perplexed Zhuanlin raised her eyes inquiringly to Auntie Lu, but Auntie Lu with an expression of mute imbecility just stood there, leaving Zhuanlin to solve the riddle by herself. That cunning vixen! Even she would bully the newcomer, not to mention how the other servants might. As she was hesitating, Fagun the butler came in.

"Madam." Fagun was a sharp one. Ever since Zhuanlin had come into the family, Fagun had never dared be remiss in addressing Zhuanlin as "madam." "The east family room is all straightened up now, and I'm ready to hang up the ancestral portraits. Now I need some tinfoil-paper. I'll have the maids fold it into sacrificial money."

Then it dawned on Zhuanlin. The annual Mid-Autumn Festival was approaching and the silversmith was making the rounds trying to drum up business. Mid-Autumn and New Year were supposed to be the seasons for making gifts of jewelry to give to all the young women, and this Auntie Lu wanted to keep her guessing in order to puff herself up.

Zhuanlin took her keys and started out with Fagun to fetch the sacrificial utensils. Turning toward Auntie Lu, she remarked icily, "Tell the silversmith to make one silver ring for each person; the silver should be of acceptable fineness, but the workmanship need not be overly intricate."

"Madam," Auntie Lu said; "for last year's Mid-Autumn and New Year, Miss Juanmin already presented us with silver rings. This year we thought something different would be nice—a little gold bell charm shaped like a fish for each person. Miss Juanmin promised us last New Year..."

"Miss Juanmin is simply the eldest daughter, and it is now I who manage the household." Zhuanlin spoke sternly and Auntie Lu dared say no more. Fish-shaped knockers, commonly used in Buddhist services, were normally made of wood, and the workmanship that would go into a gold ornament with a bell-like sound would be extremely expensive. It would be better to have the cheaper silver rings.

Having finished her business with Fagun, Zhuanlin returned, and the more she thought about the silversmith incident the more incensed she became, and could not help pouring out her complaints to her husband. "Managing your household is no easy job. Whatever I try to do, they drag out Juanmin to thwart me..."

"It's difficult to get started in any new undertaking." Jingchen was unimpressed, much to her surprise. He sat there reading the newspaper, his legs crossed, one foot wagging. "When I first took over from Mr. Wei at the bank, it was the same thing. Whatever I tried to do, they'd drag out something Mr. Wei had said in order to thwart me. I paid no attention to that sort of person: I was calling the shots now so they'd better listen, and gradually I got them under control. Ha! That's what gives it zip. You've got to have some opposition around to flavor your work."

"Will they really pay attention to everything I tell them? If they did, the maids would be satisfied with one present a year. That's the way it was in my family—my parents were only too happy to save the money."

Jingchen turned over the newspaper. "Forget it," he said indifferently. "Why be so strict with them over a little thing like that? These maids have been with us for a good many years. Back when the children were small and their mother's health was always poor, it was fortunate the maids looked after the kids and took care of the whole house." Having little interest in this line of conversation, Zhuanlin made an excuse and left. As she hurried down the gloomy stairway, for no particular reason she went into the living room, and without even lighting a lamp, just sat down in the darkness and mechanically continued with her knitting.

Finally she had become Mrs. Zhu, but what of it? Every time she went back to her old home, everybody would ooh-and-aah about how the "empress" had returned to visit her parents. Once powerful and wealthy, the Pu family today retained only a veneer of ostentation and thus it intended to acquire Zhu Jingchen as a son-in-law, whose wealth could be exploited for an instant revival of the Pu family fortunes. How could they have known that Jingchen would come up with a "simple little compact" for her. How was she supposed to explain that to her brother? Since marrying into the Zhu family Zhuanlin had grown distant even from her friends at the YW. Jingchen had a strong aversion to meddlesome people, and those in positions like Zhuanlin's at the Y were the most meddlesome of all, wasting time and spending money, like that day she returned home from a directors meeting. She had hurried back, now already past dinner time, on an evening when, it just so happened, Jingchen had also returned to have dinner at home. By the time she had finished rushing around frantically instructing the servants and getting the meal on the table, Jingchen was already behind in his evening schedule. Of course he did not utter a word of censure, but his mood upon leaving the table after a hurried meal left her uneasy for several days.

It was all due to this "Mrs. Zhu" role she had to fill—she had to act the submissive new wife even to the point of deliberately putting her own family at a distance. In broaching this matter to Jingchen just now it was really because her brother had been pestering her about the favor she owed him for having helped bring about the marriage in the first place. And in the event, Jingchen just said something about "the children's mother," which had nothing whatsoever to do with it. It had been, after all, the first marriage for both the parents. Zhuanlin felt utterly abandoned, and every last member of the Zhu household, even the servants, were conspiring to humiliate her.

"Madam, Madam!" Outside in the corridor Fagun was calling in his humble way. Zhuanlin just sat in the darkness of the living room without replying.

"Wu, where's Madam? The Shengs have sent someone over with Mid-Autumn gifts and he's waiting for Madam to accept them," he said anxiously. "The Shengs are concerned that they be delivered to Madam personally. You didn't see her leave the house, did you?"

Zhuanlin rolled up her knitting, laid it down on the sofa, and smoothed her hair. She then turned on a table lamp and said in a cold and indifferent tone, "Coming. Have him wait in the downstairs parlor."

It was a manservant wearing a meticulously ironed gray gown. One by one he placed a ham, moon-cakes, and similar things on the table, then with special flourish brought forth a package of silver-patterned lavender Nanking satin, which he held right before Zhuanlin's eyes. "A Mid-Autumn gift presented to Mrs. Zhu with the compliments of Mrs. Sheng, who says that if you are not pleased with the pattern or color, it can be exchanged at Laojiefu's—the clerks there have already been informed."

Zhuanlin took careful note of this high quality satin and was much pleased inside, and instructed Fagun to tip the servant for his trouble. The servant thanked her with many a "Madam Zhu," which pleased her all the more.

Mrs. Sheng, availing herself of the Sheng family's stature as one of Shanghai's few great families, was accustomed to conducting herself towards others with perceptible haughtiness, but with Zhuanlin she had always chatted with easy familiarity, and now to present her with so valuable a gift was, frankly speaking, simply because of the status Zhuanlin enjoyed as "Madam Zhu." Well, however that might be, being referred to as "Madam Zhu" still afforded her prestige among the people she had to associate with.

With the material draped over her, Zhuanlin posed in front of the floor-length dressing mirror. The silver-on-lavender design discreetly brought out the face of an elegant and aristocratic middle-aged lady. To have been able to marry a man of such reputation as Jingchen as she was approaching mid-life—the time when a woman's beauty starts to fade—ought certainly to be a source of contentment. At the very least, the latter half of her life would bring her blessings to be enjoyed. "Madam Zhu" would not have the hollow ring to it she had imagined. And yet while thinking these thoughts, tears welled up in her eyes for reasons she knew not, and trickled down her cheeks.

Chapter 16

Juanren was just now grooming himself with meticulous care to play the role of fiancé calling at the fair maiden's house. When Saturdays and Sundays came around he was a regular guest at the Syi household. Thunder and lightning could not have kept him away. This was the equivalent, surely, of a public announcement to the effect that "Syi Zhishuang is mine." Of course in deportment he was modest and courteous in the extreme, and extremely generous as well with his money. Every time he came to the Syis, he never forgot to bring presents for Zhishuang, her parents, even her brother Chengzu, and, yes, for Lianzi, too, who had come to fill in as maid when her mother Zhou was killed.

Just about everybody in Felicity Village knew that the Syi daughter had a beau of very high station, not only young and wealthy, but sincere and honest as well. A mother-in-law, they say, grows ever fonder of her son-in-law, the more so when the son-in-law was a fine young man like Zhu Juanren. Thus Mrs. Syi was extremely pleased.

One day when Juanren had just arrived, Mrs. Syi went to the kitchen to fix him a snack, and Chengzu, with no school Saturday afternoons, immediately started pestering Juanren to play chess with him. Zhishuang was sitting in an easy chair contentedly working at her knitting—a charcoal gray cardigan she planned to give to Juanren.

It was past three in the afternoon when the winter sun had lost all its warmth, but a cozy fire of jujube shells crackled in the pot-belly stove of the Syi's parlor. Warming himself by the stove, Juanren took off his jacket and, with the table between them, said to Zhishuang, "Next Sunday Juanying is going to throw a party at home. It would be nice if you would come."

"Well, I don't know..." she replied a little shyly. During these past two years she'd grown further apart from Juanmin, and it would be very disconcerting all of a sudden to meet her face to face.

Mrs. Syi came and pulled Chengzu away, so Juanren came around and sat on the arm of Zhishuang's easy chair. He drew close, his face touching her hair. "Tell me," he whispered, "why don't you want to come?"

"I won't know anybody there...it'll be so awkward!" She flushed so red she practically buried her head in her knitting. She was well aware of the significance that would attach to her going to Juanren's home.

"How can you say you won't know anybody when I'll be there?" He looked at her adorable expression and pulled her yet a little closer, saying softly, "Let's get married soon. There's lots of girls who continue their studies after they get married, so what difference does that make?"

"No." She struggled free of his embrace. The sweet bashfulness of a moment ago suddenly changed and she said with great seriousness, "Trying to continue an education while being married would be too much of a distraction, and as soon as a child comes, then it's all a mess. Anyway, you haven't been working for very long, so you ought to be glad to have this interlude when you have no worries or responsibilities to concentrate on your job and get a few promotions. Then if you do set up your own household, wouldn't it have a much more solid foundation?"

"That's exactly it!" said Juanren seriously. "The foreign owner has a very high opinion of me and I intend to put as much effort into the job as I can. If we get married, I'll naturally feel all settled down, and I'll be able to put even more effort into my work. Otherwise, I'll just be thinking of you from morning till night, and you can imagine the effect that'll have on my efficiency at work..."

"So, you see? You admit it yourself. It's as much to say that once we get married, you'll take me for granted..." Zhishuang seized the chance and suddenly lashed out at him. "Obviously, it's best we not get married. When you are able to regard me with some concern..."

Juanren, ingenuous by nature, became fretful and fell silent, became so fretful, indeed, that the veins on his forehead stood out like earthworms. Zhishuang was overcome with emotion. She put down her knitting and lightly caressed Juanren's soft wavy hair (people with soft hair, it's rightly claimed, are people of good temperament), and said, "all right, that's enough, I was just teasing you. But in the future...in the future, what I meant was it would be best if we lived away from home in our own place. Aside from other considerations, if we live in your family's home, the most inconvenient thing would be the telephone. Since your name and your father's name sound the same in Shanghainese, it'd be necessary to announce every time that no, this isn't Mr. Zhu senior of Cathay Republic Bank, this is Mr. Zhu junior of Bayer Pharmaceuticals. What a pain. Furthermore, your family consists of a step-mother, a younger generation of four daughters—and Juanmin is a most intractable young lady, plus an older generation of old Mrs. Zhu who bears down on me as heavily as a mountain might. And on top of all that there's Ying and Miss Yi. Being a daughter-in-law would be real tough! So my idea is that first you save some money, and I'll ask someone to find a job for me, like private tutor, so I can bring in a little money, and in the future I could still go out and find regular employment, and we could live in our own place, like rent a house in the Hardoon Garden area. Wouldn't that be wonderful!"

Juanren inadvertently smiled a smile which seemed to say that Zhishuang's talk was completely unrealistic. Then he looked at his watch and said, "Let's go out for supper. The Mandarin Club has a music combo—Philippinos, and everybody says they're real good."

That was Juanren—very slow to get angry. He just wouldn't argue with you, and in the end would return to the way he always was. But Zhishuang did not overly attempt to impose her will on him, for she well understood how within the bounds of propriety she should manage her boyfriend, now lenient, now strict.

When Zhishuang had finished changing and come downstairs, she found Juanren and Chilin chatting in the parlor. Since the war had moved to western China, the refugee shelters in the International Settlement had gradually closed down, and the various civilian anti-Japanese resistance organizations had disbanded by direction of the Municipal Council. When Chilin was doing refugee work he'd gotten to know an Englishman who took very kindly to him and introduced him to a foreign firm, which hired him on. His financial condition thus considerably relieved, he'd moved out of the Tsao home and was living in his own place, but once in a while would return to Felicity Village to see his aunt and uncle, and of course to call on Zhishuang, where he was likely to bump into her boyfriend. "I never proposed anything to her, so why should I wear so dispirited an expression? It makes me look as though I really had proposed something," thought Chilin to himself. And even while thinking these thoughts, every time he looked at Zhishuang melancholy surged up in his heart. He'd lost the campaign to marry Zhishuang, though the problem was not in his person but in his stars. Yet he harbored not the slightest resentment toward Zhishuang; rather he was resentful that he had overreached himself.

"...The English are always very conservative, and their government has adopted a very cautious attitude toward Germany—'watching tigers fight from a safe distance,' as they say. Consequently, their only move is to cast the Czechs aside, otherwise, once the Germans open fire on them in earnest, the British Isles will never survive German aerial bombardment..."

Juanren was enthusiastically holding forth on the European situation, feeling very good about himself. He was wearing a pair of brand new German-made leather shoes, polished to a high gloss, one of which he proudly displayed, as it were, by propping it atop the other knee. He offered Chilin a cigarette, then passed an ashtray to him, conducting himself for all the world as Zhishuang's fiancé. In his speech and in his manner he positively exuded both the conceit and generosity of a victor.

Seeing Zhishuang come in, Chilin immediately rose. "I've come to say good-bye, Zhishuang," he said.

"Where are you going?"

"I'm going to America to study."

"Oh!" Zhishuang was taken aback. "Have all the arrangements been made?"

"Yes, everything, including the ship booking."

Zhishuang stood there dumbly, for the moment unable to say a thing.

"Chilin, it seems to me it's not worth going abroad to study. You've already got a good job here now, and the reputation of Jiaotong Polytechnic University is plenty solid enough, so why bother going overseas and having a hard time of it there?" Juanren was sitting in the easy chair, his ankle still propped on the other knee, talking like a know-it-all. It was the affectation of a young heir, of which he was unable to divest himself, manifesting itself at every turn in a cynical don't-give-damn-about-anything attitude. Zhishuang threw him a merciless scowl, whereupon he awkwardly removed his shoe from its perch and corrected his posture.

"How is it you're rushing off so soon!" exclaimed Zhishuang, as if she might indeed be losing something. She had a sort of secret premonition that this parting would be for an entire lifetime or that at the very least it would be no easy matter to meet again.

Chilin affected an easy smile, but Zhishuang could see that the lines around the corners of his mouth, which had not been there before, concealed bitterness and helplessness. Placing his elbows on his knees, as was his habit, he said with measured gravity, "I've been thinking about it for a long time. Right now things are going fairly comfortably for me; but I do feel that at my age and lacking a good family background, it's well to have the important things in life settled early on, isn't it? I'd still like to keep developing some more but in a place like Shanghai, only in the International Settlement, which at that is no bigger than the palm of your hand, can a person get ahead. And besides, it's a small haven so all the talented people collect here—'a small temple has many sages,' as the saying goes, and without good social background and without any financial support, I'd find it very difficult to advance myself. So I might as well go abroad. All the Chinese living in foreign countries started from zero, so maybe I can put my abilities to good use there."

"It's no easy thing for a Chinese to establish a foothold in a foreign country," said Juanren.

"The question as I see it," said Chilin, "is that a person has to possess his own strengths. Since I lack family and money, my strengths can only be sought in books. That's why I want to study for a degree."

"Next time I see you, I may not even recognize you. You'll be the perfect gentleman." Zhishuang tried to make a joke, but as soon as the words left her lips, they unexpectedly turned a little sentimental.

"Actually, you two might well go abroad to continue your studies," Chilin suggested; "all the more so because it would be much easier for you than me—no need for you to save up your own tuition. And you're younger than me, too."

"Hey!" With Chilin's words barely off his lips, Juanren cut in. "I don't have any more appetite for that stuff. Anyway, my Uncle Jingwen is one of those overseas students, and his prospects aren't worth a damn; used every penny he had to set up that Verity Chemical Works, which only lost money year after year, and now with war in the Shanghai area, the buildings have been burned to the ground. I have no idea how he's going to cope with the situation."

"You shouldn't talk like that," said Chilin. "Mr. Zhu Jingwen is very well known in chemical engineering circles, and I myself hold him in very high regard. It's really extremely difficult to achieve success in life; in all Shanghai how many really great people like your father can there be? It's enough that a person be true to himself and strive for self-improvement."

"Success or failure—it's really very difficult to say, and it depends entirely on how you yourself look at it." Juanren lit up a cigarette, threw his head back and blew a smoke ring, as if to say this present conversation was not worthy of his attention. For a moment the two could think of nothing at all to say.

Perhaps because Juanren and Chilin came from different types of families or because their experiences differed, the two could never get their conversation on the same track, yet neither now had any intention of taking the initiative of saying good-bye and leaving. Maybe Juanren, recognizing that he was Zhishuang's boyfriend, could with perfect justification remain sitting there. Yet Chilin, recognizing he had for years been a close neighbor and moreover would soon be leaving for a foreign land, really wanted the opportunity to be alone with Zhishuang for a few words. Not that he had anything confidential or secret to say to her; he just wanted to say his farewells to her alone, for that would seem to make it emotionally easier for him.

With the conversational material having become obviously impoverished, Zhishuang asked, "Shall we listen to a phonograph record? What would you like to hear?"

"'Londonderry Air,'" said Chilin.

As the melody, lovely and melancholy, gently suffused the room, Zhishuang suddenly felt at an utter loss: not until today when Chilin was about to leave for afar did she apprehend that, in truth, Chilin occupied a very important place in her heart, and she ought not to deny she also loved Chilin. Alas, this word also! However, Juanren was handsomer and more stylish than Chilin, and moreover came from a well-off family and had financial resources and a good occupation as well—hardly like Chilin who'd only just started his career and had no assurances about his future. Surely Chilin couldn't blame her for snobbishness, could he? With jumbled emotions she raised her eyes and looked at Chilin, just as Chilin happened to have his eyes fixed on her. He smiled wanly: "The record's too old; it's scratchy," he said.

She really knew not what she should say to him. Flustered, she threw a sidelong glance at Juanren for fear he might be displeased. He was in fact poring over the evening paper which had just arrived—and quite without pretense, for Juanren was by nature one of those sincere and honest people who do not shield their inner feelings. His happiness or unhappiness could be read clearly on his face.

"Well, then." As if he'd resolved an issue, Chilin slapped his hand down on the arm of his chair and stood up. "Good-bye."

"When do you set off? We'd like to invite you for a meal." Juanren issued a warm invitation, couched very offhandedly in the first person plural.

Zhishuang alone saw Chilin to the door. She remembered how, when Chilin had first come from Baoshan to start college, she was still spending her days on the back stoop playing house. Now, as she was sending him off, it was as if she were at the same time sending off a part of herself. She was no longer a willful girl playing house or fooling around. From now on she would have to deport herself sure and steady, befitting of the new bride in a grand household and of the wife educated in aristocratic schools.

"That's all right, no need to see me out. Good-bye." Chilin disappeared out the main gate, firmly closing it behind him.

Chilin had gone. Would he in future fall in love with another woman? The way he now loved this woman? Yes, she believed absolutely that Chilin loved her with all his heart, but would he be able to love that future woman with his whole heart the same way? How very fortunate she would be, that future woman. Zhishuang was overcome by a wave of jealousy, and at the same time felt she was being unreasonable: on the one hand she had refused him, yet she was unwilling that he might love another.

"Don't take it so hard. At this age one always has such cares. After a while, it'll be okay." Juanren wiped away her tears. She was surprised at them: What, she thought, these are my tears?

"I'm sorry," she mumbled awkwardly. "It's just that I've always had trouble saying good-bye to people who are going away...Please don't take it to heart!"

Juanren drew her to him. "What does it matter! Such a woman as you—there must be who knows how many people who secretly love you. I sure am lucky to have beaten them all out."

So that's what is was? She had become a war trophy? Those were words not very pleasant to listen to, but that really did seem to be the fact of the matter. During those years at McTyeire, what she despised more than anything else were those society women who hadn't an ounce of individuality, but who hoped single-mindedly to attach themselves to some wealthy man so they could enjoy a life of ease and comfort, and while she of course considered that she would never be like that herself, still the reason she abandoned Chilin was precisely because he lacked that solid financial base.

"Okay, we'd better go out to eat now. If we're late, there won't be anything left." Juanren urged her on, as he pulled her coat from the hanger and draped it over her shoulders. Zhishuang obediently went with him out the door. Then Juanren rushed ahead to open the main gate for her, and as they were going down the steps, he considerately took her lightly by the elbow, the perfect image of the attentive fiancé.

The journey Syi Zhishuang had taken into love had gone very smoothly and peacefully and the journey had taken so little time to make. Now, it seemed, she was just a passenger sitting in the waiting room, waiting for the time to come to board the train and proceed to her destination—the marriage ceremony. Zhishuang had read many novels, and her mental view of love was that it ought to be a bumpier road, a more torturous road. But thinking back on the span of her love with Juanren, except for that evening when with Juanren and Juanmin they had gone to Hardoon Garden and bought cotton candy, of which she retained an image full of wonderful meaning, it seemed there was nothing worthy of recollection. Now the content of their love seemed to be almost exclusively going out for dinner, seeing a motion picture, sitting in a coffee shop, looking in furniture stores, and, in addition, hugging and kissing. Zhishuang did not know whether it was the storybook love or the love in her own life that was off track.

Juanren's work was proceeding very nicely now. Good looking, sprightly mannered, and to boot, the scion of an influential family, Juanren was perfectly suited for the work of sales engineer. From large pharmacies and dealers right up to the hospitals, just about everybody knew he was the son of Zhu Jingchen, and there was none who did not accord him due respect. On that account, although he had been at Bayer Pharmaceuticals just this short time, he had already been promoted to the post of foreign products department head. Seeing his son show some promise and realizing that stepping into the world required he do some socializing, Jingchen halfheartedly let him take his Buick in and out; Jingchen was mindful that no one would dare slight Juanren if he "walked" the modern way with exhaust belching from his tailpipe. How true it is that there is no more sympathetic person in all the world than a parent.

"Little ball, little basket, hit the ground and buds will bloom—twenty-one..."

A bunch of girls were boisterously playing jump-rope in the alley, and, being girls, they were particularly sensitive to the male-female relationship, and thus fixed their unblinking eyes on Zhishuang and Juanren as they came past. Zhishuang recalled how she had been the same way herself at that age, thinking how perfectly mysterious it all was whenever she saw a sweetheart couple in her lane.

"Hey, the young gentleman's here, he's here!"

When Juanren took out his car keys, a group of boys came screaming over. Felicity Village was a middle-class residential area and its families were only of rather modest means, so that a private automobile in this neighborhood was quite a remarkable thing.

"Those little squirts!" he said to Zhishuang. Juanren put on a stern face, honked the horn a couple times, and the kids went screaming off.

Turning the corner smoothly, Juanren drove out of the lane arrogantly sounding his horn. A few of the neighborhood mothers on their way back home from shopping had to jump aside to make way for the car, as they nonetheless gazed back enviously at it and the driver, well known to them all. A comforting warmth billowed up inside Zhishuang.

Zhishuang still had not returned when Mr. Syi came home that evening.

"Well, it's Saturday, so I suppose she must be at a party," remarked Mrs. Syi. The merry expression in her eyes was irrepressible.

But Mr. Syi thought differently. Quietly reading his newspaper, he muttered, "By the looks of things, she'll never make it to graduation before she's married."

Since the opening of Cathay's Hong Kong branch, Mr. Syi had been serving as its manager and he came home once every two weeks. Though he had been promoted, that only earned the envy of others, and there were already those at the bank who were privately circulating talk that his rise was due solely to his daughter's having taken up with the bank president's son. And he knew that the person who first let this out was their neighbor across the way, Tsao Jiusin. Early on Tsao had also had his eye on the Hong Kong position, but unfortunately that sharp Shaosying banker could hardly recite his ABCs, and that plainly would not do; yet he still wanted to take out his anger on a colleague who'd been an honest-to-goodness overseas student in England, and that just didn't make sense. Humph, her daughter could have landed anybody—there were plenty of fellows in this city—so why of all people did she have to pick the bank president's son!

"Zhensyu," said Mrs. Syi, patting her husband lightly. Her cheerful voice was touched with worry. "We really have to start preparing early for Zhishuang's dowry. The Zhus are a prominent family, with the step-mother and the daughters and all. We don't want them to make a joke of us. Everybody says jade is very inexpensive in Hong Kong. When you have the time, you'd better get some."

Zhensyu did no more than turn a page of his newspaper and keep on reading.

"Did you hear me?" she asked, poking her man.

"Let's talk about it when the time comes. In any case, we'll do what is within our capacity. You earn people's respect not by how many possessions you may have to show on the outside, but how much strength of character you have on the inside. That's the only truly valuable commodity, and it can't be destroyed by bombs or stolen by thieves." Mr. Syi laid his newspaper aside, as he spoke with a certain melancholy. The truth was, he was not altogether satisfied with Juanren.

"Oh, by the way, Chilin will be going abroad. He was here just this afternoon to say his good-byes."

"Oh? Now, there's someone with ambition. He's bound to succeed," replied Mr. Syi admiringly. Then, his tone changed, he mused aloud, "Why in fact doesn't Juanren go abroad to further his education? Let him go while the sea lanes are still open and when business prospects here are so questionable. It's not as if he didn't have the money, and I'd let Zhishuang go with him. Otherwise, as soon as they get married and have a child to bring up there'll never be another chance for advanced study."

"What an odd notion. Juanren is doing just fine now—still so young and already a department head in a big foreign firm. With his housing allowance and clothing subsidy, he makes altogether two or three hundred yuan a month. It'd be crazy to set aside a great rice bowl like that in order to acquire some stupid foreign stuff." And Mrs. Syi threw her husband a resentful look.

"That's all you know! Juanren has no real ability, he just leans on his father's reputation and in my view sooner or later he'll get weeded out. Chengzu," he said, turning toward his son, "you pay attention to your studies because later on, even if I have to pawn everything I've got, I'm going to send you abroad to study."

*   *   *

In Feng Jingsyao's apartment, meanwhile, Juanmin was busy before the coal stove. Afraid the smoke from the hot oil would get into her hair, she'd knotted a silk kerchief around her head; the kerchief's intricate, gaily colored border design set off admirably the classic beauty and appealing charm of her almond eyes.

Adroitly manipulating the spatula, Juanmin angrily spoke on. "That Pu Zhuanlin," she said, "came into our family and immediately did everything she could to act like a real Madam Zhu. Greedy as a chicken that's gotten into the rice bin. She calls in the tailor time after time to get clothes made—lined clothes, unlined clothes; silk clothes, woolen clothes. You can tell from her tone of voice that she seems to regard everyone as her enemy. Look at how she redid our dining room with brand new German oak furniture. The way she manages things it'll be a wonder if she doesn't make a ruined household of us." But with the expression "ruined household," she suddenly sensed she'd touched Feng Jingsyao's sore spot; she stole a hurried look at him, and seeing no particular indication of unhappiness, she kept talking right on. "Fortunately, Daddy's got a good head on his shoulders and he hasn't just let her do any old thing she wants..."

She'd never forgotten how, not many days after the wedding, he'd accompanied his new wife into Juanmin's room and said with great tact, "Minny, it's been real difficult for you these past few years, with all of us depending on you to manage everything and trouble yourself about us. Now a new mother has come, so from here on you can lighten your load."

Pu Zhuanlin, the new bride, leaned against her husband, smiling gently. The beauty of her full, creamy-complexioned face which accentuated her bright eyes and pearly teeth, was positively dazzling. Juanmin uttered not a word; she spun around, opened a drawer and withdrew a ring heavy with keys. Zhuanlin reached out to accept it, but Juanmin (whether by accident or intention even she was not sure) dropped the key ring on the carpet with a plunk, and, pretending not to care, stepped over it and started out the door with the remark, "Yes, I suppose it can be considered getting out from under the load. People say that after managing a household for three years, even a dog won't like you, so I'll free myself of that evil reputation, too."

It happened just then that Fagun the butler burst in. "The Syues on Syaohedu Road have a new grandson and they've sent someone over with a basket of red eggs to celebrate the event. How much should I give the servant for his tip?" How maddening: with the country mired in war, prices everywhere were going up, and even tips for servants running errands were rising by the month.

"That's none of my business." And Juanmin went on her way, slamming the door behind her.

"Juanmin, that's outrageous!" Her father chased after her, but she willfully threw a coat over her shoulders, went downstairs and out of the house. The thin ivory-colored cashmere coat billowed out bell-like behind her. She knew her father would still be in the dark hallway watching her, and in that instant she fully appreciated the outline of her figure, which, she thought, must surely be like a scene in some movie: the young damsel rushing down the steps of the castle, her clothes fluttering behind her—how very vivid! And wasn't that just her character: Juanmin seemed to conduct herself as if there were people viewing her; while she was largely unconcerned about how she herself felt, she was completely concerned about how others might feel about her.

She carefully tended the eggs she was frying in the skillet. Jingsyao was thoroughly westernized—he ate his eggs sunny-side up and the yolk had to be a little runny. Juanmin had always done well in her cooking classes, and, having put much effort into it, she was confident that the image she projected in the kitchen conformed to the modern housewife, of which Jingsyao should be most appreciative. Unable to restrain her curiosity, she turned her head to look, only to see Jingsyao still absorbed in the newspaper.

In fact, however, he was using the newspaper only to hide from view the deep worry he felt about his personal affairs. Capitalizing on the invasion of Shanghai, businesses in the secure International Settlement were enjoying a remarkable prosperity, yet the pediatric clinic where Jingsyao worked was financially depressed because its owner, the prominent Dr. Peter Gao, had gone to China's wartime capital of Chungking, and Feng Jingsyao alone did not have what it takes to keep the clinic's practice going. In the Shanghai of today there were precious few parents who would specially call in a pediatrician for their infirm children, and high-class families only viewed with disdain an obscure practitioner like himself; most educated people could themselves prescribe the right medicine for their illnesses, and when working-class people got sick they didn't send for a doctor, let alone when their children got sick. Notwithstanding all that, he still didn't want to leave this foreignized city to live in Free China. It was so nice here, and war or no war, the International Settlement had the same old gay lights and flowing wine and the whole gamut of western cuisine from Italian to French. Supposing he went to Hong Kong? Well, he just didn't know anybody there, which would only increase his uncertainties. In trying to place blame for this predicament, he could only blame his own father and uncles who had let him down. They'd had so much property and yet they'd lost it all, and the little money that was divided among the branches of the family when it split up was not much help in repaying his father's debts. If in the beginning some property had been set aside for him, he would not have come to his present impasse.

"You're so despondent again, Jingsyao. Where's your old proud self-confidence?" Quite without warning Juanmin grabbed the paper from him, and pursed her lips into an angry little pout.

Just then the telephone rang; Juanmin rushed ahead and snatched up the receiver. "Hello? This is the Feng Jingsyao Clinic..." The caller was a woman. Juanmin followed up with a "And who may I say is calling?"—posed agreeably enough but with an undertone of hostility.

"Here, for you. She's an odd one; asked her who she was, but she just mumbled something without really answering..." Juanmin grumbled loudly enough to let the caller hear her.

Jingsyao said a few words into the telephone, then hung up. "It was Peter Gao's nurse," he said, partly an announcement, partly a self-defense. "She's just back from the Philippines and asked me where Peter Gao has gone to..."

"Don't tell me! I don't want to mind your business! Come and eat before it gets cold." Although she may have appeared put out, deep down inside she was really very pleased with herself. She'd already forgotten exactly when (perhaps it was that day after she'd brought Juansi home) she had started coming regularly to Feng Jingsyao's. It had been with an almost aggressive quality that she'd intruded into Jingsyao's life, planting herself there day after day, bearing down on him like a pagoda; and anyway being a college student wasn't like living at McTyeire, because now she only had to earn unit credits, and no one cared that her class attendance resembled a fisherman's life—work one day and rest the next while the nets dry; nor did she have to worry about her household's affairs. So what she had plenty of was time. By degrees, then, she finally created in people's minds the impression that she was Feng Jingsyao's girlfriend, and it was precisely this which so irritated him. He had to admit, of course, that Juanmin was a beautiful and aristocratic woman, although he was not the type to treat a woman with respectful solemnity. Jingsyao had had a good many girlfriends. Perhaps also, having since boyhood personally witnessed far too many domestic farces, he had always had a distinct aversion to marriage, and because the women he'd associated with were mostly movie star or dance-hall types, neither party had the slightest interest in matrimonial contracts. But with Zhu Juanmin, it couldn't be the same.

"Say, next Sunday Juanying is going to give a party at home," said Juanmin. "Why don't you come too?"

"Um..." Jingsyao hesitated.

"Come on! Everyone will be performing a number for our own entertainment program. You could sing something...like 'O Sole Mio.'" Juanmin was all excited about it.

Jingsyao thought for a moment. Realizing that the Zhus had a great many social contacts, he might just be able to latch onto someone and thereby find an escape from his predicament. It was just that whenever he thought of her father, he felt a touch of cowardice.

"Will your father be there?" he asked.

"What's he got to do with it? Anyway, Daddy doesn't have the time for that sort of thing. He hardly ever comes home even for dinner," she countered.

"My family is already finished for good, and my money is also all gone, nor does the world to which I once belonged still exist. The ideal thing for me in the future would be simply to work for some missionary hospital so I could just get by, but the I of the present has been cast aside from that former order of things, and therefore I'm afraid I'm powerless to cope with the difficulties confronting me...You understand what I'm trying to say?" Suddenly Feng Jingsyao had gotten it all out, with honesty and candor.

Juanmin nodded, although in fact she had not entirely understood, or, perhaps one should say, she did not yet entirely understand life's hardships. But she had listened attentively.

He'd spoken slowly and abstrusely and, after a pause, added, "I wouldn't want anyone to think that I have ulterior motives."

Although perhaps a little muddled, that last remark she did understand. "Oh, Jingsyao, you're wrong. You have a great future. A doctor's calling is a lofty one, and you've studied abroad; wherever you go you'll be needed. If it's difficult to get by here, we could go to Chungking. Or if not there, then Hong Kong, or to Southeast Asia...I could work for you, I could do all kinds of work for you, and I know I could make you very happy...It'd be like my Uncle Jingwen and Miss Yi—she worked together with him to start up the factory, did experiments with him, followed him back to Shanghai from Germany, and has always been by his side..." Her words came out in such a torrent that Jingsyao could not get a word in edgewise.

But Juanmin was very clear in her own heart about how she felt and what she wanted. Lovingly she ran her fingers through his thick hair, which gave off a subtle hint of Yardley cologne; his shirt collar was ironed straight and stiff, and the fingernails on his long, slender hands were clean and neatly manicured. Although he had not achieved his ambitions in life, he nonetheless still preserved that same outward appearance sufficient to reveal the style of his former upbringing and student days overseas, and a wave of sympathy and affection welled up inside her. She hugged him tightly. How she loved him. Although there were plenty of moneyed scions who would send her candy and flowers and write courtship letters, she had never deigned to notice them. Compared to Zhishuang and Pu Zhuanlin, hers was a nobler, more beautiful love!

She would use her love to revitalize him, to remold him into a self-confident and successful Feng Jingsyao.

Chapter 17

As the Japanese pushed into China's heartland, enemy aerial bombing put the very existence of Bounty Textile Mill in constant jeopardy, and even though the Belgian flag atop the Bounty buildings provided temporary protection for the equipment, still, the transport of raw materials and coal had been disrupted by war. In addition, right now the Shensyin Corporation and the government-funded Yongsying Company, both Shanghai firms, had set up textile mills in Free China, thus breaking Bounty's monopolistic position. And being, in essence, public-private joint enterprises, Shensyin and Yongsying enjoyed ample financial resources, such that, whether in raw cotton, materials and equipment, or shipping, these two companies naturally enjoyed certain conveniences, putting Bounty at an even greater competitive disadvantage. Bounty's manager, Tsai Liren, uneasy for the mill's future, had gone a roundabout way via Hong Kong to Shanghai for joint discussions with Liu Tongjun and Zhu Jingchen.

"The Japs are moving westward up the Yangtze, and are now pressing on Hankou and Wuchang, and so the area where Bounty is located has been bombed time after time. After the all-clear signal following the latest air raid, we rushed out of the factory gate to view the damage: there was rubble everywhere, and a piece of shrapnel had penetrated our warehouse igniting about five hundred tons of raw cotton—a fairly sizable financial loss for us. What do you think, gentlemen—should Bounty Mill prepare to move into western China?"

Tsai Liren, not yet thirty, still had that same old apprentice manner of his, modest and patient. But now his normally close-cropped hair was long past the time when it ought to have been trimmed and his face was prickly with stubble; he was sallow and thin, and his long gray gown was badly rumpled from the long journey: he looked thoroughly travel-worn. But those small eyes of his, bloodshot though they were, were just as alert, even cunning, as ever.

"River navigation is fraught with difficulties; we'll never get a turn to use so much steamer tonnage, and if we take our equipment upriver in wood vessels, the rapids will pose an even greater risk. It's not going to be easy," said Zhu Jingchen, pondering. "And besides, Sichuan Province doesn't produce cotton. If in fact we risk all the hazards and actually do get our equipment to Sichuan only to discover there is no raw material available, well..."

"Quite so. We're better off not moving. Let's wait for the war to calm down, and then resume production." Liu Tongjun also felt that in these extraordinary times of national crisis, caution was wiser than courage. "And furthermore, flying the Belgian flag is still useful to a certain degree."

"But the present war is of concern to the people as a whole, and will affect their livelihood, indeed their very lives. If we don't move west to Free China, by the looks of things we'll inevitably end up in effect supplying the enemy, and in that event we'll destroy ourselves completely, and..."

Before Jingchen had finished his sentence, Liu Tongjun interrupted: "I'll have nothing to do with that. It would be just like killing my children with my own hand...I won't be a party to it..."

Jingchen turned toward Tsai Liren. "Well then, Mr. Tsai, what is your view?"

In a deep and somewhat husky voice, Tsai Liren ventured to advise Bounty's two principal shareholders not to entertain any illusions about the mill. "I too strongly advocate avoiding support for the enemy, so under the circumstances it is imperative to move. After relocating in Sichuan, we'll be safeguarded by the natural barrier of Wu Gorge, which pretty much prevents a Japanese advance up the Yangstze toward Sichuan. And as for raw material we could substitute Shensi cotton. The problem is getting to Sichuan, which will indeed be fraught with difficulties. I've heard that Wuhan will not be defended, and further upriver at Yichang port, already mountains of goods have accumulated, waiting indefinitely before they get shipped further. Moreover it's not as if our objective were to move a factory as part of the war mobilization effort, so it's impossible the Ministry of Industries will provide us any special facilities or subsidies."

"Is any compromise arrangement feasible?" Jingchen asked Tsai Liren. "For example, move part of the equipment while leaving part behind?"

"There is in fact one compromise arrangement, but haven't you already mentioned it yourself, sir?" Tsai knitted his eyebrows and looked up, as if to say the matter had already received their very careful consideration. "In my view, we might just as well dismantle the Bounty factory and equipment and sell it off, sell it to a public-private joint company capable of getting it to Free China and developing it there, with the proceeds of the sale to be disbursed to the shareholders at face value. We can explain to them that the deepening war crisis, the unpredictability of the mill's future, and safeguarding shareholder profits force us to take this action. This incidentally allows the rights of Bounty shareholders to be concentrated in your hands—Mr. Liu's and Cathay's. This is the only good way to arrange the matter. And by the way, eliminating those small, scattered shareholders could prove of enormous advantage to you—you could manage things more smoothly without having to worry about anyone holding you back. The reason DuPont Company in the United States has consistently grown and thrived for the last one hundred years is precisely that the DuPont family has a policy of preserving their ownership undiluted. As for us, however, we have to devise a different avenue toward development."

"Considered from this angle," said Liu Tongjun, "losing the original capital is still secondary, but if our 'Silver Dollar' brand yarn disappeared from the market and ended up a dead item, what a pity that would be!" Although he had not yet gotten to the point of desperation, Tongjun spoke with deep worry.

To auction off Bounty assets could also prove critical for Cathay Republic, likewise a shareholding partner, for financial capital must always circulate in industry and commerce in order to be effective, and if Cathay lost in the Bounty enterprise, then the bank would be like a crab with one of its pincers wrenched off—greatly weakened.

"We'll have to be extremely cautious about this," Jingchen emphasized. "I'll first have to discuss it with the board of directors."

"You needn't rush," Tsai Liren said. "I'm sure I'm right. I've been working this over in my mind for quite some time. Passing through Hong Kong on my way here, I was interested to learn that Kuiyong Co. has a textile mill there, which apparently is not doing well financially, and in addition has to contend with the competition and jockeying caused by the huge influx of inland businesses to Hong Kong. In my view, we might just as well go into a joint operation with the Kuiyong mill, putting our Silver Dollar label on the fabric just as before, and sign a short-term contract with them by which we would make an initial payment as a service charge, and then pay a certain percentage to them based on gross sales. Our purpose would simply be to try to keep the Silver Dollar brand from disappearing from the marketplace, and when we've gotten through the present hostilities, we can reconsider our position." Tsai Liren slowly twirled the glass he was holding, as he spoke in a calm, measured tone. It would appear that he had given very careful consideration to this worthwhile proposition.

"That's an excellent idea," exclaimed Jingchen. "Blindly moving further into the interior isn't worth while. And if we knock ourselves out trying to move, and the government and army unexpectedly withdraw faster than we can transport our equipment, we'd never catch up however frantically we tried."

"But they're devouring me!" said Liu Tongjun, bringing his fist down violently on the arm of the sofa. "Those Japs are cutting us to ribbons!"

"'When the moon is full it begins to wane; when the river is high it begins to flood.' Too much of a good thing brings harm, Tongjun. So if we lose some money now, just forget it," said Jingchen consolingly. "Provided we retain authority over the enterprise in our hands, we'll always be able to recover our principal. China has a lot of poor people, and if a person has too much money, sooner or later he'll be sorry because the poor people will rebel and take everything. So let the Japs devour us a little—we may lose some property now, but we'll avoid a major calamity later."

"If we really do decide to go forward with this," said Tsai Liren, "I'll need to take a trip to Hong Kong before long and arrange things with the Kuiyong Co. mill. Nowadays in doing business, one must act quickly in everything, and, if quickly, there's money to be made. But now I've got to go and check the prices of airplane tickets..." And so saying, Tsai Liren was about to take his leave.

"Mr. Tsai," said Jingchen, stopping him. "Day after tomorrow there's going to be a little party at my home. Please come and join us in the fun. The young people want to relax and visit with each other."

After Tsai Liren had left, Liu Tongjun asked skeptically, "Party? How is it, old brother, that you've now become so foreignized that you can actually think of throwing a party?"

"It was my daughter Juanying's idea. She used to be terribly quiet and withdrawn, but now that she has work outside, she's much more lively and cheerful."

"And your son, Juanren, is now in his twenties, isn't he? He's gotten to be a man of striking appearance. Does he have a girlfriend? Would he be willing to be my son-in-law? My second daughter is eighteen this year. How would it be if we made a match between our two families?" Liu Tongjun's suggestion was only half in jest.

"Aren't you 'searching far afield for what is close at hand'? Why not grab the ready-made man right before your eyes?" asked Jingchen.

"Who?"

"Who else? That factory manager of yours. If you got him for your son-in-law, your wealth would grow even greater."

"You mean young Tsai?" Liu Tongjun flicked the ash from his cigarette disapprovingly. "He's a fine person, all right; it's just that a person of his type simply isn't destined for us—incompatible family backgrounds."

"Tongjun, I don't want to be critical, but you're not being very far-sighted about this. Money is something which can be used up, but a man of talent is a treasure trove. Tsai's a fine person, whereas some other person might have used the wartime confusion to take advantage of your difficulties for his own selfish interests and make a pile of money, and how do you suppose that would make you look!"

"If you think Tsai is as good as all that," continued Liu Tongjun somewhat sarcastically, "why aren't you looking at him for one of your own daughters?"

"If my daughters were all as good as your daughters, I would indeed become a matchmaker and do my darnedest to get him as a son-in-law."

"Now you're at it too. Hey, let's not joke about this. Supposing you really do settle on Tsai, then if you, as father, say the word, how could your daughter possibly disobey?" Liu Tongjun, still under the impression Jingchen was teasing him, was surprised at the seriousness of what Jingchen next said.

"I've always been firmly of the opinion that I should not make things difficult for my children in the matter of marriage. A melon that has to be torn from the vine isn't sweet, you know. My brother's the perfect example of that, having ruined the lives of two women. And speaking of Jingwen, after the destruction of his plant and the death of over ten workers, he didn't dare remain in Shanghai, so he ran off to Hong Kong. It's already been quite a few days since I've had any news from him—I don't even know what predicament he might be in right now. Damn! The government is obviously impotent—letting the Japs take advantage of our weakness to penetrate into the interior, and then shifting the responsibility to the common citizenry. It's just too unfair. Pick up everything and move inland to Free China, they say, but it's a mass of confusion, and then later you find that it's always the government-financed enterprises that enjoy the benefits while private business suffers disaster..."

"'If you yourself have lots to eat, no need to rail when others cheat.'" And Liu Tongjun bowed deeply as he cut off Jingchen's remarks. Then, as if he wanted to shake off some vexation, he violently swung his arms back and forth a few times. Jingchen wanted him to stay for dinner, but Liu squinted at him and said mysteriously, "Do you still remember the other evening at the YW charity sale and the girl selling soda pop, Ju Beibei? Well, she did a fine job, all right, and she speaks a lilting Suzhou dialect that melts the bones in your body. This evening I promised to invite her to the Rathskeller for dinner. That's great—I'll be able to shake off some of my bad luck. Every year I'm busy from the first day of the first month to the last day of the last month and I rarely get to treat myself the way I deserve." Now that there seemed to be a way out of the factory crisis, Tongjun had recovered his spirits.

"What? You're getting ready to invite in a concubine? Will your wife put up with that?" Jingchen kidded him, not having expected Tongjun might be lucky with women.

"Huh? What would be the point in bringing in a concubine? Only a dumb ass would do a thing like that." As soon as Tongjun got on the subject of women, he became so enthused he couldn't stop talking. "Besides, that Miss Ju also comes from a good family and went to McTyeire School for Girls; but coming down to her situation today, presumably she's got some interesting stories to tell, among which there are some I probably should not inquire about in detail. But I'm not out to find a concubine. Hm, foreigners understand the heart of the matter—comfort. An overstuffed chair is more satisfying than a wooden bench, right? And an innerspring mattress is of course superior to a rope-strung bed. Similarly, the delights of a mistress greatly exceed those of a concubine! If you're pleased with a mistress you go out and have a good time, but if she's not very agreeable, well you just say 'bye-bye' and that's the end of it. So what's the benefit of having concubines? You support them from age eighteen to age eighty, every day they're planted before your eyes like a stack of lumber..." Alas, people say an ounce of gold is worth four ounces of happiness—if you have money you still need the luck to enjoy it. Liu Tongjun enjoyed just such good luck, for even though his textile mill had come to the present crisis, still, just as always, he could think of fooling around with women.

Jingchen saw Tongjun to the main gate. Returning to the house, he noticed in the downstairs parlor Juanying with her two younger sisters fixing up the room—for the party, no doubt.

"Daddy!" Juanying called to him affectionately. Previously, because her studies were not progressing particularly well, she couldn't avoid feeling rather inferior before others, but now she'd simply dropped out of school to work in a church organization; the salary wasn't much but the prestige was considerable and the employment benefits substantial. She had her own tiny office, and in winter it was even heated. A clerk's life is mechanical and lonely, but fortunately in temperament she was quiet and bookish: she not only had the patience for the job, she was in fact perfectly cut out for it. Juanying, now a self-made career woman, left early and returned late, and Jingchen had little opportunity to see her. Today she was wearing a green check mandarin dress of Austrian wool, her thick black braid was coiled as always into a bun, but from her simplicity emerged a certain charm, and the former plain-featured Juanying now had suddenly revealed her good looks.

"Juanying, I'm bringing along a guest to your party—the engineer and manager of Bounty Textiles. Take good care of him; he's a very nice gentleman." Of his two daughters—Juanmin and Juanying—who were now in their twenties, only Juanying was of an amiable disposition, and if perchance she and Tsai Liren seemed predisposed toward one another, then...

"But," (her father could not restrain a few admonitions) "throwing a party what with the war situation as it is, don't go too overboard. If the 'um-pa-pa' of the music gets too loud, people will start talking."

"Relax, Daddy. We're not having a dance party, it's just going to be people chatting and getting to know each other." Juanying's light-skinned oval face exuded animated radiance. Before, she'd been vacant and subdued, but now her lively eyes revealed a depth which connoted serenity. Could this child already have a boyfriend on the sly? Only when girls were in love did they suddenly become attractive. He felt himself getting uneasy again. So many young men today had bad intentions, and he was afraid Juanying, so honest and open, might be taken in by someone.

"Juanying, what kind of people are coming?"

"There's someone who works at the Maritime Customs College, and someone from your bank...Oh," and she mysteriously whispered into her father's ear, "and there's someone who just recently returned from southern Anhui Province where he headed up a people-to-people delegation; it's fascinating to hear him talk about his impressions there."

"Southern Anhui?" asked Jingchen suspiciously. "Isn't that the Communist area? Good heavens, how can you be bringing such people here? It'll produce calamity! You may absolutely not have any contact with the Reds."

"Daddy." She objected to his making such a fuss over it. "Does just going to southern Anhui make him a Communist? Well, fortunately you're a big banker and don't need to worry about that small gang. He only went out of curiosity to look around, and we're going to listen just to expand our knowledge a little. I'm in the Church and seek only to do the Lord's work, and other things I do no more than listen to. After all, we really should know a little bit about everything."

Jingchen looked at his daughter's pure and pious face, and could hardly believe she had the boldness—rare in any girl—to be involved with politics, and couldn't restrain teasing her a bit. "Well, you shouldn't be excessively single-minded in doing the Lord's work, either. Just look at Juanmin—what with her boyfriends sending flowers one minute and writing letters the next, she's terribly busy. Taking her as a model, you shouldn't devote all your time to that God of yours; you should reserve some attention for other men!"

"Daddy!" And Juanying, her face flushing deeply, stamped her feet in anger. Jingchen immediately felt a pang of conscience that he had for too long a time neglected this sweet-tempered daughter.

"Don't be embarrassed. Some day you'll all get married and leave home, and when you're all gone, your father will be an old man by then." And as he said it, he felt a wave of sentiment overcome him, for the whole day long he would just be busy extending loans and collecting loans, busy meeting people left and right: for whom would he then be struggling? For whom would he then be so busy?

He walked downstairs to the vestibule. Before a large wall mirror stood a half-round console table, and in a cut-glass fruit bowl were several business cards. They had been placed there the previous evening by guests who had come to call on Jingchen, but Jingchen had either missed them or had avoided them. There was also a pile of playing cards in the bowl. A good deal of social activity had been going on, but at this moment as Jingchen stood in the spacious vestibule with the rays of the setting sun stealing in through the latticed windows, a feeling of lonely melancholy welled up within him.

The unforeseen developments with Bounty signaled the difficulties that lay ahead in all things, compared to which the previous bank crisis at Cathay utterly paled into insignificance. If the entire nation was on the brink of calamity, how much more so his little bank! As if to confirm these thoughts, from among the business cards two stood out bearing Japanese names—Ono and Kagesa from Nippon Shokin Bank. They had repeatedly requested interviews with Jingchen, but had always been turned away by Fagun with a polite "I'm sorry, he's not at home." Unfortunately, however, the Japs were a persistent lot and they kept coming back to see him; forever trying to dodge them was simply not a long-term solution. As the European situation became increasingly tense due to Germany's aggression against Czechoslovakia, the Japs in Shanghai had grown more obstreperous by the day. Since Fu Youan had become mayor of Shanghai, the Japanese had been sending their military police directly into the International Settlement to make arrests so frequently it wasn't even newsworthy any more, while at the same time their puppet government continually pestered Shanghai's wealthy merchants and well known citizens with cajolery and intimidation to accept positions in various puppet organizations as chairman or consultant or the like. But this was something prominent Chinese simply did not want to get involved with. When, for example, Lu Bohong of the South City Water and Electric Company, or the "Rice King" Gu Syinyi, or others did indeed take positions in the puppet Municipal Council, they were assassinated by Chungking agents. Even without these assassinations, Zhu Jingchen would never get involved with this evil-smelling activity. Evidently the unending requests for a meeting with these two Japs only verified the saying, "those who come are not friendly; those who are friendly do not come." And once the Japs got provoked, they were capable of anything. He'd have to think of a way of "cutting the tofu without soiling either side of the knife"—and satisfying both these opposing sides would be no easy matter.

How about going to Hong Kong to hide out for a spell? The bank's board of directors had unanimously urged this suggestion on him, and while Zhu Jingchen was away, the board would choose three managers to take joint charge of bank operations and send weekly wires to the Hong Kong branch about home office conditions. But these were now extraordinary times, so how could he, Zhu Jingchen, possibly rest easy about his bank in Shanghai if he fled alone to Hong Kong? To the contrary, with conditions as perilous as they now were, he needed to attend the more closely to business right here and not be compromised by these evil influences. Alas, these were difficult days even for celestial beings!

Chapter 18

It was the first party Juanying had ever given and, rather to her surprise, it was hugely successful, and except for the thin-skinned Zhishuang, everyone came, including Feng Jingsyao and Tsai Liren. Fan Yangzhi brought along a number of his friends, among whom was a gentleman of thirty-some years with wire-frame hexagonal glasses, wearing a dark striped suit of expensive British material, who looked for all the world like a member of the English gentry. Fan Yangzhi made a point of introducing him—the man who had just returned from southern Anhui, Mr. Tang. The throng of young people now suddenly brought to life that long desolate parlor.

Feng Jingsyao opened the entertainment portion of the evening's gathering with an authentic version of "O Sole Mio." Considering he was a doctor, it wasn't bad at all. Of all the guests he attracted the most attention, wearing a serious suit of subdued color set off by a gold-color necktie with delicate black designs—the perfect outfit for an evening party. He had not for a long time participated in social activities, and was therefore particularly animated on this occasion: the dash and vivacity of that day he had lectured from the stage at McTyeire now reappeared. Following him was a succession of other entertainments, including card tricks and piano numbers.

Tsai Liren had never previously shown much interest in this sort of gathering, but considering the bank president had invited him, the bank president must have had his reasons. He was an intelligent person, and upon arrival and seeing the Zhu daughters, so elegant and detached from worldly cares, he seemed to come to an awareness of Mr. Zhu's motives—a match in the making, perhaps? Happy in his heart, he added to the fun by singing a scene from a Peking opera.

Tsai Liren had always been fond of getting himself up in Chinese garb, and for this evening, true to form, he was wearing a long serge gown with sharply pressed slacks underneath, so that among the throng of guests wearing trim western-style suits, he stood out in his elegant demeanor as both graceful and grave, such that even Feng Jingsyao could not help glancing at him more than once.

"From what quarter of the heavens does that 'traditional Chinese grandee' hail?" Jingsyao inquired softly of Juanmin, using the English phrase. He was unaccustomed to seeing men his own age wearing long gowns, and he spat out "Chinese grandee" with such contempt one might think he was himself a blond-haired, blue-eyed Westerner.

"Daddy introduced him as the manager and engineer of Bounty Textile Mill, who's done an excellent job. Daddy has a very high regard for him, and would love to have him as his own son."

"Or perhaps...son-in-law?" asked Feng Jingsyao with deliberate cynicism.

"Aha! Was he perhaps jealous?" Juanmin threw him a sidelong glance. "Well, it's hard to say," she said.

"Friends!" Juanying struck a coffee cup with a small silver spoon to get the company's attention. "Mr. Fan has brought along for us his friend Mr. Tang. He's just returned from a mysterious place. So let's listen to what he has to say, shall we?"

Mr. Tang began by introducing himself to the group. "I'm with the Red Cross. As is well known, it serves society in the spirit of humanitarianism and brotherhood, quite irrespective of whether it serves in government-controlled areas or enemy-controlled areas or even where the Communists' New Fourth Army is fighting north of here in Anhui Province. Wherever there are difficulties, we must shine the light of brotherhood there. Consequently, on this occasion and with this purpose in mind, we started out for the northern front to offer solicitude to the anti-Japanese resistance fighters. But all along the route we saw great hardship and distress. Our group of about a dozen people set out by steamer under cover of darkness, and even at that we had to pretend we didn't know each other in order to avoid provoking trouble for ourselves. Sure enough, no sooner had the ship left Wusong harbor than a Jap patrol launch overtook us from behind, forced the ship to stop, and some Jap soldiers and Chinese collaborators climbed aboard saying they were searching for guerrillas. They had us all line up on the deck and hold our hands out for inspection one by one, in order to see if anyone had thick calluses, which would mean they were actually soldiers. For our group, of course, there was no problem, but there were several people on the ship who were arrested on the spot and taken away. Later I learned that they had been among the eight hundred who had earlier held their ground defending the supply depot maintained by the Nationalists' Fourth Route Army, and after that they'd fled to the International Settlement and then boarded the ship intending to go inland to find work or be reunited with their families, when in fact they were all taken away...Presumably they are now no longer of this world..." Mr. Tang's voice cracked with emotion.

Suddenly the atmosphere in the room took on a dignified gravity, as people began discussing among themselves.

"The Fourth Route Army has been isolated and surrounded in the Jiaozhou Road area for some time now. So, far from resisting, the resistance fighters have actually gotten surrounded. Whose law will reign now?"

"Exactly. Now even the International Settlement's Municipal Council is afraid of Japanese intentions, and the Japanese are interfering with flag flying to commemorate the first anniversary of the army's defense of Shanghai...In my view the International Settlement is like a fortress built on sand—utterly unreassuring."

Feng Jingsyao, the quintessential devotee of things foreign, just stood there hands in pockets, complaining. "Do you think we'll ever beat off the Japs with only the likes of Chinese to rely on? From all indications right now, war between Britain and Germany is unavoidable, so even supposing they can set aside the Czech problem, that still won't resolve the crisis. And inevitably France, Russia, and the United States will gradually become involved, and the European war will certainly mesh with our war with Japan, and even if China then relies for help on the Big Four—I mean, the U.S., the U.S.S.R., Great Britain, and France— it's still not certain we could win."

"What a joke that in fighting her war China should place her hopes on foreigners; what a joke that..." said Fan Yangzhi expressing instant dissent. "Consider the realities. Wuhan right now is defenseless, and by the looks of things the situation in Canton is extremely critical, and if the army loses every time it fights it really makes people lose confidence."

There were others who echoed the same sentiment. Immediately a war of words ensued between two camps, while Tsai Liren stood to one side quietly smoking a cigarette. In administering any enterprise one certainly must have an accurate estimate of surrounding conditions. Because of that, throughout he just listened attentively, drawing his conclusions.

"Wait, everybody!" Juanying took a silver spoon and tapped a pot. "Quiet please. This is a question we can discuss a little later. Let's listen to Mr. Tang continue with his talk."

"You are looking at the question from too one-sided a perspective. Because China is so big, you really have no idea what a variety of regions there is. For example, on our recent trip to the Communist New Fourth theater, the morale and discipline really won our admiration. Yet their supplies and equipment were woefully inadequate, and although we'd previously brought them a shipment of medical supplies, there were still shortages. Doctors are particularly needed. And besides all that, material for clothing, rubber boots, and such are all in short supply..."

Just then Fan Yangzhi stepped over to Juanying and whispered into her ear, "Mr. Tang particularly wanted me to convey his thanks to you for arranging that shipment of medicines. You truly were doing God's work in saving the lives of so many resistance fighters. There's something else, too. I've heard that Feng Jingsyao and Juanmin are very close. Since he's a doctor, if later on I were to recommend some patients to him to treat, do you think there would be any problem?"

"But he's a pediatrician."

"In time of war we can't be fussy about the distinctions among internal medicine, pediatrics, gynecology, and so on. We'll pay his normal office call fee, it's just that...he needn't inquire in too much detail, especially when he sees that there are gunshot wounds." Having said that, Yangzhi looked long at her with implied meaning, but she was utterly stunned. "Right now they are bleeding for us," Yangzhi added; "can we remain aloof and indifferent?"

The door now swung noiselessly open and Jingchen, thinking he might sniff the air, slipped in quietly. And what he saw was Tsai Liren sitting on the sofa quite alone, and Feng Jingsyao sitting in a wingback chair with Juanmin brazenly sitting on its arm, while in front of the French windows Juanying and Fan Yangzhi were absorbed in a hushed conversation: Jingchen instantly felt ill at ease. Upon seeing him, Tsai Liren immediately moved over to let him sit down, saying quietly, "It's very interesting. The things this Mr. Tang is talking about one hardly ever sees in the papers. Evidently in the Communist area of southern Anhui there really is business to be done. Madam Sun Yat-sen is in Hong Kong doing everything she can to assist in the relief effort. Those of us in business don't care whether the cat is black or white just so long as we can make money. The Communist areas lack medicines and cloth—and that means there's a huge market there."

Just now as a photograph being passed around for general interest came into his hands, a young member of the company explained enthusiastically to Jingchen, "Here on the right is the deputy commander of the New Fourth Army, Syang Ying, and this foreigner is the American journalist Agnes Smedley..." Centered in the photograph was a banner bearing in large characters the slogan "Transforming the enemy rear into the front line;" the banner had been presented to the Shanghai group which had gone there in solidarity and sympathy.

Now Fan Yangzhi led Mr. Tang over and introduced him to Jingchen. "If you are interested, sir," Mr. Tang readily offered, "you too could go to southern Anhui and view things for yourself. Although in every respect their conditions are very inadequate, still they persist in their resistance to the Japanese. You could appeal for help in a number of ways, Mr. Zhu. The president of New China Bank, Sun Ruihuang, has already initiated a New Fourth solicitation campaign among his bank's board of directors, and I wonder if you mightn't also help. Right at present the Red Cross is encountering a lot of difficulties, particularly more and more refugees piling up in the International Settlement; with provisions and emergency shelters getting increasingly hard to come by, long-term sheltering simply isn't a realistic solution. We can only adopt a policy of 'immigration for reclamation,' whereby the refugees would be continuously evacuated and relocated to rear areas to reclaim wastelands, putting them into production and thereby supporting the front lines. But all this will require financial resources. Taigu Shipping Company's regulations limit passenger transport to 1500 persons per trip, and it charges each person one yuan. Add to that the money for food and resettlement which is allotted to each refugee, and it really amounts to a very large expense...I hope that Shanghai's prominent citizens will do all they can to aid us in this effort."

"Where exactly would the refugees be going?" Tsai Liren interrupted Mr. Tang with a point of detail.

"For right now steamers can operate easily only between Shanghai and Wenzhou," replied Mr. Tang with hidden meaning. Tsai Liren said nothing further.

"I can help," replied Zhu Jingchen unhesitatingly. "I'm on friendly terms with the foreign owner of Taigu Shipping Company, and I could discuss prices with him. About the other expenses, I'll certainly do what I can to raise money...Well then, I'm going upstairs. Please enjoy yourselves."

When Jingchen reached the top of the stairs, Tsai Liren came up behind him. "Mr. Zhu," he said, "that group which went to the lines in southern Anhui also started out by sea from Shanghai to Wenzhou..."

"That's no concern of ours. We're concerned only that Taigu Shipping send these refugees out of Shanghai, and where they go beyond Wenzhou is of no concern. We will help the Red Cross evacuate the refugees in order to gain public recognition. About other matters we do not inquire and do not care."

"It's just that..." Tsai Liren hesitated, then continued in a whisper, "...if these people were to keep coming to your residence, sir, it could be very troublesome for you. Your daughters—won't they be influenced by them?"

Jingchen nodded to him gratefully. "I've just finished observing them with an unbiased eye. Some of the young men are in fact very decent and proper and are enthusiastically involved in social work. You don't realize it, but my son and daughters, with the exception of Juanying who works for a church organization, are thereby broadening their horizons. And as for the others, they are mindless types who day in and day out understand only how to socialize or to have clothes made or to show their tempers...It can do no harm that my children listen to these people and gain an appreciation of the hardships of ordinary folk and the difficulties life presents us." Jingchen narrowed his eyes into a smile and looked at Tsai Liren with admiration in his eye. "They don't come close to having your ability!" The remark revealed a mood of depression. Jingchen was a man not easily moved, but at this moment for reasons he himself knew not, he was not altogether able to control himself.

"It's two different things," said Tsai Liren modestly. "At fourteen I began apprenticing at a yard goods store. It was difficult saving enough money to study textiles at Nantong College, so I was far from having the good fortune your children have enjoyed."

"But there are obviously certain advantages in coming from somewhat straitened family circumstances. To speak frankly, I don't feel at all easy about the children of this household. There are a lot of poor people in China, and sooner or later people with money will be unable to live tranquil lives. In view of the situation Mr. Tang has just described and according to news I pick up frequently, the Communist New Fourth Army observes strict discipline and its officers and men are equal; who can say but what one day the Communists may not indeed win the country just as they did in Russia. It may never come to pass during my generation, but who knows about yours? When the time comes, I imagine you'll be able to accommodate yourself to it. But as for my beloved children, I've no idea how they may be overtaken by it."

Tsai Liren chuckled. "Mr. Zhu," he said, "I think you are taking too long-range a view."

Jingchen likewise could not restrain a laugh. Making fun of himself, he slapped his forehead and said, "Evidently I've gotten old—I've fallen behind the times, fallen out of step with the modern morality!"

"And yet..." Tsai Liren paused for a long while before continuing. "The ancients said, 'The noble man preserves impartiality.' We who are in the business world, provided we conscientiously follow the middle course, can do business with anyone. Don't you agree, Mr. Zhu?" He stole a measured look at Jingchen's expression as he put the question to him.

Tsai Liren, who had, after all, been pursuing a business career for many years, in some ways had quicker reactions than even Jingchen. "I've heard that the New Fourth area lacks medical supplies," he continued. "Isn't your son in the medical imports division of Bayer Pharmaceuticals? There is a huge amount of business here. Taigu Shipping will be plying between Shanghai and Wenzhou evacuating refugees for land reclamation work. We could use their ships and take advantage of the Red Cross name to transport medical supplies there. For one thing, it would be doing a good work, and for another there's money to be made..."

Jingchen lowered his gaze and said nothing. For a respected bank president to engage in an activity tantamount to trafficking in contraband would be much too undignified, and it was something he had repeatedly forbidden his own bank to become involved in. And yet this was indeed a rare business opportunity. Provided he worked through that Tang fellow, this would seem to be a most welcome development. But would Fan Yangzhi be wise to what was going on? Was he in fact on close terms with Tang? Did Fan Yangzhi have any contact with the Communist areas to the north? Or had he, like Feng Jingsyao, come here tonight merely for the novelty of it? If the bank should get wind of this business, it would be most inconvenient.

It seemed unnecessary for Jingchen to say anything further. Tsai Liren was a perceptive man who had already observed the awkward position he'd put the bank president in. Jingchen felt that between the two of them there was a sufficient tacit understanding.

"Everything can be handled by me personally," said Tsai Liren. "You needn't be anxious about that, Mr. Zhu."

Jingchen narrowed his eyes and observed him closely for a moment, then drew a breath and put on a resigned expression. "I'm afraid this might not be proper for me. If it ever got out, people would really stab me in the back."

Tsai Liren offered his advice, though without in any way being overbearing. "My view, sir, is that in these extraordinary times of national emergency, you need not be overly concerned with adhering to rigid formalities; rather, you should try by every means possible first to safeguard your own resources so that if you want to go forward with this venture you can proceed aggressively, but if later you want to withdraw you'll be able to do so safely. With conditions as chaotic as they are at present, the unexpected can happen any time. You need but look at Bounty—in the beginning everyone took it for granted it would flourish and not get mired in even a moment's difficulties. But who can predict bad luck? When it comes, it comes. We'd best grasp the present opportunity. There remain only two safe areas in Shanghai today—the International Settlement and the French Concession—which provide the only air routes and sea routes out of east China. If you want to expand your business, you might well compare the situation to a turtle in a jar: all bottled up with no way to get out, he's done for any time it suits his captor. In my view if the situation keeps on developing the way it has been, it will get even more perilous for us, and it would be more difficult for a well known figure like yourself, Mr. Zhu, than for someone like me to find a niche where you could continue in business. It would be preferable to take advantage of the present opportunity to make all the money we can, so that if in the future we should find ourselves beset with difficulties on all sides and no way to solve them, we could simply give up our work, stay at home in quiet retirement, and seek fame by leading a life of unsullied purity!"

Jingchen smiled wanly. "Well, you certainly are a young man wise in the ways of the world."

"I've been compelled to it. These days anyone who does not collude with the enemy or its puppets is apt to be accused of being a Chungking agent, and there is no lack of people who have suffered for it. It's quite true, isn't it, what they say about 'It's difficult to be an upright man.' Very difficult indeed."

"All right, Liren. I entrust everything to you." And Jingchen clapped him on the shoulder. At first Jingchen had not intended to become too intimate with him, but in the end he just couldn't help himself. "Please feel free to drop in any time to sit and chat together. You young people have brains much more flexible than mine!"

Jingchen himself escorted Tsai Liren downstairs, and as they passed through the parlor he observed that the lights had been turned off and Juanying with some friends from her choral group were carrying candles and singing in full voice:

> The little place where you are is lit up bright,
> The little place where you dwell is full of light;

> Off the shore there lies a ship in wait,
> Reaching safe harbor will be its lucky fate;
> My strength is gone, my pace has slowed,
> And no one wants to take my load;
> If a single person hears on all the earth,
> Singing this song has thus proved its worth.

From the flickering candlelight which accompanied the outpouring of these noble sentiments there shone a world of purity and detachment untouched by crass reality.

As he was tiptoeing through the parlor, Tsai Liren took particular notice of Juanying. Under the candles' shimmering halo, she was absorbed in her singing, and her eyebrows—those long and graceful eyebrows—beneath her broad forehead lifted and fell with the music.

Tsai Liren was an extremely practical man, but on this occasion he could not help but let this sublime and holy picture impress itself upon his heart. In matters of music and singing he was totally untrained, but he could nonetheless discern that behind the moving melody a strong will was quietly revealed.

Outside a wind had come up, and the hem of Tsai Liren's long gown flapped in the gusts.

"Let me have my driver take you back," said Jingchen, adding, "I'll let you handle everything."

A feeling of pride and satisfaction welled up inside Tsai Liren. To have won the respect of so important a person as Zhu Jingchen was no easy matter.

The stars were twinkling in the night sky. The automobile glided over the gravel driveway with a soft crunching sound, and the gatekeeper, Old Chang, waited respectfully at the already opened iron gate.

Tsai Liren was by now able to enter freely the homes of Shanghai's prominent citizens on matters of business. From Liu Tongjun's mansion to those of the Bei and Chi families, Bounty's name and reputation allowed even him to be received as an honored guest, but none of those previous occasions at all resembled the present one, and he felt a great sense of relief and accomplishment.

Tsai Liren's father ran a yard goods store in the Changzhou countryside and could be considered a well off family in his hamlet. But there's an old saying that goes, "a small village grandee is a big city peewee," and all the more so when the big city was this foreignized metropolis of Shanghai, so when he came alone from Changzhou to Nantong to study business (old-fashioned people from the countryside believed only in studying business), the gay and colorful downtown area fairly astonished him, and he gradually came to the conviction that the lifestyle of the countryside was hopelessly behind the times. Consequently he brushed up his English and took the entrance examination for Nantong College of Textile Industry, and while Nantong College was far from being one of the prestige universities like St. John's or Dongwu, it was nonetheless a genuine seat of learning where one could learn valuable lessons. He elected a major in textiles because he was confident that the practical experience accumulated during his years of study would be a foundation for starting his career.

Now he felt he had acquired that experience and technical ability. He had helped Liu Tongjun make a very considerable amount of money, watching the figures in Liu Tongjun's ledgers grow bigger by the day. Yet he had no regrets, for he had acquired the greatest treasure of all—experience. He had devoted himself to Bounty with loyalty and hard work and had willingly endured the hardship of his position, definitely not because he entertained any deep affection for the Liu family, but because he wanted to measure his capacity to manage an enterprise and meet emergencies. And in truth, he had done well. He had escaped from that constricting environment of mediocrity and passivity.

But now he was again no longer satisfied with himself; he needed a status of his own, and financial resources too; and he wanted to be like those prominent figures with whom he had social contact, and himself possess power and prestige; he must draw even closer to them. However, that class would be extremely difficult to enter. People of that class might with kindness and courtesy entertain you in their parlor or at their dining table, but to become one of them required either an illustrious family history or some startling achievement. Tsai Liren now knew the avenue into that class. Zhu Jingchen regarded him in a new, more favorable light, to the extent of even dropping hints about marriage, which infused Tsai with a new self-confidence. He knew, to be sure, that he was not handsome, not dashing, not modish, not cosmopolitan, and not even rich. He could not compare with any of the gentlemen in the parlor, but a moment ago when he'd glimpsed Juanying bathed in candlelight, the idea occurred to him as naturally and surely as some new business trick might ordinarily pop into his head: he would marry her. The eldest sister, Juanmin, was prettier and more charming than Juanying, but there was a touch of meanness in Juanmin's expression which did not at all please him. Comparing back and forth this way, it really did seem that he was choosing between the two young women. But Tsai Liren did have this one quality—self-confidence. He believed that he could not but bring to successful conclusion any task he set before himself.

Of course he also understood that today's way of doing things was different—the matchmaker's seal was affixed to the marriage certificate now only as a matter of show, or at the conclusion of the ceremony the matchmaker would give what had now become a pat speech—so that in pursuit of the important objectives, one had to rely entirely on one's own efforts. And he had now decided to begin that pursuit, and he would begin by pursuing President Zhu.

Chapter 19

I t was the first Sunday following Christmas and the pine wreathes fastened to the doors and windows of the cathedral were wonderfully verdant and as lovely as before, but because of the dark shadow cast by war, the joy of the season had already vanished.

The great organ peeled forth the introit, brilliant and majestic:

> Holy, holy, holy Lord God Almighty,
> Early in the morning our song shall rise to Thee...

In these unsettled times such music had the capacity to console and purify the spirit.

Throughout the day the sun's rays were kept outside and declined admittance by the large stained-glass window, while within the cathedral's dim interior there shone only the pale light of flickering candles; under the high and spacious arched ceiling, the people seemed by contrast frail and impotent.

It was the first time Yangzhi had been here. It was a very prosperous church, for its congregation was made up mostly of Shanghai's westernized upper class, who had been nurtured in foreign culture. This was reflected in everything from the majestic and imposing architecture of the altar to the elegantly dressed worshippers themselves.

The deep and gentle tones of the organ's lower pipes sang forth like a mother full of love at cradle-side. Yangzhi hitherto had never believed in supernatural beings, but on this occasion, the melody, so holy and pure, so tranquil and beautiful, breached the dam of intentional indifference he had painstakingly built, allowing an ardency suddenly to well up in his heart; he thirsted to pour himself out to someone, to seek strength from someone...He felt that in this instant he himself began to float, floating out of his own corporeal shell, standing aside and observing himself.

Rays of sunlight from the stained-glass window above the altar penetrated the dim interior in kaleidoscopic patterns of wondrous color. Beneath a spray of purple lilies stood the gentle and graceful figure of Juanying dressed in pure white. Her eyes were deflected downward as she concentrated her entire self on the hymn she was singing. This good creature, modest yet dignified, was exerting herself in the betterment of society. In Yangzhi's eyes, such exertion was as infantile as the seriousness with which little girls played with dolls. But now, in the midst of this congregation of worshippers paying homage to their God, he apprehended that Juanying too was a soldier. For at bottom society was one large family which needed not only doctors, but teachers and sanitation workers and gatekeepers as well...Those who sacrifice themselves for the betterment and cleanliness of society—all were worthy of admiration.

He delighted in these half-illusory, half-lucid notions until the last lingering sounds of the introit subsided, when the pastor with dignified steps ascended to the pulpit and Yangzhi woke to full alertness.

Before the choir took their seats, Juanying was able to spot him, and when he greeted her with his eyes, the corners of her mouth revealed a barely perceptible knowing smile.

He'd asked her to bring him to a service. His supervisor at work, Syu Zhiyong, had hoped he might make some friends here, but Juanying had misunderstood Fan Yangzhi's request, thinking that she was the only cause of his coming. Since that evening when she had given lessons at the shelter and he'd accompanied her back home, Yangzhi clearly sensed that she bore very good feelings toward him.

If he had been the Fan Yangzhi of an earlier day who realized that the daughter of a wealthy and prominent household bore good feelings toward him, that surely would have swelled his manly pride even though he might not have had the slightest thought of marriage. Yes, on this matter he was always very clear-headed. He had no desire for her other than a hope to meet her regularly for conversation. But now, he knew not why, those eyes of hers, so full of trust and ardor, caused him great uneasiness.

The service concluded. Intentionally he let himself be slowed by the crowd of departing worshippers. Finally she slipped out through a side door. She'd removed her white choir gown and was wearing a three-quarter length camel-hair coat with dark brown walking shoes, and was holding an armful of music scores. She was very pretty in her gentle refined way, with very much the bearing of a woman of education.

"Hi!" she said in English, waving to him the way Americans do. "I'm so happy you came. I prayed for you." Her smile was just a little mischievous, but no less genuine for that.

"Well, I just thought I'd come and learn by looking." Under her gaze so full of hope and tranquillity, he spoke almost apologetically.

This church was under the jurisdiction of an affluent American missionary board, and following the service, according to practice, the pastor stood at the church entrance to bow and greet his parishioners.

Most of the pastors at this church were Americans, and Juanying was on very friendly terms with them all. She introduced Fan Yangzhi to today's pastor. "This is my friend Mr. Fan Yangzhi. He works at Cathay Republic Bank." This was just how Fan Yangzhi hoped she'd introduce him.

Outside the sun was shining radiantly, yet one still felt the assaults of a cold wind. Juanying tied a colorful kerchief around her hair.

"Where is the patient?" she asked quietly as they passed out of the church compound. She was going to take a patient introduced by Fan Yangzhi to Feng Jingsyao's clinic, which was the real purpose in their meeting today at the church.

A woman officer suffering from lymphocytosis had come from the communist rear area to Shanghai for treatment. Business at Feng Jingsyao's private clinic was slack and the patient would thus cause him little inconvenience, so today Fan Yangzhi wanted to ask Juanying to escort her there. Juanying, perceptive as she was, knew that Fan Yangzhi was involved in underground resistance activities which were not on the side of the Chungking government. However, she had never questioned him about it.

They stopped before a hotel entrance on Pushi Road in the French Concession. Fan Yangzhi went in, and emerged a moment later helping an ailing middle-aged woman into a rickshaw. With one hand on the rickshaw hand grip and the other holding Juanying's hand, he spoke to her softly as a husband might to his wife: "She doesn't speak Shanghai dialect, so I'm afraid things may be a little difficult for you. I'll telephone you later."

"You needn't worry." She took a blanket and covered the woman's head, as if Juanying were a family member accompanying her infirm relative to the doctor's, which would attract no suspicion. She then waved to Yangzhi as the rickshaw pulled away. From a distance Yangzhi could still see that colorful checked woolen kerchief fluttering in the breeze, so eye-catching among the bare-limbed trees which lined the street.

Today more than at any previous time Fan Yangzhi felt very deeply that although Juanying was kindhearted and devoted to public welfare activities, they were taking two very different paths through life, and while the chasm between their lifestyles might still be bridged with comparative ease, the differences in their beliefs were simply irreconcilable. He had previously regarded her only with a sort of admiration, and it was for that reason alone that he hoped to maintain this tranquil acquaintance. He sought nothing more. But now if he had to call on her incessantly, entrusting to her matters she was more suited to handle than others, he would gradually come to know her better, such that finally he would no longer be content with maintaining a mere tranquil friendship...But no, he could not develop a more intimate relation with her. Neither his underground resistance organization nor his own reason would permit such a thing.

At first he thought if he could just grit his teeth and leave, everything would be over and done with. But he needed to keep up regular contact with her, and he might sometimes even have to be very familiar with her...that simply would be toying with her feelings! But he believed that he himself from here on out would never be satisfied with any other woman.

"Read all about it! Read all about it! Romantic rumors about Wang Jingwei in Hanoi! Said to be in bed with the Japs! Read all about it!"

The shouts of a paperboy woke him up. He pulled himself together, bought a copy and hastily glanced through it. Then he folded it, stuffed it into his overcoat pocket, and hurried off.

Chapter 20

In a world this large there's nothing unusual in citing examples of families fated to be happy and those fated to be unhappy, but ill fortune can be a blessing in disguise, like the proverbial old herdsman who lost his mare only to have her wander back a year later with a new colt to boot. Before, when Cathay was suffering through the depositor withdrawal crisis and its credibility was severely damaged, not a few of its borrowers exploited the bank's weakened condition for their personal advantage: when loans came due, rather than repaying the principal, they foisted upon Cathay the properties put up as loan collateral, which had been steadily declining in value. Cathay thus got stuck with a large amount of precipitously depreciating real estate—and the bank could not utter a word in protest. Who could have guessed that later on when urban refugees began swarming into the International Settlement, real estate would surge sharply upward, appreciating in value from one day to the next, while conversely the value of currency was depreciating. Cathay reaped enormous gains, turning losses into profits. And, for the moment, Jingchen personally was smugly rejoicing, for Tsai Liren and his own son Juanren had joined forces, the one on the outside the other from inside, as it were, exploiting the inland market demand for Shanghai medical supplies. But when Jingchen read articles in the papers accusing people of war profiteering, it sent shivers of uneasiness up and down his spine.

One day a construction contractor came to the bank to call on Jingchen: in view of the fact that the housing shortage in the International Settlement was growing more acute by the day, he wanted to conclude an agreement with Cathay to construct housing in the International Settlement, and hinted that after it started to earn money he would on his own provide to Jingchen personally a twenty percent cut.

Since that occasion when Tsai Liren had advised him not to adhere too closely to outmoded rules, and, moreover, given the steadily deteriorating atmosphere in the International Settlement where even occasional terrorist incidents were occurring, Jingchen was of course always mindful of keeping open, indeed of enlarging, his own escape routes. Sometimes he would think of his family as one large troop: there were the old and the young, the unmarried son Juanren and the four unmarried daughters, whose future expenses would be very great; and if indeed the climate should suddenly change and leave him without any retreat, then, truly, he would be walking that same road to ruin the Feng family had trod. Thus, after discussing costs and terms, although they did not then strike a deal, Jingchen was inclined to go along with the building contractor's proposal.

On his way back home, he encountered a thunder and lightning storm. Pulling up to the steps leading to the main entrance, he was about to open the car door when there was a tremendous clap of thunder directly overhead that seemed to split the heavens right in two, and it frightened Jingchen into a cold sweat that soaked his shirt. "Pursuing my private gain must be contrary to the will of heaven. Heaven is warning me!" Instantly he felt a wave of uneasiness overtake him, and without waiting for Fagun to come out with an umbrella, he braved the downpour and rushed indoors.

In the downstairs parlor Tsai Liren was chatting with Pu Zhuanlin, Juanmin, and Juanying.

"Diamonds are inexpensive in Hong Kong, but I'm afraid that being inexpensive, they may be of poor quality, maybe even fake," Juanmin was saying to Tsai Liren. In the beginning she had been positively contemptuous of this man who wore the traditional Chinese gown all year round, but gradually she'd become impressed by his ability and intelligence. He was moving frequently between Shanghai and Hong Kong, and often brought back novel little gifts for the mother and daughters, and moreover the things he bought were invariably both pretty and appropriate; consequently, Juanmin began to regard him with new eyes and was always asking him to shop for things for her.

"They're very easy to distinguish," said Tsai Liren, picking up a newspaper. "All you need to do is lay the diamond flat on a newspaper, and if you can't see through the diamond to read the print underneath, that's the first step in determining if you've got a genuine diamond. But that's still no guarantee, so next you've got to look into its interior, and if it reflects a lot of rainbow colors, then for sure it's a fake. And there's an even more convenient way to tell, too—just blow on the diamond. If it's the real thing, the condensed moisture from your breath will disappear almost immediately, while if it's a fake the moisture won't go away so fast. If you listen to what I say, I guarantee you won't get cheated."

Because Juanying was there, he spoke with particular clarity and detail, which held the three women in rapt attention.

"Jingchen, you're back. I wonder why you look so upset," asked Zhuanlin anxiously as she saw her husband come in dripping wet.

"Isn't it because of all of you?" muttered Jingchen angrily as he went up the stairs. Tsai Liren, understanding the situation, hastened up behind him.

"There's good news. I've learned from our agents that 'Silver Dollar' brand has again come out in Hong Kong and is selling very nicely now. I've also heard that the Hong Kong police department will let out bids for khaki uniforms for the entire force. At one suit per officer, you can imagine how many thousands of yards of material they'll need. Mr. Liu has already gone to Hong Kong to do some maneuvering. If you have approaches you could pursue at the same time, we could win the contract."

"I could ask our Hong Kong branch manager, Mr. Syi, to pull a few strings for the project," replied Jingchen wearily as he peeled off his dripping jacket. Tsai Liren thought it strange that Jingchen seemed so unenthusiastic, when a flustered-looking Fagun came in.

"Sir, I'm afraid to say that a swarm of beggars is crowding around the main gate, saying..." Fagun hesitated as he looked toward Tsai Liren. Jingchen frowned and said impatiently, "Go on, go on!"

Fagun coughed and continued in a low voice. "They're saying that... the beggar who comes so often to the residence pestering for a handout has died and that we should go to claim the body." Fagun was discreet enough to avoid referring to the beggar as "uncle."

"Who?" Zhu Jingchen stood still as a statue even as, somber-faced, he issued instructions. "Telephone the mortuary to send a vehicle to pick up the body. Then distribute some money to the beggars. Treat them with courtesy."

"Won't they try to cause us trouble? Or take advantage of the situation to get more money than they should?" Fagun remained uneasy.

Jingchen shook his head and smiled wanly. "These beggars are a loyal lot; if we give them some money they won't give us any trouble."

After Fagun left, Jingchen turned toward Tsai Liren. "A relative of mine," he said, loosening his tie. "Cousin of my late wife's." And he put his thumb to his lips to indicate an opium pipe. "When a guy like that gets hooked on opium, he eventually sinks to begging. I was powerless to help." He took out his handkerchief and blew his nose.

Tsai Liren sat in silence not knowing what to say.

Rain pelted against the window panes. It was pitch dark outside. Only the light in Old Chang's room at the gatehouse was burning.

"He's dead, and just as well. It's a blessing for him." Jingchen's throat choked. "However, I wasn't able to look after him properly."

Tsai Liren sat there uneasily, yet felt it inappropriate to take his leave. It was most awkward for him.

"Ah, it's gotten late. You'd better go on back now." Jingchen forced a smile, a miserable smile.

After Tsai Liren had left, Jingchen stretched out his trembling hand, and, as if unsure of his decision, dialed the first number, then the second, then the others with increasing firmness. A gruff-voiced woman answered.

"Please call Mrs. Su to the phone," Jingchen said; "she's in the third-floor back room." Mrs. Su was the wife of the deceased beggar. Since her husband had forsaken his family because of his opium addiction, and because she could never get him to change his ways, she had run him out of the house and promised henceforward never to see him again. But she was still Mrs. Su, just as she had been before, and everybody referred to her as Mrs. Su.

He heard that gruff voice on the other end shouting up to the third floor: "Mrs. Su, telephone! Some man wants to... " and the sentence trailed off. That's just the way Shanghai's petty householders were—they'd never let slip by even the slightest opportunity to create a rumor.

He waited, receiver pressed to his ear. He heard a distant voice say, "Thank you"—still that same cultivated, pleasant voice. It had already been many years since they had had any contact—not even a telephone call, for he had promised himself to bring everything between them to a full stop. But today's development had to be made known to her.

"Hello?" came a puzzled greeting.

"This is Zhu Jingchen."

The other end seemed dumbstruck; there was only the sound of nervous breathing.

"I wanted to let you know that he... that Kangming has died. Died in the street. I've already instructed that he be taken to Guohua Mortuary.

Why don't you go and view him; it will be the last time. I'll go with you tomorrow."

Mrs. Su hastily expressed her thanks and quickly hung up. She no doubt was afraid of the rumors that might otherwise circulate about her socializing and chatting idly with "some man."

It was for fear of just such talk that they had long since tacitly decided henceforward never to see each other.

She was not a beautiful woman, nor was she stylish, yet she was a gentle, docile person, and she was the wife of his own late wife's cousin, Su Kangming. Before his pernicious addiction to opium, Su Kangming had worked in a counting house; the young couple lived in a front-room flat and passed their days together very happily.

When Zhu Jingchen's first wife was still living and in good health, the two of them often used to drop in at the Sus to visit. Mrs. Su, being from Suzhou, was a good cook, and had finished eighth grade at the foreign-style school in her hometown. She often spent her leisure time at home reading books and newspapers. Jingchen's former wife had not learned to read, so in this respect he was very envious of Mrs. Su. But unpredictably the scene soon changed, for not long after their marriage, Su Kangming developed his addiction, heedless of his wife's admonitions, to the point where, on one occasion, he gave her a vicious beating. She'd had to telephone Jingchen to come rescue her.

Seeing this bruised and battered woman, Jingchen angrily reproached her husband. "You don't know just how fortunate you are. You've got a wife as attractive as they come, and a wife as capable as they come. If your parents hadn't made this match for you in the first place, how could you ever have found a wife? A man should act like a man; but someone like you who accepts no responsibility for your family—you might just as well never have set up a household!"

What he said was brief, but every word made a great impression on Mrs. Su. Earlier when her husband was beating her, she had shed not a tear, but now she was shaking with sobs.

Bitterly remorseful though he was at the time, before long Kangming was again pulled away by his gang of shady pals, eventually not even returning home at night, and finally he even stole all the drafts from the counting house where he worked and exchanged them for opium. Of course he lost his job and was very nearly arrested by the police, but fortunately Jingchen intervened personally and to the last cent made good on the stolen drafts.

The Su family, of the salaried class, lived on very modest means. How could it survive this untoward turn of events? Jingchen frequently went to see Mrs. Su, consoling her with kind words and at the same time providing her with material assistance as well. When for several days Su Kangming would not come home, he'd even have to send someone to go to opium dens all over the city in search of him. When he'd been found, Jingchen would force him to get a haircut and bathe and fix himself up like a proper man before sending him home with earnest admonitions, yet within the next few days his craving would always reappear.

And dubious-looking creditors would often appear at Mrs. Su's door to press for payment, saying her husband had borrowed money, so that she felt too humiliated to look her neighbors in the eye. Overcome with despondency, she swallowed Lysol in a suicide attempt, but by good luck Jingchen had come to visit her that day, and he rushed her to the hospital thus saving her from death. It seemed to have been a coincidence, for sitting in his office that day in a state of great agitation, Jingchen had had a premonition something would happen to her, so he straightway hurried to her home and, sure enough, she had passed out on the bed.

"Why did you have to save me?" Tears filled her eyes as she lay weakly propped against a pillow in the hospital.

He gazed at her for a long while. She was the same as in the past—cultured and refined. She could not forget herself even in this deeply grievous hour, as if the gravity and frustration of her life only added to her mature charm.

"He's not worth your dying for!" he'd told her.

Jingchen was twenty-eight that year, already the head of Cathay's trust division, and, with his smooth, handsome face, resembled a gentleman working in a high-class office. His wife, according to the rural custom, was five years older than he, nor could she read, yet he strictly observed his husbandly obligations and responsibilities, and thus found it utterly incomprehensible how this scoundrel of an in-law could treat as he did a wife so kind and gentle.

Mrs. Su looked up at him. A single ray of sunlight shone through the window and fell upon her eyes, giving them unusual luster and depth, and charm too.

She wept, wept bitterly, like a child who is soothed after being unjustly scolded, wept as if she would wrench the heart from her body.

"You can't go on crying like this, it will affect your health, you can't... " His throat constricted, choking off further speech.

Suddenly she looked full at him, plaintively, helplessly, but with a trace of melancholic joy...Since Jingchen had prospered in his career, not a few women had cast him favorable glances, but no woman had ever looked at him quite like that. That gaze, thinking back on it even after all these years, still made him tremble. But the evening of that day, lying abed recalling her gaze, he felt strangely peaceful at heart, as if he'd found an answer he'd long been searching for. And washed by time, that gaze had become ever dearer, leaving a deep wound in his soul.

His wife's attempted suicide shook Su Kangming. He kneeled before her sickbed and repeatedly vowed to change his wrongful ways.

She remained unmoved, but Jingchen was delighted, for he believed the man really meant it this time. He had such a fine wife—how could he remain indifferent to her?

He took stock of the remorseful Su Kangming: he'd gotten a close-cropped haircut, was wearing a gray gown and dark cloth shoes—such a young man, such fine features—how could he destroy himself like this?

Jingchen found a job for Kangming as a watchman in the Fourth Army depot, and Jingchen arranged that every day a rickshaw pick him up as if he were a criminal under guard and take him to work, and after work have him sent home by a roundabout way so that without fail he would be with his wife. Jingchen genuinely hoped this in-law might give up his evil ways and resume a proper life, for how would she manage otherwise?

But after three months he disappeared again. Jingchen wanted to find him, but she prevented it.

"Let him go. It's as if he were dead," she'd said coldly. Such an attitude of self-restraint and detachment actually set Jingchen at ease. Without Su Kangming she could live well enough, perhaps even better.

He helped her find other living quarters. She insisted on a garret room—something small which would keep her expenses down.

From that time on, he had never again tried to find Su Kangming, and even if he happened to spot him on the street, a ragged and filthy beggar, he pretended not to recognize him because that beggar had no further role in Mrs. Su's life.

But to provide indefinite material support to Mrs. Su was not feasible, and if he visited her constantly the neighbors, moreover, would only create news of it.

"Why don't you go back to school. You're still young. Learning a skill so you can make your own living would be your best guarantee." Considering she already had some education, he offered the suggestion.

She did follow his advice and went to a vocational school to study, and found employment as an office worker in a department store. She was now quite able to make her own living.

Later on Jingchen's wife passed away. During her illness, Mrs. Su had come to look after her. Juanmin was still small then and, needless to say, unable to manage the household, so Mrs. Su also handled all the household affairs, large and small.

Back then when Jingchen got off from work, he could hardly wait to return home. He sensed she would be waiting for him.

Self-supporting and without an addict-husband interfering in her life, her face had taken on a healthy, ruddy complexion and her figure had filled out. Soft, black shoulder-length hair was clasped in back, and she always wore a solid-color mandarin dress, the very picture of a devoted and conscientious school teacher of high moral standards. With her at home quietly awaiting his return, Jingchen felt relieved and happy; she gave him spiritual sustenance.

Then, his wife died. During those days of grief, he would feel Mrs. Su's hand upon him gently caressing, not flirtingly, but as a friend offering solace.

Suddenly he was jolted by the thought that between the two of them there existed no impediments at all...

He took her hand, and though he had known her for such a long time, this was the first time he had ever touched her. With a surprised and agitated expression, she fixed her eyes on him.

But when his wife's funeral arrangements had been completed, she wanted simply to return to her home.

"That's all right. In a few days I'll call on you," he said, reluctant to see her leave.

"There's no need to. In fact, it's best that we not continue to see each other too much..." She spoke with serenity and gentility, revealing a conscious detachment.

He placed his two hands on her shoulders, and with tension in his voice said, "When the mourning period is over, we'll get married. I love you; that must be clear to you."

She shook her head sadly. "We're not suited for each other; you'll soon feel that way too. Really."

"But... " He looked at her vaguely, comprehending nothing she said.

She smiled a mournful smile. "My husband—your relation—is still living, and everyone knows he's a degenerate opium addict. Now you're a vice-president at Cathay Republic, and you'll rise much further..."

He watched dumbly as she packed her things one by one into a small suitcase.

"Goodbye," she said with great reluctance.

She picked up her suitcase, and agilely felt her way down the steep staircase—that was before he had moved into his present western-style home—feeling on the wall for the familiar location of the light switch, clicking it on at the top of the flight and off at the bottom, until she got to the kitchen on the ground floor, where she found the tea kettle hissing on top of the stove; and, as no servant happened to be about, she put down her bag, then with accustomed movements, picked up a thermos bottle and filled it with the boiling water and placed a fresh kettle of water on the stove—for all the world a perfect housewife. The sequence of actions renewed Jingchen's hopes—she'd only been just talking before without intending really to leave.

But in fact she did leave.

Later there was a constant succession of matchmakers bringing marriage proposals—all daughters of wealthy and prominent families, and if he had married any one of them, it would have been good for all concerned. He would possess a wife of reputable family background, and furthermore he needed a wife who knew English and who could entertain at social functions for him. There was no other way—this was a world where one had to be particular about profit and loss, where one had to calculate return on investment and it would be self-destructive not to go along with it. That Mrs. Su did not remain behind thus saved him a great deal of trouble.

"Jingchen." Wearing a dressing robe of embossed material, Zhuanlin pushed the door open and came in, interrupting his reverie. "Are you free? Those beggars milling around the front gate gave me a real fright. Looked like a paupers' rebellion!"

Had the episode been handled ineptly and the beggars provoked, there might indeed have been an ugly incident, for it is true enough that China had many poor people, and if the wealthy became the target of public criticism, the situation would be a haystack doused with gasoline—one touch of a match and the whole thing would explode into flames. Fortunately on this occasion Old Chang passed out generous tips to these beggars to mollify them.

The next afternoon Jingchen waited for Mrs. Su in the mortuary reception room.

She came. He had thought she might be in a very agitated state, but, to his surprise, she was unusually calm, or perhaps it would be more accurate to say, she affected detachment.

"Mrs. Su!" As he rose to greet her, he felt an indescribable sorrow: she'd aged! Not the sort of age where you lost your teeth, but the kind of dazed expression of an old person who has experienced life's hardships. Her hair which used to fall straight to her shoulders was now pulled back in a bun, and a loose-fitting black silk padded dress concealed entirely a woman's curves, while green silk socks matched her own home-made cloth shoes. She had recently begun wearing glasses, and her fair-complexioned face, accented by the hexagonal wire-framed glasses, looked strikingly similar to Jingwen's wife, Miss Yi; but on closer inspection, one could see the difference, for Miss Yi, though likewise not a modish or careful dresser, did radiate energy and enthusiasm. Why else had Jingwen not long since been able to leave her? On the other hand, the Mrs. Su before his eyes now seemed very much like the sky of approaching dusk—a veil of gray placidity.

"I'm afraid I've put you to a great deal of trouble," she said, bowing slightly.

They had already accepted with equanimity the fact of their separate lives, so he immediately led her in to view Su Kangming.

With his hair trimmed and wearing a fresh shirt, Kangming lay there serenely, a different person from that former disheveled and dirty Kangming; the cosmetician had restored the refined face and delicate features, while concealing the complexion of an addict. His cheeks appeared full and ruddy, as if his debauched vagabond years had never happened.

She wept pathetically.

He had at long last returned, returned to her; no longer would he be able to cause trouble or provoke tragedy. She forgave him. She was ready to have his coffin sent back to his village to let him sleep forever among his parents and grandparents, a prodigal returning home for the final reunion.

"I'll have someone reserve a boat ticket, and our butler, Fagun, will accompany you. Be careful during the trip...," said Jingchen as he walked out with her. He would be unable to accompany her on this occasion, for the death of Su Kangming meant that the last thread connecting Jingchen with Mrs. Su no longer existed.

The environment of the mortuary was itself suffused with a mournful atmosphere, and a nearby church was just then performing a funeral service. "...Go now to that blessed place to be in the company of our Lord, never again to sin, removed from the world of temptation and contamination..." The snatches of hymn wafting over seemed to intermix with the heavy fragrance of flowers, defining the meaning of death as it is crafted by human artifice. He believed that this parting would be for Jingchen and Mrs. Su a parting forever.

They walked down the long, dark corridor, but pushing open the solid oak door, they at once confronted the bustling, crowded street. With land worth gold, everybody in Shanghai, the dead and living alike, were all squeezed close together. They had now arrived at their final farewell.

"Take care of yourself!" he said. "I'll leave you here."

She shook her head sadly, and tried to smile at him. But the smile died before it could break through.

The streetlights were now turned on, and under their indistinct glow, her face, though showing the scars of painful wounds, was for a fleeting moment movingly beautiful and uniquely attractive.

He stood in the doorway watching her figure recede into the crowd, sometimes lost from sight, sometimes reappearing. In the soft twilight, her form, even though in the midst of a throng, gave the appearance of being all alone. On that previous occasion when she had left, if he really had pursued her, he certainly could have won her. They would have had a good life together. One might say they were kindred spirits. But no, the thing was simply impossible. So he'd let her go.

When he got back home, Pu Zhuanlin was all dressed up, ready and waiting for him. She glistened in a silver-colored silk evening gown. Then he remembered: they had a banquet this evening as guests of the owner of Taigu Shipping Company. The connection was really Pu Zhuanlin's, for her uncle had among other things acted as Taigu's comprador on a number of occasions. But Jingchen's dealings with Taigu had recently become quite extensive, so it was imperative he put in an appearance at this evening's banquet.

In her forties, Pu Zhuanlin was in the prime of her life and amply endowed with romantic appeal. Jingchen helped her into the car with suave urbanity, but at this moment his heart was occupied by the lonely form of Mr. Su. She had floated off into the vague distance, and he knew not where she might finally come to rest. He felt himself to be bad through and through. He must do some philanthropic work, he thought, to cleanse himself.

A few days later during a meeting at the bank, he completely reversed himself and withdrew his earlier proposal to construct housing in the International Settlement.

"Although Cathay Republic is confronted with the dislocations of war," he said, "our continued prosperity will be due, as before, to the exertions of our personnel, and the high cost of housing in the International Settlement is not something we should exploit for our own advantage. Consequently, I have decided that from the profits Cathay has earned and using Cathay's own land, we'll construct Cathay housing where our own employees can settle down and live. This approach both avoids the anxiety over currency depreciation and will also be a tangible benefit for our personnel as a whole."

As he was making these remarks, the sight of the clean and freshly clothed corpse that had been his in-law never left his mind, nor did the figure of Mrs. Su, broken by her hardships. Her gloomy reappearance engendered recollections of a burning, almost unendurable, shame. But anyone who has to consider worldly success would in the last analysis have had to let her go. If only his conscience at times had been stronger...In recent years in this respect he'd probably gone a little overboard, but that day when the rain was beating down it seemed, did it not, that Heaven was warning him. So he needed to perform a good work, an act of charity.

Someone raised an objection. "With the present national crisis, is it really appropriate for Cathay to undertake a large-scale construction project for its own employees?"

Zhu Jingchen stood his ground. "The present national crisis does not mean that all our work must come to a standstill. Cathay must redouble its efforts to think of ways to develop. Where we have put in effort, our foundations will be solid enough to weather whatever storms may hit. Moreover, in these extraordinary times, the bank should help its own employees in some concrete way, help them lighten their burdens a little."

This startling decision of course circulated instantly through the bank, to the approbation of all, high and low alike. Cathay proceeded to solicit bids from contractors to undertake the construction work. The bank's reputation immediately increased further, such that even graduates of university commerce and banking curricula were now vying one with another in seeking employment at Cathay.

The day for the ceremonial laying of the foundation stone was warm and sunny. Besides the bank's entire workforce, various businessmen, members of the Bankers Club, and others were in attendance. Two beauties assisted in the ribbon-cutting ceremony—one was Hong Fung, the movie star now at the height of her popularity, and the other Ju Beibei, who during the past couple years had developed into something of a socialite. To get these two young ladies to come had been no easy matter. Ju Beibei graced the proceedings, it was said, owing to Liu Tongjun's influence, while Hong Fung had come for Ju Beibei's sake. When these two beauties fluttered onto the scene carrying ribbon-decorated scissors, the attention of the crowd was turned far more to them than to the bank directors on the speakers platform.

Zhu Jingchen that day had gotten himself up in formal attire with a white silk bow tie, and was sitting erect on the platform, his expression one of classic dignity inescapably touched with self-congratulatory pride.

The site was about ten acres in area, situated in the International Settlement bordering on South City—the heavily populated old

Chinese section of Shanghai. Housing rented at market rates in such a favorable location would be beyond the means of most salaried workers. Originally, discussions had been underway for the construction of a paper mill on the site, but when hostilities began in Shanghai with the August Thirteenth Incident two years previous, prospects seemed most unpropitious and the project was abandoned.

On ten acres a whole tract of single-family homes could be put up. Jingchen swept his eyes around the horizon, catching sight of Fan Yangzhi standing in the crowd. His prominent cheekbones suddenly reminded him of that drizzly day in the gloomy front parlor, where raindrops splashed through that unclosed window wetting Old Fan, who even as a corpse had found no peace. At that moment Jingchen had vowed he would some day build employee housing. Now his intention could be said to have come to fruition, providing comfort to Old Fan's soul in Heaven. Old Fan and Jingchen had started working for Cathay as apprentices at the same time, two of a group of six new employees. Of those six only Jingchen remained, only he had distinguished himself among his fellows. Looking out over the throng of employees filling the grounds, Jingchen savored the feeling a commanding officer might have in surveying his troops from a reviewing stand.

He remembered when he had just started his apprenticeship his monthly salary was only three silver dollars, and as their only advantageous job benefit every evening the apprentices all took classes at a private continuation school which taught Chinese, English, and bookkeeping. But Jingchen was just a kid then, and working during the day while cramming at night was for an active youngster a pretty miserable existence. One evening, urged, it seemed, by an evil spirit, he slipped off all by himself to Waibaidu Bridge, playing hooky from his night school. He noticed that every time a handcart approached the bridge, there were always a few vagabonds, eager to earn a copper or two, who helped push it up the incline, and during the time he was sitting there watching, he heard the continual clink of coins tossed onto the bridge roadway by the thankful carters. On one occasion a fish wagon had just passed over the bridge and a rickshaw was coming up behind. The rickshaw coolie, seeing Jingchen just sitting there dumbly not moving a muscle, yelled at him, "Hey kid, if you wanna eat, you'd better get movin'!" So Jingchen got up and helped push him over the hump of the bridge, and the rickshaw passenger pitched him a couple of coppers.

That evening he pushed and pushed into the middle of the night, accumulating a small pile of money, and then went to a Fifth Road shop for a bowl of chicken porridge and an order of shrimp, which suited his stomach very nicely. Having tasted the sweet fruit of his own labor, the next day he again skipped class in order to push handcarts, and earned a pocketful of coins. At that time ten coppers was viewed as a sizable amount of money, and the more he made the less he wanted to give up the work.

Another day brought a different kind of good luck. He'd just pushed a rickshaw up the bridge when he suddenly discovered that the passenger was someone from his hometown in the countryside.

"Jingchen, weren't they saying you'd come to Shanghai to learn a trade? How is it you've become a tramp?" His acquaintance seemed quite surprised. Jingchen instantly felt a shame so intense he just slunk away without even pausing to pick up the coins the passenger had tossed down.

After that episode, he refused to go out to struggle for coins again, but devoted himself to eliminating his poverty by single-minded application to his studies. If he had kept pushing handcarts, he never would have gotten to where he was today.

With the sound of popping champagne corks and the martial strains of a march, the ceremony began. Cathay's Chairman of the Board, Mr. Li, presided.

According to plan, prior to laying the foundation stone, a small metal box was first placed under the stone; the box contained a roster of all Cathay employees for that year and copies of that day's Chinese- and English-language newspapers. Then, the entire board of directors gathered around the stone, and each one deposited some memento. For his part, Jingchen placed his Ronson lighter in the box, and in the instant he did so a headline on one of the newspapers caught his eye: "Germany Invades Poland; Europe Explodes Into War."

That was September 1, 1939, when war broke out in Europe as a result of Hitler's aggression against Poland; the panicky nations of the West met the attack, and the war worked its devastation. The Japanese had long since openly stood with Germany, and from this time forward the Japanese became increasingly obstreperous, and even in the International Settlement they were domineering in the extreme.

One day, a nervous-looking Mrs. Zhong came into Jingchen's office. "Two men are here from Nippon Shokin Bank. They insist on seeing you."

Well, well, now they're charging right into the bank. No doubt the same guys who'd gone to the house so many times only to meet with one put-off after another.

Zhu Jingchen stepped into his reception room. The two Japanese, their hair slicked back, immediately rose from the sofa and greeted him with an interminable succession of bows. With a wave of his hand Jingchen gestured them to their seats, while he himself remained standing to indicate he had no intention of engaging in a prolonged discussion.

The Japanese presented their business cards, and, as expected, they were indeed the same two—Ono and Kagesa. Kagesa tried to reverse the roles of guest and host, but Jingchen again motioned him to be seated.

"I'm busy in my office, so just please state your business," said Jingchen, still standing.

Speaking unexpectedly fluent mandarin, Kagesa explained in roundabout ways their reasons for coming, and Jingchen caught his meaning. Inevitably, because the Japanese occupied the Zhabei and South City districts, business couldn't recover from its slump, so Nippon Shokin Bank hoped to operate joint banking facilities with Cathay's Small East Gate branch. The naked truth was they wanted to exploit Cathay's reputation to revitalize South City's financial and commercial markets.

"Cathay is a long-established commercial bank, and in recent days it has enjoyed even greater good fortune, indeed, has started to construct employee housing. The Cathay branch at Small East Gate occupies a very favorable business location and it's only right that it thrive and develop. With Shokin and Cathay obvious banking colleagues, we want at the present time to be of as much help as possible in developing Cathay and together encouraging South City business. Therefore on this occasion in our private capacity we have come to seek an interview with you, and we wish to exert to the utmost our feeble powers."

This Jap spoke excellent Chinese, and judging from his outwardly cogent and logical presentation, he resembled not so much a banker as he did an outwardly nonpartisan politician mouthing broad global concerns.

"Well, then," began Zhu Jingchen, smiling broadly, hands folded behind his back. "We need not at present discuss South City, for beyond the border of the International Settlement, it is all your world, and you can do there whatever you like. What need was there for you to make a special trip here? In my opinion there is simply no point in forming a joint venture. In any case, what you say is doubtless true, and if you hang out the Nippon Shokin sign, it would probably be even more effective."

Those remarks turned the Japanese faces alternately red with shame and white with anger, and before they'd had a chance to recover their senses, Jingchen rang for Mrs. Zhong to escort the guests out.

In the afternoon he convened an emergency meeting of the board of directors. Hearing Zhu Jingchen's report of his interview with the Japanese, several of the directors turned pale with fright, and began to accuse him.

"Oh my god, how could you possibly have been so rude to them! Outwardly we've got to show respect to those Japs as if they were Buddhas, while secretly securing our defenses as if they were thieves."

"Don't think that just because you're in the International Settlement you're safe. Those Nips will find plenty of ways to work their evil designs. For example, wasn't Liu Zhanen, the president of Shanghai University, assassinated by Japanese right on the corner of Bubbling Well Road and Carter Road? And having gotten snubbed this morning, they certainly won't let the matter rest there. By the looks of it, there's going to be a lot of this harassment. You'd better be real careful, and it would be best if you didn't stay in your own home."

At that everyone seemed to start talking at once, but finally it was agreed that Jingchen should lie low for a while, and by good luck the chairman of the board, Mr. Li, happened to have a vacant unit in Taishan Apartments located in the French Concession, and he pressed the key into Jingchen's hand then and there.

Jingchen took it, sipped the cold dregs of his tea, and suddenly his heart sank. These developments augured ill indeed for the Small East Gate branch. Why not just close it down and be done with it? Actually, since the fall of Shanghai, Cathay's business in the enemy-occupied areas had been dismal, but, like a deaf person and his ears, the bank kept up appearances anyway. Now, however, by the looks of it, they would not even be able to do that. "In my view, our only option is to wrap up our operations there and sell off the building for whatever we can get for it, and let Cathay slap its own fanny and start running—slip away. It's just that," he said hoarsely, "for the hundred or so branch employees we don't have any new assignments!"

The room descended into heavy silence, and only after a long while did someone remark coldly, "There's no help for that; we're a bank, not a charity." It was a remark no one wanted to hear, but reality was reality.

Thereupon it was decided that, excepting department heads and higher, all branch personnel would be dismissed with severance pay and be given assistance in finding new employment. At the same time, the secretarial department would draw up a letter to depositors explaining that the closure of the Small East Gate branch would in no way affect their interests and that all banking business could be conducted at other branches located in the International Settlement or at the main office. It was also firmly agreed that before this notice of reassurance was sent out, news of the impending closure absolutely must not leak out, lest the depositors be caused unnecessary anxiety.

It was already dark by the time the meeting broke up, but because it happened to be the weekend, banking hours in the main lobby were as usual extended. One could hear the clicking of abacus beads at the tellers' counter and see the green lamps glowing atop the staff desks behind. Viewed from a distance it seemed like a sea of pale green light or a constellation of twinkling stars. "The customer is always right" and "the customer is our sustenance and parent" read two large slogans in blue lettering; hung high on the wall, they were visible throughout the lobby. The staff desks were ranged one alongside another without room to squeeze in even one more. To the right of the main entrance was the night depository, which had been installed only since the Marco Polo Bridge Incident in 1937 when war broke out in Peking. If shop owners could take the proceeds from their evening sales and drop their deposit bag into the night depository, the next day the bank could enter it onto their account and thus relieve the shop owners of the inconvenience of keeping large sums of cash overnight. Yes, one could justly say that Zhu Jingchen had done everything conceivable for the sake of Cathay Republic.

In one corner of the lobby a tiny counter, a miniature sofa, and so on, were arranged Lilliputian style. This was inspired by Jingchen's once having seen children playing bank, so he set up this Cathay Baby Bank, where one could open an account with just one silver dollar, and it attracted the children's New Year gift money and the change they might otherwise spend on candy—all of this could be deposited here and earn interest. Since its very inception, business had been pretty good, and the services Cathay provided its adult depositors it provided to the youngsters as well. How the children loved to come. But now, of course, with currency depreciation, people were exchanging their paper money to stockpile cloth, oil, soap, and such things. So where could kids get loose change any more to come and play bank? Two unoccupied women clerks on duty at that empty children's counter smiled up at him. The two had graduated from the education department of Jinling Girls' College in Nanking; they had not studied banking, but with the aim of relating socially to the young depositors at the Baby Bank, Cathay had specifically sought out these young women, only to become, unexpectedly enough, superfluous employees. Cathay had already notified the accounting department to issue them three months' salary and ask them to move on the following month, but the two women did not know that yet.

Jingchen nodded to them somewhat apologetically. Within a few days they'd be cursing him. But what could be done? It was just as that board director had said: a business enterprise is not a charity. This year it was not unusual that one salaried position be shared among three or four people. It was difficult enough for men to keep their jobs, so it was all but inescapable that women be let go to make way for them.

There was still about a month to go before Christmas, and colored streamers announcing Christmas sales in the shops along the street fluttered in the soughing wintry breeze, and though it appeared at first glance to be a bustling scene, the streamers, so tattered by the cold wind they hardly deserved to called such, seemed to wear an expression of defeat. Jingchen's heart involuntarily skipped a beat: these shop owners were too mean—why not do it right and cut strips of satin to put out rather than use these colored wax-paper streamers? But, from another point of view, nowadays everybody just wanted to be like a Buddhist monk, living a day-to-day existence with no thought of the morrow; no one had long-term plans nor, indeed, was long-term planning even possible. Although the International Settlement was still a bustling entertainment district and thriving marketplace, Jingchen, who made his living in finance, suddenly realized that though the place was aflame, as it were, with activity, it was a false flame, and what ruddied the cheeks was not benign warmth but feverish inflammation.

The Baidai Record Store was broadcasting through its open front door the perennial Christmas favorite, "Silent Night."

> Silent night, holy night,
> All is calm, all is bright...

The strains of this quest for peace and good will floated bleak and helpless above the street full of scurrying pedestrians and scattered autumn leaves.

Ah, peace. When might peace ever return?

Just look at what a fine present he had all ready for the Small East Gate branch employees. This year had witnessed a considerable loss of business—you could "see the bottom of the rice bin," so hard were the times. The Cathay housing project had just started construction, yet Zhu Jingchen's good side had already been forgotten; before very much longer, indeed, the name Zhu Jingchen would be kicked back and forth and cursed by everyone. Yes, cursed!

Sure enough, when the notification of the Small East Gate branch closure was announced publicly, it was as if a bomb had been dropped, and Zhu Jingchen not only was vilified by his employees, they actually submitted a collective petition to the main office demanding Zhu Jingchen meet face to face with the entire group for a full discussion to arrive at some understanding about the employees' future livelihood.

In a fit of anger, they'd telephoned him at his office. "If you'd had the guts, you'd've laid out the situation openly on the table and discussed it with us point by point, instead of tossing off a notification and not giving a damn about what happens to us."

"All right, I'll appear before you to confess my sins," retorted Jingchen, and he slammed down the telephone receiver in a huff. Then without so much as a "good-bye" to Mrs. Zhong, he stormed out of his office.

Stepping into the elevator, he happened to bump right into Syi Zhensyu who was on the point of stepping out. He had been in Cathay's Hong Kong branch handling foreign exchange transactions, and was now lucky to get back to Shanghai even once every three or six months. Jingchen had already gotten wind of talk about the close friendship developing between his son and Mr. Syi's daughter. In all fairness, of course, Syi Zhishuang had made a very favorable impression on him since that day she had come to solicit advertising space in her yearbook. Indeed, as it is said, "beauty and kindness go together." Though she did not come from an illustrious family, they were certainly very proper people. According to Jingchen's way of thinking, making a marriage match with one of those high-fallutin, finicky daughters from an elite family was too much like inviting a Buddhist saint into your home—they just weren't much fun. The one awkward thing about it, though, was that, as the daughter of a colleague, there would be the inevitable suspicions that advantage, not love, was the basis of the relationship. Fortunately, Mr. Syi was a man of unimpeachable character who absolutely disdained toadyism and feared most being suspected by others of toadyism. Consequently the two men purposely kept a distance from each other, besides which, since Mr. Syi had for a couple of years now been working in Hong Kong, they normally had little opportunity to see one another anyway. It was thus all the more unexpected that, despite its apparent vastness, it was a small world after all, and these two men whose families would one day be related in marriage now stood face to face.

"Mr. Zhu," exclaimed Mr. Syi, scrambling for something to say; "the bidding for Hong Kong police uniforms—the Bounty Mill's Silver

Dollar fabric won the contract. That young engineer Tsai Liren was very effective."

But at this particular moment Jingchen could not get excited about any of that, nor even pay it any attention. Seeing him lean listlessly against the elevator wall, Syi Zhensyu could tell something was bothering him, and suddenly he recalled overhearing a moment ago stormy language in his office, apparently a row over the petition sent up by the Small East Gate branch employees. Then something suddenly occurred to him.

"Are you going out, Mr. Zhu?" he asked. "Be careful. Enemy collaborators are now in the International Settlement kidnapping people. It's quite a regular occurrence."

"The Small East Gate branch—I've got to go over there and placate them," said Jingchen.

"It's dangerous. That's an occupied zone. Since you're not cooperating with the Japs, walking right up to their doorstep like that..." Now Mr. Syi was really getting concerned.

"Huh, I might just as well let some Jap shoot me dead on the street," said Jingchen despondently. "At least that would be a dignified way of getting it over and done with, and save me a lot of trouble—better than now when I've got to go and let them curse me, 'You damn bastard!'" But of course Jingchen knew that he had broken the rice bowls of those employees, and to go out and find another job in a year like this would be as hard as ascending into heaven. Even the gods were helpless to find positions for these hundred or so employees, so Jingchen, beyond seeking their forgiveness by claiming it hurt him more than them, could do nothing either.

"Don't think like that, Mr. Zhu. Everybody knows that the decision to close down the Small East Gate branch was inevitable, and that it was the decision of the entire board of directors. These are extraordinary times, and it's unavoidable that everybody accept some pain." Syi Zhensyu, a reticent man who usually kept his thoughts to himself, had no gift for speech, but when he did say something it was absolutely sincere.

The elevator came to the bottom with a clunk. This automatic elevator, though installed many years previous, was still a rarity in Shanghai. An automatic elevator of this type was reportedly to be installed in a new residence Liu Tongjun was just now having built for himself. The development of Shanghai in recent years had certainly been very rapid, and were it not for the war, it would still be developing. Those rapacious Japs!

Suddenly, in the instant before the door opened, Jingchen pressed the button and the elevator began wobbling up again.

"Mr. Syi...um...Zhensyu, old friend..." There was a certain huskiness in his voice, for in their twenty-year association this was the first time Jingchen had ever addressed him so familiarly by using his given name.

Syi Zhensyu looked at him with a degree of amazement.

Zhu Jingchen cleared his throat, and his voice resumed its former clarity. "Juanren is an honest and proper boy, though he does have a bit of the prodigal in him. After the storm over this branch closure dies down, let's announce their engagement while you're in Shanghai."

"Well, er...Zhishuang is just social climbing," Mr. Syi replied politely. In his heart of hearts, though, he was not too keen on the match, for he did indeed dislike even the appearance of social climbing.

"I've already thought of a matchmaker," said Jingchen, "Let's ask the owner of Bounty Textiles, Liu Tongjun. He's very enthusiastic about it." Although people nowadays were emphasizing that couples choose their own marriage partners on the basis of love, as a formality the matchmakers still had a nominal role; otherwise it simply wouldn't be the way these high-class families did things.

Jingchen himself had not at all anticipated that in this tiny cubicle of an elevator with his future in-law right in front of him, the complicated personnel affairs of the bank could actually flee from his mind without a trace, leaving behind naught but affection and concern for the younger generation. The entire world seemed to be distilled within this tiny elevator. Supposing that man's world really could be thus distilled, then its essence would be a sincerity of heart directed at the younger generation.

By this time the elevator was again on its way down, now already the second round. The door opened and before one's eyes again lay the perils and disorder of the world. As if someone were pursuing him from behind, Mr. Syi did no more than nod perfunctorily to Jingchen before he hurried out of the elevator, afraid people would suspect he'd gotten Jingchen all alone in the elevator with him to win favors for himself.

Jingchen did not take the bank's automobile; instead he called for a taxicab and headed toward Small East Gate.

Viewed from a distance the entrance to the red brick building of Cathay's Small East Gate branch was quite ordinary, except now the iron gate was closed, and conspicuously pasted on the doorway was the notice to depositors. The same old newsstand stood next to the entranceway, languidly minded by an old fellow wearing a battered felt hat. Jingchen swept his eyes over the scene and couldn't detect anybody suspicious, but in any case he could only resign himself to whatever fate might bring.

He had the driver stop on a nearby side street. The city streets even in broad daylight presented a cold and cheerless scene without a soul in sight. Under the house eaves in the lane opposite a nondescript youngster was tending a sweet potato oven, his hands pressed against the oven's surface to warm them, as he watched the street scene with a desultory eye. The youngster had the country boy's ruddy, weather-beaten face, yet his eyes were alert and lively. The youngster inevitably reminded Jingchen of the scene when, years before, he had come all alone to Shanghai, carrying his bedding on his shoulder, to make his fortune. Jingchen too had taken a lively interest in everything around him, and had that same ingenuous face of the country rustic across the street. Then, in the space of a finger-snap, thirty years' time had rushed by, and he at long last had become one of Shanghai's notables, but in the process he'd had to shoulder ever heavier responsibilities.

Thus musing, he couldn't help but eye the youngster a little more closely. As the boy returned the gaze, a suspicious notion suddenly occurred to Jingchen: following the Marco Polo Bridge Incident, at the iron gate on New East Bridge where Minguo Road meets the French Concession, three thirteen-year-old boys who hawked popsicles were found to have in their possession large amounts of Japanese silver dollars, and only later was it discovered that those boys were actually Japanese recruited from farm families—altogether fifty or so of them—and given special training at the Japanese encampment at Hongkou, after which they were sent to Chinese garrisons in South City, Zhabei, Pudong, and elsewhere to gather intelligence. Could it be that right before his eyes the youngster selling sweet potatoes was...

An old lady with a small child in her arms came up and bought a sweet potato. Jingchen used that moment to hurry across the street, his nerves taut from suspicion.

Jingchen bounded up the stone flight of steps and yanked open the iron gate, and except for a "He really has come," the people at the counter just stood there in utter silence nervously staring at him.

"The bank president is here." Fan Yangzhi specially brought an armchair over for him. "We had actually planned to go to the main office. It's really not at all safe for you to come here."

Jingchen was astonished that Fan Yangzhi seemed to be the brains behind this operation. He had early on felt that Fan had connections with the communists. He'd thought so ever since the day Fan had brought to his home that Mr. Tang who'd taken a goodwill trip to the communist bases. Well, all right, then, Fan: are you ready today to communize me, Zhu Jingchen? In any event, Jingchen felt ready to brave any danger. It was certainly preferable that he had personally presented himself here than having this bunch of employees come to the main office to present their petition and engage in negotiations, for there were several hundred employees at the main office, and once incited by this group in united opposition against him, then the matter might really get out of hand. He'd known deep in his heart he might as well come personally to Small East Gate; after all these employees would not dare do any harm to him. And yet, were not the communists really at the bottom of this action, and, if so, were they not likely to create some disturbance? A strike? Petitions? Sit-ins? How very irksome that would be.

Jingchen composed himself and sat down. "You asked me to come, and I have come. The decision to close this branch had my endorsement. If you have comments to make, now is the time to make them."

However, they maintained a timid silence, now altogether bereft of their initial stridency on the telephone. Finally, one of them, about forty years old, began. "Mr. Zhu, all of us have parents to care for and kids to raise. If you go through with this, how will we be able to support our families?"

Zhu Jingchen lit up a cigarette and pondered a moment. With dark bags under his eyes from lack of sleep, he looked much older than his years.

"The notification explains everything very clearly. Every person will be issued a severance payment, just as the board of directors decided, and..."

"But..." A Ningbo man, though in his fifties still just a supply clerk in the general affairs department, broke in with a quavering voice. "...How will we be able to make ends meet? My wife is ill, my two children are in high school and we've already borrowed for the tuition... I started with Cathay when I was just sixteen, and I've been a diligent worker all along...And now this...You can see for yourself, Mr. Zhu, that at my age it'll be awfully hard to find another job."

Once the discussion got under way, the other employees began their discordant grumbling.

"Sure, it's fine to talk about severance pay, but it'll be used up in no time. And when it is used up, we'll have nothing to eat except the winter winds!" Fat people always talk the loudest.

"Whose remark was that?" With a stern expression, Jingchen's piercing eyes swept across the room. "Who?" His voice was angry and authoritative, and in an instant the atmosphere of the room turned tense. "Who ever said this severance pay would last indefinitely? Even a mountain of gold wouldn't last indefinitely. Who ever said this severance pay would provide you for a lifetime? Lucky for you," he retorted through clenched teeth, "at least you're a man. Figure out some solution for yourself—scramble, go all out, find opportunities. What are you, a little kid or something? It's difficult enough as it is for the bank to give everybody even this severance pay. If you push your responsibilities onto the bank, where can the bank in turn push its responsibilities? Keep in mind you people are all well educated. And I'd be surprised if you haven't heard the expression, 'every man shares responsibility for the fate of his country.' How is it able-bodied men like yourselves can't even shoulder your own little responsibility?"

Hit head on with that angry rebuke, the employees' faces turned ashen in fright; they could only gasp and none was intrepid enough to show anger.

"It's fine for an influential person like yourself to talk about 'finding opportunities,' but where are there opportunities today for ordinary people like us?" One among them was unconvinced. "Trimming the workforce without trimming management just goes to show you'll eat us up like small fry."

"Ordinary people or influential people," said Jingchen, smiling a smile more bitter than tears, "everybody has his difficulties. I've closed down this branch and the building is to be sold, and the Japanese still will never give me any peace. The board of directors has already purchased a passage to Hong Kong for me, but to go would be unconscionable; if I did go there, what would the thousand other Cathay employees do? Of course if I had gone there when hostilities first began in Shanghai two years ago, then my turn would never have come to play the devil today." There was not a sound to be heard.

His voice was not at all loud, yet he believed that at this moment in this particular instance, he had beaten them.

"Of course whether I remain in Shanghai or go to Hong Kong, it would be solely for the protection of Cathay." Jingchen exploited his advantage by keeping up his flow of speech. "Once the opera is staged, you know, everybody's got to sing together to make it a success. But of course," he continued, flicking the ashes from his cigarette, "when you play virtuous roles in opera productions, you gain a positive reputation in real life, and when you play evil roles, you have to work hard not to bring real trouble upon yourself. In this instance I have made up myself to look the thoroughgoing villain!" Having spoken, he stood up and bowed to the group. "On this occasion, gentlemen, you have on behalf of Cathay Republic shared both responsibility and adversity, and I shall ever have you in my thoughts. When in the future peace returns, the Small East Gate branch will open for business anew. At that time I shall invite each and every one of you to rejoin us."

"Sir, even if you don't go to Hong Kong or to Chungking, you'd still be a hard man to beat. Self-sacrifice, maintaining profitability—that's all very touching; but with our salary and jobs gone, we simply have no way to get by. The way Cathay is treating us is like another Munich: you intentionally sacrifice us minor employees in order to preserve the good reputation of Cathay, with no inconvenience to yourself!" That middle-aged employee protested vigorously, and Jingchen could see that beneath those bushy eyebrows, his small eyes were full of enmity and hostility. Jingchen was not stopped, but he did feel his resolve weakening.

There was a moment of tense silence throughout the lobby.

"My esteemed colleagues," said Fan Yangzhi rising to his feet, as Jingchen listened intently to what he had to say. "We are all educated people who are capable of listening to reason. These are extraordinary times. In order to maintain Cathay's rectitude and profitability in the face of Japanese villainy, Mr. Zhu has no choice but to cease operations at the Small East Gate branch. Today Mr. Zhu has been kind enough to come here to speak to us, and we have shared alike in Cathay's responsibility and adversity. Provided the bank, for its part, knows how things stand with us, we can derive some comfort from that. Now then, in the present time of national crisis, let us go ahead regardless, and help Mr. Zhu perform his opera to a successful finale. It's just that it's hard to sing on an empty stomach!"

That last remark expressed perfectly what was on the minds of everyone present.

Cathay had never before been troubled with labor disputes, and Jingchen thought that the present matter could be amicably resolved. Since the provinces of Jiangsu, Zhejiang, and Anhui had fallen into enemy hands, Japanese interdiction had made it impossible to transport oil and grain to the Shanghai area, though fortunately there still remained a sea route by which to bring in Thai rice; but even so there were still the "rice vermin"—profiteers who hoarded this indispensable staple. Now even Cathay itself had joined the ranks of the hoarders, and indeed had for some time taken hoarding as a subsidiary banking activity. Although Cathay's assets were thus increasing day and night, Jingchen knew in his heart it was an unjustifiable and dishonest practice. Fortunately, the bank's own edible staples on store in the vault could be sold at any time to the bank employees at pre-inflation prices, and although it was only a drop in the bucket, still in a time of emergency it could afford some help to those in dire straits.

"Yes," said Jingchen, "I'll instruct Mrs. Zhong about this and immediately distribute to each employee a sack of rice and a gallon of cooking oil. Even after you've left Cathay, you'll still be on our minds, and we will always be thinking of the welfare of our Small East Gate colleagues."

His remarks were interrupted by the ringing of the telephone: the main office was sending a man over to check up on things, with orders to look out for Zhu Jingchen's safety.

"Mr. Zhu still has heavy burdens to shoulder," said Fan Yangzhi to the others. Everybody immediately became rather alarmed, for this was now enemy-occupied territory, and if by chance something should happen to President Zhu, they would all feel themselves morally responsible.

Jingchen walked out to the iron railing at the main entrance and looked around. All was as it normally was.

"You'd better go out the back way," someone suggested.

"Well, I'll just show 'em by going out the main entrance," said Jingchen with a sly smile. "Coping with the Japs is just like catching crabs—confuse them with feints and jabs, always keeping them off guard." So saying, he turned his overcoat inside out and put it on. It was a reversible coat—woolen check on one side, waterproof khaki on the other—which he had specially chosen, should he have to cope with the unexpected.

"After you've gotten back to your office, sir, please telephone here right away and inform us of it," said Fan Yangzhi, as he opened the iron door for him. Jingchen nodded gratefully. There was still that old gray-haired employee from Ningbo, looking at him with an expression of infinite gloom, causing a wave of compunction to well up inside Jingchen. He stepped out through the main entrance, telling himself over and over, "I have absolutely no other alternative, I must think only of safeguarding Cathay's interests. What else can I do besides that?"

No sooner had he left than that middle-aged employee cursed him out again. "That slippery bastard can sneak off like this!" Others took up the refrain.

"He lives in a nice foreign-style house with a garden, so it's easy for him to blandly blab away about hiring every one of us back in the future, but when the future comes and we look him up, will we be able to count on him then?"

"Okay, okay," broke in Fan Yangzhi. "They say you shouldn't press a man too hard, and the way I see it, Mr. Zhu is a man whose word can be relied on. We ought not to handicap the bank as a whole just because of Small East Gate branch." And with that he heaved a long sigh, for in assigning this duty to him, Syu Zhiyong had stressed that it would be good enough if he could secure emergency relief, and of that he was now confident.

"It's not so important for you; you're just a bachelor. But I've got parents and children!" the middle-aged employee protested.

Fan Yangzhi took no notice of him. In fact he himself was being very courageous—bed-ridden mother, widowed elder sister, plus a younger brother and sister; without this source of income, things would become very awkward indeed.

"Hey, when are you going to vacate this place? We've come to take possession!" An oldish woman, coarse in manner, overdressed in brocaded satin, yelled in from the back entrance. It was the new tenant.

"Excuse me, madam, but what will the place be used for in future?" inquired the middle-aged employee with a smile.

As the woman adjusted her hairdo, one beheld ten thick red fingers loaded with gold rings, resembling the intestinal sweetbreads hanging in the front window of a deli. "My husband's gonna make the place into a storehouse," she said. Apparently he was on the rise in the hoarding business.

"Say, do you need someone to handle your clerical and accounting work? At whatever salary you think appropriate. I'm a commerce graduate from Fudan University, and my diploma..." The middle-aged employee rambled on, full of hope.

"Are you kidding?" exclaimed the shrewish lady in exaggerated tones. "I've rented just this one floor from the landlord to operate a small business and make some money. I don't need no college people here; my husband'll take care of the accounts himself. What I do need is a few country people with a little more brawn to move stock."

The rapidity of change! In a twinkling one business had been replaced by another and even the building was now already rented out. Hardly a minute had been lost. "Time is money," all right. This year everything was going up in price—housing, rice, oil, cloth...Labor alone was getting cheaper. Fan Yangzhi and the others gloomily went out the main entrance, and, looking back, saw a large notice in bold lettering:

DUE TO CIRCUMSTANCES BEYOND ITS CONTROL, CATHAY REPUBLIC BANK HEREBY GIVES NOTICE OF THE CESSATION, EFFECTIVE THIS DATE, OF ALL OPERATIONS OF SMALL EAST GATE BRANCH,

WHICH ARE NOW TRANSFERRED TO THE MAIN
OFFICE.

THIS ACTION WILL IN NO WAY AFFECT DEPOSIT-
ORS' ACCOUNTS, NOR WILL IT...

The lower half of the notice had been torn away by somebody or
other.

On his way back, Jingchen changed pedicabs several times,
eventually arriving by a circuitous route at the bank without mishap. He
entered his office and found Mr. Li, chairman of the board, seated in
an easy chair. Zhuanlin, her eyes red and puffy, was also there.

"Finally you're back. Your wife was practically fighting with me to let
her go out looking for you. What happened? Did you smooth things
over?"

As Jingchen went into the lavatory to wash up, he said with a
scornful expression, "Those gentlemen were easy to handle. What they
say about brainy types being incapable of revolution is true. However, I
want Mrs. Zhong to notify the general affairs department to distribute
to each person one sack of rice and one gallon of cooking oil. It'll soon
be Christmas."

"It makes absolutely no sense to observe the foreign holiday," said
Mr. Li. "You might rather present these things as New Year's gifts,
otherwise you'll have to provide aid again at New Year, too."

Jingchen looked at him, saying not a word. He wiped his hands and
came out of the lavatory. "But, Jingchen, now when the Japs and their
Chinese collaborators are no longer taking seriously the rights of even
the International Settlement," continued Mr. Li, "you oughtn't stay in
Shanghai just to devote yourself to a few dozen Small East Gate
employees. Wouldn't it be better to get away to Hong Kong?"

"I'm not going," said Jingchen, adding, "as long as Cathay still exists,
I won't leave it."

After Mr. Li had left, Jingchen immediately telephoned Mrs. Zhong,
instructing her to see that the rice and oil were distributed to the
laid-off employees of Small East Gate branch. "It's on me," he told her;
"deduct the expense from my personal account."

Zhuanlin sat there looking at him, and heaved a sigh. Although
Juanren and Juanying both had jobs, the money they earned was only
enough for their own incidental expenses, while Juanmin was still in
college and Juanwei had already entered McTyeire; just paying their
hair dresser, let alone their tuition, required a considerable sum. And
then there was the elderly Mrs. Zhu, too, and Jingwen's legal wife and

her four children, also under Jingchen's care. What a shock it was figuring the daily accounts! And if she scrimped overly on the food budget, behind her back they'd curse her as "that stingy stepmother." And now Jingchen was magnanimously saying "charge my personal account." Well, however that might be, she dared not speak out.

Chapter 21

In the downstairs parlor Juanying and Tsai Liren were sitting on the sofa chatting. Tsai Liren had given her an exquisite handbag of patent leather, just the right size for carrying her piano music or notebooks, and the perfect gift for a working woman like Juanying. He certainly knew how to please her.

By this time, Tsai Liren had already openly launched his campaign for Juanying. Though outwardly expressionless, he nonetheless was pressing his advance step by step. Tsai Liren could truthfully be said to be a vibrant young man, tall of stature and striking in appearance; he was wearing a traditional serge gown over neatly pressed trousers with shoes polished to a high sheen, all of which lent him an undeniable panache.

It was the time of day when the oblique rays of the setting sun illuminated the western windows in a fiery sheet of crimson.

"For years now you've been running between Hong Kong and Shanghai. It's been exhausting for you." Juanying was very grateful for the considerations he showed her, so every time he came for a visit, she'd always sit and chat with him for a while.

"Well, I'm just a single man, so my comings and goings don't inconvenience anyone. But Mr. Liu, the owner, has dumped all the factory business in my lap, so my responsibilities have gotten to be awfully heavy. I've recently come to think that it's rather like preparing a wedding dress for somebody else's use. For example, this time I managed to recover for Mr. Liu a substantial amount in insurance payments. A few months prior to the August 13th invasion, the factory purchased some equipment from Holland, for which we had applied to a British firm for insurance coverage, and according to the terms of the policy we were to pay the insurance premium in four installments. And we did pay the first two installments, but then because of the disruptions we didn't pay the third installment. Besides, the equipment we'd purchased was delayed longer and longer and finally never did arrive. It was later confirmed that the ship met disaster and sank. But Mr. Liu never went to the insurance company to discuss the case, figuring that since he'd paid only two of the four premium installments, he didn't have a leg to stand on. But I wasn't convinced, and after a careful reading of every policy provision I realized that we were fully entitled to claim indemnification. The ship sank just before the third installment was due, so I seized on that as the basis to argue my case; the policy had already been signed and was therefore legally binding, and under no circumstances were there grounds for shifting liability onto other parties. And as for being overdue on our payment, that was an entirely unrelated issue which should not be brought into the present discussion...Oh, I'm sorry, I'm afraid you must find this all very tiresome."

"Not at all. I can broaden my knowledge by listening to you." Juanying was ever attentive to others' self-esteem, the more so when the person was sometimes a little odd or if it was a person with whom she had a good deal of contact; provided the person was not actually coarse, the more she observed him, gradually the more interesting he became, and she could discern his many good points. She was just this way toward Tsai Liren. She felt he was a capable person able to put up with hardship, and a very stable and steady person. In a man those were rare virtues indeed.

"It may be possible for me to go back to Changzhou to spend New Year with my family. It's been years since I've been able to enjoy a New Year's holiday in my hometown; I'm always so busy. And when it's that busy, while other people eat their New Year's eve dinner with their families, I just order a bowl of noodles from the local noodle shop and sit in my office and eat." As he spoke he couldn't keep a look of sadness from his face.

"Are your parents both well?" asked Juanying with genuine sympathy.

"My father is still vigorous, but my mother suffers from glaucoma and can't see at all, so she's quite inactive. Before, in her younger days, Mother could do anything; I was kind of fearful of her, not so much of my father..." With that he let out a sudden chuckle. "What a naughty kid I was. Once I made the master of our private school so mad he beat

me on the hands with a ruler—the previous evening I'd climbed onto
the roof of his house and peed down the chimney."

Juanying burst out laughing. And much to her surprise, the sound of
giggling came from behind the sofa as well. Juanying looked around,
and there was her little sister, Juansi, hiding in back of the sofa.

"And who told you to hide in here?" asked Juanying, angry but
smiling.

"Minny told me to hide here to see if Mr. Tsai was proposing to
you," said Juansi, putting on a long face, a remark which caused both
Tsai Liren and Juanying to flush deeply.

"You get out of here quick!" Juanying gave her a spank on the
bottom, and Juansi disappeared like a wisp of smoke. "Heavens! Just
see how irresponsibly children can talk," an embarrassed Juanying tried
to explain.

"In any case, Miss Zhu," said Tsai Liren softly as he toyed with the
hat he was holding, "by now we've gotten to know one another very
well, and I think you understand me as a person very well. I come from
a business background, and although you might say I have the
equivalent of a college education, still..." He quietly tucked up the folds
of his gown. "...Still I may be a little uncouth perhaps?"

"Oh..." Juanying sensed that a marriage proposal would follow, and
though she had long since prepared herself for it, she was nonetheless
quite without presence of mind.

Then, as if he were leaving her with a little something to mull over,
Tsai Liren put on his hat with exaggerated care, got into his overcoat,
and, with his usual composure, said, "Perhaps I've caught you by
surprise with these remarks, but, Miss Zhu, I do hope you'll give them
some thought. Good-bye."

He left. Although he was wearing a traditional-style gown which
made him look rather older than his years, and though the expression
he assumed seemed rather conservative, nonetheless the briskness of
his pace revealed determination and self-confidence. Such a man as he
would surely achieve success.

At the dinner table that evening, with their father out at a banquet
and Zhuanlin in her room with a headache, there were just the young
people. The atmosphere soon enlivened itself.

"I've heard that Juanren promised to invite us to the Mandarin Club
this Saturday, and he'll introduce his future wife to us. Daddy says he
has to make arrangements for the formal engagement," Juanmin
announced.

"You were a classmate of Miss Syi's for six years," remarked
Juanying; "what do you need an introduction for?"

"It's not the same. There are two quite different roles involved. And besides...I haven't gone to visit her in all this time and I want to get back into contact with her, and since we've been apart for so long, it really requires someone to push things along." Juanmin thought how at first she had been rather petty-minded about it, or, to be precise, because Syi Zhishuang had found her heart's desire before she herself had, out of that indefinable feminine jealousy she had become distant from her former friend. But now she had Feng Jingsyao, who had garnered the universal admiration of the McTyeire senior class as a true gentleman, so that her initial pique had long since evaporated into thin air, and she was indeed anxious to have her old friend share in her own happiness. Juanmin was thinking to herself that she might bring Feng Jingsyao along on Saturday, but on the other hand it might be a little embarrassing to do so—after all, he did not yet have any defined connection with the Zhu family. Thus she asked,

"Juanying, why not bring Tsai Liren along? The more the merrier."

"Well...um, what for?" said Juanying, twisting her hands.

"Mr. Tsai hasn't actually proposed to Juanying yet. He only warmed up with talk about some insurance business and about peeing down chimneys." Juansi, who up to then had been intent only on her food, now interrupted in all seriousness, causing Juanying to redden once again.

"I think Mr. Tsai is a very nice man and a very practical man," said Juanmin to Juanying thoughtfully, "and furthermore..." She was about to say "you're not very pretty," but what fell from her lips was, "you're no longer a child."

Judging from the implication of the remarks of the good-looking Juanmin, it would appear that Juanying had but this one opportunity for marriage. Of course, unlike her elder sister, Juanying did not enjoy the luxury of numerous suitors, yet she did have someone who loved her. That was a love which did not resemble Tsai Liren's love. She was quite sure that if love could be graded by degrees, then she felt only fondness toward Tsai Liren, but toward Fan Yangzhi, love. Because he had never revealed his feelings to her, perhaps he really was intentionally suppressing them, and that imparted to such a love special fascination.

"And besides, who knows but what he won't already have gone back to Changzhou by Saturday. He said he wanted to return to Changzhou for the New Year's season," said Juanying, who wanted to stall things a while.

After dinner Juanying put on her overcoat and went to Fan Yangzhi's home. To pay an evening call on a single man was perhaps quite inappropriate, but Juanying was a professional woman and had little use for such outmoded views. Besides, she had found for the now unemployed Fan Yangzhi an office job in the Shanghai headquarters of a refugee relief organization, which, being philanthropic work, would not pay much of a salary, but it was certainly better than hanging around home. And quite aside from that, today she really did want to see him, for she had some things she wanted to ask him. She felt very close to him and very trusting of him. Before making his acquaintance, she had felt a close and trusting relationship only with God, but since their acquaintance, she felt it now only with Fan Yangzhi.

She knew his address, but she had never previously gone to his home. The lane was lined with red brick houses crowded one next to the other; and under their long projecting eaves stood various peddlars' stalls—here a cobbler, there a dry goods, beyond hawkers of cigarettes and dried fruit; and standing at their back doors in knots of two and three were the maids wagging their tongues: all of this vaguely recalled warm memories of Juanying's youth before her father had begun to prosper. Although she was dressed in ordinary and unremarkable clothes, the elegant demeanor instilled by her upper class breeding inevitably attracted the attention of those gossipy servants. Their gaze followed her as she went in through the back gate of the home where the Fans lived. A woman washing dishes in the shared back courtyard eyed her as she walked through and knocked at the Fans' parlor door.

"Ah, Miss Zhu." Fan Yangzhi, wearing a turtle-neck sweater, gave rather the impression of a college student. He seemed to be somewhat surprised by Juanying's visit.

"I've found a position for you, in the refugee relief headquarters..." As she spoke, she could make out three beds arranged this way and that in the dimly lit parlor, one of them occupied by the sick old woman; sitting around an old-fashioned dining table three school-age youngsters were doing their homework, while a woman—his widowed sister presumably—was busy with her sewing. Juanying had anticipated that Fan Yangzhi's home would be humble, all right, but she hadn't expected utter impoverishment of this degree. The sister gave her own stool—as small as a domino tile—to Juanying to sit on, as Yangzhi seated himself on the edge of one of the beds.

Yangzhi's sister served a bowl of steaming porridge flakes—flakes made of paper-thin layers of glutinous rice paste cooked until crispy in the bottom of the pot, to which boiling water is stirred in just before serving.

"A local specialty from the countryside. Give it a try," said Yangzhi. Juanying's sudden appearance in his miserable environment caused him no embarrassment, nor did he, on account of his extreme modesty, feel compelled to affect an outward arrogance, and it was just this neither-humble-nor-haughty manner that lent him a certain grace. In some ways he was rather like Tsai Liren—capable, intelligent; but as far as Juanying understood him, he possessed something she could believe in, something she was seeking, and because of this she always felt that compared to Tsai Liren he was the nobler man, the more idealistic man.

"Before, when my aunt was living in the country, she'd always have someone bring us her porridge flakes. But now that she's come with her family to Shanghai, we can't get them any more."

Juanying did not go through the motions of politely declining, but went right ahead and helped herself to the snack. It was certainly one of her charms that she could make herself right at home on a backless stool without a trace of condescension, unlike those sisters of hers concerned most about projecting the airs of the beauteous young damsel. Could her attitude perhaps derive from her belief that all people stood equal before God?

Rare as it was for a stranger to come to their home, the old lady couldn't help but harp on her old theme. "...In those days," she was saying, "the Fans would normally pile in the storehouse every-day red-lacquer stools like these and would bring them out only to fill in when there was a big wedding banquet. Our house in the country had one inner courtyard after another—five altogether. And the parlor and bedrooms were all furnished in elegantly styled mahogany."

Yangzhi's young brother, doing homework at the big square table, couldn't let his mother go on in this vein, and asked derisively, "And what about that big five-courtyard house now?"

"Sold off," replied the old lady, choking with emotion.

"And all those expensive furnishings?"

"Sold off," came the faint reply.

"So, what's the point in bringing it up again?"

Juanying quickly signaled with her eyes to stop him. Her church work had accustomed her to search for and understand people's real motives, as was clear the way she provided soft-spoken comfort to Yangzhi's mother. "While a person is in this world there is natural calamity and human suffering, and we can never know how much of them a person will experience; and though it's not easy for you, Mrs. Fan, I'm sure you'll be able to bear up under it..."

Here was a young woman of crystalline purity, whose heart brimmed with love for all humanity. But in the present crisis-ridden world, a crystal was such a fragile thing!

It seemed to Yangzhi the house was awfully crowded, making it impossible to have a good talk with Juanying, and the expression in her eyes told him she had something on her mind.

"Let's go out for a walk, shall we?" he said, getting into his overcoat.

The night sky in winter was particularly clear, and although there was no wind, the air had an icy feel that made one's cheeks smart. There was no better way to enjoy such a time than to sit in a romantic spot like DDS Cafe or Charlaine's. But with Yangzhi at home unemployed, the money for two cups of coffee had to be carefully calculated. Now for the first time he could appreciate the force of what Chilin had said earlier in the year: "For us love is a luxury."

They walked along aimlessly.

"By the way, my brother is getting engaged," she said. "His girlfriend was a classmate of Minny's. She's in college now, and a very good-looking woman."

Yes, of course; the son of Mr. Zhu the bank president could be very choosy.

"What do you think...what sort of person is Tsai Liren?" she blurted out nervously as she stared at her shoes.

"Able and foxy. Why do you ask?"

"He's just asked me to marry him; it's all so sudden..." She did her best to smile nonchalantly, but it was in fact a smile full of gloom. She had opened her heart to him, but he said nothing in return.

The two walked on silently for a while. Juanying finally broke the silence. "My uncle's died. Do you remember? The uncle I once talked about as having sunk to a life of begging. He died in the streets on a cold and rainy day. Finally he was delivered from his misery."

"What a terrible tragedy. Why is it that the poor can gain deliverance only after leaving the world of man? I wonder if that heaven of yours could be moved down here to earth?" he said with feeling.

"Who says it's only the poor who find deliverance only after leaving the world?" replied Juanying, shaking her head. "Isn't everyone in fact like this? Life on earth is no more than a journey; it's Heaven which is our destination. A journey is always full of hardships and perils."

"Well, in Russia, in Bolshevik Russia, that is, everything is undergoing change..."

"Have you been there?" Her eyes were blazing and they swept across him almost in censure. "The year my Uncle Jingwen went to Europe, he traveled across Russia. It was impoverished, chaotic, and lawless. Miss Yi was wearing a sable coat and she was practically forced to sell it to them for roubles. And in that country Uncle Jingwen's Parker pen and his Rolex watch were like unheard of luxuries. So you can see just how starved they are for consumer goods."

"The question has nothing to do with Parker pens and Rolex watches. Provided they have food and work—those are the important things!" Fan Yangzhi interrupted her almost angrily.

But Juanying was not ready to concede the point. "Well if everyone in society is satisfied with just food and work, then who will there be to provide the employment and pay the salaries? Who will unearth or mine the wealth that is stored in society? Today isn't like the egalitarian society of remote antiquity when everybody worked together to hunt a single animal, like the encircling method of hunting wild boar, and after they caught it everybody enjoyed it together." Juanying had never argued with anyone before; Yangzhi was the sole exception.

"According to what you say, poor people forever have to swallow insults and hold out until they leave the world of man and seek that utterly remote and vague deliverance. Is that their only way out?" asked Yangzhi in a controlled, yet harsh tone.

"That's not what I said. Anything in the world can change. Like my father who as a child was poor but now has become a successful banker, and your grandfather who used to be a wealthy landowner but now..." She thought for a moment before going on. "...But now his descendants have become members of the wage-earning class. Poor people, provided they can get an education and find opportunities, certainly don't need to spend their entire lives in poverty."

"Juanying," he replied, shrugging his shoulders, "usually you're very sharp, but now you can't even solve a problem as simple as one plus one equals two. It is precisely because poor people are poor that they have no way of getting an education."

Juanying just stood there silently and, covering her icy nose and mouth with her gloved hand, said without a trace of diffidence, "That depends entirely on public good will. In operating schools and hospitals for the poor, our church has been very active, and I myself am devoted to such undertakings."

"How much energy does just one person like yourself have? Can you transform the whole society?" Fan Yangzhi looked straight into her eyes, without the slightest flinch.

"And what about you? Do you think you've got the energy to transform the whole society and realize the ideal of human equality?" Now she looked hard at him.

"Of course I won't be the only one striving for my goals."

"Of course neither will I be the only one striving for my goals." As she spoke she suddenly lowered her eyes. "Oh, why must we go on arguing like this? I didn't come to call on you in order to quarrel."

"No, indeed," said Yangzhi with a self-conscious smile.

They walked on for a while, in silence, shoulder to shoulder. Under the long eaves overhanging the lane were two young beggars huddled together for warmth, shivering in the penetrating cold. Juanying unconsciously began feeling around inside her handbag, but she'd already given away the last of her change. She had no choice but to snap her handbag shut and smile at them apologetically. Yangzhi, however, without a word tossed a bill into their tin cup. Yangzhi had a strong, squarish face, yet his eyes were misty.

A trolley was clattering by on the cross street ahead.

"The trolley stop is just up ahead. I'll go back home now." She raised her eyes and smiled gently. A ray of soft light from the street lamp played across her face and hair, transforming the braid wound atop her head into a serene halo.

"It's so late. Why don't I hail a pedicab?"

"Never mind. Anyway I've got a commute-ticket."

"Good night." He shook her hand. "I didn't at all mean to belittle your ideals...It's just that I'm uncertain about my own feelings. The fact is, it's only with you that I'm able to talk about these things..."

"That's quite all right, really. It's not the first time we've had this kind of argument." She let her hand remain in his. Her hands—soft and fair, hands which had never known hardship, with long and slender fingers, strong from years of piano practice. He noticed that on her smooth fingers she wore neither costume rings nor engagement ring. Yangzhi felt his heart in turmoil, and his heart told him that she was extremely precious to him and when he was together with her everything seemed to be bathed in warmth and kindness.

Another trolley rumbled to a stop; she pulled her hand away and climbed aboard. In the amber light shining from the window of the trolley car, Juanying's face appeared wonderfully creamy, and as the car started off, Yangzhi watched her face disappear into the distance.

"Is there anything I can possibly do?" He searched his heart, but he could find not a single justification by which he might win her. For she was the daughter of a bank president while he at present was still jobless. Not long before he had formally joined the communist underground movement. Would she be willing to accompany him in a life so lacking in guarantees? And even supposing she were, he would not allow it. Hers was a loving heart, rich in goodness, but a heart, after all, too like a fragile crystal. And crystals are for keeping in velvet-lined cases.

He stared vacantly at the trolley tracks glistening under the cold light of the street lamp, and felt that fate had ordained their two paths through life would be in parallel lines which, no matter that they had already approached quite close, would never intersect.

★   ★   ★

It was a few evenings later, at the Mandarin Club.

Juanying went alone, for, as it happened, Tsai Liren had gone to Changzhou. Juanmin and Feng Jingsyao arrived together. Jingsyao, who possessed self-confidence only provided he worked alongside foreigners, had now opened a clinic in partnership with a Jewish doctor of German nationality. Zhishuang, as the proud guest-of-honor, came tripping in a few minutes late, accompanied by Juanren. She was wearing a loose-fitting cashmere overcoat of pure white, whose hem was fashioned into large wave-like folds; it was complemented with a black pin-stripe wool scarf, snugly fitting gray sheepskin gloves, gray high-heeled shoes, and a gray purse. Refined and elegant, a beauty in all her glory, Zhishuang amply qualified as a daughter-in-law of the Zhu family. She went right over to Juanmin to say hello, and then began recalling the old anecdotes about their former classmates at McTyeire—Ju Beibei, Liu Tsaizhen, and the others—in order to replenish her friendship with Juanmin from whom in recent years she had grown increasingly distant. After all, the two would before long become relatives, and to be relatives more than anything else binds people together, and once having bound oneself into such a relationship, it cannot be unbound until death itself.

"I heard Liu Tsaizhen had a son," said Juanmin.

"Really?" Zhishuang arched her eyebrows. Although a person of her own generation had already marched into the ranks of motherhood, Zhishuang, still studying at the university, felt she had some time left before she joined the same ranks.

"She married into a very wealthy family. Their house takes up an entire block. At the baby's traditional 'full-month celebration,' they celebrated for three whole days." And Juanmin winked derisively.

"Are they as old-fashioned as all that?" asked Zhishuang quizzically.

"They're very pleased to have Liu Tsaizhen for a daughter-in-law. They're a perfect match, just like candy and cake, as they say." In Juanmin's view, other marriages were all utterly preposterous transactions, while her love alone was noble. "Have you run into Ju Beibei? She now enjoys some reputation as a socialite. And do you know who's stuffing money into her account now? It's Liu Tsaizhen's father!"

"Oh my gosh, she fell for an old man!" Zhishuang reacted appropriately by making a face, even though she understood perfectly well that this sort of thing was by no means unheard of. But she knew Juanmin well enough to know that she always liked her own behavior to produce corresponding reactions in others.

"So what of it? The guy's got money!" said Juanmin. And so they chatted on with never the slightest lull, as each took the opportunity to bring into harmony the subtle discords that had grown between them. Almost instantly, it seemed, they became so engrossed in their tête-à-tête that it was scarcely possible to interrupt them.

Juanren carefully hung up Zhishuang's overcoat, solicitously offered her the menu, and selected beverage and sweets for her, then with reverence and awe waited upon the charming young women seated left and right. Juanmin felt a degree of secret contempt toward her brother. Men who reverently hovered around women annoyed her. Otherwise she'd simply have plucked any one of them from the pile of her suitors, for all would be scions of important families who with bowed head and docile ear would stand before her in servile obedience. But that was not for her; she did not want to duplicate others in her choice even of dress material, let alone her choice of boyfriends.

Juanmin silently fixed her gaze on Feng Jingsyao sitting alongside. He had never proffered the slightest solicitude toward her, nor, certainly, done anything just to humor her along; he embodied many character traits which she had always found absolutely intolerable—too particular about his appearance, too impractical about money, too interested in women, too proud for...But that happened to be the way he was, and that indeed revealed a quality in him quite different from her other suitors and made him uniquely attractive. Juanmin conceived of herself as a tamer of wild animals, and while it was hard work to break in a headstrong beast, it too was uniquely enjoyable.

Everybody has some person whom he greatly admires. As soon as Zhishuang saw Juanmin, the idol of her school years, right before her, as dazzling and sophisticated as ever, radiating with her whole being those self-important Oxford mannerisms, Zhishuang assumed an expression of boundless admiration, and that much gratified Juanmin's vanity.

Juanying, sitting quietly, her chin propped on her hands, was conjecturing that no matter whether Fan Yangzhi had come or Tsai Liren had come, neither would have felt at ease with the atmosphere around this table.

Decorated with fresh flowers and candlelight, the Mandarin Club was one of those exclusive night spots without bar hostesses. On the central dance floor a White Russian was doing a belly-dance. Her fair-skinned body, wonderfully supple and powerfully seductive, was a perpetual motion of unimaginable forms, and while her figure was admittedly beautiful, to view it in such unnatural contortions inevitably made one feel rather ill at ease.

"Juanmin," asked Zhishuang; "do you still remember the White Russian selling cotton candy at Hardoon Park?"

"Russian trash of that type," interrupted Feng Jingsyao with a contemptuous wave of the hand, "are either thieves or prostitutes, and there's not a clean one among them."

"There's a Russian tailor on Massenet Road who does good western-style clothing," remarked Juanren randomly.

"Good for what?" interrupted Zhishuang. "What that Russian tailor does to expensive material is positively shocking."

"Have you ever seen that demented old Russian lady on Seymour Road?" asked Juanmin, taking a sip of coffee, "They say that when she fled here from Vladivostok she brought along two sacks stuffed with roubles, but as it turned out it became a pile of waste paper, and that's what made her go crazy."

Juanying remained silent. She never had the heart to engage in idle gossip about others' misfortunes while they were still alive, especially when the other person's life in some ways seemed so close to her own. And if you can't give the help you wish you could, you might just as well remain silent.

With a series of tumbles across the dance floor to a strong rhythmic accompaniment, the woman brought her performance to a conclusion. The band then played "Sleepy Lagoon," and Jingsyao hastened to ask Zhishuang, and Juanren Juanmin to go onto the dance floor with its gorgeous lighting of constantly changing blue and purple—a world, Juanying mused, which Fan Yangzhi would do his utmost to transform.

"I must change this inequitable social system." That was Fan Yangzhi's goal. But was it possible? Human equality! The world of mortal man was complex—people's ambitions, their virtues and vices, character and personality were of a thousand different sorts: how would it ever be possible to bring every person up even with the rest to implement universal equality?

She had once told him that such a condition existed only in Heaven, that it could be realized only in the presence of God. And everybody—rich and poor, noble and humble—must alike walk the road toward that day when everlasting equality would be truly realized.

Fortunately wealth and power were of no use in bribing Death, otherwise this world would offer even fewer options and occasion even more intriguing.

A waiter came up, bowed, and handed Juanying a note: a gentleman at table number five wished to invite her to dance. She looked over to the table, saw the tall, good-looking man, and nodded her assent.

Juanying was wearing a dark-green woolen mandarin dress decorated with black beads sewn on in a plum-blossom pattern, a dress which she had had specially made on the occasion of her father's marriage; it lent her both an appealing charm and a dignified reserve which made even her feel like a late-opening bud gaining in beauty and attraction with each passing day. The Juanying of an earlier day was timid, awkward, and colorless, and never once had a young man sent her flowers or penned her a letter, and before her stylish and lively sister Juanmin, she'd always felt herself to be without a single redeeming feature. Fan Yangzhi was the first to discover her—on that rainy evening at the children's shelter when, because she had scalded her leg, he'd taken her to the hospital and then accompanied her back home. Sitting under the rain canopy of the rickshaw, she listened intently to the pitter-patter of raindrops against the oil-cloth, and heard the wheels of the rickshaw splashing along behind, and she knew that he was near, seeing her home. Then into her life came this Tsai Liren. He had gone back to his hometown two days ago, and just prior to his departure he had specially come to speak with her, and it seemed that the two of them somehow had reached a sort of tacit agreement. He had by now accumulated for himself a sizable amount of money which he had put into a business venture of his own, and with the earnings from that he would build a new house for his parents. Figuring the time necessary for that plus the New Year's holidays, he would be away for at least a month or so, and she felt she really was missing him a little.

"Don't you sing in the Muen Church choir?" asked the gentleman with great courtesy.

"Do you go to services at Muen too?" She was surprised that anyone would have taken notice of her.

"It just so happens I do," he replied with a smile.

As they swirled over the dance floor, they seemed to complement each other perfectly, as if by some unexpressed understanding. Although she had been troubled of heart recently and often felt depressed, still, being a young and wealthy young lady, her cares could not nag her for long; she smiled a happy smile, sensing that she had now finally been able to walk away from her timidity and ineptitude.

Chapter 22

The lunar New Year celebrations had come and gone, and already the Zhu household had sent to the Syi family over one hundred high quality gilt-edged teapots with a lotus flower decoration, which bore intricately engraved characters commemorating the marriage engagement, to be presented by the Syis to their friends and relatives. In addition there was a platinum ring set with a diamond huge as a soya bean, given as an engagement present.

For the past few days the back half of the Syi family parlor had been partitioned with sliding glass doors to accommodate a work table and a woman tailor, who had been engaged to do Zhishuang's wedding wardrobe. Zhishuang was a stylish girl who patronized only such foreign boutiques as Madam Garrison's or Green House, and viewed with disdain the work of Chinese women tailors, but when it came time to be a bride, the latter seemed to be indispensable in preparing a traditional trousseau of mandarin dresses and jackets. Once the tailor had installed herself, gorgeous silks and satins began piling up on her work table, a riot of color, which connoted auspicious happiness. This year's events worthy of celebration had been very few.

Zhishuang's betrothal infected the Syis' neighbors with a certain measure of happiness, and from time to time they'd amble over to look through the colorful tailoring, and offer a few congratulatory words to Mrs. Syi. Everyone knew that the Syi family was rising considerably in status by this marriage, and the neighbors instantly began treating Mrs. Syi with uncharacteristic courtesy and respect.

On this particular day Mrs. Tsao from next door came over to present a wedding gift—a pair of embroidered silk quilt-covers of fine Suzhou craftsmanship, worth at the very least twenty yuan each.

"Oh, they're so expensive," exclaimed Mrs. Syi politely. "Nowadays marriage engagements have become such empty formalities, but this is really much too thoughtful of you; I'm afraid you must have gone to great expense."

"Well, I've watched Zhishuang grow up too, and I really ought to have gotten something for her better than this, except that now Mr. Tsao is suffering from asthma and has to take frequent sick leave from the bank, and for a long time he hasn't received a salary raise. And now what with inflation, money this year isn't worth what it was last year, but he hasn't received any supplement, which in effect means he's suffered a salary decrease, so with our financial condition pretty tight now, I've even had to let the servants go." These past few years Mrs. Tsao had indeed aged greatly, and deep lines between her eyebrows gave the impression of permanent furrows.

In recent years because of rapidly changing conditions, Cathay's business practices had witnessed corresponding change. Tsao Jiusin, for example, was an old-style banker who didn't know English and gradually just couldn't turn himself to very good account. Cathay Republic Bank, after all, had a complex personnel component where everyone was competing with each other in pursuit of his own interests. The practice was always "to use a person when there's work to be done but ignore him when there's none," and no one more so than the ever cloddish Tsao Jiusin. This being the case, he inevitably got cold-shouldered and elbowed aside; depressed in heart, his long dormant asthma was now resurgent.

"It seems to me Mr. Tsao should have his illness treated with traditional herbal medicine," said Mrs. Syi consolingly. "You wouldn't need to be so concerned then, and with his health restored—well, while there's life there's hope, you know."

"Oh my, how can I not be concerned? How can we not feel distressed when the bank persists in cutting down the work force? They fired a whole bunch at Small East Gate, and just a few days ago someone came from the bank to talk with my husband, telling him if his health doesn't return pretty darn soon, he'd be better off taking old-age retirement and leading a quiet life! How can we do that? I've still got two youngsters who can't support themselves yet. So..." She pressed close to Mrs. Syi and whispered into her ear, "I wonder if Mr. Syi mightn't put in a good word with Mr. Zhu to let my old man stay on for a while longer whatever the case. Right now it's so tough for us, we can hardly get by; so if he could stay on at Cathay at least he could be sure of getting his allowance of rice and oil at pre-inflation prices, and if he could hang on until Cathay's employee housing is built, well that would give us even more security. Please help. Oh, please!"

Mrs. Syi now realized she could not possibly accept the wedding gift. "Good heavens," she began awkwardly, "you know my husband's attitude about such things. It'd be quite impossible for him to come right out and plead your case."

"It's easy for you to talk—your daughter is as good as married." Mrs. Tsao heard a key clinking at the front door, and assuming it to be Mr. Syi returning from work, and knowing also that Mr. Syi did not look very favorably upon her, she made a quick and quiet exit out the back door.

"Those able to, should take on extra work," or so the saying goes when you're asking someone to do a favor. Since Mr. Syi's transfer to Hong Kong as Cathay's branch manager, he ought to have been able to enjoy some leisure during his visits back in Shanghai. Yet it just so happened that these days he'd met up with a general audit of Cathay's underground safe deposit holdings. Syi Zhensyu had once worked in the vault and had done a very good job of it, winning everyone's praise. Consequently he was prevailed upon to work extra and help out. It wasn't that the work was particularly demanding, but it did require him to sit there every day silently supervising the audit; he couldn't even safely go to the bathroom lest in the moment he was out something happen. As a consequence by the end of the day he was utterly spent. When he returned and saw his normally bright and spacious parlor now ajumble with material of all colors and patterns, and, furthermore, found this tailor living in his own home endlessly jabbering away about this or that, as obvious and as uninteresting a person as a door set right before his very eyes every day, an indescribable rage began to build up inside him.

"When is this pile of stuff ever going to come to an end?" he asked his wife irritably when he went upstairs.

"Come to an end?" There was a hint of rebuke in her voice. "It's too early to be thinking of that. The Zhus are an important family, so if we don't put on a good showing, we'll just earn their contempt when Zhishuang moves into their household."

"How can we compete with them? We'd never catch up, and in another three years Chengzu will be in college, and we have to budget for that."

Mrs. Syi, seeing her husband's anger on this point, did not even dare to mention Mrs. Tsao's request. Just then the tailor called up from downstairs, "Mrs. Syi, someone's come to call!"

"The manager conveys his regards to Mr. Syi, and, purely as a matter of personal friendship, hopes that in future he may continue to be favored with Mr. Syi's kind consideration." And with that greeting, the caller, an office attendant, apparently, presented a business card, then beckoned to a couple of porters, who carried in two fifty-pound sacks of rice and four four-gallon containers of cooking oil; they then hurried off before Mr. Syi, who'd heard the commotion, could even get down to the front door.

"Wow, all of this food! We sure can use it," exclaimed the tailor as she gaped at the huge pile of stuff.

Mr. Syi took a look at the business card his wife handed him and was fairly stunned. "Extraordinary!" he cried, for it was the card of Mr. Eisaku of Nippon Shokin Bank. How come he has his eyes on me, he thought. Undoubtedly Eisaku had heard of the engagement of his daughter to Mr. Zhu's son. Truly, "it's the big tree that catches the gale," and trouble was indeed on the way for the Syis, who now constituted, as it were, a branch of Mr. Zhu, the big tree. Syi Zhensyu telephoned for a taxi and that very evening had the rice and oil sent to the bank. He then reported to Cathay exactly what had taken place, and, with the bank's concurrence, immediately purchased an airplane ticket and virtually fled to Hong Kong.

The first spring of the 1940s began amid discouragement and depression. As it became daily more obvious that Germany, Italy, and Japan on the one hand and England, America, and France on the other were becoming two great antagonistic camps, the International Settlement in Shanghai became its own peculiar sort of enemy-occupied enclave within the larger enemy-occupied territory, and life became infinitely more complex as resident nationals of the two camps broke off all commercial relations with each other. This mentality was maintained right through to autumn, when Roosevelt began to order the evacuation from China of American civilians and naval personnel. With that development American and British businessmen living in Shanghai all of a sudden began making hasty arrangements regarding their own property and interests and then sailed back home. Under these circumstances, it did not seem altogether appropriate that Juanren, son of Shanghai's well known Zhu Jingchen, retain his employment at the German pharmaceutical firm. But under the perilous conditions then prevailing, finding a new position with benefits comparable with those of his present German employer would certainly not be easy. Nor did Jingchen want his son to get caught up in the wheeling and dealing required to land a good job. But as for Juanren himself, he did not really want to leave his German company, reasoning that China and Germany were not at war, and that Bayer Pharmaceuticals was merely a commercial enterprise selling medicines, healing the sick and saving lives—and was there anything wrong with that? Honestly, why was it that when ordinary people were just trying to eke out a living, their lives were made the harsher by the exigencies of international politics?

On this day Jingchen was shut in his office gloomily smoking a cigarette as he listened to the radio news broadcast: the black market price of gold had tumbled, with one bar now down from 22,000 yuan to 14,000; and the black market price for rice had fallen back to 170 yuan per pound. From these fluctuations he could surmise how speculators were appraising the Shanghai situation. Regarding Shanghai's future, a thousand people might have a thousand different appraisals, and of course you could never be sure whose observations were most accurate...These musing were interrupted when Juanmin pushed the door open and came in.

"Daddy," she announced, "I'm going to go to Chungking."

Jingchen started, and looked at his daughter doubtfully.

"Jingsyao works for the American detachment billeted at the International Chamber of Commerce building. It's being transferred to Chungking, and I want to go with him." She spoke without inhibition.

This headstrong young lady! Her gambit caught Jingchen completely off guard. Although he could see that Jingsyao was a constant visitor, yet it had never occurred to him that Juanmin had been truly smitten with love. Ever since Juanmin had grown into beautiful womanhood, she seemed to change boyfriends as often as she changed her clothes. He imagined that this Feng Jingsyao, handsome, yes, but utterly lacking in financial resources, would before long leave Juanmin quite bored. Thus Jingchen had never taken any particular notice of their contact. And besides, he'd really been so busy that he'd had no time to involve himself with his daughters' affairs.

"Uh," he said as he lit up another cigarette. He stepped over to her side. "Wouldn't it be better to wait until you've graduated from college to decide?"

"That's still a year away, and a year later, who knows what the situation will be like. I thought I'd join Jingsyao and leave now while ship traffic can still get through."

"Jingsyao! Why doesn't he come here himself to talk with me?" Jingchen started to take out his anger on Feng Jingsyao, likening him in his mind to a virtual kidnapper.

"He really doesn't want me to go with him," said Juanmin, "so he doesn't want to come here to talk with you about it. But for sure, I'm going to go with him."

"What for?" he said in a quiet voice, keeping his gaze fixed on his favorite daughter. "Are you so dissatisfied and uncomfortable staying here at home? Why must you leave? If you do leave..."

"This is your home, yours and Miss Pu's home. Daddy, all day long you're just concerned about the bank loans, repayments, investments, outlays...When are you ever concerned about me? In this family everyone is just busy with his own affairs, and nobody needs me. But Jingsyao needs me—he's practically unable to take care of himself. And besides, I'm not just a child any more, and I ought to have my own life, a life that belongs completely to me!" She spoke with real fervor, though without histrionics. Apparently she simply could wait no longer to hoist her own sail and set off before the wind on her journey through life.

Jingchen smoked on and listened, then looked up. His expression showed disappointment and there was anger in his heart. "Have I as your father pampered you so much only to have you come to detest me like this?"

"Daddy!" Juanmin threw herself into her father's arms.

"Careful of the cigarette!" Jingchen put down his cigarette and stroked Juanmin's hair. "Daddy would really love to pick you up and hold you, but Daddy's too old to pick you up any more!"

Juanmin only now realized that underneath his baggy robes her father had become thin and frail when before he had been strong and muscular. How had this happened so suddenly and why had he sprouted scraggly white hairs at his temples?

"Forgive me, Daddy!" she sobbed.

Silence filled the room as Jingchen smoothed his daughter's hair. His thoughts went back twenty-one years to the day she had just come into the world. She didn't cry when she was born; the midwife slapped her bottom but she still wouldn't cry, so the midwife very nearly gave up trying further.

"Try again," he'd anxiously implored the midwife. "Try again and let's see." Although he already had a son, Jingchen nonetheless still dearly cherished this newly arrived tiny life. Because of his anxiety, he stretched out his own hand and slapped her reddened buttocks, the slap, as it turned out, that produced the cry. Now his daughter was grown up and the palm of his hand was of no more use. A grown daughter is not meant to remain in her parents' home, indeed cannot remain there.

"You can't compare Free China with Shanghai. Will you be able to get used to life there?" he asked seriously. He took his daughter's hand in his and watched the expression in her eyes.

Juanmin tilted her head to one side and smiled. "I know."

"If you marry Feng Jingsyao, you'll be sacrificing a great deal. Is it worth it?" Jingchen cleared his throat with an effort.

"I know." Juanmin patted the back of her father's hand. Brownish age spots had already begun to appear.

"Do exercise greater care! Perhaps you should look around some more."

"Daddy, didn't you promise me not to interfere with my marriage decision?" Her voice was a barely audible whisper.

"If you're going to marry a man without any resources, you have to make a pretty thorough appraisal of things. You need to know that after getting married you'll be facing many practical problems, and to live a life always short of cash—well, will you be happy with that?"

"But Uncle Jingwen and Miss Yi have had a very happy life together! I've never seen a couple who get along better with each other than those two," said Juanmin biting her fingernails as she spoke with shyness, albeit complete conviction.

"Well..." Jingchen chuckled, as he threw up his hands in resignation. "What else can I say?" His voice was hoarse.

"Oh, Daddy." Juanmin again fell into her father's embrace. "Juanying and Juanwei and Juansi will all look after you. You won't be lonely."

"Well, I don't know about that." Jingchen shrugged his shoulders and let out a sigh. Then he stood up. "I must give you a wedding gift."

He led Juanmin into the study, opened his strongbox, and brought out that lustrous cocksblood stone, the very heirloom treasure which Jingsyao had presented to Zhu Jingchen in gratitude for so many years of concern and support for his own family.

"Now this may be returned to its original owner. But, you must have Feng Jingsyao come here personally to receive it, for in any case there are matters about which he must speak to me. For example, guaranteeing that he will not deceive you..."

"Daddy, that's impossible!" exclaimed Juanmin bashfully.

"Must you go to Chungking?" He hesitated a moment. "If you don't, couldn't I find a job for Jingsyao?"

"But Daddy, Jingsyao has a great deal of self-respect..."

Jingchen sensed there was really nothing further he could say. He opened the drawer, and wrote out a large check for her.

"Oh, thank you, Daddy!" Juanmin accepted the check with an abstract expression. If fact, however, she had a real need for the money, for she'd be setting up a small household and would have to see to furnishing it, and so on. And Jingsyao had practically no savings. Jingchen watched with doting eyes as she left. The pale rays of the western sun penetrated the window panes and fell across his face: he seemed suddenly to have aged a decade.

Juanmin passed down the thickly carpeted hallway—silent, not a soul about—and returned to her room. Juanying had not yet come home from work, and the two younger sisters were not yet back from school. The crimson rays of the afternoon sun shone on the white French-style furniture. Arranged against the north wall were four brass beds with punchwork lace bedspreads; the four sisters had shared this bedroom for over ten years. Her own bed was closest to the door because when she went out with Jingsyao on dates she usually returned very late, and so as not to disturb her three sisters she and the ever reasonable Juanying had switched beds. And now before long she would be taking her leave from here. She knew very well what her father meant when he said she'd be "facing practical problems." No nightclubs, no private car, no tailors or jewelers who'd come to call at regular intervals...Yet withal, she would have something which truly belonged to her—a family with whose cares she could immediately begin to concern herself, a family she could not do without for another minute.

One morning as he was sipping his coffee, Jingsyao had said quite casually, "I'm going to go to Chungking." It was a tone of voice which might as well have said, "I'm going to pop over to Jingan Temple."

"Why?" asked a startled Juanmin.

"Roosevelt has ordered redeployment of a portion of the American naval and land forces stationed in China, and I want to follow along with them." Jingsyao now had a job working for the U.S. Army.

He was wearing a well fitted American-style Army uniform of green wool with a matching light green necktie, which accentuated all the more his tall slender figure and his stylish bearing. An expensive FiveFiveFive cigarette dangling from his lips, he stepped over to the corner of the room to light it, and as the match flared up and illuminated the groove chiseled from his nostrils down his upper lip, a firm resolve seemed to emerge, which lent him an irresistible appeal.

"And what about me?" she blurted out. "What am I supposed to do?"

He bent over her and squeezed her hand gently. "I'll write you often, and I'll wait for you to graduate from college; then we can decide."

"You mean you're going to cast me off alone in Shanghai?" Juanmin stared at him in consternation.

"How can you call it 'casting you off in Shanghai?' You've got a family in Shanghai, a father, all kinds of brothers and sisters..." Jingsyao stuffed his hands into his pockets and spoke rather impatiently.

"Yes, but you won't be here!" she shouted back, interrupting him like a headstrong little girl.

He lowered his head and smoked his cigarette for a while, then, as if it were an effort to find the appropriate words, looked up at her and said, "Juanmin, this is not the time for bursts of anger. To be perfectly frank, a person like me might be best described as having the temperament of a prodigal and the destiny of a beggar, and I am in absolutely no position to make any promises to you about guaranteeing your happiness...I've always thought that what might be most appropriate for me would be to find an orphan who'd been brought up from childhood by foreign missionaries, pure in spirit, simple in her desires, and rather plain in looks, who could live with adversity, a Jane Eyre type in fact, who..."

"So go look for her! I'll let you go look for her!"

Not waiting for him to finish, Juanmin grabbed the half-full cup of coffee on the table in front of her and splashed it right into his face.

"You're crazy!" he cried out, caught utterly by surprise. Juanmin lifted her ashen face and stared straight at him. He was so stunned he might have been struck by lightning. He then knelt down in front of her and buried his head in her bosom and mumbled, "You know how sometimes I hate it so much—hate it that you're so beautiful, so aristocratic, yet so good to me..."

"But why?" she asked, knowing the answer full well. The fact was, Jingsyao on purpose frequently exhibited an outward indifference, arrogance, and hopelessness as if he had to be on guard at all times not to allow himself to get mired to deeply in love, yet it happened to be precisely this supercilious aloofness and intractable obstinacy that positively intoxicated Juanmin.

"Because it's so easy for wealthy people to assume a heroic posture. But me...actually I'm a very humble person intimidated by the name of Zhu and by your family and by your father who offered himself as the savior of the Feng household!"

"When we get to Chungking, none of this will exist any more. People there will simply know me as...Mrs. Feng." Juanmin closed her eyes and snuggled against him.

"Juanmin, I'm so very fond of you! I want to make you happy."

"Mere fondness?" she asked as if unjustly wronged.

"Um, well 'love,' then," he said, using the English word.

"Anything else?"

"I wonder if you really want to hear me repeat those hackneyed lines from the movies," he said gently.

"But no one has ever spoken those hackneyed lines to me before. Go ahead, humor me along; no one's ever humored me along before, nor doted on me..." She rested her head against his shoulder.

"You silly little girl! My dearest, I could treasure you because you are so important to me..." He rocked her gently back and forth as if a child being rocked to sleep, using English to talk the sweet words of love, immersing her in a hitherto undreamed of happiness.

That moving scene had forever been fixed in Juanmin's memory. She lay on the bed she'd been sleeping in for ten years and, face down on the smoothly ironed flowered bedspread, she tucked her hands between the pillow and sheet. From now on she would have few opportunities to come back to this bed of her maidenhood, which every night had embraced her in sleep. She buried her face in the pillow and rolled her head back and forth as a complex of feelings welled up within her.

Two months later Juanmin and Jingsyao traveled via Hong Kong into the hinterland. Jingsyao passed on his apartment to Tsai Liren. In recent years Tsai Liren had traveled the Burma Road quite frequently as he pursued a business venture in foreign paper products. Having made a great deal of money, he set up home in Jingsyao's apartment, as it was very comfortable and safe. Since the recent withdrawal of British forces, there remained in the International Settlement only a small American military contingent—by itself, of course, no more effective in providing security against the Japanese than one hand by itself is effective in producing a clap—yet because of the confidence people had in America's wealth and power, the population of the International Settlement continued its steady increase, causing housing costs to spiral upward with frightening speed, particularly apartments like Feng Jingsyao's which was located both within the American defense zone and near the International Chamber of Commerce building where the American troops were billeted. The rent was shockingly expensive, a fact which brought a sudden and precipitous rise in Tsai Liren's social status.

The situation in Shanghai was becoming more threatening by the day, and even the construction which had started on Cathay's employee housing had to be suspended midway because of wartime disruption of transport and resultant lack of building materials, and because of insufficient funds as well.

Jingchen more and more felt that he was living in an environment which debased the good in people, and that it would be impossible for him to remain aloof from the corrupting influences all about him. On January 6, 1941, the Nanking-headquartered Central Reserve Bank, now a Japanese-controlled puppet institution, announced the establishment of a Shanghai branch at No. 15 on the Bund—the very address of the former Central Bank of China, and Jingchen had been invited by the branch manager, Chian Dahuai, to the opening ceremony on January 20th. The invitation was delivered to his office.

"Who does this Chian Dahuai think he is!" Jingchen threw down the invitation as he began reviling the man. "He used to be just a minor character doing odds and ends at Jincheng Bank in Dairen. He engaged in speculation before the outbreak of the war with Japan and lost over 10,000 yuan of bank assets, so he lost his job in Dairen. Later, thanks to his social butterfly of a wife who built him up, he began to specialize in kissing the Japs' asses, producing juicy results as he wormed his way into their confidence. I heard later on that he wrangled his appointment as Shanghai branch manager of this puppet bank when the director general, that traitor Zhou Fohai, was setting it up. People like Chian Dahuai stink and if I have dealings with his type, I'll end up stinking too!"

"Well, remember, Mr. Zhu," advised one Cathay staffer, "'don't let small setbacks ruin large plans.'"

"One always has to maintain civilities with that type," advised another.

"Damn!" exploded Jingchen. "Bastards like him have insatiable appetites. Give 'em an inch and they take a mile. The best thing is to ignore them and treat them as nobodies."

The fact was, however, those "nobodies" were really big "somebodies" who could hardly be ignored.

Before long the Japanese-controlled Central Reserve Bank of China began to expand its sales of reserve certificates, and schemed every way possible to expand them right into the International Settlement. One day a couple of Chinese—agents of the Japanese—came to Cathay to see Jingchen, who put them off, however, with the excuse he was feeling unwell, sending in his stead an assistant vice-president who had resided in Japan. The callers, combining sweet talk with harsh threats, wanted Cathay to sign an agreement by which Cathay would redeem Central Reserve certificates, and even hinted that Central Reserve Bank had already preferred demands upon several government banks to open accounts for the redemption of these reserve certificates in amounts of one hundred thousand yuan each.

An emergency meeting of the General Affairs Department convened shortly thereafter. "According to reports," that assistant vice-president said, "the privately owned Huiyuan Bank has formally agreed with the puppet Central Reserve to redeem their bonds. Now, do we want to swim with the current and sign up for a small amount in order to maintain civility with them?"

"Don't we already understand the Japs well enough now?" asked Zhu Jingchen, impatiently tapping the table with his pen. "China has come to grief precisely because it has capitulated time after time to those Jap scoundrels, such that in the end we'll simply be letting them swallow up the whole country like a hunk of juicy meat. We'd never be able to placate them enough. Cathay Republic Bank is a bank for Chinese and those Japs had better not try to elbow their way in!" He spoke without equivocation.

Early the next morning, there came news that a Mr. Li of Huiyuan Bank—precisely the Mr. Li who had signed an agreement to buy those bogus Central Reserve certificates—had been gunned down on the street. This doubtless was the work of Chungking agents who had disposed of him as a Chinese traitor. Jingchen now secretly rejoiced in his own prescience and resolve. Then, not many days later, came news that the bona fide Central Bank of China, which had already felt compelled to move to Baikal Road in the International Settlement, had sustained a bomb explosion, perpetrated, of course, by Chinese collaborators, which had been provoked by Central Bank's refusal to redeem the certificates issued by the puppet Central Reserve Bank.

These were days when Zhu Jingchen was getting squeezed from every side. He was physically and mentally exhausted, and his hair had turned completely gray. He almost starting thinking about closing down Cathay altogether, shutting himself up at home in quiet retirement, and to hell with the rest. Tsai Liren's advice was right to the point: if you should find yourself in an impossible situation, you might just as well go into temporary retirement, and only when things had cooled down, reconsider. Fortunately, he could get along for years on a diet of quiet home life. But the present situation scarce compared with the closure earlier of Small East Gate branch; in the present case there would be several hundred employees involved who would be instantly enraged, and that would be no laughing matter. He recalled how his brother Jingwen had caused the fury of his workers, so that to this very day he had remained holed up in Hong Kong not daring to return to Shanghai. How much more fury might arise should Cathay's hundreds of employees one day be offended by that bank president who just sits in an office: would not the numerous members of the Zhu household, young and old alike, feel threatened?

Quite a few of his colleagues at Cathay had urged him to leave Shanghai and go to Hong Kong.

"Mr. Zhu, you're our boss and if anything untoward should happen to you, we'd be like a dragon without a head. It would be better for you to take advantage of the present opportunity and escape to Hong Kong; we could maintain daily telephone contact with you. Business here could be handled by the board of directors."

"No," Jingchen had replied. "As long as Cathay exists, I won't leave it. Besides, prospects aren't necessarily so pessimistic as you gentlemen seem to think. The International Settlement in Shanghai, after all, has a history of one hundred years behind it, so how could Japan be so rash as to invade and occupy it just like that? My assessment is that even if the British and Americans pull out from the International Settlement, it's quite possible that Switzerland or some other neutral nation would assume the administration of the Settlement. In my view the crisis in Shanghai is first and foremost probably an economic one. Furthermore, the black market price of gold has dropped sharply from 22,000 yuan per bar to 14,000, and the market price of rice has fallen back to 170 yuan, all of which goes to show that the International Settlement is still a relatively safe place."

Despite the fact that Jingchen himself only half believed his own argument, nonetheless to get people calmed down he could hardly say anything else.

A personal experience shortly thereafter, however, counteracted the tranquilizer he had administered to his colleagues.

One day Ayi was driving him home after work. While the car was waiting for a red light, a pedicab drew abreast in the slow-traffic lane stopping next to Jingchen's car, and he could see the profile of a woman's face, as dignified as a marble statue.

Good heavens! It was Mrs. Wei, or rather Mrs. Gong, as she should now be called. As always appealingly graceful, she was wrapped in a choice sable coat with upturned collar covering half her face, and on her knees she was carefully holding a large package in her chammois-gloved hands. In a moment the light turned green and Jingchen's car soon left Mrs. Gong behind.

He had long since heard that Mr. Gong had accompanied his bank when it moved to Chungking. But since people of his rank—assistant vice-president—could take their families with them on the retreat inland, how was it she had not accompanied him?

From the reflection in the rear-view mirror, Jingchen watched fondly as her pedicab receded into the distance. Then suddenly, by what one might call his sixth sense, he became aware that the rear-view mirror also reflected another car which, neither speeding forward nor falling behind, seemed to be following him.

He tapped the back of Ayi's seat and pointed with pursed lips toward the rear-view mirror.

"I've already seen him," said Ayi calmly.

"Let's make sure about it. Turn at the next intersection and we'll double back," said Jingchen.

As expected, the car following them also turned.

Ayi circled the block and came back to the main street where they'd just been. Now Jingchen spotted Mrs. Gong's pedicab stopped at a shop not far ahead, which Mrs. Gong was just entering.

"I'll get out right here. Don't worry about me, just drive back to the bank." And with those instructions, Jingchen jumped out of the car and followed Mrs. Gong right toward the shop. Just as he was about to push open the door, he saw reflected in the glass of the display window that the car which had been following him was also stopped at a distance.

The store he stepped into was a secondhand shop. Off in one corner at the appraisals counter he saw Mrs. Gong arguing prices with a clerk. "...Just look at this quality. Where do you see otter coats like this nowadays? One year I wore it once to a Mei Lanfang opera performance, and never had it on for more that a total of two hours. If it weren't for the fact it's out of style, I'd never think of selling it."

"Then in my opinion, Mrs. Gong," advised the clerk with an admixture of courtesy and sarcasm, "it's really not worthwhile for you to sell it. Keep it to show yourself off in. Anyway, styles these days are very much in flux—after long styles come short styles, and after marketing short styles, long one come back, a cycle of long and short, short and long. Put it away for a few years, and then it'll be right back in style. If you do want to sell it, though, it certainly won't be very profitable for you. To be perfectly honest, people who can afford to wear fine furs like this really don't want to wear secondhand goods, and people who can't afford them don't want them whether new or used. The truth of the matter is, a business like ours exists simply to spare a little money to people who are short on cash." These icy remarks so flabbergasted Mrs. Gong she turned crimson.

"Mrs. Gong!" Zhu Jingchen approached and tapped her on the shoulder, quite indifferent to her embarrassment. "Is there a back door here? Some Japanese out front have their eyes on me."

Without waiting for Mrs. Gong's reply, the clerk lifted the countertop opening and motioned him inside. "Follow me a ways," said Jingchen to Mrs. Gong, and he took her arm and groped along a dim hallway piled high with stock toward the back door, which let out onto a dark alley. The alley in turn led to a deserted narrow street. At the base of the tall buildings a cold wind soughed, confirming the truth of the saying, "a spring chill seems even colder than a winter freeze."

A pedicab happened to be standing at the cross street ahead. Jingchen pulled Mrs. Gong into it with him. Looking around to see that they weren't being followed, Jingchen finally said, "First let me take you back home. Do you still live at your old place?" Before her reply came, his gaze fell on the package she was holding on her knees. She had come to the store in the first place to sell her fur coat, but Jingchen's barging in had interrupted the transaction. By the looks of it, Mrs. Gong's lifestyle was none too affluent, and she had to rely on selling off family property to get by. Recalling how Mr. Wei had left a very considerable amount of money to her, he wondered how she had now found herself in such a plight as this.

"Is Mr. Gong well?" he probed. "Do you occasionally get letters?"

"Yes," she replied simply.

"And how are the children?" he asked, referring to the two children by Mr. Wei's first marriage.

"One is in high school, and the other will soon graduate from junior high." Mention of the children brought a gratified smile to her lips. "They're very good at their school work. The boy is at St. John's High School, and his younger sister is at McTyeire."

Naturally her children would be studying at the best schools, but why did Mrs. Gong herself...He looked at her, so carefully holding that package containing her otter coat. Sitting close by, dark though it was, he could still make out the lines around her eyes and the drooping bags beneath. A woman bringing up two children without a cent of income—that was tough.

Mrs. Gong's home was on a broad and quiet lane in the French Concession, a home Mr. Wei had bought particularly for the installation of the then Miss Mary Luo.

She stepped down from the pedicab, and asked without really meaning it, "If you like, Mr. Zhu, why don't you come in and have a cup of tea." She was still holding her package, a light package, to be sure, but even so she hardly seemed to have the strength for it.

"Another time, thank you," he said, declining politely. As the pedicab moved down the lane he looked back at that house which he used to visit so often. It was a hybrid Sino-western residence of three stories, each with three main rooms. Inexplicably for this time of day, the place was pitch dark, with not a single light burning in any window on any floor. When Mr. Wei was still here, wasn't the place always abustle with friends and callers? Sometimes they were playing mahjong, sometimes singing opera, or maybe discussing market trends—the place would be brightly lit every night. But after the passage of just these few years, another man, hardly expending even a breath of effort, majestically took over as master of the house. Such men are shameless! If Mr. Wei in his after world could know of it, oh, how he would weep! When you think about it, man's life in this world is utterly fruitless: while living, there is hardship as one labors for the financial benefit of one's family, and when it is time to be laid out in one's coffin, how do you know but what someone else won't ruin your enterprises and squander your property. Pity is, Zhu Jingchen, who had seen so much, could not yet figure it out. Since he was still living in this mortal world, he still had a few more bouts to fight as best he could so as not to incur other people's ridicule.

As evening deepened, he began carefully turning things over in his mind, and sensed that he absolutely must not return to his own home, that it would be much better to hide out a few days in Tsai Liren's apartment. Located near the American military compound, it was relatively safe there.

Starting that day Jingchen took extended sick leave and did not go to the bank, staying instead at Tsai Liren's where he directed daily bank operations by telephone.

The winter days in Tsai's apartment seemed very long, and even the daylight hours were dreary; and because coal was in short supply, the building's steam heat had long since been turned off. Jingchen perforce hardly ever took off his long padded gown, which further added to his depression and made him feel old age was setting in.

One morning, following his normal routine, he was in the bathroom scrubbing his chamber pot, a white enamel chamber pot with a blue rim, which he scrubbed until it gleamed without a speck of soil remaining. This was one of the few vestiges of Jingchen's apprentice years, when it had been his job to clean the chamber pots of the dozens of senior apprentices. Another habit retained from that earlier life of his was to eat while standing. Jingchen intentionally preserved these two habits both as a matter of personal discipline and as a reminder of those hard times before he started prospering, which thus afforded him a certain happy self-satisfaction.

"Mr. Zhu," said Tsai Liren coming into the apartment with the newspaper he'd just gone out to buy. "It says here that a Japanese employee of the puppet Central Reserve Bank was assassinated."

"What?" Jingchen took the paper and began reading intently. Just then the telephone rang.

"For you, sir," said Tsai Liren to Jingchen. In his big three-room apartment there was neither maid nor manservant, so it was Tsai Liren himself who kept everything neat and tidy. He disliked that in his private life there should be outsiders with whom he had no connection, and the trouble of looking after himself was preferable to having a maid around.

When Jingchen had finished his telephone call and reappeared, his face was deathly pale.

It seems that a Japanese employee of Central Reserve had been murdered just as, by chance, he was returning from Cathay Republic, and the Japanese were threatening to take three Chinese lives as compensation; indeed they had already sent men from the dreaded "No. 76" to break into the homes of Cathay personnel on the Chinese stretch of Robison Road, where they summarily arrested twelve employees including the infirm Tsao Jiusin, who was pulled out of his sickbed and taken off.

Zhu Jingchen hurriedly dressed himself.

"Mr. Zhu!" exclaimed Tsai Liren tugging at him. "You can't go out, it's too dangerous. It's obvious that Chinese collaborators are trying to provoke something with Cathay. The International Settlement hasn't the slightest power or influence now. You mustn't go."

"Right now the families of those twelve employees are at the bank terribly distraught; of course, as head of the bank, I've got to go and try to calm them down. How could I possibly turn a blind eye to them? I've simply got to find some way to rescue them."

"Rescue them..." Tsai Liren furrowed his brow. "If you're going to rescue them, you've first got to see if anybody at Cathay might have close private connections with some high-ranking officer in the Nanking puppet government or its Central Reserve Bank who might intercede for us in the matter."

"How could I find such a person?" asked Jingchen, throwing up his hands in despair. "Every one of our employees is perfectly innocent of any dealings with the puppet government."

"Yes, but later on..." Tsai Liren was silent for a while, then continued. "Mr. Zhu, you can't go on hiding here forever trying to evade the Chinese collaborators. You've got to find someone with private connections to the puppet government in Nanking and at the very least ask him to assume a nominal title at Cathay. Everything would be so much simpler that way."

Jingchen felt chills go up and down his spine. Could it really be that he would have to wallow in the mire with them?

"Otherwise," added Tsai Liren confidently, "you'll never know what's going on with the Japanese, and you'll end up suffering for it."

Jingchen said nothing as he let out a long sigh.

"Let me go with you," Tsai Liren offered, pulling his car keys from his pocket. Since his business success, he'd bought a secondhand Ford.

For the next several days Jingchen, disregarding any danger he might bring upon himself, personally took up the matter, passing out his business card as he rushed one after the other to the police stations in the International Settlement and in the French Concession, then to the chambers of commerce and to foreign firms, everywhere appealing for help, but whenever he mentioned the involvement of No. 76, no one dared to act on his own to help. Even his wife made an effort by paying calls on important American and European figures in the YWCA—vain exertions in every case.

Once when he happened to pass by Mrs. Gong's lane he suddenly recalled that Mr. Gong of Bank of China seemed to have an especially close connection with a Chamber of Commerce director who had studied at a Japanese military academy: mightn't Jingchen ask Mrs. Gong to intercede for him? Since Mr. Gong was not in Shanghai, it might well be that it would be easier for Mrs. Gong to get something accomplished, for in some matters Mrs. Gong could intercede with greater effectiveness.

Mrs. Gong's home, like all the homes on this upper class lane, had a small flower garden, a lush velvety front lawn, and a narrow black-graveled path leading from the metal gate to the front steps. The entire lane had a western flavor to it, especially the wonderfully pleasant flower garden of this home—formerly Mr. Wei's—which used to be kept in luxuriant condition by Mrs. Wei, the present Mrs. Gong. Not so today, however. In just the few months since Jingchen had last come here, the courtyard at Mrs. Gong's home had become overgrown with weeds and it was now piled with boxes tightly covered with oil cloth. As he was about to lift his hand to ring the bell, he saw a large notice posted on the main entrance gate: PLEASE USE REAR ENTRANCE, which instantly aroused an ominous feeling in him.

He wended his way to the rear door. Mrs. Gong was inside with her back to the window, busying herself over a briquette stove. Jingchen tapped on the window; she turned around to look. Not having made up her face or put on any jewelry, she appeared pallid and aged in the extreme.

"Oh, Mr. Zhu!" She hurried to open the door, then returned to her stove, where a pot of dough-drop soup was boiling. "Dough-drop soup," she said apologetically as she stirred the sticky stuff with a long spoon; "it's just like milk—once it boils over you can't get it up again." The air was laden with the smell of burned dough, reminding Jingchen of the odor of glue when the maids at home cooked starch to stiffen his shirts.

Because the price of rice and vegetables was going up every day, many Shanghai residents had taken to substituting dough-drop soup for rice at meal time, but Jingchen had never imagined that Mrs. Gong would have to resort to such fare! How could she swallow the stuff?

"You've doubtless come to call because you have some particular matter to discuss, Mr. Zhu?" she asked as she added a few stingy drops of her precious vegetable oil to the soup. "Are the Japs tailing you again?"

"Just a moment ago I was at the front gate but with the entrance closed off I was wondering if you'd moved away, perhaps to Hong Kong or Chungking to rejoin Mr. Gong." Jingchen opened the conversation by probing discreetly.

"Rejoin him?" queried Mrs. Gong with a tragic smile. "Since he went to Chungking, he's written only twice, and, I hardly need say, he's sent no money. My money, every last cent of it, he took to Chungking with him, telling me that financial markets in Free China were stable and dependable and safe. And I believed him. Too much. Men just aren't to be relied upon. Isn't the Chungking government now saying that because of the excessive population losses during the war, if wives have not been with their husbands for two years, then husbands may remarry? Now they're not even calling them concubines; they're called war-brides..." Her voice was full of resentment, as she vehemently stirred the pot, panting as she spoke. Jingchen offered her a cigarette, but she'd given up smoking, she said.

"And now you've got the two children to bring up. It certainly must be hard for you." Jingchen sighed as he spoke, noticing now for the first time that her hands were not those same soft white hands that used to play mahjong.

"It certainly is! In the beginning I could presume on my old friends for help so I managed to get by more or less, but later on...Those old acquaintances have been avoiding me like the plague...Can't blame them, though—people are all like that. Anyway, I now take it one day at a time. To begin with, I've rented out the house to someone who's made it in war profiteering, and now the two children and I are squeezed into a front room on the third floor, and if that doesn't do it, I can still sell off property—the piano, the refrigerator, leather chairs—I can get rid of them all. I'll sell what I can sell even though money isn't worth what it used to be. You've got to stay alive," she exclaimed with an icy smile. Then, suddenly remembering, she turned toward him and asked, "What is it you want?"

"Nothing in particular. I just happened to be passing by and thought I'd call on you. Bank business has been a terrible headache for me recently, so I haven't been able to come around to see you." Saying this, he drew from his coat pocket a wad of bills and pressed it into her hand. "Take this little bit of money and use it for yourself; it's not enough to solve all your problems, but it is a token of my concern for you."

She wasn't at all politely demure about it. She took the bills and began nimbly counting them. "Later on when Mr. Gong returns," she said, "I'll have him repay you. He'll certainly come back at least once to see me. 'Even blood brothers settle their debts,' you know, so let's keep track of the amount."

Jingchen felt a momentary grief, stayed the hand counting the bills and said, "It's just a trifle, don't worry about it."

"No," she said with dignified reserve, "I'll certainly have him repay you."

"I've got to be going now. Do take care of yourself." He wanted to rush out of the place.

"It's just as well to leave. I'm afraid I can't ask you in to visit. To be honest, out of the whole house there's only one room left to me, so there's no place to sit and chat anyway."

As he was going out the back entrance, Jingchen felt a little faint, and he remembered he'd not only missed his noon meal, but hadn't eaten any breakfast either. It would seem that the option of using Mrs. Gong was no longer a viable one.

A week passed and still there was no good news resulting from his attempts to help the Cathay employees under arrest. One day he went to foreign-owned Huifeng Bank in quest of assistance, only to be put off with a "Sorry"—they'd like to help but couldn't.

With intermingled sadness and indignation Jingchen quickened his weary pace across the bank's main lobby toward the exit. That in his own country he should have to approach foreigners with flattering words trying to secure their intercession and in the end still come up empty-handed! Chinese law, Chinese police, Chinese government— where had they all gone? The nation was too weak to resist, was so weak that even these contemptible Japanese could run rampant in complete disregard of the law. Ignored by his own government, Zhu Jingchen, who had worked hard his whole life and was now getting old, had to shoulder the responsibility by himself. What injustice!

"Hello, Mr. Zhu!" In the bank lobby a gentleman with hat pulled low reading a newspaper called to him. Jingchen stopped and cautiously looked his way. The face, half hidden by the hat brim, was strong and square and his eyes sparkled with intelligence.

"Fan Yangzhi!" Since the closing of Small East Gate branch Jingchen had not once seen Fan Yangzhi, so that beholding him now, smartly dressed in a gray pin-striped suit with a fine-grained German leather portfolio clasped against his side, he was to all appearances in circumstances far better than those when he was at Cathay. It was obvious that any intelligent young man could find employment if not at one place, then certainly at another. How true it was, "when a person returns after an absence we must look upon him with new eyes."

"Mr. Fan, you've done very well for yourself! Where are you employed now? Still in banking?" asked Jingchen courteously. If today's parvenus weren't speculators, then they were collaborators, and he wondered which path Fan Yangzhi was walking.

Fan Yangzhi responded with the name of his company—a collaborationist trading company devoted to business with the Japanese.

"Ah...no wonder!" sneered Jingchen.

"I had no alternative," replied Fan Yangzhi, twisting his fedora in his hands. "A person's got to eat, and I still have my mother and widowed sister to support, so it's unavoidable that I go where the work is. But in here," pointing to his breast, "there beats the heart of a Chinese." His reply was composed and relaxed, and his intelligent eyes glistened with tears as he looked at Jingchen. "Mr. Zhu, if you have an opening where you might be able to use me, I should be forever obliged to you."

"Thank you," said Jingchen, nodding to him icily, while in his heart he cursed him, "Thanks a million—but if I have anything to do with you, it'll be bad luck for me!"

"Here is my card, showing my address and telephone number," he said, offering his business card to Jingchen.

"Oh..." Suddenly remembering, Jingchen took the card and asked hesitantly, "Are you free now, Mr. Fan? Let's go out for a cup of coffee, shall we? There's something I'd like to ask of you."

At last there seemed to be a solution to all his problems. It really was a case of "searching far and wide only to chance upon it close at hand." The owner of the company where Fan Yangzhi worked was friendly with Wu Sibao of No. 76, and Wu Sibao also appeared to be beholden to Du Yuesheng. Thus one could attack the problem from both angles—on the one hand ask Fan Yangzhi's collaborator boss to plead the case with Wu Sibao, and on the other ask Du Yuesheng, now in Hong Kong, to wire his Shanghai protégé, Gao Lansheng, to visit Wu Sibao and apply a little pressure, so that finally No. 76 would agree to release the men. But this plan would certainly require Zhu Jingchen and that collaborator boss to act as personal guarantors.

Finally, on the day for the release on bail of the detainees, Fan Yangzhi and his employer, along with Jingchen and Cathay's board chairman Mr. Li as well, all went to No. 76 Jessfield Road. While Jingchen could be said to be a long-time Shanghai resident, this was the first time he had experienced a place like No. 76. As the great outer gate opened, one saw guards shouldering loaded rifles, all dressed in green uniforms, lacking only insignia on their caps. Before the inner entrance a ceremonial archway had been erected, from which a horizontal plaque was suspended bearing the government's grand-sounding slogan, "Brotherhood of Mankind." As the callers stepped inside, Jingchen noticed that Chairman Li's legs were trembling like vibrating fiddle strings.

The procedures for securing the release of the detainees were handled in a room just to the east of the inside entrance, where Chinese puppet personnel brought out a sheaf of guarantee papers—one for each of the twelve detainees—to which, one by one, the guarantors had to affix their personal seals.

Twelve guarantee papers—it seemed they were stamping them forever still without getting through them all. How anxious they were to wind up their business and leave this evil lair.

Everyone was jittery. Silence reigned in the room, save for the sound of stamping documents.

"The life span of this riff-raff's gonna be over and done with!" Everybody started as the silence was suddenly shattered by a woman's voice. Then the woman herself charged in, her face caked with make-up, her hair done up in curls, the perfect image of some hoodlum's moll. Even the side slits in her mandarin-style dress ran all the way up to her thighs. Propping her foot up on a bench, she swept her cold and indifferent eyes across the group and began arrogantly ranting at them. "Lemme put it to youz people straight. If anyone gets in my way again, I'll kill 'em one by one and toss 'em into the Huangpu River so you'll become just so many corpses floating in the water, so putrefied your bodies won't even be fit for proper burial!" So saying, she gesticulated wildly, smoothed out her dress, glared at no one in particular, and swaggered out. She was none other than Wu Sibao's wife, Yu Aizhen.

Neither Jingchen nor Mr. Li in their long years of being surrounded by hangers-on had ever endured such ill-bred taunts. And how much more so when it came from a moll the likes of her. But considering she was the wife of Wu Sibao who kiss-assed the Japanese, there was nothing for it but to swallow one's outrage.

It was close to dusk by the time the twelve Cathay employees, all silenced by fright, were finally released. Escorted by MPs, they shuffled out single file, oldest among them being the piteous Tsao Jiusin whose asthma had flared up, so terrified he was barely able to walk. Jingchen did not dare make a move to help him, praying only that this whole nightmare could soon be put behind them.

"Hold it!" One of the puppet clerks stopped them with a gesture, and Jingchen's heart pounded as he nervously observed the man, fearful the Chinese puppets would go back on their word. "This won't do for Mr. Tsao here; we'll have a car send him home," said the clerk.

Quaking with fright, Tsao Jiusin waved his hand as if to say don't trouble yourselves, but the fact was he was so weakened he couldn't even talk, and he just leaned against the wall panting.

Well, at bottom they were still Chinese, and their hearts had not been entirely devoured by dogs. Jingchen nodded to them gratefully, and whispered to Tsao Jiusin, "'It's best to show one's respect by obedience,' you know, so let them drive you home; anyway your wife is anxiously waiting for you."

Tsao Jiusin's eyes seemed to glaze over, giving him a vague and distant look. Imprisonment for over a week had turned the already debilitated Mr. Tsao into a befuddled and dazed old man. After he gets back home, thought Jingchen to himself sadly, he'll never be to resume his work at the bank.

A glossy black sedan pulled up in front of them, lights on, engine running; the driver—a puppet soldier—opened the car door and said to Tsao Jiusin, "Please get in."

Jingchen was about to offer his arm when another of the puppet soldiers rushed ahead to help him into the car. Tsao Jiusin's filthy gown seemed terribly baggy, flapping loosely and getting in his way. As he stepped onto the runningboard, he turned back toward Jingchen to smile in appreciation, but the smile that appeared on his pallid, blood-drained face was an involuntary grimace of misery. He dug his fingers, emaciated as chicken feet, into the driver's seat-back and pulled himself into the automobile. The soldier assisting him also slipped in and sat down close beside him. Jingchen suddenly sensed something ominous about the soldier's manner, and the purring of the engine had a somehow frightening quality. Then, almost before he knew it, the Chinese turncoat waved through the car window. "My apologies to the rest of you gentlemen," he said, and the car whooshed off in a cloud of exhaust. Hardly had he spoken those words than the others hurried away from No. 76 without so much as looking back.

Few pedestrians even at normal hours walked the street where this hellish house was located, and at this time of day, there was hardly a soul about. The deserted street was a stretch of black silence, not, however, the ordinary kind of quiet tranquillity, but rather a deathly hush. A lighted street lamp or two only accentuated the sinister bleakness. Jingchen looked up and swept his gaze across the gray heavens, and sighed a deep sigh of relief.

But it proved to be a false relief.

That night he was wakened with a start by the jangle of the telephone: it was Tsao Jiusin's daughter. It seems that after the soldiers had driven Mr. Tsao back to Felicity Village, they shot him three times in the back and left the body right there in his own lane. These were days when, faced with desperate crisis, people dared not meddle in other's business, so that even the sound of three gunshots could not bring anyone out to inquire. Thus the murderers were allowed to do their murdering, then simply drive away. It was the Tsaos who, anxiously waiting throughout, finally sensed that those three shots boded evil and they rushed out into the lane to see what had happened; by then Tsao Jiusin had already breathed his last.

Those monsters, those faithless monsters! No wonder Zhu Jingchen had thought it odd that those brutes should all of a sudden be so solicitous as to send Tsao Jiusin home by car! He reflected how during his long forty-odd year career he had met and dealt with people of every stamp, only to be deceived now at the hands of such people as these! Consumed with indignation, he telephoned Fan Yangzhi, asking him to have his employer go to No. 76 to protest. But the answer he got back was, "The rule is, three of your lives for one of ours, but at this moment it's only one of your lives for one of ours, which already redounds very much to your advantage. Furthermore, Mr. Tsao was chosen on special orders of Wu Sibao's wife Yu Aizhen, since the other gentlemen were all still young and healthy, while Tsao Jiusin alone was old and sick. In short, it would seem you should thank her for her consideration."

"Thugs and gangsters!" exclaimed Zhu Jingchen later to Tsai Liren. Jingchen was overcome with rage, yet there was nothing he could do about it. Juanmin and her fiancé were right after all in going inland to the government-held area, he thought—at least they won't have to endure the miasmal atmosphere around here.

The man had died, and nothing more could be done than to comfort his family. Cathay's board of directors immediately decided that since Tsao Jiusin had died while in service to the bank, his monthly salary would continue to be paid and in addition all customary welfare benefits would continue as before, and the bank would assume the responsibility for all tuition payments incurred by the three Tsao children still pursuing their education. When this news became known, there were those who were secretly envious of Tsao Jiusin. After the closure of Small East Gate branch, that "superannuated trainee" from Ningbo who had issued stationery supplies for the General Affairs Department was unable to secure other employment, and soon found himself pressed by both penury and illness; but hearing of the generous treatment with which the bank had favored Tsao Jiusin following his tragic death, the man pounded his sickbed and wailed, "I wish No. 76 would pump its bullets into me like that, then at least my family would have something to show for it."

Yes, his death did seem a matter of grief and of rejoicing and of envy...Yet a murder was after all a murder, and from here on out, everyone at Cathay felt a heightened sense of personal danger.

Before long the Cathay board of directors formally invited Fan Yangzhi's employer, Lu Zuyao, who resided in Japan, to accept an honorary directorship at Cathay in order to facilitate future dealings and contacts with the Japanese and their Chinese puppets.

Chapter 23

The winter of '41 was particularly severe. Already by December cold currents were rolling in. When Juanying finished her choir rehearsals and pushed open the large front door of the church, she was greeted by a piercing wind which seemed to freeze the very blood in her veins. She turned up her overcoat collar, buried her mouth and nose in it, and proceeded at a quick pace.

Cold as it was, precious few people were abroad, and only the clanging of a distant trolley car could be vaguely heard. Around the corner ahead a young man and woman—sweethearts, apparently—were in the midst of a reluctant good-bye. For some reason or other, Jyanying's gaze seemed fixed on the man. He was wearing a wide-brimmed fedora and a dark green gown, which accentuated his slender, graceful build. He was just now tucking up his gown and reaching into his trouser pocket, as he bent close to the woman saying something to her. In the dim light of evening, Juanying did not so much see as feel she recognized the man to be Fan Yangzhi.

After Fan Yangzhi lost his job when Cathay's Small East Gate branch closed down, Juanying had found for him another job paying a very meager wage, and after he'd worked at it for a while, he quit.

And no wonder, for the work was appropriate only for a girl who needed a little spending money. Later on, she heard he had set up a company and was going into business for himself. These days everyone under the sun seemed to be engaged in one sort of speculative enterprise or another, but that Fan Yangzhi of all people should be involved in such work was to Juanying utterly unexpected, for in her heart she viewed Yangzhi as a young man of high aspirations with a sense of social responsibility.

"I'm going to set aside my political activities and give up the attractions of the city and just concentrate on earning a living." That's what he had in effect told her on one occasion.

She had once gone to his office. Supposedly a "company," it was nothing more than one room in an office building where he shared the rent with a couple of leather handbag businesses, his own business consisting of the desk he'd set up there. The entire room was a thick cloud of cigarette smoke and ceaselessly ringing telephones, and there he was squeezed in among the others busy as could be. Frankly speaking, in view of Juanying's family status and outward appearance, Yangzhi had absolutely nothing going for him, but he did possess an inner light so lacking in today's mundane world—the spirit of self-sacrifice to one's calling—that made Juanying feel she had a deeply confiding friendship with him; but now even Fan Yangzhi had sunk to speculative hoarding, and having become this grasping merchant his attractiveness to her was irrevocably lost.

Of course there were a lot of people in the hoarding business nowadays, and she didn't mind that Tsai Liren was making so much money he couldn't count it all, so why should she be so disappointed just because Fan Yangzhi was in the same line?

Later on, when Tsai Liren happened to mention in passing that Fan Yangzhi was working in a business run by Chinese collaborators and, indeed, had a rather good position there, she was practically dumbstruck. Well, perhaps he was just growing distant from her, and after her initial shock she very quickly recovered her composure: after all, people do change.

Now as she watched him say his fond good-byes to this other woman, she suddenly realized she was actually jealous. Lest he catch sight of her, she thought of darting across to the other side of the street, but just then he turned and saw her.

She could see he was genuinely happy to meet her after so long a time. But he did no more than just quietly call to her, "Juanying," then, smiling absent-mindedly, added, "It's been a long time."

"Yes it has. You've been very busy recently." She spoke rather coolly, quite a change from her kindness and consideration of a previous day. He just smiled wanly, without in the slightest catching her sarcasm.

On account of the cold, Juanying tucked her hands up into her coat sleeves and was pressing her music scores against her chest, half concealing her face. She could easily have ended the matter then and there by simply walking off, but for reasons she herself did not know, she just stood there in the cold, right in front of him, seemingly waiting for something...

"Shall we go over there and sit down?" he said, pointing to a coffee shop across the street. "It's awfully cold out here." How the times had changed: now he had money to spare.

It was a tiny coffee shop, run by a White Russian. Frugal as always, Fan Yangzhi ordered two cups of coffee from the big pot—cloudy unfiltered dregs, gritty and acidic.

Juanying lifted her eyes and looked at him inquiringly, not knowing what to say but feeling disappointed about him, very disappointed.

"Juanying." Her hand was on the table. Covering it with his own hand, he pressed it softly, and said in a low voice, "The real world is different from what your church says. Whether it's paradise or whether it's hell, it's just like the cup of coffee you're holding—there is the bitterness of the coffee and the sweetness of the sugar, but there still remains the acidity, and we all must live with it. It's difficult to retain one's own purity, just as the water in the coffee does not retain its purity. But you must believe me, I'm not a three-year old child, and I understand what self-respect is." He clamped his mouth shut and smiled a bitter smile of resignation.

What he was referring to was his employment at that company of his. How odd—why was he talking with her about such things? Everybody enjoys the right to arrange his own life. It was just that Juanying felt Fan Yangzhi's choice of life to be unworthy, and this made her feel that his fall had been precipitous indeed.

He looked at her in silence and she at him, and both sensed a chasm had started to open between them.

"Well, good-bye, and take care of yourself!" he said as he got up from the table. It's as if he were announcing the termination of something. She understood: what she had been standing in the cold street waiting for was this. Although Juanying's school grades had never been particularly good, she'd been a hardworking student, never setting down her pencil until she had worked out the answers to every last homework problem, and only then taking up a new exercise. And precisely because she was this way, she never finished her examinations within the prescribed time. But she was invariably very conscientious.

He left, again with his gown tucked up and one hand shoved down into his trouser pocket, the other clasping a package of books or something. It was a mannerism he had developed while in college, where all the men students habitually had one hand in their pocket and carried books in the other, whether they were walking to the classroom or to the laboratory or to the chapel...

Well, if it's to be a termination, let it be terminated. She'd still had the dream, though, that she might somehow convince him to quit that dishonorable company, but she had overestimated herself. For it was now quite clear to her that her dream was impossible.

She remembered that rainy evening after the August Thirteenth Incident when the two of them were squeezed together in the tiny office of the children's emergency shelter; she'd scalded her leg with boiling water and reproved herself with, "I'm always doing things like that." "But I'm here today and wouldn't feel right if you went back home alone," he replied. Heavy bean-sized raindrops pelted the rickshaw's oil-cloth canopy. That evening possessed all the charm of a musical nocturne. She was only eighteen that year, though she felt she was already so very old, too old to attract the interest of any man, and then in a twinkling four years had passed. Now she really was old. Emotionally she had never resembled Juanmin's suavity and boldness. Although she projected an outward coldness, in fact she had a heart of love, and it had started to throb early on. But of course that was forever a secret known only to herself.

Once, long ago when she was just a sixteen-year-old high schooler, Juanying fell in love with a recently ordained priest of her own church. He had graduated from Yanjing Theological Seminary, then studied for two years in the United States. He spoke perfect Peking dialect and had a wonderfully pleasant voice—soft and deep. Listening to his sermons, Juanying would sometimes feel as if she were hearing the voice of God Himself—tolerant, loving, profound.

He had once said with great pride, "I went abroad as a self-supporting theology student." Most theology students who went abroad for advanced study were supported financially by the church, but he studied theology abroad using his own means, clearly showing the firmness of his religious convictions. He was from a wealthy family: his father, it seems, was an Overseas Chinese who owned a sugar business. But he gave up all of that to devote himself to the church. It was from his example that Juanying learned the meaning of the word "sacrifice."

His young figure was draped in solemn black vestments, and around his forehead was tied a bright red ribbon symbolizing a yoke—the yoke that hangs heavy around a bullock's neck just as life weighs heavy upon mankind; of his own free will this young priest would unburden mankind by placing that yoke around his own firm neck. When not officiating at services, he invariably wore a conservative suit over a black shirt with a stiff, dazzlingly white roman collar—the ageless badge of priestly status. He also liked keeping one hand in his pocket while holding books in the other, a mannerism young men picked up during their years as conscientious university students. Juanying's own firm faith was in large measure due to this priest of such unusual bearing, a fact which he himself would never know.

When she advanced to the third and final year of high school, he got married, the bride none other than the church organist. Not long thereafter the two of them were transferred to a mission in Kunming, far to the southwest. He would never know how this timid, unexceptional girl had loved him so deeply. She lacked Juanmin's pluck principally because she'd always felt inferior, felt she'd grown up to be ugly, and she certainly wasn't a lively personality...This was the first time she had been disappointed in love.

With regard to the present instance, however, she couldn't say whether or not it constituted a disappointment in love. During the four years she'd known Fan Yangzhi, she was in the church while he remained an atheist, yet the two of them got along perfectly—a very well matched couple, one might say. She felt that he very much resembled that priest, that he too would willingly place around his neck a heavy, onerous yoke. It was just that he had no magnificent identifying symbols. Between the two of them there seemed to be mostly quiet and congenial conversation, as if Fan Yangzhi was always engaged in a balancing act to maintain this calm and peaceful relation, but sometimes even he would look at her with a blazing gaze...Anyway it was now terminated. Everything would become a memory, just like that young priest.

As soon as Juanying stepped through the front gate into the front garden of her home, Old Chang told her that Tsai Liren was inside, apparently waiting specially for her.

She pushed open the heavy parlor door. Because of a coal shortage, they were not lighting the stove in the parlor this year. Tsai Liren, wearing a padded silk gown, was gazing out the window, his hands clasped behind his back.

"Mr. Tsai," she greeted him, and then, without knowing why, tears began to stream down like rain.

"What is it? What's the matter?" he said gently as he sat down beside her.

"I feel very tired, too tired. Let's get married." Twisting her handkerchief, she amazed herself that she could actually on her own initiative put forth such a proposition, and yet her tone of voice was such that she might just as well have proposed, "I'm hungry, let's get something to eat."

But he wasn't the slightest taken aback, and certainly wouldn't fuss about her indifferent tone of voice, for he seemed to have anticipated that sooner or later this scene would occur.

"All right. I'll see Mr. Zhu and broach the matter to him. We should first announce our engagement, then, after the war situation improves a little and Mr. Zhu comes back here to live, we can have the marriage ceremony."

At a moment like this the man and the woman invariably have feelings to express to each other, and he began by tentatively putting his arm around her waist. "This time," he smiled, "I hope there's no one hiding behind the couch." Seeing that she put up no resistance, he gave her a kiss on the cheek. This was the first man who had ever kissed her. How odd when you think of it: she'd always considered love and marriage to be unimaginably marvelous, when in fact it simply turned out to be something primly waiting for her in the parlor.

"Mr. Tsai...Oh, Mr. Tsai." It was Fagun the butler knocking at the door. For some time now—nobody seemed to know just when—if something came up in the family that couldn't be handled, Mr. Tsai was always sought out. "Mr. Fan Yangzhi has telephoned and insists on speaking to Mr. Zhu; says it's important." Zhu Jingchen's telephone number, as a security precaution, was not even known to the servants. Tsai Liren went out to take the call, and Juanying wondered why Fan Yangzhi would be calling at this particular hour when she had just seen him, and he didn't appear then to have had anything special he wanted her to convey to her father. She was thinking how odd it all was when Tsai Liren came back in wearing a grim expression. He had his overcoat on and was about to go out.

"What's happened? Dinner will be served in a moment; why not eat first?" she asked worriedly.

"Fan Yangzhi's present boss is well connected, so his information may well contain an element of truth. He says that this very evening it's possible something untoward may happen and Cathay should take precautions. But today happens to be Saturday and everybody's left work by now, so how can we take precautions? What a predicament! Anyway, I'm going to hurry over to see Mr. Zhu, and I might as well tell him about us, too." And with that he patted Juanying on the cheek and rushed out.

"Fan Yangzhi's employer has connections so his information may contain an element of truth." Tsai Liren's remark echoed in her ear.

Could it be that Fan Yangzhi was...? But the notion only flashed into her mind then disappeared, for the relationship between the two was now terminated.

★   ★   ★

Tsai Liren rushed into his apartment, where Zhu Jingchen was playing a game of mahjong solitaire to ease his boredom. After hearing Tsai Liren's news, Jingchen immediately telephoned to Li Chengpeng, chairman of the board. He could hear the clicking of mahjong tiles at the chairman's end. The two discussed the matter for a while and concluded there were no other precautions to take than to send someone over immediately to move the vault keys and lock combination codes to a more secure place. After putting down the phone, Jingchen thought about it some more and, still uneasy, he called a number of his friends in the old counting houses and asked them to see what they could find out. Before long they were calling him back. "I phoned a member of the Municipal Council," said one, "to find out what was going on, but he said he hadn't heard anything special."

"We'd best be careful," said Jingchen after he'd finished his telephone calls, "and not go to sleep tonight." He took off his silk bathrobe and dressed himself, and then prepared two cups of strong coffee. "Is everything okay at home? Juanren certainly isn't likely to be there. On a Saturday night, he'll be out with Syi Zhishuang."

"Apparently there's a dance at the British Navy Club sponsored by the British Huangpu River squadron," said Tsai Liren, "and Juanmin and Miss Syi will be there joining in the fun."

"Oh? The British navy is still holding dances ashore? If that's the case, it wouldn't seem as though any untoward event might occur, otherwise they'd be the first to know about it." Jingchen breathed more easily.

"There's another matter, to be regarded as a happy event—marriage." Tsai Liren stared at the coffee cup his was holding and smiled.

"Happy events like marriage are a rarity this year."

"Juanying and I are planning on becoming engaged," he said blushing shyly.

"Good," replied Jingchen, nodding, for he had long been expecting this day. Yet it also occurred to him that it would be painful for another of his daughters to leave him. "The children are grown up and one by one they are flying off. Juanmin has gone to Free China, so I hope you won't be taking Juanying to distant parts, too?"

"Please rest assured I won't, sir."

Jingchen surveyed him with an impartial eye, and sensed a person of unflagging perseverance. Among Tsai Liren's forebears, there was not one who had attained wealth or name or stature, indeed, to put it bluntly, his family was no recommendation for him at all. But now things were all right: he had prepared himself by achieving the necessary qualities on his own. This marriage might well provoke a good deal of social gossip, with everyone remarking that, yes, Tsai Liren was a fine and able person, but the Zhu daughter was marrying below her status and accepting second best. Shanghai people are quirky that way. The powerful and influential Feng family, for example, was like that fermented bean curd dish known as "smelly tofu"—smelly but still a welcome addition to the dining table, while Tsai Liren, even though on the ascendant himself, was of such unremarkable origins that he would never be allowed even on the sideboard. Although Jingchen had done everything he could to bring about the match, once it had become a reality, he suddenly felt he'd been hoodwinked by Tsai Liren. His two daughters—the one to marry the heir of a ruined family, the other to marry an upstart—caused him a certain dissatisfaction. Fortunately his future sons-in-law, quite aside from their status or appearance, were really quite acceptable as individuals. And in these disruptive times when Syi Zhensyu so rarely was able to get back to Shanghai, it would be up to Jingchen to select an auspicious day for Juanren's marriage and handle those arrangements, too.

The night wore on and Jingchen could hold out no longer; he lay down on the sofa to nap. He was startled out of his drowsiness by the rumble of bombers flying overhead. He looked at his watch—only about four o'clock. Could it be the Japs carrying out another predawn exercise?

The residents in the entire building seemed all to have been roused from their sleep, as one could tell from the sound of windows opening here and there and from the uneasy inquiries going back and forth. Beyond the windows a misty drizzle was falling.

"Something's happened all right," stammered Tsai Liren, bursting into the apartment dripping wet. "The Japs have invaded us!" His hand clutched a soggy leaflet with the heading, "International Settlement under Japanese Imperial Army Occupation." He had gone out to see what was happening just as the airplanes were dropping these leaflets. What suddenly struck Jingchen was that the information Fan Yangzhi had given him was so prescient, yet the International Settlement was all the while so apathetic! Now finally the day had come when Shanghai no longer had an island of safety, save one tiny patch—the French Concession.

As these thoughts were racing through his mind, Board Chairman Li telephoned. "The Petrel, that British gunboat anchored off Shanghai, has just been attacked and sunk," he exclaimed, "and the American gunboat Wake has hoisted a white surrender pennant. The Japanese have already declared war on Great Britain and the United States."

By now it was already daybreak. Jingchen washed up and combed his hair, called Zhuanlin to reassure each other, then put on his overcoat and started out.

"Mr. Zhu, you're actually going out today?" asked Tsai Liren in astonishment.

"I'm going to the bank. With conditions like this, it's all the more important that I go there and take personal charge of things. Anyway, it hardly makes sense to speak of an International Settlement any more—it all amounts to the same thing now." As he spoke he knocked his two fists together. "Everything depends now on who can push the harder."

To get a better on-the-spot view of just what had happened, rather than going by automobile he braved the rain and walked a ways on foot, and soon discovered that armed Japanese sentries were posted at every intersection. Standing there impassively, they gave the impression of so much statuary.

Jingchen hailed a rickshaw, and started toward Cathay Republic Bank. After a distance, he realized that every single bridge across Suzhou Creek had been sealed off. Moreover, the French trolley line and the public busses were not operating. At conspicuous places along the route large notices had already been posted, and though soggy with rain and blotched from running ink, the bold-face heading easily caught the eye:

> Issued under the Authority of the Supreme Commander
> of the Japanese Imperial Army in Shanghai

The notices were inescapable, and utterly depressing in their effect. The shops along the streets were all shut up tight, bringing paralysis to the entire business district.

As he passed along Edward VII Ave., he could see large detachments of Annamese policemen at work on the French Concession side of the avenue setting up sandbag and wire barricades on the streets leading into the International Settlement.

When Jingchen arrived at Cathay it was already past ten, and the great iron door of the bank was tightly shut. He went in through a side entrance, and discovered that notwithstanding it was a Sunday, the bank employees were all sitting silently in the main lobby. Seeing Jingchen come in, everyone stood up in silent greeting, a scene that reminded him of the atmosphere of Tsao Jiusin's funeral at the mortuary. Jingchen could only return the greeting with a mute nod. On a day when the situation had changed so suddenly, each employee, just as always, had, to the extent possible, come to work on time—moving testimony that Cathay still enjoyed a loyal and conscientious work force; that alone gave Jingchen a ray of solace in an otherwise bleak picture.

Jingchen settled himself in his office, although there was in fact scarcely any more business to attend to. Gazing through the rain-splattered window to the British-owned building across the street, he saw the Japanese Rising Sun fluttering above its rooftop.

"Mr. Zhu," said Mrs. Zhong softly as she came into his office. "An aide to Colonel Kuniguchi, the commandant of the Japanese military police battalion, has just telephoned—he's summoned the heads of all banks, public and private, to a meeting right now in the International Hotel."

The hour of reckoning had now finally arrived. Well, anyway, Jingchen could say with a clear conscience that for the past two decades he had done everything humanly possible for Cathay.

He assumed a resigned expression and looked at Mrs. Zhong. "I'd better go," he said. He rose from his chair and looked through the rain-streaked window to the Japanese flag flying above the British building across the way. "Mrs. Zhong," he said slowly, "please record the following for me in today's log: 'In the early morning hours of December 8, 1941, the Japanese invaded the International Settlement.'"

"Yes...And?" With a practiced hand, Mrs. Zhong wrote the entry onto her writing pad, then looked up waiting for the next sentence.

Jingchen sighed lightly. "That's enough. 'The Japanese invaded the International Settlement.' My colleagues will forgive me for not explaining what followed. It is not an offense which can be summarized in one line." He shook his head and smiled tragically, signaling Mrs. Zhong to withdraw.

Mrs. Zhong lowered her eyes and straightened up the papers on her lap, slowly and deliberately as if something was weighing on her mind, as if she had something she needed to say. Finally she spoke. "Mr. Zhu, last Sunday I had my fiftieth birthday."

Huh? Mrs. Zhong already fifty? Amazed, Jingchen turned toward her, and could make out a bit of scalp showing through her thinning hair.

"Oh, I apologize for not sending you a birthday present, but these days I've been terribly distracted," he said apologetically.

"A birthday present is something that can be sent any time," she said, looking at the sheaf of letters she was holding for his perusal, as well as two thick piles of stock quotations which Jingchen had to check every day. She was silent a moment, then finally spoke again. "I'm thinking of retiring."

A perplexed expression crossed his face. "How's that? You're not in good health? Are there employees here who don't think highly of you in some way?"

"Of course, it's nothing like that."

"So why all of a sudden do you want to resign? You've been with Mr. Wei and me for so many years. You've been an outstanding secretary and have eased my burden of work a great deal. I really do need you..."

"To be perfectly frank about it, Mr. Zhu," she said slowly, "I've worked as secretary to the president at Cathay for a very long time...But now the Japanese have invaded the International Settlement, and the British building across the street is flying the Japanese flag; Cathay's future seems very ominous. I've been the secretary now to two presidents, and I have no desire to be the secretary to some Japanese president. I've lived for fifty years and I have no desire in my later life to befoul myself with their dirty work. You do understand me, don't you, Mr. Zhu?"

Indeed he did. To a certain degree one could say that Mrs. Zhong was the very soul of the president's office at Cathay, and she understood her job perfectly. Here was an exemplary secretary, and if one day the Japanese should take over Cathay, they'd certainly want to take her over as well.

The telephone on Jingchen's desk rang. Her pencil poised, Mrs. Zhong answered it, as she might on any ordinary day. For a moment the room was perfectly still, then she repeated crisply: "I understand; that's 5:45 on the morning of the ninth, at..." When she had finished taking down the message, she unconsciously straightened the stack of signed letters on top of the desk.

"You're quite correct in what you say," Jingchen finally said. "Thank you very much for serving Cathay for these many years. I hope that when the war is over, those of you who can return to the bank will do so." Jingchen's throat began to choke up.

Jingchen followed Mrs. Zhong with his eyes as she silently left his office. Then he slumped heavily into his chair.

It was not until four in the afternoon that Jingchen was released from the meeting at the International Hotel. The "meeting," in fact, had turned out to be more of a lecturing. That MP commandant, Colonel Kuniguchi, scolded them as if they were errant grandsons, berated them for relying on the loathsome authority of the International Settlement and propping up the currency of the Chungking government, upbraided them for not redeeming the bogus Central Reserve Bank certificates of the Wang Jingwei puppet regime, etc., etc., etc. Finally, as if issuing an ultimatum, he said, "Such errors as have been committed up to now have resulted from lack of mutual understanding, but hereafter we shall meet frequently so there can be no question of unresolvable problems arising. Consequently each bank must resume normal operations immediately..."

Seeing the despondent and discouraged expression their own president was wearing, the Cathay employees themselves could hardly help from harboring dark thoughts about their very uncertain future.

Jingchen sat down at his desk and began drumming his fingers on the empty desktop. It would seem that Cathay Republic Bank, so painstakingly built up over two generations, had now come to the end of its days. He lifted the glass desktop panel and slipped out the print of the bank's coin-shaped emblem—round in circumference with a square hole in the center; it bore the bank motto in the vigorous calligraphy of its founder, Wei Jiusi:

> If business slumps, we take no risk
> Nor are we flurried when it's brisk;
> Cathay's transactions with the public
> Regard this coin to be symbolic:
> The round outside means flexibility,
> The inner core is four-square honesty.

He felt a sudden pain in his eyes. He pressed his hands against his temples as hot tears began trickling down. He thought how in the beginning they'd managed to avert Chinese government take-over by exercising extreme ingenuity, only to find that now in the end they would succumb to a Japanese take-over. If they could in the beginning have known of today, perhaps they might just as well have let Cathay be absorbed by the government, in which case the onus of handing over his bank to the Japanese today would not be his to bear.

"Mr. Zhu, there are three Japanese gentlemen here to see you," came Mrs. Zhong's voice over the intercom. She was an excellent secretary, and notwithstanding she would leave the bank tomorrow, she was as attentive as ever to today's work.

"All right, show them in." Jingchen pulled himself together, took out a pocket comb and smoothed back his thinning hair.

Of the three Japanese who had come to the bank, one was in full-dress uniform, though with a pleasant looking face. He was the same Mr. Kagesa who had earlier come to discuss (in that fluent Chinese of his) a cooperative arrangement with the Small East Gate branch.

"President Zhu," began Mr. Kagesa. "You Chinese have an ancient proverb that goes, 'To know at first what later will befall, prevents us starting mistakes at all.' In short, sir, it is too late for regrets, for are we not at last seated here together?"

Without waiting for Jingchen's invitation this time, the three Japanese sat right down and made themselves at home.

Kagesa began. "Finance—it is the key which directly affects the market, and we do not wish that the present war should affect the Shanghai market too long. Whether the Shanghai market soon returns to normal or not, Mr. Zhu, is entirely in your hands."

Strange indeed! What complete and utter nonsense! How should this responsibility actually devolve upon me, Zhu Jingchen? He shook his head again and again. "Mr. Kagesa, I am quite unequal to the challenge."

Kagesa sighed. "There have always been two types of power in this world—one is destructive power, the other constructive, and we of course belong to the latter type."

Pure duck piss! thought Jingchen to himself. He was just about to ring for Mrs. Zhong to notify all departments to prepare the ledgers to be turned over to the Japanese.

"Ah, no need to rush!" said Kagesa, gesturing him to stop. "We have by no means come here to take over Cathay Republic Bank. To the contrary, we are going to let you have Cathay, just as always. But my two colleagues, Mr. Ono and Mr. Sekiya, and I will serve here under your supervision, all of us striving together for the sake of the Greater East Asia Co-Prosperity Sphere and for the restoration of Shanghai's status within it as an international metropolis." And so saying, he fixed his cold, hard gaze directly on Jingchen.

So that was it! The Japanese idea was to pressure Cathay to reorganize and resume operations. Were the Japanese simply to take over the bank outright, then it would be clear to everyone that Zhu

Jingchen had been intimidated by superior force, or, to put it more crudely, raped. Regarding reorganization and resuming operations, whatever positive aspects that might have, it still amounted to complicity with the enemy, and if he went along with it, he would never be able to show his face anywhere.

"That's a very large matter," said Jingchen, trying to put him off, "and I certainly could not make a decision about it on my own authority. I'll have to discuss the matter with the board of directors before making a decision."

"That's fine. We can give you three days, Mr. Zhu. And please bear in mind that old Chinese proverb, 'To know at first what later will befall, prevents us starting mistakes at all.'" Having thus spoken his piece, Kagesa and his two aides swaggered out, their riding boots clicking along imperiously.

Jingchen leaned back in his chair. From beyond the window next to his desk dusk was gradually closing in. He looked at his reflection in the window pane—a specter, it seemed, floating in a cavern. He slowly opened the desk drawer, took out a sheet of writing paper and began to compose his letter of resignation to the board.

Well, he was nearly fifty and approaching retirement anyway, he thought, so the best option was just to leave. It was fortunate he had joined so perspicacious a gentleman as Tsai Liren in a business partnership, for he had created a sizable savings from his investment. And so what of it—he had enough to get by on, so why should he proceed with fear and trepidation on the tightrope of life making a fool of himself? Why not just retire? Wasn't Mrs. Zhong's solution after all the right one?

His letter of resignation completed, he locked the desk drawer, pulled at it a couple times, as was his habit, to test the lock, then took down from the windowsill the snapshot of Zhuanlin, slipped out the bank motto from under his glass desktop, and carefully tucked them into his briefcase. Then, finally, in the dark, he lit up a cigarette and smoked moodily.

There was a knock at the door. He hastily turned the resignation letter face down. "Come in!" he said with his old authoritative voice.

It was Fan Yangzhi. Since his employer had been appointed honorary member of the Cathay board of directors, Fan Yangzhi was himself also a frequent visitor to the bank. Just now Cathay was actually in great need of a person who could mix with the Japanese.

"No lights turned on?" queried Fan Yangzhi, seeing Zhu Jingchen sitting in the dark.

Jingchen switched on a lamp and said wearily, "Kagesa and some others came. Kuniguchi had earlier given us a real lecturing. 'What course should you follow?' he asked us exactly as if he were delivering an ultimatum. Anyway, I don't care any more. I'm taking old-age retirement."

Fan Yangzhi was dumbstruck.

"In the past few years I just haven't been up to doing the things that need to get done," Jingchen said despondently. "It's age. I've been performing on a tightrope for twenty or thirty years, and now I just can't do it any more."

"Mr. Zhu, at a juncture like this, you can't just run away. Cathay has hundreds of employees and if you go, they'll be a leaderless crowd. This is no trivial matter!" Fan Yangzhi's impressive features revealed his former earnestness, and his eyes a deep commitment.

Jingchen sat motionless as he stared at the floor, hands folded, fingers tightly interlaced. They were silent for a long while before Fan Yangzhi finally asked, "Can you really tear yourself away from Cathay? Do you really have the heart to let the Japs willy-nilly run rampant over the bank?"

Jingchen had the sudden feeling that this Fan Yangzhi seemed to be showing excessive concern, and whatever one might say, it was he, Zhu Jingchen, who was still the head of Cathay Republic Bank, so how was it Fan Yangzhi might take it upon himself to come and offer big-brotherly advice? He looked up with a frown on his face and glared at him. But when he started to speak, his words gushed out at will like a breach in a dyke. "I can't give any consideration to that; I only feel that the past few years have been nightmarish. I'm half dead already, and now if I have to work under the noses of the Japanese, I just won't be able to stand it. When I think how I've lived to be nearly fifty years old, I can only hope that the rest of my life will remain unsullied..."

"But Mr. Zhu," interrupted Fan Yangzhi, as he pulled up a chair and sat down next to him. "Why hasn't it occurred to you that since the Japs are claiming they want us to resume operations rather than talking about outright confiscation of the bank, that means Cathay still enjoys at least a little leverage, and since that's the case why should we abandon that leverage for free? We should at least exploit it as much as possible for the sake of the employees, and help them along until the new dawn arrives. If we do that, sir, then I think that your achievements on behalf of the bank will go down in history." It was an impressive speech, spoken without excitement yet in tones of deep conviction.

Almost imperceptibly, Jingchen nodded in agreement.

"And furthermore, should Cathay actually be compelled to reorganize and resume operations, it would be the equivalent of rape, for which the employees would be forgiving of you."

Fan Yangzhi's brief remarks, sincere and sensible, held Zhu Jingchen's closest attention and he could not help eyeing Fan Yangzhi from head to foot as if he were meeting him for the first time. This fellow appeared to be getting smarter and abler by the year—on the one hand muddle-headed enough to join a collaborationist business firm, and yet, on the other, perspicacious beyond a doubt in his handling of affairs and in his judgment of men.

Yangzhi's squarish face, now illuminated by the lamplight, seemed more than ever cleanly defined in feature and resolute in its contours, and Jingchen could make out an expression of trust and hope.

"But if operations are resumed under Japanese supervision, what little would there be for me to do?" asked Jingchen skeptically.

"Mr. Zhu. You're well known for your intelligence and ability. Whatever the circumstances, you'll continue to give full play to what you are best at—accomodating to circumstances and exploiting new opportunities. So, as much as possible, you'll use the resumption of business to bring some measure of benefit to your fellow workers and to the nation, and you'll actively push toward the new dawn rather than passively wait for it to come. There are many things you can do. For example, because of the present commodity inflation, the employees are having a very difficult time getting by, especially the ones who got laid off two years ago at Small East Gate branch. A lot of them simply haven't been able to find work again, and it's been a long two years of struggle for them. Others, for sheer survival, have had no alternative but to climb aboard with the enemy and work for the puppet Central Reserve Bank. But if, after Cathay's reorganization and right under the very noses of the Japanese, you could appropriate a sum for employee assistance, well then, sir, that would be an act of great philanthropy."

"Well..." said Jingchen uncertainly, propping his chin between thumb and forefinger.

"Mr. Zhu, I remember as a country boy the story they used to tell about an old woman curing vegetables in the sun—I wonder if you've ever heard it? It seems a robber burst into the home of this old woman who was hanging out vegetables to dry in the sun, and although she was well along in years she wasn't about to give in to the man, and besides she had a few what you might call 'little friends' around who secretly helped her. Like a hedgehog hiding in a cistern who stuck the robber with its quills, and chestnuts roasting in the oven which exploded in his face, and honeybees hiding in the kindling wood who flew after him.

And so in this way with everyone combining their efforts and working together, they chased off the robber. Our bank, Cathay Republic, is just like that old lady's house. And I also believe that there are a lot of the same sort of 'little friends' here too. In your future dealings with the Japanese, you can rely on my boss, Mr. Lu, to handle things for you. He used to live in Japan as a student and he's now an honorary member of the Cathay board. This could be very important to you in directing bank operations. So, as you can see...Mr. Zhu, stay on for a while longer to see how such an arrangement might work out."

"In my view," replied Jingchen, "the idea of resuming business under their reorganization scheme positively stinks. But right now, after hearing what you've had to say, the phrase 'sudden enlightenment' really does take on new meaning for me. My personal reputation might get smelly, but at least I'll have a clear conscience, just as you have, and one day people will understand."

Chapter 24

Over the kitchen stove a bare electric bulb was burning dimly as Mrs. Syi busied herself with the meal. Her bottle of cooking oil looked more like a bottle of cough syrup, what with the graduated lines etched into the medicinal plaster smeared up one side. She poured a few stingy drops into her wok. Clever Mrs. Syi, a housewife for decades, knew all the tricks for stir-fry cooking in a hot wok. But "even the cleverest cook can't get up a meal without the makings," they say, so nowadays, when you had to stand in a long line to buy price-controlled oil and coal, you inevitably used them very sparingly to stretch them as many days as possible. Thus a plateful of vegetables, stir-fried with too little oil over too slow a fire, came out looking pretty sick. Alas, in all her years, she'd never before encountered times like these.

Since the Japanese had invaded the International Settlement, sea transport into Shanghai had been completely cut off, making it impossible to ship Thai rice into the city, where all rice was limited to three pints at a single purschase—more than that and they simply wouldn't let you take it away. And what's more, the price had gone up to four or five yuan. Three pints of rice—how could that possibly be enough? Chengzu had already developed into quite a big fellow and was at an age when he really knew how to eat.

There was a knock at the back door: a rice peddlar (a profiteer, really, selling black market supplies) had come into the neighborhood. Mrs. Syi scooped up a handful from one of the peddlar's sacks and saw that the rice was adulterated with broken grains and millet seeds.

"How much is it?" she asked.

"Five hundred yuan per ten-peck sack." The peddler was a woman in her thirties, though she had very fair skin; if instead of that baggy lavender padded jacket she were wearing a fur coat, she would pass very nicely for a proper Shanghai matron.

"Five hundred for this grade of rice? That's unconscionable," exclaimed Mrs. Syi, shaking her head as she brushed the rice dregs from her hands.

"Don't be so fussy, ma'am. We risked our lives snatching this rice out from under the noses of the Japanese. And there were three others today who were bayoneted to death by the Japanese. Those merciless Japs. One of them who was murdered was a pregnant woman, but the Japanese insisted that she was profiteering, so they bayoneted her right in the stomach and pulled out the fetus—oh! what an ungodly sin...Its arms and legs were still twitching!"

The story made Mrs. Syi's flesh creep. She abruptly began to haggle over the price of the rice to change the subject. "Five hundred is rather expensive. My husband isn't here, and for a woman raising two children by herself it isn't easy balancing the budget. Make it four ninety."

"Really, ma'am." And the woman heaved a long sigh. "I'm not kidding when I tell you that I once was the wife of a good family, and my husband had a good office job. But then war all of a sudden broke out and my husband lost his job, and without any income we eventually exhausted our savings. And on top of it all my husband developed TB, so what choice did I have but to take up this dangerous business."

The world had crashed down upon her, in a tale of woe for which the depredations of the Japanese were all to blame. When Hong Kong came under attack, all communications between Mr. Syi and his family had been cut off, and then eighteen days later the Hong Kong government hoisted the white flag of surrender. Mrs. Syi learned that a ship had left Hong Kong for Shanghai, but one had to scramble fast to make arrangements for passage, and needless to say Mr. Syi missed his turn. Liu Tongjun of Bounty Textiles did manage to get aboard and return to Shanghai, and he brought back news that Mr. Syi was safe and sound, and with a few of his friends had gotten a flight into Free China. Mrs. Syi was one of those old-fashioned types who knew her proper place, and felt that if her husband went here or went there, he would of course have his own good reasons for doing so. But with his financial support cut off and with only the meager subsidies provided by the bank here in Shanghai, it was no easy matter maintaining a household of three persons. The Syi family was, after all, a family living on salary, and while Mr. Syi enjoyed a high salary, it could not stand comparison to the large incomes earned by independent businessmen, and consequently the Syis had no great reserves of savings. These past few years prices had been shooting up, her daughter was engaged and still studying at the university, and Mrs. Syi had already long been dipping into their modest savings. And now she was up against this. How hard it was just getting through the day!

The two women haggled back and forth for a long time, and only with the greatest difficulty settled on 495 yuan for a ten-peck sack. Mrs. Syi didn't dare buy more than two sacks, and at that nearly one thousand yuan was gone forever. Not long before this Mrs. Syi had sold a few pieces of jade jewelry to get some money, among them a green jade ring of a quality whose excellence one rarely saw these days. She sold them to the rice profiteer at No. 34. That woman had been stockpiling rice for years and now that rice could no longer be brought into the International Settlement, she set all scruple aside and began selling off her hoard (made the larger by its adulteration with tiny pepples)—a nefarious business which very quickly made her a wealthy woman. How true it is: "a sixty-year cycle brings a complete change in fortune!"

When it was just about meal time, Zhishuang telephoned to say she wouldn't be coming home to eat. She would be graduating from the university this summer, but with present conditions as they were, graduation meant subsequent unemployment. The headmistress at McTyeire, her old alma mater, had expected to hire her after she graduated from the university, but that was one time and this was another, and now the American flag which used to flutter above the McTyeire campus had been replaced by the Japanese flag, and Miss Syu, the new headmistress, was powerless to do anything. In order to get settled in some sort of job after graduation, Zhishuang was dashing about every day seeing people who might help her, and on this day it happened that she'd bumped into Ju Beibei downtown, who dragged her off to a western restaurant.

Ju Beibei was as beautifully dressed as ever, resplendent in a gray fur coat over a purple velvet mandarin dress. The war seemed not to have affected her one jot, so pleasant and carefree an expression was she wearing.

"Tell me, Zhishuang, when will you be inviting me to your wedding banquet? Has Juanmin written? I wonder if she and her dashing prince have brought a little angel into the world." When she learned that Zhishuang was rushing around trying to line up a steady job, Ju Beibei was utterly astonished.

"Good heavens, poor Miss Syi! You've abandoned your ready-made role as rich man's wife to run around madly looking for work? Do you think the Zhu family can't feed another mouth?"

What could she say? Syi Zhishuang since childhood had accustomed herself to a proud independence and she was strongly disinclined that in the future she should have to approach her husband with outstretched hand whenever she might want, say, to buy material for a dress. Their maid, Zhou, always used to tell her, "In money matters, it's better to rely on a husband than on parents, but it's better yet to rely on yourself than a husband," which did indeed make sense. What's more, the drafts her father had been sending had been cut off now for several months, making household finances suddenly very tight, so both her mother and the maid were scrimping, and they hired in only an old woman to help with the washing. And Zhishuang herself had even experienced the crush of lining up for the household rice ration, and she liked it not one bit.

"But, Miss Syi," she said, affectedly using the English word, "you've always been an advocate of women's independence." Then, withdrawing a hand from her fur muff—a delicate white hand with nails buffed to a beautiful gloss, Ju Beibei snapped her an impish military-style salute: "Oh, how I do admire you!"

Zhishuang was disinclined to argue with her. These two women had traveled through life by very different paths, so why not just enjoy the chance meeting and not fuss about minor annoyances. To Zhishuang's surprise, Ju Beibei asked her with genuine warmth, "Didn't you say you're looking for work? I know of a real good job—there couldn't be anything more suitable for you. Remember that movie star, Hong Fung? She's married now, married to a rich elderly widower with a son and daughter who need a governess. They've been looking for a number of days now and haven't found anyone suitable. But you, Zhishuang, you'd be perfect for the job."

Seeing Zhishuang's skepticism, she added, "Hong Fung may have a movie world background, but her husband is really a very proper sort of person, so there's absolutely nothing to be concerned about."

A few days later Ju Beibei took Zhishuang to Hong Fung's home. It was located on Edinburgh Road, a foreign-style residence with an exquisite garden in front. Ju Beibei was on very familiar terms with Hong Fung, who immediately invited Zhishuang upstairs into her own room. In days like these when most Shanghai residents were counting one by one every coal briquette they burned, Hong Fung's room was heated very comfortably by a proper coal stove such as they use in Peking. Since the previous time—before the outbreak of war—when

Zhishuang and Juanmin had gone to see Hong Fung in her apartment in Rose Mansion, four years had passed in just a twinkling, and Syi Zhishuang felt that she herself had changed significantly, that her happy-go-lucky school-girlish temperament which took a bright-eyed interest in every new thing had long since vanished. The Hong Fung who now appeared before her eyes was no longer a big star, and indeed it had been a very long while since she had done any acting at all. She was now the wife of a wealthy man, nothing more.

But even at home Hong Fung as always attended to her looks, so that Zhishuang was quite unable to determine her age. The room was appointed with a set of mahogany furniture of a modern style, and on the walls were mirrors in brightly burnished frames. Exquisite though the furniture was, the bedside table was cluttered with all manner of stuff, for this popular star had been unable to change her slovenly habits of yore. Zhishuang felt a certain pity as she roamed her eyes over the quality furniture and comfortable room. If she herself possessed so elegant a room as this, she would certainly keep it much tidier. Movie stars like Hong Fung simply didn't understand the real importance of life, so perhaps she ought to tell her that real life and the silver screen were actually very much the same: they were at once truth and untruth played out on a stage.

Hong Fung had thrown a dressing robe over her shoulders—a padded silk robe with a brocaded design—and on her feet low-heeled slippers decorated with a flower pattern of lustrous pearls. Yes, she was a wealthy woman, but she still had the movie star's style—the perfect image of a frivolous socialite. By all appearances, the war hadn't affected her in the slightest as she passed her days in utmost comfort. Women like her always had a way, and whatever happened, they always survived.

"This is Miss Syi. Do you remember her? Once we went to Rose Mansion specially to pay a call on the great star Hong Fung. She's engaged now to the son of Mr. Zhu, the president of Cathay Republic Bank, but nonetheless she wants to learn what a working woman's life is all about. So, I thought I'd introduce her to you."

Hong Fung put on a vague can't-seem-to-place-you look as if to say, "important ladies easily forget trifles," though Zhishuang sensed she was only feigning lack of recognition.

With an extreme of reserve toward Zhishuang that seemed to be intentionally stand-offish, Hong Fung lit up a cigarette. She cocked her head toward Ju Beibei and asked, "What kind of favor are you doing Miss Syi? This is tough work, especially with kids like these." Whereupon she scowled contemptuously, clucked her tongue, and shook her head. "The old man's first wife was a country hag who didn't know what manners are, so these two kids are a couple of wild brats without an iota of breeding. Liu!" she said, calling to the maid, "bring the kids in to see their new teacher."

After that Hong Fung propped her feet up on the edge of the bed, revealing under her dressing robe two very shapely legs in fiber-glass stockings whose ankles bore a black pagoda logo—the finishing touch identifying them as a prestigious brand of hosiery.

Women are always sensitive to such delectable goods as fiber-glass stockings, which had only just come out, and the more so considering American and French products had simply vanished from the Shanghai market since the Pacific war began. Even Zhishuang could not restrain her ogles, while Ju Beibei, ever unrestrained, gasped audibly.

"Wow, imported goods—where did you find them?"

The self-satisfied Hong Fung looked at her stockinged legs appreciatively. "I bought 'em on the black market," she said in a tone of affected indifference. "Two ounces of gold per pair. I bought two pair so I'd always have a fresh change. The stockings available in the shops nowadays, well," (and here she clucked her tongue again) "they could appeal only to ordinary housewife types." Still propping those shapely legs on the edge of the bed, she conspicuously crossed one over the other.

Zhishuang unconsciously looked down to inspect her own stockings of flesh-colored Japanese rayon, which in comparison were painfully coarse and ill-fitting. Her ears instantly turned red in embarrassment.

Before the war her father had once bought her some good quality fiber-glass stockings, but she was always afraid she'd catch them on something riding a trolley or just walking around, and get runs in them. Now such foreign accessories as these had become real luxury items. Zhishuang had always prized such things, all the more so her own favorite clothing accessories. But today, lacking the slightest forewarning, she'd let this vulgar parvenu wife lord it over her. Yet at bottom what did she amount to? She'd merely married some man of unsavory wealth, could not even be sure she was wife number what, a woman to whom learning was unknown and family background unnoted, while Syi Zhishuang could honestly claim to be from a prestigious girls academy and a graduate of a top-ranking university; so by what right was it Hong Fung's turn to be so ostentatious?

The door opened just then and a woman with a lustrous head of hair came in dragging behind her two children aged about ten.

"Here. This is your teacher," said Hong Fung to the children. Her legs remained propped on the bed, and she didn't even bother mentioning Syi Zhishuang by her proper name. It was a lazy, offhand introduction indeed.

"Come over to me," said Zhishuang, with the kind and pleasant look that befits a teacher. "Won't you write your names for me?"

How could she have known that these two children would have not a bit of breeding, would not even know how to address her properly, but would start rough-housing in the doorway? Syi Zhishuang grimaced.

"The children are kind of on the naughty side, otherwise it wouldn't hardly be necessary to engage a governess for 'em," put in Hong Fung. "As for salary, whatever you say is okay. But no goofing off, mind you; you've gotta teach 'em..."

Zhishuang again found intolerable that supercilious expression of hers. She arose brusquely from her chair. "Excuse me, " she said, "but you'll have to find someone better than me," and marched right out the door.

"Why did you have to be like that? Movie actresses like her are all on that level..." said Ju Beibei as she followed Zhishuang out to the main gate.

"Upstarts like her—let her spend a few extra ounces of gold to hire someone else, because I've got no stomach for it," said Zhishuang still feeling her anger.

Ju Beibei could only offer repeated apologies. She was certainly intelligent enough to know that Zhishuang would be rising, not declining, in future social stature. A young lady especially of Zhishuang's beauty and education would have market value, as it were, in the world of high society, so out of a sense of simple precaution she wanted to remain in Zhishuang's good graces. It was for that reason she'd been so enthusiastic about recommending her for the job in the first place, though Hong Fung's degree of arrogance today had caught even Ju Beibei quite by surprise and was acutely embarrassing to her.

Juanren had earlier made a date to meet Zhishuang for lunch this day at Golden Gate Restaurant. Zhishuang, full of pent-up resentment, stormed into the restaurant and spotted Juanren sitting in a booth reading a paper. His hair was carefully brushed in a foreign style, and he was wearing a well tailored wool tweed sport jacket and a white shirt with contrasting black necktie. A cigarette dangled from his lips, and the curling smoke caused him to squint slightly, giving him an unintended expression of reserved elegance. This was her fiancé. Neither parvenu nor merchant, he was upper class, well-bred, and the scion of a prominent family—a man, in short, whom Zhishuang would not at all be embarrassed to admit was her fiancé. As soon as this thought occurred to her, her nose twinged and grateful tears began rolling from her eyes.

Juanren listened attentively, or, more accurately, relished with an air of satisfaction, the "job-hunting blues" that Zhishuang related to him through her sobs. Zhishuang impressed people as beautiful, charming, and intelligent, but not in the slightest fragile. Today, however, he was indeed witnessing her fragility.

"That insufferable movie star—she's too dumb to remember her own birthday, belittles others just because she has money..." She nibbled on her knuckles as resentful tears came down in torrents, just like a high schooler who gets a D.

Juanren caressed her cheek gently, and smiled. "But you and Juanmin were full of such pious admiration when you went to pay your respects to Hong Fung a few years ago."

"Don't you dare mention that. I was young then, and immature." Zhishuang turned her head away and pouted.

"Of course." Juanren reached out and rubbed the engagement ring on her finger. "You're grown up now, grown up enough to become Mrs. Zhu. There's no need for you to go looking for a job and getting all upset again. After you graduate, let's get married, and you can be the home tutor for the child we'll make ourselves. Okay?"

"No." She pursed her lips to signal her displeasure. "I told you long ago I want to be a career woman, and even though we'll get married I still want to have work outside. I don't want to be like my mother who has to ask my father for money every time she wants to have a dress made. Besides, we can't hold the wedding ceremony until my father gets back."

"All right. We'll do it your way. But may I say something further?" He smiled charmingly and looked around to see that no one was near, then leaned across the table and planted a kiss on her cheek.

"Good heavens, everyone's looking!" she scolded him gently. Seated in the comfortably heated room in the company of her own wonderful fiancé, she had now fully regained her composure, just like a child wading at the beach who suddenly gets a mouthful of foul-tasting sea water and is gradually calmed down by her comforting parents.

In the afternoon Zhishuang went to the university for two classes. When she got back home, her mother already had the evening meal on the table and was waiting for her.

"The neighbors told me a good way to conserve on coal briquettes," said a pleased Mrs. Syi across the eating table. "The water used to rinse the previous evening's rice is poured into a thermos bottle, then you fill it to the top with boiling water, put the stopper in, and the next day it's turned into a nice thick porridge. I think I'll give it a try."

Syi Zhishuang was just lifting her rice bowl to her lips when Mrs. Tsao's voice could be heard calling in from the back door. "The rice shop's got in a fresh supply, and they start selling tomorrow morning at nine o'clock. Praised be Buddha. Let's go out now so we can be at the head of the line." Since Mr. Tsao had met with his tragic demise, his family was receiving special death benefits from the bank, but still it was the old case of "when you're not around you get ignored," so with the head of household no longer there, the bank wasn't paying a salary and Mrs. Tsao was perforce having a very hard time making ends meet.

Mrs. Syi reacted quickly, noisily punted down the remains in her rice bowl, then started off to queue up the whole night long.

"Mom!" Chengzu called her up short. "Didn't you just buy some black-market rice today? Going out on a cold night like this isn't worth it."

"You silly boy. We have to have rice at every meal How many days can just a few pecks last?" And so saying, Mrs. Syi wrapped a knitted shawl snugly around her neck and shoulders.

"I'll go, Mom." Chengzu stood up and restrained his mother.

"It's better if I go," said Zhishuang, getting up from the table. "You've got classes tomorrow, Chengzu."

"You...?" Mrs. Syi said skeptically.

"I'll go. The wind's going to be bitter tonight, Mother, and if you come down with a cold, it'll be a nuisance for everyone." Zhishuang picked up the rice sack and headed out, and no sooner did she open the back door than she was met with a wind so cold it made her eyes water.

A long line already extended from the shuttered store-front of the rice shop, snaked along the adjacent eave-covered alley, and turned the corner. A sharp wind blew down the alley, cutting knife-like through heavy overcoats and padded jackets to stab painfully right into the flesh, lending poignancy to the phrase, "oppressed by heavy debt and numbed by arctic winds."

This was the first time Zhishuang had ever competed for rationed rice and the first time she had ever associated with these maids and housewives; a few of them, who lived at the head of the lane and ordinarily watched her comings and goings with considerable interest, seeing her on this occasion join the queue, very particularly eyed her up and down. The proud Zhishuang normally would not condescend to associate with their type, but now she had no other alternative than to steel herself and squeeze in among them. Accustomed, as they were, to waiting in long lines, they'd all brought along pieces of cardboard to sit on or even little stools, while Zhishuang at first forced herself to stand erect. But Zhishuang was used to a comfortable life, after all, and before very long she felt her legs growing stiff and numb, and when the icy wind blew up again, she felt virtually paralyzed with cold. She looked at her watch—still only 3:00 a.m. Mindless of its grime, she leaned against the wall running along the alley and pulled her woolen shawl up over her head leaving only her eyes uncovered. Someone tugged at her coat sleeve: the old lady who was just ahead of her in line was considerate enough to offer a newspaper to Zhishuang to spread underneath her to sit on. By now too weary to pay much attention to prestige and appearances, she unceremoniously plopped herself down on it.

"They say that this time the limit is one pint per person," remarked someone dolefully.

Zhishuang's mouth dropped. Endure the suffering of queuing an entire night to buy one paltry pint?

"One pint?" someone immediately chimed in. "How many people is one pint supposed to feed? Three weeks ago you could get three pints at a single purchase, and now, not a month later, it's down to one pint? How is that possible?"

"What isn't possible nowadays? Anything's possible and everything's impossible, too. It all depends on what those Japs happen to be jabbering about at the moment, and then..." But someone's cautionary "Shhh!" cut off the woman's hoarsy voice in mid-sentence.

The old woman sitting next to Zhishuang began talking to her, sticking up her unsightly ink-stained fingers as she recounted the figures. "The price isn't right either. Last month price-controlled rice was selling for just one yuan sixty for one pint, but now it's jumped to five yuan for one pint and a half, and I've heard it'll go up to six yuan thirty per pint...Good heavens, there's just no way to survive."

"What's happened with your fingers?" inquired Zhishuang curiously, as she looked at the old lady's hands.

The woman smiled. "You're a young lady who hasn't had to scramble for rationed rice. Hey, this is on account that some people may try to buy more than their allotted share. So, look here, people who bought rice on Monday get their thumb stained with ink, and for Tuesday the index finger, and Wednesday I didn't buy any so my middle finger is clean, and Thursday I was able to get through without buying more, and today's Friday so the turn has come for my little finger..."

So that's why Mother has recently taken to wearing those old knitted gloves, thought Zhishuang. If that's the way it was, then her own finger would get stained with ink today. No, no! Zhishuang looked at her fair, slender fingers, the middle finger revealing the writing calluses that marked her as a privileged student. She clenched her hand into a fist and plunged it into her overcoat pocket. "How can they do that, how can they do that to me!" she fumed.

"It's a great system," said the old lady with a toothless grin.

"Without any trouble at all, you can know who's made how many purchases, or who hasn't even had a single turn..."

Zhishuang looked with horror into the black hole that was the old lady's mouth and at her head full of disheveled white hair, and felt a poignant sorrow for her—hunger lowered people's self-respect to zero.

Zhishuang shifted her sitting position, easing for a moment the numbness in her legs and sticking her hands deeper into her pockets, as she recalled her visit that morning to Hong Fung's home—the cozy heated room, the outrageously expensive fiber-glass stockings—everything about it in such contrast to the people here, beset with cold and hunger as they patiently waited in the dark of night: it hardly seemed possible the two scenes could exist within the same city.

The icy wind had now chilled Zhishuang to the bone; even the tip of her tongue, as it felt around her gums, seemed frozen through. Fortunately, before having gone out her mother had made her drink a cup of sweetened ginger tea. How she regretted now having been swayed by personal pique this morning, tossing aside that governess job. At the very least she could have used the extra income to buy black market rice so she wouldn't have to suffer the cold here and, to boot, get her fingers inked as if she were being fingerprinted...

Another gust of icy wind whistled past, penetrating her to the very marrow and bringing pain to her cheeks. It hardly seemed believable even to herself that the present moment and the previous noon at Golden Gate Restaurant could have been experienced by the same person. The Miss Syi who had been sitting in Golden Gate was the elegant and respectable Miss Syi, escorted by an equally elegant and aristocratic gentleman friend, whereas the Miss Syi who was right now queued up under these eaves waiting to buy her rice ration, wearing her mother's ancient otter coat and an old lady's style shawl wound around her head, had all the appearance of a slum dweller. If Juanren should chance to see her at this moment, he would not even recognize her.

Zhishuang rested her head on her knees and gazed up at the rectangle of gray sky visible between two red brick houses; the waning half-moon emitted a cold light which played off luminously against the frost-covered roof tops in the distance.

Well, then...get married? That would be the best way to extricate herself from her present financially awkward straits, and it was the path of least resistance as well. With the family situation so difficult as it was at present, however, to marry into the Zhu family would have a very deleterious effect on her subsequent position in their household. And without question her own sense of self-respect also forbade it.

Would the day soon break? How was it the darkness of the night sky was actually deepening? Even the faint rays of the moon had vanished. This interminable night—would it never come to an end?

Chapter 25

"This is the last of our money." Jingwen placed a stack of U.S. dollars on the table. "I had originally planned to use it for a trip to America to purchase an acid-resistant centrifuge."

Following the recent cease-fire in Hong Kong, Jingwen and Miss Yi had squeezed aboard a steamer and returned to Shanghai. With the outbreak of hostilities back in August 1937 he and Miss Yi had fled to Hong Kong where they rallied their spirits, and, taking advantage of Kowloon's economic resurgence, tendered a successful bid for land, on which they constructed a make-shift wooden factory building of some ten rooms. As it happened, after the Japanese occupation of Canton, supplies of hydrochloric acid became unavailable, so he and Miss Yi in partnership with some friends set up this workshop to maintain the supply of the product. The Hong Kong authorities were very concerned about environmental pollution, however, and because of chlorine gas emissions and acidic effluents, the factory had been fined god knows how many times. Due to shortage of capital, the factory substituted kerosene ovens for high-pressure glass chambers in the decomposition process, used water kettles in place of acid-resistant vacuum evaporators, made do with...Anyway, after the most painstaking efforts, they finally got the factory operating, and were satisfied enough that at least it wasn't losing money. But who could have foreseen the surprise attack on Pearl Harbor and the renewed shelling of their own factory, which instantly reduced the wooden structure to a sea of flames. There was no alternative but to fold up the business and pay off the employees. With this development Jingwen and Miss Yi had used up the last of their savings, and, lacking the means to stay on in Hong Kong, in the end there was nothing for it but to return empty-handed to Shanghai.

"I swear I'll never try to set up a business again as long as I live," he said to Jingchen. His graying head propped in his hands, Jingwen looked ten years older than his brother.

Upon their return to Shanghai, Miss Yi was obliged to stay temporarily with friends, while Jingwen stayed in Jingchen's house, though definitely not in the same room as his wife, Ying. In recent years old Mrs. Zhu had lost much of her physical vigor and knew she would be unable to convince her son to treat his wife with the consideration due her, so she made a pretense of befuddlement and simply looked the other way. The present living arrangements scarce constituted a long-term strategy, however; Jingwen's own children had already reached college age, and it would hardly do to rely forever on his elder brother. Moreover, as Jingwen was well aware, Jingchen himself did not have unlimited amounts of cash, because most of his U.S. currency and negotiable securities had been deposited in an American bank, which had now been frozen by the Japanese as their own private property. Thus to take on the added burden of Jingwen's household would really be too great a weight.

"The way I see it now, my only recourse would seem to be speculative investment," said Jingwen, pressing the stack of bills under Jingchen's hands. Then, mocking himself, he smiled, "Already old but still a student of braggadocio. This Ph.D. of mine is really an advanced degree in brag-ology, which has never brought me success but only allowed me to boast. I talk about my ventures loud enough to rock the very heavens, but the results have proved ruinous to my standing and reputation. Now I want to begin studying investment. Oherwise I simply won't be able to earn a living." That stack of U.S. bills represented the last of Miss Yi's private savings. Imagine—here was a man who had made such a mess of everything yet Miss Yi still stuck with him, and they had never enjoyed a day of comfort or satisfaction.

"Slow down a bit, Jingwen," his brother urged. "How do you think an impractical academic of your type can possibly make it trading securities? You'd better rest quietly for a few days then go out and look for some job that will allow you to get by." And he took the stack of bills and pressed in into Jingwen's hands. "Anyway, we're all family—if there's food for one, there's food for everybody. You don't need to be concerned on that score." With that, afraid his brother would urge the money on him again, Jingchen got up and hurried out.

After Cathay reopened for business, three Japanese were stationed there to supervise operations, one of them being Kagesa. They inspected the blueprints of the building, verified the contents of the vault, and audited the loan accounts. They also required withdrawal customers to sign for the amount in the presence of the Japanese supervisor on duty before payment would be made. Why did banking have to be conducted this way? Was this not tantamount to the bank's cheating its customers? Cheat people by taking in their money on deposit only to restrict their withdrawal of it later on?

But today the world belonged to the Japanese, and this once imposing bank president was now like a Buddhist saint sculpted of sand fording a river to reach the haven beyond—it would be difficult enough to save himself, let alone lend a saving hand to others. Thus, the bank carried on with its business with palpable lack of enthusiasm, and banking activity itself, because of the Japanese restrictions, was also very slack. Jingchen frequently returned home early, though he actually preferred it before when he was always extremely busy.

Returning to his own room, he found Zhuanlin sitting before the mirror doing her make-up. Jingchen sat in an easy chair and watched her as she primped. How rare it was since their marriage that the two of them could enjoy together such leisure as this.

Although they had been married already for quite a few years now, even upon closer observation Zhuanlin did not at all look her age. Knowing, however, that Jingchen rather disapproved of her involvement in those women's social functions of the YWCA—for fear only that he might have to contribute funds to them—she had gradually withdrawn from active social life. With her activities reduced, she'd gradually filled out more, as she spent her days at home playing mahjong and card games with old Mrs. Zhu. She'd been told that this evening, unusual enough, they were going out to a dinner party, so she'd started getting ready for it early. He watched her as she carefully arranged the curls of her hairpiece over her bangs in front, while at the sides she fashioned two full, fluffy buns, enhancing the graceful elegance of her facial contours. A wife, they say, basks in the glory of her husband. Although the husband—Zhu Jingchen—had entertained apprehensions about marriage beforehand and would not allow his wife to interfere with his work, nevertheless outsiders fully accepted her as Madam Zhu; moreover, because Jingchen was fond of affecting a "she's the boss" role, Zhuanlin had accustomed herself during these several years to being a matron of proud reserve.

"Is this dress a little too tight?" Seeing her husband come in, she stood up and turned around to model the dress for him. It was a sleeveless, high-collared mandarin-style dress, made of a colorful silk velvet, and it fit perfectly. "I've gotten a little heavy this year, so I had my tailor let it out, but I wonder if it was enough." And she scrutinized herself anxiously in the mirror.

Aren't women just this way—they forever consider that they will become the center of attention and imagine that others will carefully observe every last detail from the tips of their shoes to the rouge on their cheeks and the strands of their hair.

"If it's a little loose, so be it; if it's a little tight, so be it. Who cares?" remarked Jingchen indifferently. There was a woman for you, all right: even in a year like this she could be worried about the fit of her dress.

"Good heavens, how can you be so insensitive? These theater people have particularly sharp eyes. One year Mrs. Liu from the YW went to an opera especially to see how a young male role was sung, but because she wore a wool check overcoat instead of a fur coat, she was almost turned away by the stagehands when she went backstage to congratulate the actor, and was the butt of jokes for a long time after that."

"Don't make foolish comparisons. Mr. Mei's our host tonight and he isn't like that."

Zhuanlin made a scornful face into the mirror, but was disinclined to argue the point.

The situation was this: Mei Lanfang, the Peking opera star famous for his women's roles, had been intimidated by the Japanese into returning from Hong Kong to Shanghai, where the Japanese hoped to sponsor performances by him, thereby implying his support for Japanese policies in China. But being wise with years, Mr. Mei cited illness as a tactful pretext for declining to go on stage, then let his beard grow out to be doubly sure he could not be used by the Japanese to play his women's roles. But even an opera singer has to eat, so the Shanghai banks put on a special charity exhibition of Mei Lanfang books and photographs to raise money for him, and this evening Mr. Mei was hosting a dinner in his own home to express thanks to his benefactors. Alas, all Chinese were likewise trying to play it safe under the Japanese occupation while at the same time maintaining their moral integrity and a clean conscience; but society as a whole had become a kettle of turbid water making it more and more difficult to preserve oneself uncontaminated.

The Mei residence was a neo-classical structure on Rue Marche. A large room on the left front of the second floor was the dining room, the right front being a sitting room, with a spacious parlor taking up the central portion. The parlor was furnished with a refined elegance, and other than a western-style sofa, everything else, including the small objects d'art and wall scrolls, was in the classical Chinese style.

Mei Lanfang was wearing a woolen pinstripe suit of British cut, and not a strand in his meticulously styled western haircut was out of place; his teeth were pearly white, and above the corner of his mouth there was even a small black mole. He radiated elegance. On stage a graceful maiden, off stage he had the imposing appearance of a real man.

"Mr. Mei, you never seem to get old." As Jingchen shook his hand, he realized all the more how much he himself had aged these past few years.

"None of us here is so old we can't still lock horns...or," he added, "give the Japs a hard time." He took Jingchen's hand in his own hand, soft as silk. His voice had the same sweet sonority now as did his stage voice.

Because of his connection with Cathay as one of its board members, Liu Tongjun had also been invited to the dinner party. Zhu Jingchen had not seen him for quite some time, and to judge from his emaciated figure, he seemed to have suffered a serious illness.

"Tongjun, my friend, how is it you've gotten so thin?" inquired Jingchen solicitously. "Have you been ill?"

"He's been suffering massive haemorrhages," broke in someone sarcastically.

It seems that due to the efforts Tsai Liren had made among the right people, Bounty Textiles had underbid the competition and thus won the contract to supply its "Silver Dollar" brand fabric for manufacture of Hong Kong police force uniforms. Supplying khaki cloth for police uniforms was a very large-volume transaction, and at the time Liu Tongjun was wildly elated. Earlier, when the Bounty mills had been damaged during the fighting with the Japanese, he felt his business was in real trouble; thus to have won the opportunity so soon for a turnaround in his affairs was a matter of extreme good fortune. But who could have known that while waiting for delivery of the cotton yarn to be used in manufacturing the khaki fabric, the Pacific war would break out: the cotton yarn became a precious commodity to be hoarded, and due to spiraling inflation, the money he had earned depreciated so fast in value it was no longer even convertible. Then, quite contrary to expectations, the other party, on grounds the yarn had not yet actually appeared on the market, himself hoarded the yarn to sell later at a big profit. Thus Liu Tongjun's mood of delighted self-satisfaction turned to anger, and right before one's eyes his weight daily decreased until now his clothes flapped loosely on his emaciated frame.

"I just hope that a loser like me can be reincarnated in my next life as the manager of a successful business," said Liu Tongjun with an expressionless face.

"At this juncture," someone advised, "don't be thinking about setting up a business, because whatever anyone does, it'll be difficult. Now even writing up an order for goods specifying payment and delivery date costs an extra 30%, otherwise the order form is just scrap paper. And no one's even speaking of credit purchases any more. Even breakfast crullers have shriveled in size. When things are like this, the only way to make it is to speculate on hoarding. If the other guy's merciless, then I've gotta be heartless. Therefore, Tongjun, my friend, you'd best engage in speculation. Just give a free hand to the able Tsai Liren, and you've got a sure thing. He's conducting business on the exchange right now, and making a pile of money. In a world like this even saints get forced into prostitution."

Tsai Liren would have been better left unmentioned, for, once mentioned, Liu Tongjun's expression turned ugly. He threw a glance at Zhu Jingchen and remarked cynically, "Now Tsai Liren himself has become a precious commodity, while I have become a brainless loser. And it's the guy who's a brainy schemer that makes the money."

In fact Tsai Liren had long since resigned his position at Bounty Textiles in order to free himself to concentrate on his own business dealings in preparation to become Zhu Jingchen's ideal son-in-law.

Jingchen was in temperament a generous man, perhaps because his circumstances were so much more favorable other people's. He thus affected not to understand Liu Tongjun's remark, and immediately turned the conversation to a new subject. "There are an awful lot of rumors flying around out there," he said to Mr. Mei, "and it's now widely reported that you're preparing to take to the stage again in a performance of 'The Fairy Maiden's Birthday Celebration' to commemorate the birthday of that gangster-collaborator Huang Jinrong. The rumors are so prevalent they're practically deafening."

Mei Lanfang smiled indulgently. "Well I'm not going to argue with the rumor mongers. Those tabloid reporters seem to be speculating—seizing on a little rumor to make a big story, trying to sell long, as it were. But times are difficult and they have to eat too, you know. So I composed a couplet for the newspapers:

> The peach and pear to bloom require a warming sun;
> Defying cold winter's tyranny here am I the plum.

Since my surname in fact means 'plum' and plums bloom in winter, I think that'll do it. No one will hassle me any more."

"To be sure, no one will tease you with rumors any more," said someone with a deep sigh.

"The household registration and surveillance system has come back already," remarked another. "Has it started where you are? There's no escaping it. And we've had to turn in our radios to have the wires of the short-wave band cut. And people are forbidden to listen to Voice of America broadcasts. Traffic cops hold you up to extort tolls, and tax officials go into stores to demand gratuities. The prewar price of grade "A" rice was ten yuan per hundredweight, and now it's jumped to one thousand. In all my life I've never experienced anything like the mess Shanghai is in right now."

Rain suddenly began to fall, pelting the windowpanes and casting a pall of depression over the company. The scene was so moving one among them could not restrain himself from humming the Peking opera tune, "I've picked up the realm and loaded it onto my carrying-pole; the day is done and my road is ended; the life of man..."

The thin and doleful voice sang on, to the accompaniment of the pattering rain. "...We raised no defense, and for the rest of my years, we'll be separated by war..." Every word, every note was permeated with the vicissitudes of life and the hardships and misery it held in store for mortal man.

*   *   *

Not going to his office on the pretext of ill health had become Zhu Jingchen's daily routine recently. Today he again languidly kept to his bed, eyes closed, seeking tranquillity. He had Zhuanlin telephone the bank to report his absence. He'd never been this way before. What with having to work under the supervision of those three Japanese, however, just stepping into the bank as president made him feel sick to the stomach, and he actually wished he could come down with a serious illness so he could take extended sick leave.

He lolled in bed, expelling puffs of cigarette smoke toward the ceiling. Then, abruptly addressing his wife, he said, "Zhuanlin, what about all that silverware in your dowry?" Herself the daughter of a prominent family, Zhuanlin's trousseau had included whole trunk's full of silver trays, silver fruit dishes, silver compotes, and so on.

"What about it?" Zhuanlin turned and looked at him with a startled expression.

"You know, it's awfully tough getting by nowadays, and business conditions are only going to worsen. It would be best to hold Juanying's wedding right now. We can all have a real good time—these last few days at home have been gloomy as hell. So I was thinking about that silver of yours, all piled up somewhere not being used, and anyway it's of a design that may go out of style before long. Wouldn't it be best to select some pieces to give to Juanying for her dowry? It would save us from having to spend money to buy things for her. Anyway, what's the point in keeping it?"

Zhuanlin brushed her hair in silence. She got her husband's drift—keeping it is useless when you don't have children of your own! They'd been married several years, but perhaps Zhuanlin had passed her most productive child-bearing years, or perhaps the upheavals of the times had forced Jingchen to concentrate on his business responsibilities to the neglect of his conjugal duties. In any event, at the present moment she sat absolutely still. And what could she do? In this large and tangled household, she had only Jingchen to rely on. And so she forced herself to nod in assent.

Jingchen sensed she wasn't very pleased about it, but that didn't bother him. He clasped his hands behind his head, and with apparent casualness began chatting. "Didn't you say a few days ago that you'd taken a fancy to a fur coat at Siberia Furriery? How much do they want for it? Why don't you buy it? Present from me." The price of a fur coat, of course, would certainly be cheaper than a silver trousseau. But Zhuanlin had indeed been itching the last few days for a fur coat, so wouldn't both be getting what they wanted?

Her eyes reddened and only with an effort did she restrain her tears.

It's not that she was petty. The truth was she really wanted to be like Miss Yi, offering her complete support to her husband. It was just that Jingchen adhered to the principle, "He who promptly pays his debt will ne'er have cause to fret," so that in whatever aspect of their lives he owed her nothing. That was his character: he had never liked being indebted to anyone for anything. But toward one's own wife such an attitude could really be very painful. For the sake of Jingchen, Zhuanlin had abandoned her own social circles and her charitable work for the YWCA to become Mrs. Zhu the dutiful wife. And of how many fur coats was that the equal?

"You're just walking out? Not a word of thanks to me and you're just walking out?" queried Jingchen as she started out the door. She turned and came back in, sitting on the edge of the bed. Though now well into her forties, Zhuanlin was as alluring as ever with those smooth shoulders and soft flesh. Jingchen embraced her. "There is no permanence in life," he said softly. "A daughter goes off to get married, and money depreciates in value. You alone never change; you'll always be mine." His eyes, hard and keen, which always gave him such a commanding presence, were now intoxicated with desire.

The bedside telephone rang most inopportunely. It was Fan Yangzhi saying there was urgent business he needed to see Zhu Jingchen about. Jingchen quickly rose and concentrated on washing and dressing. As he lathered up his face to shave, he studied his puffy eyes for a long while in the mirror. No, this would not do at all; he would not let the young Mr. Fan see him in such a decrepit state as this.

He carefully shaved his lower jaw, which left a virile bluish tinge behind, rubbed an elegantly scented Yardley pomade into his hair, and knotted his tie with particular precision. Despite the heat of the past few days, he carried a sport jacket over his arm, then drove to the Cantonese restaurant where he and Fan Yangzhi had arranged to meet.

Since the reorganization of Cathay Republic under Japanese control, Zhu Jingchen had become powerless as president, though Fan Yangzhi still respectfully referred to him by his formal title.

"I've received information, President Zhu, to the effect that both Bank of China and Bank of Communications are to issue large overdrafts drawn on the puppet regime's Central Reserve Bank, and will use the funds to help their own employees get through this long crisis. You might say it'll be doing business without putting up capital. Why don't we issue such an overdraft, too?"

Yes, it made sense. Right now currency values were eroding on a daily basis, so that using today's money to hoard goods for future sale had become extremely profitable. Jingchen's eyes brightened. But he'd have to consult those three Japanese overseers at Cathay, and that would necessarily involve some ass-kissing for which he had no enthusiasm.

"We oughtn't simply to wait passively during these dark days, sir. Cathay's employee housing is half built already, and construction has had to be suspended only because of present financial uncertainties; so why not make use of puppet funds to complete the construction? The buildings are being put up on Shanghai soil and the Japanese can't very well take them away when they leave, so when in the future their game is up, the apartment buildings will still be the property of Cathay Republic Bank. All you have to do is borrow the money from their bank to construct your own housing. It'd be foolish not to engage in a venture like this which doesn't require a cent of capital. It'll be like boosting the family belongings of the Chinese people! Since the successful landing of the allies in north Africa, the German army has never been able to regain its superiority, and after the Battle of Stalingrad everybody, from their commander, Marshal von Paulus, on down, were taken prisoner by the Russians! Don't you think the Japanese, seeing these developments, must be getting awfully nervous? For our part then, we should seize the opportunity to benefit ourselves."

"Where did you get this information?" asked Jingchen doubtfully. "Radio and short-wave broadcasts are all jammed now. You should be more cautious!"

Fan Yangzhi smiled slyly. "Do you want to see the actual Battle of Stalingrad? The whole thing was captured on film. There are open-air showings of the film, courtesy of the Soviet consulate, in an alley near the intersection of Avenue Joffre and Avenue du Roi Albert. If you're interested, sir, I'll get a complimentary ticket for you." He paused, then resumed the original subject. "Anyway, sir, with the international war situation the way it is, the puppet regime under Wang Jingwei will start squabbling internally, and because of those factional struggles, the days of the puppet government are numbered, so we'd better get ready for it right now and secure as much property as we can for the Chinese."

Their conversation was short but very sensible and of long-range significance. If it really was possible to complete construction of the Cathay housing project by issuing low-interest overdrafts on the puppet Central Reserve Bank, that would definitely be one good thing for China to come out of this economic depression brought on by the Japanese occupation.

"All right, I'll go argue with them," said Jingchen with a nod. His spirits had revived and he was ready to go at it. Already some little time had passed since he had given any thought to financial affairs. Due to the withdrawal restrictions imposed by the Japanese at Cathay, and due as well to the jumble of currency conversions—first from the national currency to military scrip and then to puppet government currency—the value of the money in customer savings accounts had dropped by fully one third. And precisely because those deposits (which were calculated in the old national currency prior to any of the conversions) had depreciated substantially, the bank itself had actually made money. But if the money thus earned was allowed simply to sit there without circulating, wasn't it just being eroded away for nothing? At present housing construction was the most lucrative thing to do, for speculation in material goods enjoyed far greater advantage than speculation in currency or securities. By concentrating Cathay's capital in the purchase of land, he could construct housing on it while at the same time defraying the costs of construction with the proceeds derived from separately selling the dwelling units to their occupants on an installment payment basis. Thus the investment of capital would not be particularly great but the profits would be very considerable. In addition, one could even trade the Cathay-created construction company stock on the securities exchange, working both angles simultaneously—like "painting a picture with two brushes," as the saying goes. Really, what good was there in allowing that large amount of money deposited in Cathay just to sit there idle?

In the short space of a few seconds a jumble of thoughts suddenly flashed through Jingchen's mind like a series of movie scenes: everywhere ferro-concrete buildings towered over him—English style, French style, hybrid Sino-western style structures, alleys and lanes filled with apartment buildings, towering, solemn, heavy...Ha! If you Japanese think you're so smart, let's see you pick those buildings up one by one and ship them back to Japan!

"And how is Miss Juanying these days?" Fan Yangzhi asked the question as if incidentally, articulating his words through a mouth half full of tea.

"Okay, I guess. When girls get to be her age they always want to travel down a new road—marriage," replied Jingchen absently while his mind still worked away on the previous topic. "This housing investment is really something of a gamble, isn't it? I wonder if I should deal myself into it?"

"Who's the groom?" asked Fan Yangzhi, staring.

"Who else? Tsai Liren. That gentleman has made piles of money the past few years," said Jingchen with mixed admiration and envy. "A shrewd cookie."

"And after their marriage, will Miss Zhu continue working?" The less Jingchen's mind seemed to be on that subject, the more insistent were Yangzhi's stares and queries.

"Work at what! That organization of hers has long since closed up, and the foreign boss is locked up in a concentration camp. So now she's thinking of marriage—there's no other option to follow." He spoke in a jocular tone, but what Yangzhi heard made him feel lonely and sorry.

"Well, then," Jingchen resumed; "if I'm going to do it, I'd better go do it. I'll go now and call on Kagesa and get him to help mediate with the Reserve Bank." With a gulp, Jingchen swallowed the remains of his tea, patted Yangzhi good-bye on the shoulder, and left. Yangzhi remained behind, alone and gloomy, remembering that evening when he and Juanying—Juanying, with her lithesome figure and that delicate look about her—were standing on a deserted street corner facing one another. He knew that Juanying was very disappointed in him, and he had caused her a great deal of emotional pain. Yet he had not in the slightest been able to explain himself to her. As he fixed his mental gaze on the memory of Juanying's pale and pretty face, how he wanted to explain to her that he was not at all the shameless economic collaborator she imagined, that he was not seeking to spend the rest of his life with her in marriage, but that he did want to maintain a relation between them of sincerity and trust, to be able to confide in one another, to be kindred spirits...Of course, that would never happen.

Two months later he heard that Juanying had gotten married.

Chapter 26

"**Z**hishuang, Juanmin is a mother now and Juanying is married, too. But this elder brother of theirs has been left hanging right up to this very day. When are we going to get married? Dad spoke with me about it recently, saying Grandma was getting awfully old and was anxious to hold a great-grandson in her arms."

Juanren was seated in the small parlor of the Syi's home, talking quietly. In the twinkling of an eye it was again the depth of winter and its icy winds bore down with a vengeance. Zhishuang's home lacked even a charcoal burner, to say nothing of a Peking-style pot-belly stove. Aside from the homes of such prominent families as the Zhus and the Lius, most people now viewed home heating as an extravagance, and had simply done away with it. When the cold got to be insufferable, Zhishuang would ward it off by clasping the hot-water bag next to her. It was covered on the outside with silk, now worn threadbare by Zhishuang who kneaded it to extract the warmth, ever reminding her of her childhood when she used to hug her doll.

"However that may be, we still have to wait until Daddy returns to Shanghai," said Zhishuang softly yet firmly as she eyed her rose-colored felt shoes.

"But if we keep waiting like this, we'll be waiting forever, and I can't wait that long." He added his hands to the hot-water bag, caressing Zhishuang's while he was at it.

"Humph," she smiled. "If you can't wait, then suit yourself and look for other options."

"You're terrible!" Juanren took her hand and kissed it, but she'd rubbed Sparrow Spirit Cold Cream into her skin, and the cheap smell fairly stung his nostrils.

"Imported goods are simply unavailable," she moaned. "Foreign brands like Hazeline Snow and Pond's are worth their weight in gold."

"Oops, I almost forgot. I have a little gift for you." As if it had only just occurred to him, Juanren drew a small package from his coat pocket.

"Oh, Max Factor!" exclaimed Zhishuang gleefully. It was a small tube of American lipstick.

"Try it right now and let's see," urged Juanren.

"No, I'll wait till later to use it..."

"Wait until you're a bride?"

"There you go again. Oh yes, there's something I want to give to you, too." Zhishuang mischievously squinted her eyes into a smile, and ran upstairs.

Zhishuang's uncle had recently started a small department store and was doing very well financially. Merchants who had hoarded goods were now making a lot of money; it was a form of commerce requiring neither capital outlay nor business experience but which was sure to reap huge profits. Zhishuang's uncle had always remembered when her mother had been so helpful to him and his family years ago, and now that he had prospered, he would for his part be helpful to the Syi family. So he had opened a bank account in Mrs. Syi's name from which she could make withdrawals for herself. It was by this means that Mrs. Syi had finally been able to hire a maid, so at least she no longer had to do cold-water washing. Furthermore, the Syis no longer had to vie for rationed rice or price-controlled cooking oil.

The new maid, Lianzi, came down the stairs, struggling with a large box.

"At first I was thinking of giving you a surprise, but I just couldn't stand it any longer." She turned her head aside and laughed with child-like charm, adding softly, "I bought it with money I earned myself."

What had happened was that, because a large number of the British and American missionaries at McTyeire had been put into concentration camps, the school suddenly had a severe teacher shortage, which Zhishuang turned to her advantage by getting a position as instructor of first-year English.

She carefully undid the satin bow on top of the box, then opened it up, revealing a set of ten silver compotes.

"Wow...you must have been saving a long time for these!" Juanren picked up one of the matching silver lids, then carefully replaced it in the box.

"I want to make my own marriage dowry," said Zhishuang with more than a touch of pride.

"What for? If you have something, then add it to the dowry, and if you don't have very much, then it doesn't make any difference anyway. Who's going to be fussy about it?" Juanren knew that Zhishuang had always been a proud girl, yet these years when her father was not in Shanghai, inevitably the household income was less than generous, and he did not want her to feel she had to bear so heavy a burden.

"I'm going to be fussy about it!" said Zhishuang seriously. Yes, indeed; how could she be compared to the daughters of the Zhu family? Didn't she after all want to show that there were areas where she was different from them? She could at least show that she was capable of putting together part of her own dowry. She had made her decision, but her pride was tinged with depression all the same.

Because Zhishuang had to go out very early the next morning to teach her classes, Juanren returned home from the Syis right after supper.

Since Mr. Syi had left, save for occasional visits by Zhishuang's uncle, hardly anyone came to call at the Syi home, not even the widowed Mrs. Tsao. As a consequence, the Syi family had long since withdrawn from the pleasant diversions of city life.

Evenings Chengzu had his homework to do and Zhishuang her class preparation. On especially cold days, Mrs. Syi would have Lianzi light a pan of charcoal in an upstairs bedroom and the family would squeeze into the room to get the fullest benefit from the warmth. Those lonely few pieces of faintly red charcoal emitted but a stingy heat as they turned into white ash. To absorb the charcoal fumes, pieces of orange peel were placed at the edge of the pan, and they gave off a pleasant fragrance. Well, however one might complain, still, when the family huddled around that pan of charcoal in the dead of winter and the dark of night, it really did seem like a little bit of heaven on earth. No wonder, then, at these times Mrs. Syi would more that ever think about her long-separated husband.

Mrs. Syi was sitting by the bed lamp stitching cloth shoes. "I wonder how your father is getting along right now all by himself out there," she mused aloud. "In weather as cold as it is here in Shanghai, the interior must be even more so. They say that Chungking now is very hard pressed. I wonder exactly where he is."

"Don't worry, Mother," said Zhishuang consolingly. "Daddy's got a good head on his shoulders and he's such a capable man that if there's a withdrawal, no way are they just going to cast him off."

"When the new day finally dawns and your father can return, we'll be able to finish up the plans for your marriage. And then when Chengzu gets into college, finally I'll be able to stop worrying." Mrs. Syi heaved a deep sigh.

Days are bright and nights are somber, just as, so they say, "some families are happy, some families are troubled." And during these hard times the great families of Shanghai all quipped that the thickest smoke was issuing from the chimney of the Zhu residence, so extravagant was their consumption of coal.

Jingchen had already brought to completion the construction of Cathay's employee housing, and had now started the second phase of his housing business—Yongye Mansions, comprising three four-story apartment buildings in the English manor style, also located on Robison Road, which even in its present unfinished state was fully rented. There had now developed in Shanghai a sizable new aristocracy of wealth, and housing had become for such people a much sought after means of off-setting the constantly depreciating value of currency. This being the case, Jingchen himself exploited the opportunity by constructing several apartment buildings, and, having been the first to jump into this business, he could build them for less and thus reap a greater profit.

"The more the lice get into your hair, the less concerned you are to scratch them," as the saying goes. After Cathay's resumption of business under Japanese supervision, Jingchen had at first been very passive, but he forced himself to resume his work, trying to get Cathay back under his own control. Having been unexpectedly jolted to his senses that day by Fan Yangzhi, and having in addition witnessed such bullish securities markets and commodity speculation, was it worth his while to sit idly by preserving his moral chastity—keeping the lice out of his hair, if you will—when everyone else was exploiting the chaos of the times to grab up his share? Due to the difficulties of raw material supplies and the unending depreciation of currency ever since the outbreak of the Pacific War, there was simply no way to carry on normal banking operations; but with Cathay employees leading such desperate lives, as they were, it might well prove advantageous to the bank, its employees, and to himself as well to engage in outside business activity. According to puppet government financial regulations, of course, no bank, whether the modern banks or the old-fashioned counting houses, was permitted to engage in any non-banking business. But Cathay Republic Bank had surmounted that hurdle by establishing a separate Cathay Republic Enterprise Company, which drew its funds from Cathay Bank; Fan Yangzhi was appointed by Zhu Jingchen as its director. At first Jingchen had to bear up under those three Japanese supervisors, who bore down on the bank as oppressively as Mount Fuji, and it was unavoidable that he always turn a smiling face toward them—especially that Kagesa fellow—in a smoke screen of obsequious subordination. So he'd had to transform his inherent Chinese spirit of radiant courage, and, like a truly great man, show how really flexible he could be! Thus Jingchen began to toady and fawn.

"Right now you have all of Shanghai in the palm of your hand," he'd said to Kagesa, trying to win him over, "including, of course, Cathay Republic Bank. What need is there to keep Cathay's funds buttoned up so tight? Aren't you just tying your own hands?" Kagesa, realizing that what he said made sense, loosened his grip on Cathay operations.

These two years since the outbreak of the Pacific War had been extremely difficult to get through. Prices were spiraling upward one day to the next so that even a thick stack of bills couldn't buy much. Everything depended on Jingchen's finding ways to convert currency into negotiable securities, while holding in store his gold and U.S. dollars. Employee salaries were issued in half-year lump-sum payments lest inflation erode their value to nothing. Then after a certain interval he'd see if the employees again complained of a shortage of money, when he would again sell off some gold or dollars and pay another few months of salary. That Cathay employees managed to get by better than those of other banks was due, in the last analysis, to Jingchen's devoted attention to them, which earned for him the praise of the entire financial community.

And as for those three Japanese supervisors at the bank, Jingchen managed one way or another to get them to restore to himself a little authority over bank operations. That had been his biggest headache. Fortunately, the three Japanese after all these years had themselves gotten awfully tired of the war, and no longer lorded it over the employees with that same intimidating arrogance they had displayed on first taking charge of Cathay.

One day when Jingchen went into Kagesa's office to urge him to invest a sum in another housing project, he discovered him with his head drooping, despondently drinking alone. Seeing Jingchen enter, he gestured with annoyance for him to leave, mumbling, "Don't come in any more to bother me; I haven't any more interest in managing your affairs. My wife and two sons set out three months ago from Japan to come to China and ever since that time I haven't heard a word from them...they must have lost their lives...drowned at sea..." He broke down sobbing, and Jingchen felt genuinely sorry for him.

Thereafter Kagesa really seemed uninterested in continuing to play his role as devil. And with Kagesa himself in such a state, the other two were only too happy to shirk their work. As a consequence the pressure on Jingchen disappeared and he was free to transfer money and securities, making business ever more profitable for the bank.

If you want to do business and take advantage of the opportunities it offers, you've got to maintain contacts with people from all walks of life, and that's why the parlor at the Zhu residence was night after night occupied by distinguished guests who kept at least four tables of mahjong going. On this particular evening a Peking stove, burning shiny black chunks of high quality Vietnamese anthracite, was placed in the middle of the parlor giving off a cozy warmth. Pu Zhuanlin, wearing only a plum-colored mandarin dress which revealed her supple, white shoulders, sat behind Jingchen studying his mahjong tiles and lending advice.

Jingwen had recently changed his former detached indifference to good grooming, and was wearing an ivory-colored wool vest and a white shirt with cuffs held properly in place with shiny buttons. He too had finally struck it rich. That an impractical idealist like himself could actually strike it rich just goes to show that striking it rich was not at all hard.

And while speaking of his riches, it should be noted that they came quite accidentally. After war broke out in Hong Kong, he and Miss Yi had managed a frantic return to Shanghai, but since their home contained nothing but a jumble of useless chemistry equipment and various colors of chemical compounds, one could justly claim they had not a cent to their names. But "unexpected rescues often occur in times of direst need," they say, and it just so happened that many of the hospitals set up by the British and Americans in Shanghai had been expropriated by the Japanese as enemy property and either reorganized or put to different uses. Those Chinese who needed medical attention could easily find private doctors instead of going to a hospital, the only major difficulty for them being the matter of laboratory analysis, for private clinics did not normally house such facilities. Seeing with his own eyes all the inconvenience resulting from this state of affairs, the bookish Jingwen got a bright idea: he rented a room, bought a used refrigerator, and putting to use the chemicals and equipment he'd stored in his home, hung out a sign proclaiming Verity Medical Laboratory, and with barely the effort it takes to lift a finger he had resolved for thousands of patients a problem of crisis proportions. That is how he found his road to riches. How true it is: "Anxious that the flower live, it dies; indifferent to its fate, it thrives."

When Jingchen finished the round, Jingwen caught his eye; Jingchen got up from the mahjong table, yielding his place to Zhuanlin, and stepped with Jingwen over to the French windows. The two brothers had counted on each other for help during these turbulent years, and Jingwen had come to place a great deal of faith in his elder brother.

"Jingchen," he began softly, "she...that is, Miss Yi, is pregnant. What do you think—should we have the child or not?"

Because Miss Yi had previously led so unsettled a life lacking both money and energy, she had secretly miscarried several pregnancies. Now, however, she and Jingwen were enjoying a well earned stability in their lives, and the new laboratory business was doing well, too, bringing in a virtual blizzard of money. Jingwen might thus wish to add another child to his family, but in the present case Miss Yi seemed obviously to be some sort of lover—for how else explain the pregnancy? Yet since such a status was in general tacitly recognized already, it would not be any cause of embarrassment to Miss Yi to carry the pregnancy to term. But if, then, the child were allowed to be born, should it after all be regarded as the child of Jinwen's legal wife or the child of a mere mistress?

"She shouldn't have the child unless you decide to divorce your legal wife," said Jingchen without moving his lips.

"That's just not possible. I'd never be able to face her," said Jingwen, shaking his head. "She's been very good to me, except for the fact she can't read and so could never help me in my work. When I was abroad studying all those years, she shouldered the entire responsibility for the children."

"Well, that's the way it's always been," countered Jingchen after a pause.

"But Miss Yi is already thirty-four. And besides...she'd really like to have a child. She and I have shared a lot of joys and sorrows these past few years, and now finally we have a stable career..."

Jingchen frowned. "Hm. Miss Yi's only thirty-four?"

"Yes, twelve years younger than me. What about it?" asked Jingwen somewhat warily. He was now making good money, true enough, but he still had the same old pensive, tired look about him.

"Remember Wei Jiusi, the former president of Cathay? After his first wife died, he married a much younger woman, then when Mr. Wei himself passed away, his entire property—every last cent of it—went to her, and she lost every last cent of it; now she's completely impecunious. Understand?" And he nodded meaningfully at Jingwen.

Jingwen, almost imperceptibly, nodded in return.

"Your oldest boy, Juanfeng, is graduating from the university, isn't he? Why not have him help you with your laboratory business and take over from Miss Yi. She's had a hard enough time already; let her return home and enjoy a happy life." Having spoken, Jingchen corrected the position of the chair next to him, turned, and walked off.

His arms dangling at his side, Jingwen just stood there dumbfounded. He was an intelligent man and of course had got his brother's meaning: concubines are not reliable transmitters of family property. But if he did what Jingchen suggested, how could he ever face Miss Yi? He had five children, and now that Jingwen, who had been waging a struggle half his life, had finally won some wealth, he naturally began to think of his children, and even granting the children were cool and distant with him, that simply reflected the truth of the saying, "at thirty the husband loves his wife, at forty he loves his children." He did truly hope that his lab business, now so prosperous, could be handed down to his children and grandchildren. Miss Yi was his financial partner in the business, and the problem was she was more than a mere concubine but less than a real wife; and being young it was entirely possible that she might leave him at any time. Leave, that is, and take half of the property with her...Well then, what about letting her have the child, which would tie her to him? Wouldn't Jingwen with his impressive Ph.D. degree in chemistry, wouldn't Jingwen who was laboring so assiduously in a calling related to the national salvation effort—would he not ruin his name and reputation by maintaining a concubine? These were modern times, the Republican era, after all, when maintaining a concubine had lost its respectability—among the intelligentsia, at any rate. Of course, a fellow lacking money and reputation, such as the Jingwen of yore who operated a money-losing chemicals factory, had no need to give much thought to these matters. But now his Verity Medical Laboratory was attracting ever more attention in Shanghai, which was itself already bringing a new set of worries to Jingwen and was likely to bring even more as time went on.

"Jingwen, what are you doing standing here all by yourself?" Someone was tapping him on the arm: it was Miss Yi who had approached unnoticed. She had a black cashmere shawl thrown over her shoulders. "Why don't you play mahjong?" she asked thoughtfully.

Jingwen looked at his watch, took her hand and said he wanted to return home. He had in mind urging her not to have the baby. He felt the smooth flesh of her fingers—a woman of her age ought long ago to have had a wedding ring slipped onto her third finger.

Jingwen had already bought a three-story house for Ying and the children, while he and Miss Yi lived in a rented apartment. But that, he knew, was no long-term solution.

Chapter 27

One end of a thread held clumsily between her teeth and the other end wound around her finger, Zhishuang was using the taut thread as a knife to cut—rather ineptly—a preserved egg into slices. Normally, if it was to be seen by her husband, she would be very precise, but this time she'd made a mess of it from the first: the slices were all different sizes and her fingers all smeared with the yolk.

Juanren could meanwhile be heard in the bathroom gargling noisily and clearing his throat. Zhishuang stole a glance at the bedside clock: she'd have to hurry and give breakfast to Juanren, but looking at the ill-cut jumble of preserved egg slices, she felt she was at the end of her rope.

Having finished his washing and dressing, and cheerily humming "Yankee Doodle," Juanren emerged from the bathroom. He'd thrown a coarse-weave brown-checked dressing robe around him, and though he was not near-sighted, he was wearing wire-frame glasses with flat lenses. With a light workload and with things going very much to his satisfaction, he had recently been putting on weight, and had replaced that earlier air of casual elegance with the settled maturity of a typical upper-class husband.

"Today I'll wear that brown necktie with the rounded ends," he said as he buttoned his shirt cuffs and stretched out his neck expectantly.

"Coming," Zhishuang called, licking the yolk from her hands as she went to wash up first. Juanren grabbed her in an embrace as she passed, but Zhishuang, her hands all sticky, exclaimed coyly, "Just see what a capable wife you've married!"

That spring Zhishuang had become the young bride of the Zhu family. But because, one, old Mrs. Zhu had been so insistent about it and, two, being a career woman in these troubled times was very difficult, Zhishuang had had no choice but to submit to custom and dutifully fulfill her role as housewife on a full-time basis.

Although Mr. Syi never did make it back to Shanghai to preside over the nuptials, the family had long since prepared for Zhishuang a dowry consistent with the standards of the socially more elevated Zhu family. Moreover, Zhishuang's uncle, who in recent years was practically wallowing in money, generously put up a portion of his niece's trousseau. Thus it could be reckoned that Zhishuang was married off with a full measure of respectability.

The marriage of Zhu Jingchen's son was a major event within the financial community. Although by disposition Jingchen disliked extravaganzas, still he normally maintained broad social contacts; and besides, he was a warm and generous person who liked to please others. Then too, there were those who wanted to settle social debts with Jingchen, those who wanted to curry favor with him, those who wanted to forge a connection with him, those who...Anyway, for these various reasons there was a steady stream of celebrants to the event, which surpassed in ostentation even Jingchen's own marriage to Pu Zhuanlin.

With still a month before the wedding, two thousand invitations were sent out, and an even greater quantity of wedding gifts was received in a ceaseless flow, whereupon it became necessary to send out more invitations. Gratuities were given to the servants who delivered the gifts—all manner of things from silver trays and tea utensils to furnishings such as hanging lamps, table lamps...—all piled in the small downstairs north parlor which had been specially set aside for the purpose and was now getting to look like a department store warehouse. All the gifts were carefully recorded by Fagun, who was kept so busy with it he scarcely had time to go to the bathroom. Not only Fagun, but the entire Zhu household domestic staff from high to low were madly dashing about. Old Mrs. Zhu was so happy she went every day to the newly furnished apartment on the third floor just to look around. Since Jingwen had purchased his own home and moved Ying and their children into it, and considering, too, that both Juanmin and Juanying had married and left home, all of a sudden there were a lot of empty rooms in the house. Consequently, the third-floor rooms had been fixed up for the exclusive use of Juanren's little household. Its furniture had been carefully made-to-measure by Mao Chuantai, Shanghai's best furniture maker. Juanren disapproved of mahogany as too reminiscent of the flashy, nouveau-riche taste, preferring instead the present furniture set in high-grade chestnut-stained teak, which included features like invisible hinges on the armoire doors, a framed dressing-table mirror of German manufacture, and the like. There were besides a sitting room and a small parlor, likewise furnished with tasteful elegance. Old Mrs. Zhu was so happy and excited that she forgot all about her aches and pains.

Of course not everyone in the Zhu household was equally happy, least of all Pu Zhuanlin, what with the appearance of a new generation Mrs. Zhu, younger and of course prettier. This was a development which could not occasion Zhuanlin any joy, for Zhishuang, unlike the four Zhu daughters who could all be expected to move out sooner or later, was likely to remain indefinitely. Outwardly, however, Pu Zhuanlin was the busiest person in the Zhu home assisting in the wedding preparations. And another thing that she was none too happy about: Juanwei had gradually come to understand the human heart. She was now a young lady of eighteen and this fall she would start college. With the two oldest sisters already married, her time had come to be the spoiled little mistress of the family, but now the family was unexpectedly revolving around the new bride as its center. Since her childhood Juanwei in many ways had imitated her eldest sister, Juanmin, and thus without even being aware of it, she had come to be similarly headstrong and imperious. Once she discovered she would no longer be the cynosure of household attention, she had a fit of jealousy, which, on the pretext of Juanren's upcoming marriage, she vented with single-minded purpose by purchasing fabrics and clothes for herself—a dress of silk crepe and another of velvet embossed with miniature flowers, and a western-style evening gown, too; then she added a cashmere jacket, and finally topped it all off with an ermine coat. She knew full well that during these joyous and busy days her father would be too distracted to put up much of a fuss.

The large banquet hall occupying the entire eleventh floor of the Jinjiang Hotel had been reserved for an afternoon reception and because there were so many guests only light refreshments were served; but there was in addition to be a thirty- or forty-table wedding banquet in the evening to entertain near relatives and close friends. As many as a thousand guests came in a steady stream to the afternoon reception. At precisely three o'clock when the bride appeared, already there were many more guests than could be accommodated, but most of them, fortunately, were urbane people who would be little concerned if the amount of refreshments they consumed was not commensurate with the value of the present they'd given.

Jingchen had attired himself for the occasion in formal black tailcoat with satin lapels and he sat erect in the seat of honor flanked by society's most prominent personages. His formal wear was the very same he had had made when a bridegroom to Pu Zhuanlin, which he had never worn since, though not for lack of opportunity, by any means; it was rather that since the outbreak of this protracted war he had been preoccupied with other things. He had then suddenly lost considerable weight so that his clothes didn't fit well and this tailcoat, when he'd once tried it on, flapped loosely on his thin frame, lacking all shape. He thought he might have a new tailcoat made for the present occasion, but, much to his surprise, when a couple weeks beforehand he rummaged up this old one and tried it on anew, it happened to fit quite nicely, for this was a period when things were going very smoothly for him, when he was enjoying peace of mind and good health and thus had been able to put back on all the weight he had previously lost.

He sat in the seat of honor savoring the experience. Recently it seemed that he'd been unexpectedly rescued from a desperate situation—the Cathay housing project had been completed and the first group of employees, practically wild with joy, had already moved in, and the second phase of housing construction had already started. Besides all that, designs for a new Cathay Republic Bank Building were in the drafting stage and within days they would lay the foundation stone...And now he was adding a new member to his household, his new daughter-in-law.

Although the Syis were not a prominent family, ever since Zhishuang had come to his office selling advertising space in her school yearbook and had impishly plunked down a piece of candy in front of him, he had taken a real liking to her. And in terms of good looks, she was not inferior to any of his own daughters, while at the same time embodying, each in its proper degree neither a fraction too much nor a fraction too little, both the charming innocence of a child and the dignified reserve of an adult. Jingchen, experienced in worldly affairs as he was, understood perfectly that such palpable good breeding required native intelligence and strong family values, qualities that could not be feigned however much one might try. Especially after hearing she had accumulated a set of silver compotes using her own savings, Jingchen's respect and admiration for this young woman only increased.

With the piano playing the wonderful strains of the wedding march, the bride approached with dignified steps, leaning on her uncle's arm for support; the long train of her veil, held with utmost care by four little children, was a limitless expanse of whiteness in which she resembled a carefully wrapped gift to be presented to the Zhu family by the hands of God himself. She would add a subsequent generation to carry on the Zhu family name.

The sound of admiring applause arose in the banquet hall.

The son, Juanren, also wearing a dark tailcoat, was dashing, handsome, and of exceptional bearing. Although not more intelligent than most people, he was by no means unworthy of the pains his father had taken in his upbringing: he neither gambled nor womanized and in conduct he was responsible and honest. At his German pharmaceutical firm he had worked his way up to department head, had a black sedan which chauffeured him to and from work every day, and earned a monthly salary sufficient to support a wife and family. Even though he might not make much of himself, he had at least made himself into a man. As his son accepted the bride from her uncle, signifying acceptance of the responsibility for her as new family head, Jingchen felt a lump in his throat, and though he himself had twice been a bridegroom, he had never been quite so affected as on this occasion, and it made him acutely aware of the weighty responsibilities, whether in the family or in the larger society, one bears when born into this world as a man. Son, carry on to the end your responsibility for this young woman!

This thought led him to the marriage of his two daughters. Juanmin was now already a mother of two; in a letter from Free China delivered a few days previous, she described a congenial household and a smooth life, working alongside her husband Feng Jingsyao at the American USO. How love can change a person: pampered since childhood, Juanmin had transformed into the capable director of a service organization and a good housewife. And Juanying, who with abdomen bulging and soon to give birth ought by tradition to have cut her hair short, still preserved, impending motherhood notwithstanding, the church custom of keeping it long—wound into a large flat bun at the back of her head, held in place by a lustrous green jade clasp, a present, of course, from her husband Tsai Liren. By comparison, she enjoyed much greater good fortune than her sister Juanmin, for Tsai Liren earned a great deal of money. Formerly, because of her plodding diligence, her plain looks, and her lackluster personality, even Jingchen himself unconsciously tended to ignore her. The entire household all along had been terribly snobbish toward her, and even Fagun, Auntie Lu, and other old servants treated her with a certain scoff. But now that Mr. Tsai had attained such wealth, of course it was all quite a different story, and whenever Juanying now visited at her former home, she heard nothing but honey-coated language and respectful forms of address; even Pu Zhuanlin made a point of instructing the kitchen to prepare special dishes for her.

As one of Juanren's older-generaton relatives, Mrs. Su, his aunt, came to join in the wedding celebration. Time had passed so swiftly it had already been several years since Mrs. Su and Jingchen had seen one another. The last time they had met was when Juanren's uncle had died in the street and Jingchen had made the funeral arrangements.

Perhaps because her husband finally had a home to return to—the tranquillity of death—she seemed to have put on some weight; and with her hair combed up in a top-bun held with an amber-colored clasp, and wearing a loose-fitting brown satin dress, she looked elegant and dignified. Only Jingchen among the entire company could read into her appearance a lonely widowhood. She would traverse that brown wasteland of her remaining years, eating alone, sleeping alone, enduring a cheerless existence.

Jingchen spotted her at a distance. Once she had been very precious to him, indispensable even. But after he'd reached high station in life, he had to endure, however much he would have wished it otherwise, the inevitable emotional scars for himself and to accept that he had inflicted an equally unpreventable inner anguish on her. In the last analysis, everything had to pay a price. He had even ceased bemoaning the fact he had virtually no time for himself, that he still had to rush forward like a machine which, once set in motion, kept spinning by the force of its own inertia. Even though he was at his son's wedding ceremony, he still felt compelled to circulate endlessly among the guests, observing them shrewdly, sounding them out about business matters, sorting out who was now enjoying power and who behind a façade of strength was really weak...

As he raised his glass in toasts to his friends, he took advantage of the flickering candlelight in the banquet hall to look at her solicitously. "It's been a long time since we've seen each other," he said. "Have you been getting along satisfactorily?"

She cocked her head and smiled. There was a tragic look in her eyes as she said, "I hope only that you yourself are getting along well." And she turned away and disappeared into the crowd of other guests. Jingchen did not again seek her out.

He discovered that Mary Luo Gong had not come. At the time he was sending out the invitations, he wondered if he ought to invite her, knowing that her circumstances in recent years had been none too favorable. An invitation would impose on her the expense of a gift in return, but if he did not issue an invitation, news of so important a social event would sooner or later reach her ears and that would cause certain anger. The self-respect of a defeated and frustrated person is particularly sensitive and fragile. Having mulled it over, he decided to send an invitation to her. As expected, her daughter came, delivering a pair of silver toothpick holders, which was very creditable of Mrs. Gong, but she never did appear at the ceremony. Jingchen felt very much ashamed of himself for having thus put her to the needless expense.

Among the throng of celebrants in the hall, some were complimentary, others envious; some had favors to plead, others wanted to make use of him; there were those who wanted to destroy him, and those who loved him...The people here were of all hues and colors, and they constituted the world in which he had placed himself these many years, where he had circulated and socialized, and where he had sought opportunities to expand his business interests.

Zhishuang's gown had been custom tailored at great expense by Madam Janet's Fashion Boutique. Most brides, wearing such gowns only a few hours for this once-in-a-lifetime occasion, rented them from formal-wear stores, a matter of only ten or twenty silver dollars. But a streak of pride ran through Zhishuang: she had never before worn borrowed clothes and she certainly was not going to start now with a wedding dress worn by god knows who—the notion was positively nauseating. She might limit the number of her other clothes, but the wedding dress—well, that had to be special ordered. It was to symbolize her farewell to youth, and how could she possibly wear someone else's old clothes for that?

And so it was that, advancing in time with the stirring strains of the wedding march, a blizzard of confetti blanketing her head and shoulders, accompanied by unbroken applause, she bade farewell to the springtime of her youth. With Juanren's soft warm hand folded around her own, the two wielded the beribboned silver knife and cut the first slice of wedding cake; the cake was coated with a hard sugary icing which at first required a little pressure to cut through, but having broken through that layer, the inside was soft and fluffy. In that instant Zhishuang sensed how closely this resembled her own marriage: her love for Juanren was this icing—sweet to the taste, smooth in texture without a trace of graininess, firm yet brittle. She believed that true love ought not be like this. True love should be like wine—not merely sugary sweet, but richly mellow; her intellect told her all too clearly, however, that she would have to abandon all of that for the sake of the permanent comfort and contentment that would later come...But now, she had finally broken through the hard outer coating and cut down to the soft fragrant interior. By the time the ceremony was over and she'd managed to get out of her white gossamer gown, she was nearly exhausted. As she spread out the stiffly starched wedding train on the carpet, the rustling of the material seemed in Zhishuang's mind to echo the utter bleakness of her life.

She didn't know how the practice had come about, but all the expenses of Juanren's little family were naturally included in those of the general household, except for breakfasts which Juanren took responsibility for. That responsibility was a very limited one, considering Juanren's ample income, but managing just the morning meal involved much trouble, especially for Zhishuang who had never before even touched housekeeping chores; perhaps the Zhus intended by these means to urge the new bride toward a greater fulfillment of her obligations. After managing to get her husband off to work, she really felt she had nothing to do, for although the huge Zhu mansion contained well over ten rooms, the only place where she could live with unconstrained freedom was this third floor.

She yawned vacantly and stepped over to the window. Its curtains were made of gold-colored poplin, rather crass, to be sure, but she had yielded in deference to the joyous occasion. That Zhishuang should yield on any point was quite out of character, but when she had actually arrived at the Zhu home, she necessarily had to be careful about everything and attentive to her every action. Looking down onto the steps leading toward the garden, she could see several of the maids, all wearing blue tunics and black pants—Lu, Sun, and some others whose names she couldn't remember, so closely did they resemble one another—just now carrying out broad rattan flats of rice to dry in the sun. The rainy season would soon be upon them and the rice insects would soon appear. The whiteness of the rice in flat after flat caught one's gaze, resembling, as it did, a pond of lotus flowers in full blossom. Zhishuang was reminded of that piercingly cold winter evening when she was huddled together with the neighborhood housewives waiting for rationed rice, sitting on the freezing pavement with only a newspaper under her, sitting the whole night long, just so she could buy three pints of price-controlled rice! Poverty was indeed an abominable thing, and while Zhishuang's contact with it had been slight, still it had made a powerful impression on her. Of course from here on it was scarcely likely that she would ever be touched by poverty again.

She glanced at the clock: it was only eight-thirty. Normally at this hour she would have been sitting properly in the teachers' room. The life of a working woman was far from soft: whether windy or rainy, every day she had to rush to get to work and rush to get back home, but it did include, of course, the pride that comes with earning one's own living. In her last year of college, aside from having to cope with the customary graduation thesis and comprehensive examinations, and with sentimental activities like the class yearbook and farewell parties and dates with men students, she additionally had to cope with prospects of "commencement for unemployment," as they mordantly quipped. After the outbreak of the Pacific War and the discontinuation of her father's remittances, she seemed suddenly to have reached adulthood. First she was employed as a secretary, stationed at a high counter just outside the door of the business office, not unlike working at a hospital admitting desk, where a sign overhead announced "No Entry Without Authorization." Her responsibilities included drafting correspondence, typing English-language materials, and answering the telephone. She could have handled such trifling work as this quite without five years in the home economics department. A good-looking working girl always seems to get better treatment, so not surprisingly the manager was very considerate toward her. But Juanren was not overly pleased about her taking this sort of job: where he worked he always had a secretary, so how could his own fiancé actually be someone else's secretary? Although he didn't say anything directly, his expression indicated clearly enough his displeasure. Zhishuang paid him no notice. She knew perfectly well when she should yield and when she could not yield. At last, however, she gave up the job, not because of Juanren's unspoken disapproval, but because of the insufferable attitude of the manager's wife when she telephoned. Her wary and supercilious tone of voice made one feel that the position of secretary was as uncomfortable as lying on a bed of nails. After several such encounters, Zhishuang up and quit. Later on, she was invited to join the faculty at her alma mater. She would never forget her life as a teacher during that semester. But who could have predicted that during this period of disorder, sudden and unexpected change would become the norm? Because McTyeire was owned by an American missionary board, the Japanese army before long forcibly occupied the campus buildings and turned them into a hospital, which compelled the school to relocate to a foreign-style house on a city lane, where it carried on as best it could. By dint of these circumstances, the headmistress talked the matter over with Zhishuang and requested her to give up her position in favor of an instructor whose family was dependent on him for its livelihood; Zhishuang assented. Thus it was that her college commencement was indeed followed by unemployment, which left her with little choice but to marry. Anyway, for a twenty-four-year-old woman not to be married just wasn't right.

Having gotten her husband off, she stayed in her room whiling away the time reading the newspaper until it was eleven o'clock, her time to "strike a pose," to use the Peking opera term. Otherwise she would give the servants cause to sneer at their new "young mistress" for being a positive scaredy-cat. Zhishuang arose languidly from the couch, slipped into a gold-patterned black dress, threw a honey-colored sweater around her shoulders, and went down to old Mrs. Zhu's rooms to pay her respects.

Because her two sons were now both very prosperous, and with a granddaughter-in-law come into the family, the elderly woman felt great peace of mind, and her face had become rosy in color and lively of expression. On this particular day Jingwen's wife, Ying, had dropped by and was now with the elder Mrs. Zhu talking, trying to dispel her own gloom. Although her husband was now doing very well, she was the same old Ying: a worn indigo jacket over a summer-weight poplin mandarin dress, and, showing through the side slits, thick flesh-colored woven stockings, and embroidered slippers on her feet; only her wrist showed any attention to style—a lustrous, deep-green jade bracelet. She had accustomed herself to her husband's living openly with another woman virtually as wife, indeed accepted it as her destiny; such a woman as Ying required only the recognition of her priority status in Jingwen's family as his first and only legal wife; all else was open to discussion. Since moving into the spacious two-story, six-room house her husband had bought for her, she actually felt very lonely and depressed, and it was on that account she would go for a walk along Great Western Road almost every other day. Anyway she now had her own rickshaw, so the coolie could take her over to the main house in the morning and fetch her back home after supper. Thus she passed her days, one after another.

When Zhishuang stepped into the room, she felt the atmosphere was not quit right: old Mrs. Zhu was wiping tears from her eyes, though Aunt Ying's face revealed definite happiness as she bent over the old woman, offering comfort.

"Zhishuang!" exclaimed Ying, beckoning her in as soon as she saw her. "What a happy occasion. The Zhu family has had such good fortune these past few years!"

What had happened was that at Jingwen's laboratory, quite by chance Miss Yi was looking over a lab order and noticed the patient's name was Zhu Juanming; since the custom in Chinese families was to give similar names to members of the same generation, she mentioned it to Jingwen who in turn happened to mention it to Ying, who, for her part, told the story to old Mrs. Zhu. Mrs. Zhu's first son, Jinglian, had joined the army at an early age and to the present day there had never been any news of him—it wasn't even clear if he was still alive—a matter which had always been very distressful to her. Particularly now that things were better than ever for the family, what with her two sons doing so well, during the still of night her thoughts turned even more to her first son who had never enjoyed a day of happiness. Thus, suddenly hearing this account, she gazed wide-eyed at Ying and asked her to have Jingwen make inquiries and find out what the situation was. So Jingwen sent someone to follow up on the information in the lab order form, and, sure enough, on the basis of place of birth and generational position it was confirmed beyond doubt that the father of the patient was none other than Zhu Jinglian. Pity was, Jinglian's circumstances had throughout been none too favorable: during his period in the army, he had been through untold dangers and on any number of occasions had very nearly lost his life at the hands of warlord armies; in addition his unit was transferred from one place to another on an almost daily basis, and sometimes he received his pay and sometimes he didn't, but he never had any way of keeping in touch with the family. In any event, he was tossed about for all those years and of course there was the chaos of war throughout that time, and consequently all news was completely cut off. Who could have guessed that he would finally end up in Shanghai, living in South City with his wife's parents who owned a soy sauce shop. For over ten years Jinglian and the rest of the family had been in Shanghai together and neither ever had the slightest inkling of it. And to think that everyone knew the name Zhu Jingchen! Unfortunately theirs was a family of only very limited means which had no dealings with the world of finance and thus no knowledge of its leaders. Jinglian himself had died of hematemesis at the beginning of the Anti-Japanese War, leaving two sons, the younger of whom had come to the laboratory for a sputum analysis. Not long before he'd discovered he too was spitting up blood, and because his father had been taken off by this ailment, the son was naturally concerned and thus had gone to Jingwen's laboratory for tests. Jingwen knew that since both he and his brother had now become important public figures, it was unavoidable that there would be impostors fraudulently claiming kinship. So, an academic through and through, he felt strongly that the family not be rash in recognizing any claimant until there was scientific verification by means of blood tests. Old Mrs. Zhu, however, complained she just couldn't wait for that, so she had Ying go personally to South City to investigate, and one look at the two sons told her that there was no need for a blood test, for their faces were perfect replicas of Zhu family features: high-bridged nose, broad forehead, general bearing—practically carbon copies of Jingchen and Jingwen when they were young. It was this which Ying had hurried back to report to old Mrs. Zhu.

Zhishuang had heard only snatches of the developing story. She was still very new in the family and consequently she could not immediately share in the family's joys and sorrows. She was, however, overcome by the notion that so great a chasm of luck and fortune could separate brothers of the same mother—proof, she thought, of the maxim, "humans plan but fate decrees." Suddenly she felt an awe before the inexplicable power of destiny.

Before long Pu Zhuanlin came in to pay her respects to the elder Mrs. Zhu. She was wearing an unlined mandarin dress of rippling light-gray silk, while thrown around her shoulders was a lavender cashmere shawl with a crocheted flower pattern, and on her feet matching embroidered white slippers: even though she was just relaxing at home, Zhuanlin did not slacken her attention to good grooming. She was perfectly courteous toward Zhishuang, courteous to the point that Zhishuang tried her best to avoid her, but it was, after all, impossible to escape these daily morning and evening encounters. Since becoming Mrs. Zhu, Zhuanlin had taken her husband's hints and almost entirely withdrawn from her activities at the YWCA, retaining only a nominal membership on its board of directors. Thereafter she had been devoting her intelligence and abilities entirely to the maintenance of the household and attentiveness to her husband.

Old Mrs. Zhu and Ying related to Zhuanlin yet again the saga of the long-lost relatives, which she listened to without any particular show of either enthusiasm or indifference. The story concluded, she pulled the corners of her shawl a little more snugly around her and said matter-of-factly, "All right, we'll have the two boys and their mother over for dinner sometime."

Zhishuang, casting a furtive and apprehensive glance at her step-mother-in-law, felt that she should say at least a little something more, be a little more expressive, but she had already dumped the box of mahjong tiles onto the table and started shuffling them for a game. The fact was, Zhuanlin had very little to talk about with either her mother-in-law or her sister-in-law, and it was solely to avoid offending etiquette that she attended these morning musters, as it were, to fritter away a couple of hours. Zhuanlin's behavior caused Zhishuang inward uneasiness for it implied that she too had to fritter away two hours here every day for god knows how many years into the future.

Luckily, going over the whole long-lost relative story again consumed quite a bit of time, and before she knew it, it was time for the noon meal. That eaten, Zhishuang could finally relax, as if delivered from a predicament, and although she had to pay another visit to the old woman's room in the evening, her husband and father-in-law were now at home, so the atmosphere was entirely different.

Unlike most Chinese, Zhishuang was not in the habit of taking a midday nap. After finishing the noon meal, therefore, the matter of getting through the interminable afternoon was quite a problem. She looked into the mirror and thought her hair needed doing, so she decided to go out and, while she was at it, wander around the streets. She climbed into a pedicab and headed straight out Bubbling Well Road to White Rose Hairstyling Parlor, where she was a regular customer of the number three hairdresser.

No sooner had she settled herself into the high barber's chair than someone called, "Zhishuang, Zhishuang!" and, turning her head to look, she saw a woman sitting under a hard-bonnet hair dryer nodding toward her repeatedly, a broad round face nearly concealed by the dryer. That face seemed familiar, but on the spur of the moment Zhishuang couldn't place her. With much effort the woman moved her head out from under the dryer and, with a twitter, unwrapped the towel from around her head. "Zhishuang," she said, "have I gotten so old you don't recognize me any more? I'm Liu Tsaizhen!"

Liu Tsaizhen indeed! Since that day when she had been hastily fetched home by the maids, already six or seven years had flown by—not that Liu Tsaizhen's added years had caused Zhishuang's momentary failure to recognize her, but, to the contrary, the fact that she was even prettier now than she was as a girl. Or, one might say, in bearing and demeanor she had developed a natural grace.

"Zhishuang, Ju Beibei says you've gotten married. And I never even got an invitation to the wedding banquet." Patent-leather handbag clasped under her arm, ring finger sporting a dazzling diamond in a platinum setting, Liu Tsaizhen looked every inch a woman of wealth. She seemed very content with life. She had married into the rich and powerful Li family, her home occupied fully half a block, and her little boy had already started nursery school. The boy, being the eldest son of an eldest son, had conferred on Tsaizhen an immediate and considerable rise in stature in the Li family, and the Liu Tsaizhen of today was far removed from the inarticulate, self-deprecatory student at McTyeire.

But she preserved her simple honesty of those years, and, more than just vying with Zhishuang to pay the hairdresser for her, she insisted on waiting until Zhishuang was through, sitting in an empty chair alongside, keeping up a flood of patter about their life at McTyeire.

When Zhishuang was finished and they emerged from the salon it was already dusk. Thus another afternoon had been whiled away.

Recently, because the Japanese were limiting the supply of gasoline, the number of taxis and private cars had declined. The two women hailed a pedicab, and much to her surprise, Zhishuang discovered that Li Tsaizhen lived only one block away from Zhishuang's new home.

"You should come over often to visit—it would cheer everybody up, and you live so close by," said Liu Tsaizhen, holding her friend's hand, reluctant to part. Was she too perhaps lonely and bored?

The Li family mansion of Liu Tsaizhen's husband was one of those stern and forbidding-looking foreign-style residences with formal gardens. The grounds were enclosed by a red brick property wall, jagged shards of glass imbedded along its top, interrupted only by a black sheet-iron gate; just to the other side was a row of dense shrubbery, which made the interior seem particularly dark. According to Liu Tsaizhen, back in the twenties her father-in-law had been kidnapped by hooligans, and on that account the family had ever since been extremely cautious. From the pedicab Zhishuang watched as Liu Tsaizhen rang the bell; a peephole opened, then the gate parted a crack, Tsaizhen disappeared inside, and the gate clanged shut before Zhishuang could even get a good view of the scene within.

By the time Zhishuang got back to the Zhu residence, it was already late enough for the lights to be on. Since electricity restrictions had come into force with violators subject to fine, the light bulbs in the dining room chandelier had been removed save for a single forty-watt bulb, which cast only gloom in such a large dining room as this.

Juanren had a dinner party this evening and did not return home, so Zhishuang sat at the dining table reserved and withdrawn, carefully taking food only from the dishes right in front of her. Unusual though it was, Jingchen was eating at home that evening.

The story of Jinglian's son and his whereabouts formed the principal topic of dinner conversation, and that gradually extended to various anecdotes about the earlier years of the Zhu family. This was all very new to Zhishuang, so she just sat there without adding a word, sullenly punting down her rice, though necessarily keeping an appropriate smile on her face to forestall any innuendo about "the new mistress with the glum appearance."

"Zhishuang," said Jingchen, abruptly breaking off the idle chatter. "How have things been going for you here? Are you enjoying yourself?" he inquired considerately.

Zhishuang was taken quite by surprise. She felt a little panicky, then smiled graciously. "Everything's wonderful," she replied.

Well, whatever the case, she really did appreciate even this slight concern shown by her father-in-law.

Past nine and still Juanren hadn't come back. Zhishuang picked up an English-language novel, propped herself up on the bed and started aimlessly flipping through it. Liu Tsaizhen telephoned, inviting her over the next afternoon to play mahjong, to which she readily assented, for otherwise how would she while away that time?

Oh, how she recalled the day at McTyeire when Liu Tsaizhen was reviewing English history under the lamplight, and a couple of her household servants had come to fetch her home, and when she later heard Tsaizhen had returned to get married, Zhishuang regarded her with sympathy admixed with resentment. But after the passage of six or seven years, was she not herself, except for the addition of a college degree, virtually indistinguishable from Liu Tsaizhen?

She laid her book aside; she felt she couldn't read another word of it. The notion that she would have to pass the rest of her life like this—the rest of her life!—was positively frightening. She was only twenty-five years old, but in fact she had already begun "the rest of her life;" and what expectations did she have, what hopes could she cherish? Tears began to roll down her cheeks.

One day she finally said to her husband, "Juanren, why don't we move out and set up our own little household? We could rent an apartment—a two-room apartment would be enough."

Juanren looked at her in astonishment. "Rent an apartment? Hey, I don't make the kind of money Tsai Liren does; and besides, what about the household expenses if we lived independently?"

"I could go out and get a job again," said Zhishuang.

"Stop joking. If it got out that the young mistress of the great Zhu family was holding down a job, well, it would look as though the Zhus couldn't even support the new bride."

Zhishuang said no more. Quite of her own volition she had walked into this circle of life, and besides herself there was not a soul she could blame.

"I imagine the days drag pretty slowly for you, don't they? But we won't just be two people forever. You'll be having your busy day," he said, tweaking her nose. Yes, perhaps if they just had a baby, everything would be different.

Chapter 28

In view of the frenzy of speculation and profiteering in the marketplace, which directly affected the puppet government's wartime economic controls, the puppet Central Reserve Bank began intensifying efforts to recall its loans. At the same time it also constricted loans to financial institutions, temporarily reduced the money supply, and dumped onto the market the huge supplies of commodities it had been stockpiling. Especially after the puppet-controlled General Chamber of Commerce began implementation of a directive for compulsory purchases of cotton yarn and textiles, many speculators, faced with five-year prison sentences and fines of up to 50,000 yuan for non-compliance, felt compelled to sustain heavy losses by selling their hoarded stocks at artificially deflated prices, as a result of which a great number of them went bankrupt and committed suicide. Needless to say, the new business climate affected Mr. Tsai Liren, the speculator.

One evening Juanying, her stomach bulging with pregnancy, braved the rain and took a rickety pedicab to her old home to talk with her father. It seems that Tsai Liren was planning on smuggling his stockpile of cotton cloth to Free China to avoid having to sell it at a loss. But a smuggling operation like this would be quite impossible without Japanese military or collaborator personnel to provide bodyguards and escorts.

"Liren says that at your bank they always have goods and documents they ship inland, and he wonders whether it would be possible to squeeze in his stuff and ship it together," asked Juanying anxiously.

People—how unpredictable they are. Initially Juanying's intention in marrying Tsai Liren was no more than to fulfill a young woman's duty to start a new family, but once she had in fact become his wife, she identified herself with him, promoting his interests with a single-minded devotion, and whenever she talked it was always "Liren says this" and "Liren says that."

Although Jingchen was an expert in making money, he always did so by taking advantage of areas unexploited by others; no opportunity escaped his eye, but every advantage gained was for the sake of Cathay's prosperity—about that he had a clear conscience. Indeed, he was even a little cowardly about the notion of lining his own pockets at the expense of the public. Tsai Liren knew his wife's character perfectly, and so he specially sent this pregnant woman to seek the favor, for she could move the old fellow better than anyone else.

Jingchen frowned. But Juanying just smiled. "Liren says," she went on, "that you're a little on the over-cautious side. You know the Jia household in Dream of the Red Chamber—there wasn't an untainted person in the whole place except for the pair of guardian stone lions at the entranceway. Really, isn't the Shanghai business world just the same right now? Everybody's saying that, except for the bronze lions in front of Huifeng Bank, there's not a clean thing to be found in the whole of Shanghai. So why do you need to be so careful, Daddy?"

Notwithstanding she was still a pious Christian, since becoming a housewife and seeing with her own eyes the price of rice spiraling upward from four yuan a bushel before the war to twenty thousand yuan today, or hard coal from about one yuan per basket to one thousand per basket, inevitably she too, like everybody else, hung on tightly to what little money she had. And besides all that, of course, she was pregnant, and once the baby came into the world there would be many large expenses. Because the apartment building where they were presently renting was originally British-owned, it had now been designated "under military control," and for the past few days the Japanese authorities had been ordering the residents in five separate moves gradually to vacate the building so it could be put to other use. But rents and deposits were shockingly expensive, so finding other housing this year was simply impossible. Under such financial pressure as this, she no longer had the time to participate in missionary activities. Anyway, the foreign pastors of the church where she had always done her charitable work were now in concentration camps and the church building had been converted into a Japanese garrison. Selfless service to others was thus no longer feasible, and besides she belonged now first and foremost to her husband and to that new life which would be coming into the world.

Having finished the conversation with her father, she passed through the dark corridor to look in on her grandmother. To conserve electricity the light bulbs in the wall lamps along the corridor leading from the entranceway to the stairway had been purposely removed lest someone inadvertently break the "turn off the lights when not in use" rule, for there were a lot of servants in the Zhu household, and if one person were inadvertent, everybody would be inadvertent and electricity consumption would shoot up. Feeling her way up the staircase, familiar to her, of course, since childhood, she sensed a deathly stillness throughout the whole house, which now lacked that gentle, tranquil atmosphere retained in her memory. Juanmin had married and moved to distant parts; she had been the very soul of the home, and once she had gone, there was no way of recapturing the former liveliness of the place. And Juanying herself had married, and her two younger sisters were living in their school dormitories, and Auntie Ying and the children had moved out. As she thought about it, she realized there was hardly anyone left in her old home. Indeed, it was precisely for this reason that Juanying rarely returned. For one thing there was much to occupy her with her own family, and for another the old home was getting less pleasant but more complicated. Her stepmother, Pu Zhuanlin, was mistress of the household and could not be offended. The new bride, Zhishuang, was courteous enough, but, as the younger mistress of the household, of course, could not very well be neglected. And her grandmother, who was accorded more respect than a Buddhist saint, had to be kept amused like a little child, in addition to which grandmother had always doted on her more than anyone else, which made it all the more impossible to slight her. So on those rare occasions when she visited her old home, she had to visit all three and sit and chat, lest suspicion arise that she was partial to one and cold to another.

Reaching the second floor landing, she noticed a faint shaft of light issuing from the opened door of her grandmother's room, although it was perfectly quiet inside. She walked in and looked around, and saw her grandmother, as always, sitting in her rattan chair. When old people doze off, they really doze off with their head sunk into their chest. Around the little mahogany coffee table in front sat her new sister-in-law, Zhishuang, and a maid, Shen, who specially attended on the old woman. Juanmin's former maid, Auntie Lu, was also there. They had been accompanying the old woman in a game of mahjong, for which an overhead gourd-shaped 15-watt lamp with a flowery white ceramic shade provided half-hearted illumination. It was now the old woman's turn to play, but she'd unexpectedly dozed off, and the unfortunate Zhishuang did not dare wake her up, so there was nothing for it but, very gingerly, to pick out tiles from the old woman's pile and play them for her. Auntie Lu, also getting drowsy and dull-witted in the dimness of the lamp light, was throwing out any old tile and then letting her head flop to one side as she closed her eyes and succumbed to torpor.

The scene before her eyes suddenly filled Juanying with sympathy for her beautiful new sister-in-law. Hearing someone enter the room, Zhishuang twisted around in her chair. "Oh, Juanying's come!" she exclaimed, and simultaneously the old woman's eyes opened again.

"Juanying's here. What good luck. Lu, get the photograph of the young lady and show it to her."

"Photograph of whom?" Juanying seemed to have not the foggiest notion of what was going on. Zhishuang smiled wryly at her.

What had happened was that after the old woman had found the two children of her lost eldest son, she bought for them (inevitably at Jingchen and Jingwen's expense) a rowhouse on a charming little lane off Avenue Road, a distinct improvement on the virtual bird cage they'd inhabited in South City. Due to straitened family circumstances, Jinglian's younger son had had to drop out of college, and it was only with the assistance of Jingchen and Jingwen that he was now able to continue his studies. The older of the two boys, Juanguang, had suffered a high fever as a child, which, it was said, had affected his intelligence and he had never been a very good student, indeed, had never even finished elementary school. Not that he was actually dim-witted, but he was, certainly, rather slow. For such a person to find outside employment would be very difficult, so Jingwen had pretty much to take him under his wing. Fortunately Jingwen was now his own boss, and the reputation of Verity Medical Laboratory was widely known, which had enabled him to open a branch lab in the Jingan Temple neighborhood; he let the boy help out by washing beakers and test tubes, putting in as much time as he liked, for which Jingwen gave him a monthly salary. It was, in a way, Jingwen's repayment to his eldest brother for the latter's sacrifice to the family those many years ago. That ought to have been enough, but unfortunately the old woman was intent on seeing things through to the end, and since it just so happened that Ying, with the heart of a saint, was practically going crazy with idle time, old Mrs. Zhu had suggested she act as an informal go-between for Juanguang.

"But...Juanguang is retarded," said Juanying tactlessly. She picked up the photograph and scrutinized it; it was obviously the product of a photography studio: standing next to a flowering plum tree a young lady in a printed mandarin dress was holding a sprig of plum blossoms as she stared into the camera with a wan smile, and although she had the look of a typical daughter from a modest household, she nonetheless possessed very fine features. "What delicate beauty. Does she really agree to the match?" asked Juanying.

"Having your father go personally to request the match, who wouldn't agree? If she could fly here, she still couldn't get here fast enough!" said the old lady, bursting out in laughter. As soon as Juanying had come in, her drowsiness had vanished.

"Fine. So let's discuss it with her and see how things go," added Juanying with a polite smile. But in her heart she felt that there was something downright mean about it, that the old woman was getting too old, that her arrangements were getting increasingly old-fashioned, even perverse. How could her father and Uncle Jingwen actually pursue this marriage idea just to please the old woman? But having married out of the family, she herself was not in a position to argue the point. After endless chatter about nothing in particular, Zhishuang invited Juanying up to her third-floor rooms for a visit. The old woman imagined Zhishuang, the new bride, had much to ask Juanying, the mother-to-be, and so did not detain them.

Besides his work Juanren also had many dinner parties, and again this evening he was not at home, so the two sisters-in-law went into the sitting room to chat. Zhishuang fixed a cup of good rich coffee for Juanying—a tin of premium coffee left over from before the war. It was such a treat to have someone over she could talk with that Zhishuang always entertained guests with special generosity.

"You've seen it all," said Zhishuang, choking with emotion as soon as she started to speak.

"There's really nothing that can be done about this family," said Juanying, trying to comfort her, while at the same time inwardly rejoicing in her great good fortune that Tsai Liren had none of his family living with him here in Shanghai.

"Juanying," her friend probed, "renting an apartment on the outside the way you do and hiring a servant, how much does that cost?"

It would have been better not to have raised the subject, for it practically made Juanying sick to her stomach. "At first, Liren paid six gold bars for the apartment, in accordance with his discussion with the foreign landlord. Then the Japanese came and completely repudiated that arrangement and demanded we pay an additional sum. We could put up with that, but now these past few days they've been evicting the residents so they can put the building to some other use. And trying to get a new place now is frightfully expensive...Really, Zhishuang, would it be worth the trouble for you to move out of here? Here you can eat and sleep for free—what can you possibly have against that?"

"Where in the whole world is there really a 'eat and sleep for free'!" Zhishuang took the lid off a jar of something she'd bought at Guansheng Food Fair—sugar-coated preserved sour plums, which made Juanying recoil in disgust, but which Zhishuang began nibbling without so much as batting an eyelash. "I'm thinking of going back to McTyeire to teach. Headmistress Syu telephoned me the other day to say she could arrange a position for me."

"Will Juanren agree?"

"Let him mind his own business. Otherwise I'll die of boredom." Zhishuang spit out a pit, then picked out another plum and popped it into her mouth.

"Zhishuang," her friend asked suspiciously, "you wouldn't be pregnant, would you?"

Zhishuang was taken by surprise, then nodded sort of vaguely.

"Really, just look at yourself," Juanying scolded; "about to become a mother but still talking nonsense like this. Once the baby is here and you have to provide for your little family, you'll be spending everything Juanren makes for the child and it still won't be enough." Advanced in pregnancy as she was, it was tiring for Juanying to sit long, so she rose from her chair and walked a few paces, then looked around at Zhishuang who was still sitting dumbly, her eyes glistening with tears.

"Enough of such talk, Zhishuang. We've both been through that period—working for the betterment of society, bringing credit to the female sex...but now it's time for Juanwei and Juansi to take their turn at those things. Honestly, isn't that what being a woman is all about?" And she threw up her hands in a gesture of resignation. Seeing it had by now gotten pretty late and thinking of her husband at home waiting for a reaction to his request, Juanying said a hurried good-bye. As she started toward the front door, she remembered she hadn't dropped in to visit with Pu Zhuanlin, so she thought she'd pass by her room and chat with her a minute or two for form's sake, trying though that always was. No wonder Zhishuang was insisting on moving out and setting up her own household. Seeing Zhuanlin's door ajar, she started to push it open and go in, only to hear, much to her surprise, her father's stern voice ask, "Who's there?" followed, apparently, by a shoulder leaning against the door to force it shut. Juanying was startled into a heavy sweat. "Daddy," she stammered, "I just wanted to tell you I'm going back now."

Her father thereupon opened the door a crack, enough for Juanying to catch a glimpse of two gentlemen seated on the sofa, one of whom being Fan Yangzhi—not that she recognized it was he so much as she sensed it. For a while the two of them had been very close, so that she could distinguish even the atmosphere about him. But that was a thing of the past and this was a different day. She'd heard he was now making a good living, had moved from that cramped alley, had even gotten married. That was all very normal, of course; after all there had never been any pledge of love between the two of them.

"Okay. Be careful on the way back. Your stepmother is in the small parlor downstairs." Jingchen spoke with her through the door without letting her in. Juanying thought it very odd: whenever guests came, except for family like Uncle Jingwen or Miss Yi, they never came up directly to her father's bedroom, but today Fan Yangzhi and that other gentleman were there. What was going on, anyway?

In the downstairs parlor Pu Zhuanlin was sitting by a lamp cracking open lotus seed shells, the pretext, obviously, by which Jingchen had sent her out.

"Mother, who are the two people in your room?" asked Juanying suspiciously. "And why so mysterious?"

"Something about discussing business with your father. Doing business with the interior is now under strict control, so they've got to be extra cautious. Without thorough preparation, the whole project could just collapse." Zhuanlin spoke off-handedly, and Juanying figured that's all these was to it. So she had a pedicab called to take her home. But on the way back she couldn't help thoughts of Fan Yangzhi from welling up in her mind, though it was a vague feeling that did no more than simply provide flavor to her ordinary and tranquil life, just as pepper flavors a bowl of soup.

Meanwhile in the upstairs room, Jingchen was talking to Fan Yangzhi. "Never mind, it was only Juanying, and she's never been gossipy. Where were we? Oh, yes. I know there were plenty of people cursing me behind my back when I got 150 million yuan from the Reserve Bank to construct more Cathay housing units. But that's all an accomplished fact, isn't it? That hundred fifty million, one could always say, was business I won for Cathay without using any of our own capital. But the way things are at present, the more you do the more mistakes you make, while the less you do, the fewer mistakes you make. So by holing up at home and doing absolutely nothing, you won't make even the slightest mistake."

The gentleman next to Fan Yangzhi was dressed in tunic and trousers of plain white silk. He was Syu Zhiyong from Cathay

Republic's home office. Forty-some years old with emaciated features yet with alert and piercing eyes, he seemed very much the perspicacious business man.

He listened quietly until Jingchen had finished his grumbling. "Considering Cathay's scale" he began, "it might seem like doing business without capital, but if thieves broke in, would they bring their own money with them to steal? Obviously not: Central Reserve has lent you money because it wants to use you and thereby harm the entire nation, just as thieves, after all, murder people to get their money. Mr. Zhu, you have accepted the trust reposed in you by all the Cathay employees, and you have maintained your steadfast loyalty to them while coping with the present situation, as is obvious to everybody. It's just that, aside from safeguarding Cathay's assets from loss, you still have to be careful not to unintentionally help the Japanese or their puppets manage the wartime economy. Right now both are hell bent on expropriating goods and materials in order to implement their war policy. Cathay will have to be especially alert not to jeopardize its great achievements because it tried to gain petty advantage. For example, according to our information, the Japanese authorities plan to ask you to take the directorship of the General Chamber of Commerce, replacing the bed-ridden board chairman of Yongfa Bank in that position. You should be careful about this, Mr. Zhu."

Zhu Jingchen smiled as he listened. "Please, gentlemen," he replied; "you may rest easy on that point. The General Chamber of Commerce is the agency the Japanese army is using to carry out its expropriations. I have examined my conscience and I shall not do this work."

A meaningful expression passed across Syu Zhiyong's face. "You're a figure of critical importance, Mr. Zhu, and of course you have deemed it best not to accept the directorship yourself. But it would be all right if you recommended someone else for the position." And so saying, he inclined his head toward Fan Yangzhi. "Him!"

"Mr. Fan? Aren't you afraid that others would get the wrong idea about him if he became director of the General Chamber? How could he hold his head high if he did that?" In his anxiety Jingchen felt that this was almost inconceivable.

The two callers looked at each other and smiled. "Just as you've said, sir," said Fan Yangzhi, "it's like singing opera. You need someone to play the hero and someone to play the villain, otherwise it just isn't opera. Playing the villain on stage earns the jeers of the audience, but there's no help for that. Fortunately, however, after he exits and gets out of his stage attire, everyone praises his acting skill."

Finally, Syu Zhiyong drew from his tunic three glistening gold bars. "What the northern Jiangsu area lacks most acutely are medicines, bandages, sterile gauze, and so on. We've worked with you a number of times before, and we hope you will be able to continue supporting us. We'll always remember how much you've done for the people there."

Jingchen was much moved by this. He took those precious gold bars and laid them on the table, then pushed them resolutely toward Syu Zhiyong. "I can't accept these. As long as we're fighting the Japanese even while short of medical supplies, and as long as fine young men like Mr. Fan willingly endure public humiliation in their struggle against Japan without considering their personal losses, I shall consider myself honored simply by your trust in asking me to be of help in any way possible. I absolutely cannot accept any money." He stammered a little as he spoke, and his voice was husky with emotion. Finally he cleared his throat and said with a trembling voice, "I won't touch it!" And having said it, Jingchen himself could hardly believe it, for, having climbed up step by step from the very bottom level of society, he had throughout his whole life felt he could not have an unshakable faith in anything. And yet with these two gentlemen right before him, particularly Fan Yangzhi, he could now say he understood the meaning of true conviction. He used to think that Juanying was quite extraordinary in the piety of her Christian faith, but it was all too evident that during these times and with the changes in her personal circumstances her former enthusiasm had gradually cooled. But Fan Yangzhi...With an impartial eye Jingchen had observed him become day by day a stabler, more mature person of unshakable tenacity—no easy accomplishment.

"Oh, if only we had more people like you, the war against Japan would never have dragged on so long," said Jingchen with real emotion.

"The fact is, there are lots of people like us—in Shanghai, up north—and they need prominent citizens like yourself, Mr. Zhu, who are friends of the Chinese people; otherwise, if they are left to operate on their own without help, it will be difficult to accomplish anything significant." Syu Zhiyong shook hands firmly with Jingchen, by no means the perfunctory concluding handshake Jingchen was accustomed to in his social dealings, nor was it the limp, toadying handshake of one who, basically insincere, is afraid his hand might get squeezed painfully. This handclasp, so full of trust and gratitude, had occurred, so far as Jingchen could remember, only once before in his life. That was the year he had been entrusted by Wei Jiusi to go to Japan, accompanied only by a secretary and an accountant, hand-carrying the huge sum of one million Japanese yen to establish a Cathay Republic branch in

Kobe. Wei Jiusi went all the way to the dock to see him off, and as they parted he shook his hand firmly—no windy repetitions of instructions, no words of encouragement or felicitation, just that firm, silent handclasp. That was already close to twenty years ago, though it seemed only an instant; Mr. Wei had passed away long since, survived by his beloved wife who was now suffering through hard times. And now he, Zhu Jingchen, had a young and idealistic successor who would become by his middle years a man scarred by the experiences of life's vicissitudes. Although leader of the bank, Jingchen had never since Wei Jiusi's time witnessed such heart-felt trust, such sincerity of word. Then, unexpectedly, on this day, a man whom he'd never even met before was entrusting him with so important a matter as this. Jingchen's eyes began to smart with emotion.

Syu Zhiyong scribbled a few words on his note pad, ripped the page out, and handed it to Jingchen. "This is a receipt for you. When you have completed the job for us, we'll always remember it."

Jingchen took the piece of paper and read it. The signature made his flesh creep: this was the very same gentleman who, some twenty years previous, was on the police wanted list as a "communist gangster chief" with six hundred silver dollars offered for his arrest, the same man who subsequently served as a reliable employee at Cathay for over ten years. How, then, could he possibly be thought of as a "commie gangster?"

"I'm sorry, but when Mr. Fan introduced me earlier, he used my alias." He smiled easily, expressing an uninhibited self-confidence.

"Interestingly enough, there is in fact a slight family connection between us, Mr. Zhu. Jingwen's wife, Miss Yi, is a cousin of mine, but she went overseas when she was young and I went to Peking to study as a young man, so she was never able to leave much of an impression on me. I graduated from Furen Catholic University."

Small world, indeed!

It thus appeared that this Syu Zhiyong was the child of an aristocratic family. They say that only the impoverished turn to rebellion, but he had suffered neither poverty nor hardship, so why in heaven's name was he embarked on such a journey? Syu Zhiyong seemed to have guessed Jingchen's thoughts. Getting to his feet, he said, "What this world needs, I think, is a lot of people devoted to remaking it, to perfecting it. A person can't just be out for himself. In reality, Mr. Zhu, you are a person of that kind of devotion, for otherwise you could just hole up in your house and live a life of retirement. Wouldn't that be a lot better than endangering yourself in these activities? You and I have simply chosen different means to improve the world, that's all. Looked at from that angle, you can understand the means I've chosen."

They then agreed that five days hence Jingchen would arrange to send a shipment of medical supplies by Syu Zhiyong to northern Jiangsu.

After the two visitors left, Jingchen studied the note Syu Zhiyong had left with him, or perhaps one might call it a receipt, or even evidence. Finally, he snapped on his cigarette lighter and burned it. Although, as Syu had just said, they had chosen different means, in Jingchen's estimation his two visitors were on a level of selflessness from which Jingchen himself was far removed.

Zhuanlin pushed the door open and came in. "What a stink in here," she said, holding her nose. "What were they here for? You talked for so long."

"Just talking business," Jingchen replied nonchalantly.

"That Fan Yangzhi doesn't have a very good reputation. Everybody says he's a collaborator in business matters. It would be well to have less to do with him," she offered hesitantly.

"What do you know about it!" exclaimed Jingchen roughly. He told her to draw a bath in their adjoining bathroom, and covered by the noise of the running water, he pulled out a little Westinghouse radio from under his bed pillow and pressed it to his ear while adjusting the tuning knob. Although the Japanese had ordered all radios to be turned in to have their short-wave wires cut, he had secretly withheld this set, so the Japanese, of course, never did modify it. After all, he was a financier; how could he manage if he didn't keep his eyes and ears alert to all that was going on?

"...And the island-hopping strategy of the Allied forces in the Pacific is making steady progress. Following their successful landing on Luzon, Allied forces have continued their drive toward Manila...In the battle of the Japan Inland Sea, the Japanese fleet sustained a crushing defeat..."

It would appear that the Japs' boastful myth assuring "total elimination of American power in the Pacific" had been exploded.

Zhuanlin looked at the time—already past eleven. She set about fixing the dark air-raid cover over the lamp shade, then closed the dark drapes hung in front of the curtains. Japanese MPs often patrolled this area, and if by chance they discovered a family not abiding by black-out regulations, it could be very troublesome.

In the darkness of the night sky one heard only the drone of warplanes passing overhead. They were American planes which had taken off from Chungking, flying over Shanghai as they headed toward Japan to bomb targets in Kyushu. For the past several months whole squadrons of American planes had been regularly flying past Shanghai and then back again. Shanghai people were a practical lot and they liked to cite the old adage, "If in your dishes dwells a rat, you daren't assault him with a bat," to reassure themselves that Shanghai would avoid the catastrophe of American air attacks. But war is war and bombs have no eyes, and peaceful Shanghai citizens did indeed end up as sacrificial objects. On one occasion a plane was shot down over South City, which produced casualties numbering in the hundreds.

"I'm going to look in on Mother," said Jingchen, as he stood up and threw a dressing robe around him.

"I'll go with you." Zhuanlin too got up, and lit a candle for them.

Jingchen felt he'd been a little rough with her just now, so he took her by the hand. Her hand was cold and sweaty from nervousness. "Are you afraid," he asked gently?

"Not when I'm with you," she replied, leaning close to him.

"You're right. When I'm here, there's nothing to fear." And he squeezed her hand gently. He himself felt a great comfort to have her with him just now.

On the floor above, in Juanren's apartment, Zhishuang was standing bare-footed before the window, gazing out through the wispy curtains into the blackness of the night sky.

"Bomb them! Hurry up and bomb every last Jap to death!" Then, looking back toward Juanren, she said, "You have good eyes; how many planes would you estimate are in this formation?"

"You'll catch cold," said Juanren fondly as he threw a wrap over her shoulders.

"I hope our child is lucky enough to come into the world after the arrival of peace," she said as she peered into the black sky, full of the roar of warplanes. "When that time comes, conditions will be stable and everything will be getting back to normal, and we can rent an apartment outside and hire a nursemaid and a servant. Then I can go back to my teaching job at McTyeire and if prices return to prewar levels, we'll be able to meet all the expenses of our own family. How's that, Juanren?" She looked up at Juanren supplicatingly. She considered her demands not at all onerous—she simply wanted her own home. But why did it seem to her as if she was asking such a big favor?

"We'll talk about it later," answered Juanren. Then, as if he were humoring a child along, "Now off to beddy-bye, otherwise you'll catch cold."

The American planes flying over Shanghai this night seemed especially numerous, and under the black sky all the people of Shanghai waited uneasily, waited apprehensively. Wasn't time up now, they felt?

Chapter 29

Whatever people's hopes may have been, the fact was conditions in Shanghai got even grimmer. Soon after New Year's Day 1945 a large contingent of Japan's Kwantung Army began moving southward toward Shanghai, a plague of dogfaces in fur caps whose rapid advance allowed no escape. Their commander, Okamura Neiji, had publicly indicated in the newspapers that the Japanese would fight to the last man rather than give up Shanghai: "Better to die in glory," he said, "than live in dishonor." It would thus appear that Shanghai sooner or later would see battle, and those who had family in the countryside or could otherwise get away to a safe distance made arrangements to flee this perilous den. As people began gradually moving away, housing prices in the Shanghai area started to decline.

But whatever the conditions, there was something about Shanghai that attracted people to it like a magnet. At the very least there was always the type of person who clung with inflexible tenacity to the principle that "despite unceasing change without, the changeless essence endures within." Mrs. Syi, for example, had made up her mind to move nowhere.

Since Mrs. Syi had married off her daughter in such grand style, she felt as though her shoulders had been relieved of a great weight, and she was now breathing much easier.

With one person fewer, the house seemed rather cheerless, on top of which Zhishuang, recently suffering from morning sickness, seldom went out and rarely came visiting. Chengzu, now in his last year of high school, was preoccupied with his preparations for the college entrance exams. So Mrs. Syi was in charge of the whole place all by herself, and in the end the household did manage to survive. She had never been one for socializing anyway, and since her husband had gone inland to Free China and since, too, her neighbors the Tsaos had moved, there were even fewer callers with whom to idle away the time. Well, that was all right, for she could save the money otherwise spent on entertaining guests. But sometimes idleness really did hang awfully heavy on her hands. Even then, however, she'd do no more than call on her brother's family and play a few rounds of penny-ante mahjong, necessarily returning home before dark. Recently, lighting and heating restrictions had become even harsher, which was terribly disconcerting to everybody, so as soon as dusk gathered, Mrs. Syi would seclude herself indoors lest something untoward happen.

Her brother was now living quite prosperously, but held firmly to the ancient teaching that "frugality converts with ease to prodigality, but not the other way around," and consequently the family still lived in that cramped row house, except that now the interior had been whitewashed upstairs and down and some mahogany furniture had been added.

Because Zhishuang had made a match with a rich and powerful family, when Mrs. Syi visited her brother, she naturally came with added luster.

"My husband's sister here is no less than the mother of a daughter who married into the Zhu banking family. The wedding was quite an affair, and without her husband here, Mrs. Syi had only herself to rely on, and she brought her daughter's wedding arrangements off splendidly." That's how Mrs. Syi's sister-in-law, whenever seated with new mahjong friends around the playing table, always liked to introduce her. Amidst the ooh-ing and aah-ing Mrs. Syi felt that, whatever previous wrongs or hardships she may have suffered, she now had her consolation.

Some of those mahjong friends, however, were tactless enough, or perhaps too lacking in self-restraint, to inquire, "Oh, Mr. Syi is in the interior? How long has he been away? Do you hear from him often?" What they really meant was, is there "another woman" in his life? No wonder they should ask, for wasn't the government implementing a "war bride" policy, which allowed men who'd fled with the government inland to take another wife? And besides, getting through the tribulations of the past few years had considerably aged Mrs. Syi.

"You're all unaware that my brother-in-law Mr. Syi is one of the finest husbands under the sun, always 'true to his word and resolute in his deeds,' as they say..." Her sister-in-law hastened to provide the explanations, letting Mrs. Syi sit there smiling indulgently, knowing in her heart that her husband was not the kind of man to play around. Inevitably, however, time had dragged on and people were talking, and hearing rumors about how this person or that person had taken a war bride was troubling and could not but give cause for worry, and, unable to talk openly about such worries, her mood only worsened.

On this particular day just as Mrs. Syi settled herself at her sister-in-law's mahjong table, she heard the insistent ringing of a handbell at the back door. It was the chief of the neighborhood surveillance association, here for some damn nonsense or other.

"Collecting for the air defense fee," said the surveillance chief as he walked into the house.

This nonsense was that residents of the lane where Mrs. Syi's brother lived had been told they had to dig their own air-raid shelters, one at every intersection, and the fee in question was in effect a forced contribution.

"Collecting again?" asked Mrs. Syi's sister-in-law, angrily slapping down a white mahjong tile. "Nowadays you have to pay a fee to get an I.D. card, have to fork over a fee to the meter reader when he comes to the door just to look at the water and electricity meters, and now we've got to cough up this air-raid shelter fee. I don't have enough money for all this. I'm not paying, and if they actually start dropping bombs I won't even go into your damned air-raid hole. Let them bomb me to smithereens, I still won't go!"

The surveillance chief forced a smile as his eyebrows drooped pitifully. "Everybody's depending on the prominent members of the neighborhood to help out. If I can't collect all the donations it'll be bad for me, too. Didn't I make it plain in the beginning that I'd act on behalf of the neighborhood only if everyone would help me do the job?" This surveillance chief was a lane resident who ran a small hardware store and had always been a cautious and honest man, only to find, quite unexpectedly, he'd "hit the jackpot" (as the Japanese and their Chinese collaborators conceived it to be) by getting himself appointed to this luckless surveillance association job. At first he'd tried a hundred times to decline, but unfortunately for him the whole thing was rather like that children's handkerchief game, where one kid drops the handkerchief behind another kid's back, who's now "it," much to the relief of all the others. Thus, all the neighbors one after the other drummed up support for him to get admitted into the surveillance organization. For one thing it got the other neighbors off the hook, and for another the fellow had always been a decent and honest shopkeeper, so rather than let the job go to some bad egg who'd end up terrorizing the neighborhood, wouldn't everyone rest a little easier if they let the hardware man do it?

Mrs. Syi's sister-in-law was well aware of all this, of course; it's just that she had accumulated a great store of pent-up resentment with no place to vent it. But then she opened her purse, counted out the money for that abominable air-defence fee, and handed it over to him. "First, we had to donate our metal gates and street address plates as scrap iron because the Japs had lost so much metal in the fighting, and now we have to dig air-raid shelters. Doesn't that mean the Japanese have made a botch of their war in Southeast Asia?" she asked cautiously. "How can they still be so crazy?"

The hardware man nervously fingered the handbell he was holding, and in a hushed voice confided, "By the looks of it the Japs' days are numbered, but you know what they say about a cornered beast doing desperate things. According to what I've heard, these air-raid shelters are preparation for the Japs to carry on street fighting."

"Gracious! The Japs are actually preparing for a fight to the death?" A cold shiver overtook Mrs. Syi and the mahjong tiles she was holding clattered to the table. If there was a repetition of the August Thirteenth Incident, when the Japanese started their invasion of Shanghai back in 1937, it would be much worse now, for there was no longer an International Settlement to flee to. And on top of that, she had to take care of Chengzu all by herself—an old woman with feeble legs that wouldn't let her flee anywhere.

"There's even more startling news," said the hardware man, lowering his voice still further. "I've heard the puppet government is going to start press-ganging. The Japs have lost all their men in the war, so they've got to press-gang them from China. Not that they'll necessarily end up fighting—there's also road construction, digging trenches..."

This was something people just didn't know about. Mrs. Syi was horrified. "Will they come to Shanghai?" she asked, all color drained from her face.

The surveillance association chief, seeing how shocked she was, tried to offer consolation. "It's probably just rumor. All kinds of rumors are flying around now, so there's no way of knowing if this one is accurate or not."

Mrs. Syi was too agitated to sit still after the hardware man had left. "Our son Chengzu just turned eighteen, and if he gets impressed and something terrible happens to him, how could I ever explain it to Mr. Syi!" So distraught was this woman, who had for years now endured a thousand hardships alone, that she finally burst into tears.

"Oh well, that hardware man picks up talk from every quarter, and it's not necessarily true," said her sister-in-law reassuringly.

"But if those Japs have some tricks up their sleeve, we'd better be prepared for them." Mrs. Syi's brother, who had been standing there without saying a word, now finally offered some remarks. "What's to be feared is that they should come all of a sudden catching us without time to prepare."

"Why don't you just let Chengzu go inland to be with Zhensyu?" asked her sister-in-law. "The very safest thing is for a son to be at his father's side. Let him study at an inland university in Free China."

"Go inland?" Mrs. Syi shook her head back and forth. "I'd never stop worrying. Chengzu's only eighteen and he's never been away from home before. How could I rest easy if he went inland?"

"Eighteen isn't young any more," said Mrs. Syi's brother with a shake of the head. "When I was sixteen I left home to apprentice in a business."

An uncomfortable silence followed. Then Mrs. Syi's brother slapped his knee and exclaimed, "Ask Zhishuang's father-in-law. The bank's smuggling activities into the interior are an open secret. Ask Mr. Zhu. He goes to the interior on a regular basis to conduct business; let Chengzu go along with him. And their traveling expenses for the whole trip will be taken care of by others, rest assured of that."

Mrs. Syi couldn't make a decision right away—the matter had come up far too abruptly. Nor was she now in the mood for mahjong, so she just up and went back home. Fortunately Chengzu was at home. At eighteen Chengzu looked exactly like his sister Zhishuang, with the dash and energy of a young man to boot. Mrs. Syi mentioned the matter off-handedly, and he was in fact entirely willing to go to the government-controlled area. Even if there weren't this talk of impressment into puppet labor gangs he still wanted to go if he had the chance.

"The atmosphere in the Japanese-held area here is so oppressive you can't even breathe," he said. "I've already been talking with the other students about taking the entrance exam for Southwest Associated University in Free China."

His voice was deep and husky. Her son had already grown to manhood.

"Shouldn't you talk it over with your sister and Juanren?" she asked tentatively.

"Okay. But," he said, yielding no ground, "I'll make up my own mind about it."

And so it was that Chengzu left. Well that he might be with his father.

As Mrs. Syi had walked her son out to the main street that evening, she'd discovered that there was another young fellow also going into the interior to be with his father. Or, rather, to be with his step-father. For it was none other than Mrs. Gong's son.

★   ★   ★

While these events were transpiring, a marriage had occurred in the Zhu household. Under old Mrs. Zhu's prodding, Juanguang, the retarded son of Zhu Jingchen's deceased elder brother, had taken a wife. Just as the old woman had said, "There's a war going on, all right, but you still have to go on living." The wedding banquet was held in Kangle Restaurant, and since the bridegroom was the nephew of the prominent brothers Jingchen and Jingwen, there was a very large number of guests. Jingchen and Zhuanlin attended of course, even though of a different generation, but the rest of the family, being snobbish to one degree or another, had difficulty developing much enthusiasm for this very unremarkable relative who had dropped from the sky. Consequently of guests representing the bridegroom's own generation there was but Juanren alone. Tsai Liren did not come, declining on grounds his wife was in her post-partum confinement.

The bride's family operated a food store specializing in delicacies from south China, and though rather uncultured, she was the daughter of good and decent parents. Even if gaudily dressed in a bright red brocaded mandarin dress with a bright red silk flower atop her head, she did nonetheless reveal a certain beauty. By contrast, Juanguang, despite a new suit, looked dull and dumpy—the perfect image of a bumpkin bridegroom from the boondocks. Jingchen, acting as formal witness, looked him over with an objective eye and felt real pity for the bride. He couldn't understand why he had ever let the matchmaker put together a marriage such as this.

Old Mrs. Zhu was in high spirits throughout the evening. She had a red velvet flower stuck into her gray hair to indicate she felt she had finally done right by her deceased son. She realized that the bridegroom was rather simple-minded, but so long as the bride's family didn't gossip about it, the old woman need not be overly concerned. But sometimes thoughtlessness by even a good person can harm others.

According to restrictions imposed by the puppet government, the restaurant had to close no later than eleven when a curfew was enforced on the streets. The wedding banquet thus wound up early.

With gasoline now a controlled commodity, Jingchen had long since switched from automobile to pedicab.

"The new bride is actually very nice. How can she willingly get married to that dim-witted Juanguang," asked Zhuanlin as they were returning home in the pedicab. "Didn't she agree to it only because of the reputation you and Jingwen enjoy? It's unconscionable; the matchmaker gets them married and then within a couple of months the truth about him will get out. It just doesn't make sense to rush into this sort of thing so quickly." By now Zhuanlin was feeling quite indignant.

"Forget it. Just so long as the girl's family was willing," said Jingchen with a yawn.

The normally deserted streets this evening seemed somehow different, particularly as their pedicab passed through the intersection of Avenue Joffre and Père Froc Rue, where he noticed a lot of foreigners about (the only foreigners these days not in concentration camps were White Russians, it seemed) in knots of three or four, arm in arm, laughing aloud, conversing about something or other in Russian, beaming with smiles—just as if it were a holiday. And the strangest thing was that there weren't any Japanese MPs out meddling.

"Is Russia putting on an entertainment today?" asked Jingchen. Zhuanlin replied with a bewildered shrug of the shoulders.

There were even some people playing accordions in the street.

"Dad!" As soon as Jingchen stepped into the vestibule, Juanren, who'd reached home ahead of him, told him the news. "The Soviets have captured Berlin and Hitler's committed suicide. Voice of America just reported it."

So! Jingchen was stunned for a moment, then ran up the stairs two at a time to his bedroom where he immediately turned on the bathroom water faucet and switched on his radio. A moment later Juanren and his very pregnant wife rushed in, crowding around him, listening.

"...Thus this long six-year European war has finally been brought to an end by the defeat of Germany. And our eight-year struggle against Japan must also reach a successful conclusion..." Jingchen suddenly felt overcome with fatigue; he slumped into a chair.

"Dad, are you all right?" asked Juanren anxiously.

"I'm so tired." Jingchen kept sitting there with his eyes closed. Tears began to trickle down his cheeks. He pulled out a handkerchief and wiped them away. His eye caught Zhishuang's swollen womb.

"When the child is born, whether it's a boy or girl, let's choose Shengli—'victory'—for a name, shall we? I think the child is a good omen, for the day he comes into the world will certainly be the day peace comes to China." He closed his eyes again and mumbled, very much as if it were a prayer, "May the day come soon, may the day come soon!"

The next day all of Shanghai was wild with joy. People piled into Nanking Road and Avenue Joffre, especially the Russians who were dancing Cossack folk dances in the street, again without any interference from the Japanese MPs.

At the dinner table that evening, Juanren, all a-bubble, related a story he'd picked up on the street earlier in the day. It seems that at the corner of Avenue Joffre and Rue Père Robert there was a storefront, though hardly bigger than the palm of your hand, which actually housed two shops, one a tiny coffee shop run by a White Russian, and the other a tiny photography shop run by a German. Since the start of the war in Europe, the German had hung a portrait of Hitler on his wall and the Russian, not to be outdone, hung up Stalin—diametrically opposed, trading blow for blow. When the German armies invaded Stalingrad, the German shopowner had strutted around arrogantly. But today the Russian shopowner, his chest all puffed up, stormed into the German's shop, ripped the Hitler portrait from the wall and hurled it into the street with a crash. That German shopowner without uttering so much as a word of protest just slipped away without a trace. "And the really odd thing," said Juanren, trying to restrain his laughter, "is that the German was a Jew expelled from his country by the Nazis, and the other was a White Russian living in exile following the revolution in his country. Yet there they were, each standing up for his own country!"

"Oh, that's not so very odd," said Jingchen, taking a sip of Johnny Walker he'd saved unopened ever since prewar days until now. "The affection one retains for his native soil is part of his very blood, just as the child who is neglected by his own parents is still reluctant to leave them."

Zhishuang suddenly recalled how long ago she'd bought cotton candy from a street-corner vendor who was a White Russian. That was the evening she'd met Juanren. The monotonous and desolate sound as the man banged his spoon to attract customers seemed still to be floating about her ears. Eight years had passed since then, time enough to have squeezed in a whole war.

Just then Jingchen was called to the telephone and when he returned his color showed something was amiss; naturally everyone supposed it was just another vexation at the bank, so no one inquired particularly. It wasn't until he returned to his own room that he spoke in an almost inaudible voice to Zhuanlin:

"Juanguang's bride—she's hung herself."

Zhuanlin broke into a stunned sweat. "How is that possible?"

"That pitiful bride," said Jingchen, deeply moved. "It was only on the day of her marriage that she discovered the groom wasn't quite right, and that night she wouldn't let him in the bedroom. Early this morning she sent the maid out on some pretext, then hung herself right there in the room."

"What was the need for it?" asked Zhuanlin, with a look of incomprehension. "If she felt she'd been wronged, why didn't she just come out and say so, or even sue them for breach of contract, or get divorced. Really, how could that bride be so...so narrow-minded!"

"You're blaming her?" Jingchen looked askance at her and shook his head. "A girl like her from a poor family like that, with hardly any education—how can you talk of divorce, let alone sue in court? You take her for a modernized graduate of the McTyeire type?"

Zhuanlin felt put out. "Then blame the matchmaker for doing a poor job," she scowled, "or for not explaining the real situation. That matchmaker was a damned liar."

"Don't you think the Zhu family must bear some of the responsibility? At the very least it was a case of exploiting our wealth to get our way." Jingchen paced around the room depressed and agitated. He despised his own family, and he too had unconsciously absorbed its evil influence. Although he had not been aware of the details about engaging a professional matchmaker for Juanguang, nonetheless he had been the formal witness solemnizing the union. In his heart he felt a stinging remorse. Such a fine girl, a bright red dress and a bright red flower in her hair, had suffered a grievous wrong through no fault of her own, and now had quietly died.

Beyond the window the streetlights were shining brightly—lighting restrictions and air-raid controls seemed now to be utterly disregarded throughout Shanghai. With the war in Europe over, the Japanese could not last long. Every single home in Shanghai was now rejoicing. But there was one pure girl who had died this morning, a girl of virginal purity taken away. In a moment victory would be achieved and the day soon would arrive when the Chinese people could lift their heads high again; yet she had died. When daylight broke, she would still sleep. Jingchen shook his head vigorously, trying to shake her out of his mind. Jingchen's thoughts turned from her to his own favorite daughter, Juanmin. He hadn't seen her for years, and now that pampered child was already the mother of two. For years now without influential people to rely on and lacking financial resources of her own, how had she managed to get by, he wondered. Judging from the few letters he had received from her, she seemed to be very happy; even reading between the lines he could discern no complaints. The most unpredictable thing in life was the marriage of one's children. As the daughter of a wealthy Shanghai family, Juanmin could confidently have had the pick of the lot and could thus have become a very comfortable Shanghai matron, like Zhishuang or Juanying, yet of all things she'd picked this foreign-worshipper Feng Jingsyao and had thereby gotten her fill of hardship. Fortunately, she had married him of her own volition, and if it wasn't an equal match, well then it wasn't an equal match.

Fully eight years now. Life hadn't been easy.

Jingchen stepped over to the mirror. May in Shanghai is a very humid month and the mirror was misted over. He could only vaguely make out his broad shoulders. Now nearly fifty, spiritually and physically exhausted from the strain of the past few years, he scarcely possessed the courage to inspect himself in the mirror. He hesitated a moment, then wiped away the mist with his hand. His features were now clear: strong character revealed in the bluish trace of beard on his cleanly shaven jaw, pride implied in his tightly compressed lips; though time had ruthlessly etched lines in his brow and wrinkles around his eyes, still those eyes, he felt, were as bright and animated as ever. Although at this moment he had only a velvet smoking jacket casually thrown around him, his slacks were smoothly pressed and sharply creased as always, such that in overall appearance he might attract attention as a man of power and ability.

"I'm good for another twenty years," he thought. He stroked his chin and smiled a pleased smile into the mirror.

Chapter 30

August 15: Japan surrendered.

The same day high- and middle-ranking officers of the Japanese army contingent stationed in Shanghai assembled in a three-story building behind Guotai Theater on Avenue Joffre to hear the speech broadcast by their emperor. One officer of mid-rank upon hearing the surrender statement was said to have committed suicide on the spot by traditional disembowlment.

The day following, Chiang Kaishek in Chungking announced the conclusion of the war.

And at Cathay Republic Bank, sobs of joy could be heard throughout the night until the very break of day.

Although Cathay Republic was a privately owned bank, it had nevertheless been infected by the Japanese and by the puppet government, and forced to reorganize under their supervision. Consequently, a directive was issued by Chungking to the effect that all accounts and vault holdings were to be maintained in their present condition to undergo inspection and audit by Chungking agents. This order caused Jingchen, in the midst of his rejoicing over China's victory, to feel some little resentment. Having endured eight years of Japanese depredations, it seemed, finally, he must now undergo screening by Chungking. Five years ago he had to hand over the books to the Japanese and now five years later he would have to hand the books over to some Chungking agent. That being the case, what then did the managerial skills of this impressive bank president, Zhu

Jingchen, count for? What, indeed, did his arduous eight-year ordeal count for?

Nor had it ever occurred to him that the big man from Chungking sent to conduct the audit would be that former assistant vice-president, now vice-president in charge of business operations, at the quasi-official Bank of China, Mr. Gong.

And he came so soon! On the eighteenth Jingchen had received the Chungking directive to "await instructions" and Mr. Gong flew in on the afternoon of that very day, appearing in Zhu Jingchen's office just as if he had dropped from the sky. He was wearing a high-collared uniform-like tunic-suit of gray faille with a gleaming gold watch fob dangling from his pocket; his thick hair, carefully combed back in a western style, showed streaks of gray. Compared to the Mr. Gong of eight years ago at the YWCA charity sale, he seemed to be an entirely different person. The present Mr. Gong was reserved, composed, seasoned, and, what's more, rich.

However that might be, Mr. Gong's appearance seemed to represent Cathay's golden age of the past. Although Mr. Gong at that time had done his utmost to force Cathay to its knees, his reappearance today for Jingchen wiped the slate clean of the bad feeling and discord of those former days. What remained was only regret about the fluctuation of affairs and resentment over the loss of time. Moreover, Mary Luo Gong had very much been looking forward to the return of her husband.

"Ah, Mr. Gong!" Hand outstretched, Jingchen stepped forward to greet him, so moved he could say no more.

Who would have believed that this new aristocrat from Chungking would merely take two fingers of the proffered hand and squeeze them with cold arrogance all the while looking this way and that as he took stock of the office.

Jingchen retracted his hand, and offered him a cigarette.

"To facilitate our audit, commencing tomorrow entry and departure of all bank personnel will be via the side door," announced Mr. Gong officiously.

"The side door!" Jingchen was astonished. Even under the Japs the employees hadn't been relegated to the side door.

"It will be more expedient to use the front entrance to move out enemy property," retorted Mr. Gong.

Move out enemy property? What holdings of enemy property did Cathay have? It appeared that the people from Chungking planned to load up a big truck. But my god, was it not the truth that Cathay's every brick and every tile had been snatched back from the very jaws of the Japanese and their puppets by Jingchen and his colleagues practically at the cost of their lives? How could that be construed as "enemy property?"

"Mr. Gong, a careful examination will clearly show that we were coerced into a reorganization, but we were never absorbed into the puppet government." Jingchen licked his lips and stammered nervously. "This cannot be categorized as enemy property!"

Mr. Gong sat there, one ankle arrogantly propped high on the other knee. Using the official mandarin dialect rather than his native Shanghainese, he began lecturing Jingchen in condescending tones. "Mr. Zhu, although we have been friends for many years, I must execute my official duties unswayed by personal considerations. Mr. Zhu, you have worked in the financial world for many years and I therefore need not elaborate on the principles by which it is governed. During these eight years of war, countless numbers of righteous men and women have laid down their lives for their country. Chinese patriots came to Free China during these past eight years truly in wave upon wave, so how can you appeasers who stayed in the enemy areas explain youselves? In view of this, I hope, Mr. Zhu, that you will appreciate the larger issue, consider the total picture..."

Jingchen scarce heard what followed, for when Mr. Gong mouthed the words "patriots" and "appeasers," a piercing chill gripped his whole being.

The auditing work at Cathay Republic went on for several months. The bank suffered grievous losses in its real estate holdings. Eventually, homes acquired by Cathay in the Rue Courbet and Avenue Road neighborhoods were completely confiscated as enemy property. Since the laying of that first foundation stone until the completion of all the Cathay housing projects—everything was categorized as enemy property. Bank of China also withdrew a large quantity of gold bars from the Cathay vault which were then sold at auction. Thus the bureaucracy with no great difficulty insinuated its control over Cathay Republic Bank.

"Pirates! They storm in during full daylight and plunder us!" Jingchen was so enraged he dared not speak out because of the party from Chungking; he dared only shut the door and curse the heavens. Yet he was still both the leader of the bank and the voice of his aggrieved colleagues, and he felt urged on by both, particularly one day when a former employee of Small East Gate branch who had been laid off years previous came into the president's office.

"Mr. Zhu," he began. Despite the heat of this summer day, the man was immaculately dressed in a very refined looking long gown of silk pongee, but the weary and dejected facial expression bespoke the hard life he had endured since leaving the bank. Notwithstanding the care and concern—widely praised in Shanghai banking circles—which Cathay showed its employees, it was nonetheless difficult to get by relying only on the relief aid which the bank had extended. From the moment he joined the bank, any employee could at least be assured of the means to provide his family with food and clothing; consequently, when an employee left the bank, he was likely to feel that other employment was arduous and intolerable.

"It was made quite clear in the beginning," the man continued, "that we employees of Small East Gate branch should take the larger picture into consideration and see that Cathay, in order to survive its adversities, had no alternative but to let us go. You must remember, sir, that day when you stood in the lobby of Small East Gate branch and stated with perfect clarity, 'In the future after victory, I promise to hire back each and every one of you.' How I relied on your word, Mr. Zhu, as I endured one day after another until right now. Imagine, at the time you made that promise I was only thirty-five years old—in my prime. Then in a twinkling, the years rushed by and now I feel my age. They say, Mr. Zhu, that a person should be true in word and resolute in deed, and how much more so when the person is the head of a bank. During that dark long night of Japanese occupation the bank nonetheless often thought of us and from time to time provided us with emergency rice and cooking oil. Now the new day has dawned, but how is it you have not raised the matter of rehiring us?"

Having gotten to this point, the employee was bold enough to lift his eyes and look straight at Zhu Jingchen, only to discover the president had turned ashen white and was so stunned he could hardly form his words.

"Yes, um...I did say that...," mumbled Jingchen, as his trembling hands mechanically creased into ever smaller pieces a sheet of paper he was holding. He never made rash promises; he would always honor a commitment however difficult that might prove to be. So now the resentful reproach delivered by this employee was like being publicly slapped in the face, and he felt an acute embarrassment. But what could he say? Mr. Gong, dispatched by Chungking, was even screening those employees who had remained with the bank through the Japanese occupation, first processing separation papers for everyone across the board to leave the bank, and then processing papers for new people he was hiring; so what hope could there be for the Small East Gate employees who had been laid off many years ago!

"Sifting out appeasers from patriots" was a fine-sounding phrase, but there seemed little doubt it was just an excuse to make room for those

Chungking carpetbaggers. In effect, Mr. Gong was simply throwing people out of their jobs.

"If I'd known it was going to be like this, we might just as well have gone the way of Tsao Jiusin and let ourselves be shot dead by the Japanese. Our families at least could have lived comfortably off of the bank's death benefits." In the midst of his confusion, Jingchen heard the man's lament; but didn't the man know that even the financial consideration Jingchen had shown Tsao Jiusin's family had already been canceled by the Great Expropriator, Mr. Gong? It was as if to say Tsao Jiusin was not worthy of the consideration he enjoyed for being a patriot. Damn, could this actually be called the dawning of a new day? He had lived on hope all these years, but now those hopes had vanished. Now he could see only dull gray before his eyes; in face of these Chungking agents, Jingchen was again experiencing the bitter taste of a people subjugated by conquest.

"Swine! The dirty swine!" And his fist came down hard on the table. Then he suddenly realized he had lost control of himself.

By the time he had pulled himself together he discovered that the room was empty; the former employee had disappeared. Atop a side table, an electric fan was blowing into the emptiness: it rather seemed the man's spirit was haunting his office. He thought of Tsao Jiusin. He thought also of how not long after he'd left Small East Gate branch, pressed by both poverty and illness, that overaged apprentice from Ningpo had passed away. And in that instant Jingchen felt that all those people were returning as evil spirits one by one demanding money of him. His skin became gooseflesh, his back broke out in cold sweat.

"I'm not going to let it be so easy as that!" He picked up the telephone and dialed Mary Luo Gong's old home, now also Mr. Gong's residence, for it could be assumed they hadn't been able so quickly to find new quarters for themselves. If he didn't have any pull with Mr. Gong, at least Mrs. Gong could put in a good word for him. He thought of the hardships she'd suffered, and who but himself had shown her any concern? And while Zhu Jingchen was certainly not the type to expect a favor in return for every little favor done, if it seemed convenient for both sides, then he felt absolutely no qualms about it. Pity this woman, once the great beauty Mary Luo, then the former Mrs. Wei, and now Mrs. Gong, who had waited expectantly for the present day when at long last her husband returned home unscathed. Her step-son—Mr. Wei's son—had gone off with Zhishuang's brother Chengzu to Free China, a journey made possible only through the aid and support provided by Jingchen himself. Yes, he had helped Mrs. Gong.

Jingchen listened with mounting vexation as the telephone rang interminably and still no one answered it. After a long while the harsh voice of an old woman servant came over the wire. "Who is it? Who do you want?" she asked in a heavy up-country accent. If Mr. Gong kept uncouth maids like this, all his guests would feel they were being shooed away.

At bottom a parvenu, Mr. Gong here simply revealed his basic flaw—a shaky foundation. Things that required particular attention he was not particular about, while things that did not especially matter he was very fussy about. Jingchen threw down the telephone and decided he'd personally call at the Gong home after work and take the opportunity to discuss the matter face to face with the Great Expropriator. If he couldn't get his views across, he'd go over his head and talk with H. H. Kong or T. V. Song—both in the highest echelons of government finance. In any event it simply wasn't right to practice such discrimination against the entire Cathay workforce because it had stayed behind in the occupied territory. In order to catch the man off guard, Jingchen decided to go unannounced. And should the Great Expropriator not be at home, well he'd just sit in their parlor and wait for him. He would present his reasons and argue forcefully, and not let that man bully the Cathay employees who had remained in Shanghai.

Himself at the wheel, Jingchen drove to the Gong residence in the French Concession. He had come here on a previous occasion. That was when the Japanese had trumped up an accusation against twelve Cathay employees for the murder of a puppet Central Reserve Bank employee, and Jingchen, attempting to secure their release, had come to call on Mary Luo Gong. She was then in very straitened circumstances. But with the return of her husband might she not now be overbearing and presumptuous?

The small front garden was as disarranged and tangled as before, and still posted by the main gate was that "Please Use Rear Entrance" notice, its lettering now barely discernible. Of course, the restoration of family finances and normal appearances couldn't happen overnight. Jingchen circled around to the back door and rang the bell. A perfectly charming young woman opened the door; he guessed her to be the daughter left when Mr. Wei passed away.

"Is Mr. Gong at home?" Jingchen carefully sized up the girl standing before him. From her smooth white skin to her beautiful sparkling eyes she was a virtual carbon copy of her mother at that age.

"And you are... ?" she asked warily, looking him over.

"I'm Zhu Jingchen." He thought he might tease her a bit with something like "I used to bounce you on my knee," but the girl's expression of detached seriousness made him think better of it.

"Oh, Uncle Jingchen," she said familiarly. "Mother frequently mentions you." She perked up a bit.

"Is Mr. Gong at home?" he repeated.

"Mother's here. But...please wait a moment..." She hesitated, as if embarrassed, apparently weighing whether she should or should not invite him in, while Jingchen stood there in the doorway resolved not to turn back.

"Madam wants to know who the guy is." From behind the girl came the crass voice of a stocky old woman, the very one who had earlier answered the telephone.

"Tell Madam that Mr. Zhu has come." Then, turning to Jingchen, she said with a worried smile, "My mother's not too well... up here." And she gestured toward her own head. Jingchen was stunned, for he'd never had any inkling that somehow Mary Luo might be mentally unbalanced.

"Has Mr. Gong taken her to the doctor?"

"Gong?" She frowned contemptuously. "For a long time after returning from Chungking he didn't even come to see Mother. He brought back a war bride with him and they live in an eighteen-story apartment building. If it hadn't been for an acquaintance who happened to bump into him on the street and told Mother about it, she still wouldn't know he'd returned to Shanghai. Only because of that he finally came to call..."

That Gong had taken a war bride was not an unexpected development, but that he should not even visit Mary Luo upon his return to Shanghai had never entered Jingchen's mind. What a scoundrel! What a con artist!

"The day he came, Mother wrapped a towel around her face to show she didn't want to see him. He just threw some money down and left. A few days ago he came again, and Mother again wrapped herself in a blanket, and from that time on, she hasn't done up her hair or gotten dressed..."

"Madam says," came the hag's harsh voice interrupting them unawares, "she's returning this money to you." And she held out a red envelope to Jingchen. "Madam says to give her thanks to the gentleman. The house is small so she can't invite you in."

Miss Wei smiled apologetically. "I'll see you out, Uncle Jingchen."

Although already past seven, the dusk of a summer evening always drags on for a very long while, especially, it seemed, here in newly developed West District. In the twilight the silhouette of the rooftops of the lane's western-style homes was dim and indistinct, just as when he'd last come here. Some late-returning crows, always omens of ill, flew over the rooftops; their cawing seemed particularly sad and shrill. Jingchen glanced at Miss Wei, subdued and disconsolate, and could only feel ashamed before Mr. Wei and before Mary Luo. When he had first heard that Mary Luo was to marry Mr. Gong, a man beneath her station and eight years her junior, he thoroughly disapproved of it, and yet he did subconsciously feel that this choice of hers contained an element of pique and resentment toward himself, for it was he whom she had really wanted to marry. Alas, he ought not have revealed to her his admiration and affection... yet he was a man, and it was just at a period in his life when he was a lonely widower... perhaps it would have been natural for him to marry her? But he couldn't, it was all too complicated... Alas, during his lifetime he had come to owe too much to women—Mrs. Su, Mary Luo, even including his own wife Zhuanlin—for all of whom he felt both a certain remorse and a lingering affection. Well, whatever the case, he considered that his past had by no means been a blank, that he had truly endured a lifetime of experience.

"Good-bye, Uncle Jingchen." Miss Wei's reedy voice aroused him from his reveries.

"You have a brother—is he a younger brother or older?—who traveled to Free China with some others all on their own; did your step-father look after him when he arrived there?" Jingchen suddenly remembered Mr. Wei had had a son.

"At first he was a student at Southwest Associated University, but I think he might now have transferred to Furen Catholic University. He doesn't want to return to Shanghai and has no interest in rejoining the family."

"And you? Are you still studying or do you already have a job," he asked.

"I still have another year and a half of college, but I really can't afford the tuition now so I've dropped out. A few days ago some student friends and I agreed we'd go to America to pursue our studies, and Mr. Gong is actually willing to pay my expenses. But what will become of Mother?" She smiled placidly.

Jingchen looked at this frail girl whom he had known since her childhood, and shook his head slowly. "Just let her be," he said, patting her on the shoulder. "You're still young. Don't waste the springtime of your youth in a place with no hope. You listen to Uncle Jingchen—you're very fortunate, the war is over and there is still much that you can do in life, still much you can learn. You young people ought not atone for the crimes or be burdened by the tragedies left by war." Only with effort was Jingchen able to keep his own emotions under control as he spoke.

He said good-bye to Miss Wei and climbed into his car, then slumped against the steering wheel as utter exhaustion suddenly overwhelmed him. How he had longed for the dawn of the new day, confident it would bring boundless light and unlimited happiness, only to find that the enemy had not laid down its arms, that the government had not returned to its capital at Nanking, and that the joy of victory would so soon be dissipated by corruption, rapacity, and shameless reality.

*   *   *

When he arrived home, Juanren, full of excitement, came out to meet him. "Dad, there's a letter from Minny. As soon as she can get her hands on boat or plane tickets she and Feng Jingsyao and the kids will be coming back to Shanghai. Trouble is, it's extremely difficult to get tickets. Dad, you could help her by giving her introductions to some big shots so she can get tickets as soon as possible."

Near four years since he'd seen Juanmin! How wonderful it would be to have the family together now that this long struggle was behind them. Although Jingchen had many children, he dearly loved every one. After all, they say, the skin on the back of the hand is as precious as the skin on the palm. But Juanmin was his real favorite. When she got married, she was determined to leave home and go with Jingsyao to Free China. As her father, Jingchen felt he should not prevent her from leaving. Now she was returning and that was wonderful. Not until now did Jingchen feel his icy heart begin to warm. He anxiously opened the letter. It began with a parody of an ancient verse.

> Year in, year out reside your kin in Chungking's slime,
> Cut off from natal home by peaks too high to climb.
> We righteous patriots angrily brand it as a crime:
> Ten thousand planes soar overhead, but still 'tis not
> our time!

> Dear Daddy, We're just itching to fly back to Shanghai
> on the wings of victory, but right now it's even harder
> getting from Chungking to Shanghai than it was getting from
> Shanghai to America before the war broke out. Of course it's

not difficult if you're relatives of the emperor or a high-ranking
official—then for sure you can soar through the
clouds. But for us ordinary mortals, we either have to go
by wood-plank boat or use our own two feet. Daddy, I've
heard that Mr. Gong is now pretty high in government and is
well connected in Shanghai. Please ask him or Mrs. Gong to
telephone or wire someone here in Chungking who's in a
position to help us. Oh, how I want to go home!

Jingchen sighed audibly and put the letter aside. "I'm afraid your
father," he said to no one in particular, "doesn't have what it takes any
more." And he went upstairs.

Zhuanlin saw the icy expression on his face, and realized that
something was troubling him, but she was careful and knew she
shouldn't press him with questions. Jingchen took off his jacket and
drew from its pocket the stiff red envelope he'd been given at the Gong
house. Tearing it open, he found a thick packet of fresh green
bills—American currency. This was money which Mary Luo was
returning to him. Ah, Mary Luo—the ablest woman of them all. What a
pity fortune had not favored her. She was being too conscientious.
Other than looking to Mr. Gong to provide her with a little money,
what extravagant hopes could she have?

Before going to bed, Jingchen took a sleeping pill. As soon as he
opened his eyes the next morning he'd have knotty problems to
confront, and without a good night's sleep he simply wouldn't have the
energy for them.

He was roused from a deep slumber by Zhuanlin's frightened
summons: "Wake up, Jingchen! A whole bunch of armed American
G.I.s are in the parlor. Quick, go down and see what it is." He looked
at his watch—only six o'clock in the morning.

Temples throbbing from the effects of the sleeping pill, Jingchen
threw on a robe, instructed Zhuanlin to look in on his mother and not
let her get upset, then went down to the parlor.

As soon as he entered the room a soldier wearing the uniform of an
American officer peremptorily demanded, "You are Zhu Jingchen?"

"I am. What is it?" One look around and Jingchen could tell
immediately what it was all about: of course they were here to shake
him down.

"If you have business to discuss, it can be discussed at the bank. This
is my private residence and you have no right to barge in like this.
Furthermore, my elderly mother is here and a daughter-in-law soon to
give birth, and they mustn't be upset by you people." His face crimson

with anger, Jingchen flung open the doors giving onto the garden. There he was stunned to see a double file of twenty or thirty American-outfitted troops, and he immediately apprehended that their presence was for the sole purpose of coercion. And the blame for it all was that during the past few years Cathay had made too much money, had gotten too fat, and there were others whose mouths were watering for a share of it.

"I'll speak with you and no one else," said the soldier arrogantly. "Give me the names of each and every employee who remained at Cathay Republic Bank during the Japanese occupation. Be precise, and don't conceal anything or make excuses." Then he added with an icy smile, "While we were at the front fighting the Japs, you guys were back here lining your pockets!"

Jingchen was livid, but he kept his head high and bravely stood his ground.

"How dare you speak to me in this fashion." His voice trembled in quiet rage, and his eyes burned with anger.

"Why shouldn't I dare? Who do you think you are? You're a banker turned traitor," he yelled ruthlessly, "and this is the day you pay for it!"

"You have to have proof for what you say," retorted Jingchen. "I reject your accusation. I reject it absolutely!" Jingchen was shouting in desperation now.

As this was going on, the entire household was thrown into commotion, some crying, others screaming.

Jingchen calmed himself. "Let's go into the study," he said. "And please order your men not to disturb my family." He stuck his hand into his bathrobe pocket; it hit against a stiff envelope—yes, the envelope of American bills Mary Luo had given him, money he could now put to good use. He pulled it out and pressed it into the officer's hand.

The officer took the money and stuffed it into his pocket, and said (now with a measure of courtesy), "Fine; but you'll have to cooperate with us." Then he went through the doors into the garden and barked some orders at the twenty-odd soldiers. Jingchen took the moment's opportunity to comfort the family, whispering special instructions to Juanren: "You're eldest son—take good care of your grandmother, mother, and your sisters. I'm afraid I may be in for some trouble."

"Father!" exclaimed Juanren anxiously.

"Act your age! All of thirty and you still can't keep yourself under control?" Jingchen furrowed his eyebrows and gave his son a stern look as he unceremoniously berated him.

From this time on, Jingchen was confined to his study under house arrest, not allowed to go outside or to receive telephone calls.

★   ★   ★

As soon as it got out that President Zhu Jingchen was being held under house arrest awaiting investigation, his colleagues at Cathay one after another wrote letters and signed petitions to the judicial authorities and even to officials in Chungking detailing Zhu Jingchen's life during the enemy occupation. Finally the entire Cathay workforce staged a sit-in in the bank's main lobby, completely disrupting banking activities, to demand that the proper officials clear up Zhu Jingchen's case based on the true facts. They also protested Chungking's sending agents who were unjustly discriminatory toward those Cathay employees who had remained in Shanghai during the Japanese occupation. The sit-in stretched on for three days and immediately became one of Shanghai's major news stories.

It happened to be during this time that the Ministry of Finance announced a two-hundred-to-one exchange ratio between the puppet currency and the national government currency. This announcement rocked Shanghai just the way those bombs had which exploded in Great World Entertainment Center. In an instant the black market price of gold shot up, currency depreciated, and inflation set in. A sea of people again swarmed about the entrance to the securities exchange building on Hankou Road. At this point, doubtless due to the exacerbation of the financial crisis by the sit-in at Cathay, the municipal authorities issued the following statement: "In the matter of suspected traitorous activity alleged against Zhu Jingchen, it has been determined that there is insufficient evidence to warrant investigation and that the band of troops holding Zhu Jingchen in custody is itself engaged in blackmail and extortion. It is hereby ordered that said troops release Zhu Jingchen and withdraw. Case closed."

The unexpected ordeal had so debilitated Jingchen, however, that he required hospitalization; he stayed behind closed doors in a first-class private room in Washington Hospital in West District declining all visitors, save for Zhuanlin who alone remained in attendance at his side, in order to concentrate on his recuperation. Nonetheless, a bedside table was weighed down with a thick pile of Chinese- and English-language newspapers.

The very next evening Zhishuang was admitted to the hospital for her delivery, and Zhuanlin stayed close to her, lending moral support; consequently Jingchen was by himself in his room for the entire morning, a period of quiet which he put to good use paging through recent issues of the newspapers.

But his anger rose when he saw the papers full of phrases the likes of "one people, one leader," or "people first, nation first, leader first." And what was this "great people of a victorious nation" and this "China—ranked among the world's Big Four?" Even China's leader was touted as "one of the three outstanding men" in the contemporary world. What the actual conditions were, heaven only knew, but it was safe to say that this victory against Japan was in actuality a tragic victory.

A nurse came in to say a gentleman bearing a letter from a Mr. Fan wished to see him.

A Mr. Fan. Fan Yangzhi? How long it had been since he had received word of him. At a time when accusations of traitor were flying about wildly and with Zhu Jingchen personally confronting serious difficulties, it had not been expedient to have any contact with him; nor did Jingchen know what sort of conditions Fan Yangzhi himself might be in.

The gentleman bearing the letter was a refined and educated person. He presented Fan Yangzhi's letter. Jingchen read it, and learned that Fan Yangzhi had gone to north China, and, furthermore, that the petitions and large-scale sit-in demonstration at Cathay had come about through agitation by members of his clandestine organization. Had there not been this large-scale popular movement, Jingchen might very well not so easily have been released: at best there would have been repeated extortion demands, while at worst he might well have ended up in prison.

"My thanks to everybody," said Jingchen, visibly moved. "I understood from the first that if I were the only person caught in a jam, it'd be unlikely anyone would take notice, and even more unlikely anyone would speak up for me..."

"The fact is, sir, any man who is in the public eye and who in his speech and action does good for the people will always be remembered." The caller spoke with a steady voice, which gave much comfort to Jingchen.

"That's easy to say," replied Jingchen, angrily slapping the pile of newspapers by his side, "but there are always some people shameless enough to speak lies on the assumption there are other people dumb enough to believe them."

"These things—these newspaper stories—are of course absolutely without foundation. Here, these are magazines our publishing firm puts out; you'll find them a more interesting way to pass time than flipping through those others." As he spoke, the caller pulled out a couple issues of World Knowledge and an issue of Great America. It seems the gentleman worked for World Knowledge Publishers.

Jingchen took the magazines and looked through them. "I've read a few of these before," he said, gesturing to World Knowledge. "The editorial position is rather novel, and it's nicely put together. Who might its editor be?"

"Feng Bingfu, the son of Feng Junmu."

"I see. Feng Junmu—" he said, musing aloud, "—the well known classical scholar. Really, a good case of the son's following in the footsteps of his illustrious father."

"Yes, indeed. But these days the winds of putting profit first are blowing hard, with the result that the cost of paper has escalated sharply, making survival extremely difficult for a publication like ours which tries to report the facts and tell the truth. I hope, sir, when it will be convenient for you to do so, that you might lend us your help."

Although the caller spoke with tactful indirection, Jingchen understood his meaning perfectly: he was intending to approach Cathay Republic for a loan. And the fact that he had brought Fan Yangzhi's letter told Jingchen something about the background of World Knowledge Publishers. Jingchen recalled the adage, "a drop of kindness deserves a wellspring in return," and gave his promise.

After the man had left, Jingchen picked up one of the magazines and began reading more closely.

The telephone on the bedside table rang. It was Juanren who with uncontrollable excitement exclaimed, "Dad, Zhishuang's just had a boy!"

"That's nice," he replied mechanically in a flat, tired voice. But after he'd put the receiver down, he suddenly clapped his hand to his forehead—Juanren had a son, so he, Zhu Jingchen, had a grandson. A grandson! A bouncing baby boy born into the family. A grandson! Now there were father, son, and grandson: the flourishing Zhu family now had its third generation. They say that a millionaire can be made overnight, but it takes three generations of effort to create an aristocrat. Now for the first time the Zhu family truly had an aristocratic member. He would certainly do everything he could to foster the boy's development, and would in the future send him to a western-style boys' academy to experience dormitory life, so he would grow up to be a true gentleman.

He felt his throat tighten in a sweet poignancy. He stepped over to the window. Beyond, the scenery had already turned autumnal. The warm rays of the sun played over the fallen leaves, which had scattered into a design such as an abstractionist might have painted. Everywhere the eye could see there was a golden resplendence set against the limpid purity of the azure sky—a panorama of wonderful fall color without a trace of the sad decay so characteristic of the season.

Jingchen, who had never believed in gods or ghosts, now felt welling up in his heart some ardent emotion, and, more than that, he began with unquestioned sincerity to murmur a silent prayer.

★ ★ ★

Zhishuang was lying in bed. Now slimmed down after her birth and covered with only a thin blanket, to look at her one would think her just a girl.

The family had reserved for her the most comfortable room, which was rather like a small apartment. There was an oriental rug and figured pastel curtains—none of the normal hospital atmosphere which so disquiets people. The bedside table and the coffee table in her own room, the small parlor beyond, and even the balcony were all piled so full of fresh flowers which kept coming in a steady stream day after day that even the nurses were saying they reckoned this delivery to have been the most important ever. Not to mention the packages—too many for all even to be opened—containing dainty and expensive nourishments. During her month of post-partum confinement the gifts were given to the new mother, and only thereafter were gifts presented to the new-born. And if Juanying and Juansi hadn't taken home a batch of gifts every day, the two hospital rooms would have burst from the flood of flowers and presents. Zhishuang could only feel smothered in love as she suddenly became the center of the world—the feeling a sixteen-year-old schoolgirl might have who'd scored A-plus on all her exams. When she had been crushed in that line waiting for rationed rice, half dead, half alive, she really did feel under tight siege by a kind of death-fear. In a way she believed she really was dead, for she discovered she had never really lived, nor had she ever really loved. The road that had led her from love to marriage was no more than a trolley track already laid and waiting to take her there; yet what she was yearning for was to race across the open fields—wildly dancing, barefooted, hair flying, in quest of an embrace almost violent in its ardor...And the man in that hazy vision was not Juanren, no not Juanren, nor even Chilin; rather, he somewhat resembled that White Russian selling cotton candy—bold and brave and searing hot... she felt her own body to be searing hot, she wanted to burn, she wanted to burn up! She screamed, not merely because she was in pain, but because at any ordinary time she simply could not willfully shout aloud. She screamed herself hoarse and sobbed aloud, and cried that she had made a mess of everything. She suddenly realized that she bore not the slightest love for Juanren, that weak, useless, albeit opinionated man; and yet she was fated to spend the rest of her life with him... Her cries rose louder.

"Oh, it's a boy." In her confusion she heard a soft and kindly voice.

Paying no heed, she went on with her wails.

"Congratulations. A boy," said someone else, shaking her lightly. Just then a warm towel was pressed against her forehead. Thereupon everything vanished as if it had been just a dream world, and she realized she'd awakened and had returned from the very brink of death, and was now lying in the delivery room. She even understood that the delivery had been performed by one of the most celebrated obstetricians in all China, Dr. Wang Shuzhen. She stopped her crying, not because it was no longer painful, but because she was the young mistress of the Zhu family. She had enjoyed a superior education, and would not allow herself to cry aloud like some country woman.

"This baby is the eldest son of an eldest son. What excellent good fortune you have, Mrs. Zhu," said one of the nurses enviously. At the time Zhishuang had not at all felt she enjoyed any good fortune. She felt only that life's three great events for a woman—love, marriage, and childbirth—had already passed by, and now she felt only the tranquillity of being relieved of a heavy burden.

But now, as her body was gradually recovering, lying in this fancy hospital room full of flowers, receiving unceasing congratulations from well-wishers some known others unknown to her, she did truly feel herself most fortunate. Most of those well-wishers were refined women, elegantly and fashionably dressed, the wives of Shanghai's prominent citizens and wealthy businessmen, and all close friends of her parents-in-law. She recalled years ago when the YWCA was holding its charity bazaar how she hadn't dared to look them straight in the eye. But now they would even sit gushingly on the edge of her bed and talk women's talk with her in complete confidence, which made Zhishuang feel that there was now no longer the slightest distance between her and them.

She felt wonderfully happy.

One day Ju Beibei came to visit. Being very westernized, she brought along a basket of American tangerines. She didn't realize that the Zhus, for all their outwardly modern ways, were still old-fashioned in their bones and did not allow that new mothers during their month of confinement eat cold or uncooked foods.

"Wow! Some family you married into," Ju Beibei blurted out as her eyes took in the roomful of flowers. "Your father-in-law sure survived the war well. He seems to have turned every crisis to his advantage. And your husband is such a good-looking and even-tempered man, and earns good money, too. And now that you'll be raising a grandson for Mr. Zhu, for sure he'll treat you with great deference."

Ju Beibei, to the contrary, had always treated the men in her life if not with cruelty then with fickleness; toward Juanren alone did she evince a proper maidenly attitude. Zhishuang listened to these remarks and felt very self-satisfied. What Ju Beibei said was correct: Juanren was an absolutely faithful husband, quite incapable of getting involved in any kind of affair with the women who worked with him. The German firm previously employing him had now been confiscated by the Chinese government as enemy property, though this had not in the slightest affected his own fortunes. Based on his status as son of a prominent family and on the skills acquired through work experience, he remained in the same organization and continued as department chief; indeed the pedicab that used to take him to and from work was now upgraded to a Cheverolet sedan—the very car formerly belonging to the German assistant manager.

"That's what you say." Zhishuang felt she had to be modest, at least outwardly. "People like me are so ordinary—we only want to get married and lean on our husbands the rest of our lives, that's all. But you—you've led such a romantic life all these years, and you actually get younger and prettier. Any fish you'd land of course would have to be refined and quite extraordinary."

"Stop, stop! What romantic life? It's dead! Even I know that. In a flash I was already well into my twenties and I really wanted to settle down—like you—and raise children." As she spoke, Ju Beibei's eyes reddened. Zhishuang was quite overcome by it all and momentarily didn't know what to say that might comfort her, so she quickly waved a box of chocolates in front of her eyes. "Have one," she offered.

"No thanks, I'm afraid of putting on." Ju Beibei pushed away the chocolates, spun her pretty hips around and stepped over to the dressing table and looked at herself admiringly in the mirror. "Still okay? Not too old, huh? Hong Fung's way out of shape—looks like a beer barrel."

"Hong Fung married wealth, all right. Peace of mind and fat of hind." Zhishuang recalled how in her high school days she had positively worshipped that movie idol, and had once with great expectancy rushed to her home to seek her autograph; thinking back on it now, the Zhishuang then with her green school uniform seemed quite a different, charmingly innocent girl. Ridiculously naive, even. She had come a long way since then, and there was no going back, either.

"Yes, she married wealth. But she's really just a concubine." Ju Beibei shrugged her shoulders and smiled with reserve. Turning the conversation to a new subject, she exclaimed, "Say, Juanren's Uncle Jingwen has done well these past few years. It's really amazing the way he treats his concubine just as nice as ever."

"You mean Miss Yi? She's quite different from an ordinary concubine. She's really very helpful to Uncle Jingwen's career. And besides she's very well educated with genuine intellectual ability, and..."

Without waiting for her to finish, Ju Beibei interrupted with a wave of the hand. "I know, I know. If a woman, just because she's married to some guy, thinks she can rely on him for support and sustenance the rest of her life, then she's the silliest woman in the whole wide world. I don't include Juanren in that, of course. You can certainly rely on him. I guarantee it."

"What you're saying is that Juanren won't take a concubine?" Zhishuang giggled.

"Concubine...!" Ju Beibei muttered in return, then whirled around and demanded, "Zhishuang, if I were to be someone's concubine, would you look down on me? Would we still be friends?"

"Beibei, what on earth?" exclaimed an anxious and flustered Zhishuang, still rather naive about worldly ways.

"There's a gentleman who wants to take me in as his concubine. You know him. I'm thinking of agreeing to it." Ju Beibei leaned against the dressing table.

"But...why don't you find a regular husband instead? A proper person? A beautiful woman like you..."

"Beautiful! Lots of people have called me beautiful, but not even one man have I seen who really wants to marry me. Proper men all view me as improper, men of Juanren's caliber, for example... I don't know what the solution is. I can only blame myself—once I made my first mistake, the rest of my life has been just one mistake after another. I'm exhausted. The war's all over now and the world's at peace, and I want to settle down, just like you, taking care of a baby boy. If I had a little boy, then there'd be nothing to be afraid of."

"So what are you afraid of?"

Beibei threw up her hands in frustration. "I don't know," she said, shaking her head. "Maybe it's loneliness or isolation or feeling forsaken...I just don't know. But this gentleman is very honest and sincere. I guess it's okay if I tell you. It's Liu Tongjun—Liu Tsaizhen's father."

Zhishuang was astounded.

"He's a little on the old side, but from a medical point of view that's fine, because a woman fifteen years or so younger is sexually more compatible." Ju Beibei's off-hand remark caused Zhishuang, now a mother, to flush a deep red. But Ju Beibei went right on. "I feel so sorry for him. During the bombing of Pearl Harbor, he lost a lot of his property, and of course as soon as a person starts failing in his career, his supporters dwindle fast. And as for his family life...well, if I were a man I certainly wouldn't have any interest in that wife of his. She doesn't do anything except play cards all day long. She really hasn't the vaguest idea about how to take care of a man. If only she were like Liu Tsaizhen, it would be fine. To have to be with such a boring wife every day is a real drag."

"You first ought to make him divorce his wife," offered Zhishuang, rather upset.

"She had a proper and formal wedding ceremony, and she's the daughter of a prominent Suzhou family. She's done nothing to deserve a divorce, so how could Liu Tongjun possibly initiate one?" It had never occurred to Zhishuang that Ju Beibei could be so considerate of other people.

"So then, you and Mr. Liu would live together in another home?" asked Zhishuang.

"No, I'd move into the present house," Beibei replied almost indignantly. "I insist on moving into the main residence. I've made it clear—every Monday, Wednesday, and Friday he can be with his wife, and on Tuesday, Thursday, Saturday, and..." (here she smiled slyly) "...and on Sunday too, he'll stay with me." This talk again had Zhishuang quite flushed.

"And if I could have a son with my first pregnancy the way you have," she repeated almost as a prayer, "then there wouldn't be anything to be afraid of."

A son? Was a son really so important?

The nurse brought the tiny fellow in for his breast-feeding. Zhishuang couldn't stop looking at his little red face with its tightly closed eyes, until an angry wail reminded Zhishuang to stuff her nipple into the baby's greedy mouth. He sucked strongly, bringing pain to that soft and sensitive nipple, pain enough to make perspiration drip from the tip of Zhishuang's nose. How difficult motherhood was!

As soon as Juanren got off work, he rushed straight over to the hospital, his daily routine, rain or shine. He had already put on some weight and a slight pot-belly was prematurely bulging; dressed in a carefully tailored western-style suit, he looked like a model husband. As he leaned over to kiss his wife and son, his cleanly shaven face gave off the pleasantly lingering fragrance of his shaving cream. Zhishuang immediately recalled how she herself had sunk into that preposterous hallucination. Thank the Lord that He had laid a ready-made and unobstructed track for her through life. She gave Juanren a tight hug.

"I've got some good news for you," he said, fondly smoothing the fuzz on the nape of her neck. "Your father is arriving tomorrow, along with Juanmin and the family, all on the same flight."

Oh, her father was coming back! Zhishuang gazed at the newborn child in her arms, and suddenly felt that she herself had not accomplished much, that besides the son she was cradling, it seemed she had nothing else to show her father. And yet her father had always cherished for her the highest expectations.

Chapter 31

It has always been true in China that one utterance from some notable can change a person's entire life.

The government's number one official in charge of finance happened to see the petition submitted by the Cathay employees when Jingchen was in such trouble, which enumerated the many ways he had shown his care and concern for the employees and how he had contended with the Japanese and their puppets in a battle of wits. As a consequence the government issued a special invitation to Jingchen to go to Chungking and report on his experiences in war-time Shanghai and receive official commendation. The government even placed at his disposal General Tang Enbo's personal aircraft to convey Jingchen and a few of his fellow "heros of beleaguered Shanghai" to the capital. Really, from traitor to hero in the short space of two weeks even Jingchen felt to be unnatural in the extreme.

As Zhuanlin was packing her husband's suitcase shortly before his departure, a thought suddenly occurred to her. "In just a little while the baby will be exactly one month old. If you leave now will you be able to get back for the big 'first month' celebration?"

Problematical, indeed. Jingchen hesitated a moment. "Might as well take my being out of Shanghai as an excuse not to hold the celebration at all. Putting on a party like that is a complicated matter. To invite this person but not that person simply won't do; but if we invite everybody to our home, I'm afraid we'll need upwards of a hundred tables. That would be too extravagant and ostentatious, and there's no point provoking nasty talk."

"Well...We've received gifts from so many people, how can we repay them?" Zhuanlin found the prospect quite embarrassing. "Besides, it would be difficult to explain to the Syis."

"We'll talk about it later," he said, waving her to silence, and he went out, intending to visit a while in his mother's room. But as he passed by Juanmin's room, he noticed the door was ajar, so he thought he might go in first to chat a bit. Just then he heard Juanmin's angry voice.

"...Why not go and ask them? For their sake we slaved away in Chungking all those years. Aren't they just writing us off with a stroke of the pen? Aren't we getting a raw deal?"

"Calm down, calm down," Jingsyao sneered in reply. "Something will turn up...Hey, here's a love poem written by an ancestor of mine. It's very reserved, not at all like those I-love-you-you-love-me poems foreigners compose. And listen to these lines from Tao Yuanming's 'Ode on Stilling the Passions':

> To be the collar of your dress is my desire,
> and breathe the fragrance of your flowered hair;
> To be the ceinture round your skirt is my desire,
> encircling thus your slender willowy waist...

The lavish repetition of the word 'desire' lends this poem a wonderful sentimentality, yet there is still much that is unsaid. What beauty wouldn't be moved by this? Chinese poetry sure is interesting."

"Oh, stop that!" she interrupted angrily. "Who's in the mood to listen to you talk about poetry? If I'd known it would be like this, we never should have gone to Chungking in the first place, putting up with all the hardships only in the end to find that no one regards us any the higher for it, while the people who stayed in the occupied areas spent the years as contented as ever. Just look at Juanren's belly—that guy's had such an easy time of it, all fat and soft. And he actually ends up with his own set of wheels to run back and forth in. Even Juanying's got status now, all because Tsai Liren's made a pile of money. Did you hear what she was saying at the dinner table this evening? They've spent nine thousand U.S. dollars to buy an English-style manor house so big it covers nearly a quarter acre. Just look how smug she is."

She paused briefly, then continued her diatribe. "And that sister-in-law of mine. People are fawning all over Zhishuang as if she were a Buddhist saint. She's produced a grandson for the Zhu family and everybody thinks it's so extraordinary. I remember back at McTyeire when she was a loud advocate of women's rights, and yet now she's betrayed all that, sacrificing her years of education and dreams to become a prisoner of the home..."

Juanmin, already with two children yet as pretty and lissome as ever, had a gold-patterned black dressing gown thrown about her. Made of Burmese silk, it was a gift she had received as soon as she'd arrived back in Shanghai, an extravagance to which her life as a working woman these past few years had made her an utter stranger. But her latent desire for beautiful things of this sort was instantly rekindled with nearly uncontrollable force. For so many years when she would wend her way from the high cobbled streets down to the river's edge below and see Chungking's huge rats walking the streets as if out for a leisurely stroll, then she would invariably recall the familiar Shanghai scenes she had grown up with—bustling Avenue Joffre, the one and only Mandarin Club, Greenhouse Fashion Boutique...while here in Chungking these ceaseless stair-step streets of stone were like monotonous avenues whose end was always just out of sight. And when it rained, this hilltop city was transformed into a sheet of mud. Even the sedan-chair bearers with their incomprehensible utterings were nothing like Shanghai's rickshaw pullers, uniformly clad in brown sleeveless jackets. For all their coarseness, at least the rickshaw pullers of Shanghai observed such courtesies as "good day, sir" or "take care, ma'am;" and if you gave them a little extra for the fare, they'd never stop thanking you—a far cry from these half-naked, apparently only half-civilized coolies.

In Chungking both she and Jingsyao had worked in an American military guest house where they looked after the needs of the American pilots. Jingsyao seemed destined to thrive in life only if employed by foreigners. From the start, both Jingsyao and Juanmin changed into American olive-drab khaki uniforms, giving them a fresh sense of pride. Especially Juanmin: tan khaki shirt matched perfectly by the green wool necktie, hair fixed into permanent curls, peaked hat set jauntily on her head—all of this lent a bit of dash to her already pretty looks, and not infrequently turned the heads of those American flyers when she was walking along the street. At such times she felt very good about herself, both psychologically and physically. The springtime of her youth was not empty, she felt.

Chungking's equivalent of Shanghai's DDS Cafe was Double Hearts, where she and Jingsyao often went. It served milk, lemon tea, and, surprisingly enough considering it was wartime, butter, even if the patties were of only miniscular proportion. Notwithstanding the addition of two children to their family, Juanmin and Jingsyao, just like sweethearts, would frequently go to Double Hearts to relax and relive for a moment the sweet tenderness of a young couple in love.

But the charm of all that vanished upon their return to the realities of Shanghai. Juanmin on the one hand cursed Zhishuang for her "betrayal" and mocked the now despised Juanying for her wealth, when in fact what she resented was her own poverty and misery.

Shanghai was the same old Shanghai: pretentious, faddish, snobbish. Just so long as you had money in your pockets, you were a big shot, praised to the sky. As for those in their prime of life like Juanmin and Jingsyao, who, having no desire to work as subject peoples, had gone to Free China to try to better their lot, no one expressed the slightest solicitude for them upon their return; to the contrary, they were disdained by Shanghai people for the rural vulgarity and poverty they evinced. The agency in Shanghai where they now worked was in the process of a major staff reduction and it was even rumored it would close down, so it was quite possible that the two of them would find themselves without any salary at all. Juanmin, as a woman, might live at home, all right, but what about Jingsyao? Could he really sponge off his in-laws forever? And since Jingsyao had fashioned a career for himself apart from his own family, there wasn't any prospect of their lending a helping hand.

Juanmin's reproachful outburst toward Juanying and Zhishuang was borne not so much of contempt as of sour-grapes envy.

"Really!" she continued to grouse. "Even Uncle Jingwen has gotten wealthy. Did you see that fancy diamond ring on Miss Yi's finger? It's the real thing, too. Who would have imagined that an egghead like Uncle Jingwen would ever make money? And Miss Yi waited for it to the end."

"What you're really saying," said Jingsyao flaring up, "is that everybody else has made piles of money, which means you're blaming me for not making any! Right? In the beginning I made it perfectly clear to you that Feng Jingsyao was a man without means, and it was you who insisted on marrying me."

Juanmin stomped her feet in anger. "I've never blamed you," she sobbed in injured righteousness. "It's just that now you're not making any effort to do anything about it. If you just keep loafing around this way, how will you ever be able to hold your head high?"

She threw a resentful look at Jingsyao. He was as handsome and dashing as ever, with the same graceful build. Men really don't change much with the years. But a man's true attraction lies in his ability, and, difficult to describe though it may be, the status implicit in his professional environment—for example, a fancy private office with a good-looking secretary—confers upon the man generous proportions of animus, perspicacity, and wisdom. Take away all that and the dash of the dashing young man loses its luster. Feng Jingsyao, for example. Alas, as a young man he possessed irresistible romantic allure and experienced unanticipated good fortune, but not satisfied with passing his days in happy pleasures, of all things he concocted a multitude of useless illusions! Little did he know that once he awakened from his dreams, all would be emptiness.

"I just can't believe that with my fluency in English I can't find any work in this city." Jingsyao massaged his wife's back, by now jerking with her tearful sobs, as he tried to calm her.

"It's not hard to find employment," she needled. "It's just that nobody's going to hire you to be in top management and you refuse to be a petty functionary."

His face instantly turned ashen with anger. "If I were still a single man," he said hoarsely, "would you be so afraid I couldn't get a decent job? You know, there's an American passenger liner looking right now for a doctor. Salary and benefits are calculated in American dollars. But I can't take a great job like that because you keep me so tied down!"

Following that came the sound of shattering dishes. Jingchen tiptoed away and went back to his own room. What manner of victory was this, alas? Those who had remained in Shanghai boiled with resentment, while those returning from Chungking nursed their grievances.

Juanren pushed the door open and came into his father's room.

"Dad, you're going to be away for a few days, but the baby doesn't have a name yet. I wonder if you'd choose one for him before you leave."

This youngest generation of Zhus ought all to use yong, or "eternal," in their names. But this little fellow enjoyed special good fortune in having come into the world upon the restoration of peace, welcoming victory after eight years of war. Whatever else one might say about it, it was after all victory. A great many people had died so that the day might arrive, and the baby must always remember this hard-won victory. Jingchen would break with family tradition.

"Let's just call him 'Shengli' for victory. Zhu Shengli—Victor Zhu in English. That has a real ring to it." Jingchen repeated the name a few times, savoring the sound.

"It's too ordinary," Zhuanlin interrupted. "Half the babies born this year will be named 'Shengli' or some such."

"Never mind that. Anyway, there's an old maxim that a child with an ordinary name is easy to raise." Jingchen was sticking to his choice.

"You know," Jingchen said, suddenly slapping the arm of his chair, "according to the laws of nature, with the war now over there'll certainly be a baby boom. I propose that instead of having the traditional first-month celebration for Shengli, Juanren you look around for a small house with a yard—something in the vicinity of the bank—and I'll present it to the Cathay employees for use as a kindergarten. We'll call it Victory Kindergarten. It'll be free of charge for the children of Cathay employees—a way of repaying those who gave gifts to the new baby."

"What a generous heart you have, Dad," said Juanren, genuinely moved.

"No need to put it in terms of generosity," Jingchen said, absently cracking his knuckles. "To be perfectly candid, I'm doing it out of selfishness. As I view the situation, corruption and decay among the Nationalists have already reached an extreme, and it will be the Communists who actually unite the nation and serve the people. I think it a certainty that it will be the Communists who will rule the country. Don't you agree?"

Juanren only smiled vaguely; he felt his father's views were far removed from reality. Jingchen heaved a depressed sigh. As in chess, one has to think three or four moves ahead; pity Juanren had no such gift!

"Is the little fellow sleeping?" asked Jingchen. "Let's go take a look."

"The wet-nurse coaxed him to sleep just a moment ago. Her milk is very good. The baby will get chubby in no time, and he doesn't fuss at night, either. Grandma told the butler to have the wet-nurse eat more noodles made of flour from wild rice stem, with brown sugar mixed in. She says that will make her milk flow even better."

"Sweet noodles?" Zhuanlin practically wretched at the thought.

Juanren took his father up to the third-floor nursery on the east side. The wet-nurse, of delicate features, was sitting by the lamp busy with her needlework. Little Victor was tucked into his cradle, painted with scenes from Snow White and the Seven Dwarfs, sweetly sleeping, gentle and serene. Now almost one month old, the baby's facial features were already well defined, and his high forehead was cast from the same mold as Jingchen's.

This Victor was still so tiny and delicate—a tender shoot, it seemed, which invited everyone's care and concern. Be that as it may, Victor's little form embodied hope unlimited, even if the present reality was for some sadly disappointing.

Through the eastern window from the lonely narrow lane beyond came the old and doleful voice of a street peddler calling out his flavored porridge; the sound echoed back and forth, lingering in the murky darkness of the night sky.